T0367846

# GREEK MYTHIC HISTORY

# GREEK MYTHIC HISTORY

SPENCER CLEVENGER

**GREEK MYTHIC HISTORY**



*iUniverse books may be ordered through booksellers or by contacting:*

*iUniverse*
*1663 Liberty Drive*
*Bloomington, IN 47403*
*www.iuniverse.com*
*1-800-Authors (1-800-288-4677)*



*ISBN: 978-1-4917-7228-7 (sc)*
*ISBN: 978-1-4917-7230-0 (hc)*
*ISBN: 978-1-4917-7229-4 (e)*

*Print information available on the last page.*

*iUniverse rev. date: 11/3/2015*

# Contents


Preface ........ xi

1 Creation of the Cosmos ........ 1

2 Golden Age ........ 12

3 Silver Age ........ 14

4 Bronze Age ........ 27

5 Rise of the Hellenes ........ 53

6 Rise of Mycenai ........ 61

7 Fall of Krete to the Rise of Dionysos ........ 83

8 First Heroes ........ 106

9 House of Pelops ........ 129

10 Eternal Year ........ 159

11 Sack of Cities ........ 205

12 The Wanax, King of Kings ........ 246

13 The Trojan War ........ 258

14 The Returns ........ 306

15 The Fall of Mycenai ........ 330

16 Iron Age ........ 363

17 Conclusion ........ 374

Addendums

1 Clevenger Chronology ........ 385

2 List of Kings ........ 475

3 Anatolia Prehistory and Bronze Age ........ 485

4 Minoan Krete ........ 493

5 Procession of the Stars ........ 503

6 Important Mythic Sources and Early Poets ........ 505

Bibliography ........ 515

Exhibits (chapter and number)


1.1 Hellenistic Cosmos Theory
4.1 The Pleiades – Star Nymphs
5.1 Tribal Dialects and Their Founder
5.2 Minyan and Mycenaian Pottery
6.1 The Rise of Mycenaian Civilization
6.2 Descendants of Phorbas and Peiras
6.3 Tholos Tombs
6.4 Mycenaian Palaces
7.1 Wedding Gifts for Harmonia
7.2 Tholos Tombs of Boiotia
7.3 Tragic Lives of the Daughters of Kadmos
8.1 Mycenaian Warfare
8.2 Historic Seeds of Perseus, Bellerophontes, and Pelops
9.1 Early Mycenaian Era History of the Western Peloponnesos
9.2 Early Kings of Thebes
9.3 First Wave of Sea Peoples
9.4 Teiresias the Seer
10.1 Mycenaian Walls
10.2 How Athens Was Forced to Sacrifice to the Minotaur
10.3 Marriage of Idas and Marpessa
11.1 The Rainmaker Aiakos
11.2 Marriage of Peleus and Thetis
11.3 Fate of Hypsipyle
12.1 Argeian Kings after Perseus Traded Mycenai for Tiryns
13.1 History of Wilusa (Ilion/Troy)
13.2 Telephos and Teuthrania
13.3 Fate of the Palladium
14.1 Where the Akhaians Settled after the Trojan War
14.2 Early Mythic Settlers—The Sea Peoples of Near Eastern Texts
15.1 Jason and Medeia
15.2 The Akhaian Migration
15.3 The Dorian Migration

15.4 Palace of Pylos
15.5 The Ionian Migration
16.1 Pottery Dating
16.2 Horseback Ridding
A1.1 Clevenger Chronology
A1.2 Dating the Trojan War
A1.3 Ephorian Generations
A1.4 Dark Age Dates from Ephoros's Sequence of Events
A1.5 Dating Pheidon by the Orthagorids
A1.6 Argos Dating of the Herakleids' Return
A1.7 Cyrene Dating of the Herakleids' Return
A1.8 Descendants of Akrisios
A1.9 Major Chronological Events
A1.10 Korinthian Kings Timeline
A1.11 Dating Dorian Attack on Athens
A1.12 Athenian Kings Timeline

Images (chapter and number)

1.1 World Map
1.2 Map of Cosmos
3.1 Map of Early Farming Cultures
5.1 Map of the Tribes of Hellas
6.1 Descendants of King Argos of Mycenai Genealogy Chart
7.1 Map of Kadmos's travels
8.1 Significant MH-LH 111B Sites of Hellas
9.1 Map of Western Peloponnesos Bronze Age Sites
9.2 Map of Pelopid Ruled Cities
10.1 Map of First Six Labors of Herakles
10.2 Map of the Last Six Labors of Herakles
11.1 Map of Important Sites in the Later Life of Herakles
11.2 Map of Cities Attacked between Trojan Wars
12.1 Map of Important Sites of Argeia and Korinthia
13.1 Map of Troas and Surrounding Area
14.1 Map of the Returns
14.2 Map of Late Bronze Age Mycenaian/Minoan Migrations
15.1 Map of the Mycenaian Kingdom
15.2 Map of Important Dorian Invasion Locations
15.3 Map of the Twelve Ionian City-States
A3.1 Map of Bronze Age Anatolia

# Preface

What is the connection between Greek mythology and Greek history? Many have expressed opinions on this topic since Western historians first began writing. Exhaustive discussions of the historic and mythic aspects of the Trojan War exist. Historic perspectives of other mythic events, such as the Dorian invasion and the migrations of war heroes after the Trojan War, are available. Therefore it is surprising to learn that a comprehensive retelling of the various myths concerning gods, kings, and heroes in their intended physical place and historic perspective does not exist.

*Greek Mythic History* is the first book to provide a concise retelling of Greek myths from a historic perspective of time and place. All surviving text versions of Hellenic myths from ancient writers beginning with Homer in the seventh century BCE and ending with Hyginos in the second century C.E. were studied to see if they could be read as historic narrative. Then each myth was compared with known facts.This book is neither history nor mythology, but rather myth told as if it were history. It is an original retelling and provides modern facts and knowledge that frame the canon in a new context. This is the main objective of the work.

Greek mythology is a topic that has been covered extensively. Ancient Greek poets drew on rich oral traditions to provide an explanation for how the cosmos came to be, their religious beliefs, and vibrant tales of great heroic exploits in the not-too-distant past. When men turned to philosophy and history, poets soon stopped providing inspired new poems on the subject. While Greece was part of the Roman Empire, handbooks of mythic narratives providing synopses were written to preserve the old myths. Nevertheless, the subject was not widely read until the nineteenth century CE, when an American bank clerk named Thomas Bulfinch reintroduced the myths with an English-version narrative. More recent updates by Robert Graves, Edith Hamilton, Richard Buxton, and others have all followed Bulfinch's approach of narrating each myth individually. The same is true for writers seeking to provide deeper psychological or social interpretations: Sigmund Freud, Carl Jung, and Joseph Campbell, for example.

## Mythic History

*Greek Mythic History* provides a concise "history" of Greek mythology. The story is told in chronological order, starting with the creation of the cosmos and ending in the Dark Age that separated the mythic heroes from the poets who immortalized them. The detailed timeline of mythic events was calculated using ancient genealogies. Genealogies compared from various city-states provide the timeline, cross-referenced. Obviously there are many conflicting versions and genealogies to consider. Usually one version fits best within the overall sequence. Those that did not were discarded. If there were multiple versions that fit, the oldest version available was most often used.

In the beginning, order was established out of chaos, the formless expanse. Primordial powers, such as time, came to be. So did heaven (Ouranos) and earth (Gaia). Heaven covered the earth and produced the Titans, wild gods of nature. The youngest Titan, Kronos, emasculated his father, Ouranos, and ruled heaven and earth as the king of the Titans. The Titans were the first of three important generations of gods. Kronos added to the earth her most wondrous creature, man. Hesiod believed that this first race of men lived in a Golden Age. Carefree, they roamed, living off the bounty that the earth provided.

Zeus overthrew his father, Kronos, and replaced the earlier people with a new race in his own image, the men of silver. The older gods of nature were not dead. Zeus and his siblings represented a new, greater power, the unique power of the human spirit and mind; their unique facilities allowed them to consciously alter their environment as no creature had been able to do beforehand. This control over nature is most profoundly demonstrated through the invention of agriculture; flax, cereals, and pulses were grown, and sheep, goats, pigs, and cattle were tended.

The arrival of the younger generation of Olympian gods marked the transition from the Neolithic Era to the Bronze Age. Zeus willed that there be a new race of men—men of bronze. The most instrumental of the younger gods who educated the men of bronze were

- Hephaistos, who taught metalworking;
- Athena, who provided all sorts of crafts and indispensable olive cultivation;
- Dionysos, who taught viniculture (wine was considered a hallmark of civilization); and
- Apollo, who uttered the gods' prophecies to men.

Technical advances from the youngest generation of gods provided mankind with the means to build the first cities around the Aigaian Sea. Yet the bronze men were inferior to the races before them because they fought incessantly.

Alone, Deukalion and his lovely bride Pyrrha survived the great flood Zeus sent to destroy the evil race of bronze. Thankful to be alive, but stunned by the devastation they had witnessed, the pious couple timidly approached the holy Delphic oracle with solemn prayers, beseeching the gods to create a new race of men to share the earth with them. Their prayers were answered, and a new heroic race was created. Deukalion and Pyrrha were the first "Greek" couple.

Most of the surviving Greek myths describe important events of the Heroic Age. This age was a glorious time when men and gods interacted and accomplished great things. Phoroneus was the first Greek to build a city. For twenty generations, Phoroneus and his successors ruled strong built Mycenai. Other city-state kingdoms sprouted up throughout Greece, many built by children of the gods. Kings built great palaces and tombs and led stout warriors who fought for glory and loot in gleaming bronze chariots beneath cyclopean walls. Mycenai held the place of honor, and its kings forged a great empire that commanded respect far beyond the boundaries of Greece.

When Gaia complained to Zeus that the greatly expanding multitude of men was becoming a burden to great too bear, the king of the Gods devised war plans to decimate mankind. Within a generation, most of the cities of Greece were sacked, many by the indomitable Herakles. The sieges of cities culminated at Troy. Many died in the fighting, others at the fall of Troy, others trying to get home. Many choose to flee the turmoil in Greece and settle abroad. The fall of Mycenai a century later spelled the end of the Heroic Age.

Hesiod provides a depressing account of life during the subsequent Iron Age. These were the few men of iron who survived the great calamity. They lived in modest huts outside the crumbling great-halled palaces. The gods had withdrawn from the daily affairs of men. Might was right, and shame ceased to be. Men survived in backbreaking toil, and they grieved unceasingly. The age of myth was over.

## Correlation to Greek Prehistory

Once the mythic history was compiled, it was compared to Greek prehistory. The detailed myths of the Heroic Age fit extremely well into a tightly knitted story. The myths readily lent themselves to a consistent historical approach. Was that because the myths were grounded in history?

As mentioned above, studying the relationship between history and myth is not new. As far back as the fifth century BCE, Pherecydes of Syros (in the Cyklades) and other early mythographers attempted to rationalize and integrate city-state stories into a coherent mythic Hellenic prehistory. Writing a century later, the historian Ephoros drew a line between myth and history with the return of the Herakleids (Dorians). Ironically, the return of the Herakleids is the most important mythic event not substantiated by archaeological finds.

After the fall of the Roman Empire, the historic value of myth was lost. The great Bronze Age sites such as Troy and Mycenai gradually disappeared from sight and were forgotten. Greek religion and philosophy were replaced by a Christian theology that disapproved of pagan myths. The understanding that myths contain historical information was gradually lost. It took the drive of the intrepid German merchant Heinrich Schliemann to show a skeptical modern world that Troy existed.

So how much history is contained within Greek mythology? Myths accurately describe the general outline of Greek prehistory uncovered by archaeologists, linguists, and other scientists. Hesiod provided a poetic description of three generations of gods that correspond to important human technologies. The men of gold, silver, and bronze represented the three broad human time periods: preagricultural hunters and gatherers, Stone Age farmers, and civilized men using advanced metal tools.

The Mycenaian Age, which Hesiod calls the Heroic Age, is described in mythic details that fit remarkably well with prehistory. The era began after a time of turmoil brought on by migrations and warfare. It was during that time that the Greek language developed. Soon cities arose throughout *Hellas,* the largest at Mycenai. The most important myths were centered at the largest discovered sites, including places that were not important later, such as at Pylos. The documented fall of the Minoan civilization on Krete is both explained and set in time by the myth of the rape of Europa. The myths indicate, and modern scholars believe, that the city of Mycenai flourished for some five centuries. Troy was sacked twice. Most of the palace cities of Greece were sacked between the two times Troy fell. Mycenai peaked in the generation before Troy was sacked for the second time. A great depression followed, and many settled overseas. However, the myths do not always get it right. There was no big migration into central and southern Hellas at the end of the Mycenaian Age, Pylos was sacked before Troy VII, and Lakonia (Sparta) was largely deserted before Troy was sacked.

The Greek myths provide a solid explanation for why the Mycenaian Age ended. They blamed environmental changes, the "burden to Gaia," for being the catalyst for civil strife. Greek city-states fought and destroyed each other's cities. The Mycenaian civilization collapsed, and many emigrated abroad. Modern scholars have proposed many theories for the collapse, but none better.

## The Long Dark Age

When I started writing this book, I accepted the conventional view that there was a yawning gap of time between the fall of Mycenai and when Homer wrote, a dark age. That unquestioning acceptance was shattered by Peter James's book *Centuries of Darkness.* Consequently, I searched the myths to see if the ancient Greeks provided any information about this issue. While most ancient historians provide long timelines that support a long Dark Age, it is also evident that they have inflated the antiquity of their own heroes. James's assertion is validated using the genealogies found in Herodotos and Ephoros. This assertion has no bearing on mythic retelling of myths of the Late Bronze Age, but it does mean that Homer may be separated by only six generations from someone who lived when Mycenai fell. In other words, Homer's grandfather may have known someone who survived the fall of Mycenai.

## Qualifications

So why did I feel qualified to write a mythic history of Greece? After all, I am not a trained classics scholar. I do possess academic credentials, but they are within the disciplines of economics (bachelor of arts, University of California–Los Angeles) and business (master of business administration, University of Southern California). I believe there are four main reasons: perspective, flexibility, science, and originality.

Perspective: I have studied the subject matter from a unique perspective. I have read and reread an exhaustive list of sources in trying to find the version of each myth that best fits within the overall mythic historical framework. That focus, or perspective, has allowed me to discover mythic insights that were not apparent to other writers. When you know what you are looking for, it is easier to find it.

Flexibility: I may take liberties to interpret myths in a way not possible for scholars, who must adhere to exacting scientific standards. I am not bound by the constraints, traditions, and structure of academia. My book reads as history, and its conclusions are logical and original but fanciful; no one should mistake it for fact. I believe my unique perspective will appeal to readers with a deep love of the ancient history and myths of Greece.

Science: The work resolves some problems regarding the canon with respect to what is now known about the subject, and this is something that earlier works from the twentieth century CE cannot do. Many modern discoveries about the ancient Hellenes—for instance, discoveries about their environment, their language, and their metallurgical knowledge—have revealed facts that provide a new context for the myths. The book accounts for known facts about the real, physical world of ancient Greece, and it places the myths into context.

Originality: I am the first to write a comprehensive rendition of Greek mythology from a historical perspective. The work is revolutionary in that it attempts to place nearly the entire canon into context. Contemporary works on Greek mythology tend to focus on a singular age or, even more narrowly, a singular myth. They follow the narrative approached employed in Thomas Bulfinch's *Age of Fable*, first published in 1855.

The book is a compelling mythic history of Greece from the beginning of time until the time when poets began to write down their myths and stories. The gods, early kings, and great heroes are all featured. It is not history, just what history might be if the myths were interpreted more literally. There are some interesting results that will surprise and challenge commonly held assumptions regarding myth's place in history. The subject is timeless, but the approach, which capitalizes on modern discoveries, makes the work both timely and unique.

# Creation of the Cosmos

Much the poets lie.

—Politician Solon of Athens, sixth century BCE

Homer and Hesiod have attributed to the gods all things which among men are reproach and blame: stealing, adultery and mutual deception.

—Philosopher Xenophanes of Kolophon, sixth century BCE

Shepherds of the wilderness, wretched things of shame, mere bellies, we know how to speak many false things as though they were true; but we know when we will, to utter true things.

—The Muses to poet Hesiod of Askre,
*Theogony*, seventh century BCE

## Creation Myths

The Oceanides Eurynome rose naked from chaos and divided the sea and sky, dancing lonely on the waves. Her movement set the wind into motion and she caught the north wind in her hand. Rubbing it in her hands – behold - the serpent Ophion appeared! She continued to

> dance more and more wildly until Ophion grew lustful and coiled around her divine limbs and was moved to couple with her. She changed into the form of a dove and laid the Universal Egg. Out of the egg came the sun, moon, planets, and stars. Eurynome and Ophion ruled until they were supplanted by Kronos and Rhea. Then she slipped into the *sea.* [1]

There were, no doubt, many mythic explanations for the creation of the cosmos or universe that circulated among the ancient Greeks,[2] all believed with a healthy skepticism. The great poets were not oblivious to the obscure version above, and they gave Eurynome a place of honor as well; Hesiod says she bore the Kharities (Graces) to Zeus, and Homer says she attended to Hephaistos when he was thrown from Olympos.

Another early creation myth is preserved in the *Rhapsodic Theogony* of the early first century BCE. The *Rhapsodic Theogony* records the influential sixth- and fifth-century BCE Orphic cult creation myth. It states that out of the primeval abyss came a winged serpent with heads of a bull and a lion on either side of a god's countenance. Its name was Khronos (meaning "unaging time"). Khronos created the One, represented as the silver egg of the cosmos. From it burst out Protogenos (meaning "firstborn"), the creative principal, also called Eros (meaning "love"), and the bisexual god Dionysos-Phanes. Phanes ruled during the Golden Age and created Nyx (meaning "night") and with her produced Ouranos (meaning "heaven") and Gaia (meaning "earth"). Ouranos and Gaia gave birth to the Titans, and one of them, Kronos, castrated his father and ruled until Rhea saved Zeus, her sixth child, from being swallowed by his father. The Orphics say Zeus swallowed Phanes, embodying in himself the previous Golden

---

[1] Obscure creation myth recounted by the third-century BCE poet Apollonios of Alexandria, surnamed the Rhodian, in *Argonautika*, i.503–506. Also discussed by the Roman Pliny, *Natural History*, vi.35 and vii.67.

[2] The words "Greek" and "Greece" come to us from Romans. Will Durant's *The Story of Civilization*, volume 2, *The Life of Greece*, provides an explanation for the name. He states that the Graikoi were a small tribe from Boiotia who settled in Cumai. More specifically, these Graikoi were from Graia, a Boiotian Plain mentioned by Homer and identified by Aristotle with Oropos. They were the first Greek speakers the Romans came in contact with. The term became universally applied to all like speakers. Perhaps Graikoi and Hellenes may have been early names and Delphic Hellenes won out as a term over Dodona Graikoi. The Greeks called themselves Hellenes after Hellen, ancestor to most of the tribal founders. Henceforth, the Greeks will be referred to by their own name.

Age. Through his daughter Persephone, Zeus gave birth, or rebirth, to the creative principal—Dionysos-Zagreus. Goaded by jealous Hera, or by envy, the Titans dismembered, roasted, and ate Dionysos-Zagreus. Zeus's thunderbolts brought swift retribution, and from the ashes of the Titans came the human race. Thus man is part evil-natured Titan and part divine Dionysos, whom the Titans ate. Lord Zeus was only able to recover the heart of his son. He swallowed it and, through the womb of Semele, gave birth to Dionysos. Orphics evoked Dionysos to help them purge their Titan nature so that their Dionysian soul could be liberated.

The most influential version of the creation myth, the one most commonly believed, is provided in Hesiod.[3] Hesiod is the first historical Hellenic poet, and the concise myths in his magnificent poem are largely consistent with the then evolving oral epic poetry and hymns attributed to the name of Homer. Hesiod gave an orderly account of the cosmos, heavenly battles, and succession myths which all have Hittite parallels.

> Chaos was first of all, but next appeared
> Broad bosomed Gaia, sure standing-place for all.[4]

From Chaos also sprang Tartaros (meaning "underworld realm"), Eros, black Nyx, and Erebos. Nyx in turn bore Hemera (meaning "day") and Aither (meaning "divine air"),[5] whom she conceived in love to Erebos. She also bore Moros (meaning "doom"), Thanatos (meaning "death"), Hypnos (meaning "sleep"), Nemesis (meaning "indignation"), Eris (meaning "strife"), Geras (meaning "old age"), and other unpleasant powers that were not personified by the Hellenes. Meanwhile, without embrace, Gaia bore Pontos (meaning "the deep" or "sea"), Ourea (meaning "hills"), and Ouranos. Pontos was the sea itself over which other gods ruled (much

---

[3] Hesiod's *Theogony* is the main source. Eumelos of Korinth's *Titanomachy* was the other important early cosmology source. Eumelos's work is lost, but it is thought to be the source behind the Roman-era mythographer Hyginos's *Fabulai*, preface 1–3, and the Roman-era Hellenic mythographer Apollodoros's *Library*, i.1–44. The Roman poet Ovid's *Metamorphoses*, i.1–75, provides additional details. The Roman-era Hellenic travel guide writer Pausanias's *Guide to Greece*, iv.4.1, says Eumelos lived two generations before the First Messenian War, but the early Christian theologian Clement's (ca. 150–215 CE) *Stromateis*, i.21.131, says Eumelos was a contemporary of Arkhias of Korinth, who lived at start of First Messenian War.

[4] Hesiod, *Theogony*, 116-117

[5] Eumelos says Ouranos was the offspring of Aither.

as Zeus later ruled the sky, the body of Ouranos).[6] Gaia intended starry Ouranos to be an equal to her, to cover her all over and be a resting place for all the blessed gods.

Heaven (Ouranos) came nightly to cover the broad earth (Gaia), and their union produced three one-eyed giants known as the Cyklopes (meaning "orb-eyed"): Brontes (meaning "thunderer"), Arges (meaning "bright"), and Steropes (meaning "lightner"); as well as three Hekatonkheires (meaning "one-hundred-handed ones"), who had a hundred arms and fifty heads each: Briareos (meaning "strong"), Gyes (meaning "earthborn"), and Kottos. Ouranos hated his monstrous sons and shut them away in Tartaros, enraging Gaia.

Next Gaia bore to Ouranos lovely gods of gigantic proportions: the Titans, divinities representing the forces of nature. The firstborn Titan was Oceanos, followed by Coios, Krios, Hyperion, Iapetos, Theia, Rhea, Themis, Mnemosyne, Phoebe, lovely Tethys, and finally the crooked schemer Kronos, who hated his lusty father.[7]

Still, Gaia was furious over the treatment of her elder children, and when she could bear it no longer she approached her lovely Titan children, asking, "children of mine and an evil father, I wonder whether you would like to do as I say. We could get redress for your father's cruelty."[8] All were seized by fear at her proposal except for the youngest, Kronos. With a great flint sickle[9] provided by his mother, Kronos hid and waited for his father

[6] The deep, Pontos, should not be confused with the far-off Pontos (Black) Sea, which the Hellenes also called the inhospitable sea, which is only one of the seas in the deep. Confusion between the two came about from one tradition that said Pontos was pushed aside by the Titan Oceanos as king of the (Mediterranean) sea and he went to dwell in the sea named for him (Pontos). More likely Nereus was the first sea king of all the seas (as Kronos was in heaven), then Oceanos (or perhaps he always was identified only with the circling steam—the ocean), and then Poseidon.

[7] This account varies from Hesiod's in the order of the birth of the children of Ouranos and Gaia to fit with Apollodoros, who follows Eumelos. It seems to make more sense for the monsters to come first, followed by the more refined anthropomorphic Titans. However, Apollodoros's addition of Dione as a thirteenth Titan does not fit with the widespread belief in councils of twelve—a Hittite notion. Homer calls Dione the mother of Aphrodite by Zeus (*Iliad*, v.370–416).

[8] Hesiod, *Theogony*, 116-117

[9] Hesiod actually says a sickle made of adamant, a mythical substance of great hardness. Given that it was the Stone Age, flint or obsidian would have likely been the hardest substance used as a tool.

to come and cover his mother. When his father arrived, Kronos grabbed his genitals with his left hand and sliced them off with the sharp sickle he held in his right hand. The left hand has ever since been a sign of ill omen. Kronos flung the severed genitals into the sea. The blood drops that fell to earth created the Erinyes (meaning "avengers"), Gigantes, and Meliai nymphs. In the rich sea, a white form enfolded the severed manhood of Ouranos, and from it emerged Aphrodite (meaning "sensual love").

The reign of the Titans under King Kronos ensued. Kronos took his father's power and ruled over his emasculated body, while his cousin Nereus ruled the inland sea and his brother Oceanos ruled over the circling ocean—two portions of the body of Pontos, the sea. The twelve eldest Titans, brothers and sisters, lived in council above Mount Othyrs.[10] Kronos greatly displeased his mother by continuing to keep his monstrous brothers locked up in dark Tartaros.

The Titans mostly married each other: Oceanos to Tethys, Hyperion to Theia, Coios to Phoebe, and Kronos to Rhea. Krios and Iapetos married non-Titan deities, while Themis and Mnemosyne remained unmarried. Oceanos and Tethys ruled the far-off circling ocean and raised three thousand river gods and three thousand nymphs called Oceanides. Hyperion and Theia bore glowing Helios, the sun; rich-tressed Selene, the moon; and rosy-armed Eos, the dawn—three beings of titanic stature like their parents. Coios and Phoebe raised two beautiful Titanesses: Leto and Asterie (meaning "starry"). Krios married flint-hearted Eurybie, ancient daughter of sea (Pontos) and earth (Gaia). Though not a Titan herself, she raised three Titan sons: Asterios (meaning "starry"), Pallas, and Perses, who shone out among them because of his wisdom. Iapetos married one of the eldest Oceanides, Klymene (also known as Asia), and raised four strong Titan sons: stern-hearted Atlas, violent Menoitios (who rejoiced excessively in his own manly strength and was struck by a thunderbolt during battle against the Olympians), Prometheus (meaning

[10] Marija Gimbutas interpreted Hesiod's Theogony to mean that the earthborn Titans were the gods of the people living in Hellas before the coming of the Indo-European Hellenes with their sky gods. The discovery of Hittite and Near Eastern succession myths proved this was not the case. Both sets of deities existed within an Indo-European pantheon and within neighboring cultures. In the Indo-European Hittite cosmogony, there is a divine struggle for heavenly supremacy in which the top god is castrated by his successful challenger. However, there are differences: two separate families fight in the Hittite version, the challenger vanquishes his foe by biting off his manhood, and new gods arise from the loser's genitals.

"forethought"), and Epimetheus (meaning "afterthought"). By his mistress Thorax, Iapetos was the father of the giant Bouphagius (who was killed by Artemis when he tried to rape her on Mount Pholoe in Pisatis). Perses and Asterie bore the only third-generation Titan, the witch Hekate. In all, there were fourteen Titans and eleven Titanesses who ruled over heaven and earth.

The Titan Pallas married the Oceanid Styx (the implacable underworld stream by whom the gods swore oaths) and fathered four aspects of success that later surrounded Zeus. Asterios, the god of the starry night and predawn wind, was married to Eos, the dawn. They raised the winds and the morning and evening stars—ornamental orbs for Father Heaven (Ouranos)—and also begat a goddess who was identified with the constellation[11] Virgo. Atlas too was the father of star clusters: the Hyades (meaning "raining") and Pleiades (meaning "doves"), as well as the sea nymph Kalypso, by his wife, the Oceanid Pleiones. Atlas also sired the Hesperides, who tended the golden apples for Hera. The Hyades had once acted as wet nurses for young Dionysos, and several of the Pleiades were lovers of the Olympians.

The briny sea, Pontos, embraced his mother, just as Ouranos did. Gaia bore to Pontos the ancient sea gods Nereus, Phorcys, and Thaumas, as well as Eurybie and the archetype sea monster Ceto. Pontos's children must have been on friendly terms with the Titan rulers, since they intermarried.

Nereus was the eldest son of Pontos and possibly the first prophet; he may have held considerable power before Poseidon, possibly ruling the inland seas (Mediterranean and Pontos). He was a kindly and just god who represented the bounty of the sea. He married the Oceanid Doris and sired fifty mermaid daughters, important and lovely sea goddesses called the Nereides, who lived with him. One of them, Amphitrite, would marry Poseidon and become the queen of the sea. Nereus had great prophetic powers, and those who bound him could learn much about what they asked.

The ancient powers of his kindly brother Thaumas are forgotten, but his children by the Oceanid Elektra were not. They were Iris and the Harpies,

[11] The Hellenes developed surprisingly few star myths of their own. See Addendum 5, "Procession of the Stars" for more detail.

and they served Zeus. Iris was the rainbow messenger of the Olympians, and the Harpies punished impiousness.

As mentioned above, Thaumas's sister, Eurybie, whose heart was like a sharp stone, married the Titan Krios and bore the Titans Asterios, Pallas, and Perses. Asterios married the Titaness Eos, the dawn. They raised the three winds: Boreas, Zephyros, and Notos (there were no prevailing winds from the east in Hellas).

Image 1.1
World Map
Hekataios of Miletos
Early fifth century BCE
(based upon earlier Babylonian maps)

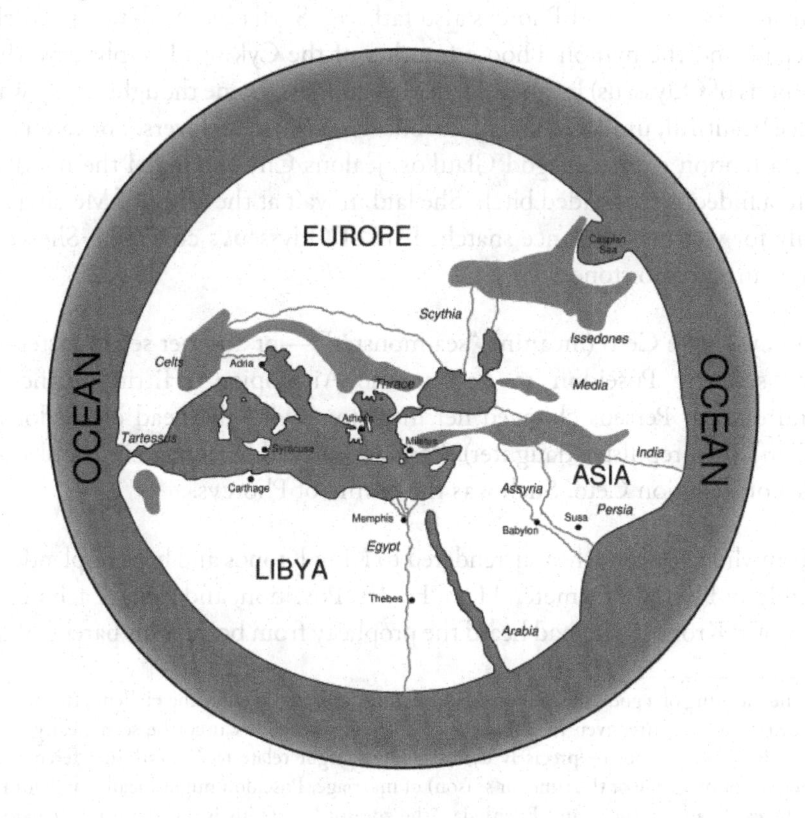


Whereas Nereus and Thaumas represented the bounty and friendliness of the sea, their brother Phorcys represented another aspect, its terrors. He married his sea monster sister Ceto and sired the Gorgons, Graiai,

Echidna, and the serpent Ladon. The Gorgons (Stheno, Euryale, and Medousa) were so hideous that a glimpse of them turned man or beast to stone in fright. The Graiai hags were Enyo, Pemphredo, and Deino; grey-haired from birth, they possessed only one eye and tooth between them. The Gorgons and Graiai lived far to the west near Oceanos, beyond the Atlas Mountains, where the dragon Ladon guarded the golden apples of Hesperides that Gaia gave to Hera as a wedding present.

The speckled serpent Echidna married the most fearsome land monster Typhoeus, son of Gaia. Their monstrous children were hardly more attractive: the goat/lion/serpent Chimaera, the poisonous seven-headed Hydra, the three-headed hound Cerberus, the two-headed hound Orthos, the Sphinx, the Nemean Lion, and the Krommyonian Sow.

The terrifying sea god Phorcys also fathered Scylla by the Titaness witch Hekate and the nymph Thoosa (mother of the Cyklops Polyphemos, the nemesis of Odysseus) by an unidentified goddess. Some thought Scylla was once beautiful, unlike her relatives, but she scorned all lovers. For catching the attention of the sea god Glaukos, jealous Circe changed the maiden into a hideous six-headed bitch. She laid in wait at the Strait of Messina in Italy for victims. She once snatched six of Odysseus's crewmen. She was later turned into stone.

Phorcys's wife Ceto (meaning "sea monster")—or another sea monster—was sent by Poseidon to devour the Aithiopian (Hittite) princess Andromeda. Perseus changed her into stone with the head of Medousa (Ceto's own repulsive daughter). Poseidon placed her image in the sky as the constellation Ceto. Such was the family of Phorcys.

Meanwhile, Queen Rhea surrendered to King Kronos and bore resplendent children: Hestia,[12] Demeter, Hera, Hades, Poseidon, and Zeus. Each birth troubled Kronos, who had heard the prophecy from both of his parents that

[12] The meaning of a god's name is profound in most religions, yet for the Hellenes the names of deities are obscure, even to the ancient Hellenes. The gods cannot be seen clearly, and so their names cannot be precisely defined. Hera might relate to "Horai" in reference to ripeness for marriage or the time (or season) of marriage. Poseidon might mean "earth lord"; Demeter, "grain mother"; and Eileithyia, "the coming." Artemis is a Lydian proper name, and Hephaistos is clearly non-Hellenic, possibly Lemnian. Only Hermes is clear; his name derives from "herma," the word for a heap of stones set up as a crude demarcation, and he was the god of boundaries—most importantly as the conductor of souls across boundaries from this life to the next.

a son of his was destined to depose him. So he swallowed and suppressed the infants as they reached their mother's knees from her holy womb.

Rhea suffered terrible grief and resentment over the loss of her children. So when she came to term with her sixth, Zeus, she begged her dear parents, Gaia and Ouranos, to devise a plan so that she could bear her child in secrecy and make the crooked schemer Kronos pay for his vile actions. In the wild, mountainous hinterland of the Peloponnesos Peninsula known as Arkadia, the Thunderer-on-High, Lord Zeus, was born. Immediately after his birth, he was washed in the stream of Neda, third eldest of the Oceanides (only the previously discussed Eurynome and the implacable underworld stream Styx were older), and then Rhea whisked him away to Krete, to avoid his terrible father, and it was there he grew to manhood. She followed the plan her parents suggested and deceived the crooked schemer Kronos into swallowing a stone wrapped in swaddling clothes.

Once, while Rhea was secretly attending to Zeus,[13] Kronos slipped away to visit lovely Philyra in her faraway island home beside the inhospitable Pontic Sea. Philyra was the fourth daughter of Oceanos and Tethys (after Eurynome, Styx, and Neda). There the strutting Kronos mounted Philyra in the form of a horse in a botched attempt to avoid his wife's detection. Watchful Rhea was not deceived, and when she appeared unexpectedly, Kronos ignobly galloped away. Wise Kheiron was conceived from that union, and he chose Mount Pelion in Thessalia as his home.

The birth of the children of the Titans and the Pontids basically completed the development of the physical cosmos (thankfully the children of Nyx did not conceive a third generation of underworld gods, and as yet there was no king in the undergloom since there were no dead souls to rule over). Conditions were right to nurture life and for the creation of the most wondrous creature in the cosmos.

---

[13] On Krete the Korybantes protected Zeus, drowning his cries by banging on their swords. They were said to be descendants of the Dactyls and were credited with inventing swords and bronze-tipped arrows. It was fitting that these magical smiths should become the guardians of the new king of heaven, the civilized god, the one who brought a new world order. Agricultural bounty (surplus) represented by Rhea made this possible, and so it is she who gave birth, foundation, to this new god, Zeus. He was able to seize heaven from the Neolithic Titans thanks in large part to the superior weapon (thunderbolt) provided to him by bronzesmiths called the Cyklopes. The rise of Zeus's children corresponds with the beginning of the Bronze Age; his son Hephaistos taught bronze-making to the magical guilds that taught mankind.

Exhibit 1.1
Hellenistic Cosmos Theory

The first-century BCE Roman poet Ovid began his masterful mythical poem *Metamorphoses* with a poetic recap of Hellenistic scientific belief on the creation of the cosmos:

> In the beginning there was a shapeless uncoordinated mass, nothing but a weight of lifeless matter, whose ill-assorted elements were indiscriminately heaped together in one place. Men have given it the name of chaos. The strife was finally resolved by a god, a natural force of a higher kind, who separated heaven from earth, and the waters from the earth, and set clear air apart from the cloudy atmosphere. When he had freed these elements, sorting them out from the heap where they had lain, indistinguishable from one another, he bound them fast, each in its separate place, forming a harmonious union. The fiery aither, which has no weight, formed the vault of heaven, flashing upward to take its place in the highest sphere. The air, next to it in lightness, occupied the neighboring regions. Earth, heavier than these, attracted itself the grosser elements, and sank down under its own weight, while the encircling sea took possession of the last place of all, and held the solid earth in its embrace.[14]

Next the Creator shaped the earth into a ball. With conditions right, either the Creator or Prometheus created mankind.

[14] Ovid, *Metamorphoses*, i. 5-31.

Image 1.2
Map of Cosmos
Eudoxos of Knidos
Early to mid fourth century BCE

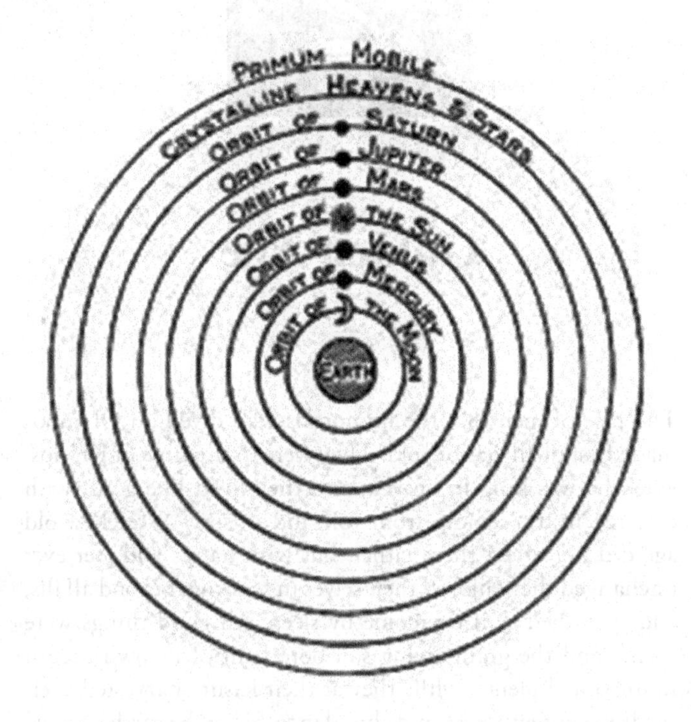

# Golden Age

> The race of men that the immortals who dwell on Olympos made first of all was of gold. They were in the time of Kronos, when he was king in heaven; and they lived like gods, with carefree heart, remote from toil and misery. Wretched old age did not affect them either, but with hands and feet ever unchanged they enjoyed themselves in feasting, beyond all ills, and they died as if overcome by sleep. All good things were theirs, and the grain-giving soil bore fruit of its own accord in unstinted plenty, while they at their leisure harvested their fields in contentment amid abundance. Since the earth covered up that race, they have been divine spirits on the face of the earth, watchers over mortal men, and bestowers of wealth: such is the kingly honor that they received.
>
> —Hesiod of Askre, *Works and Days*, seventh century BCE

Hesiod recorded the Hellenic belief that there were five ages of men: Gold, Silver, Bronze, Heroic, and finally Iron, the men of his day. The five ages correspond well to important stages in the development of mankind, but his description of the ages was pure fantasy.[15]

The first, or golden, age came after Kronos used a sickle to emasculate his father and permanently separate heaven from earth. Then Kronos added to the earth her most wondrous creature, man. Hesiod waxed poetically

[15] Perhaps during the early nineteenth century CE, we moved from the Iron to the Energy Age.

about a time when men did not live in cities but instead lived carefree upon the bounty earth provided. Kronos ruled the natural forces, and his people lived as hunters and gatherers without civilization. These men knew no penalties or laws; it was through their own good faith that they kept right action. They did not have ships, as they had no need to sail across the barren sea for profit; nor had they need for weapons of war.

Even Hesiod admits elsewhere in his poem that things were not nearly as idyllic as he elsewhere suggested. Three revelations demonstrate trouble was present. First, when Ouranos was castrated, his blood created the Erinyes (although Aphrodite was also created from that act). Second, Kronos continued to imprison the Cyklopes and Hekatonkheires—the action that caused Gaia to overthrow his father, Ouranos. Finally, by swallowing his own children, Kronos invited future trouble.

While it was true that the earliest inhabitants of Hellas did not toil to till the soil and wretched old age did not afflict them, it was a difficult time. Hesiod surmised that the time before warlike and greedy nobles and landlords must have been great. The reality is that survival was always precarious for the hunter-gatherer groups and that none lived long enough to face any kind of old age. On the other hand, hunter-gatherer groups lived healthier lives than farmers did up until very recently. The first people of Hellas were brutes like the Titans; they were the powerfully built Neanderthal. Modern humans arrived later, and the two coexisted for millennia. Eventually the Neanderthal died out and the humans hunted alone. There were never very many of them. Hesiod says the souls of the race of gold were the daemons, spirits occupying the mythic station between gods and men.

# Silver Age

Good mother, mankind must take the gifts of the gods even when they bring pain, since gods are truly much stronger.

—Homeric Hymn to Demeter, sixth century BCE

If the gods do anything shameful, they are not gods.
To such a god who would pray?

—Euripides of Salamis, fifth century BCE

## Rise of the Olympians

A rise in consciousness challenged the old order in heaven. The rule of Gaia's Titan children, epitomizing the forces of nature, was challenged by younger gods. King Kronos resisted, and a great commotion filled the heavens as his freethinking children rebelled. Kronos had maintained control by swallowing his children upon their birth until finally his exasperated wife Rhea wrapped a stone in baby clothes to save her youngest, Lord Zeus. (So the youngest became the eldest since the others were born a second time). Then, from Olympos, Zeus led his brothers and sisters into battle against the Titans.

Young lord Zeus's courage and resplendent limbs grew fast. Upon reaching manhood he persuaded a daughter of Oceanos named Metis (meaning "wisdom") into telling him that he should give Kronos an emetic provided by Rhea. When he did, the slow-witted Kronos vomited the deceiving stone (which was called omphalos, meaning "navel" or "center"), followed by Zeus's immortal siblings.

For ten years the challengers from Olympos, whom lovely-haired Rhea had born after sleeping with the crooked schemer Kronos, fought continually against the proud male Titan deities from high Orhrys in fierce combat. Both sides displayed powers of awesome brute force, causing the boundless sea to roar terribly while great waves rolled about, the earth to shake violently, and the broad sky to quake and groan. An amazing conflagration prevailed, and the din from the terrible conflict was immense. Long Olympos was shaken by the onrush of the immortals. The fight gave them heartache; neither side came to solution or end to bitter strife, and the outcome of the war hung equally in the balance.

Then, upon Gaia's advice, Zeus sent Hades to free her mighty children, the Cyklopes and the Hekatonkheires, from dank Tartaros.[16] They had suffered long with great pain in their hearts, for Kronos had bound them in powerful fetters, indignant at their overbearing strength and aspect and stature. The Cyklopes, bronzesmiths, created great weapons for the Olympians: thunderbolts for Zeus, an helmet of invisibility for Hades, and a trident for Poseidon. The Hekatonkheires pummeled their enemy with rocks.

Zeus held back his strength no longer. Straightaway his lungs were filled with fury, and he displayed his full might. Amid thunder and lightning, the Titans were finally vanquished. For nine days they fell into the great chasm. On the tenth day, they hit bottom in the black abyss of Tartaros. The Hekatonkheires went down willingly to guard them in that dark and dank place that even the gods shudder to think about. Kronos was eventually released, a mere shadow of his former greatness, and became king of the Island of the Blessed. Strong Atlas was brought up to hold an unwieldy load that pressed down upon his broad shoulders. He is the pillar keeping heaven (Ouranos) and earth (Gaia) apart, and he groans mightily under the strain.

---

[16] Apollodoros, *Library*, i.1.2, says Zeus killed the guard Kampe and freed the monstrous brothers of the Titans himself.

Zeus was chosen as king and lord of the heavens, and he danced in their midst.[17] His brother Poseidon took dominion over the sea, and Hades the underworld. Earth and Olympos were shared, though no one dared challenge the will of Zeus. Hades rarely visited heaven or earth, preferring to stay within his own shadowy realm. The Cyklopes established their forge on either the Lipari Island or nearby Mount Aetna on Sicily, where they crafted precious things for the Olympians.

Zeus wanted to erect the omphalos stone as a monument to his victory at the center of the earth. To discover where the center was he ordered the release of two eagles, one at the easternmost part of the earth and one at westernmost, and they flew toward each other at full speed until they crossed paths above a chasm below the glens of Mount Parnassus. There the serpent Pytho guarded a holy oracle that Gaia had given to Themis. In triumph, Zeus set up the omphalos stone, the hearth and center piece of the world, as the first war memorial. He willed that henceforth it be a sign and a marvel to mortal man. Themis graciously gave the Olympian Poseidon a share of the holy oracle.

Not all the Titans had chosen to fight with Kronos. Prometheus advised his Titan brethren not to resist Zeus, for the earth had foretold that not brute strength, not violence, but cunning would give victory to the rulers of the future. In their pride of strength, the Titans foresaw easy victory and the continuing rule of might. So they found Prometheus's words not worth one moment's heed. Among the Titans, only Prometheus, his brother Epimetheus, and far-off Oceanos remained neutral. Rhea sent her daughter Hera to Oceanos, to be raised safely away from the battle. None of the Titanesses fought on either side, but victorious Zeus slept with those maidens he desired (the only married Titaness he sought was Asterie, and she was the only one to elude him; she changed herself into an island).

To the victor went the women, and Zeus chose to wed the Oceanid Metis first. Though she assumed various shapes to avoid lying with Zeus, his stronger will prevailed. After prevailing, he was warned that any son he sired by Metis would supplant him. So Zeus took a cue from his father and swallowed Metis; wisdom thenceforth resided in his thoughts. Later their

---

[17] The first-century BCE historian Tallos said Zeus defeated Kronos 322 years before the siege of Troy. This fits well with the beginning of the Mycenaian era. In fact, the Olympians brought about farming millennia before the Trojan War.

daughter, Athena, sprang from his head. Alone among Zeus's daughters, Athena received paternal prerogatives, for no woman had born her.

Armed with wisdom, all-seeing Zeus set out to establish order for his kingdom. His first Titan tryst was with the all-wise earth goddess Themis (meaning "order or meaning "justice"), goddess of order, and she bore him two sets of goddesses, each representing an aspect of divine order. The first set consisted of the three Horai (meaning "seasons"): Eunomia (meaning "order"), Dike (meaning "justice"), and Eirene (meaning "peace"). The second set consisted of the three Moirai (meaning "fates"):[18] Klotho (meaning "the spinner of life"), Lakhesis (meaning "assigner of destiny"), and Atropos (meaning "she who cuts the thread of life").

With order came grace. The father of gods and men bedded the lovely Oceanid Eurynome (the creator of the cosmos in one version of the creation myth). Eurynome bore him the three Kharities (meaning "graces"): Aglaia, Euphrosyne, and fair Thaleia. They became attendants of the love goddess Aphrodite, born in the sea off Cyprus from the severed genitals of Ouranos; Zeus saw fit to invite her into his snowy Olympian palace. Next Zeus entered into sacred union with the lovely haired Titaness Mnemosyne (meaning "memory"), from whom the nine Muses sprang. Memory was vital to civilization in the time before written records. Children with exceptional memory were employed in high art and science. The Titaness Selene bore to Zeus the nymph Pandia.

## Demeter's Fury

After bedding the Titanesses and Oceanides of his choosing, all-seeing Zeus went to the bed of rich-haired Demeter, and she bore him slim-ankled Persephone, whom he secretly promised as a bride to his merciless brother Hades, who was also known as the Host of Many.

Demeter, whose golden hair shone like grain, raised her daughter, Persephone, near Henna on the fertile island of Sicily. Lord Hades of the undergloom was captivated by the well-endowed maiden and asked Zeus, the loud-thunderer, for her hand in marriage. Zeus was pleased that she

[18] Elsewhere in the *Theogony*, Hesiod calls the Moirai daughters of Nyx "Night." There are different accounts and names for the Horai; Karpo (meaning "fruit") is an example.

should marry so well and agreed. But Zeus knew golden-haired Demeter would not like to lose the company of her daughter, especially since it meant Persephone would disappear from the face of heaven and earth to live in the undergloom. So Zeus told dark-haired Hades to secretly abduct the girl.

With Persephone leading the world into full bloom, she blissfully gathered wildflowers with the deep-bosomed daughters of Oceanos. Grim Hades caused the cosmic flower to appear in front of the blossoming child: "A thing of awe whether for deathless gods or mortal men to see: from its roots grew a hundred blooms and it smelled most sweetly, so that all wide heaven above and the whole earth and the sea's salt swell laughed for joy."[19]

Persephone, naturally, stooped to pick it, and immediately the ground split open beneath her and the Host of Many, Hades, appeared riding in his royal chariot. Against her will, he grabbed the wailing girl and in his golden chariot carried her down from a life of beauty. A nearby swineherd and his pigs were inadvertently swallowed too. (Henceforth, sacrificing pigs into chasms was an important part of Demeter's mysteries).

For ten days golden-haired Demeter frantically searched for her lost daughter. Each night, Hekate carried a torch as the search continued. Hope charmed her mind, despite her grief. None of the gods could bear to tell her the truth, and none of the birds of omen came to her as trusted messenger. Finally rich-haired Demeter and Hekate, who had heard Persephone's cries, gave up the search. Together the goddesses went to the all-seeing sun, Helios. Helios told them that it had been dark-haired Hades, not an unseemly bridegroom, who had abducted Persephone and that Demeter should be pleased for her daughter, for she was now a queen. Instead Demeter sank further into despair.

Aimlessly, dark-robed Demeter wandered the world, lost and without purpose; her daughter was gone. She left Sicily and landed in Hellas at the Peloponnesian city Sicyon. From there she roamed into wild Arkadia, where Poseidon saw her. Filled with desire for this vulnerable beauty, he approached her. Demeter, as Poseidon would have realized if he had not been so blinded by lust, was in no mood for sex. Golden-haired Demeter changed herself into a mare to escape his amorous advance. Dark-haired

[19] Hesiod, "Homeric Hymn to Demeter," 11-14, in *The Homeric Hymns and Homerica*

Poseidon was neither deceived nor deterred. He changed into a stallion and caught and mounted her. In due time, Demeter gave birth to the fabulous horse Arion and to a goddess so mysterious that the Arkadians know her only as Despoina (meaning "mistress").

Demeter was so enraged with her brothers Zeus, Poseidon, and pitiless-hearted Hades that she refused to return to Olympos. Instead she took on the guise of an old woman and, unnoticed by mortals, for whom immortality is hard to see, continued wandering. All the while she withheld fertility and drought conditions prevailed. She visited the great palaces at Mycenai and Knossos. Still miserable, she took a boat across to Thornikos in southern Attike.

Sullen Demeter arrived in Eleusis and demanded that the Eleusinians build her a temple. She shut herself inside it for one year. Demeter did not forget her fury over Persephone's disappearance, and the drought she induced reached crisis proportions.

Finally all-seeing Zeus, not wishing to lose the sacrifices of men, relented. He sent for Persephone to be returned to her mother. A complication arose because anyone who has eaten in the underworld is forbidden to leave. Persephone had been tricked into eating some pomegranate seeds. So the dark-clouded son of Kronos decreed that Persephone would spend part of the year with her mother and part with her husband. Persephone learned to love her days in Hades, a place of knowledge and insight, mystery and paradox, as well as she loved her life on earth, a place full of passion and warmth, beauty and wonder.

Demeter, bringer of seasons, accepted the compromise, and her own mother, Rhea (identified by the Hellenes with the great Anatolian goddess Cybele), escorted her out of the misty gloom to join the gods on Olympos again. The Titan Hekate, who had led the nightly searches and was most familiar with the underworld chthonic deities, became the attendant and tutor of Persephone.

The drying death of summer ended, except for the time while Persephone is away. Demeter did not forget the kindness shown her by the Eleusinians and taught the Eleusinians her mysteries.[20] They spread knowledge of the mysteries throughout the world.

The earth shaker, Poseidon,[21] was usually more circumspect with women than he had once been with Demeter. He (and Zeus) honored Hestia's wish not to marry. It pleased Zeus to grant Hestia her wish to remain a virgin and tend the holy Olympian hearth. When Nereus's stately daughter, loud-moaning Amphitrite, refused to marry Poseidon and fled to the Titan Atlas, giving one more worry to the one who strains mightily under the weight of the heavens, the dark-haired sea lord showed restraint. Instead of force, Poseidon sent a playful dolphin to find her and convince her to marry the lord of the waves. The reluctant bride rode on the back of that dolphin to her wedding in the magnificent undersea palace the loud-roaring earth shaker had built near the Akhaian seaport of Aigai. Poseidon and his bride raised great Triton.

Dark-haired Zeus chose his white-armed sister Hera to be his wife, though she was even more reluctant to assume the role of wife and queen than Amphitrite had been. Her refusal was steadfast, but the will of scheming Zeus was not to be denied. The lord of dark clouds created a great storm and changed himself into the pitiful shape of a drenched cuckoo. Hera took pity on the poor creature and sheltered it beneath her skirt. There

[20] Sir James Frazer, in *Golden Bough*, described this common Near Eastern myth as an explanation of the cycle of nature. The eastern Mediterranean is wet and green in winter and hot and dry in summer (with vegetation dying off). More recent research has identified other motifs, such as life and death. The earliest preserved account is provided by the Sumerians. The goddess Inanna resists her suitor Damuzi, but then he awakens her desire. She marries him, but after a while he ignores her, spending his time ruling the universe—a position he received as her husband. Her sadness turns bitter and she has him carried off to the Place of Darkness, the land of the dead, for it is her will that whatever lives will die. Without his special purpose, the world withers. She begins to miss him and goes to the Place of Darkness and recovers him after first placating her angry sister, the queen of the undergloom. Damuzi then perform his sweet task, and the fecundity of nature returns. Other examples of the cult include Cybele and Attis (Anatolia), Demeter and Persephone (Eleusis and elsewhere in Hellas), Demeter or Cybele and Iasion (Thebes and Samothrace, Hellas), Apollo and Hyacinthos (Sparta, Hellas), Isis and Osiris (Egypt), Atargatis and Hadad—or her son Ikhthys (Syria), Astarte and Baal (Phoenicia), Ishtar and Tammuz (Babylonia), and, of course, Aphrodite and Adonis (Cyprus). Ironically, it was Persephone, who is herself identified with the earth's fecundity in Hellas, who blocked Adonis's return, and he must split his time above and below in the Cypriot version. Aphrodite is identified with Inanna and Astarte.

[21] His name is probably an Indo-European term for "consort of Da (or Demeter)." Thus he may have once been her consort. Many of his powers did relate to earth, such as being the lord of earthquakes and horses.

Zeus returned to his glorious form and ravished the startled goddess. Afterward, Hera agreed to marry him, not wishing to bear the shame of having sex outside of holy marriage.

The Kretans say that Zeus and Hera were married beside the Theron River. They blissfully spent a three-hundred-year honeymoon on either Krete or Samos. Meanwhile, time rolled on uneventfully among the race of men Zeus created to replace the race of gold.

## The Race of Silver (Neolithic Agriculture)

The victorious Olympian gods represented in new order the unique power of the human spirit and mind, the unique facilities of which allowed them to consciously alter their environment as no creature had been able to beforehand. All-seeing Zeus replaced the earlier people with a new race in his own image—the men of silver. The older gods of nature were not dead, but instead they were forced to bend their will, to a point, to a higher will.

Hesiod describes the race of silver in *Works and Days* as

> a second race after that, much inferior (to the golden race), the dwellers on Olympos made of silver. It resembled the golden one neither in body nor in disposition. For a hundred years a boy would stay in the care of his mother, playing childishly at home; but after reaching adolescence and the appointed span of youthful manhood, they lived but a little time, and in suffering, because of their witlessness. For they could not restrain themselves from crimes against each other, and they would not serve the immortals or sacrifice on the sacred altars of the Blessed Ones, as is laid down for men in their various homelands. They were put away by Zeus, son of Kronos, angry because they did not offer honor to the blessed gods who occupy Olympos. Since the earth covered up this race in its turn, they have been called the mortal blessed below, second in rank, but still they too have honor.

Hesiod's views aside, mankind greatly benefited from the Olympian ability to conquer and shape brute nature. The most profound aspect of this ability was the invention of agriculture, "the mysteries of Demeter." As best we know, farming, which gave rise to the Silver Age, first came into being in southeastern Anatolia, between the Tauros and Zagros Mountains in the hill country above the Syrian Desert (the Great Goddess– and bull-worshipping people). Agriculture developed slowly over two millennium, starting during the eleventh millennium BCE. Farming allowed man to congregate in larger numbers and to build villages. Catal Huyuk was the first permanent town of Anatolian farmers (eighth millennium BCE). Catal Huyuk (and not Eleusis, as the Athenians proclaimed) was probably responsible for spreading farming throughout the Hellenic world. Agriculture spread slowly westward through Anatolia, taking nearly two millennia to reach Hellas.

The earliest known agricultural settlement in Europe was discovered at Nea Nikomedia in Macedonia, and soon afterward farmers separately reached Knossos on Krete (early seventh millennium BCE). Archaeological evidence indicates that farming techniques came to Hellas from Anatolia (from northwest Anatolia via Thrace into Macedonia and from southwest Anatolia in the case of Krete). There are different theories regarding the ethnic background and language of the first Hellenic farmers. Genetic research strongly suggests that the earlier hunter gatherers of Hellas were replaced by farmers from Anatolia.

The farmers found the broad, fertile Macedonian and Thessalian plains ideal. The population density in these plains became fairly thick, even before the cultivation of grapes and olives (which are native to Hellas). Still, the villages were small and the lifestyle crude. Most of the early farming communities of Hellas never numbered more than a few hundred, and there was very little social stratification.

Because the soil in central and southern Hellas is of lower quality than that of the northern plains, they were not settled extensively. Most of the islands were too small to support permanent settlement because of the inefficient farming techniques employed. At first all European farms were indistinguishable; they were run by subsistence farmers who ate the same foods, used the same materials, and shared a common religious background. The farmers grew three kinds of wheat, barley, pulses (lentils, peas, and, primarily for fodder, vetch), figs, apples, pears, cherries, and flax (linen). Acorns, nuts (pistachio, almond, walnut, and chestnut), berries, and wild grapes supplemented their diet. Wild grapes may have been fermented for alcohol. They brought domesticated sheep, goats, cattle and pigs; the latter two supplemented with wild local stock. Hunting was rare, though boar, hare, and deer were eaten when they could be caught. Those living near the sea supplemented their diets with seafood.

The influential twentieth-century CE archaeologist Marija Gimbutas believed the first farmers were a relatively peaceful earth-worshipping group. The Supreme Being was a bountiful Mother Earth goddess. Large numbers of earth goddess stone images have been found around the lands bordering the Aigaian Sea, as well as in Anatolia and on Cyprus. A creator goddess, her ample girth demonstrated that she was both bountiful and satiated. Few early farmers ever had a surplus of food, so being fat was the ultimate symbol of wealth. While important, Gimbutas and others probably exaggerated the importance of the earth mother. The Hellenes called the earliest inhabitants of Hellas Pelasgian (meaning "earthborn" or meaning "ancient ones").

With time and distance, the farmers of Hellas (Sesklo culture), Illyria (Starcevo culture), and Thrace (Karanovo culture) developed distinct cultures. The three cultures met in Macedonia. This early farming culture flourished for three millennia; this was the longest uninterrupted cultural epoch of Hellas.

Image 3.1 Map of Early Farming Cultures

A slow, unbroken development progressed through two significant Neolithic (Stone) Age epochs; the first one was called the Sesklo Age after a Thessalian village (6500T/6250R-4300T/4050R BCE).[22] While Sesklo may have been unusually large, it was still typical of the small, unfortified villages of the time, which were usually little more than farm dwellings for extended families with some social structure for trading parties, festivals, and manufacturing crafts. During climatic change a significant number

[22] There are two conventions used for dating in this book. The T stands for traditional dating of the Hellenic Bronze and Early Iron Ages. The traditional dates derive from long held assumptions about Egyptian chronology developed by William Petrie using two Sothic calendar dates calculated by Eduard Meyer. The R stands for revisionist; the dates are principally based upon Peter James's *Centuries of Darkness*. Both dating systems are discussed at length in Addendum 1, "The Clevenger Chronology."

of new Anatolian farmers migrated into Hellas. They brought the first pottery into Hellas (6200T/5950R BCE).

The Sesklo Age in Hellas ended during a period of turmoil throughout the Balkans. Most of the villages burned and new villages arising with a related, though distinct, culture. This new Neolithic Age epoch is called the Dhimini Age (4300T/4050R BCE through the early third millennium BCE) after a Thessalian village just south of Sesklo. Climate change was likely to have been the cause of the disruption. There is no evidence of foreign invasion, but there is evidence that the weather became drier and less stable. The arrival of the bow and arrow is one key marker for the transition to this new era. A general decline followed and the population shrank significantly. Ditches or stone walls were added at the previously unprotected hamlets of Sesklo and Dhimini (they may have been defenses or just fences to mark property lines between neighbors).

Did the Silver Age Pelasgian farmers of Hellas speak an Indo-European language, and if not, when did they arrive? Professor Colin Renfrew's assertion that the earliest farmers were Indo-Europeans has been refuted. Most of the place names in Hellas do not have Hellenic roots (Hellenic is an Indo-European language). Linguistic evidence suggests that Indo-European languages developed later. Finally, genetic markers for the Indo-Europeans are not found in Hellas at this time.

So where did the Indo-Europeans come from, and when did they arrive in Hellas? The archaeologist Marija Gimbutas was the first to identify the Kurgan Culture of the Volga steppes and the northern slopes of the Pontic Mountains (in what is now Ukraine) with the original proto-Indo-European speakers. Linguistic evidence in support of Gimbutas's theory was provided by J. P. Mallory. Technical terms evident in the proto-Indo-European language led Mallory to date its emergence to ca. 4500T/4250R BCE.

The first group of Indo-European speakers to leave their homeland on the steppes crossed the Danube into lands where farmers had settled long beforehand (4200T/3950R BCE). The impetus may have been climate change here, as in Hellas. The farming population in the Balkans was in great decline and many had migrated into western Europe in search of better farming conditions. Over time, Indo-European languages and genetic markers came to dominate in the Balkans.

Over time the language of these migrants evolved into the first distinct Indo-European language group; proto-Anatolian. Following them were speakers of the Hellenic/Thracian/Phrygian/Armenian branch. The once popular theory, espoused by Gimbutas, that Indo-European hordes conquered the peaceful farming communities of Hellas is not supported by archaeological discoveries. The compelling image of terrifying horseback riders wielding superior weapons must be discarded. The horse was domesticated by other Indo-Europeans after the Anatolian and Hellenic/Thracian branches had departed from the steppes. Also, the Indo-Europeans did not introduce the most formidable weapon of the time, the bow and arrow. That technology arrived in Hellas much earlier. However, the Indo-Europeans did bring two important technology improvements; dairy farming and metallurgy (the ability to make copper tools and jewelry). Meanwhile, the proto-Indo-Europeans remaining on the steppes domesticated the horse, invented the wheel, and developed the first nomadic pastoral society (3600T/3350R BCE).

The movement of these tribes caused disruptions in the Balkans that impacted the Dhimini culture of Hellas, but there is no evidence of immigrants arriving in Hellas at that time. More pronounced changes occurred in Hellas during the late forth millennium BCE, when bronze tools were first used in Hellas. The technology came from Anatolia and was adopted by the local population; there is no evidence of a cultural change.

Though bronze arrived earlier, its impact became pronounced as proto-Anatolians arrived in Anatolia and cities first appeared around the Aigean Sea during the early third millennium BCE. The local population adopted the more warlike nature of the people living in Thrace. This heralded a new age and a new generation of Olympians. The god Ares, the eldest son of Zeus and Hera, came from Thrace with bronze-tipped weapons and a thirst for war to lead the charge.

# Bronze Age

## Early Helladic Bronze Age

### The Younger Gods

> You Sir (Apollo), who knows
> The appointed end of all and all paths:
> How many leaves in April the earth puts forth,
> How many grains of sand
> In the sea and in the rivers
> Are troubled by the waves and the swirling winds,
> What shall be, and whence it shall come,
> You see with clear eyes.
>
> —Pindar of Thebes, *Pythian Ode,* iv.45–49, fifth century BCE

> I would not celebrate a man nor give him a place in my tale …
> Not if he were famous for everything save stubborn courage.
>
> —Tyrtaios of Sparta, sixth century BCE

After a long, harmonious honeymoon, cloud-gathering Zeus and white-armed Hera ruled as king and queen from lofty Olympos. Cities first arose in the Bronze Age and they espoused a radically different way of living, requiring men to revise their view of the cosmic order. Cities require great social organization, and the heavens were now viewed as embodying this. Zeus founded the heavenly city, Olympos. He ruled over gods with coordinated, orderly purpose, quite unlike the unpredictable, seemingly disjointed forces of nature that had prevailed before. This order could be seen in the stars, which were so very different from the chaotic events on earth.

All-seeing Zeus sired powerful deities that brought even further refinement and improvements to the human condition, and they represented various aspects of civilized society. The eldest of these new gods were the legitimate offspring of Zeus and golden-crowned Hera. Joined in love with the king of gods, large-eyed Hera fittingly brought forth the birthing goddess Eileithyia (meaning "the coming" or "the birthing") first. Eileithyia, goddess of the sore travail, lived on Olympos along with her siblings Ares (meaning "war") and Hebe (meaning "youth") and her parents. Stout-hearted Ares, an exceedingly strong chariot rider, was the ally of Themis; and he governed the rebellious.

Ares, king of manliness, was the first of the new generation of Olympians. He brought bronze weapons, chariots and warhorses, and brutal war to Hellas. Ares was the first of Zeus's children admitted to the great Olympian Council of great gods. Other gods, Ares's siblings, followed, bringing greater refinement and sophistication, and softening the harshness of the age.

## Apollo of the Silver Bow and Artemis, Mistress of Animals

When the magic of Zeus and Hera's honeymoon ended, awful Zeus began his philandering ways. His first tryst was with the Titan Leto.[23] The rage of Hera, queen of heaven, goddess of holy marriage, was unfathomable. She persecuted poor Leto so effectively that no place would give her rest. The mover of earth and fruitless sea, Poseidon, had to release tiny Delos Island from the depths to allow gentle Leto a place to give birth.

> In the center of the Cyclades lay Delos. When all the lands of earth refused her (Leto), fearing the wrath of Hera, Delos took her in. Upon finding haven on Delos, Leto was wracked for nine days and nine nights with pangs

[23] Hesiod clearly says Zeus slept with Leto before Hera, but the wrath of Hera paramount in the *Homeric Hymn to Apollo* must indicate he slept with her afterward.

beyond wont. Though goddesses and Titanesses stood by her, jealous Hera detained her daughter Eileithyia on Olympos. The goddesses sent Iris, the messenger goddess, to secretly talk to Eileithyia and bring her to Delos. Iris moved the heart of Eileithyia and they left Olympos together, like shy wild-doves in their going.

As soon as Eileithyia, goddess of sore travail, set foot on Delos, the pain of birth seized Leto and she longed to bring forth; so she cast her arms about a date palm tree and kneeled in the soft meadow while the earth laughed for joy beneath. Then the child leapt forth to the light, and all the goddesses raised a cry. The earth laughed and the sea rejoiced. Straightaway, great Phoebus, the goddesses washed you purely and cleanly with sweet water and swathed you in a white garment of fine texture, new-woven, and fastened a golden band about you.

Now Leto did not give Apollo, bearer of the golden blade, her breast; but Themis duly poured nectar and ambrosia with her divine hands: and Leto was glad because she had borne a strong son and archer. But as soon as you tasted that divine heavenly food, O Phoebus, you could no longer then be held by golden cords nor confined with bands, but all their ends undone. Forth-with Phoebus Apollo spoke out among the deathless goddesses:

"The lyre and the curved bow shall ever be dear to me, and I will declare to men the unfailing will of Zeus."[24]

Artemis too sprang forth. Over the shadowy hills and windy peaks she draws her golden bow, rejoicing in the chase, and sends out grievous shafts. The tops of the high mountains tremble and the tangled wood echoes awesomely with the outcry of beasts: earthquakes and the sea also where fishes shoal.[25]

[24] Hesiod, "Homeric Hymn to Delian Apollo," in *The Homeric Hymns and Homerica.*

[25] Hesiod, "Homeric Hymn to Delian Artemis," in *The Homeric Hymns and Homerica.*

Zeus's luminous son Apollo immediately sought out a place to build an oracle in order to change the way gods and men communicate. He decided upon holy Delphi and struck the serpent named either Pytho (meaning "to rot") or Delphyne that lived there with arrows when she refused to relinquish her allegiance to the goddesses Gaia and Themis. The wound festered, and she died of gangrene. Apollo buried the serpent beneath the omphalos stone, which Zeus had erected to commemorate his victory over the Titans; he also initiated the Pythian Games to placate the serpent's spirit, but Gaia remained angry until Zeus, holder of the Aigis, soothed her.

While still exuberant over slaying the serpent Pytho, Apollo observed young Eros bending his taut bow. He angered Aphrodite's mischievous child by chiding him, saying the boy should leave weapons such as those to broad-shouldered gods like himself, as he could aim his shafts unerringly to wound wild beast or human foe, just as he had recently felled the bloated Pytho.

With a wicked smile, the god of love stalked Apollo and Daphne (meaning "laurel"), daughter of the Thessalian river god Peneios. In his quiver were sharp golden arrows to kindle love and blunt leaden ones to put love to flight. With one he cruelly struck Apollo; and with the other, Daphne.

Along her father's river, Daphne wandered without a care for marriage, though her father wished it. When he pushed it, she replied:

> "Let me enjoy my state of maiden bless forever! Artemis' father granted such a boon in days gone by!" Her father did, indeed, yield to her request, but her very loveliness prevented her being what she desired, and her beauty defeated her own wishes.[26]

As soon as Apollo saw Daphne, the poison of Eros's secret shot caused him to fall deeply in love with her. Desire clouded his own great prophetic powers, and he deceived himself with hope. For the only time in his immortal life, Apollo proposed marriage. Gazing at Daphne's lips and looking deeply into her eyes, which were sparkling as bright as stars, he professed his desire, his whole heart aflame. But she darted off and did not hear him imploring her not to run away.

---

[26] Ovid, *Metamorphoses*, i.486.

They sped on, one fueled by hope, the other by fear. Though she was fast, he was swifter, his steps lightened by love. He ran just behind her, his warm breath touching the locks that lay scattered on her neck as he tried to sooth her. When at last her strength was spent, she desperately prayed to her father, or to Mother Earth, to destroy her beauty. Her legs sank into the ground and her body became stiff, wooden. She became the laurel tree, and only her shining loveliness remained.

Apollo embraced his changing love, still feeling her pounding heart beneath the hard exterior. Sadly he proclaimed that if he could not make her his bride, she would become his tree; he made his lyre and quiver from her wood and garlanded his head with her leaves.[27]

Meanwhile, young Artemis went to sit upon the lap of her father, Lord Zeus. She asked him for what she wanted: to be a virgin huntress with a band of nymphs as attendants. With an Olympian nod, Zeus gave her what she asked for and more. The Cyklopes fashioned her a bow and shafts of gold. She represented wild animals and the wild nature within mankind.

Her childhood desires were challenged the day she met the great hunter Orion on Krete. They hunted so successfully that Orion, handsomest of men, boasted that together they would kill all the wild animals of Krete. The broad earth, Gaia, was alarmed by the prospect that they might just accomplish what he proclaimed. The Olympian gods were no happier with Orion than all-nourishing Gaia was, for as always, it displeased them for a goddess to choose a mortal lover. Far-shooting Apollo was particularly vexed by the thought that his virgin sister was falling in love. With Gaia he plotted to bring Orion down.

On a rare day that virgin Artemis and Orion were not hunting together, Gaia placed a giant scorpion in Orion's path. Orion issued a barrage of arrows that bounced harmlessly off the scorpion's bony shell. Undaunted, Orion drew his sword and advanced. But again his mighty blows were unable to penetrate the scorpion's thick shell. Exhausted, and unable to repulse the monster, Orion jumped into the sea and swam away.

---

[27] In another version, provided by Pausanias, *Guide to Greece*, viii.20.1-4, Daphne is a maiden who hunts with her attendants along the Ladon River in Arkadia. The correlation with Artemis is striking. In the Arkadian version, she kills Leucippos of Pisatis and spurns Apollo.

When he had swam so far offshore that his head appeared on land to be just a piece of driftwood, long-haired Apollo appeared beside his sister. Phoebus Apollo taunted her by saying he doubted her archery skill was sufficient for her to strike the floating object way out at sea. Competitive Artemis, who delights in arrows, accepted the challenge and unwittingly killed Orion. When she discovered what she had done, she placed his broad-belted image in the heavens. He follows the star cluster of Pleiades (daughters of the Titan Atlas, one of whom was his grandmother, Alcyone, who resides in the zodiac constellation of Tauros). Pythian Apollo placed the scorpion in the skies to chase Orion and remind him to stay away from his sister.[28]

## Owl-Eyed Athena

Order on Olympos was upset when the Thunderer on High was troubled by an excruciating headache. Lord Zeus called upon clever Prometheus to extricate him from his predicament. It was with great trepidation, and only at the insistence of the loud-thundering Zeus, that the mighty son of Kronos was struck with an axe blow to the head. With a mighty shout, out sprang auburn-haired Athena, fully dressed in armor. The gods were profoundly alarmed at this imposing prodigy until she removed her helmet and revealed herself in a less formidable aspect. Her mother, Metis (meaning "wisdom"), had born her inside Zeus, for he had swallowed Metis when he learned that a son of Metis would be stronger than his father.

Zeus ordered nymphs to escort owl-eyed Athena to the sea god Triton, eldest son of Poseidon, to be raised beside Lake Tritonis. There the nymphs hid her nakedness while she shed her armor and clothes to wash off the afterbirth, a reversal from every other deity, all of whom had been born naked, washed, and then clothed (metaphorically illustrating that stripping the mind of ego and preconceived notions is required to see "naked" wisdom). Born from the head of Zeus, Pallas Athena embodied shrewd,

---

[28] The Hunter and the Great Bear were the earliest Hellenic constellations. Homer did not identify Orion with The Hunter; that association came later. Scorpius was adopted by the Hellenes from the Assyrians. Since Orion sets as Scorpius rises, it was said that Scorpius chased Orion.

scheming intelligence; only later was she associated with philosophical wisdom.

Bright-eyed Athena became the companion of Triton's daughter Pallas (meaning "maiden"), a beautiful and wise girl. Once, while they enthusiastically played war games, all-seeing Zeus feared for his daughter and struck Pallas dead with a thunderbolt or by shaking the Aigis at her. To honor her dead companion, Athena or Hephaistos sculpted her likeness in wood and erected the statue on Olympos. Dark-clouded Zeus would later cause it to fall from the sky so that it might protect the great city of Troy. Called the Palladium, it stood in Athena's temple in Troy until the Hellenes stole it.

## The Limping God, Hephaistos

> Hera, without union with Zeus - for she was very angry and quarreled with her mate - bare famous Hephaistos, who is skilled in crafts more than all the sons of heaven.
>
> —Hesiod of Askre, *Theogony*, seventh century BCE

White-armed Hera produced Hephaistos, blacksmith of the gods, by herself, in anger over Zeus's affairs or in a jealous response to Athena springing unaided from the head of Zeus.

Hera was not pleased with her offspring, for he was not perfect in form, and she threw him out of heaven. The silver-sandaled Nereid Thetis and the Oceanid Eurynome, mother by Zeus of the Kharities, found and cared for wounded Hephaistos in Nereus's palace at the bottom of the sea, halfway between Imbros and Samothrace.[29]

While living with the lovely Nereides, hobbled Hephaistos developed his immense skills. Finally he sent a beautifully crafted golden throne to his mother. She had never seen a more beautiful, ornately designed throne; there was none more fitting for the queen of heaven. But when she sat upon

[29] Homer's *Iliad* includes two accounts of Hephaistos's birth. One agrees with Hesiod—the account presented herein. In the second account, Hephaistos was conceived in the normal manner and it was his father, Zeus, who threw him from heaven for meddling between the lord and his wife Hera, and that was how he became lame.

it, invisible bonds snared her and upended her in ignominious fashion. For a while Hephaistos ignored the many pleas sent to him. Then he relented and returned to Olympos. There he released and was reconciled to his mother.

Hephaistos was thrown from Olympos a second time. Once, but only once, while Zeus and Hera quarreled violently, as they oft did, did Hephaistos dare to intervene on his mother's behalf. Angry Zeus grabbed him by the foot and flung him out of Olympos. Hephaistos fell for a whole day, finally crashing to earth on Lemnos. Although Hephaistos was permitted to return to Olympos, he maintained a forge and a wonderful palace inside the volcano Mosykhos on Lemnos.

## Golden Aphrodite

Zeus invited laughter-loving Aphrodite to join the Olympians; she was alone among the gods who were not the siblings or offspring of Zeus[30] (a testimony to the power of love). She rose out of the foam surrounding the genitals of Ouranos floating in the fish-rich sea off of Cyprus, and from there she became known to the Hellenes as golden Aphrodite. The second-century CE travel guide writer Pausanias of Magnesia says the Assyrians were first to worship Aphrodite, and the Cypriots of Paphos second.[31] On Olympos she was attended to by Eros and Desire.

[30] Although Homer says she was the daughter of Zeus and the sea nymph Dione.

[31] In truth, long before the Assyrian civilization came to be, this love/fertility goddess was worshiped as Inanna in the world's first civilization—that of the Sumerians. To the Assyrians and Babylonians, she was Ishtar; to the Phoenicians, Astarte; to the related Canaanites (which included the Hebrews), Asherah; and to the Amorites of Syria, Atargatis. With Demeter and Persephone already filling the roles of commanding nature's cycles; her worship in Hellas became more narrowly focused on her role as the goddess of love and sex.

Aphrodite and Apollo were the only major Homeric gods not mentioned in Mycenaian texts uncovered so far. This discovery was a surprise for Apollo, but not for Aphrodite, whose Near Eastern roots were obvious. Near Eastern traders from places like Ugarit introduced Aphrodite's cult to the Cypriots. Hellenic traders and colonists who had visited and settled on Cyprus during the twelfth century T / tenth century R BCE were probably responsible for carrying the cult back to Hellas. In her ritual, the use of myrrh and frankincense became almost universal from India to the western Mediterranean during the eighth century BCE. Apollo's background is Anatolian. Some of the lesser gods listed in Mycenaian texts include Eileithyia, the Erinyes, the Titaness Theia, and Theia's children Helios and Selene.

Hephaistos married laughter-loving Aphrodite, but the sweet-garlanded goddess could not find it in her heart to love the god of crafts, he who hobbled on skinny legs that carried his monstrous bulk. She found the dashing war god Ares more to her liking, and they made love secretly in the Olympian house of Hephaistos. Ares gave her much and fouled the marriage and bed of Hephaistos. When their passionate embraces carried on beyond the dawn, all-seeing Helios (the sun) observed them at their sport and promptly told Hephaistos.

Seething in anger against manly Ares, the craftsman plotted his revenge. Inspired rage brought sweat to his brow as he stood by the billows and built a snare to trap the lovers in the act. When he had spun his treacherous device around the lordly posts of his massive bed, he started off to visit the Sintians in the strong citadel of Lemnos, which of all the places on earth was far dearest to him. Ares kept no blind watch and entered the house of the limping god Hephaistos lusting after the love of the sweet-garlanded Cyprian. She was well pleased to lie with him as he led her by the hand to the handsome bed. When their ardent desire was fulfilled, they found it impossible to rise out of bed. Then did the glorious strong-armed smith turn back before reaching Lemnos. He returned to Olympus and found them in their predicament.

Hephaistos cried out in his anger and anguish for the other Olympians to come see. Standing by the bed, his heart grieving, Hephaistos demanded back the bride's price he had paid. Far-shooting Apollo turned to luck-bringing Hermes and asked if he would change places with Ares. Hermes said that he would without hesitation. The two gods laughed. Dark-haired Poseidon was not amused and promised that either Ares would make restitution or he would cover the debt himself. So Hephaistos released them. Aphrodite flew off in her dove-drawn golden chariot for Cyprus to refresh her spirit and let her embarrassment pass. Meanwhile, golden-throned Hera secured Hephaistos a new wife, the youngest of the richly dressed Kharities, Aglaia. Aglaia was the daughter of Zeus and Eurynome, the Oceanid who had once cared for wounded Hephaistos, and according to one myth, the one who had danced on the waters to create the universe.

To Ares and Aphrodite were born Terror and Fear, who pierced men's shields and served as attendants to their violent father. (Sometimes Terror and Fear accompany their mother as well). Ares and Aphrodite also bore lovely Harmonia.

## Luck-Bringing Hermes

Bound by sweet sleep, Hera did not notice Zeus visiting the shy star nymph Maia, and he sired stealthy Hermes. The eldest and fairest of the Pleiades was

> Maia of the lively eyes: Atlas fathered her, outstanding in beauty among his seven dear violet-haired daughters.[32]
>
> A shy goddess she. Ever she avoided the throng of the blessed gods and lived in a shadowy cave, and there the Son of Kronos used to lie with the rich-tressed nymph at dead of night, while white-armed Hera lay bound in sweet sleep: and neither deathless god nor mortal man knew it.[33]
>
> And when the purpose of great Zeus was fulfilled, and the tenth moon with her was fixed in heaven, she was delivered and a notable thing was come to pass. For then she bore a son, of many shifts, blandly cunning, a robber, and a cattle driver, a bringer of dreams, a watcher by night, and a thief at the gates.[34]

Maia's son Hermes was born at dawn and tarried not long by his mother's heavenly womb. Remarkably precocious, he sprang up and, at noon of his first day, stepped outside of his mother's cave and encountered a tortoise. He killed it and pulled out its soft parts. Tying seven strings (in honor of his mother and the six other Pleiades) of sheep guts to the tortoise shell, he invented a new musical instrument, the lyre.

All afternoon he played sweet music as he pondered sheer trickery in his heart—deeds that unscrupulous people pursue in the dark nighttime.

[32] The mid to late sixth-century BCE poet Simonides of Keos, "quoted by Athenaios, Scholars at Dinner", in *Greek Lyric.* Translated by David A. Campbell.
[33] Hesiod, "Homeric Hymn to Hermes" xviii, in *The Homeric Hymns and Homerica.*
[34] Hesiod, "Homeric Hymn to Hermes" iv, in *The Homeric Hymns and Homerica.*

When golden Helios retired, luck-bringing Hermes put down his lyre and slipped out of the sweet-smelling cave. He went to far-off Pieria and stole Phoebus Apollo's cattle, which he drove to the Alpheus River near sandy Pylos while cleverly hiding their tracks. There he slew two for a sacrifice and hid the rest.

He passed through the keyhole of the hall like an autumn breeze and came to the rich interior chamber as rosy-fingered dawn approached. Walking softly and making no noise, he hurried to his cradle and slipped back into his swaddling clothes. Maia, undeceived by his tricks, warned him that the gods would be angry. Young Hermes was unrepentant.

Far-shooter Apollo discovered the theft and divined that the culprit hid on Mount Cyllene in Arkadia. Unable to spot his herd, he grabbed the precocious infant Hermes,[35] who was pretending to sleep in his cradle. Shooting quick glances, Hermes denied the theft despite his older brother's threats. Though he had many wiles, he found the other had as many shifts, so finally the two went to Olympos and stood before their father. Zeus laughed heartily at the audacity of his newborn son, who still cunningly denied the deed. All-seeing Zeus ordered keen-eyed Hermes to give back the cattle, and he readily complied.

Stern Apollo was furious when he discovered that two of his prized cattle had been slaughtered. Hermes very easily softened Apollo's heart when he took to playing his awesome-sounding music. Delighted, Apollo gave the cattle back to Hermes for the pleasure of his music. Giving gift for gift, Hermes gave Apollo the lyre.

The two hastened back to snowy Olympos, delighting in the lyre. Zeus was glad to see them friends and made Hermes herald and guide to mortal travelers in life and in death. He wore his famous winged sandals[36] on his journeys and carried the caduceus (which means "herald's staff"), a golden rod presented to him by Apollo.

[35] Hermes is one of the few Hellenic gods whose name can be clearly traced. Perhaps by intent the gods' names were ambiguous, for they could not be pinned down with a name. But Hermes clearly derives from herma, heaps of stones that were placed on roads, usually at boundaries. Later, a phallic herma was used for demarcation, hence his role as god of travelers and boundaries. His name appears in Mycenaian Linear B texts.

[36] There was a Hittite prototype for winged sandals.

Hermes's son Pan was also born in mountainous Arkadia. His mother[37] had been so frightened by his unexpected appearance (he had goat legs, horns, and an uncouth face already covered with a full beard), that she sprang up and ran away. Then luck-bringing Hermes took his infant son into his arms; very glad at heart was he. The swift messenger Hermes took his infant son to Olympos and proudly showed him off to the delighted gods.

Pan's place was not in the heavenly city of Olympos, but rather in the mountains, where he danced and sang with the nymphs. They sing of the blessed gods while Pan, dressed in a lynx pelt, plays high-pitched songs on pipes while reclined in soft meadows where crocuses and sweet-smelling hyacinths bloom at random in the grass. He invented his instrument, the pan pipes, or syrinx, after pursuing the Arkadian nymph of that name and failing to capture her. On her prayers, she was changed into reeds to avoid him. He made pipes from those reeds and played them as if kissing a dying lover.

---

Exhibit 4.1
The Pleiades—Star Nymphs

In the clear skies above travel seven heavenly sisters, the Pleiades, daughters of the mighty Titan Atlas, who holds broad Ouranos on his powerful shoulders, away from his onetime consort Gaia. Upon lofty Mount Cyllene in Arkadia, the Oceanid Pleione bore these lovely nymphs.

When these nymphs grieved so at the death of their half sisters, the Hyades,[38] the gods honored them with a place in the heavens. Their cluster of stars (one is now invisible) is found in the constellation of Taurus. The lusty hunter Orion chases them nightly across the broad sky.[39]

---

[37] Hermes's mother was usually called a daughter of Dryopes. Her name might be Penelope, and she might later have been confused with the wife of Odysseus.

[38] The Hyades were seven nymphs who earned a place in the skies as the constellation Hyades after they grieved over the death of their brother, Hylas (meaning "to rain"). Hylas was killed by a boar or a lion. Zeus placed them among the stars. Thus, this is a weather metaphor: the death of rain is a clear, star-studded night. Both Homer and Hesiod mention the Hyades.

[39] Hyginos says that for seven years Orion chased lovely Pleione and the Pleiades before they were placed in the skies to save them. The story was not grounded in myth and probably arose to explain why the constellation Orion follows the Pleiades in the night skies; after all, one of them was Orion's grandmother.

In the years before they ascended into the heavens, the exceedingly beautiful Pleiades attracted the gods as lovers. We have already encountered Maia, eldest and fairest of the Pleiades, mother of Hermes by Zeus, and dark-faced Elektra, who had the dubious distinction of being the only rape victim on holy Olympos. She clung to the Palladium carved by virgin Athena for protection, but to no avail. Zeus bent her will to his desire and flung her and the Palladium away. They landed on the island of Samothrace, and there she bore Dardanos (an early king of Troy). Again Elektra stirred the great lord's desire and in time bore a second son, Iasion.[40] Lovely Taygete's flight from the Thunderer on High was assisted by the huntress Artemis, who changed her into a doe to escape him. Cloud Gatherer Zeus merely changed her back, and she raised the son she bore him, Lacedaemon (an early king of Sparta), on the mountain range named for her.

Poseidon found willing lovers among the Pleiades and kept them on opposite sides of the Straits of Euripus. Alcyone lay in wait on the Boiotia shore for Poseidon's saltwater kisses. She was a favorite of his, and often he came to her. She bore him Hyperes and Anthas, two early kings of Troizen, and later Hyrieus, Anthedon, and a daughter named Aithouse. The Pleiades Celaino also slept with earth-shaking Poseidon, and their son Lykos of Euboea was among his favorite children. Poseidon saw to it that Lykos received a home on the Isle of the Blessed after his earthly life ended.

The two remaining Pleiades married mere mortals, although they were at least of royal blood. Merope married death-cheating Sisyphos and raised her family in Korinth. Bright Asterope married violent king Oinomaos of Harpina, son of Ares, and their daughter Hippodameia was far-famed for her beauty.

As to which was the dim star,[41] there is no agreement. It could have been Merope, blushing in shame for having married a mortal—and a scoundrel at that. It might have been Elektra, hiding her face in grief over the fall of Troy, the city her son Dardanos built. It could have been Asterope, dimming in grief for her dead husband.

---

[40] The Hellenic historian Diodoros, in *Library of History*, v.47, adds Harmonia as an offspring of Zeus and Elektra, perhaps an allegory to the promise that the mysteries bore harmony in one's life. Most authors identify Ares and Aphrodite as the parents of Harmonia.

[41] One of the stars burned out in ancient times. There is no agreement as to which one of the Pleiades it was.

## The Olympian Council

Once precocious Hermes joined the Olympians, the supreme council of twelve was complete.[42] Most of them dwelt with Zeus on heavenly Olympos. The males were Zeus, Poseidon (who spent most of his time beneath the Aigaian Sea, ruling over the oceans from his splendid palace—golden chambers he shared with his queen, the Nereid Amphitrite), Apollo, Ares, Hephaistos, and Hermes. Hades chose not to be involved in the affairs of the living and was not on the council. He rarely left his pale palace even though his wife Persephone spent half the year with her mother, Demeter. The six goddesses on the council were Hera, Demeter, Hestia, Athena, Artemis, and Aphrodite. It was Themis's duty to call the Olympians to council, and she always received the first cup at festivals.

## Terrible Typhoeus

Gaia was as furious with the new sky-king Zeus as she had been with Kronos and Ouranos beforehand. Her rage against the Olympians was for imprisoning her beloved sons, the Titans.[43] By Tartaros she conceived Typhoeus, who embodied the power of his all-nourishing mother Gaia's terrors; he was the biggest and tallest monster ever. His body was covered in wings, and jets of fire shot from his mouth.

Typhoeus attacked Olympos, and the trembling gods fled to Egypt, cowering in the guise of animals.[44] Athena alone held her ground and taunted Zeus until he returned to fight, armed with thunderbolts and a sickle. He pummeled Typhoeus with thunderbolts and in close quarters struck him down with an adamantine sickle. Typhoeus fled and dark-clouded Zeus pursued him back to Mount Kasios on the Syrian side of

[42] The council of twelve has Anatolian parallels. Twelve supreme Hittite gods are mentioned, and the Lycians of Xanthos built a temple to the twelve supreme deities in their marketplace.

[43] Hesiod says Gaia was infuriated over the Titans' treatment, while others say it was the death of her sons the Gigantes that angered her. Either way, it was the strong forces of nature being subdued that she objected to. Apollodoros's *Library*, vi.3, and Nonnos's *Dionysos,* i, tell the myth.

[44] As the Roman historian Lucian pointed out, this part of the myth was added in an attempt to map the Greco-Roman gods to the Egyptian pantheon. Egyptian deities were routinely displayed with animal faces. The myth of Typhoeus borrows heavily from Egyptian, Mesopotamian, and Hittite themes.

the Amanos Mountains.[45] Overconfident Zeus grappled with the monster until Typhoeus overpowered him and got hold of the sickle. Typhoeus cut out the sinews of the god's hands and feet and carried the helpless god to nearby Cilicia, where he hid him in the Kercyrian cave of his speckled serpent spouse Echidna.

While Echidna stood guard, keen-eyed Hermes and Aigipan arrived and tricked her. After they restored the sinews of awful Zeus, the king of the gods and men returned to Olympos for a fresh supply of thunderbolts. He rushed back into the fray, this time riding in a chariot drawn by winged horses. Carefully staying out of the monster's reach, Zeus pelted him relentlessly until he withdrew to mythical Mount Nysa (possibly in Phrygia). There the Moirai persuaded Typhoeus to eat ephemeral fruits to increase his strength. Instead it weakened him, and he fled to Mount Haimos in Thrace. The hissing monster was still powerful enough to break off boulders as large as mountains and fling them at his tormentor. Zeus deflected them back with thunderbolts, and the monster's blood spilled out. Staggering, he fled through the sea to Sicily. Relentlessly Zeus pursued the terrible monster until he threw Mount Aetna on top of him, pinning him helplessly below.[46]

At his fall, Typhoeus's semen mixed with earth, and from it sprang the mighty dragon that guarded the Golden Fleece in Colchis. Sometimes Typhoeus struggles to break free and the earth shakes; at other times his venomous breath melts rocks that then spew out of the mountain. Zeus must be wary lest angry Gaia raise up another great monster.

Troubles with the Titans did not end with the great battle for supremacy. Prometheus chose to champion men, whom the son of Kronos held in contempt. He beseeched Zeus to end the gods' requirement that during a sacrifice the whole slaughtered animal must be burned as an offering for the gods' pleasure. Prometheus asked for Zeus to share the spoils with men.

---

[45] The site is now called Hebel-el-Akra. It is the same mountain where the Hittite stone giant Ullikummi resided. Ullikummi fought against the Hittite pantheon. Mesopotamian Gilgamesh defeated Huwawa, (meaning "whose breath was fire"), in the nearby mountains of Lebanon. It marked a boundary between Indo-European and Semitic language speakers.

[46] Another myth says the Gigante Encelados is pinned under Mount Aetna. Typhoeus seems to have personified the terrors of natural phenomenon, especially volcanoes. Ancient Hellas was ringed by active volcanoes, none more fearsome than the volcano of Thera, which devastated the island during the time of the Minoan civilization.

Zeus agreed. Prometheus then deceived Zeus into allowing mankind to keep the better portion of the spoils. Zeus quickly realized his error.

> "Son of Iapetos, clever above all! So, I see you have not forgotten your cunning arts!" So spoke Zeus in anger, whose wisdom is everlasting; and from that time he was always mindful of the trick, and would not give the power of unwearying fire to the Malian race of mortal men who lived on the earth. But the noble son of Iapetos outwitted him and stole the far-seen gleam and unwearying fire in a hollow fennel stalk.[47]

Zeus, enraged at the audacity of Prometheus, ordered him chained in the Caucasian Mountains.[48] Then loud-thundering Zeus saw to it that man did not long profit from these more comfortable conditions. He ordered the limping god Hephaistos to build Pandora (meaning "all gifts"), the first woman, to be created with craftiness, deceitfulness, and a generally vile nature; she was the price to be paid for beneficial fire. Athena girded and clothed her with silvery raiment, and down from her head she spread over Pandora an embroidered veil, wondrous to see. They presented her to gullible Epimetheus, Prometheus's brother. Epimetheus accepted the alluring gift despite repeated warnings from his now absent brother not to accept the gifts of the Olympians. She brought to earth as her dowry a jar or box filled with other "gifts" from the Stronger Ones. When Epimetheus opened the box on their wedding night, a swarm of troubles was released, along with a single gift—hope.

## Olympic Myths

Only once was there rebellion on Olympos. Hera, Poseidon, Apollo, and the other Olympians hid Zeus's thunderbolts and tied him down with rawhide thongs as he slept. While they taunted and laughed at him, the

[47] Hesiod, *Theogeny*.

[48] The Hellenes were absolutely right that the domestication of fire separated men from beasts, bringing a new world order. However, it would fit better chronologically if it were Kronos, god of brute nature, who punished Prometheus for giving man that advantage. Fire was domesticated in the Age of Gold. It does make sense that it would be the civilizing god Zeus who eventually freed and restored Prometheus. Another interpretation is that the fire Prometheus gave to mankind was the spirit of self-conscious knowledge.

Nereid Thetis brought the hundred-handed one, Briareos, to Olympos, and he untied the knots. For instigating the revolt, Zeus hung Hera upside down, and Poseidon and Apollo were forced to serve King Laomedon of Troy for an eternal year. The other gods were pardoned because they had acted under duress. Zeus made them all swear never to rebel again.

Apollo, god of the silver bow, was forced to serve a mortal a second time, in punishment for murder. Hades had vehemently complained to Zeus about a new order, introduced by Asclepius, in which mankind could return from the house of Hades. In support of his brother, Zeus killed Asclepius with a thunderbolt. Enraged at Zeus for striking down his son Asclepius, who had cured the dead, Apollo sought to deny Zeus of his advantage, the thunderbolt. Consequently, Apollo slew the Cyklopes, crafters of the thunderbolt, and their spirits still haunt the caverns of Mount Aetna on Sicily to this day.

## Age of the Race of Bronze

The arrival of the younger generation of Olympian gods corresponds to the time when the Neolithic Age was replaced by the Bronze Age. Zeus willed that a new race be born. Most instrumental among the younger gods were the smithy god Hephaistos, who taught man about metalworking; the craftsman goddess Athena, who gave the olive to mankind; and the oracular god Apollo, who uttered the gods' prophecies to men. But the era opened with the birth of bloodthirsty Ares, the Thracian-born god of war. Archaeology has indeed proven that the Early Bronze Age was a far more violent than the era before it, just as Hesiod says.

> Then Zeus the father made yet a third race of men, of Bronze, not like the silver in anything. Out of ash trees he made them, a terrible and fierce race, occupied with the woeful work of Ares and with acts of violence, not eater of grain, their stern hearts being of adamant; unshaped hulks, with great strength and indescribable arms growing from their shoulders above their stalwart bodies. They had bronze armor, bronze houses, and with bronze they labored, as dark iron was not available. They were laid low by their own hands, and they went to chill Hades' house

> of decay leaving no names: mighty though they were, dark
> death got them, and they left the bright sunlight.[49]

Bronze tools were preferred to stone tools because they were sharper, thus making agriculture tools more efficient and weapons more formidable. The Bronze Age saw significant technological advances: superior metal tools; improved farming yields; intensive cultivation of grapes, olives, and figs; and improved animal husbandry. These advances led to rapid population growth. Soon the potter's wheel was invented in response to the need to store and transport goods in better and cheaper containers. As a result, the first cities developed. Grapes and olives complemented grain production because they grow in soils poorly suited for grain and require attention at times when farmers do not need to tend to cereals.

The first Aigaian basin cities arose at Troy in Anatolia and Thermi on Lesbos (2920T/2670R BCE). Within a century, cities at Lerne and Tiryns in the Peloponnesos, Knossos on Krete, Poliokhni on Lemnos, and other sites began developing.[50] The metal-rich Cyclades were also permanently settled for the first time. Southern and central Hellas gained prominence due to more its more abundent metals and because the area is well suited for olive and vine cultivation.

This time of economic and cultural growth resulted in the first palaces being constructed. Early palaces were built at the famous House of Tiles in the walled Peloponnesian city of Lerne, and a larger palace was built at nearby Tiryns. Kretan palaces were built, somewhat later, at several sites. It was probably at the Kretan palaces that olives were first cultivated in Hellas—a skill learned from the Semites of Syria. Besides serving as the residence for the royal family and their retinue, the palaces also functioned in the administration of the nation, in state religious ceremonies, and in business activities, such as manufacturing, warehousing, and trade. A

---

[49] Hesiod, *Works and Days*.

[50] The first city-states grew out of the mud-hut villages of Sumer in modern Iraq (3500T/3250R BCE), and within a few hundred years they had a hierarchical order to them. They began using valuable new inventions, such as the wheel, writing, mathematics, bronze, and, of course, taxes. This new civilized order evolved from farming villages. It may have taken as long as a millennium for the technology to reach the Aigaian Sea basin and for cities to rise there. The palaces had the resources necessary for long-term care of olives and the storage facilities needed for large-scale olive and wine production.

division of labor began, and it grew throughout the Bronze Age until huge social inequities developed.

The cities of Hellas were destroyed around 2265T/2015R BCE and again around 1900T/1650R BCE. It has long been argued by Gimbutas and others that Indo-European speaking tribes were the destroyers. The first wave did not arrive with the horse, which was introduced into Hellas with the second wave of destruction. Both times the invaders arrived in Hellas by way of Thrace—the birthplace of Ares and home of Indo-European tribes.

After both disasters, the sites were reoccupied, each time on a smaller scale than before. Hellas endured a long depression after the second disaster (the mythic flood), while the islands were spared disaster. Consequently, the uninterrupted Minoan culture surpassed its related neighbors on the mainland. The Minoans of Krete performed architectural feats unheard of around the Aigaian; they built multistoried palaces with windows and balconies. In addition, the first beehive-shaped tombs, called tholos tombs, were constructed in the Mesara Plain of Krete and used by whole clans over many generations.

Hesiod provided the prevailing Hellenic belief that members of the Early Bronze Age race were not the ancestors of their own Heroic Age ancestors, and Hellenic myths are full of stories concerning the pre-Hellenic Bronze Age inhabitants of Hellas—the Pelasgians. The Hellenes did not know where the brutish men of bronze came from and indirectly indicated that they were in Hellas before the Hellenes by calling these ancient inhabitants earthborn.

## Hesiod's Bronze Age Myths

The superior technology of the earliest bronzesmiths was considered magical, a craft that surely came from the gods. They were the followers of Hephaistos. When Hera cast Hephaistos from Olympos, he was cared for by the earliest Lemnian inhabitants—the Sintian tribe. The limping god Hephaistos rewarded the Sintians with the knowhow to cast hard metal alloys, and an important Early Bronze Age city arose on Lemnos at Poliokhni. "Magical" craftsmen tribes were identified with places where some of the earliest cities arose; namely Krete (Kouretes and Dactyls), Lemnos (Sintians), Lesbos (Heliades), Rhodes (Telkhines and Heliades), Samothrace (Kabeiroi), and Troy (Kouretes and Dactyls).

Some thought that metallurgy was first developed by the Dactyls at Troy or Krete.[51] The nymph Ankhiale was said to have born them on nearby Mount Ida (there is a Mount Ida in both places). The Dactyls Celmis, Damnaimeneus, and Delas (Scythes) discovered smelting bronze while visiting Cyprus.[52] The Dactyls left their home in Troy for Krete (or vice versa). Along the way they stopped on Samothrace, where they dedicated the first Samothracian mysteries to Rhea/Cybele. The female Dactyls remained on Samothrace and bore the Kabeiroi. The males continued on and spread the Bronze Age throughout the Aigaian Sea basin.

Eldest Herakles (Akmon) was the leading Dactyl. He led his brothers Epimedes (Celmis), Iasos, Idas, and Paionaios (Damnaimenos) to the Peloponnesos and celebrated the first Olympic Games. The Dactyls Titias and Cyllenos became dispensers of doom and assessors for Cybele in Phrygia (central Anatolia).

---

[51] Krete and Troy each had ancient, but distinct, Bronze Age cultures that show little interaction. However, storytellers knew both places held important ancient civilizations, and many concocted a connection between them. In such stories, the Dactyls move to Krete, and according to first-century BCE historian Strabo of Amasia in Pontos, it is a Kretan who founds Troy. Diodoros's *Library of History*, v.64, quotes the fourth-century BCE historian Ephoros of Cyme in saying they were from Mount Ida in Troas and on the way to Krete they founded the Samothracian mysteries. Apollonios's *Argonautika*, i, suggests that Ankhiale bore them on Krete by saying that she clutched the earth of Oaxos (Tylissos) while delivering Titas and Cyllenos. It is very possible that the Teukrians (Trojans) were first to smelt bronze in the Aigaian and that they received knowledge of it from mineral-rich central Anatolia via Cilicia (where the earliest known copper tools have been found at Mersin) and Cyprus. On the other hand, it is possible that metallurgy spread across the underbelly of Anatolia from Cilicia/Cyprus and reached Krete before it did overland to Troy.

[52] The third-century BCE stela known as the Parian Marble says that the Dactyls invented iron smelting on Mount Ida, but Pliny's *Natural History*, vii.56, states that Celmis and Damnaimeneus learned it on Cyprus—where the Hellenes probably learned it. Either way, it was bronze, not iron, they smelted. Cyprus was the leading supplier of copper, which when combined with tin makes bronze (the name Cyprus probably derives from the Semitic word *kpr*, meaning "henna-colored"—the color of copper. The Hellenes rendered the name as Kupros; the Romans, Cyprus. The word "copper" comes from the Latin *cuprum*, from Kupros). Iron smelting first developed on Cyprus, but not until after the Mycenaian era. Clement (in *Stromateis* i.16.75), like Pliny, quotes Hesiod's poem "The Dactyls" as his source, but he gets the metal right (bronze).

## Athens Becomes a City

Very few myths deal with the time before the Hellenes. Athens provides us with an important one. According to the Athenians, Kekrops, one of the earthborn men, succeeded Aktaios at Athens. Kekrops had married Aktaios's daughter Agraulos. Kekrops was born of the sea and earth, the son of Oceanos and Gaia. During his thirty-year reign, Athens rose from village to city. He renamed the region from Akte to Cekropia. He was the first to call Zeus supreme and honored him with a bloodless sacrifice of honey cakes. Kekrops and the Heliades of Rhodes first recognized the birth of Athena, the birth of the cultured spirit of wisdom. While the Heliades hastily sacrificed to her in order to be the first men to do so, Kekrops carefully prepared his sacrifice. Pallas Athena smiled upon the Heliades and taught them to use bronze, but she smiled even more so on Kekrops.

## Kekrops Arbitrates

It was customary for Indo-European gods to claim as their property nations as they first developed. In Attike, Zeus appointed Kekrops as arbiter, tasked with deciding between the rival claims of Poseidon and Athena. Kekrops[53] stood on the acropolis before the two great spirits—an impressive figure himself, for he had a man's body ending in a coiled snake's tail rather than legs. Kekrops calmly told the contestants that true patronage shows in the benefits bestowed upon the people. He then asked what each contestant offered.

Elder Poseidon stepped forward first. Pointing his trident at a nearby rock, a salt spring called Erekhteis erupted to symbolize the sea power that would belong to Athens. Next it was bright-eyed Athena's turn, and she caused an olive tree to sprout nearby, and the Classical Athenians believed the same one survived into their time. Classical Athenians debated the wisdom of

[53] Hyginos, *Fabulai*, ii.29, quoting the fourth-century BCE Athenian orator Eubulos, identifies the constellation Aquarius (meaning "water bearer") with Kekrops because in his time water was used in religious ceremonies because men had not yet learned about wine.

the decision, but Kekrops chose the versatile olive,[54] which provided food, cooking oil, lighting oil, soap, and a perfume base and was used in treating wool and linen cloth.

Loud-roaring Poseidon was furious. His raging seas flooded Cekropia. The sea god eventually relented and allowed his gift of sea power to come to fruition.

Kekrops and his shapely wife Agraulos bore a son named Erysikhthon and three beautiful daughters. While his father still lived, Erysikhthon died at sea while returning from Delos. Cerkrops's lovely maiden daughters attracted the attention of the gods. The eldest daughter, Agraulos, named for her mother, danced into the passionate embrace of manly Ares. She bore him Alcippe.

## Miraculous Birth of Erikhthonios

During the reign of Kekrops, bright-eyed Athena came often to visit her beloved city. Once, the smith-god Hephaistos became filled with desire and tried to forcefully deflower the great maiden when she would not consent willingly. The pure virgin Athena struggled mightily against him, and he prematurely ejaculated upon her thigh. Disgustedly, she wiped his semen off with wool and flung it to the ground. It was not Hephaistos's nature to behave so grossly; he was the victim of a malicious joke played

[54] Wine and olive cultivation were considered the hallmarks of civilization, and along with metallurgy, they brought southern and central Hellas into ascendancy over the grain-growing regions of Thessalia and Macedonia. The first palaces in Hellas were built on Krete, and they afforded the resources necessary to grow grapes and olives in mass quantities.

Since wild grapes and olives grow in Hellas, it is difficult to determine when they were first cultivated there. The first evidence of olive cultivation comes from Syria ca. 3000T/2750R BCE. Pollen samples clearly indicate olives were widely produced by ca. 2000 BCE. Symbols representing wine, olives, and figs are among the earliest written symbols uncovered in the first palaces of Krete (1800/1550 BCE).

Neolithic winemaking from wild grapes is attested to in many areas, including Hellas. However, since the Hellenic name for wine is derived from a word common throughout the Near East, the technology to produce wine commercially was probably imported. Grape cultivation and wine production may have first developed in Georgia, Armenia, or Anatolia (ca. 6000T/5750R BCE, about the time sheep were domesticated in the nearby Zagros Mountains). It was in the earliest palaces that large-scale production first arose around the Aigaian Sea.

upon him by still-smarting Poseidon. The sea lord had told Hephaistos that Athena was on her way to see him and that she secretly hoped to have violent love made to her. In truth she wanted him to make her some weapons. From the earth of the acropolis and the semen of Hephaistos, Erikhthonios (meaning "much earth")[55] was conceived.

Wise Athena wrapped the miraculously conceived Erikhthonios in warm blankets and placed him in a chest that she gave to Kekrops's daughters. The newborn baby resembled Kekrops in appearance; his human body ended in a snake's tail. Bright-eyed Athena did not tell her chosen keepers what was inside but warned them not to look in. But man is a curious being, and if he is forbidden to do something, the more he desires to do it.

Curious Agraulos tried to convince her sisters to disobey. Agraulos ripped off the lid of the chest, hoping to find some valuable treasure inside. Herse looked on. Pandrosos, who had chosen the call of Athena and virginity, had argued against the plan and wisely looked away, though she too was very curious. Immediately, snakes darted from the basket. Agraulos and Herse were frightened and jumped back in terror, falling to their deaths off the north face of the acropolis. Athena heard of the transgression while she was carrying a large rock to buttress the acropolis. Stunned, she dropped it, and the Lykettos remains close by the acropolis but of no use to it.

In *Metamorphoses,* Ovid disputes Pausanias's report (*Guide to Greece* i.18.2–3) that Agraulos and Herse fell to their deaths. He says that Agraulos accepted gold from Hermes in exchange for opening the chamber to her youngest sister, Herse, but at the appointed time, jealous Agraulos kept the doors barred. Hermes turned Agraulos to stone and forced his way into Herse's bedchamber, and she conceived beautiful Cephalos.

Athena rewarded Pandrosos's obedience by appointing her high priestess while the goddess raised Erikhthonios in her Temenos. Pallas Athena then cared for Erikhthonios so tenderly that she was often thought of as his mother.[56] Also on the acropolis, Kekrops raised his beautiful orphaned grandchildren, Cephalos (Herse's son) and Alcippe (Agraulos's daughter).

---

[55] Erikhthonios and Athena might have originally been the local version of the goddess and her dying consort—the god who is born in winter and dies every summer. Erikhthonios was the divine child, the newborn spirit of vegetation.

[56] The Athenians made their goddess's virginity a symbol of the city's invincibility. Originally Athena was probably raped by Hephaistos and the mother of Erikhthonios in the usual way.

Cephalos's beauty attracted rosy-fingered Eos (meaning "dawn"), who carried him off to be her lover on Cyprus.[57] There she bore him a son, Phaethon. Young Phaethon became as lovely as his father and suffered a similar fate. Laughter-loving Aphrodite carried him off to be her lover, and he kept watch over her Cypriot temples. Erikhthonios was believed to have invented the war chariot during his conquest of Eleusis.[58]

## King Kranaos

Because old Kekrops died without a male heir, the kingdom was given to Kranaos, a leading elder in Kekrops's court. Kekrops was buried in a style not afforded to men before his time. Kekrops was buried in a tomb located in Athena's sacred acropolis Temenos, near where the Erekhtheion would later be built.[59]

Ares, god of the blood-curdling yell, brought violence to Attike. Always passionate, whether as a warrior, father, or lover, stout-hearted Ares was devoted to his motherless daughter, Alcippe. Her beauty intoxicated Haliartos (meaning "sea foam"), Poseidon's son by the nymph Euryte, and as he tried to rape her, Ares interceded and slew the youth. The earth

---

[57] The story of Hermes's son Cephalos is often confused with Phocian Cephalos. The more ancient sources of the story (in Hesiod's *Theogony* and the fifth-century BCE Athenian playwright Euripides's *Hippolytos*) do not say which Cephalos was abducted but clearly separate the myth from Phocian Cephalos, eponym of Cephallenia Island. Ovid's *Metamorphoses* and *Art of Love* ingeniously combine the stories of Eos's abduction of Athenian Cephalos with the infidelity of Phocian Cephalos's wife.

[58] Although carts pulled by donkeys, asses, or cattle appear much earlier, the first war chariots (two-wheeled with spokes and pulled by horses) appear much later. The war chariot was quite likely introduced by the Indo-Aryan Mitanni tribe, who began to dominate the Hurrians of Eastern Anatolia ca. 1800T/1550R BCE. War chariot use spread rapidly from Anatolia as far as Hellas in the west to India in the east and to Nubia in the south. The first evidence of chariots in Hellas comes from a stele in one of the earliest shaft graves dug at Mycenai (mid sixteenth century T / late fourteenth century R BCE). Before that time there was not enough wealth in Hellas for chariot warfare to thrive.

[59] If Kekrops introduced olive cultivation, he could not have been buried in a tholos tomb, as the earliest tholos tombs were built more than a millennium later. However, it was logical for the Athenians to identify their first king with the most ancient building on the Akropolis.

shaker, Poseidon, demanded that the Deathless Ones of Olympos try Ares on the Areiopagos.[60] Ares was acquitted.

## Pelasgians of Arkadia

The men of bronze became known as Pelasgians for an early leader who was taller and wiser than the rest. Pelasgos married the Oceanid Meliboia and fathered Lykaon (meaning "wolf"), Temenos (meaning "holy place"), and Phrastor. Lykaon succeeded his father and founded the first Arkadian city, Lykosoura.

Besides the introduction of civic life, Lykaon also instituted the local worship of Hermes and Zeus Lykaios. Though primitive, Lykaon was a pious man who initiated the Lykaian Games.[61] However, his sacrifice of a child was unacceptable to mighty Zeus. Lord Zeus punished him by changing him into a wolf. Lykaon regained his human form after an eternal year (eight years) by abstaining from tasting human flesh. Lykaon fathered many sons by many wives, and they spread out across Arkadia, gathering the Pelasgians into towns and villages.

Word spread about the heinous crimes (specifically human sacrifice) of the savage sons of Lykaon, and eventually word reached the halls of lofty Olympos. So poorly did the men of Bronze behave that the gods withdrew one by one from the affairs of men. The last to abandon mankind was the

---

[60] The Areiopagos was generally believed to be the first court for homicide. Several mythic trials took place here: this one, Daidalos's conviction for killing his nephew, Cephalos's acquittal for killing his wife Prokne, and Orestes's acquittal for killing his mother.

[61] Originally, a primitive rain-making cult dedicated to Zeus celebrated upon Mount Lykaios in Arkadia. Their solemn ceremony occasionally included human sacrifices. According to Pausanias (*Guide to Greece,* ii.6) and the first-century BCE Roman Varro (*FGrHis,* 320), quoting the Hellenistic writer Euanthes, the flesh of the human sacrificial victim was mixed with other sacrificial meat, and the one who ate of it became the werewolf priest until the next sacrifice. He was then relieved unless he was the one who ate the human portion again. Euanthes said the period between sacrifices was an eternal year (eight years), while Pausanias says it was ten years. Rain-making rituals were also performed on other mountaintops, such as Parnassus near Delphi and Laphystios in Boiotia, as well as in Thessalia. Human sacrifice is hinted at in those places as well. Such a great sacrifice, which continued very late, attests to the importance of water in dry Hellas. More sophisticated Hellenes of later times were aghast at the human sacrifices and added that Zeus was repulsed by them and responded with the great flood.

shy virgin goddess Astraia (meaning "starry"). She withdrew to the heavens as the constellation Virgo. She was either a daughter of Asterios and Eos or orderly Themis's daughter Dike.

Zeus rose in righteous indignation, commanding his Arkadian-born son Hermes to join him in an investigation. At Trapezos they saw the eldest son of Lykaon, Mainalos, suggesting to his brothers that they test the divinity of all-seeing Zeus by serving the flesh of their youngest brother Nyktimos in a soup. Hot-tempered Zeus turned the men into wolves and restored Nyktimos to life.

Back on Olympos, Zeus remained infuriated by the actions of base men, particularly the sons of Lykaon. Angry storm clouds poured out a deluge, as it was his will to cleanse the earth of mankind. The flood was devastating, but the king of gods and men relented somewhat and allowed a pious remnant to survive. The great flood to erase evil men occurred during the reign of Kranaos of Athens.

## Demise of the Bronze Age Men in Hellas

Though chained in agony, Prometheus warned his only son, Deukalion, born by the Nereid Pronoe, of the impending storm. Deukalion ruled as king over the people living in the glens below the former Titan mountain stronghold of Othyrs. The Titan Prometheus told Deukalion to build an ark and prepare for the deluge. Deukalion heeded his father and floated safely with his bride, Pyrrha, during nine days and nine nights of driving rain. They were a pious couple, and Zeus had compassion upon them. Finally the rain stopped, and when the waters receded, their boat beached on Mount Parnassus.[62]

Safely aground the couple gave thanks and prayed to the Titan goddess of order, Themis. They grieved for their lost friends and family and were sobered by the destruction they had witnessed. They approached the Delphic oracle with solemn prayers to restore mankind.

[62] The Deukalion flood myth is the Hellenic version of the Mesopotamian flood myth, which dates back at least as far as the third millennium BCE. This story is included in the Sumerian epic poem *Gilgamesh*, in which the ark is built by Utnapishtim. To the Hebrews, he was Noah. The Hellenic and Hebrew belief that such a destructive flood must have been the act of an angry god is a late addition.

# Rise of the Hellenes

## Middle Helladic Bronze Age (MHI–II); Beginning of Hesiod's Age of Heroes

> After the earth covered up this (Bronze) race too, Zeus son of Kronos made yet a fourth one upon the rich-pastured earth, a more righteous and noble one, the godly race of the heroes who are called demigods, our predecessors on the boundless earth. And as for them, ugly war and fearful fighting destroyed them, some below seven-gated Thebes, the Kadmeian country, as they battled for Oidipous' flocks, and others it led in ships over the great abyss of the sea to Troy on account of lovely-haired Helene. There some of them were engulfed by the consummation of death, but to some Zeus the father, son of Kronos, granted a life and home apart from men, and settled them at the ends of the earth. These dwell with carefree heart in the Isles of the Blessed. Once, beside deep-swirling Oceanos: fortunate heroes, for whom the grain-giving soil bears its honey-sweet fruits thrice a year.
>
> —Hesiod of Askre, *Works and Days*, seventh century BCE

While Hesiod says the men of the Bronze Age died by war (and certainly the early to mid Bronze Age culture perished as a result of the violent destruction of their cities), the Hellenes gradually came to accept the Near Eastern motif that the earlier race had died in a great flood. The time of the flood was when the Helladic cities were sacked and the population of Hellas sank to its lowest level since the Stone Age. It was a time of extreme poverty. Marija Gimbutas and many scholars afterward presumed the destruction was due to invaders and in synthesis with the decimated native population (Pelasgians) giving rise to a new tribe—the Hellenes.[63] Certainly Hesiod believed the birth of the Hellenes was now—and with them the beginning of the Heroic Age. Their glory came with horses, swords, and chariots.

There was certainly a great decline in Hellas after the cities were destroyed. What followed was a time of melding of Pelasgian and Indo-European elements into a new Hellenic culture. According to Hesiod a new age began after the disastrous flood subsided, and the population of Hellas began to rebound under Deukalion ca. 1835T/1585R BCE. The nineteenth-century CE archaeologist Heinrich Schliemann labeled the new era of recovery the Minyan Age after a distinctive pottery style first discovered at the city of Orkhomenos in Boiotia (where mythic King Minyas of Orkhomenos would rule later). Homer calls only three cities rich: Troy, Mycenai, and Orkhomenos. We know that this new race of men were Indo-European and Hellenic speakers because they left written records; they were the first literate society on the European mainland (their Linear B texts have been deciphered).

## Deukalion, Father of the Hellenes

Deukalion, son of clever Prometheus and his wife, the Nereid (sea nymph) Pronoe (meaning "foresight"), and his lovely bride Pyrrha, daughter of Prometheus's dim-witted brother Epimetheus and his wife, Pandora, bringer of evil omens, survived the great flood Zeus sent to destroy the evil race of bronze. Thankful to be alive but stunned by the devastation they had witnessed, the couple approached the holy Delphic oracle with

[63] The introduction of the horse at this time has led many archaeologists to believe that there were invaders at this time and that they were the Indo-European ancestors of the Hellenic language (although they admit there could have been other earlier Indo-European tribes in Hellas as well). Professor Mallory, author of *In Search of the Indo-Europeans*, and other linguists agree, indicating that this timeframe fits for the development of the distinct Hellenic language. Hesiod seems to support this position as well by claiming that the Hellenes came into being at this time.

solemn prayers, beseeching the gods to create a new race of men to share the earth with them.

Their sorrow magnified when they received a cryptic answer calling on them to throw the bones of their mother over their shoulders. Believing the request to be an outrage against their ancestors, they held back; literal-minded Pyrrha was especially offended at the demand. Then bright Deukalion surmised that the oracle meant for them to throw the stones of Mother Earth over their shoulders in order to repopulate the world. Hesitantly at first, Deukalion tossed boulders over his shoulders, and happily, men sprang up. Pyrrha followed his lead, and women sprang up behind her. So without the joy of blessed wedlock, these two sired a new earthborn race at the very center of the earth; they were simply called the Leleges (meaning "people").

Joyfully Deukalion led his new tribesmen down from the mountain and settled in the open hill country that came to be called Lokris, nestled between towering Mount Parnassus and the sea. Deukalion built the seaside city of Opus as his new capital. He also traveled to far off Dodona, in Epeiros, to establish a shrine in thanks to all-seeing Zeus.

With Deukalion we have the first "Hellenic" man, a man whose culture and language have been well documented. His descendants naturally considered the new race to be superior to the brutish men of bronze. Their heroic ancestors retained the admirable warlike spirit of those that came before, but they also enjoyed refinements of civilization.

Deukalion and his wife, through wedlock, did their part as well to repopulate the wild land. Their descendants led Leleges colonists throughout Hellas. Their eldest son, Hellen, married the nymph Orseis and built the great palace city of Iolkos not far from the Thessalian birthplace of his parents. Hellen was the eponym of the Hellenes (meaning "Greek speakers"). His second son, Amphiktyon, was the first man to interpret dreams and the first to mix water with wine. The Hellenes believed that wine was one of the hallmarks of civilization; its cultivation made a great distinction between their heroic forefathers and the brutish men of bronze. After hearing about the wealth of Athens, Amphiktyon led many Leleges south into Attike. He became the king of Athens, where the family of serpent-legged Cerkrops once ruled.

Exhibit 5.1
Tribal Dialects and Their Founder
(Descendants of Hellen are in italics)

| Dialect Group | Tribe | Eponym | Eponym's Lineage |
|---|---|---|---|
| *Aiolic* | *Aiolians* | *Aiolos* | *Son of Hellen, son of Deukalion* |
| | *Boiotians* | *Boiotos* | *Grandson of Aiolos, son of Hellen* |
| | *Magnesians* | *Magnes* | *Son of Aiolos, son of Hellen* |
| | *Minyans* | *Minyas* | *Son of Aiolos, son of Hellen* |
| | *Phlegyans* | *Phlegyas* | *Great-grandson of Sisyphos, son of Aiolos* |
| | *Thessalians* | *Thessalos* | *Descendent of Aiolos, son of Hellen* |
| Arkadian-Cypriot | Arkadians | Arkas | Son of Zeus, no relation to Deukalion |
| *Doric* | *Dorians* | *Doros* | *Son of Hellen, son of Deukalion* |
| *Ionic* | *Ionians* | *Ion* | *Son of Xouthos, son of Hellen* |
| NW Hellenic | Aitolians | Aitolos | Great-grandson of Protogeneia, daughter of Deukalion |
| | *Akhaians* | *Akhaios* | *Son of Xouthos, son of Hellen* |
| | Epeians | Epeios | Great-grandson of Protogeneia, daughter of Deukalion |
| | Lokrians | Lokros | Grandson of Amphiktyon, son of Deukalion |
| | *Myrmidons* | *Myrmidon* | *Son of Xouthos, son of Hellen* |
| | *Phocians* | *Phokos* | *Son of Aiolos, son of Hellen* |

With so many tribes derived from Hellen (in italics above), it is easy to see why "Hellenes" became a "pan-Hellenic" term for all Greek speakers. However, there were other tribes not descended from Hellen. In a mythic admission that Deukalion was not the only survivor of the flood, the speakers of one of the five major Hellenic dialects (Arkadians) were not considered to be his descendants, but they were still considered to be

Hellenic. The mythic lineage of these tribes was probably derived from the similarity of speech between tribes. In other words, tribes speaking similar dialects were given founders who were closely related. The Hellenes also recognized the speech of several tribes that they did not quite consider Hellenic. The mythic founders of these semibarbarian tribes living on the fringes of Hellas (including Centaurs, Epeirots, Lapiths, and Macedonians) were not considered to be descendants of Deukalion.

Alternatively, the Akhaians were believed to have originally been called Danaans after Danaos, son of Belos and a direct descendant of the first king of Mycenai, King Phoroneus. He too was unrelated to Deukalion. Material evidence strongly suggests that the Mycenaian culture of the Heroic Age was overwhelmingly uniform in nature, and therefore it is doubtful that there were separate dialects at that time. The original dialect of the Mycenaians (Danaan/Akhaian) probably did not splinter into the historic dialects until the civilization began to decline rapidly at the end of the Heroic Age. (Evidence for this has been gained from pottery dating to the Late Helladic [LHIIIC].) The differences magnified during the isolation of the Early Iron Age, which followed. Mythic explanations pushed their development back into the Early Heroic Age.

---

Image 5.1
Map of the Tribes of Hellas
Fifth century BCE

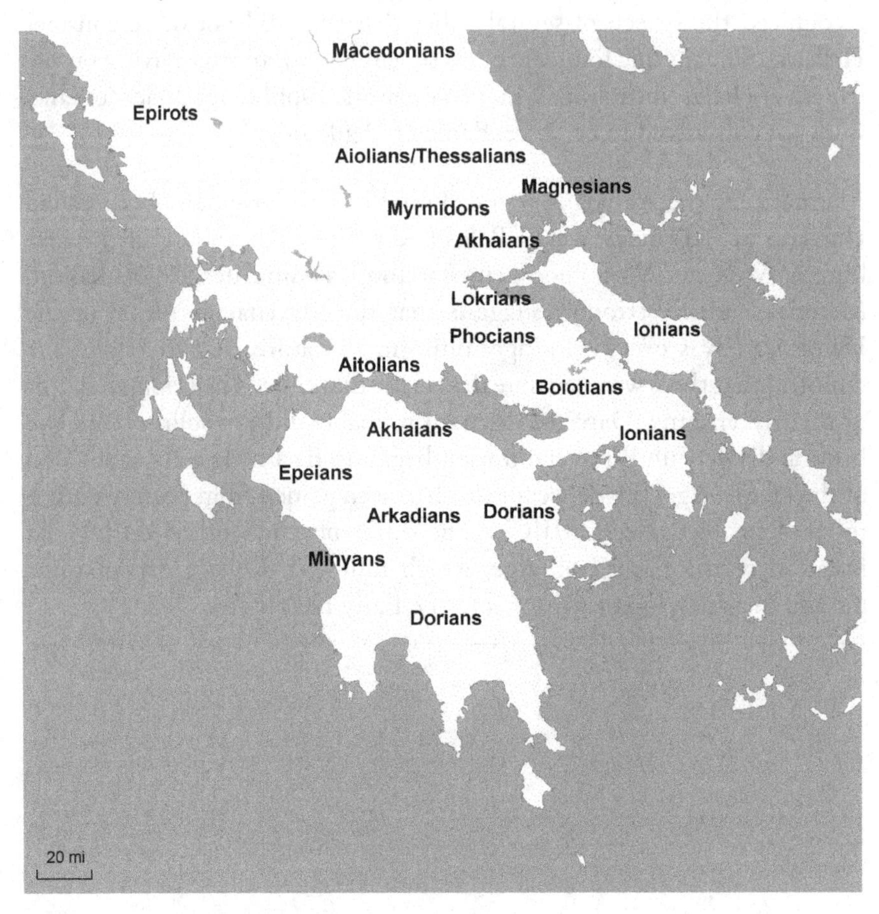


Archaeologists have determined that the first city to arise after the flood was not Opus, as claimed in myth, but Orkhomenos, a few miles to the south (middle seventeenth century T / end of the fifteenth century R BCE). Orkhomenos was located on the fertile Boiotia plain, which was then occupied by the Ektenes. According to legend the Ektenes sprouted from the Boiotia soil that was fertilized by the receding floodwaters. The Ektenes tribesman Alalkomeneus (meaning "guardian"), son of King Ogygos and the nymph Thebe, was considered to be so wise that rumor has it he raised young Athena and that Zeus once sought his consul concerning his marital strife. According to legend, most of the Ektenes died in a plague, which may explain why, after a century of leadership,

Orkhomenos was surpassed by Mycenai and other Peloponnesian cities. Only then did the Minyans settle at Orkhomenos.

---

Exhibit 5.2
Minyan and Mycenaian Pottery

Minyan pottery was once thought to have been brought to Hellas by invaders. It is now known to be a clear descendent of Early Helladic (EHIII) pottery—the pottery of Hesiod's brutish men of bronze. Although it is descended from earlier local wares, Minyan pottery is clearly superior in quality. The special technique used for its rather dull glossy finish is thought to have been developed to imitate metal wares. The first examples of this monochrome blue-grey pottery style were found by Schliemann at Orkhomenos and, unfortunately, named for the mythical inhabitants of Orkhomenos during the Late Helladic Era (eponymous king Minyas of Orkhomenos was a descendent of Deukalion). Despite its scholarly label, the creators of this distinctive pottery would have been the Ektenes, not the Minyans. The oldest examples of grey Minyan pottery uncovered thus far come from Lerne in the Argeia, and these are used as a marker separating the Early Helladic Age from the Middle Helladic Age. Similar wares are found at the earliest levels of Troy VI, suggesting the inhabitants of Hellas and Troy were related.

The Middle Helladic Age, the time of the flood, began in extreme poverty. There were no horses, chariots, or swords and very little metal use in Hellas at the start of the age. Monumental construction ceased, and the population plummeted.

As the Middle Helladic Age progressed, during the time of Deukalion and his family, civilization began to recover. Conditions rapidly improved with the introduction of the horse and, later, the chariot; resumption of construction projects; increased metal use; development of other pottery styles, such as lusterless lilac or green-black on a light background (matte-painted pottery); and a rapidly growing population. Matte-painted pottery developed about the time the first shaft graves were dug in Mycenai. The Athenian king Erikhthonios is believed to have overthrown Deukalion's son Amphiktyon in Athens and to have invented the war chariot.

Matte-painted pottery combined with yellow Minyan pottery to form a distinctive Mycenaian pottery style that was produced for several hundred years. Mycenaian pottery adopted the dull brown to black glazes of earlier pottery styles, but the themes and shapes of the wares changed. Both were heavily influenced by Minoan and, to a lesser degree, Cycladic products. However, besides the floral and marine designs so popular in Krete, Mycenaian pottery also displayed themes of chariots and war. It spread uniformly over Hellas.

---

# Rise of Mycenai

## Middle to Late Helladic Bronze Age (MHII–LH IIIA); Part of Hesiod's Age of Heroes

> Moderation
> O my soul, my soul - you are mutilated helplessly
> by this blade of sorrow. Yet rise and bare your chest,
> face those who would attack you, be strong, give no ground.
> And if you defeat them, do not brag like a loud-mouth,
> nor, if they beat you, run home and lie down to cry.
> Keep some measure in your joy - or in your sadness during crisis -
> that you may understand man's up-and-down life.
>
> —Arkhilokhos of Paros, sixth century BCE

The city of Mycenai in the Argeia (Argolis) valley of the Peloponnesos quickly grew larger than all other cities of Hellas. On first brush, the hot, dry Argeia valley seems an inhospitable place for a great civilization to arise. Precious little water flowed in the local rivers, and the stony hills were barren. Nevertheless, there was enough water to irrigate extremely fertile valley soil and foster impressive civil growth. Inakhos, the premier river and river god (river gods were descendants of the Titans, the forces of nature), reigned as king of the valley during the early ages of man, when everyone was a farmer.

While Inakhos ruled over the sleepy valley, two Olympian deities approached him for patronage of his land. As we have seen with Athens, it was customary for the Indo-European gods to claim as their property nations as they first developed. The Olympian Hera and dark-haired Poseidon vied for patronage of the Argeia. After consulting with his two major tributaries (Asterion and Cephissos) and also with his son Phoroneus, Inakhos chose white-armed Hera. The vote for Hera was due in part to Hera's close association with the river Asterion's daughter Euboea. Queen Hera stayed safely in the palace of the Titans Oceanos and Tethys, king and queen of the swirling ocean that encircles the broad bosomed earth, while the Olympians and Titans fought furiously. There the nymph Euboea attended to cow-eyed Hera.

Dark-haired Poseidon, a vengeful god, punished the three insubordinate rivers for choosing Hera over their watery lord. On his command the yearlong flowing of their waters ceased, their flow thereafter restricted to the time of the winter rains.[64] Nevertheless, the decision held, and Inakhos vigorously instituted Hera's worship.

The river god Inakhos's wife, Melia, was one of the Oceanides[65] (water nymphs and, like the river gods, children of Oceanos and Tethys). This union of freshwater (masculine) and saltwater (feminine) deities produced the first Hellenic civilization (which required fresh water for sustenance and the salty sea for fish and trade). They bore five children: Phoroneus, Aigialeus, Mycene, Phegeus, and Philodice.

---

Exhibit 6.1
The Rise of Mycenaian Civilization

Archaeologists have established that the first flowering of Mycenaian civilization occurred during the period called the Middle Helladic II, which took place in the early sixteenth T / middle fourteenth R century BCE. The first important structures built in the city were two circles of shaft graves. George Emmanuel Mylonas dated Circle B to 1580T/1330R BCE

---

[64] Hellas was a lot wetter after the Ice Age than it is today. It became progressively drier. Perhaps this myth recalls an earlier time when the rivers flowed more regularly.

[65] While the Hellenes identified salt water as feminine they originally identified the Oceanides with fresh water because they believed the world circulating Ocean stream was fresh water. The discovery of the Atlantic Ocean changed that belief, and thereafter there were both salt and fresh water Oceanides.

and Circle A to a half a century later. The latest one dates to 1500T/1250R BCE. There is no contemporary evidence for the city.

The steady improvement in technical and artistic skill is obvious. The first graves were simple plots with pebbles placed upon them. Subsequent shaft graves were larger, with wooden roofs covering them. Although the Mycenaian civilization quickly outshone anything seen before in Hellas, it still paled in comparison with contemporary cities of the Near East.

The Circle A shaft graves would have held the second and third Mycenaian kings, Argos and Phorbas. They were dug five to seven feet deep, covered with a wooden roof to shelter the remains, and then covered up with dirt. The riches found in these tombs have led scholars to believe they held the families of noblemen; they all show Egyptian influence. Because artisans became heavily influenced by the alien Minoan civilization of Krete, and because Egyptian goods begin appearing in the graves, accurate comparative dating is possible. Their wealth derived primarily from the export of wool, linens, pottery, oil, wine, timber, drinking cups, ivory and metal jewelry, horses, weapons, and mercenary wages, which paid for metals, such as copper, tin, and gold, as well as ivory, gems, and grain—not unlike Classical Hellas.

---

## Phoroneus Founds Mycenai; First Ruler of the House of Inakhos[66] (1580T/1330R–1412T/1162R BCE)

Because Inakhos was of Titan descent, a force of nature, it was up to his mortal children, guided by the Olympian gods, to found cities built upon the bounty his waters made possible. He withdrew into his riverbed when Phoroneus built a city out of the farming village of Mycenai. Hermes gave Phoroneus the prerogative to be the first human ruler. Men of later times worshiped him as the god of civilization, the first civilizer.

Phoroneus built the first Hellenic city at Mycenai. The original name of the city was Phoroneia, but the king renamed it for his sister Mycene. He instituted the first great building program in Mycenai, the building of shaft graves to house the remains of his royal family (1580T/1330R BCE).

Although Ektenes (Minyan) Orkhomenos was bustling nearly a century earlier, the rest of Hellas underwent rapid development only after Mycenai did (as the myths corroborate). Not long after Mycenai was built, Phoroneus's younger brother Aigialeus took settlers over stony northern hills to build Sicyon (1572T/1322R BCE). Meanwhile, Phoroneus married Cerdo and begat Kar, who, like his uncle Aigialeus, moved abroad and founded a city (1555T/1305R BCE). Kar left to found Megara because his father promised the kingdom of Mycenai to his regal grandson Argos, the son of his daughter Niobe. Phoroneus had other bastard children as well,

[66] Phoroneus, like Kekrops and Lykaon, could easily be placed in the earlier age of the men of bronze, because according to some, he was an ancestor of Pelasgos—eponym of the ancient ones that inhabited Hellas in earlier times. However, the kings list of Mycenai fits so well with the archaeological record for the site of Mycenai that he must be considered as a man of the Heroic Age. The kings list for the House of Inakhos is derived from lists provided by three late writers: Apollodoros (*Library* ii.2.1–5), Pausanias (*Guide to Greece* ii.15.5–16.3) and Diodoros (*Library of History* iv.58). The fifth-century BCE genealogist Akusilaos of Argos appears to be the source of all three lists, although he moved the kings' residency from Mycenai to his own city. Apollodoros says Phoroneus's son Apis was the second king. The Roman-era author Pausanias excludes him, and the fifth-century BCE Athenian playwright Aiskhylos, in *Supplicant Women*, says he was a healer, not a king, a son of Apollo. Three dynasties followed the Inakhids: Danaides, Amythaonids, and Pelopids. Unlike the Inakhids, these kings were very well known and consistently listed by numerous writers. Hyginos, in *Fabulai*, 124, gives an abbreviated list (see also *Fabulai,* 143 and 145).

such as Europs, the father of Hermione, eponym of the city of Hermione.[67] Uniform Mycenaian culture spread from Iolkos in the north to Pylos in the southwest corner of the Peloponnesos.

## The First Mortal Affair of Zeus

From his perch upon lofty Olympos, Lord Zeus looked down with excitement on the rising city of Mycenai. Observing his mortal subjects, Zeus became attracted to the noble girls he saw in the newly built city. First to catch his eye was stunning Princess Niobe, the king's daughter by the nymph Teledice. He secretly seduced her (1593T/1343R BCE). It was Niobe's good fortune that jealous Hera did not discover the liaison. Affairs of the gods are not without issue, and in due time Niobe bore Argos.[68] Hera began to suspect Zeus's infidelity but did not catch him until his second mortal affair, which produced Niobe's great-granddaughter Io.

The grandson of the god of civilization lived up to his pedigree. Argos, son of Zeus (1570T/1320R–1535T/1285R BCE), succeeded Phoroneus and consolidated Mycenaian control over the Argeia Valley, and it has been called Argeia after him ever since. Neighboring rival cities (Berbati and Prosymna) were destroyed, and allied cities grew in their place. Presumably King Argos played a direct role in the founding or enlarging of Argos[69], his cousin Hermione founded Hermione, and his sons Epidauros and Tiryns[70] founded eponymous cities. A new pottery style (LHI) arose and was nearly universally adopted in Hellas and exported widely.

---

[67] Another of his reputed bastards was Sparton, whose life was undistinguished except as the father of an otherwise unknown Myceneus. Both personages were late fabrications to explain the name of two great cities (another invention is his great-aunt Mycene). As the civilization god Phoroneus was, according to one version, the father of Klymenos and Chthonia, chthonic deities celebrated in Demeter's cult in Hermione.

[68] Apollodoros, *Library*, ii.1.2 says that the early mythographer Akusilaos of Argos considered Pelasgos as the full brother of Argos but adds that Hesiod said Pelasgos was earth born (native).

[69] Apollodoros, *Library*, ii.15.4, says everyone knows Perseus founded Mycenai. However, that belief was spread at a time when Argos was the premier city of the valley and had appropriated earlier Mycenaian myths. King Argos must have ruled Mycenai, which was clearly the dominant city of the Late Bronze Age.

[70] Archaeological evidence concurs with the timing, identifying Mycenaian-era monumental construction at Tiryns beginning in 1500T/1250R BCE—somewhat later than at Mycenai.

King Argos married the nymph Euadne, lovely daughter of the great Macedonian river god Strymon and the nymph Naira. The couple had other sons besides those listed above: Phorbas (whom Apollodoros calls Ekbasos), Krisos (Krinos), and Peiras (also called Peirithoos, Peiren, and Iasos).

King Argos was interred in a more elaborate shaft grave site, labeled Circle A. This new shaft grave site was near the simpler, older one that King Phoroneus had constructed.

## Zeus Desires Io

While King Phorbas, son of Argos, ruled (1535T/1285R–1510T/1260R BCE), his uncle Peiras raised a frenzied daughter who fired Zeus's heart with love. Night after night he whispered in her dreams, repeating his seductive words:

> Most blessed maid, why live a virgin so long? Love waits for you - The greatest; Zeus, inflamed with arrows of desire, longs to unite with you in love. Do not reject, my child, the bed of Zeus. Go out to the deep grass of Lerne, where your father's sheep and cattle graze, that the eye of Zeus may rest from longing and be satisfied. [71]

Io told her father about her disturbing reoccurring dream. Prince Peiras sent repeated inquires to the venerable oracles of Dodona and Delphi. After many quibbling responses, he received a clear reply: exile Io or Zeus would destroy him and his people. Sorrowfully, he banished his frightened daughter (1522T/1272R BCE).

Zeus overtook the fleeing girl and ravished her on Euboea (the Argeian hill, not the island). After satisfying his lust for Io, Zeus felt a rush of guilt when he observed Hera approaching.

[71] Aeschylus (Aiskhylos), "Prometheus Bound", in *Prometheus Bound and Other Plays*. Translated by Philip Vellacott.

> Being discovered by Hera, Zeus touched the girl and changed her into a white cow,[72] while he swore that he had no intercourse with her. And so Hesiod says that oaths touching the matter of love do not draw down anger from the gods. "And therefore he ordained that an oath concerning the secret deeds of the Cyprian should be without penalty for men."[73]

Hera was not deceived and asked for the cow as a present. Sheepishly Zeus agreed. The site of Io's miraculous transformation became one of Hera's most holy precincts, the Heraion. Hera's anguish and rage over Zeus's philandering was intense. Hera could not directly punish the powerful perpetrator. So she vented upon the poor girl who had been raped, a scapegoat, blaming Io for enticing Zeus rather than believing ill of him.

Io's ill-fated tribulation was ironic given that she was serving as the reverent priestess of Hera when she became the object of desire for the Thunderer-on-High; she was a mortal image of Hera. Strong devotion to Hera did not save her from Zeus's lustful desire or from Hera's fury.

## The Labors of Argos Panoptes (meaning "all-seeing")[74]

The furious Hera entrusted a giant herdsman of ungoverned rage, Argos Panoptes, with guarding the heifer Io, and he tied her to an olive tree in the Heraion. Argos Panoptes was the son of Prince Ekvasos, the nephew

[72] According to some sources, Hera was directly responsible for driving the daughters of Proitos of Tiryns mad and changing them into cows. Like Dionysos, she had powers to drive people mad.

[73] Hesiod, "Aigimios", in *The Homeric Hymns and Homerica.*

[74] "Labors" were very ancient mythic material and usually involved fighting wild beasts and monsters during the time before heroic deeds were equated with war. These were the stories of men before they build cities. Herakles alone prevailed and became an Olympian. Herakles obtained immortality while Argos Panoptes was too brutish and both Theseus and Bellerophontes failed in their labors to gain immortality (Theseus could not escape Hades and Bellerophontes could not reach Olympos). Because Herakles (who wore the pelt of a lion he killed) became so famous, he stole or obliterated most of the labor cycles of other heroes. Vestiges remain in Argos Panoptes, Theseus, Bellerophontes, and a few others.

of King Phorbas, and the cousin of his prisoner Io.[75] Watchful Argos Panoptes was a remarkable hero, physically unlike any other man who ever lived. Argos Panoptes was covered with one hundred eyes, and they slept in shifts, so he could always keep an eye on Io. With eyes all over his body, he could see danger approaching from any direction. He was an incredibly strong man who was devoted to Hera, and he was the great protector of her land.

While watching over Io, all-seeing Argos Panoptes managed to perform heroic exploits. Coming to the aid of settlers in Arkadia, he killed a savage bull that was ravaging the district. He wore the tough hide of that bull for the rest of his days. The Arkadians called on him again to fight and kill a Satyr that was stealing from them. His most famous exploit, however, was the slaying of the serpentine Cilician monster Echidna (meaning "viper"), the widow of terrible Typhoeus, whom Zeus had vanquished with great difficulty.

All the while Argos Panoptes faithfully guarded the cow Io for Hera, the goddess smiled—no doubt at the rough treatment he gave Io during the years he guarded her. Zeus pensively allowed the torture to continue until he felt Hera's temper subsiding. Then he determined to free Io. Since Argos Panoptes was the consummate guard, Zeus entrusted the task to no other than the god of guile, Hermes. Hermes found Io tied to an olive tree in the Heraion but could not get close because wary Argos Panoptes watched all approaches with tireless eyes. Slippery Hermes could not elude his attention, neither in the bright daytime nor in the holy night. Changing tactics, the clever god approached Argos Panoptes openly and befriended him. He pulled pipes (invented by his son Pan while roaming the nearby Nemean Mountains) from his sack and played sweet lullabies. One by one, the alert eyes of Argos Panoptes drifted off into drowsy sleep. When the last eye closed, the swift-footed messenger quietly pulled out a concealed dagger, cut off the head of Argos Panoptes, grim child of earth, and unfettered Io (1519T/1269R BCE).

---

[75] Apollodoros, *Library*, ii.1–2 lists numerous alternatives for the parents of Argos Panoptes besides Ekvasos, including: he was earthborn (Akusilaos of Argos), a descendent of Inakhos (Asklepiades of Samos), the son of Arestor (Pherecydes of Syros), or a son of Argos and Asopos' daughter Ismene (Kekrops of Miletos). To add to the confusion Ismene is also called the wife of Argos Panoptes.

## Wandering Io

Zeus soon realized that he had underestimated Hera's fury. When Hera saw her sacred shrine polluted by murder, she reacted quickly. To continue punishing her rival for daring to be a temptation to Zeus, she sent a gadfly to repeatedly sting free roving Io. To honor the achievements and devotion of her slain knight, Hera spread Argos Panoptes's many eyes into the tail of the peacock, thereafter a bird sacred to her.

Driven on by the relentless gadfly, Io went down to the Inakhos River to drink. There, with sad eyes and lowing tones, Io was somehow able to let the god know of her pitiful predicament, and she pleaded for help. Inakhos was powerless to help and could only counsel her, suggesting that the Dodona oracle or the wise Titan Prometheus (who too suffered unjustly from the actions of Zeus) might be able to give her good advice. Then the watery god sank back into his riverbed.

Stung mercilessly by the persistent gadfly and haunted by the ghost of Argos Panoptes, plodding Io trudged onward. She was chased away from the holy Epeirot oracle of Zeus in Dodona without consideration for the question in her sad eyes. With quiet resolve she walked on, past Mount Haimos in Thrace, across the wheat plains of Scythia and Cimmeria, and into the snowy Caucasian Mountains. There she found some comfort in the words of another tortured soul. With ears perked and big cow eyes rimmed with tears, Io observed how the great Titan Prometheus had been laid low in agony for supporting hapless man against the rash god-king Zeus. Only the knowledge that he would one day be released from his suffering comforted proud Prometheus. With compassion he told Io her future so that she too might be consoled; but he could offer her no help.

Io traversed the highlands of Anatolia and crossed the deserts of Syria before dropping in exhaustion and despair at Canoibos or Memphis in the land of the linen-robed Egyptians. Moved by her distress, Zeus finally pleaded with Queen Hera to let long-suffering Io go. On Hera's demand, Zeus promised never to have relations with Io again. Hera was appeased, and Io's curse was lifted. Zeus returned to Io, and not with force, but instead by the gentle touch of his hand, she was restored to her beautiful human form. That same touch awakened his long-dormant seed in her womb. She bore him a son she named Epaphos (meaning "god's touch"; 1516T/1266R BCE).[76]

The story did not end there, as both Zeus and Hera found loopholes in their promises. Zeus did stay away from Io, but he undertook numerous affairs with other mortal women. Hera stopped punishing Io directly, but she sent the magical bronzesmiths known as the Korybantes or Kouretes to steal her child.[77] They hid him in their home on Minoan Krete, and poor Io again wandered through Syria, this time looking for her lost son. When Zeus discovered their crime, he killed the sorcerers and returned the child to his distressed mother. Io returned to Egypt and became one of the wives of the Egyptian pharaoh Amenhotep I (1525T/1275R–1504T/1254R BCE), whom the Hellenes called Telegonos, and who graciously accepted the boy as his own. As a man, Epaphos returned to Krete and prospered by leading Mycenaian traders on Minoan expeditions to Egypt. Eventually vengeful Hera caused him to die in a hunting accident. One of his descendants, Danaos, would return to his ancestral land of Mycenai and become king.

## Growth of Mycenai under Inakhid Kings

While Io wandered the world, tormented by the gadfly, her uncle Phorbas, the eldest son of Argos, ruled Mycenai (1535T/1285R–1510T/1260R BCE). Phorbas married the nymph Euboea, daughter of the Argeian river god Asterion, who eons earlier had attended to young Hera in seclusion from the warring Titans and Olympians.[78] Euboea bore Phorbas an heir named Triops (1545T/1295R BCE).

Io's father, Peiras, brother of King Phorbas, grew concerned by her long absence and requested that Cyrnos, the admiral of the fleet, be dispatched to find Io. Cyrnos failed to find her and chose not to return. Instead he

[76] The myth of Io incorporates a Hellenic explanation of the cult of the Apis bull at Egypt. Herodotos, in *Histories*, ii.153, says that Apis is the Egyptian name for Epaphos. Io's initial arrival in Egypt occurred during the reign of the pharaoh Ahmose, who drove the Hyksos from Egypt with the help, possibly, of Hellenic mercenaries.

[77] These same spirits were said to have hid infant Zeus on Mount Ida on Krete at the request of Rhea to protect him from Kronos. The Hellenes identified Io with the Egyptian goddess Isis.

[78] Only the Argives say Oceanos and Tethys raised Hera; others followed Hesiod's lead in saying Kronos swallowed her too.

founded the port of Cyrnos on the coast of Karia; he was the first of many Hellenes to settle upon the shores of Anatolia.[79]

---

Exhibit 6.2
Descendants of Phorbas and Peiras

| Descendants of Phorbas (all Mycenaian kings) | Descendants of Peiras |
|---|---|
| Phorbas | Peiras, younger brother of Phorbas |
| Triops | Io (loved by Zeus) |
| Agenor | Epaphos (husband of Memphis, daughter of the Nile) |
| Krotopos | Libya (lover of Poseidon and wife of Triton) |
| Sthenelos | Belos, Agenor, and Lelex |
| Gelenor | Belos's sons, Aigyptos and Danaos; Agenor's son Phoenix |

The lineage displayed in the chart above most closely follows the Hellenic mythologist Apollodoros (*Library* ii.9–11 and iii.1–4), with input from Pausanias (*Guide to Greece* ii.15.5) and Diodoros (*Library of History* iv.58) for the kings list. The fifth-century BCE Argive historian Akusilaos is probably the source of the kings list for all three. However, there are two places of disagreement regarding the family of Peiras: who was the father of Io and whether Agenor or Phoenix was the father of Kadmos and Europa (whose lives are discussed in the next chapter).

Apollodoros (*Library* ii.2) says that both Hesiod and Akusilaos identify the otherwise unknown Peiren as the father of Io. He could be the same as Peiras, whom Apollodoros (*Library,* ii.1) says was the son of Argos and Euadne. The Athenian tragic poet Aiskhylos and others say the river god Inakhos was her father. Still others say Io's father was Argos's son Iasos by a daughter of the Sicyonian river god Asopos. This Iasos is not to be confused with the same-named son of Argos Panoptes and his wife,

---

[79] The first Mycenaian colony in Asia was at Iassos in Karia; this colony is presumably the same as Cyrnos. In agreement with the myth, Mycenaian goods have been discovered at Minoan trade posts, such as Iassos and Miletos, concurrent with the construction of the shaft graves, although these Anatolian cities did not become Mycenaian until after the Minoan civilization was conquered (ca. 1450T/1200R BCE).

Ismene, daughter of the river god Asopos, or with the brother of Agenor who served as regent-king for Krotopos.

The second discrepancy is who sired Kadmos and Europa. Possibly following the fifth-century genealogist Pherecydes, the Roman poet Ovid (*Metamorphoses* ii.840–875) and Apollodoros (*Library,* iii.1.1) state that Agenor was Kadmos's father even though Homer (*Iliad,* xiv.321), Hesiod (*Catalog of Women,* 19), Bakkhylides (xvii.29), Asios (referenced in Pausanias's *Guide to Greece*, vii.4.1), and Moskhos of Syrakuse (ii.7) all say it was Phoenix. Hesiod (*Catalog of Women,* 20) adds that Agenor was the father of Phoenix. The number of generations in the more ancient poets' claim fits exactly with the generations of Mycenaian kings, but it is one shy if Kadmos was the son of Agenor. Therefore, the more ancient claim is followed here.

---

Image 6.1
Descendants of King Argos of Mycenai Genealogy Chart

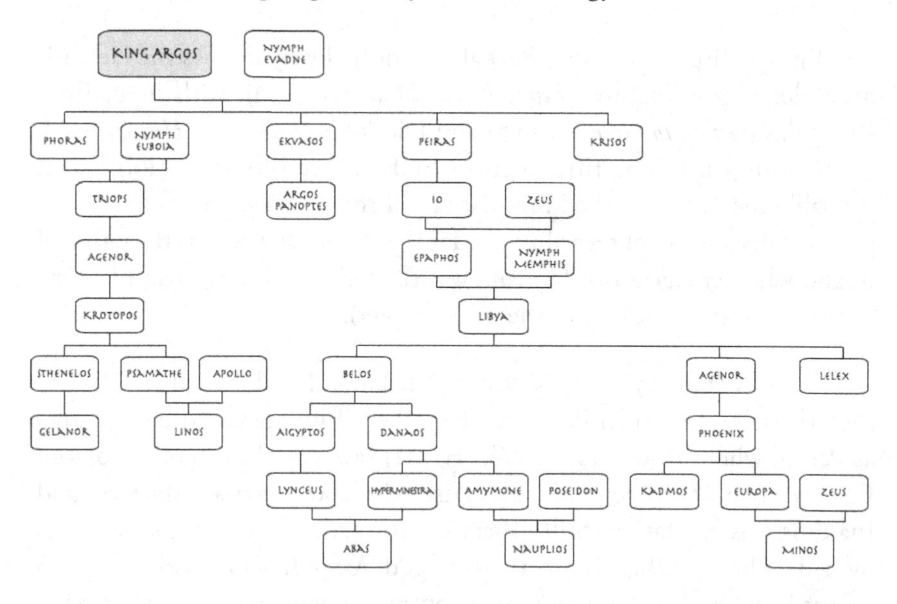


Economic growth and prosperity continued during the reign of King Triops, son of Phorbas (1510T/1260R–1485T/1235R BCE). The overwhelming majority of the trade was conducted with the Minoans. As a result, Minoan themes came to dominate Mycenaian culture. One of the king's younger sons, Pallen, founded Pallene in Akhaia, near the earlier Phoroneus-era

Mycenaian colony of Sicyon. Triops's strong-willed daughter Messene and her husband, Prince Polykaon of Lakonia, settled on the west coast of Messenia, where the Mycenaians competed with the Minyans of Boiotia for trade (primarily in metals) with Sicily and Italy (1481T/1231R BCE).

Mythological claims that sons of Triops founded colonies on Aigaian Islands and on the Anatolian coast correspond closely with evidence for early Mycenaian overseas trade colonies. Triops's bastard son Xanthos settled first in Lycia before moving on to Lesbos (ironically not one of the islands the Mycenaians settled on). Some consider Mycenaian Triops the father of Syme, patron of an Aigaian Island. These early "colonists" would have been partners of Minoan merchants in ventures to Egypt, Anatolia, and the Near East. These trade colonies helped the Mycenaians learn the mercantile industry from the seafaring Minoans.

When Triops died, he was laid to rest in the first tholos tomb built in Mycenai—a magnificent domed structure built to impress. He was survived in Mycenai by three legitimate sons: Agenor, Iasos, and Pelasgos. His eldest son, Agenor, succeeded him. Agenor's reign was short and uneventful (1485T/1235R–1475T/1225R BCE). His untimely death left his son Krotopos, who was only a boy, as king. His uncle Iasos, brother of Agenor, ruled as regent for ten years.

---

Exhibit 6.3
Tholos Tombs

The earliest domed tholos (round building) tombs in Hellas appeared on the west coast of Messenia ca. 1500T/1250R BCE. Scholars debate whether the tombs are of indigenous design (Dr. Oliver Dickinson) or under influence of the Minoans (M. S. F. Hood). Whatever its inspiration, the design was quickly adopted by the nobles of Mycenai and the rest of Hellas. These tombs were normally used for a series of burials and not, as later Hellenes thought, used for the burial of a single nobleman.

Tholos tombs grew more impressive as wealth increased and building techniques improved. During the early fourteenth century T / mid twelfth century R BCE, the building of tholos tombs largely gave way to the building of great-halled megaron palaces. The superbly crafted tomb of Klytaimnestra was the last tholos tomb built at Mycenai, ca. 1250T/1000R BCE.

---

The long reign of Krotopos (1475T/1225R–1433T/1183R BCE) was anything but uneventful. During his rule the Hellenes, and in particular Mycenaian warriors, sacked the Minoan cities of Krete. Sea power made the conquest of the island possible. Krete and Rhodes began receiving heavy Mycenaian colonization soon after their conquest. Two sons of Poseidon were among the leading Mycenaian warlords of Krete—Belos and Agenor. Their brother Lelex became the king of the Hellenic city of Megara. The mother of these men was Libya, the daughter of Io's son, Epaphos.

With an eye for gain, the Mycenaian invaders wisely did not kill off the Kretan inhabitants with whom they had long traded and from whom they had learned so much. Instead they chose to rule over the artisans and traders of Krete and prosper from their industry. No Mycenaian lord held mastery over the whole island; instead warlords established themselves in the hundred Minoan cities of Krete.

The Egyptians were anxious to conduct business with the new masters of the Aigaian. To learn more about the Mycenaians and to establish friendly trade relations, they sent a diplomatic envoy to Hellas. King Krotopos entertained this first known Egyptian envoy to Hellas.[80]

Despite these great events, Krotopos is known in myth principally for his infamous treatment of his daughter and grandson. The trouble started when Psamathe bore Linos (meaning "flax") to Apollo (1447T/1197R BCE). Rightfully fearing her father's wrath, she secretly bore and exposed the child. Shepherds found the child, but unhappily, Krotopos's sheep dogs had torn the infant to pieces. Psamathe grieved so mightily that Krotopos surmised that it was her child. He responded by kicking his daughter to death for disgracing him by bearing a child out of wedlock.

[80] Egyptian records document a diplomatic contact between the Mycenaians and Egyptians around 1445T/1195R BCE, during the reign of the pharaoh Thutmose III (1479T/1229R–1425T/1175R BCE). Unfortunately no individual Mycenaian was named in the document.

Apollo was understandably upset with Krotopos's actions and sent a Harpy-like creature named Poine (meaning "punishment") to Mycenai. Poine snatched away children until a local man named Koroibos killed her. Apollo responded by sending a plague (no doubt brought back by bold sailors). Koroibos went to Delphi and confessed to killing Poine. The local priestess of Apollo uttered the wishes of the far-shooter, and Koroibos obeyed. Upon divine order he founded the colony of Tripodisci and a shrine to Apollo below Mount Geraneia (in Megaris).

Although the plague passed, Apollo's anger was not abated until after he shot old Krotopos with an arrow of illness, from which Krotopos died after prolonged agony. His son Sthenelos (1433T/1183R–1413T/1163R BCE) and grandson Gelanor (1413T/1163R–1412T/1162R) ruled while the Mycenaian civilization rapidly advanced. Gelanor was the eighth and last Mycenaian king from the House of Inakhos.

## House of Danaos (1412T/1162R–1306T/1056R BCE)

The heroic tribesmen of Argeia became known as Danaans (and later Akhaians) after the founder of a new ruling house, which was related to the previous dynasty. The founder of the new dynasty sailed to Hellas in what some ancients thought was the first two-prowed vessel. The captain of this ship was Danaos, son of Belos and a member of one of the Mycenaian families ruling Krete. His family lived in Kommos, a port facing Egypt on the underbelly of Krete.[81] He circumvented Krete and landed on Rhodes, where he sacrificed two or three of his daughters in order to gain safe passage to Mycenai.

Danaos's trip to Mycenai was either a bold plan to use the wealth and power he had accumulated abroad to make a play for the kingship of Mycenai or a way for him to flee Krete in order to avoid his twin brother, Aigyptos, who demanded submission. Although Danaos had no issue from

---

[81] Although the Minoans were the only foreigners to profoundly impact Mycenaian culture, ancient writers usually identified Danaos with Egypt and other ancient foreigners with either Egypt or Phoenicia, important Near Eastern states of the historic Iron Age. A few early writers did allude to Kretan connections, but later writers knew nothing about the Minoans. Danaos was then said to have been born at Khemmis in Egypt and to have ruled in Libya rather than Krete.

the stronger gender to protect him, he was prosperous in female offspring (the Danaides). The lusty sons of Aigyptos demanded them as brides.

Upon safely landing at Apobathmi, near the important town of Lerne, Danaos sent his daughters to fetch water in that thirsty land. Danaos knew of Poseidon's curse, the one that made all the rivers of the Argeia dry up during the hot summers, and so he desperately told his daughters to use any means necessary to get the precious liquid.

## Poseidon and Amymone

Only Amymone (meaning "blameless") returned successfully from the quest for life-giving water. Her happy sisters eagerly gathered around her to listen to how she obtained it. She said that while searching for water, a sleek deer crossed her path. Hoping to bring back both food and water, she tossed a javelin at the buck, but she missed and instead struck a sleeping Satyr. Angry and slightly wounded, the lusty Satyr leapt up and gave chase. Upon her prayers, Poseidon arrived and hurled his trident at the racing Satyr, who dodged it and fled. With exuberance, Amymone showered her rescuer with heartfelt gratitude. Pleased, Poseidon told her to pull his trident out from the rock it had stuck in. When she did so, three springs gushed out. Called the Amymone springs, they still feed the Lerne River, which flows even during the searing summer heat. For this, Hesiod (*Catalog of Women,* 16) credits Danaos with making the dry Argeia well-watered (a rational explanation is that Danaos's kinship group, the Danaans, developed the earliest irrigation system).

In due time, Amymone bore a son she named Nauplios, the offspring of trident-bearing Poseidon. One day their son, with the sea flowing in his veins, would build strong fleets that would maintain Mycenai's status as the principal sea power in the Aigaian. Nauplios was the first to boldly sail out into the barren sea, out of sight of land. He confidently navigated by the Great Bear and reached his destinations faster than others. As a reward for his ingenuity and service, Nauplios received a land grant not far from Lerne. There he built the port of Nauplia. Most of Danaos's soldiers obtained local wives and settled with him at Nauplia.

Backed by a loyal army, Danaos marched inland toward his ancestral home. News of his arrival reached the lofty citadel of Mycenai long before he did. The Mycenaians certainly considered him one of their own and respected his large force of chariots. An assembly of knights was convened to decide who should rule. Both King Gelanor and Danaos gave persuasive speeches to the knights. Danaos backed his claim by reminding the aristocrats assembled that he was a direct descendent of Zeus and Io's son, Epaphos, and therefore more deserving than Gelanor.

Apollo sent a sign indicating the gods' concurrence with Danaos's claim (a lone wolf bringing down the herd's lead bull). The Mycenaians understood that Danaos was like the wolf and might take similar vengeance on Gelanor if frustrated. The knights backed Danaos, and young Gelanor[82] was forced to abdicate. As his first act as king, thankful Danaos (1412T/1162R–1403T/1153R BCE) built the temple of Apollo Lynceus (meaning "god of wolves") in Argos.

## Danaan Brides

The new king had little time to celebrate. When the sea-lanes opened after winter, Aigyptos's sons arrived to claim the maidens for their unlawful love. Danaos resisted, rightly suspecting that Aigyptos was planning to kill him. The mighty walls of Mycenai kept the invaders out, but thirst eventually forced Danaos to surrender and marry his daughters to them. Before the ceremony, Danaos made each bride swear an oath to cut the throat of her husband before the wedding night ended.

After the passion, then violence, of that night was spent, all of the bridegrooms except for one had descended into the underworld. Danaos's eldest daughter, Hypermnestra, alone disobeyed, because her husband, Lynceus, respected her request for continued virginity. Under night's cover, she told Lynceus to flee into the mountain village of Lyrceia while she fled in the opposite direction toward Lerne. They each lit beacons to announce

[82] Aiskhylos's *Supplicant Women* identifies Gelanor Pelasgos as being "Of the Ancient Lineage," suggesting that leadership changed from Pelasgian to Danaan (Hellenic). He says Danaos came to Pelasgos as a supplicant and that Pelasgos offered him protection from the sons of Aigyptos. The transition from Pelasgian to Danaan occurred earlier; there is no archaeological evidence of a cultural break at this time.

their respective safe arrivals. The next day, the heads and bodies of the sons of Aigyptos were buried separately—the heads on the acropolis of Argos (Larissa) and the bodies near Lerne. The Danaides superstitiously believed that by maiming the corpses their ghosts could not harm them. Zeus sent Hermes and Athena to purify the murderous maidens.

Soon Hypermnestra returned alone, willing to be called a coward but not a murderer. Her father put her on trial for not fulfilling her oath to him. Aphrodite was her defense, for

> this goddess, various and subtle,
> Is honored only with most solemn rites,
> Where, joined with their dear mother,
> Come first Desire, then soft Persuasion,
> To whose enchantments nothing can be denied;
> While Music and the Loves, who play in whispers,
> Have their parts assigned then by Aphrodite. [83]

Danaos put Hypermnestra in prison, but love overcame him and he quickly forgave her. Hypermnestra persistently pleaded her husband's case until aging Danaos permitted Lynceus to return and become his lawful heir.

Meanwhile, Danaos tried to marry off his other daughters. At first there were no takers. None were willing to risk their neck for a night with a princess. Danaos then offered their hands without demanding the customary bridal gifts. That failed to entice enough suitors, so he held races with his daughters as prizes. Still there were brides left over. When the first winners were not killed in their beds, the remaining daughters were quickly married off after subsequent races.

If the Danaides got off easy in this world, it was not so in the afterlife. They were punished for their crime in the underworld, where they were

[83] Aeschylus (Aiskhylos), "The Supplicants", in *Prometheus Bound and Other Plays*. Translated by Philip Vellacott.

required to perpetually catch water in broken urns.[84] By this the gods showed that right action is more important than oaths—even those given to one's own parents. The purification these girls received saved them from the Erinyes only during their lifetime. Because Amymone had been the lover of Poseidon, she was acquitted. Hypermnestra was, naturally, exempt.

Lynceus eventually put old Danaos to death to avenge his brothers. He would also have killed the Danaides, but the citizens refused him this. After avenging his family, he settled down and ruled as a just king (1403T/1153R–1382T/1132R BCE). During his reign, the Mycenaian forces in Anatolia came into direct contact with the rising Hittite Empire for the first time.[85]

## The Great Warrior Abas

Abas, eldest son of Lynceus and Hypermnestra, earned his reputation as a great warrior. He succeeded his father as king of Mycenai (1382T/1132R–1355T/1105R BCE).[86] Abas was conceived when his parents were reunited in Mycenai (1410T/1160R BCE). In Hellas, Mycenai's preeminence was recognized as far away as Phocis, where a city was named Abas in the king's honor. There was no great poet to extol the exploits of Abas, but it can be assumed his reputation as a great warrior had much to do with the expansion of his kingdom in Hellas and in Anatolia.

---

[84] Until Hellenistic times, they were not punished for their crime (Amymone's name even means "blameless"). Professor Martin Nilsson, author of *Mycenaean Origin of Greek Mythology*, surmised that this was because the Danaan women, wives of the Sea Peoples, were caught by Egyptians and made concubines. They rose up and slew their oppressors, and that is why it wasn't a crime. Many of the Sea Peoples, which included the Denyen (Danaans), settled in Palestine. The closeness in name of the Danaans to the Israeli tribe of Dan has led to speculation of a connection.

[85] Hittite royal archives state that when they first campaigned in western Anatolia they came in contact with an army of infantry and one hundred chariots under Attarsiya (meaning "man of Ahhiyawa (Akhaia)," who was conducting a military campaign there during the reign of Hittite great-king Tudhaliya I (1400T/1150R–1380T/1130R BCE). Mycenaians (Danaan/Akhaians) were probably active in western Anatolia beginning in the late fifteenth century T / mid twelfth century R BCE.

[86] Hyginos, *Fabulai*, 244, states that the warrior-king Abas (of Mycenai) killed Megapenthes to avenge his father, Lynceus. Nothing else is known of that myth. Since Megapenthes, son of Proitos, lived during the rule of Abas II of Mycenai, son of Melampous, perhaps it was Abas II who slew Megapenthes.

The rising importance of Mycenai was not lost on the great powers to the east. Egypt was well pleased to see Mycenaians harassing the western Anatolian vassals of their rivals, the Hittites. They sought alliances with the Mycenaians.[87] The Hittites too interacted with the Mycenaians, sometimes in cooperation and at other times in competition. Mycenaians were no longer content to trade and raid along the coast of Anatolia; they began colonizing, especially in the area around Miletos. The importance of Anatolia to the kingdom is evident in the marriage of one of Abas's sons to a Lycian princess.

Wealthy Abas initiated the construction of a great palace in Mycenai—one to rival the sumptuous Minoan palaces of old. He lived in the kind of splendor his ancestors could only afford to be buried in. Abas married the Mantinean princess Aglaia (also called Okaleia) and fathered twin sons Akrisios and Proitos (1385T/1135R BCE), who fought in the womb and incessantly thereafter.

It was fitting that King Abas and the Mycenaians were the first to be taught Demeter's mysteries when Demeter ordered her priest, Triptolemos of Eleusis, to tell the world her mysteries (1373T/1138R BCE). Triptolemos arrived in a chariot drawn by winged dragons loaned to him by Demeter, the bringer of the seasons.

---

Exhibit 6.4
Mycenaian Palaces

The construction of impressive royal palaces was the third great building program of Hellas (shaft graves and tholos tombs were the first two). Krete was already famous for its impressive palaces, and on the mainland modest palaces had existed since the Middle Helladic Era (2025T/1775R-1550T/1300R BCE), most notably at Lerne and Tiryns in Argeia. However, nothing remains in Mycenai of any palace before the Late Helladic (LHIIIA) palace of Abas and Akrisios (if there were any before).

Numerous Mycenaian palaces have been discovered, from Iolkos in the northeast (Thessalia) to Pylos in the southwest (Peloponnesos). The best

[87] Egyptian royal records mention an envoy sent to Hellas during the reign of Pharaoh Amenhotep III (1391T/1141R–1353T/1103R BCE).

preserved palace was found at Pylos, where no later construction occurred. The palaces of Mycenai and Tiryns are also fairly well preserved.

Mycenaian palaces were generally smaller and less impressive than Minoan palaces, but they shared a similar outline with a few fundamental differences; the more warlike Mycenaians surrounded their palaces with great walls built of large stones, and at the center of their palaces was a great hall or megaron. The megaron was a Mycenaian design developed from earlier mainland architecture. The megaron was roughly square and was usually entered from a courtyard. A large hearth stood toward one end, and on the opposite wall was a platform with a throne upon it. Their palaces confidently stood several stories high and included bathrooms and royal apartments.

Mycenaian palaces were established as centers of power after the fall of the Minoans and flourished for several hundred years (LHIIIa–LHIIIc; 1375T/1125R–1075T/850R BCE). Palace walls were decorated with frescoes of Minoan style and technique. The painters also borrowed many Minoan motifs, although depictions of war, royal hunts, and heraldic animals often replaced Minoan nature scenes.

Palace economies required stability, and the warlike nature of the Mycenaians depicted in art and literature is overstated. Like Minoan palaces, the Mycenaian palaces supported mostly self-contained elaborate societies based upon agriculture, crafts, and, to a lesser degree, trade. There were many small, unfortified villages and towns surrounding the palaces. The fortifications at most palaces were minimal until late in the period, and some palaces—notably those at Pylos and Orkhomenos—were never walled. Linear B was used primarily to inventory goods and prescribe religious rituals. Piracy and plunder did not play a significant role but became more widespread as palace economies began to collapse.

---

It is not surprising that a great warrior was responsible for constructing a great palace. Through conquest he would have gained the power and resources to undertake the great building project. Although we know nothing about Abas other than his prowess and his children, he must have revolutionized society. We know little about the early, prepalace Mycenaian kings or their neighbors. However, starting with Akrisios and Proitos, mythic details bring alive the personalities of Mycenaian kings and warriors, and the interactions between city-states.[88]

---

[88] If the volcanic eruption on Theras occurred between 1650 BCE and 1600 BCE—as radiocarbon, Greenland ice core, and tree-ring analyses indicate—then the building of the shaft graves would be pushed back by up to 150 years. The earliest shaft graves were built (Middle Helladic) before the eruption of Theras (Late Minoan). If the palaces are also pushed back by the full 150 years, then Danaos or even Phoroneus would have to be considered the builder of the earliest palace instead of Abas.

# Fall of Krete to the Rise of Dionysos

## Late Helladic Bronze Age (LHII–LHIII); Part of Hesiod's Age of Heroes

> No man has seen nor will anyone know
> The truth about the god and all the things I speak of.
>
> —Xenophanes of Kolophon, fifth century BCE

> And so hail to you, Dionysos, god of the abundant clusters!
> Grant that we may come again rejoicing to this season,
> And from that season onwards for many a year.
>
> —"Homeric Hymn to Dionysos" xxvi, sixth century BCE

The rape of the Minoan princess Europa by the supreme god of the Hellenes symbolizes the conquest of Krete and the beginning of the Heroic

Age on Krete.[89] Zeus, yielder of the flaming three-pronged bolt, saw lovely Europa gathering flowers in a meadow while accompanied by rich-haired nymphs, and he desired her. Where the god had once changed the maiden Io's form into that of a cow, for Europa he changed his own shape into a gentle white bull with a dignified streak of black running between his horns. When the bull-god appeared near Europa, she marveled at the beautiful and tame beast before her, and she was bold enough to approach. The deceitful bull allowed her to pet and scratch him. Then, to her astonishment, he dropped to his knees and turned his head as if to ask her to mount him. Entranced and exhilarated, she threw caution aside and climbed onto the beast's muscular back.[90] Immediately he sprang up and bolted, the poor screaming girl clutching onto one of his horns for dear life (1388T/1138R BCE).

Only when the galloping bull reached the far side of the island did he stop in a grassy meadow. There, beneath an evergreen tree, the frazzled girl dropped off his back and onto her hands and knees. Immediately the god in bull form amorously assaulted her. Then he departed from her, and alone she regretted her loss of virginity. But laughter-loving Aphrodite

---

[89] Hellenic writers consistently identified Europa and the House of Phoenix with Phoenicia/ Canaan. Babylonian seals uncovered in Thebes that date to the mid fourteenth century T / late twelfth century R BCE suggest an early literary link to the east. Thebes was certainly active in the trade to the east, and the members of the Sea Peoples may have colonized Canaan and become known as the Philistines.

However, the rape of Europa is a clearly a metaphor for the Hellenic conquest of the first European civilization, the Minoans of Krete. Classical Hellenes had forgotten the Minoans and their demise, but their myths held a recollection of them. Europa was a descendent of Epaphos, the son of Zeus and a Mycenaian princess. Her uncle was Danaos, the eponym of the Danaans. When Homer refers to Mycenaians, he calls them either Danaans or Akhaians. It seems likely that this prominent Mycenaian (Danaan) family played a key role in the conquest of Krete. They may have settled at Kommos, an important Bronze Age Kretan port facing Egypt. Once the Minoans were forgotten, later Hellenes moved their homeland to the Egypt (port of Khemmis) and to Phoenicia—important places during historic times. Finally, the Linear B writing style Kadmos (Europa's brother) brought to Hellas was derived from a Minoan script. Phoenicians did not invent their alphabet; nor did they actively trade around the Aigaian Sea until after the collapse of the Minoan and Mycenaian civilizations. Herodotos, in *Histories*, 5.58, mistakenly assumed that Kadmos brought the Phoenician alphabet into use during his time. See Addendum 4, "Minoan Krete" for more on Minoan Krete.

[90] The rape of Europa, first recorded in Hesiod, *Catalog of Women*, 19, and more elaborately described by the fifthe century poet Bakkhylides of Keos, in *Oxyrhynkhos Papyri*, may have been inspired in part by Minoan frescoes showing dancing acrobats leaping over bulls. The seeds of the ancient Bull-Horned god of the Neolithic Anatolian site of Catal Huyuk are present too.

appeared to comfort her and she told the girl that Zeus was the one who had loved her and that their union, like Zeus and white-armed Hera's, was a sacred marriage. Because dark-haired Zeus no longer feared discovery or concerned himself with angry Hera's feelings, he came to Europa again and again. He also commemorated his action by placing the image of his white bull form in the heavens as the constellation Taurus.

For protection Zeus gave Europa the Bronze Age giant Talos, the last of a mechanical race either built by Hephaistos or sprung from ash trees. He also gave her the superlative hunting dog Lailaps. Europa bore Zeus three sons: Minos, Rhadamanthys, and Sarpedon. Once his desire was fulfilled, the Thunderer-on-High gave Europa in marriage to Asterios, who adopted and raised her semidivine children. Europa bore her mortal husband a daughter named Krete, eponym of the island.

Meanwhile, Europa's frantic father, Phoenix[91] (a cousin of the Mycenaian king Danaos), sent his sons to find his beloved daughter Europa with stern instructions to return either with her or not at all. Phoenix ruled Phoenix, a city he built on the south side of Krete, farthest from Mycenai and closest to Egypt. Europa and her brothers—Kadmos, Cilix, Thasos, and Phineus—were the offspring of Phoenix's linen-robed Egyptian wife Telephassa (or Argiope), daughter of the undulating Nile.[92] The sons of Phoenix all assumed their sister had been taken off the island and sailed away. None found her or returned. Cilix headed east and became the eponym of Cilicia. The seer Phineus eventually settled on the Thracian coast of the Propontis Sea just before the narrows of the Bosporos. Kadmos was joined by his mother, Telephassa, and his brother Thasos and sailed northward. Once his sons departed, Phoenix's daughter Astypalaia was abducted by earth-shaking Poseidon and embraced upon the Cycladic island bearing her name.

---

[91] Phoenix is often thought to mean "Phoenician," but it doesn't have to. Literally it means "dark red" or "purple." Akhilleus's mentor was named Phoenix, and he was never associated with the Near East.

[92] See also Exhibit 6.4 for the lineage of Phoenix.

Image 7.1
Map of Kadmos's travels

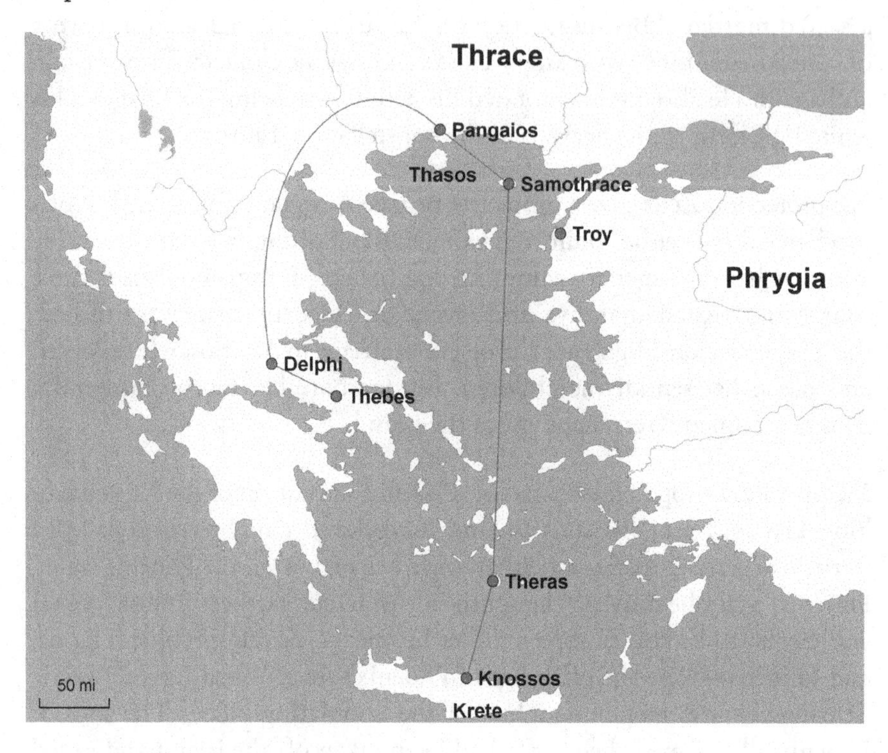


## Kretans Found Thebes

Prince Kadmos and his followers first landed on the Cycladic island of Thera. There he left a small party with his kinsman Membliaros to repopulate the island, which long ago had been devastated by a tremendous volcanic eruption. Sailing on to the north, Kadmos stopped on Samothrace Island and was initiated into the mysteries of Cybele (Rhea) by the Pleiades Elektra. Tan Elektra, whom the son of Kronos carried off, was the daughter of the Titan Atlas and the Oceanid Pleione. Understanding the mysteries, however, did not help Kadmos find Europa.

Kadmos continued sailing north until he landed on the mainland of Thrace. Exhausted and discouraged by their search, Kadmos and his weary band settled down for a time. There Kadmos discovered the gold mines of Pangaios. After his old mother died, Kadmos resumed the search. His brother Thasos and some of the men stayed in Thrace (Thasos is eponym of gold-rich Thasos Island, off the coast of Thrace) while Kadmos left his ships behind and wandered overland, clueless, into Hellas, finally stopping at Delphi for guidance.

Kadmos was told Europa would be found where a cow was laid low by fatigue. "Give up looking for a girl, your sister, and settle in the land to where you are led," said the prophetess. So Kadmos bought a black-and-white cow from King Pelagion and drove her on until, finally, she dropped near the sacred spring of Thebe.

Kadmos too dropped to his knees and gave a prayer of thanks for the end of his journey. He prepared a sacrifice to Athena for finding him such a bountiful and yet unoccupied land. Servants were sent to fetch water for the rite. Soon they came upon a deep well, and not knowing of the dragon that guarded it, they began to drink. The dragon awoke. He rushed to protect the holy precinct and killed the terrified servants. When they did not return, Kadmos became concerned. He set out to look for them and found the dragon feasting on their bloodied bodies.

Kadmos confronted the serpent, not realizing it acted upon the order of bronze-belted Ares to protect his precinct and fountain. As the dragon charged, Kadmos threw a well-aimed rock that killed the beast. Then tall Athena appeared and directed Kadmos to pull the dragon's teeth, give half of them to her, and sow the remainder. No sooner had the teeth entered the soil than men dressed in flashing bronze arms began to spring forth from the ground.

Kadmos feared that these numerous and fierce looking Aones warriors would overpower him. Thinking quickly, he hid and threw a rock into their midst. Believing one of their own had caused the offense, they began to battle among themselves in Ares's precinct. Eventually only five remained: Ekhion, Odious, Chthonios, Hyperenor, and Peloros (1386T/1136R BCE).

Ekhion then listened to the wise council whispered into his ear by bright-eyed Athena. Throwing down his sword, he proposed peace. His weary brothers quickly agreed. These five warriors were appropriately called the Spartoi (meaning "sown men") and they were the ancestors of the top Theban families. Kadmos reappeared and promised each an important position in his court. Then, to atone for killing the dragon, Kadmos was commanded to serve stout-hearted Ares for an eternal year.[93]

Serving the war god for an eternal year meant constant warfare. Finally Kadmos defeated local Hyantes and Aones tribesmen. The Hyantes fled to Phocis and founded Hyampolis. The Aones sued for peace and were allowed to remain, most choosing to live in the hills around the Theban Plain. After the long war, peace and harmony returned. Kadmos, with the help of the Spartoi, built his city, Kadmeia, around the sacred spring.[94]

## Marriage of Kadmos and Harmonia

After faithfully serving manly Ares, Kadmos was rewarded by Athena, who secured Harmonia, the third child of Ares and Aphrodite (Terror and Fear preceded her), as his bride (1378T/1128R BCE). Their wedding was the most splendid ever witnessed by mortals. All the Olympian gods attended—an honor they would later bestow on only one other mortal (Peleus, who married the Nereid Thetis). Lyre-playing Apollo provided spirited music, and the Muses sang melodically for the happy guests. Peace and harmony prevailed in Thebes.

---

Exhibit 7.1
Wedding Gifts for Harmonia

King Kadmos and his bride received splendid wedding gifts from the gods (the warlike Hellenes understood they were the gifts of harmonious living). Crafty Hermes presented a lyre; Hephaistos, on Aphrodite's suggestion, crafted for Harmonia a gorgeous necklace that made the wearer irresistible;

---

[93] Apollodoros, in *Library*, iii.24, says any god who broke an oath bound by the Styx had to observe a year of silence and fasting followed by an eternal year (eight solar years) banished from Olympos. The Roman grammarian Servius said Apollo served Admetos for an eternal year, and the Hellenistic writer Euanthes says Lykaian Zeus werewolves of Arkadia remained in that grievous state for an eternal year. Herein Herakles's labors are assumed to have taken an eternal year.

[94] Foundation myths, which tell how a city was located and from whence came its king and noble families, were out of place in Hellas, where most of the sites were settled since the Early Bronze Age or before. The only foundation myths we have are this story about Thebes and possibly Athamas' founding of Halos in Thessalian Akhaia. Troy also had a foundation myth, but it is a late invention and borrows from the Theban one.

and Athena presented a robe that gave the wearer the appearance of youthful yet divine countenance.

Probably the best gifts came from Demeter and the Pleiades Elektra. Demeter brought sustenance (grain), and Elektra brought knowledge from Samothrace of the ancient agricultural mysteries of Rhea (Cybele).

During the wedding, Demeter became enamored with Elektra's mortal son Iasion. This charming, gentle man made her forget the loss and humiliation she had suffered at the hands of the Olympian gods over her daughter Persephone. Eager Demeter slept with Iasion discreetly, away from the wedding guests, in a trice-plowed field called Kabeirion.[95]

In time Demeter bore Iasion two children and raised them on Samothrace. The Olympian gods were shocked upon discovering that Demeter's lover was a mortal, even though they regularly slept with mortals. So the god of the dark, furrowed brow killed Iasion with a thunderbolt as a warning for men to stay in their place and not enter into relations with goddesses.

---

[95] In a variation of this Theban myth told at the Samothracian mysteries, the marriage of Kadmos and Harmonia occurred on Samothrace because Harmonia was the daughter of star nymph Elektra and the sister of Iasion. The Kabeirion, near Thebes, was founded in the sixth century BCE, although by Pausanias's time (*Guide to Greece,* ix.23.5) it was believed that Demeter founded it herself for the Kabeiroi Prometheus and his son Aitnaios.

Kadmos's marriage to Harmonia meant that peace reigned in the previously war-torn land. Kadmos ruled long with the blessings of the people. He brought with him to mainland Hellas the knowledge of writing.[96] Kadmos was fortunate, and as Pindar, the most famous Theban poet said,

> If any man is fortunate, either
> In glorious prizes or in the strength of wealth
> And keeps down odious pride in his heart,
> He is fit to be wedded to his townsmen's praises.
> Zeus, from you mighty qualities
> Come to men. If they honor you,
> Their happiness lasts longer,
> But when it consorts with contorted minds
> It flourishes not in like measure all the time.[97]

During this happy time Kadmos and Harmonia raised five children: noble Polydoros and four beautiful daughters—Agave, Autonoe, Ino, and Semele. Kadmos wisely married his eldest daughter Agave to one of the leading Spartoi, Ekhion, and she bore him the future king Pentheus. To ensure peaceful relations, Kadmos gave his second daughter, Autonoe, in marriage to the prominent Lapith chief Aristaios of Thessalia and his third daughter, Ino, in marriage to Athamas, the Lapith king of neighboring Orkhomenos, the other great Boiotia palace city-state (besides Thebes). His youngest and fairest daughter attracted a divine lover.

---

[96] The Classical Age Hellenes (525T/500R–323 BCE) were unaware of the writing (Linear B) of their own Mycenaian Age ancestors, which was forgotten once the palaces fell (there was a palace at Thebes, but it has not be excavated). The alphabet used by later Hellenes to record their epic past was originally a Canaanite alphabet that was adapted by the Phoenicians and introduced into Hellas by them (ca. 750T/705R BCE). Following Herodotos's *Histories*, v.58, the Hellenes assumed incorrectly that their early ancestors also learned to write from the Phoenicians, and therefore they incorrectly associated Kadmos with Phoenicia. However, that a Hellen from Krete brought knowledge of Linear B back to the mainland is factual.

Linear B texts have been uncovered in the palace of Thebes starting with the time the Hellenes built elaborate shaft graves (in Thebes probably during the mid fifteenth century T / late thirteenth century R BCE). The city of Thebes is referred to by name in those texts.

[97] Pindar, "Isthmian Ode iii", in *The Odes*. Translated by C.M. Bowra.

## Rise of Orkhomenos

Orkhomenos was a great city worthy of Kadmos's respect. It was an older city that was well established before Thebes was built; this is a mythic claim supported by archaeological evidence. In fact, Orkhomenos was one of the first cities to rise during the Middle Bronze Age (2025T/1775R–1550T/1300R BCE). A century before Mycenai and other Peloponnesos cities rose in importance, Orkhomenos was already bustling (mid seventeenth century T / late fourteenth century R BCE).

A band of nearly-Hellenic Lapith tribesmen from Thessalia were first to arrive from the north after a plague caused the demise of most of the earthborn Ektenes. Their leader was Andreus, the son of the swirling Thessalian river god Peneios and his lovely wife, Kreousa. He called the area Andreis after himself, and Orkhomenos prospered as Mycenaian and Minyan sailors replaced the Minoans as masters of the Aigaian Sea.

Andreus was succeeded by his son Eteokles (meaning "true fame") as king of rich Orkhomenos. Some said his mother was a daughter of the nearby Cephissos River. Eteokles was the first man to realize that there were three Kharities and to name them. He built the first shrine to these goddesses, and Boiotia remained their chief center of worship thereafter. By grace, Orkhomenos prospered.

Eteokles named his people the Cephissians and Eteokleans. When Aiolian immigrants from Thessalia arrived (descendants of Hellas, father of the Hellenes), Eteokles felt it prudent to welcome them rather than risk defeat in war. When Eteokles died suddenly before he had the chance to start a family, the Aiolian commanders Athamas and Minyas, sons of Aiolos and Enarte, took over the city. The city grew rapidly in part as a result of immigration and also in part because of expanding trade. Minyan merchants were among the first to establish trading posts in Anatolia and were most active in the Pontos (Black) Sea trade.

Athamas, the elder Aiolian chief, was chosen to rule prosperous Orkhomenos (1357T/1107R BCE). He married the cloud nymph Nephele (Nebula)—an attendant and look-alike of Hera. The rainmaker king Athamas slept upon a cloud and seeded Helle and Phrixos.

While his first family was still young, Athamas was offered a second wife as part of a political marriage. Kadmos of Thebes had built a strong city to the south and wanted to keep peaceful relations with the new ruler of larger Orkhomenos. Kadmos offered his third daughter, Ino, to Athamas. Because Athamas's marriage with Nephele was not going well, for she looked down upon her mortal husband, Athamas accepted Kadmos's offer (1354T/1104R BCE).

## Children of a Cloud

As to be expected when a man has two wives, strife arrived. When Ino became pregnant, she worried about the fate of her unborn child, knowing that Nephele's son Phrixos was already heir to the throne. Secretly Ino began poisoning the wheat crop, and Athamas feared that famine would strike the land. He sent an envoy to Delphi to find out why the crops were failing. Ino bribed the envoy into saying that if Phrixos were sacrificed, all would be well again.

Nephele prayed for white-armed Hera to save her family. Hera did not disappoint her servant and sent clever Hermes with a marvelous, speaking golden-fleeced ram. Just like the Israelite Abraham, Athamas agonized while preparing to sacrifice his son. At the last minute, Nephele snatched her young children away and put them onto the back of the golden ram, which quickly flew off (1354T/1104R BCE). As the ram headed toward Colchis, the younger Helle fell off and drowned in the strait between Asia and Europe, which has been called Hellespont ever since. Phrixos safely landed in Colchis and sacrificed the ram upon its own advice. The Golden Fleece,[98] guarded by a dragon, became the object of the Argonaut quest.

---

[98] Hellenic trade with Colchis (in modern Georgia) during Mycenaian times is well documented. Precious tin and gold were traded for Minyan pottery and other manufactured goods. The tin, a critical and scarce ingredient of bronze, came overland from Afghanistan. The gold came from the local Phasis River, as it still does today. It is very likely that rather than panning for gold, the early miners used fleeces, "golden fleeces," to catch the precious mineral. Minyan wares have been found at Troy beginning in the sixteenth century T / fourteenth century R BCE, and direct trading with Colchis by the fourteenth century T / twelfth century R BCE is likely. Orkhomenos appears to have played a dominant role in this trade, and it likely made her rich. A faded memory of this trading relationship is preserved in the story of the Argonauts.

Anguished Nephele left earth for her home in the tearful rain clouds surrounding Olympos (later, when great Zeus brought mortal Ixion to visit heaven, the ungrateful guest seduced Nephele, gleefully thinking she was Hera.) With Nephele out of the way, Ino safely delivered her first child, Learkhos.

---

Exhibit 7.2
Tholos Tombs of Boiotia

Tholos tombs were built throughout Hellas during the early fifteenth century T / mid thirteenth century R BCE. Later Hellenes were profoundly impressed by those massive domed structures. The most impressive one in Boiotia still stands today (in 1870 CE locals heard an explosion inside a hill and rushed to find that the weight of earth had finally caused the roof to cave in). The Hellenes speculated that the building must have been a treasury (the first treasury ever constructed, they thought), built to house Minyas's considerable wealth (remember, Homer called only Mycenai, Troy, and Orkhomenos rich). The building attributed to Minyas was actually a tholos tomb built in the early thirteenth century T / mid eleventh century R BCE. It is from the same era and roughly equivalent in size and scale to Atreus's marvelous tholos tomb in Mycenai. Pausanias saw both but preferred Minyas's "treasury," calling it Hellas's greatest wonder, on par with the pyramids of Egypt. Fabled king Minyas was the subject of a now lost epic.

The famous Minyan architects Agamedes and Trophonios,[99] twin brothers, were thought to have built Minyas's treasury. To them were also attributed Poseidon's first shrine at Mantinea, Apollo's temple in Delphi, and Hyrieus's treasury (tholos tomb). To honor their great skill, Apollo rewarded them with quick deaths.

These architects died after completing their best work, the "treasury" of King Hyrieus of the nearby Boiotia port of Hyrie. The brothers had placed a trap door in the treasury and were stealing from it. Eventually Hyrieus realized he was being robbed and set a trap. Agamedes was caught in the snare, and Trophonios cut off his brother's head so that he would not be

[99] It was said that King Erginos of Orkhomenos fathered the famous architects Agamedes and Trophonios. However, he ruled during a later generation.

tortured (or talk). Trophonios then fled back toward home, but the ground swallowed him near Lebadeia. An oracle dedicated to Trophonios arose on the spot.

---

## Birth of Dionysos and Wrath of Hera

The youngest of the apple-cheeked daughters of Kadmos caught the attention of the roving eye of the Olympian Zeus. While powerless Hera seethed, Semele was only too happy to embrace the king of the gods. Zeus returned often to his radiant, expecting lover. As Semele's[100] body changed, she lost confidence in her beauty. Soon she convinced herself that Zeus despised her and begged him for a favor. Lovingly, Zeus promised her anything.

White-armed Hera took this opportunity to vanquish her rival. Appearing before Semele in the guise of her old nurse Beroe, Hera suggested that Semele ask to see Zeus in his full splendor. Hera knew full well that no mortal could the naked face of god and live. When Zeus appeared again, Semele made her request to see him as he really is. Zeus begged her not to ask for this, but she was blind to reason. Sadly Zeus obliged, and Semele went down in flames.

Quickly Zeus tore the six-month-old fetus from her lifeless body and sowed it into his own thigh. In this manner, Dionysos (meaning "son of Zeus") was carried to term; he is called "twice-born" for this reason (1353T/1103R BCE).

After Dionysos's miraculous birth, Zeus instructed Hermes to take the child to Semele's sister Ino to nurse. Ino and her husband, King Athamas of Orkhomenos, were instructed to disguise the child as a girl, in a vain attempt to deceive Hera. Ino had just delivered her first son, Learkhos, and she pretended to have born twins. With Hera's attendant Nephele out of the way, Ino accepted further risk of Hera's wrath by nursing the divine offspring of Zeus and her deceased sister.

---

[100] The identification of Semele with the Thracian/Phrygian fertility goddess Zemalo, because of the similarity of their names, appears to be unfounded.

Things went well for a few years. Ino gave birth to a second healthy son named Melicertes. Soon after Dionysos was weaned, cloud-gathering Zeus sent the messenger god Hermes to their glorious palace to say it was too dangerous for dark-haired Dionysos to stay with them any longer. Sadly the couple kissed their adopted son goodbye. Ino was particularly saddened by losing Dionysos.

As Ino and Zeus had feared, Hera figured out that Dionysos was in Orkhomenos; but she arrived too late, for Dionysos was gone. In rage Hera sent the Fury Tisiphone to punish Athamas and Ino with madness for having harbored her enemy Dionysos (1349T/1099R BCE).

Crazed Athamas hunted down his son Learkhos like a wild beast. The poor, panic-stricken boy screamed in vain for his father to stop. Learkhos died not understanding what caused his formerly loving father to abuse him so. Meanwhile, Ino threw her infant son Melicertes into a boiling cauldron to cook. Then, clutching her dead baby, Ino ran to the seashore in Megaris and jumped off a cliff at the Isthmos. Aphrodite asked Poseidon to grant divinity to her poorly treated granddaughter Ino. Poseidon obliged, and Ino became Leukothea (meaning "white goddess"). Together with Melicertes, whose divine name is Palaimon, Ino often left their home in the palace of the Nereides to assist sailors in distress.

Athamas's brother Sisyphos, ruler of Korinth, found the tiny, lifeless body of Melicertes crumpled on the beach and realized the child's essence had become divine. Sisyphos started the Isthmian Games in honor of the child's divine rebirth.

Athamas groaned heavily after coming to his senses. The ascension of his wife and son did little to ease the vivid memories of Learkhos's betrayed look and hideous screams. The Minyans exiled Athamas for his heinous crime, and his brother Minyas became king (1349T/1099R BCE).

Through trade and plunder, King Minyas became richer than all of his predecessors. At home he initiated a great building program to drain Lake Kopais and provide additional farmland for his growing population.[101] To

[101] The Late Bronze Age drainage of this lake was an engineering marvel not repeated until nineteenth century CE, but by the Archaic Age, the visual evidence of the dikes had largely disappeared.

keep up with the growth and prosperity of Orkhomenos, many architects and builders were employed.

Under Minyas, the earlier Lapiths, Aiolians, and Ektenes merged, and he called them Minyans. Minyan settlers helped found the first Hellenic colonies in Asia: Iassos and Miletos. Two daughters of Minyas married Thessalian kings, and so many of his descendants were among the Argonauts that the crew were often referred to as Minyans.

Meanwhile, Dionysos was spirited away to his cousin Makris, daughter of the beekeeper Aristaios and Kadmos's second daughter, Autonoe (who was one of Dionysos's aunts). Dionysos remained in constant danger from Hera. Soon Dionysos was disguised as a goat by Hermes and taken to the Nymphs of Mount Nysa in far-off Phrygia. The nymphs were aided by a Satyr named Seilenos, who became Dionysos's foster father. Meanwhile, Makris fled heavenly queen Hera's wrath to Kercyra (Corfu) Island, where she became a cave nymph and the lesbian lover of golden-haired Demeter.

As a youth, black-eyed Dionysos was forced to flee again. Alone this time, Dionysos left Phrygia and reached the island of Ikaria. There he paid some sailors for passage to Naxos. Out at sea the pirates stole his expensive clothes and prepared to rape the handsome youth.

> First throughout the swift black ship sweet and fragrant wine formed a gurgling stream and a divine smell arose as all the crew watched in mute wonder. Next on the topmost sail a vine spread about all over, and many grapes were hanging down in clusters. Then round the mast dark ivy twined, luxuriant with flowers and lovely growing berries the those-pins were crowned with wreaths. When they saw this they bade the helmsman put the ship to shore. Now the god became a fearsome, loud-roaring lion in the bow of the ship and then amidships a shaggy bear he caused to appear as a portent. The bear reared with fury and the lion scowled dreadfully on the topmost bench. The crew hastened in fear to the stern and stood dumbfounded round the helmsmen, a man of prudent mind, as the lion swiftly lunged upon the captain and seized him. When they saw this, they escaped evil fate by

> jumping overboard into the shining sea and were turned into dolphins.[102]

Such a powerful display caught the attention of cow-eyed Hera. At last she had found the little bastard she had long sought. Despite the youth's display of power, he was no match for the queen of heaven. She drove him insane, and he fled through Egypt, Assyria, and on to India. Hounded by his madness, as Io once was by a gadfly, black-haired Dionysos finally returned to Phrygia seeking shelter from the storms of madness.

The concerned Nymphs of Nysa comforted the madman. They placed him on two donkeys and escorted him to the great (Phrygian) goddess Cybele. Cybele, whom the Hellenes identified with Rhea, the mother of Zeus and Hera, purified her grandson Dionysos and presumably cured his madness. The transfigured wine god Dionysos rewarded the two asses with human speech. He also set up his own rites, many of which were similar to Cybele's.

Ivy-crowned Dionysos gave grape cultivation and the pleasures of wine to his followers.[103] His rites were often orgiastic communions performed on mountaintops at night. Under religious fervor and perhaps the intoxication of wine, the revelers often saw visions of their god. As Euripides says[104] "The soul grows great, overcome by the arrow of the vine".

Dionysos attracted a strange company of wild women called Mainades (meaning "mad ones"; the root for "maniac") and Satyrs (woodland spirits). He was reunited with Seilenos, who was now an old, wise Satyr. Seilenos led the Satyrs under Dionysos while the Nymphs of Nysa led the dancing Mainades. The Mainades were often joined in their orgasmic rites by local women, to the chagrin of fathers and husbands.

---

[102] Hesiod, "Homeric Hymn to Dionysos" vii, in *The Homeric Hymns and Homerica.*

[103] Before his identification with wine, "Dionysos" may have been one of the names given to the minor fertility god that was born each winter and died each summer and who was consort to the Great Goddess (Cybele/Rhea in Anatolia and her daughter Demeter in Hellas). With wine and the leisure time needed for contemplation, Dionysos's status rose to that of a civilization god and a representative of man's deep psychological nature. The Hellenes considered him the youngest Olympian. Thus it came as a surprise to find his name appearing in Linear B documents, while Apollo was not mentioned. What is agreed upon is that his name is not Hellenic.

[104] Euripides, "Bacchae" 1160, in *The Bacchae and Other Plays.* Translated by Philip Vellacott.

Wine can be an impetus to love, and so it was that Aphrodite was charmed by twice-born Dionysos and slept with him. But the offspring of their lust was not so beautiful: radiant Aphrodite bore the ugly, Satyr-like Priapos, a Phrygian fertility god. Priapos had extremely large genitals, and outside of Anatolia his worship was not taken seriously. Once, Priapos and one of the asses Dionysos had bestowed speech upon debated as to who had the largest erect penis. The donkey won, and furious Priapos beat him dead. Dionysos put both of the speaking donkeys in the stars as thanks for carrying him to Cybele.

## Triumphant Return of Dionysos

Dionysos led his followers on a triumphant return to Thebes (1331T/1081R BCE). Along the way he encountered resistance among a Thracian tribe called the Edonians; King Lykourgos drove the god's ragtag band away. Dionysos fled to Thetis, who lived in the palace of her father, Nereus, at the bottom of the sea offshore. There he was joyfully reunited with Ino, now deified as Leukothea, and her son Palaimon. They comforted Dionysos and restored his resolve. Then he returned to his followers and drove Lykourgos mad, bringing about his brutal death, and continued on his journey.

The long-haired god Dionysos passed through Thessalia and past Halos, a city founded by Athamas, the former king of Orkhomenos. After killing his son in a madness inflicted by Hera, Athamas had consulted an oracle for guidance. He had been told to travel to where a wild beast showed him hospitality. Not understanding the prophecy, he traveled north, toward his ancestral lands, until he came upon a pack of wolves. The startled canines fled and left behind their meal. Athamas realized that he should settle upon that spot. He sent for Minyan supporters to help build the city of Halos (in Thessalian Akhaia). He also built the Minyan port of Teos across the grey Aigaian Sea in Ionia.

Old Athamas had recently escaped being sacrificed in Halos as part of a rainmaking ceremony by the timely arrival of his grandson Cytissoros (son of Phrixos, who had ridden the golden-fleeced ram). Young Cytissoros had been raised in Colchis and upon his arrival was given rule over Halos. Athamas followed Dionysos back to Orkhomenos with his third wife, the

Lapith princess Themisto, and their four young sons: Leukon, Erythrios, Ptoos, and Skhoineus. The wild band passed by Thermopylai, the pass that guarded the entrance into Hellas, and stopped in the palace city of Orkhomenos.

The god was not well received; Alkathoe, Arsippe, and Leucippe, the younger daughters of King Minyas, scorned him, refusing to participate in his emotional rites. They remained at home, worshiping Athena and weaving fine clothes. In punishment the young god drove them out of their home by causing vines to rapidly grow around them. With their controlled facades ruptured, their powerful repressed feelings exploded uncontrollably. These berserk ladies cast lots to choose their victim, and they agreed to sacrifice Leucippe's young son Hippasos. They ripped him up limb by limb and ate him. Then they joined the Mainades on Mount Laphystios. Afterward, either Hermes or Dionysos turned them into bats.

So the cult of Dionysos was adopted in rich Orkhomenos, where King Minyas decreed an end to the banishment of his long-absent brother Athamas. The Orkhomenians now appreciated his role in Dionysos's early life, and Minyas commissioned his brother Athamas to supervise the construction of dikes and canals on the south shores of Lake Kopais.

Ivy-crowned Dionysos continued on and triumphantly returned to the place of his birth, holy Thebes. There too he met resistance. The city was then ruled by Pentheus, the brash, aristocratic nephew of Kadmos. Old Kadmos had stepped down in favor of Pentheus. Although Pentheus was young, he clung to his belief in traditional, rational gods extolling the virtues of warriors. Dionysos was rejected.

Kadmos, his uncle Athamas, and others warned Pentheus not to resist the cult. Arrogant Pentheus would not listen. He forbade the women of Kadmeia (Thebes) to participate in the rites. When his injunction was ignored, Pentheus imprisoned the bacchantes. But the prisoners' chains fell off of their own accord and the jail doors opened mysteriously. The joyous revelers returned to the hills to continue their rites.

When King Pentheus of Thebes followed to spy upon the devotees, Dionysos exacted a terrible revenge. Pentheus's mother, Agave, and her sisters saw Pentheus hiding in a pine tree and imagined in their madness that he was a wild beast. They pulled him down and in their frenzy did not hear his pleading cries. Pentheus was torn apart limb by limb. In the sober light of day, the sorrow-filled women were exiled from Kadmeia (Thebes). Pentheus was succeeded by his uncle Polydoros, Kadmos's only son.

Dionysos's followers continued on throughout Hellas, spreading the new religion. The last bastion of resistance was found at Tiryns. Dionysos drove the daughters of the king of Tiryns mad and continued his journey through Hellas. On Krete Dionysos took as his wife Ariadne, the daughter of his half brother, King Minos of Knossos, whose mother was Europa (1328T/1078R BCE). They married on Naxos Island and received the good news that King Proitos of Tiryns had capitulated in order to recover the sanity of his daughters and that Dionysos was now honored throughout all of Hellas. Dionysos and Ariadne raised their children—Thoas, Oinopion, Staphylos, and Peparethos—on Lemnos Island.

After raising his children on Lemnos, Dionysos achieved what no other mortal Hellen had ever done beforehand and only Herakles did afterward; he became an Olympian god. While Herakles had to die physically before achieving that Olympic stature (his mortal parts burned away on a funeral pyre), Dionysos's death was strictly symbolic. To achieve immortality, Dionysos had to pass through the undergloom. The depths of Lake Alcyonia near Lerne in the Argeia were believed to be unfathomable, and its waters sank down into an entrance to Hades. For this reason Dionysos went there looking for the way into the underworld. Being a god (and therefore not having knowledge of death), he needed a mortal to help him find the gates of death. A local man named Prosymnos agreed to show him the way if he could make love to the god like a woman. (Since the gods could not die, prostituting themselves to lowly humans was the required price for favors. Demeter underwent the same treatment in Eleusis.) Dionysos agreed, and Prosymnos rowed the god out onto the lake and told him to dive below. Dionysos descended into the underworld and bribed Persephone with myrtle to release his mother. When Dionysos returned with his mother, he found that Prosymnos had died. To honor his debt, Dionysos went to his graveside with amorous intent. He cut a branch from a fig tree shading the grave and pushed it into himself.

Dionysos was offered a home on snowy Olympos. Before accepting the offer, he requested that both his wife and mother be granted immortality. The Olympian Zeus gave a nod of his great head, and Semele became a fertility goddess. Her divine name is Thyone. Angry Hera accepted them with resigned silence, but gracious Hestia gave up her seat among the council of the twelve supreme deities to Dionysos, tipping the balance of power to the males. So, with woman's consent, males have dominated society ever since.

Dionysos's return and Pentheus's death propelled Kadmos and Harmonia to leave Thebes. The gift of harmony bestowed upon Kadmeia (Thebes) had ended, and they no longer belonged there. While strife returned to the city of Ares, the aging couple headed north, toward Illyria, accompanied by their grieving, clear-headed daughter Agave, who had been banished for murdering her son Pentheus. They settled among the Illyrian tribe of Enkheleans, just beyond the boundary of Hellas. Soon Kadmos killed a serpent and was immediately changed into a magic serpent himself. So was Harmonia. Kadmos was worshiped in a benevolent serpent cult.[105] On Ares's command, the two lived on the Isle of the Blessed. Harmonia was one of the few Hellenic women to receive hero cult worship.

---

Exhibit 7.3
Tragic Lives of the Daughters of Kadmos

Ironically, the lives of the four daughters of Harmonia (meaning "harmony") were engulfed in tragedy. Agave and Ino killed their own sons, Semele died as a young woman, and Autonoe was abandoned by her husband and lived to hear of her son's brutal death.

Aristaios, husband of Autonoe had a miraculous birth. Apollo was attracted to the wild Lapith maiden Cyrene,[106] who, like Daphne before her, was fiercely proud of her maidenhood. She hated walking to and fro before the loom and feasting with docile companions who kept the house, for she was a tomboy, a wild outdoors girl, a horse tamer. Because of her skills, she became the shepherdess of her father's flock and a great huntress, tracking game without a chaperon from the Vale of Tempe all the way to

[105] Serpent cults were fertility cults of rebirth. Snakes are an excellent representation of vegetation's cyclical death and rebirth in that they shed their old skins and are born anew. Snakes and serpents were also identified with another aspect of rebirth—healing. Since Kadmos was from a country that worshipped the Great Goddess and his daughter and grandson were fertility deities, it is understandable to think of him as one as well.

[106] The rise of the Hellenic colony of Cyrene in Libya lent importance to this myth.

Mount Pelion. Once, when she unflinchingly challenged a lion without her spears to save her father's sheep on Mount Pelion, Apollo, God of the Broad Quiver, observed her and became hot with desire.

Apollo called out to Kheiron, saying, wise Centaur come and observe the marvelous courage and great strength of the woman, yeah a girl who fights lions with her head unflinching, her maiden spirit high. Kheiron saw, and as his eyes softened, he foretold that Apollo would carry her off and experience what she had to offer. Apollo wasted no time in fulfilling that prophecy:

> When Gods are once in haste,
> Their work is swift, their ways short:
> That day, that day determined it.
> In Libya's rich golden room
> They slept together.[107]

In far-off Libya, the god stripped the fierce, willing maiden of her virginity (1382T/1132R BCE). There, far from Hellas, she bore him a son, Aristaios. Apollo returned after she delivered their son and took the baby from her breast. He instructed luck-bringing Hermes to take the child to Olympos, where the Horai waited to grant him immortality by feeding him ambrosia and nectar. Then the robust baby was given to the wise teacher Kheiron, a Centaur who roamed the hills of Magnesia where Cyrene once hunted, to be raised. Apollo rewarded Cyrene by bestowing upon her a long life and by making her a powerful water nymph with attendants. Strong-willed Cyrene did not remain in Libya; she chose to return to Thessalia with her attendants. There she lived in a grotto palace below the surface of her grandfather's river.

Cyrene's divine child Aristaios received a fabulous education from Kheiron and became a minor divinity responsible for various rustic pursuits.[108] Hermes's daughter, the nymph Myrtle, suckled the infant Aristaios. Kheiron taught Aristaios the arts of the hunter and the shepherd, and

---

[107] Pindar, "Pythian Ode" ix.66–69, in *The Odes.* Translated by C.M. Bowra.

[108] His cult bestowed upon him the status of god for teaching man so many agricultural arts. The cult began in agrarian Thessalia but was biggest in rural Arkadia. Both states, coincidentally, were Pelasgian strongholds and the first king of the Lapiths was the brother-in-law of Pelasgos.

especially the agricultural practices of beekeeping, olive and other fruit-tree growing, and cheese making.

Apollo's musical attendants, the Muses, found Aristaios a bride and taught him to be a healer and prophet. To pay back their kindness, Aristaios became shepherd of the Muses' rich flocks, which he herded from the Athamanian Plain of Phthia to Mount Othrys and as far as the Apidanos River of Thessalia. Their daughter Makris secretly cared for young Dionysos.

Aristaios grew tired of his simple, rustic wife and abandoned her as well as the flocks of the Muses. He moved south into the great city of Thebes, where he married Princess Autonoe, daughter of wise Kadmos. The marriage was fruitful, and among their children was the hunter Aktaion. Civil life did not suit Aristaios; he abandoned the princess and returned to his rustic homeland with his son Aktaion. The great teacher Kheiron raised the child to be a peerless hunter like his father and his grandmother.

One day while walking through the Vale of Tempe, Aristaios saw a lovely dryad nymph and was filled with desire. She ran away, and he followed in hot pursuit until she accidentally stepped on a poisonous serpent and was bitten. She died almost instantly, and the angry dryads vexed his bees.[109]

Aristaios became both heartbroken and perplexed when, despite his immense skill and best efforts, his bees began to sicken and die. Once all his bees had perished, distraught Aristaios abandoned his home in the lovely Vale of Tempe and stood at the brink of sacred Peneios's utmost fountainhead and loudly complained to his mother. Deep down beneath this pool, Cyrene and her attendants heard his distressed cry and bade the river to part, and the waves gathered him in their vastness and sent him down beneath the flood.

After Aristaios finished marveling at the caverns his mother called home, the nymphs washed his hands and laid dishes and cups on a table beside burning incense. Then Cyrene told her son about the old man of the sea, Proteus, the honored seer of the water deities, knower of all that has been, is now, and lies in store. She told her son to catch and bind him with fetters

[109] The myth involved Orpheus because his wife was a dryad who lost her life in the same manor. But Aristaios' son Aktaion lived a hundred years before Orpheus.

and he will reveal to you the cause of this calamity and we will bring a prosperous close to this issue. But, it will not be easy, only by constraint will he give answer.

Cyrene bathed Aristaios in ambrosia to supply him with vigor and led him to where Mount Pelion meets the sea.[110] There they waited for the noonday heat to bring shape-shifting Proteus and his wave-weary seal herd to sun themselves on the rocky shore. Sheltered in a receding cove, Proteus fell fast asleep. Quickly, Aristaios sprang upon him and, with a mighty shout, surprised him with shackles where he lay. Just as Cyrene had warned, Proteus changed into numerous forms, but Aristaios bound him all the more tightly. When no trickery won him escape (and he knew it would not), Proteus resumed his divine shape. Then he rolled back his sea-green eyes and saw the cause of Aristaios's plight.

Cyrene spoke truly in saying the anger that pursues his son is divine, grievous the sin he must pay for. The piteous dryads seek this penalty - though it is far less than deserved for the bitter anguish caused them by bringing about the death of their sweet sister. Having said this, Proteus plunged safely into the depths below. Cyrene appeared beside her shaken son and said, "Now rid yourself of all your cares, you must become their supplicant and ask with gifts for peace from these venerated spirits. For they will grant you pardon as you pray and will forget their anger."

Without delay, Aristaios carefully followed his mother's instruction; he sacrificed four splendid bulls and four unblemished heifers at an altar he raised in the grove of the dryads, and he waited for nine days before returning. Then he gave poppies of forgetfulness as a funeral offering and sacrificed a jet-black ewe. As he looked on in astonishment, there came from the carcasses of the oxen a cloud of buzzing, swarming bees that landed on a tree overhead.

Aristaios's good fortune was short lived. Soon he fell into despair again when he heard news every parent dreads; his dear son Aktaion was dead. The matter of his son's death gave Aristaios no comfort, for his son had been torn apart by his own hunting hounds because of Artemis's anger.

---

[110] Or on the Pallene Peninsula jutting out off the coast of Thrace according to the first-century BCE Roman poet Virgil, *Georgics*, iv; which provides the fullest account of the story. See also Pindar, *Pythian Ode*, ix and Apollonios, *Argonautika*, ii.500–527.

After receiving a splendid education from Kheiron, Aktaion had returned to the land of his mother, Princess Autonoe of Thebes, and boasted of his superior hunting skills. One day he chanced to see Artemis and her nymphs bathing at a spring in the Cithairon Mountains. Instead of turning his gaze away in modesty, Aktaion leered at the naked goddess. Angry Artemis changed Aktaion into a stag, and his hounds chased after him. When exhaustion overtook him, his hounds devoured him. Not understanding where their master had gone, the befuddled hounds howled until, in pity, Kheiron made a statue of Aktaion to soothe them (1321T/1071R BCE).[111]

Aristaios could find no solace in his own pastimes. Everywhere he went, the rustic countryside reminded him of his dead son. The summer was unbearably hot. Apollo wished to end his son's suffering and instructed destitute men from the islands to enlist Aristaios's support in their endeavor to improve the harvests in the parched islands. Unmoved in his grief-stricken state, it took a direct order from his father to make him go.

On Apollo's command, Aristaios assembled the Parrhasian[112] tribe and settled them on Keos Island. In that place Aristaios prayed to the Dog Star, Sirius, whose rise was accompanied by the summer heat, but most of all he prayed to all-seeing Zeus, who sent cooling Etesian winds that now blow each year for forty days, alleviating the heat that accompanied the Dog Star's rise.

Then Aristaios traveled to the land of his birth, Libya, where nymphs told him to go on to Sardinia, the huge footprint-shaped island off the Italian coast. There he taught the inhabitants his agricultural arts. Restlessly he sailed to Sicily and then moved on to live for a time near Mount Haimos in Thrace. There he met up with Dionysos and disappeared from the sight of men.

---

[111] Artemis is usually identified with the aspect of the great goddess called the Mistress of the Animals. Aktaion was originally her male aspect, the Master of the Animals. Both these deities represented the life force found in nature. The Hellenistic poet Kallimakhos of Cyrene may have invented the story that his death was caused by seeing her naked ("Hymn V. On the Bath of Pallas"). This is contrasted with the story of Teiresias, who did not leer and received both punishment and blessing.

[112] This might be an ancient corruption of "Perrhaibi," the name of the ancient serf tribe of Thessalia. Apollonios says they were a tribe dwelling around Othyrs, a mountain where Aristaios once grazed the Muses' flocks. Others identified them with the Arkadian tribe of the same name.

# First Heroes
## Late Helladic Bronze Age (LHIIIA); Part of Hesiod's Age of Heroes

Life is brief, and winged hope undoes the thinking of mortals. Lord Apollo said to the son of Pheres: "Since you are mortal, you must foster two thoughts: that tomorrow will be the only day on which you see the sun's light, and that for fifty years you will live out a life steeped in wealth.

Bakkhylides of Keos, fifth century BCE

The god's power makes it easy to win
What is beyond oath and beyond hope.

A prophet to Bellerophontes in Pindar of Thebes,
Olympian Ode xiii, fifth century BCE

### Madness of the Daughters of Proitos

When the unruly band following Dionysos reached the Argeia, they were opposed, as usual, by the conservative nobles in power. The devotees engaged in drunken orgies, which did not sit well with the conservative kings. They doubted effeminate Dionysos's divinity and extolled the virtues of warriors. When the Mainades arrived, they found Mycenai and Tiryns ruled respectively by Akrisios and Proitos, twin sons of the great

Mycenaian warrior-king Abas. They had been feuding since they shared their mother's womb, but the two found rare common cause against the new Dionysian religion. Dionysos punished Proitos for his resistance by afflicting the women of his kingdom, particularly his daughters, with madness.

The women ran off into the mountains of Arkadia and madly celebrated wild Bakkhinad rites. Then bull-like Proitos sent word to the holy man Melampous of Triphylian Pylos[113] asking that he come and cure the women. When Melampous offered to do so for one-third of the kingdom, Proitos flatly refused. The hideous wantonness of the women of Tiryns deprived them of their beauty, and the men became desperate. Their demands for action prompted Proitos to agree to Melampous's revised terms: one-third of the kingdom for himself and one-third for his brother Bias (1328T/1078R BCE).

Melampous enlisted the aid of his brother, and together they captured the possessed women led by the daughters of Proitos in the wild Aroanian Mountains near Pheneos in Arkadia. He was able to temporarily cure them by a purification cleansing at the site of Lousai (meaning "Washing") in Arkadia. Melampous brought all the girls home safely except for Proitos's incurable daughter Iphinoe, who died in Sicyon during the long walk home.

Upon his triumphant return, Melampous insisted that Proitos institute Dionysian rites in Tiryns. Proitos readily agreed, and once Dionysos was honored, the bouts of madness ceased. Proitos's daughter Maira joined the Mainades and spread the Dionysian gospel throughout Arkadia. This holy woman was honored in Arkadian Mantinea with a spring named for her, and she was buried in Tegea. Grateful Proitos not only held up his part of the bargain, but he also gave Melampous and Bias

[113] The myth of Melampous's curing of mad women is ancient (Homer and Hesiod mention it) and well documented by many writers (Apollodoros, Bakkhylides, Herodotos, Ovid, Strabo, and others). Only in a few sources is the cause of the madness mentioned. Apollodoros, in *Library*, ii.2.2, states that Hesiod (*Catalog of Women* 18) names Dionysos as the culprit but adds that the mythic historian/genealogist Akusilaos of Argos (fifth century BCE) claims Hera caused it because the girls belittled the wooden image of the goddess. Hera was the patron goddess of the Argeia, and the women were said to have behaved like cows. Both Hera and Dionysos were thought to have caused madness; for example, Hera caused Herakles to kill his own children in a fit of madness.

his daughters in marriage. Melampous received the city of Argos and Proitos's eldest daughter, Lysippe. Bias received the citadel of Midea, and upon the death of his first wife, he married Proitos's daughter Iphianassa (1309T/1059R BCE).

## The Wise Sons of Amythaon

Melampous and Bias were raised in wealth in the rich countryside of Amythaonia, a coastal region on the western shores of the Peloponnesos. The region was named for their father, Amythaon, an Iolkian prince[114] who fled dynastic disturbances upon King Aiolos's death.

Hesiod said that Zeus gave might to the sons of Aiakos, wealth to the sons of Atreus, and wisdom to the sons of Amythaon (Melampous and Bias). As a young man, Melampous once visited Polyphontes, king of a neighboring Mycenaian state in the western part of the Peloponnesos. When a snake bit one of Polyphontes's servants, the king killed it. Melampous noticed her offspring nearby, piously buried the mother serpent, and cared for the orphaned snakes. When the snakes were grown, in gratitude they slithered beside Melampous as he slept and purged his ears with their tongues. Melampous jumped up startled but thereafter understood the language of the birds and the animals.[115]

A richer understanding of the world inspired Melampous to seek Apollo, the spirit who reveals divine revelation in terms humans can understand. After many sacrifices, Melampous met this god by the banks of the swift-flowing Alpheus River. The luminous son of Zeus taught him the

[114] Amythaon was called the son of King Kretheus of Iolkos, but he clearly resided in an earlier age, based upon the timeline of his children.

[115] Apollodoros says Melampous's servants killed the snakes in their lair beside an oak tree near his house. Melampous piously burnt them and raised their offspring. Helenos and Kassandra of Troy received the power of augury in the same manner.

prophetic art of studying the entrails of sacrificial victims; he was the first Hellenic seer to do so.[116]

Melampous became the most celebrated seer in all of Hellas, and some thought that he was the first to use drugs in healing (those who had forgotten Apis, the ancient son of Apollo, a master of cures and divinations who crossed the waters from Naupaktos and by cleansing rituals once restored the land). Although not the first, Melampous certainly improved upon this ancient craft. However, like his father before him, he was forced to leave his home after incurring the enmity of a king; one who was jealous and fearful of Melampous's mystic powers. The king of Pylos became jealous or fearful of Melampous's good fortune, confiscated his property, and exiled him. Melampous's brother Bias tried to patch up the rift with a marriage alliance to the king's beautiful daughter Pero, whom he dearly loved.

Pero had so many suitors that her father demanded a great gift for her. Her father promised her hand to the man who could fetch the far-famed cattle herd of King Phylakos of Akhaian Phylace.

Exiled Melampous was undaunted by the difficulty of the request and gladly undertook the task on his brother's behalf. Confidently he proceeded, understanding that the Stronger Ones would grant him success. This noble man was willing to face great hardship, for his brother's happiness and his own were the same to him. Bias proved worthy of the gift.

Melampous traveled to Phylace, where the cattle of Phylakos grazed. He tried to steal them, although he had foreseen that he would be unsuccessful. When caught, Melampous was imprisoned in a small cell in the barn (1330T/1080R BCE).

[116] Ancient seers used various methods to seek divine understanding. Hellenes were particularly fond of bird watching and studying the entrails of sacrificial victims. Watching birds, usually birds of prey, is an Indo-European tradition. It is a form of prophecy called augury. The seer faces north and waits for a bird of prey to appear. If it appears on the right, it is a good omen; on the left, a bad omen. The art of studying entrails, especially livers, is Near Eastern in origin and appears to have reached Hellas during the eighth or seventh century BCE from Anatolia—where Apollo was originally worshipped. Augury always remained more popular among the Hellenes.

Melampous was detained for one year. Then one day he overheard the termites saying that they had nearly chewed through the beams supporting the prison. Melampous emphatically pleaded with his prison guard to be moved. Although the guard did not really believe this crook, he was impressed by the concern and sincerity of Melampous's prediction that the prison walls would fall that very night. Prudently, they moved elsewhere that night, and the prison fell as predicted.

The guard sent word to King Phylakos, who demanded that Melampous be brought before him immediately. Phylakos promised Melampous his freedom and the cattle if he would cure his son Iphikles's impotency. Melampous sacrificed two bulls and invited the birds to feast. One old vulture recalled seeing Iphikles run in terror when he saw his father racing toward him with a bloody sacrificial knife he menacingly wielded in his strong right hand. Iphikles had believed that he was to be sacrificed. The fear unmanned the boy even though his father rushed to comfort him and show him that a ram was the intended victim. Melampous used rust from the old knife to cure Iphikles. *Aha!* Iphikles thought as he realized that his childhood fear was unfounded. With that, Iphikles was cured.

After a celebration, Melampous drove the lowing cattle to Pylos, where the king gladly took possession of them. Melampous claimed the bride and presented her, still a virgin, to his brother (1329T/1079R BCE). After a great wedding celebration, Bias and Pero settled down to raise a family, but Melampous was sent back into exile. The couple was blessed with many children.

Because his ears could hear the language of the irrational, non-human world of other living beings, Melampous readily embraced the Dionysian cult spreading throughout Hellas. He understood, or was at least aware, that these same irrational powers also dwelled within every man. Melampous believed that intoxicants had their place and used drugs in healing. He was the man most instrumental in spreading the new Dionysian religion into the Peloponnesos. He was the first to build temples to the new god and reputedly the first to mix water with wine.

## Akrisios and Proitos Fight

Although Akrisios and Proitos agreed about Dionysos, they constantly fought among themselves for power. The twin princes fought before they were born through the day that they died. They fought over the Mycenaian crown even though the cultural norm dictated that the eldest son should rule. Yet aggressive Proitos was barely younger than his brother and had amassed plenty of supporters. So when King Abas died, the town nobles divided their support between slightly older Akrisios and more aggressive Proitos. Civil war ensued (1355T/1105R BCE).

Men marveled at the mighty forces mustered by each side. Some believe it was the first battle in which foot soldiers carrying shields were used. Akrisios prevailed, and Proitos fled overseas with his supporters.

---

Exhibit 8.1
Mycenaian Warfare

Early tacticians speculated that during the war of succession between Akrisios and Proitos, foot soldiers using leather-and-wood shields played a prominent role in support of chariot-riding warriors for the first time. In reality, throughout the Mycenaian era warfare was primarily chariot based, a unique battle formation used only during the Bronze Age. Besides the descriptions given by Homer, the chariot may have also been used to transport aristocratic warriors to the battlefield, or it may have been used to get close to and shoot arrows into infantry. Aristocratic chariot warriors dominated chaotic battles in which the valor of a single combatant could change the outcome.

The importance of foot soldiers came during the subsequent Iron Age, when cheaper weapons were available to outfit men of modest means with shields and swords. The Spartan poet Tyrtaios extolled the phalanx battle formation:

> Fear not the number of the enemy, nor be afraid, but let each man hold his shield straight toward the front …
> Of those who are bold enough to advance shoulder to shoulder to close quarters against the van of the enemy

> fewer are killed, and they save the fall behind, but all the
> merits of cowards is lost.[117]

---

Proitos sailed east to the Akhaian/Danaan cities of Rhodes. By now Mycenaians had ruled the Cyclades Islands for over a century, and they were also settling along the Anatolian coast. Proitos sailed to these settlements and gathered additional forces with which to wrestle Mycenai away from Atreus. He also received important backing from a Lycian king named Iobates. King Iobates thought that by having a Mycenaian king as an ally he could keep Danaans from ravaging his shores (just as the Mycenaians had tried to settle in Lycia under King Triops's son Xanthos). He also thought that with Mycenaian allies he could defy the imperialistic Hittites, who were exerting growing power over western Anatolia. Iobates promised an army and the hand of his young daughter to the rebel prince Proitos.

The next summer, Proitos returned to the Argeia with his troops laden with booty captured during skirmishes with Hittite allies in Anatolia. Akrisios met the invading forces near Nauplia. The great armies battled to a draw; the Lycian reinforcements were enough to balance the rival brothers' strength. During a truce, the combatants agreed to divide the kingdom (1352T/1102R BCE). Akrisios kept Mycenai but gave Proitos control over the smaller cities of Tiryns, Argos, Midea, Prosymna, and the coast. In exchange, Proitos accepted Akrisios as his overlord. With much of his power base overseas, Proitos established his royal residence at the port of Tiryns.

With civil strife at an end, Akrisios (1355T/1105R–1325T/1075R BCE) largely completed construction of the grand palace his father started. Proitos paid the mighty Cyklopes to build massive walls around Tiryns.[118] Who else but the Cyklopes could lift those massive stones?

Proitos also built a splendid palace and devoted considerable energy to securing a source of tin. Afghanistan was a major source of tin, which

---

[117] Tyrtaios of Sparta, in *Greek Lyric*. Translated by David A. Campbell.

[118] The massive walls of Tiryns remain impressive today and certainly were a source of awe to early Hellenes. Proitos was credited by later Hellenes for having built the walls, but those built during Proitos's reign were relatively modest. The surviving massive walls surrounding Tiryns were built during the mid to late thirteenth century T / end of the eleventh century R BCE, when the states of Hellas were constantly at war with each other.

was transported to Hellas through Colchis and the Bosporos. The rich Minyan Orkhomenos dominated that route. A second important source was Britain, which came to Hellas by way of Iberia and Sicily. In order to compete with the Minyans, who were already active in the western tin trade, Proitos required a western-facing port. He seized the two closest western-facing ports: Aiolian/Minyan Korinth and Akhaian Sicyon. King Proitos also sent colonists to strategic islands perched between Korinth and Italy, such as Delikion and Kercyra (where Proitos sent Eurysaces of Nauplia to build a settlement). This activity attracted the attention of the watery lord Poseidon, god of the shimmering sea, and in his excitement he carried off the Tirynian noblewoman Hippothoe. On Delikion Island she bore him Taphios, a great Danaan pirate (1350T/1100R BCE).

When Princess Stheneboia of Lycia (whom Homer called Anteia) reached maturity, her father, Iobates, sent her, as promised, to Tiryns (1344T/1094R BCE). Proitos eagerly consummated his marriage to the bright-eyed girl. Stheneboia presented Proitos with four lovely daughters: Lysippe, Iphinoe, Iphianassa, and Maira. These lovely girls grew into desirable young princesses. The couple was joyfully surprised years later by the birth of a son, Megapenthes.

Meanwhile, his lord, King Akrisios of Mycenai, married Princess Eurydice of Lakonia. Tragically their only son, Apesantos, died of a snakebite while he was only a boy. The mountain on which he died was renamed Apesas in his honor. The royal couple's eldest daughter, Evarete, married Oinomaos, the war-loving king of Pisa (1340T/1090R BCE) and was the grandmother of future king Atreus. Their younger daughter Danae (meaning "Danaan maiden") was named for her mother's sister and caught the attention of all-seeing Zeus.

With the ascension of Akrisios, the mythic history of Hellas underwent a significant change. The number of city-states grew dramatically and began to undertake constant interaction, whereas before this change, the few cities of Hellas grew in relative isolation. Great heroes and warriors were born after this change occurred.

## Danae and Gorgon-Slaying Perseus

Without strong sons to succeed him, Akrisios was vulnerable. Ambitious Proitos was moved to act when he learned that an oracle had decreed that his brother's youngest daughter, Danae, would bear a son who would one day kill his grandfather. When Proitos's wife died, he decided to help fulfill the prophecy by sending expensive gifts to his brother Akrisios and asked to marry fair-haired Danae. Akrisios obviously refused his offer. So Proitos went to Mycenai and raped the young maiden during the dark night (1345T/1095R BCE). Akrisios's guards nearly caught and killed Proitos, so he never tried that trick again. The king was relieved to learn that Danae had not conceived. Akrisios, fearful of another incident, placed Danae in a bronze underground chamber.

The will of the gods could not be denied by mortal means—not even the precautions of a great king. Zeus transformed himself into golden rain that showered down upon the dispirited princess through a crack in the ceiling, thereby illuminating her damp, dark chamber. Later, when the trembling guards informed Akrisios that they heard a baby's cry from within Danae's cell, he demanded they bring her to him. The furious Akrisios refused to believe her story. Because he did not have the stomach to kill his daughter and grandson outright, he had them locked in a chest and thrown out into the barren sea.

> While in the intricately-carved chest the blasts of wind and the troubled water prostrated her in fear, with streaming cheeks she put her loving arm about Perseus[119] and said, "My child, what suffering is mine! But you sleep, and with babyish heart slumber in the dismal boat with its brazen bolts, sent forth in the unlit night and dark blue murk. You pay no attention to the deep spray above your hair as the wave passes by, nor to the sound of the wind, lying in your purple blanket, a lovely face. If this danger were danger to you, why, you would turn your tiny ear to my words. Sleep, my baby, I tell you; and let the sea sleep, and let our vast trouble sleep. Let some change of heart

[119] The correct spelling may have been "Pterseus," which means "destroyer." Because the name "Perseus" is so similar to "Persia," he quickly became identified with that nation once it arose.

> appear from you, father Zeus. If anything in my prayer is audacious or unjust, pardon me."[120]

Miraculously the seas slept, and Danae and Perseus floated safely to Seriphos Island, where the fisherman Diktys found the chest bobbing on the waters. It was the sea nymph Klymene, in fulfillment of the will of Zeus, who ensured that the precious cargo fell safely into the hands of her benevolent son Diktys. Hopeful that he had found a treasure chest, the astonished Diktys found something better than gold inside, for peering up at him were a terrified Tirynian princess and her crying infant son. Diktys provided them with shelter and respected Danae's honor.

Years later, King Polydeuces, Diktys's lustful brother, met and instantly desired well-built Danae. When she refused his advances, the king assessed her young son's budding might and withdrew, leaving his dignity behind. Twisted Polydeuces falsely announced to his subjects that he planned to sue for the hand of lovely Hippodameia. Oinomaos had promised his daughter to the one who could beat him in a chariot race. Polydeuces requested that his noblemen contribute horses as bride gifts. Perseus owned no horses and rashly promised to bring something else, perhaps the head of Medousa.[121] Polydeuces eagerly accepted his rash offer (1326T/1076R BCE).

Perseus sought advice from his father, Zeus, at the oracle of Ammon in the Libyan Desert. There bright Athena, wily Hermes, and local nymphs helped him obtain the helmet of invisibility and winged sandals—property of Hades. Hermes also presented him with a sickle. Armed appropriately, Perseus flew confidently to the end of the earth, landing in Tartessos, Spain.

To discover Medousa's exact whereabouts, Perseus surprised the swanlike Graiai (meaning "grey ones"). These sisters shared one eye between them, and they knew the whereabouts of the heinous gorgon Medousa. Donning the invisible cap of Hades, Perseus silently approached the sisters and stole the common eye as they passed it among themselves. He refused to return the precious eye until they told him the location of the monster's lair.

---

[120] Simonides of Keos, "quoted by Dionysos of Halikarnassos", in *Greek Lyric.* Translated by David A. Campbell.

[121] Perseus's deeds were popular during Homer's time, and all three great Athenian playwrights wrote lost plays about him. Our knowledge of his exploits came primarily from Apollodoros's *Library*, ii.4, and a romantic version in Ovid's *Metamorphoses*, iv.

Determined Perseus flew off to the vile Gorgons' lair. Since her hideous stare could turn the stoutest of hearts to stone, Perseus did not fly directly at her. Wisely he flew backward, passing many men and animals turned to stone by her stare. Perseus quietly entered Medousa's lair and sidestepped her sleeping immortal sisters. Looking into his highly polished shield he beheld the image of hideous Medousa, a ghastly sight, deformed and dreadful. He marveled at her bronze hands and golden wings. Her huge tongue rolled from her mouth between swine's tusks and hair of snakes. By good chance, not one strand of her snaky hairs was awake. Perseus calculated the best angle to strike from and severed her head with one mighty swipe. Then, as he averted his eyes, he put her bloody head safely into a bag.

The two immortal Gorgons rose into the air, but unable to pursue an invisible attacker, they returned to mourn their sister. Miraculously, from the blood that spurted from Medousa's lifeless head sprang the winged horse Pegasos and the warrior Khrysaor (meaning "he of the golden sword"). That night Perseus landed to drink and rest at a fabulous oasis where the Atlas Mountains met the Libyan Desert.

The anxiety-filled Titan Atlas, who lived nearby, rushed at Perseus as he drank from the cool waters to quench his thirst. Atlas had fought against the Olympians during the cataclysmic war between the Olympians and Titans. His punishment for supporting the losing side was to carry a great weight upon his broad shoulders. Each night he holds Ouranos when he comes to cover Gaia. The gigantic Atlas was in no mood to befriend a son of the Olympian Zeus, and besides, he was a blood relative of Medousa. As gigantic Atlas rushed at him, Perseus drew Medousa's head from his bag, and immortal Atlas was temporarily frozen like a statue in fright. With the Titan Atlas immobilized, Perseus rested peacefully throughout the night.

The next morning, Perseus flew off toward the rising sun. Over Libya the shaggy head of Medousa shed some "hair." The poisonous snakes multiplied and infested the desert of Libya, where they remain to this day.

By nightfall Perseus arrived on the shores of Aithiopian (Hittite) territory. There, in either Cilicia or Joppa, he observed a beautiful princess chained to the rocky coast; she was adorned with jewels but nothing else. He watched the distressed princess as she wriggled helplessly while a sea monster approached. Perseus fell immediately in love with her but prudently wished to discover the nature of her crime before saving her. He landed among a crowd that mourned nearby, and he discovered that she was being punished because her mother had boasted that her daughter was more beautiful than the Nereides. Perseus quickly struck a deal with her father, the local Hittite king Cephalos; Perseus would obtain her hand in marriage if he could save her. Once the king had agreed to this, Perseus took off flying on the back of Pegasus.

Perseus flew at the serpent until, annoyed, as a man becomes at a persistent gnat, it turned to strike him. When the huge serpent's rolling eye looked directly at him, Perseus pulled the head of Medousa from his sack. Instantly the serpent turned to stone and sank into the sea.

Cephalos prepared a great wedding feast for his daughter and new son-in-law. Perseus sat beside his glowing new bride Andromeda, who was every bit as charming as she was beautiful. However, the celebration was ruined when Andromeda's uncle Phineus, who had earlier been promised her hand, arrived and declared the marriage illegal. Cephalos sided with Perseus. The king asked his brother Phineus where was he when the sea monster claimed his daughter? The king said to his brother that he lost his claim to marry the princess when he did not defend her. Phineus vehemently disagreed, saying that a king's oath was binding, with no exceptions. Still denied, Phineus led a surprise attack upon the wedding guests. King Cephalos slipped out a side door, leaving Perseus to defend himself. Perseus and a few supporters fought valiantly, but they were grossly outnumbered. Nearly overwhelmed, Perseus shouted for his supporters to shield their eyes and drew out Medousa's head. His rival Phineus and his thugs were turned to stone. Perseus and Andromeda lived happily within her father's home during a yearlong honeymoon.

## Dashing Bellerophontes

While Perseus was conducting his exploits, King Proitos was approached by an athletic young Korinthian prince named Hipponoos (1326T/1076R BCE). Hipponoos, son of Poseidon, received a nickname, Bellerophontes (meaning "killer of Belleros") after a murderous Korinthian he vanquished. His mother was the Megaran princess Eurynome, praised for her wisdom, who conceived Bellerophontes on the night she was married to King

Glaukos of Korinth. The good name of the great youth was tarnished when he killed his half brother, Prince Deliades, in a fight. Angry and distraught, King Glaukos of Korinth, stepfather of Bellerophontes, ordered him to report to his lord, Proitos, the king of strong-built Tiryns (1325T/1075R BCE). Proitos was impressed with the size, strength, and royal demeanor of Bellerophontes and gladly invited him into his palace. To honor the House of Glaukos, the king dismissed the scribes without reading Bellerophontes's letter of introduction and instead extended his hospitality. The young man's god-given qualities of beauty, charm, and bravery were obvious to Proitos. He did not notice that strife accompanied Bellerophontes as well.

In time Proitos's wife, Stheneboia, became more enamored with their handsome guest than with her aging husband. Poor Stheneboia was a foreigner, sent as a frightened girl from her native Lycia to marry Proitos. The marriage was purely political, and she had dutifully raised their children. Now she was bored and lonely, and the difference in age between her and her husband became increasingly pronounced. Aroused by the heroic young Bellerophontes, she tried to seduce him. He would have none of it.

Spurned Stheneboia raged. She told Proitos that Bellerophontes had tried to rape her. Although Proitos believed her, he would not kill a guest, as that was a taboo act.

Belatedly, Proitos called for a scribe. The scribe read Glaukos's accusation that Bellerophontes had killed his own half brother Deliades, the king's only son, in a childish fight. Glaukos begged his lord Proitos not to extend hospitality, but rather to do away with the strong youth. Since honor-bound Proitos had already extended hospitality, he could not do so without violating the Hellenic code of hospitality (one taboo was killing a man you had broken bread with). The quick-thinking Proitos decided to send Bellerophontes to the one man who could share a husband's fury—his father-in-law. So he sent Bellerophontes to Iobates, who was not bound by Hellenic honor codes, being a Lycian (Luwian). "The strong king drove Bellerophontes out of Tiryns: this because the queen lusted to couple with him secretly, but he was honorable, she could not lure him, and in the king's ear hissed a lie. "Oh, Proitos, I wish that you may die unless you kill Hipponoos: he desired to take me in lust against my will."[122]

---

[122] Homer, *Iliad* vi.

Only once does Homer mention Bronze Age literacy. He says that Proitos presented Bellerophontes with a folding tablet stamped with his royal seal. We now know that folding tablets, primitive books, were in use during the Bronze Age, especially among the Hittites and the Luwians. King Proitos dismissed Bellerophontes with one of those folding tablets. Illiterate Bellerophontes was unaware of its contents.

Knowing that Proitos sent him, Iobates welcomed Bellerophontes into his home and for nine days honored him with nine parties, each beginning with the sacrifice of consecrated beasts. When the rosy fingers of dawn made the tenth day bright, Iobates questioned his guest and then privately asked the royal scribe to read aloud the words that were written on the tablet stamped with his son-in-law's seal. The poisonous words revealed that the guest was no friend of Proitos. It falsely accused him of making an unscrupulous advance toward his wife, Iobates's affronted daughter. Furthermore, this reprehensible young man had killed his own brother. Iobates decided the best way to dispose of this powerful young man was to send him on an impossible quest.[123]

Lycia had long been plagued by the ghastly and inhuman monster called Chimaera.[124] It was a fearful creature—great, swift-footed, and strong—a marvelous creature to behold. It was unique among beasts, as it had three heads—those of a lion, a goat, and a dragon. Its body was equally strange; it had the powerful shoulders of a lion, the tail of a snake, and the body of a she-goat between. The dragon's mouth exhaled jets of rolling fire.

Iobates asked Bellerophontes to rid the land of the terrible beast. Bellerophontes was eager to please his host and demonstrate his might, but he did not know how to proceed. As Bellerophontes was experiencing troubled sleep, Poseidon appeared in a dream to council and encourage him. A seer interpreted the dark-haired lord's message. He told Bellerophontes that a great hero, a grandson of King Akrisios of Mycenai, had recently

---

[123] Bellerophontes, like Argo Panoptes before him and Herakles and Theseus after him, preformed heroic labors. Bellerophontes's labors are found in Apollodoros's *Library*, ii.3, Pindar's *Olympian Ode*, xiii.60–91, Homer, *Iliad*, vi.154, and elsewhere.

[124] The Chimaera appears to be a mythic creature of Anatolian origin; its likeness is found on a Hittite temple in Carchemish. The Anatolians believed this monster held some power over storm clouds. The Mycenaians were familiar with this fabled creature; its likeness appears in art recovered in the palace of Midea, a Bronze Age city located a few miles inland of Tiryns. The earliest Hellenic writers, Homer and Hesiod, mention the Chimaera.

slain the ugly gorgon Medousa, and from her severed head had sprung a marvelous winged horse. The seer told him that if he rode the flying horse against Chimaera he would succeed. Bellerophontes wandered around Lycia looking for the fabled horse until he met an excited man claiming to have seen a winged horse grazing in lush meadows nearby.

Bellerophontes, whose given name was Hipponoos (meaning "horse-minded"), stood a better chance than anyone of catching a wild flying stallion. His innate ability as a horse tamer was the gift of his father, the god of horses. His stepfather, Glaukos, was a skilled horseman who had refined Bellerophontes's great talent. Still, catching a flying horse proved difficult, and Bellerophontes suffered much along the streams and meadows, longing to yoke the snaky gorgon's child. Then Athena spoke to him in a dream, revealing the whereabouts of a soothing drug. Bellerophontes sprinkled the sweet-smelling herb in the horse's meadow, and it could not resist the tasty plant. Calmed by the drug, Bellerophontes was able to catch the noble steed.

Bellerophontes lovingly tamed Pegasos, who flew unwearyingly, for like the gales he could course along. Now prepared, Bellerophontes flew off to find the Chimaera. It did not take long for him to find his fearless prey. The strong beast had no defense against the well-aimed arrows shot down upon him by the hero on a winged perch. Iobates and his court were astounded to see Bellerophontes return on a winged mount, proudly displaying his terrible trophy (1320T/1070R BCE).

Promptly Iobates ordered Bellerophontes to accompany his army in battle against the troublesome Solymoi. Eager Bellerophontes flew to the front of the battle on Pegasos, where he proved to be a better fighter than anyone among the savage Solymoi. Defeated, the terrified Solymoi fled into the mountains. Bellerophontes repeated his exploits when ordered to fight against the warlike Amazones.

Iobates was pleased but still wanted to avenge the insult to his daughter. Secretly he sent his best warriors to ambush the godlike Bellerophontes. Alert Bellerophontes slew them all. Angry at his mistreatment, Bellerophontes prayed for his father to flood the Xanthian plain behind him. As he advanced on the capital, he was followed by seawater that no man could stop. It was left to the seductive young Lycian women to stop him. Hitching their skirts to their waists, they waded out to offer themselves to the hero.

Blushing Bellerophontes backed away, and the waves receded. Iobates decided to forget Proitos's request and befriended the divine youth from a godly line. The king gave him his youngest daughter, Philonoe, and gave him a slew of royal privileges as well. The Lycians, for their part, set aside their best lands for him. When Iobates's lying daughter, Stheneboia, heard of these events, she committed suicide (or was thrown to her death from the back of Pegasos by Bellerophontes).

Bellerophontes's beautiful wife, Philonoe, bore him an heir named Isandros (meaning "impartial man"), as well as two other children, Hippolokhos and Laodameia. Bellerophontes continued his heroic ways, defending his adopted land against enemies like the fiery and boastful Karian pirate Kheimarrhos. When Iobates died, Bellerophontes became king.

Bellerophontes was a few years older than Evandros, king of the other great Lycian kingdom. Evandros had succeeded his father, Sarpedon, as king of Xanthos and he married Bellerophontes's daughter Laodameia, sealing a vow of friendship between the two great kingdoms.

Bellerophontes lived happily in Lycia for many years, but few Hellenic myths end happily. In time Bellerophontes incurred the gods' wrath, and so he spent his final days homeless, wandering alone, eating his heart out, shunning the beaten track of scornful men. The cause of his affliction was the loss of his precious children.

First it was Isandros who took over leadership on the field of battle when his father's aging frame could no longer withstand the rigors of war. Though the youth was his father's match in courage and fury, he was not as gifted a warrior. While leading an army against the rapacious Solymoi, he was killed in battle by Ares. Soon Laodameia joined her brother in the dark realm of Hades. Darling young Laodameia died of Artemis's anger, the arrow of sudden illness.

The fall of Bellerophontes was the subject of Euripides's lost play *Bellerophontes,* a subject the fifth-century BCE poet Pindar of Thebes (*Olympian Ode* xiii) says he would not talk about, although he implied his fall was due to pride. In distraught contemplation, Bellerophontes grew disillusioned with a world where evildoers prosper while the pious either die young or grow old and helpless. Bellerophontes decided there could be no gods if such outrages exist. Wanting to know for certain, he dressed in his finest armor, mounted Pegasos, and ascended toward Olympos, ready to demand the reason (if he found the gods) that they had created such a world.

Bitter Bellerophontes did not reach Olympos; he did not gain the insight he sought. Instead his indignation led him to fall into destruction and madness, for Zeus alone determines who enters Olympos, and he had not willed it so for Bellerophontes. The Cloud-Gatherer sent a gadfly to bite Pegasos, and in reaction he threw his unworthy rider. Pegasos continued on to heaven to live in Zeus's stable. Bellerophontes fell hard and dislocated his hip. The Lycians (Luwians) shunned him because he had displeased the gods. He wandered alone, lame, as an outcast, until he died in Cilicia. He received no burial, and the site of his grave was not even remembered.

## Gorgon-Slaying Perseus Returns

Meanwhile, the summer following his marriage, Perseus decided it was time to return home. They left behind their firstborn son, whom they called Perses, eponym of the Persians. As Perseus explained it, Cephalos had no heirs and wanted Andromeda's child to succeed him. Cynics believed Cephalos demanded a hostage to ensure that the great Danaan king would give him no trouble. At any rate, Perses never came to visit Hellas, and Perseus never attacked the land of his wife.[125]

The couple said their tearful goodbyes, and the court watched in awe as Perseus cradled Andromeda in his lap and flew off home to tiny Seriphos Island. Andromeda cradled the bag containing Medousa's head carefully in her lap as he flew off using Hades's helmet and sandals. Perseus had been gone so long that Polydeuces figured he had died. Without fear of retribution, Polydeuces had acted upon his unlawful passion and tried to force Perseus's mother, Danae, into bed with him. Danae and her loyal supporter Diktys fled to the altar of the gods, which Polydeuces did not dare violate.

[125] It is possible, as was then the custom in the Near East, that the king of the Hittites gave one of his daughters in marriage to a Mycenaian prince in order to establish friendly relations with the pesky Hellenes. His aim would have been to reduce the attacks on his allies in western Anatolia.

Upon his return, Perseus immediately went to Polydeuces's palace and announced that he had returned successfully with the head of Medousa. Perseus presented to him Medousa's head, which naturally turned the maleficent king into stone. With his mission complete, Perseus gave Athena Medousa's head, which she embroidered onto her breastplate. Hermes came to take back his sickle and Hades's possessions (the magical helmet and sandals). Polydeuces's brother Diktys became king of Seriphos.

With his fabulous adventure complete, Perseus returned in glory to his native Mycenai, a land that had cast him out in fear as a baby. He sailed to Tiryns with his mother and young bride (1325T/1075R BCE). It was not hatred or revenge that brought Perseus home. Perseus had heard of the dark prophecy concerning him, and he wanted to prove that his intentions were honorable and that the prophecy was wrong.

Rumor has it that Perseus killed Proitos, his grandfather's rival, upon his arrival in Hellas, though he may have died of old age. [126] Either way, Akrisios did not stick around to gloat over his rival's death. Old Akrisios feared that the prophecy would now be fulfilled and fled for his life to Larissa in Thessalia.

It was important to Perseus that his grandfather knew his true intentions, and so he followed him to Larissa. In Thessalia Perseus tried to coax Akrisios out of hiding. Failing at this, Perseus entered into funeral games then being held. Akrisios attended the games in disguise, compelled to watch his famous grandson compete. During the discus competition, Perseus threw a discus so far and so wildly that it crashed into the spectators. Old Akrisios was struck and died instantly. (One cannot change the will of the gods; only one's intent can be changed while carrying out one's fate.) Perseus buried the old king with honors in Larissa and returned to his ancestral lands.

Perseus did not wish to live in the palace of his grandfather, because he had killed him. So Perseus arranged a three-way swap that gained him Tiryns. Megapenthes, Proitos's son, obtained Argos, and Melampous received

[126] Pausanias, in *Guide to Greece*, ii.16.3 (following the Argive genealogist Akusilaos) insinuates that Proitos was already dead when Perseus returned. Ovid, *Metamorphoses*, iv says Perseus killed him.

Mycenai.[127] Melampous gladly gave up Argos for the largest city in Hellas. Megapenthes, who was only ten, was in no position to resist great Perseus, so he ruled smaller Argos. Perseus did not relinquish his birthright to the title of great-king, which had hereto been held by the kings of Mycenai. Melampous was his vassal. The Romans believed Perseus's mother, Danae, migrated to Italy and founded the city of Ardea.

---

Exhibit 8.2
Historic Seeds of Perseus, Bellerophontes, and Pelops

The Hittites often arranged political marriages to strengthen ties with neighboring states. Both the Hittites and the Akhaians (Ahhiyawa in Hittite texts) were very active in western Anatolia at this time. Most of the native Arzawan states were vassals of the Hittites, although the Akhaians had founded numerous independent colonies and one palace state (at Miletos [Milawata in Hittites texts]). Hittite records indicate that they carried on diplomatic relations with the Mycenaians, whom they also fought with at times. These records indicate Hittite respect for the Mycenaians; they address the Akhaian king as a great-king, or king of kings. In that context it is not hard to see Perseus's marriage to Andromeda as an arranged marriage between powerful kings.

The exploits of Bellerophontes may explain why the Hittites seized the Mycenaian palace city of Miletos (1318T/1068R BCE). The annals of the Hittite Great-King Mursili II (1321T/1071R-1295T/1045R BCE) indicate the attack was in retaliation for Akhaian attacks on Lukka (Lycia). According to the Hittites, the Mycenaian general Eteokles fled home across the sea when the Hittites seized Miletos. Eteokles was a common name among the Mycenaians; who specifically this was is unknown.

---

[127] Pausanias, in *Guide to Greece*, ii.16.3 (following the Argive genealogist Akusilaos) says that Perseus traded crowns (Tiryns for Argos) with Megapenthe, daughter of Proitos, and that he founded Mycenai. Apollodoros, in *Library*, ii.48, follows the same tradition in saying that Megapenthes was the son of Proitos and that Perseus traded Argos for Tiryns and that Perseus walled both Midea and Mycenai. Argos was the key historic city-state of Argeia, and its historians usurped Mycenaian myths. The crown swapping espoused above relates to the four Argeian palace cities of note during the Bronze Age. The four cities play prominent roles as kingdoms in mythology, which reflects the city-state political reality of the sixth century BCE, not the Bronze Age. The king of Mycenai once ruled the whole valley, but it is likely that the king's extended family governed the other cities—just like in the myths.

Perhaps the Hittites had patiently endured Proitos's assistance to his Lycian father-in-law against Hittite allies in Lycia, but the exploits of Bellerophontes became unbearable. The Hittites supported rebellions in Lycia and seized Miletos as a warning to the Mycenaians. They quickly withdrew. The Solymoi and Amazones attacks on Lycia may be a mythic remembrance of historical struggles with the Hittites, but the myths are silent about Miletos (which later Hellenes did not even know was occupied by their ancestors at the time). The apologetic letter Mursili II sent to an unnamed Akhaian great-king would have been sent to Perseus. Mursili II would have had an open line of communication with Perseus, whose wife was a Hittite princess.

The Hittites were much more concerned with a rebellion by the Arzawan nations of western Anatolia. When the Hittites defeated the rebels, the Arzawan king Uhhaziti fled to Hellas and, with Perseus's blessing, became the king of Pisa under the name of Pelops (1316T/1066R BCE).

See Addendum 3, "Anatolian Prehistory and Bronze Age" for additional details.

---

The warrior Perseus, like his regal ancestors, did not like the earthy new Dionysian cult. As a son of Zeus himself, Perseus felt justified in returning Hellas to the conservative religion of the sky gods, and he suppressed the cult of his half brother. Perseus persecuted Dionysos's followers and killed most of them in a pitched battle near Argos. Zeus intervened between his sons and checked any thought Dionysos might have had for revenge while seeing to it that Perseus relented.

Perseus and Andromeda ruled as the Argeia continued to prosper. Closer to home Perseus had fortifications built around Midea, and he lavished Tiryns with building projects. Later Perseus conquered nearby Ionian territory and established the port of Troizen around a fountain dug out by a kick from the winged horse Pegasos taking off. Mycenaian influence in Asia Minor continued to grow even though the Hittites temporarily occupied Miletos (Milawata).

Perseus and Andromeda were blessed with many healthy children:

| | |
|---|---|
| Elektryon | Succeeded his father to the throne |
| Alcaios | Inherited Troizen and lived in Tiryns serving as polemarch for his brother |
| Sthenelos | Seized the throne upon Elektryon's death |
| Mestor | Possibly the absentee landlord of Hermione |
| Gorgophone | Married King Perieres of Arene and then King Oibalos of Lakonia, becoming the first widow to remarry |
| Heleios | Founded Helos in Lakonia |
| Polydora | Married the bastard son of Gorgophone's husband Perieres and moved with him to Iolkos in Thessalia |

Perseus also raised a bastard son, Cynuros, who settled in nearby Cynuria to the south. Cynuros received the land on a grant from his brother, King Elektryon.

Perseus was not blessed with a long life. Sadly, he suffered from a debilitating illness. Many came to pay respects to this once mighty warrior.

Image 8.1
Significant MH–LHIIIB sites of Hellas
This map clearly show that the Argeia and Messenia were the most important early Hellenic regions; just as early myths key on Melampous and Perseus.

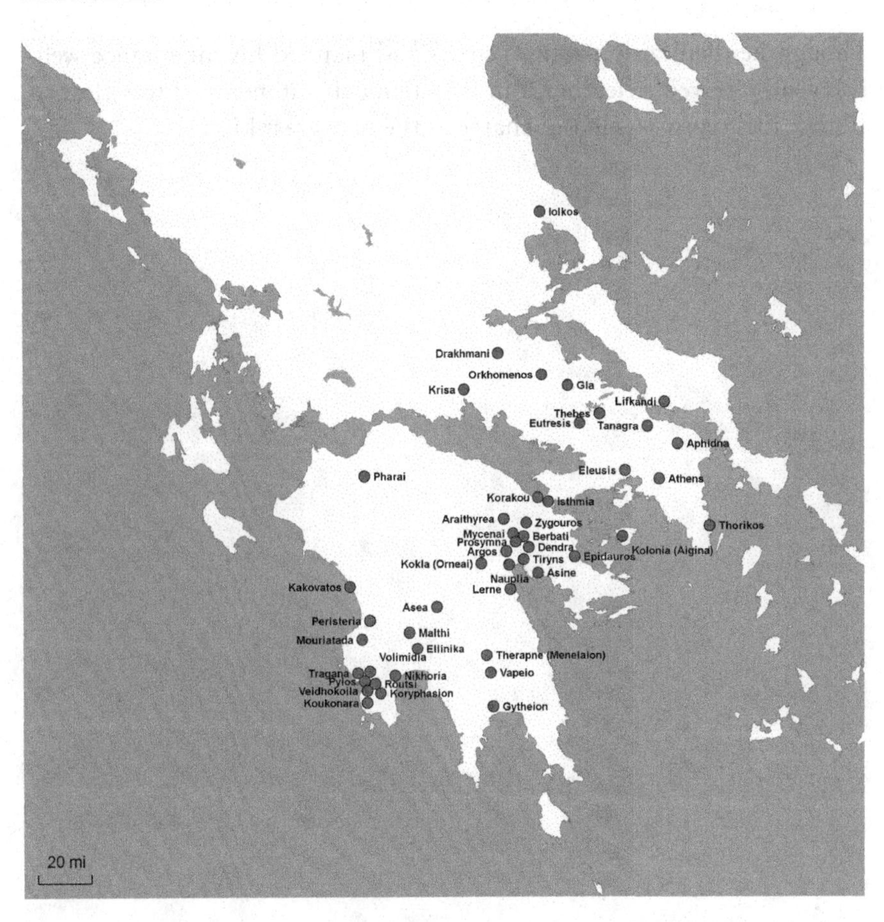


As the first truly heroic figure of Hellas, Perseus was rewarded with a place among the stars as a constellation upon his death (1297T/1047R BCE).[128] So were the sea monster he vanquished, his faithful wife Andromeda (fittingly near his celestial side) and Andromeda's parents. For her mother it was a dubious distinction; Poseidon arranged it that for much of the

---

[128] The playwrights Aiskhylos and Euripides were the first to identify Perseus with a constellation, and it became a very important constellation. See Addendum 5, "Procession of the Stars" for more details.

year Kassiopeia was lying flat on her back with her legs spread wide apart in the sky. The indiscreet pose was her punishment for boasting. Perseus's divine-hero cult was naturally big in the Argeia (he had a shrine between Mycenai and Argos), but it was especially important on Seriphos Island and in Hellenistic Tarsos in Cilicia.

Though he died fairly young, Perseus had planned his inheritance well. Each son received a fiefdom. But despite much autonomy, it was clear to all that Elektryon was left in charge as the new great-king.

# House of Pelops

## Late Helladic Bronze Age (LHIIIA–LHIIIB); Part of Hesiod's Age of Heroes

> There are many wonders described in the world, and many are embroidered tales that overpowered time true accounts and tricked men's talk with their enchantment of lies.
>
> —Pindar of Thebes, "Olympian Ode" i, fifth century BCE

> I could not hope to touch the sky with my two arms.
> From all the offspring of the earth and heaven, love is the most precious.
>
> —Sappho of Lesbos, sixth century BCE

### Pelops's Arrival

The greatest ally of Perseus was an Arzawan lord called Pelops[129] by the Hellenes and Uhhaziti by the Hittites. The Hellenes say the draw of

[129] The name Pelops ends in "ops," a common ending for Hellenic tribes. The myth of the eponym of the Peloponnesos was quite possibly grafted to the historical king Uhhaziti of Arzawa (Lydia), who rebelled from the Hittites with the aid of Hellenes, lost, and fled to Hellas. One problem in matching the two is that in myth Pelops was a young man looking to marry while Uhhaziti had grown sons. A synopsis of early Anatolian history is included in Addendum 3, "Anatolian Prehistory and Bronze Age."

love pulled Pelops across the wine-dark domain of Poseidon to Hellas. The Hittites say Uhhaziti fled across the sea to an unnamed Ahhiyawan (Akhaian) lord (probably Perseus) after his forces were defeated by the Hittite great-king Mursili II.

Perseus and Pelops were first connected, unknowingly, by beautiful Hippodameia, daughter of the war god's scion and the Pleiades Sterope, daughter of the Titan Atlas and the Oceanid Pleione. When Hippodameia grew into a beautiful maiden with many suitors, King Oinomaos of Harpina (Pisa) could not bear to part with his daughter and proclaimed a challenge to all suitors.

Polydektes of faraway Seriphos Island told his subjects he planned to win Hippodameia's hand and needed a contribution of fast horses. He knew young Perseus, nephew of Oinomaos's first wife, Evarete, was too poor to own horses but still demanded a gift. Prideful Perseus promised him the head of Medousa and went off to get it. Polydeuces never intended to race Oinomaos; he just wanted to get rid of Perseus.

In far-off Lydia, Pelops too had heard of Hippodameia, but unlike Polydeuces, he was seriously interested in her hand in marriage. The love of Hippodameia inspired him (as did the need to flee after leading an unsuccessful rebellion against his Hittite lords). The Arzawan king Ilos of Troy and the Phrygian king Adrastos of the Sangarios River, loyal Hittite vassals, helped drive him out (1316T/1066R BCE).

## Tantalos's Punishment

The Hellenes recorded rich myths regarding the Bronze Age inhabitants of Lydia and their most famous kings—Tantalos and his son Pelops. The power ascribed to them is placed in the time of the Late Bronze Age but reflects the political power of the seventh- and sixth-century BCE kings of Lydia. Homer and the fifth century BCE historian Herodotos of Halikarnassos say the Lydians were once called Maionians. They lived around Mount Sipylos and Mount Tmolos, inland of the seaside-dwelling Tyrrhenians. Their king, Tantalos, reputedly ruled over the Phrygians and Paphlagonians as well. King Ilos of Troy conquered Paphlagonia from him.

The Maionian king Tantalos was obviously one of Zeus's favorite children. He was the son of Zeus and Pluto, representing leadership and wealth. Pluto (meaning "wealth") was either an Oceanid or a daughter born to Kronos and Rhea[130] after they lost rule over the heavens to the Olympians. Tantalos married the star nymph Dione the Hyad, daughter of the Titan Atlas. She bore him Pelops and Niobe.

Tantalos ruled Maionia from below Mount Sipylos and was the first human ever invited to dine with the Olympians (the equally notorious Ixion of Thessalia was a later invitee). Tantalos so amused his hosts that they offered him anything. True to his mortal roots, he turned his back on heavenly potential and asked only for earthly pleasures.

Tantalos indeed became a wealthy and sensual man. He invited the gods to dine with him in his sumptuous palace. When they arrived, he decided to test them. He did so by cutting up his son Pelops, boiling him, and serving him as an entree. The man who thinks he can do anything and expects the gods not to see it is wrong; only Demeter, who was still distracted and mourning the loss of Persephone, was deceived.

The Olympians determined to restore Pelops to life. They placed his dismembered parts, and an ivory shoulder constructed to replace the one eaten by Demeter, into a bronze cauldron. Herbs were added, and incantations uttered. Then Cybele[131] lifted Pelops out of the cleansing cauldron, his healed shoulder ivory-white and fine. The gods had made him more handsome than before, a youth of unrivaled beauty. The mighty earth-shaker Poseidon instantly fell in love with him and carried him off in a gleaming chariot to his bedchambers on Olympos. It was by Poseidon's side on Olympos where Pelops became a man.[132]

---

[130] Or Cybele. It is interesting to note that most of the deities mentioned associated with Tantalos were either Titans, older gods representing the forces of nature, or Hellenic equivalents of Cybele (Rhea and Demeter). His children Pelops and Niobe dealt with the Olympians, who represented civilization.

[131] Bakkhylides (*FGrHis,* 15) says it was Rhea, and she is here substituted with the Lydian equivalent. The most comprehensive account of Pelops is found in Apollodoros's *Library*, Epitome 2.3–2.9. Living in a later era, when the role of fate was considered paramount, Apollodoros says it was the Moira Klotho who raised Pelops.

[132] A recorded custom in Athens had older men abducting youths on the verge of manhood, with parental approval, to spend a few days or weeks as lovers. The custom was apparently ancient and widespread.

Tantalos remained an impious man. He stole the golden dog of Zeus from his shrine in Miletos on Krete with a son of the giant Pandareos of Kos Island. When his pleasurable life ended, Hades commanded that he be sent to Tartaros. Tantalos's crime was to be unworthy of the extraordinary favor the gods showed him. Besides affronting the gods, who came to him as guests, he had tattled the gods' secrets and shared ambrosia with those unworthy—his mortal friends. Tantalos's punishments were four: hunger, thirst, fear, and that the first three punishments would last for eternity.

The theme of Tantalos's punishment was present pleasures that cannot be enjoyed. Homer (*Odyssey* xi.582–592) describes a place where Tantalos is surrounded by pleasure, just as he had asked for on earth; cool water brushed below his parched lips and luscious fruit dangled before his eyes from above. But alas, when he bent to quench his thirst the waters receded below, and no matter how high he reached, the wind pushed the fruit just beyond his grasp. Apollodoros (*Library* Epitome 2.1) says that Zeus added to his misery by placing a rock over his head, on the verge of falling on him at any moment. The fourth-century BCE Sicilian king Dionysios of Syrakuse is an example of Tantalos. Dionysios said that kingship is like having a rock hanging over your head. The longing to cast the rock away exiles one from delight. When Pelops came to the sweet flower of his growth and down covered his darkening chin, Poseidon released him from his loving bondage and let him return to claim his inheritance—dominion over the lands surrounding Mount Sipylos. He did not stay long.

To have far-famed Hippodameia of Harpina, daughter of formidable Oinomaos, Pelops cried out beside the grey sea in the darkness, alone. His prayer did not go unanswered; Poseidon lent him winged horses and a golden chariot to seek his bride. He won her and the city of Harpina (Pisa) too. Because his descendants ruled most of the peninsula he settled on, it became known as the Peloponnesos after him.

After Pelops fled across the sea, aided as he was by his ex-lover Poseidon, his ugly half brother Broteas became king of Lydia (Arzawa). Broteas was the son of Tantalos, and his second wife, Euryanassa, was the daughter of the river god Paktolos. In Asia, unlike Hellas, polygamy was an accepted custom. Broteas reputedly set up the oldest shrine to Cybele in Magnesia and served as high priest too. He also commissioned the first image of

Cybele to be carved on Coddianian crag, north of Mount Sisyphos.[133] Broteas, a great hunter, abandoned the worship of Artemis, the patron goddess of Lydia. Jealous Artemis drove him mad. Thinking he was immune to fire, Broteas threw himself onto flames and perished. His son Tantalos succeeded him, careful to worship both Artemis and Cybele.

## Formidable Oinomaos of Harpina, Son of Ares

King Oinomaos named the city he built after his mother, Harpina. Chariot-riding Ares had carried off a daughter of the river god Asopos to lie with in a field by the swift flowing Alpheus River. Unfortunate Asopos was powerless to stop the Olympians from carrying off many of his lovely daughters. After the stout-hearted war god departed, a local man named Alexion took in Harpina and helped her to raise her semidivine offspring. Ares, god of the bloodcurdling yell, did not forget a son with his own warlike nature and gave him a splendid suit of armor. Oinomaos loved the cry of battle and carved out an impressive kingdom for himself.

In a testament to his power and wealth Oinomaos secured a daughter of King Akrisios of Mycenai as his wife (1340T/1090R BCE). By this princess, Evarete, Oinomaos sired Dysponteus and Leucippos. Dysponteus founded the local town of Dyspontion, but Leucippos's fate was unlucky.

Leucippos fell in love with the nymph Daphne, who loved to hunt with her companions along the Ladon River in Arkadia. Because Daphne would have nothing to do with men, Leucippos, who had already grown his hair long in honor of the river Alpheus, dressed himself as a girl to be near her. Daphne's new friend's prowess as hunter won admiration, and the two became close companions. Apollo soon arrived as a rival for Daphne's affections and convinced the girls to bathe naked. When Leucippos refused on some pretense, the girls playfully stripped him and then indignantly stabbed him to death. Apollo, even without a rival, was no more successful at winning Daphne's affections.[134]

[133] This is the westernmost representation of Hittite rock carvings. It is possible that Cybele was introduced into Lydia during the Late Bronze Age, when the Hittite Empire stretched from Lydia to Carchemish, seat of the goddess Kubaba (Cybele).

[134] In the other famous version regarding Daphne, she was the daughter of the Peneios River. In that Thessalian version, Apollo fails to woo her but there is no mention of Leucippos.

Oinomaos was a great horse breeder and driver. He went so far to keep his breed pure that he forbade mating stallions with jennies to make mules—a taboo that remained in Eleia for centuries. His best mares, Psylla and Harpina, were the fastest in all Hellas, begat by the north wind Boreas and given to Oinomaos by Ares.

When Queen Evarete died and the time for mourning passed, Oinomaos married the Pleiades Asterope. He loved their daughter Hippodameia dearly, possessively. When Hippodameia came of age, many suitors were willing to risk their lives for the chance to marry this widely renowned beauty.

Oinomaos offered to let lovely Hippodameia ride in the suitor's war chariot, and Oinomaos would give them a head start, long enough for him to sacrifice a black ram. If he could not overtake the suitor, his daughter would be the prize. But if he caught them, he would kill the suitor and reclaim his daughter. The race was held in the countryside where the Olympic Games would one day be held. Hippodameia loved her violent father and assisted him by purposely distracting her suitors as they raced.

Pelops flew to Harpina, a worthy town on the west coast of the Peloponnesos and confidently challenged King Oinomaos for the hand of his far-famed daughter Hippodameia. However, when Pelops saw the sixteen skulls of those that had failed before him hanging in the war temple and noticed the speed of Oinomaos's horses, he lost hope of winning without cheating.

## Pelops Wins Hippodameia[135]

Hippodameia fell for the handsome suitor with an ivory shoulder blade. She suggested Pelops bribe Myrtilos, Oinomaos's charioteer and top administrator, to pull the linchpins from Oinomaos's chariot. Myrtilos was the son of Hermes and a Danaan woman named Phaithousa or Kleobule. Myrtilos loved Hippodameia but dared not compete for her hand. When

[135] This is a popular ancient story included in Hesiod's *Great Eoiai* (only fragments remain) and Pindar's *Olympian Ode*, i, a lost epic by Epimenides of Knossos (sixth century BCE), and Pausanias's *Guide to Greece*, vi.21.9. There are other examples of chariot races conducted to win brides from fathers. In another famous race, Poseidon loaned out his chariot again, this time to his son Idas.

Pelops offered Myrtilos half the kingdom for his treachery, Myrtilos agreed on the condition that he also would get to spend the first night with Hippodameia.

Oinomaos gave Pelops the customary head start, and the race began. Pelops's concerns were valid, for as they approached the finish line, Oinomaos closed in eagerly with outstretched spear in hand; frightened Myrtilos clutched tightly onto both reigns and car. At last the sabotaged wheel fell off and Oinomaos tumbled out. Asterope rushed to her mortal husband's side and cried as his life ebbed. Oinomaos became a ghost who spooked horses at Olympia, and Asterope dimmed from the night sky in shame at having married a mortal and in mourning for suffering the loss of her man.

The new couple invited Myrtilos to climb into their chariot with them. Myrtilos agreed, and Pelops's charioteer, Sphairos, stepped out. Pelops had treacherously pushed Myrtilos out near Euboea Island into the sea, which was renamed Myrtoan. As Myrtilos fell toward his death, he cursed Pelops and his descendants.

To appease Myrtilos's father, Hermes, and to rid himself of the curse, Pelops recovered the body, buried it with honors in a great tumulus, instituted a hero worship for Myrtilos, and built the first shrine to luck-bringing Hermes in the Peloponnesos (at Pheneus in Arkadia). Then Hephaistos purified him of murder. Meanwhile, keen-eyed Hermes placed his son's spirit in the skies as the constellation Auriga. Though the curse passed Pelops, it plagued his descendants up to and including his great-grandson Orestes of Mycenai.

In thanks for her marriage, Hippodameia initiated a race performed by virgin girls to Hera, the goddess of marriage, prior to the Olympic Games. In addition to the race, dances were initiated by Hippodameia and the Epeian heroine Physkoa, as well as the custom of annually weaving a new peplos (robe) for the statue of Hera in Olympia.[136]

---

[136] Annual festivals where the image of a goddess was removed from the shrine and ritually bathed were celebrated in many cities for at least a millennium. Afterward, a new gown was put upon the idol and it was returned to the temple. Hittite-Hurrian influence can be seen in this ritual. It was a discomforting event to move the goddess and interrupt the normal flow of life; consequently, the procession was a solemn occasion.

Exhibit 9.1
Early Mycenaian Era History of the Western Peloponnesos

It comes as no surprise that the first monumental construction of the Mycenaian Age occurred in Argeia, just as the myths say (with shaft graves of Mycenai, ca. 1580T/1330R BCE). The Argeia is full of impressive ruins, like the Lion Gate of Mycenai and the great walls of Tiryns, and Hellenic myths clearly identify the region's preeminence. Because none of the important Mycenaian cities of the southwestern Peloponnesos survived into classical times, their myths were largely forgotten or stolen by historical cities to the north: Pisa and Elis—cities in regions with few Mycenaian settlements. Therefore, it is a bit surprising that almost immediately after developments grew in Argeia, Mycenaian buildings began appearing along the southwestern coast of the Peloponnesos in the regions of Triphylia and Messenia.

Early Mycenaian settlements clung to the western coastline and have not been found very far inland, except along the ridge overlooking the Suplima Plain of Messenia. Important cities rose at Malthi, Mouriatadha, Peristeria, Kakovatas (Triphylian Pylos), and elsewhere. The sites show evidence of early megarons (palaces) that do not show any influence from the larger palaces of Minoan Krete.

The first tholos tombs built in Hellas, whose vaulted, beehive-like structures were unlike anything seen before, were built here (just after 1500T/1250R BCE). More tholos "beehive" tombs are found in the Mycenaian settlements here than anywhere else, even more than in Argeia. They may have borrowed from Minoan designs and quickly became popular in Mycenai and elsewhere in Hellas (the first one in Mycenai dates to ca. 1485T/1235R BCE).

Archaeological evidence shows that Triphylia declined after the mid fifteenth century T / late thirteenth century R BCE. Probable causes for the decline were the fall of their trading partners the Minoans, the rise of Mycenai and Pylos, and the coming of the Aiolian/Minyan settlers.

According to myth, the earliest seafaring settlements of the western Peloponnesos were built by the Leleges, an ambiguous name for ancient tribesmen flourishing after the flood.[137] Leleges prince Polykaon of Sparta, youngest son of King Lelex, eponym of the Leleges, married Princess Messene, the strong-willed daughter of King Triops of Mycenai, and settled in the territory he named Messenia in her honor (1481T/1231R BCE).[138] Messene played a powerful, unprecedented role in the government, and she is the only woman of her era to receive a hero's worship. Their kingdom flourished on the growing trade, particularly in tin, that was carried out with Italy.

Prince Aithlios of Lokrian Opus was another foreign-born Leleges who settled in the area (1375T/1125R BCE). Aithlios was the son of Zeus and Protogeneia, daughter of first couple Deukalion and Pyrrha. He settled in the fertile Peneios river valley and became the first king of Eleia. His marriage to Aiolian Kalyce of Iolkos suggests a intermingling of the Leleges and the later arriving Aiolians/Minyans. Their beautiful son Endymion became the lover of the moon goddess Selene.

The prosperity of the Leleges attracted Aiolian/Minyan tribesmen from northern Hellas, possibly to strengthen their position on the trade routes to Sicily and Italy and to provide a route to Krete not controlled by the Mycenaians (Danaans). First to arrive was Amythaon of Iolkos, a distant relative of Kalyce. He settled on the Triphylian coast, which was thereafter called Amythaonia (1349T/1099R BCE). The great seer Melampous, who became king of Mycenai, was his son. Next to arrive was Salmoneus, the grandson of Aiolos and Enarte who founded Salmonia in Pisatis, near the headwaters of the lovely Enipeus (1305T/1055R BCE). Perieres of Iolkos, a descendent of Aiolos and Enarte, settled in Triphylia (1295T/1045R BCE), and finally, Aiolian Pyttios settled in Eleia (1277T/1027R BCE).

Oinomaos, Pelops, and Neleus were later kings of great power. Oinomaos and Pelops ruled Harpina, though they were later placed in Pisa. Neleus

---

[137] The first Hellenic couple, Deukalion and Pyrrha, was the ancestors of the Leleges tribe. However, "Leleges" is a generic term applied to others that were not related to Deukalion, and some might not even have been Hellenic, such as those of coastal Karia, where Pelops once ruled.

[138] The Dorians believed Polykaon settled at Andania in the Messenian plain; however, few Mycenaian settlements have been found on that plain. Most likely Polykaon settled on the west coast of Messenia, where Mycenaian settlements thrived. Later, when the Dorians ruled, they assumed that Polykaon lived where most of the historic cities were, and they placed him at their own stronghold, Andania.

turned Pylos into one of the greatest Bronze Age cities of Hellas. Many of the sons of Amythaon and Pelops migrated to the Argeia and helped enrich Mycenai.

---

Image 9.1
Map of Western Peloponnesos Bronze Age Sites

- • Important as both a mythic and archaeological site
- X Important mythic site
  Rest are important archaeological sites

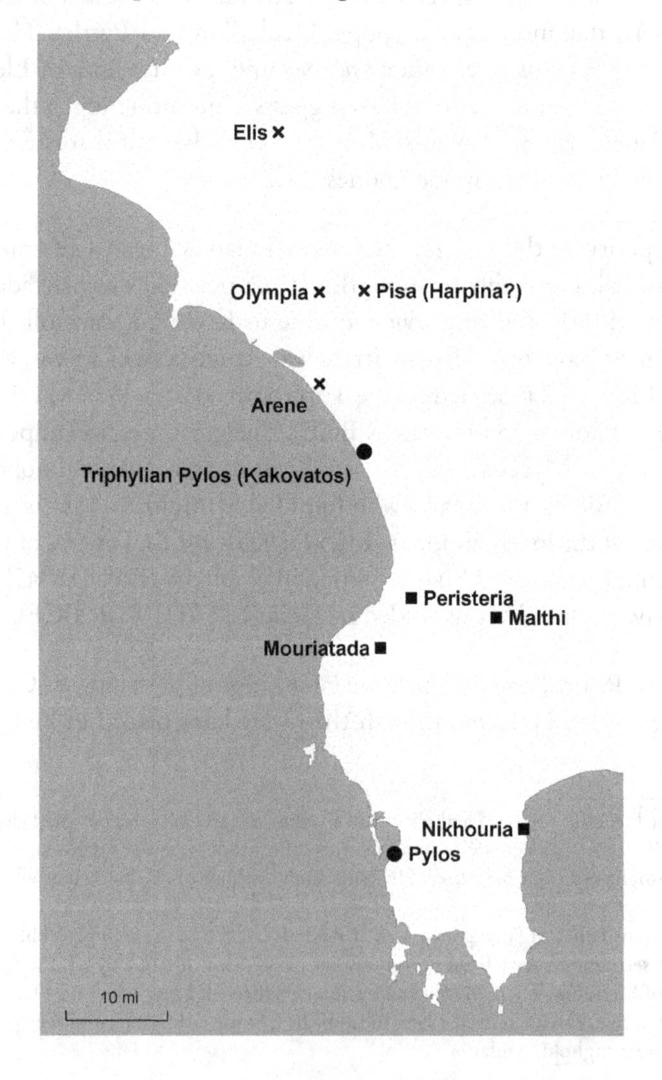

## Exploits of King Pelops

Pelops attacked Eleia when he saw an opportunity at the death of King Epeios. The young king Eleios enlisted Lapith mercenaries and defeated Pelops (1299T/1049R BCE). The Lapiths were a mountain people, kindred to the Centaurs. Lapith prince Phorbas led the Epeians to victory. Rebuffed to the north, Pelops turned inland and began a long campaign against the Pelasgians of Arkadia.

The first Arkadian city to fall was Phineus (1283T/1033R BCE). His widowed daughter Astydameia eventually moved there. Upon the death of Arkadian king Kleitor, Pelops seized Azania (1276T/1026R BCE). Pelops then pushed his conquests all the way across Arkadia to Stymphalos, which he failed to sack. The unrelenting Pelops deceitfully killed King Stymphalos and took the city by guile (1273T/1023R BCE). The angry gods sent a drought as punishment.

Pelops was more famous for his ubiquitous descendants who eventually ruled most of the great cities of Hellas than he was for his own exploits. The peninsula of Apia was renamed the Peloponnesos in their honor. Hippodameia bore to Pelops thirteen children of note: Astydameia, Alkathoos, Kreon, Pittheus, Troizen, Lysidice, Nicippe, Broteas, Dias, Kopreus, Kleones, and the twins Atreus and Thyestes. Many lesser-known individuals were said to be his children (Hippalkos, Cybosoros, Hippasos, and Ailinos, for example), and the later writers created names out of cities and made them his sons (such as Korinthos). Pelops also sired numerous bastards (Letrinos and Khyrsippe were the most famous ones).

Hephaistos made Pelops's royal scepter on Zeus's order either while he ruled Arzawa or later, when he ruled Pisa. When he died, the coveted scepter was given to his son Atreus at his coronation ceremony in Mycenai.

## Amphion and Zethos

Pelops had a noble sister named Niobe. Their proud father, Tantalos, who had once entertained the gods, insisted that his lovely daughter marry a man of the same station as his (a son of Zeus and a king of an important state). King Amphion of Thebes was such a man. Tantalos married

Niobe to him and also arranged for Thebe (or Aidon), the daughter of his notorious companion Pandareos of Kos, to marry Amphion's twin brother and co-king Zethos. Tantalos and Pandareos once stole a sacred image of Zeus, and their daughters would suffer for it.

Majestic Amphion and strong Zethos, descendants of the Spartoi who built Thebes with Kadmos, did not gain the kingdom easily. In the form of a Satyr, Zeus ravished their mother, Antiope, the beautiful daughter of Nykteus of the Spartoi, one of the men who had sprung from dragon's teeth Kadmos sowed. When Antiope realized she was pregnant, she fled in a panic, justifiably fearing a harsh punishment from her stern father. Not knowing where she would be safe, she ran to her father's enemy, King Epopeus of Sicyon. Epopeus was unaware that Zeus had been with her. He was taken by her beauty and became her lover and protector. He thought her unborn babies were his own.

Epopeus had become an enemy of Kadmeia (Thebes) when he conquered Korinth from the Sisyphids. The Korinthian royal family, sons of Sisyphos, fled to Kadmeia and were given land in Potniai by Kadmos. Sisyphos was the brother of Athamas, who had married Kadmos's daughter Ino when he was king of Orkhomenos.

Nykteus gathered an army to attack Sicyon and reclaim his daughter (1319T/1069R BCE). Naturally, the sons of Sisyphos joined him. They marched on Sicyon, where they were defeated by Epopeus. In the battle, Nykteus faced Epopeus and wounded him slightly. Epopeus dealt Nykteus a mortal wound. On his deathbed back in Thebes, Nykteus made his brother Lykos swear to avenge his death and bring Antiope back and punish her.

During the winter, Lykos prepared a second invasion. On the way to Sicyon, Lykos helped restore Glaukos, son of Sisyphos, as king of Korinth (1318T/1068R BCE). Epopeus had died during the winter because he had neglected his wound. Without him the Sicyonians were in no mood to fight over Antiope and the twin sons she had delivered. They handed them over to Lykos. During his triumphant return to Thebes, Antiope gave birth to twin sons who were exposed near Eleutherai in the Cithairon Mountains and left to die. Back in Thebes, Antiope was imprisoned and gleefully tortured by Lykos's wife, Dirce, for bringing shame to the family (via her unwed pregnancy by Zeus).

Zeus willed that his sons be found and raised by cattle herders. The foster parents named the twins Amphion and Zethos.[139] Zethos was an exceedingly strong man who devoted himself to the cattle-herding ways of his adoptive parents. Amphion (meaning "native of two lands") showed musical promise and was taught by Hermes to play the lyre. Amphion modified the design of the lyre (invented by Hermes) by adding three strings to the original four. Like a later, more famous musician named Orpheus, Amphion's music was so magical that the rocks and stones themselves were enchanted.

As men, the twins built a following of supporters. When they felt strong enough, they left the mountains and seized Kadmeia (Thebes) from the regent Lykos and the crown prince, the child Laios. Lykos was killed or escaped. His wife Dirce (meaning "double"), a devotee of Dionysos, was tied to the horns of a bull and gored to death for torturing Antiope. They sent the rightful heir, Laios, to King Pelops, the brother of Amphion's wife, Niobe, to be raised in supervised exile. Happy Antiope was reacquainted with her sons.

The twin kings decided to build protective walls around the city. Everyone marveled at the huge stones Zethos carried on his back to build the walls. But awe struck all when they saw his brother Amphion march by with stones twice as large, following the tune on his lyre. Zethos no longer scoffed at his brother's music. Soon the two completed a magnificent fortress with seven towering gates. Secure behind their great walls in a rich palace, Amphion and Zethos raised their families.

[139] The myth of twin gods ridding on white chargers has parallels among other Indo-European peoples, such as the Asuin of the Indic Vedas and the Thracians living to the north of Hellas. In Hellas the Dioskouroi most famously filled that role and Amphion and Zethos were a less popular version. In Hellenic myth, the greater of the twins was usually the son of a god, while the other was considered the son of a mortal. Therefore, Zethos was sometimes said to be King Epopeus of Sicyon's son. Examples of the divine twins include Polydeuces and Kastor (the Dioskouroi), Amphion and Zethos, Herakles and Iphikles, Idas and Lynceus, Pelias and Neleus, and the conjoined twin Moliones.

Exhibit 9.2
Early Kings of Thebes

| King | Revisionist | Traditional | Lineage |
|---|---|---|---|
| Kadmos | 1136–1085 | 1386–1335 | |
| Pentheus | 1085–1081 | 1335–1331 | Grandson of Kadmos; son of Ekthion of the Spartoi |
| Polydoros | 1081–1070 | 1331–1320 | Son of Kadmos |
| Nykteus/ Lykos | 1070–1056 | 1320–1306 | Regent for Labdakos; sons of Khthonios of the Spartoi |
| Labdakos | 1056–1037 | 1306–1287 | Son of Polydoros |
| Lykos II | 1037–1035 | 1287–1285 | Regent for Laios; son of Lykos |
| Amphion & Zethos | 1035–1017 | 1285–1267 | Sons of Zeus and Nykteus's daughter Antiope |
| Kreon | 1017–986 | 1267–1236 | Son of Pelops |
| Lykos III | 986–985 | 1236–1235 | Son of Poseidon and usurper to the throne |
| Laios | 985 | 1235 | Son of former king Labdakos |

## Niobe's Tears

One day Pelops received news of his sister's tragic death. Pelops's sister Niobe had not heeded bright-eyed Athena's warning against hubris. Niobe was excessively proud of herself and her husband, Amphion—their noble backgrounds, his talents, and the pomp and power of his Theban kingdom, birthplace of Lord Dionysos. But above all she prided herself as a mother. She boasted that she was more accomplished a mother than Leto, having twelve children to the goddess's two.[140] The mighty Titaness became highly indignant upon hearing Niobe's boast. Standing on the birthplace of her children—the summit of Mount Cynthos (on Delos)—she cried out to them. Apollo, Artemis, listen; Niobe has shown herself to be her father's daughter in matters of blasphemy. Apollo cut her statement short,

[140] This story reminds one of Aisop's fables about the conversation between the vixen and the lioness. The vixen chides the lioness for having only one offspring and the great cat retorts "One only, but a lion".

saying, "Enough, the longer you complain, the longer we are kept from punishing her."

A rain of deadly arrows brought down a dreadful plague upon Thebes. Homer (*Iliad* xxiv.605) says all of Niobe's brood perished—six young girls and six tall boys. Apollo made his silver longbow whip and sing; he shot the boys while Artemis rained arrows down upon the girls. Theirs were arrows of illness. Tall Niobe cried out loud, begging them to leave the little one, her youngest, and she cradled him in her arms. Like his brothers and sisters before him, he died anyway. Then Niobe stood up, and the blood drained from her colorless face; her eyes stared in an expression of fixed sorrow.

All of Thebes blamed Niobe, a foreigner, for the plague. Only her brother Pelops shed a tear for her upon hearing what had happened. She returned home to Arzawa (Lydia), and upon her own prayers, Zeus turned her into a weeping stone. Her husband, by contrast, flew into a grief-induced rage. He died trying to avenge himself on Apollo by sacking Delphi. Perhaps not all of her children perished. Their orphaned daughter Khloris (meaning "pale") survived because of her prayers and was sent to be raised by her uncle Pelops.

## Pelopids in Thebes

Laios greeted the news of Khloris's tragedy with quiet glee. Pelops had taken in toddling Laios, the crown prince of Thebes, when Amphion and Zethos seized the city. Niobe, wife of Amphion and sister of Pelops, wanted this potential rival to be supervised and controlled by someone she trusted. Pelops raised Laios as well as he did own children. To Laios, the death of King Amphion and his sons meant he was again heir to the throne of Thebes, which was recovering from a plague.

On being summoned back to Thebes, Laios offered to teach Pelops's beautiful young bastard son Khrysippos how to drive a chariot and then rode off to Thebes with the handsome youth beside him (1267T/1017R BCE). Khrysippos's mother, the Danaan nymph Axiokhe, wept bitterly to Pelops, who had once been treated in the same manner by Poseidon. Pelops reacted by cursing Laios and then assembling his army. To avoid conflict, the Thebans negotiated a settlement; Pelops's second son, Kreon (meaning "ruling"), became king of Thebes and Khrysippos was returned to Pelops, but Laios was allowed to remain in his native Thebes unpunished (1267T/1017R BCE).

## Pelopids in Pylos

Amphion and Niobe's pale daughter Khloris grew into a beautiful girl skilled at various crafts while living in her uncle's palace. She even won the running games of Hera, which had been initiated by her aunt Hippodameia. Many suitors were interested in marrying this beautiful former princess (1251T/1001R BCE). Pelops awarded her to Neleus, who would later conquer sandy Pylos, the greatest Peloponnesian palace city outside of the Argeia.

Neleus was a truly miraculous man. His story begins with Salmoneus, the king of Salmonia, one of the important kingdoms of the western Peloponnesos. King Salmoneus married an Arkadian princess from Tegea.[141] His wife died during childbirth, but their daughter Tyro survived (1299T/1049R BCE).[142] Salmoneus remarried the priestess of Hera, Sidero. Sidero kept distinctive bull horns in her shrine to Hera, and Sidero cruelly mistreated her stepdaughter Tyro.

When Tyro came of age, her desires awakened. As was then the custom for marriageable maidens, she prayed to the river that her virginity be taken away. She became enamored with a dream that perhaps it would be the river himself who would be her husband. She would often splash its running waters into her lap and utter her pliant prayer to

> a river, godlike Enipeus, by far the handsomest of all those
> rivers whose streams cross over the earth, and she used
> to haunt Enipeus' beautiful waters; taking his (Enipeus')

[141] Diodoros's *Library of History*, iv.68, calls her Alcidice, daughter of Tegean king Aleos. To fit Tyro's generation, she would have to have been Aleos's sister.

[142] Tyro was the heroine of two lost plays by Sophokles, both dealing with her romantic love and her sorrows. The fourth-century BCE comic playwright Menandros of Athens wrote a play about her following a different tradition. Eustathios of Antioch and the Scholast on Homer add details. Hyginos adds the story of Tyro's seduction by her uncle Sisyphos, which doesn't fit well with the myths of Sisyphos or Salmoneus. Her story was tied to both Iolkos in Thessalia and Triphylia in the Peloponnesos.

> likeness, the god (Poseidon) who circles the earth and shakes it lay with her where the swirling river finds its outlet and a sea-blue wave curved into a hill of water reared up above the two, to hide the god and the mortal woman; and he broke her virginal zone and drifted a sleep upon her. But when the god had finished with the act of lovemaking, he took her by the hand and spoke to her and named her, saying:
>
> "Be happy, lady, in this love, and when the year passes you will bear glorious children, for the couplings of the immortals are not without issue."[143]

Her father and stepmother refused to believe her incredulous story and mistreated the innocent girl. When her term ended, she delivered twin sons—Neleus and Pelias. She placed them on a small ark and sent them floating down the Enipeus River, hoping Poseidon would save them (1281T/1031R BCE). The god of horses did not fail her or their sons.

The ark ran aground in a pasture where a horseman was tending his herd. One of the mares kicked one of the infants, leaving a livid mark on his face. The child's howl caught the herdsman's attention, and he took them both in and reared them. Alone without women, the herdsman did his best. The marked one, whom he named Pelias (meaning "livid"), was suckled by a mare; and the other, Neleus, by a bitch.

Tyro had been forced by her hard-hearted parents to abandon her babies. They greedily demanded that she fetch a bride-price worthy of a virgin princess. Tyro was sent far away, to her father's homeland, where no one knew her past. There she was married to King Kretheus of Iolkos. She bore to her king a son named Aison (father of Jason the Argonaut) and a daughter called Phalanna, who was the eponym of a Thessalian city.

Salmoneus and Sidero were rainmakers who presumptuously imitated Zeus and Hera. They drove through town in a four-horse chariot dragging bronze kettles covered by dried hides to imitate thunder while they lit oak

---

[143] Homer, *Odyssey* xi.235.

wood torches to simulate lightning. Zeus was not amused and hurled a bolt of lightning to kill the impostors and destroy Salmonia.[144]

Pelias and Neleus survived Salmonia's demise since they were raised far away from the destroyed city. As young men the twins presided over contests held at the holy Olympic site. When the two learned of their pedigree, they traveled to Iolkos and were reunited with their mother, Tyro. Pelias seized the kingdom of Iolkos upon King Kretheus's death, and he banished his brother Neleus (1252T/1002R BCE). Neleus returned to the land of his birth, western Peloponnesos. As a supplicant he approached King Aphareus of Arene. The king was impressed with godlike Neleus and gave the ambitious young man the fort of Thryoissa to manage. While Neleus was living in Thryoissa, he married Khloris, the pale daughter of Amphion and Niobe who was raised in the court of Pelops. Sometime afterward Neleus convinced his overlord to supply him with an army he used to conquer sandy Pylos.[145]

## Pelopids in Megara

Pelops's broken-hearted eldest son Alkathoos left his native Pisa (and the kingdom he would have inherited) upon the unexpected death of his young wife, Pyrgo, perhaps during childbirth. The grieving Alkathoos headed north, perhaps to visit his brother Kreon, who ruled Thebes. Along the way he stopped in Megara.

He found Megara was in crisis. The city was plagued by a troublesome lion known as the Cithairon Lion, a man-eater who terrorized the citizens. Among the adults and children lost to this fearsome beast was the king's young son Evippos. Desperate king Megareus promised two things to the man who slew the lion: his lovely virgin daughter Eurskhme and the kingdom as her dowry. Despite two wonderful rewards, not one local man

[144] The myth of Salmoneus as a rainmaker is very ancient. His brother Athamas preformed a similar function in Minyan Orkhomenos. Aiakos of Aigina was another famous rainmaker. Salmoneus's odd behavior was a ritual performance to entice the sky god to deliver rain. The late mythographers Apollodoros and Diodoros were unfamiliar with the ancient custom and presumed the unorthodox actions evoked a punishment for hubris.

[145] That Pylos and Iolkos, the most distant of the palace states, were once ruled by twins is a mythic affirmation of the archaeological findings that Mycenaian culture was very homogeneous.

found the courage to face the fierce lion. Instead it was a foreigner, Pelops's son, who accepted the challenge. After killing the lion, he married Princess Eurskhme and stayed in Megara (1266T/1016R BCE).[146] Alkathoos became king when Megareus died unexpectedly (1262T/1012R BCE).

Image 9.2
Map of Pelopid-Ruled Cities

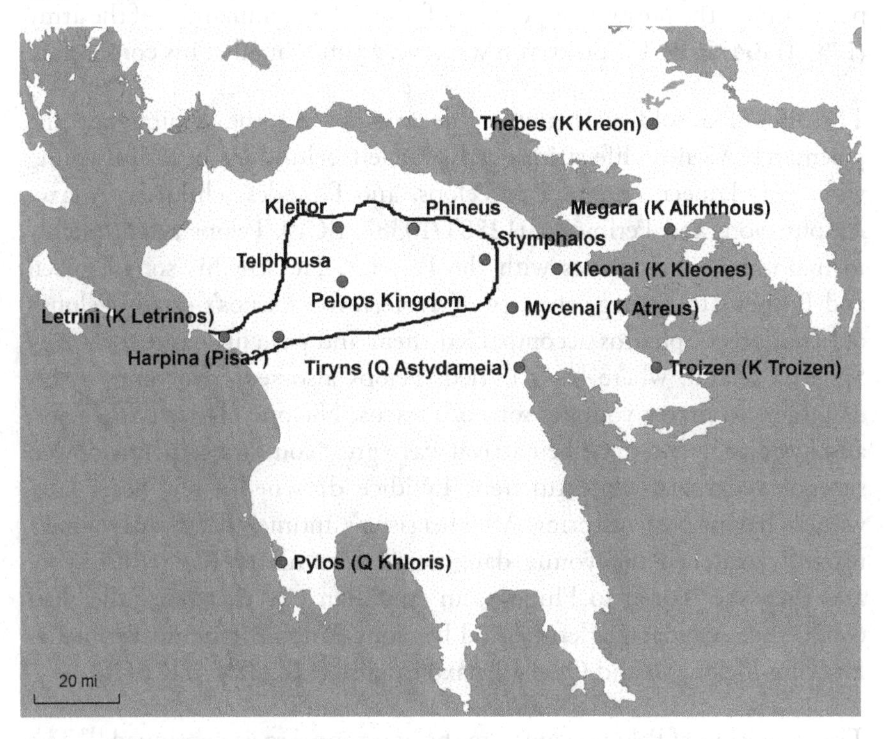


King (K) or Queen (Q) is the son or daughter or niece of Pelops

## Pelopids (and Perseids) in Argeia

The two greatest families in the Peloponnesos intermarried freely. The first of these marriages was arranged while Pelops was visiting his dying overlord and benefactor, the great hero Perseus. Pelops's eldest daughter,

[146] Alkathoos may originally have been a primitive, prepolis hero who performed heroic deeds against monsters and wild beasts, like Herakles and Theseus. Herakles and Theseus overshadowed Alkathoos, and his labors are largely lost. In Megara, however, his cult thrived.

Astydameia, became enamored with Perseus's son Alcaios. The two powerful monarchs were pleased, for they both wished to bond their families together through a political marriage. A great wedding feast followed (1298T/1048R BCE).

When Perseus died, his eldest son, Elektryon, became king of Tiryns, while his younger brother Alcaios inherited the fief of Troizen and became polemarch—the prestigious position of warlord or commander of the army (1297T/1047R BCE). Elektryon was a very young man at his coronation.

The life of a soldier is always precarious, and the Moirai cut the polemarch Alcaios's life strings early. He left behind his beautiful young wife, Astydameia, daughter of Pelops, and fatherless children: Anaxo, Amphitryon, and Perimedes (1288T/1038R BCE). Pelops acted quickly to maintain his close ties with the Perseids. He sent his sons Troizen and Pittheus to manage the city of Troizen for Alcaios's estate. Pelops's old charioteer Sphairos accompanied them and gave his name to nearby Sphairia Island, where he is buried. Pelops also sent two more of his daughters to marry younger sons of Perseus; Nicippe married Sthenelos, and Lysidice,[147] Mestor. Their arrival was a great comfort to their widowed sister Astydameia. Unfortunately, Lysidice drowned a few years later without having born offspring. After her sister's untimely death, Astydameia tearfully watched her young daughter Anaxo marry King Elektryon, and then she retired to Phineus, an Arkadian city that her father had conquered. Astydameia left behind her sons Amphitryon and Perimedes for King Elektryon and Queen Anaxo to raise (1282T/1032R BCE).

The migration of Pelopid youths to the booming Argeia continued.[148] The Perseid Sthenelos, who became king of Tiryns after his brother Elektryon's death, accepted the petition of Pelops's eighteen-year-old son Kopreus for work. Kopreus fled to Tiryns after murdering a man named Iphitos and was purified by the king, his brother-in-law Sthenelos (1263T/1013R BCE). Kopreus served Sthenelos as courier and became the chief herald

---

[147] She could not have borne Hippothoe to Mestor (Apollodoros, *Library* ii.4.5). Hippothoe was abducted from Tiryns nearly a century earlier.

[148] Archaeological finds indicate a relative decline in importance of the western Peloponnesos while the cities of the Argeia grew during the mid fourteenth century T / late twelfth century R BCE. Perhaps many of them migrated to Argeia, as the sons of Pelops (originally a tribal name) did.

in the court of his son Eurystheus. Kopreus later acted as go-between for Eurystheus and his servant Herakles.

The youngest legitimate sons of Pelops, Atreus and his twin brother Thyestes, were fortunate far beyond expectations. The youngest do not usually do so well. They were born long after it was thought that Hippodameia could still conceive (1280T/1030R BCE). They remained at home after most of their siblings had left. Atreus married Kleolia, the daughter of his older brother Dias (1258T/1008R BCE). Kleolia died young, leaving behind a sickly son named Pleisthenes.

Old Hippodameia grew jealous because Pelops favored his bastard son, Khrysippos, over all the legitimate children she had born. She secretly convinced her twin sons to murder their half brother Khrysippos (1256T/1006R BCE). Pelops discovered their guilt and exiled them. Quite naturally they went to where their other siblings had prospered. About one year after their arrival, King Talaos of nearby Midea died before his son Adrastos was old enough to rule. The nobles of Midea accepted King Sthenelos of Midea's recommendation to employ his brothers-in-law Atreus and Thyestes as regents (1255T/1005R BCE).

## Taphian Raiders

The great Perseid king Elektryon married Anaxo, who was both a Perseid and a Pelopid. The title of queen came at a heavy price. Her childhood ended at sixteen, and by seventeen she was a mother herself. Twins ran in the family, and she had several sets. The honors bestowed for bearing many sons was offset by a heavy toll on her young body. She was dead by age twenty-five, leaving behind nine sons: Amphimakhos, Anaktor, Arkhelaos, Celaineus, Khirimakhos, Gorgophenos, Lysinomakhos, Paylonomos, and Stratobates. She also gave birth to daughters named Alkmene (their firstborn) and Midea (eponym of Midea). Alkmene was a tall, dark-eyed beauty of rare intelligence. She blossomed into the most beautiful women of her day, which was just fine for her fiancé Amphitryon, the son of her uncle Alcaios and his successor as polemarch.

With so many children, the future of the Perseids in Tiryns seemed secure. After his wife's death, Elektryon kept company with concubines, and one of his bastards by a Phrygian slave[149] became his favorite. The child was named Licymnios.

The Danaans regularly supplemented their income with plunder, but they were caught unprepared for the tables to be turned. A ship of Taphian raiders saw Elektryon's cattle grazing close to the sea, guarded by only nine boys and a few herdsmen. The pirates landed and were surprised, as the nine boys fought them like men. The boys were all princes, sons of a burly king. Alas, after a savage battle, the outnumbered Danaans were defeated and the princes were dead (1263T/1013R BCE).

The young polemarch Amphitryon (son of Perseid prince Alcaios and the Pelopid princess Astydameia) was responsible for vengeance. While Elektryon assembled the army, Amphitryon took off in pursuit of the bandits. Amphitryon found the stolen herd in Elis and ransomed it. When Elektryon found out, he was furious that Amphitryon had paid for what was already his.

The ensuing argument grew so heated that both men lost their wits. The unbalanced Elektryon lunged at his nephew Amphitryon, who reacted like the powerful warrior he was, and the middle-aged monarch crumpled in death.

The king's brother Sthenelos seized the opportunity to become king. He claimed the crown because he was the eldest remaining son of Perseus, and he promptly ordered that the popular Amphitryon be banished for murder.

---

Exhibit 9.3
First Wave of Sea Peoples

Taphian raiders were not the only warriors active at sea. Royal inscriptions from the pharaoh Ramesses II of Egypt declare that he destroyed the warriors of the great green sea ca. 1278T/1028R BCE, the first known Egyptian reference of the Sea Peoples. So many Sea Peoples were captured

[149] Linear B texts and Homer both attest to the sacking of cities to gather women slaves (Troy was sacked for a woman). The women were put to work performing industrial and domestic chores around the palace. Although most of the slaves came from Anatolia, they could not have been Phrygians, since that tribe did not settle in Anatolia until the end of the Late Bronze (Heroic) Age.

that they were used as auxiliaries in the great battle at Kadesh against the Hittites (1274T/1024R BCE). These two states battled for supremacy over Syria. They battled inconclusively by the Orontes River. Tensions remained high between the two states for a long time afterward, but neither side could afford another great battle. Among the Hittite allies were Arzawan tribesmen. These events occurred during the reign of Elektryon.

---

## Exile of Amphitryon

The assembled army was loyal to Amphitryon, and a tense moment passed as Amphitryon weighed his response. Amphitryon knew he was responsible for Elektryon's death, even if he had killed him in self-defense, and decided to accept his punishment. His brother Perimedes and a large band of supporters fled with him to Thebes, where his uncle Kreon ruled. One of Sthenelos's younger brothers, Heleios, chose to leave with Amphitryon. With much of the army departing, Sthenelos abandoned the planned expedition against the pirates of Taphios.

Young Princess Alkmene faced the toughest choice of all: whether to honor her parents' pledge to marry Amphitryon or join those condemning her father's killer. Her understanding heart knew Amphitryon had not planned his deed, and so she left with him. Still, she was a strong-willed maiden who dared to stand up to her husband. She set one condition before she would consummate the marriage: Amphitryon had to complete the will of her father and avenge the death of her brothers. Amphitryon readily accepted the challenge. It gave him the chance to redeem himself.

## Exploits of Amphitryon

Once in Thebes, the exiled warlord offered to rid the land of a particularly pesky vixen if King Kreon would supply him an army for an exhibition against the pirate island nation of Taphios. His uncle Kreon agreed and purified him of the murder.

When all of Amphitryon's tricks failed to catch the fox, he sought another alternative. Having heard that the Athenian Cephalos had a hound that never failed to catch its prey, Amphitryon sought out Cephalos. Old Cephalos had been banished from Athens years before for accidentally killing his wife, and he agreed to hunt the vixen in exchange for an island should the Taphians be defeated.

The chase was on between what the gods decreed could never be caught and what they decreed could never fail to catch. Zeus ended the quandary by turning both into statues. No matter—the Thebans were delighted, for the vixen was gone. The grateful citizens purified Cephalos of the murder of his wife.

Before Amphitryon could attack Taphios, Thebes came under attack (1262T/1012R BCE). Thebes had grown so powerful behind the sturdy walls built by Amphion and Zethos, twin sons of mighty Zeus, that she began rivaling Orkhomenos for supremacy of Boiotia. The war started during a confrontation at the sanctuary of Poseidon in Onkhestos. King Klymenos of Orkhomenos was performing a rite when Menoiceus of the Spartoi, descendent of Ekhion—one of the fierce warriors who had sprung up from the dragon's teeth sown by Kadmos—rode up in his chariot.

Menoiceus was the leader of the Spartoi in Thebes at the time, the polemarch, and he argued with King Klymenos. Hot tempers led to bloodshed when Menoiceus's charioteer Perieres struck the Orkhomenian king with a rock. The king staggered back while Menoiceus and Perieres fled the scene. Klymenos died shortly thereafter in Orkhomenos, but not before demanding revenge.

Klymenos's young son Erginos immediately led the army against Thebes. The Thebans were defeated despite the support of Amphitryon and his followers. The Thebans were forced to pay an annual tribute of one hundred cattle to Orkhomenos. The fate of Menoiceus is not specifically recorded, but since Amphitryon soon became polemarch, it can safely be assumed he was killed during the battle. His children, Kreon and Jokaste, survived him.

Amphitryon rallied Theban spirits by focusing their attention on his project. He assembled a large force of Tirynians, Thebans, Phocians, Athenians, and others. Kreon gladly provided his promised troops, hoping to restore the fortunes of his disgruntled subjects. The stout warrior Panopeus led Phocians and a few Lokrians. Cephalos led Athenian allies and also convinced wise king Aiakos of Aigina to provide a contingent. Heleios, the youngest son of gorgon-slaying Perseus, joined the expedition, and Amphitryon led his own considerable contingent of Tirynians. Fearing squabbles among the unruly allies, Amphitryon demanded that each commander swear that they would peacefully share the spoils. Then he led the expedition.

The king of Taphios, Pterelaos, was a treacherous and dangerous man. He possessed a golden strand of hair that made his kingdom impenetrable, a gift from Poseidon. Try as Amphitryon might, he could not bring down the kingdom until Pterelaos became a victim of treachery himself. His daughter Komaitho plucked his golden hair for the promised love of Amphitryon. Then the forces stormed the citadel and Amphitryon killed Pterelaos (1262T/1012R BCE). He showed no mercy to Komaitho and ran his sword through her heart, a path laid open by the piercing arrow of love.[150]

During the sack of Taphios, only the rash young spearman Panopeus ignored his oath and embezzled some of the booty. Accused of theft, he swore his innocence by Athena. The gods punished him by making his son Epeios a poor soldier. The victorious army divided the spoils without further issue and celebrated. Eager Amphitryon had other matters on his mind and quickly dismissed his forces. Some of his Akhaian followers from Tiryns, as well as Cephalos and the Athenians, chose to settle in the conquered islands. The remainder set sail for Thebes, where the Tirynian refugees settled down. King Kreon announced that henceforth Amphitryon would be the polemarch of Thebes, a position held previously only by Spartoi.

## Miraculous Conception of Herakles

Amphitryon led the army homeward at double speed, anxious for the love of the virgin Alkmene. Zeus, meanwhile, took the opportunity to lie with the most beautiful and intelligent woman of the day, disguised as her valiant husband. Alkmene threw open her chamber doors and enthusiastically gave him his reward. So satisfying was her lovemaking and

[150] The same story is told of King Nisos of Megara and his daughter.

his desire to sire a strong hero that Zeus ordered the sun to remain below for the day and the moon to travel slowly. Sleep was sent upon mankind so that they would not notice that the night was three times longer than normal.[151] Then he departed.

Exhausted, Alkmene dropped into a well-deserved sleep. Her blissful repose was soon interrupted when the real Amphitryon came knocking upon her door. Amphitryon was chagrined at the chilly reception he received. His exasperated wife said enough! I cannot keep up this amorous embrace with you. Amphitryon was puzzled and angry. He asked the great Theban seer Teiresias how it was that while he swore the marriage had not been consummated, Alkmene adamantly swore that it had. Teiresias correctly perceived that Zeus had been there and convinced Amphitryon that Alkmene had abandoned her virginity in innocence, though prematurely. The flattered Alkmene found renewed energy and did not disappoint her rightful husband. As his pregnant wife grew larger, Amphitryon wondered if his wife carried the god's son or his own.

---

Exhibit 9.4
Teiresias the Seer

One of the five Spartoi who sprang from the dragon's teeth that Kadmos sowed in Thebes was Odious, who fathered Evenes. Evenes was lucky enough to marry a lovely nymph, an attendant of Athena, Khariklo. Khariklo bore to Evenes a marvelous son they called Teiresias. At the age of seven Teiresias went looking for his mother and found her at an inopportune time while Athena and Khariklo were bathing in the spring of Hippokoon after a hunt on Mount Helikaon. Athena immediately blinded the boy, saying that no mortal may see divinity against divine will. The brilliance of naked Athena (the goddess of wisdom) blinded Teiresias, and poor Khariklo howled in anger.

> He (Teiresias) stood there, speechless, pain gluing to his knees, his voice paralyzed.
> "You have spoken in anger, divine woman. Take back your words.

[151] This myth may be borrowed from an Egyptian legend in which the god appears to the queen in the form of the pharaoh in order to sire the next pharaoh.

It was not I who struck your son blind.
Putting out young eyes is not sweet to Athena,
but the laws of Kronos demand
that whoever sees an immortal against the god's will
must pay for the sight and pay dearly."

"You mustn't grieve so, darling. Your son will be honored,
all for your sake, by divine gift to him.
I will make him prophet, his fame will be mythic."[152]

Then, to please Khariklo Athena gave the lad numerous gifts to compensate for his lost eyesight: a magical staff to guide him, prophetic powers of mythic proportion, a lifespan three times normal, and the unique ability among mortals to keep his wits (his memory) in Hades (the Argeian seer Amphiaraos later received the same boon).

---

On the day Herakles was fated to be born, proud Zeus proclaimed in the lofty halls of Olympos that the next descendent of his born that very day from the House of Pelops would one day rule Tiryns. Hera, pretending disbelief, asked Zeus to swear that what he declared was true. Zeus had no sooner made his unwary vow than Hera forbade her daughter Eileithyia (the goddess of sore travail) from visiting Alkmene, in order to make her labor long and difficult. Eileithyia and Hera flew off instead to Tiryns, and Queen Nicippe of Tiryns, wife of King Sthenelos, delivered Eurystheus (who was a Pelopid and a descendent of Zeus) prematurely, at seven months. That day Zeus learned that even he should not boast prematurely. Zeus was not powerful enough to undo his own word, and so Herakles never gained the kingdom. He would have ruled a magnificent kingdom, for the busy port of Tiryns was by now the second largest city in all of Europe. Only Mycenai was larger.

Hera would have liked it very much if Alkmene and her child were to die in childbirth. Finally distressed that Alkmene might die, her midwife, Galanthis, tried a ruse. She left Alkmene's bedchamber rejoicing the birth of a son. The birthing goddess Eileithyia was so surprised that she uncrossed her fingers and legs and entered the bedchamber to investigate.

---

[152] Callimachus (Kallimakhos) of Cyrene, "Hymn v; Bath of Pallas", in *Callimachus Hymns, Epigrams, Select Fragments.*

Alcaios (later called Herakles [meaning "glory of Hera"]) was born upon her arrival, and he was named for his grandfather, who had once been the polemarch of Tiryns (1261T/1011R BCE). His mortal half brother Iphikles, son of Amphitryon, followed. Eileithyia was furious at being tricked and changed Galanthis into a weasel. Hera returned to Olympos and sported a discrete, smug smile while furious Zeus blustered about.[153]

Unable to give his son a kingdom, Zeus placed the infant at sleeping Hera's breast to give him nourishment to befit a god. Herakles bit her nipple so hard she awoke and pulled away. Her milk spread out across the skies as the Milky Way.

Iphikles and Herakles looked much alike, and who was who was soon forgotten. When they were eight months of age, jealous Hera sent an azure-colored snake to devour the babies in their crib. Hearing frightful cries, Alkmene rushed to the crib to find Herakles strangling the snake while Iphiklos recoiled screaming in the corner. Teiresias was called in to explain the significance of the snake; he told of Hera's deed and foretold Herakles's greatness. A rumor spread that Amphitryon had let loose the venomous snake to discover which child was his. Thereafter no one ever confused the twins again, for Herakles embodied the power and wonder of his conception.

Amphitryon and his good wife Alkmene raised their boys by the Elektra Gate, surrounded by his followers. Polemarch Amphitryon proved his worth when King Khalkodon of Khalkis attacked Thebes. Amphitryon led the Thebans to victory and killed Khalkodon in single combat (1246T/996R BCE).

[153] Herakles's connection to the great goddess Hera is open for interpretation. He became the archetype of the hero. The Herakles Cycle was an important oral narrative. Although none of the early poems about the cycle survives, Homer quotes it. Peisandros of Rhodes established that there were twelve labors (a subset of the Herakles Cycle) during the sixth century BCE. Panyassis, uncle of the historian Herodotos, writing in the middle of the fifth century BCE, wrote the fifth (and last known) ancient work on Herakles, titled *Herakleia*. His fourteen-book story, like the four before it, is now lost. Only excerpts survive. Panyassis is the first to identify Herakles with the constellation The Kneeler. Matris of Thebes (author of *Praise of Herakles*), and the fifth-century BCE mythographer Pherecydes were key sources of Diodoros of Sicily's summary on Herakles. Apollodoros and Hyginos give versions that closely follow the accounts of Diodoros, and the famous third-century BCE pastoral poet Theokritos of Syrakuse wrote two short poems about Herakles. Hellenic and Hellenistic cities all wished to claim a piece of Herakles, so many, often conflicting, exploits were added to his story.

## Kingdom for Eurystheus, Fame for Herakles

Sickly Eurystheus, born before Herakles, was the only son of King Sthenelos of Tiryns and his Pelopid wife Nicippe. He was raised in splendor as heir apparent in Tiryns. His royal parents had grieved often at her difficulty in carrying a child to full term. Only three of their children survived: Medousa, Alcyone (who is sometimes mentioned as the girl the Centaur Homados tried to rape, though usually the intended victim was called a daughter of King Eurystheus; Herakles killed Homados before he could complete his aim), and Eurystheus.

When Sthenelos died, his eighteen-year-old son Eurystheus became king in fulfillment of Zeus's prophecy (1243T/993R BCE). Hera had so often been humiliated by Zeus's philandering that she was well pleased to watch him powerlessly fume over what might have been for Herakles. The same year, Herakles obtained glory by leading the Thebans to victory over the Minyan Orkhomenos. It started when an Orkhomenian envoy arrived in Thebes to collect the annual tribute. Herakles's pride would not be checked, and he outraged the envoy by cutting off their noses, hands, and feet. He sent word back with them that Thebes would no longer pay.

As expected, King Erginos of Orkhomenos led his army on the attack. A local oracle proclaimed victory to Thebes if their noblest would die. All eyes turned to Antipoinos, a descendent of the Spartoi. When he hesitated, his daughters Androkleia and Alcis agreed to be sacrificed, and they have been honored in Artemis's Theban temple ever since. After the two sides fought to a draw, Herakles suggested to his countrymen that they sabotage the channels draining Lake Kopais. The resulting flooding ruined their enemy's farmland. Orkhomenos sued for peace, and the Thebans imposed twice the tribute on Orkhomenos that they had themselves previously paid (1243T/993R BCE). So Herakles gained through cunning what he could not by brute force.

King Kreon rewarded Herakles with the hand of his daughter Megara. Kreon also appointed Herakles polemarch to succeed his dead foster father, Amphitryon, who had fallen during the inconclusive battle. The king also arranged for Herakles's brother, Iphikles, to marry his niece Automedousa, daughter of King Alkathoos of Megara (the son of Pelops who gained his kingdom by slaying a fierce lion).

Even the gods were impressed by Herakles's prowess and showered him with gifts. Hephaistos presented him with a shield, Apollo with a bow and arrows, Hermes a sword, Poseidon horses, and Athena a robe. Herakles settled down and sired three sons.

While living happily with his young family, the Moirai appeared before Herakles with a choice between a long happy life of obscurity (an unmemorable life) and a difficult but glorious life (eternal fame). He chose the latter. Soon after his decision, Hera struck Herakles with insanity, and he slew his own children. In punishment he was sent to serve the weakling who ruled his rightful inheritance. Herakles arrived in great-walled Tiryns alone in a chariot pulled by fast horses, one of them being the immortal Arion (1239T/989R BCE). Herakles, the anvil of Tiryns, was tormented by his own gruesome deed and his belittling servitude. He spent an eternal year (eight normal years) performing tasks for King Eurystheus.

# Eternal Year

## Late Helladic Bronze Age (LHIIIB); Part of Hesiod's Age of Heroes

Listen to me. All men have to pay the debt of death, and there is not a mortal who knows whether he is going to be alive on the morrow. The outcome of things that depend on fortune cannot be foreseen; they can neither be learned nor discovered by any art. Hearken to this and learn of me, cheer up, drink, reckon the days yours as you live them; the rest belongs to fortune.

—Herakles in Euripides's *Alcestis,* fifth century BCE

May Leto, nurturing Leto, give you fine children
And Cypris, goddess Cypris, equal love for each other
And Zeus, Kronian Zeus, prosperity without end.

—Theokritos of Syrakuse, *Helene's Wedding Song,* third century BCE

The Heroic Age peaked during the eternal year in which Herakles earned immortality by successfully completing twelve seemingly impossible labors. Gods and men never interacted more often than they did during this eternal year (eight solar years).

**1239T/989R BCE**
Herakles begins his labors in the service of King Eurystheus.

## Herakles Begins His Labors

**1) Nemean Lion:** Herakles hunted a fierce man-eating lion terrorizing the Argeia for thirty days before finding it listless after a large meal. Herakles shot the lion, but the thick hide of the baleful monster was impervious to the arrows. When the annoyed lion leapt at his tormentor, Herakles struck him on the head with a mighty blow from his massive club made of wild olive wood. The club broke into two pieces while the lion fell, midleap, to the ground. The lion stood on unsteady feet, shaking his head in befuddled pain. Quickly, before he recovered, Herakles jumped on the beast's muscular back and strangled him. During the struggle, Herakles lost a finger. Herakles skinned the lion and wore its tough hide for protection. King Eurystheus of Tiryns was so terrified at his cousin Herakles's appearance when he returned in the hide of the beast that he commanded that henceforth Herakles was to display his trophies outside the city gates. Moreover, all communication would be conducted through his herald Kopreus, son of Pelops.

Image 10.1
Map of First Six Labors of Herakles

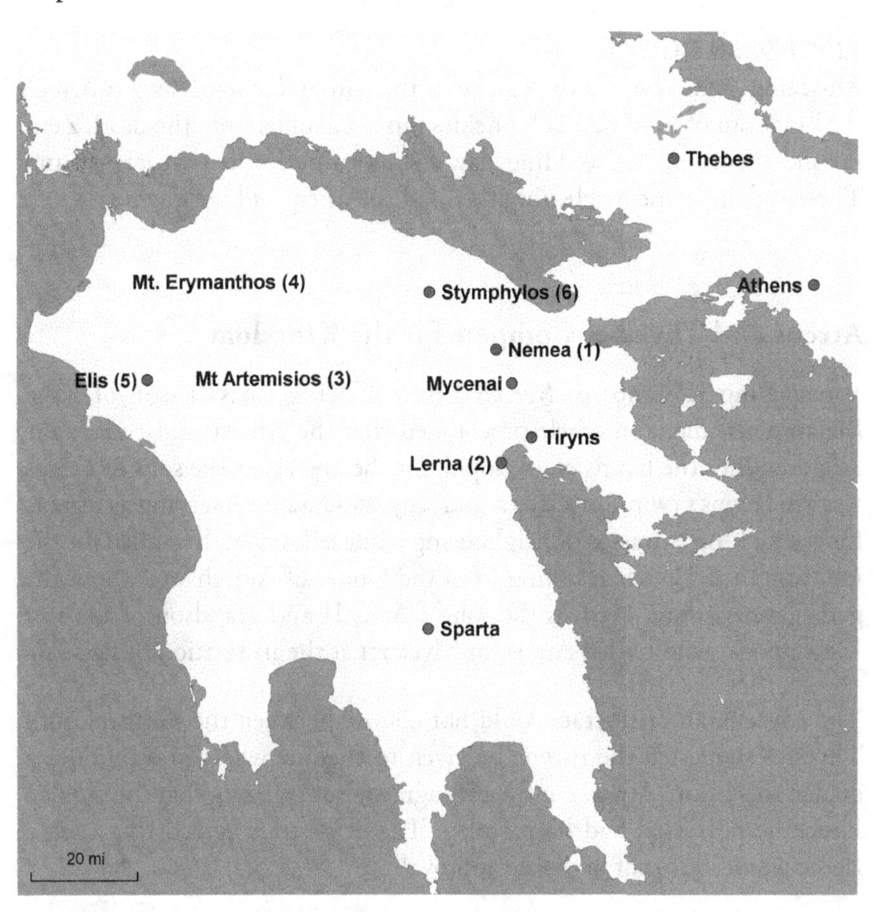


**2) Hideous Hydra:** Next Herakles boldly drove his chariot into the Lerne swamp, which had been created by the waters Poseidon caused to flow for the Danaid Amymone. He leapt out of the car, grabbed the seven-headed serpent by the neck, and cut off the first head that lunged at him. But alas, every time Herakles cut off one of its heads, two heads grew in its place. The situation became increasingly grim until the great hero bellowed to his squire Iolaos (Iphikles's son), asking him to quickly bring burning brands. Then every time Herakles cut off a venomous head, Iolaos cauterized the wound before new heads appeared. In this manner the beast was killed. Herakles buried the immortal head. Then Herakles smashed an annoying crab that Hera had sent to pinch his heel the whole time he fought the

Hydra. Golden-throned Hera put her loyal subject into the heavens as the constellation Cancer.

**1238T/988R BCE**

All-seeing Zeus reverses the course of the sun and stars to award Atreus the kingdom of Mycenai, Polypheides raises Glaukos from the dead, Zeus ravishes Leda on her wedding day, Herakles performs two labors, and Theseus gains fame by clearing the road to Athens of highwaymen.

## Atreus and Thyestes Compete for the Kingdom

When King Koiranos of Mycenai (son of King Abas II, son of King Melampous) died, an oracle proclaimed that the citizens must place the kingdom into the hands of a Pelopid, for the gods gave the sons of Pelops wealth. Pelops's twin sons Atreus and Thyestes had been serving as regents for young king Adrastos of neighboring Midea. They both applied for the job. Koiranos was the last king from the House of Amythaon, whom the gods gave wisdom. He was the son of Abas II and grandson of the seer Melampous, who traded Argos for Mycenai at the instigation of Perseus.

The Mycenaian aristocrats could not choose between the brothers until Thyestes suggested the throne be given to the one who could produce a golden sheepskin. Atreus confidently agreed, not realizing that the Golden Fleece he possessed had been stolen. The aristocrats agreed that such a fleece would be proof of divine approval.

Atreus and Thyestes had inherited rich Akarnanian pastureland filled with a great flock of sheep from their father, Pelops, who had passed away while they were regents of Adrastos (1242T/992R BCE). In thanks Atreus vowed to sacrifice the finest sheep in the herd to Artemis. Sly Hermes took this opportunity to sow seeds of discord between the brothers, for he held a grudge against Pelops for treacherously murdering his son Myrtilos. Fulfilling Myrtilos's dying curse, scheming Hermes aimed to tear apart Pelops's descendants with bitter hatred. To do this he made a wondrous golden-fleeced ram appear among the flocks that grazed in rich pastureland of Akarnania. Atreus, mindful of his oath to wild Artemis to sacrifice the best in the herd to her, slaughtered the ram and offered the meat to Artemis, but he kept the fleece in a box instead of presenting it to the goddess.

Artemis was livid over the ingenuous sacrifice and turned Thyestes against his brother, reminding him that he was entitled to the fleece as well. Atreus's second wife, Airope, had scandalously slept with lovers before her marriage and had afterward made advances toward Thyestes. Hereto he had brushed aside her advances, but he now slept with her in exchange for the box that contained the hidden fleece. At the appointed time, Thyestes produced the fleece, which duly impressed the Mycenaian nobles, and he was anointed king. Scheming Hermes was well pleased.

Atreus cried foul but had no proof that the article had been stolen from him. But the son of Kronos, Zeus, favored Atreus and sent his messenger Hermes to suggest that Atreus propose a new challenge. Atreus complied and proclaimed that the lords should reverse their decision if he could reverse the sun's flight and change the course of the Pleiades.[154] Confident that his brother could not perform such a feat, Thyestes sarcastically agreed. To everyone's astonishment, the sun and stars changed just as Atreus predicted. The people were amazed and gave Atreus the illustrious title of wanax (meaning "great-king"). All of the sons of Pelops agreed that Atreus deserved to wield the royal scepter of their father. Hephaistos crafted it on lordly Zeus's command and gave to the bright pathfinder Hermes to present to Pelops.[155] Seated on his jewel-studded throne in the great hall of his palace, Atreus stamped his scepter on the polished tile and proclaimed his first decree—Thyestes was to be banished.

---

Exhibit 10.1
Mycenaian Walls

Despite its great and growing wealth during the reign of Atreus, Mycenai was a less confident place than before. Instead of palaces or tombs, the

[154] The second-century BCE statesman/historian Polybios of Megalopolis, in *Histories*, suggested the rational explanation that Atreus was the first to realize that the heavens moved in reverse order from the sun's revolution.

[155] So says Homer (*Iliad* ii.102–104). Perhaps Pelops/Uhhaziti brought his awe-inspiring scepter from Anatolia, the likes of which had never been seen in Hellas, where he had been an Arzawan king. His descendants wielded that scepter when they ruled Mycenai, which may have borrowed concepts of kingship from the Arzawans.

great construction project of the era was the building of massive new walls to protect the city. They replaced older, smaller walls and enclosed both the citadel (where the palace was) and the Circle A shaft graves, but not the older Circle B shaft graves. The crowning achievement of the fortifications was the famous Lion Gate, the only example of monumental sculpture found in Bronze Age Hellas. It took twenty years and a great expenditure of resources to complete this fourth and final major building program of Mycenaian Hellas. During this time the shaft graves and older tholos tombs were restored and became public cult sites for the first time.

---

## Polyeidos Raises Glaukos from the Dead

As the eldest son of the dead king Koiranos of Mycenai, Polyeidos should have become the king of Mycenai. He lost that title when an oracle proclaimed that the kingdom must go to a Pelopid. Polyeidos, who was an excellent seer, left Mycenai and arrived in Knossos on Krete during a crisis. King Minos Deukalion had ordered a frantic search for his missing son Glaukos. The magical smiths called the Kouretes told the king that the seer who could figure out a simile for a miraculous heifer that changed from white to red to black could find the boy. Polyeidos likened the heifer to a ripening blackberry, and Minos ordered him to find his son.

Polyeidos observed an owl sitting over the wine cellar and cleverly discovered clues leading to the boy's whereabouts. The little boy had fallen face-first into a vat of honey and drowned. The grieving Minos Deukalion would not accept the outcome, and on the Kouretes' advice, he demanded that the seer restore him to life. Polyeidos protested, but to no avail. In helpless despair, the astonished Polyeidos saw a snake restored to life after its mate rubbed a particular herb on its skin. Polyeidos applied the same herb to Glaukos, and the boy miraculously revived.[156]

The demanding Minos Deukalion was still not satisfied. He commanded that Polyeidos remain in court and teach the child his divining and healing skills. After Polyeidos did as he was commanded, he was showered with many gifts and allowed to leave. As he departed, Glaukos came to see him

---

[156] The Lydians tell almost an identical tale about the death and subsequent restoration of a local hero by an herb discovered through the observation of snakes.

off. Polyeidos told the boy to spit into his mouth. Glaukos obeyed and promptly forgot everything the seer had taught him. Polyeidos sailed away before Minos found out.

## Marriage of Leda

A few years earlier, King Oibalos of Lakonia died, and two of his sons struggled over the throne. The bastard Hippokoon claimed the throne on account of his being older. The rightful heir, Tyndareos, was defeated and fled (1242T/992R BCE). Tyndareos wandered abroad, worried about assassins. When he reached Aitolia, he and his brother Ikarios eagerly served King Thestios of Pleuron in a successful battle against his Akarnanian enemies.[157] In reward Thestios gave Ikarios provisions necessary to establish a colony. Tyndareos was given the hand of his youngest daughter, Leda.

Leda was so beautiful that she attracted the attention of the lusty Lord Zeus. As she waited for the ceremony to begin the dark-clouded Son of Kronos bent her to his will and made ardent love to Leda in the form of a swan, hoping his form would avoid detection from Hera. Unsuspecting Tyndareos entered the bridal chamber second.[158]

When Leda delivered her burden, it was clearly no mortal occurrence, for Leda delivered first a golden egg and then a baby boy, born in the usual way. The egg burst open from the angry blows of the strong-lunged infant within, a boy. The egg-born baby, an immortal son of Zeus, was named Polydeuces, while his mortal twin brother was called Kastor. They loved each other as few brothers have and are known together as the Dioskouroi.[159]

---

[157] If this myth wasn't started when the Aitolians and Spartans became allies against the Akhaian League, it was certainly expounded upon when that alliance developed (third century BCE). The Roman-era mythographer Apollodoros is our source. The close connection in myth between Eleia and Aitolia may derive from their similar dialects or their alliance during the third century BCE.

[158] Apparently by an ancient custom widespread throughout the Mediterranean, a king had a right to lie with any bride he wished to before the bridegroom had his chance. This myth is probably a recollection of that custom, which had been abandoned by historic times.

[159] See note 139 on divine twins.

## Theseus Goes to Athens

Not far from Lerne, in the town of Troizen, the second most accomplished of the Hellenic heroes made a name for himself. Upon the sixteenth birthday of her strapping son, Aithra decided that he was ready for the manly test his royal father had set for him before his birth. Theseus easily lifted the heavy stone and removed the sword and sandals his father had placed beneath it. Only then did Aithra tell her son of his birth.

She started by telling what he already knew: that Pittheus was one of the wisest and most eloquent men of his day. He and his brother Troizen, sons of King Pelops and Queen Hippodameia of Harpina (Pisa), had been invited by gorgon-slaying Perseus, king of Tiryns, to build nearby settlements. Troizen had long since died, and Pittheus named their settlement after him.

She continued with what he did not know. King Aigeus of Athens heard of Pittheus's wisdom and courted his understanding after visiting Delphi. Aigeus had consulted Delphi to find a cure for his inability to conceive children. The king was left dumbstruck by the riddled answer given him. So Aigeus returned home by way of Troizen and asked Pittheus to interpret the Delphic riddle: "Do not loosen the wineskin spout before you get home." Pittheus correctly understood that the oracle requested that he not spill his seed until he returned home (1255T/1005R BCE).

Pittheus did not tell Aigeus the true meaning. Instead he arranged a rendezvous between Aigeus and his only daughter, Aithra. Pittheus thought it would be best for his daughter to receive the seed of the powerful king and thereby gain his protection. He told Aigeus that the oracle meant he was destined to father a child by Aithra.

On the nearby island of Hiera, where Myrtilos, the charioteer of Pelops, fell to his death when pushed out by his lord, Aithra dutifully awaited her fate. She was sent by her father on the false pretense of sacrificing to the ghost of Sphairos (Pelops's charioteer). Before Aigeus arrived, dark-haired Poseidon took the opportunity to lie with the lovely virgin maiden. Soon Aigeus arrived for his turn. Upon his departure to his home and wife, Aigeus laid his sword under a huge rock and told Aithra that if she conceived a son, someday he would be able to lift the rock. If he did, she was to tell him who his father was and send him without haste to Athens. The sword would serve as proof. Of course, Aigeus knew not of Poseidon's appearance and Aithra knew not which one was the father.

Immediately upon hearing of his royal lineage, Theseus left for Athens to claim his birthright. He was inspired by the feats of Herakles (whom he had met as a small boy) and wished to demonstrate his own heroic nature to prove himself worthy of Athens. [160] Despite his mother's and grandfather's pleas, Theseus did not sail to Athens. Instead he took the dangerous land route, determined to clear it of highwaymen.

Theseus dispatched his reprehensible opponents in the manner in which they killed their victims. First he dispatched Periphetes in Epidauros in single combat. Periphetes was called Korybantes (meaning "club-bearer") for his formidable weapon, which Theseus confiscated and used thereafter. Next he defeated strong Sinis, the pine binder, at the Isthmos and dispatched him by tying him between two bent pines and then releasing them. Then Theseus hunted a sow or boar ravaging Krommyon and brought it down. Next, at the Skeironian Rocks, he defeated the robber Skeiron and kicked him off the cliff. At Eleusis, he agreed to wrestle King Cerkyon for his kingdom; the loser was to die. Theseus's skill and quickness were too much for Cerkyon's brute strength. Cerkyon was executed, and Theseus was anointed king of Eleusis. Theseus continued onward and killed the scoundrel Damastes at Erineus on the Cephissos River in a bed of his own making. Damastes used to place people in a bed and cut off parts of them to fit if they were too tall or stretch them on a rack if they were too short.

When the young man who had cleared the notorious Isthmos road of outlaws reached Athens, the town was abuzz. Aigeus felt obligated to invite this heroic stranger to a splendid state feast. Out of courtesy, neither Aigeus nor Theseus inquired of the other regarding his lineage.

---

[160] Theseus was a folk hero who was later added to the heroic myths because of the rising importance of Athens. Arkhaic art from Athens shows that Herakles's labors were popular, while Theseus is rarely noted. With the rise of Athens as a great state under Pisistratos, Theseus's labors were awarded greater importance. His fight with the bull of Marathon and rape of the fertility spirit (Ariadne, Helene, or Persephone) were added to his exploits on the highway between Troizen and Athens. But whereas Herakles defeated Hades and subdued Cerberus, thereby overcoming death, Theseus failed in his attempt at immortality (the rape of Persephone).

Aigeus feared that the young man was bent on the pastimes of Ares. He thought Theseus would dispatch him as he had the other powerful men he had encountered. Fearful Aigeus was too old to fight, and he treacherously had poison mixed with wine. As Theseus raised the poisoned wine goblet to his lips, Aigeus noticed the sword under Theseus's belt and recognized it.[161] Aigeus quickly struck the cup from Theseus's hand and joyously embraced him as his son.

The king's brother Pallas was furious when he heard the news that Aigeus had an heir. He had been waiting for old Aigeus to die, but now he decided to seize the kingdom by force. An informant told Aigeus, and Theseus led a successful ambush. Many of Pallas's sons were killed, and the rest fled. Some of Pallas's supporters fled to King Cepheus of Tegea and settled in the Arkadian city of Kaphyai.

---

Exhibit 10.2
How Athens Was Forced to Sacrifice to the Minotaur

**Birth of the Minotaur:** Minos was the hereditary title of several rulers, the first a child of Zeus (Hellenic) and Europa (Minoan). Zeus had given Europa in marriage to a Kretan named Asterios once he had sired three children by her. When Asterios died, Minos, the eldest of Europa's three sons, claimed the throne.

Since Minos was not Asterios's son, there were other challengers for the kingdom. Minos prayed for the bull-god Poseidon to send him a magnificent white bull in support of his claim. In his prayers, Minos fervently promised to sacrifice such a bull at his coronation. Poseidon, patron of Knossos,[162] sent the bull as proof of Minos's worthiness, and he was awarded the kingdom. Minos, however, found the bull so beautiful that he kept it among his cows and sacrificed a number of his best bulls instead.

---

[161] Ovid, Apollodoros, Pausanias, and other late writers say that the sorcerer Midea became Aigeus's wife after leaving Jason and that she mixed the poison. This doesn't make sense, as Theseus was considered an Argonaut crew member and Midea first came to Hellas with the Argonauts.

[162] Poseidon is the deity most often referred to in Linear B documents found at Knossos, although the limited number of references does not make that statistically significant.

It was to punish Minos for not keeping his bargain that the earth-shaker Poseidon afflicted his wife Pasiphae, daughter of the sun god Helios, with an unnatural attraction to the bull, just as Europa had once mated with one. When Minos left on business, Pasiphae secretly paid the Athenian craftsmen Daidalos to construct a hollow wooden cow convincing enough to seduce the white bull. Within it she was able to have her passion consummated by the powerful bull. From that union sprang a mingled form in which two strange shapes combined and different natures, bull and man, were joined. He was Asterios, the Minotaur, a dim-witted monster with a bull's head and the body of an incredibly strong man. In shame Minos locked the Minotaur within the Labyrinth, a maze he had Daidalos build within the palace complex. Because of his own guilt, Minos could not punish Pasiphae, who also felt ashamed.

**Athenian Tribute:** Many years later, during the reign of Minos Andraimon, there was an athletic Kretan prince named Androgeus. He was the eldest son of the king and much beloved. Thirteen years before Theseus's birth, Androgeus came to Athens to compete in the Panathenaic Games (the games actually date from the sixth century BCE). The Kretan prince won great glory by winning every event he entered (1268T/1018R BCE).

Androgeus did not celebrate for long, for life is fleeting. Only the murderer knows for sure how he died. King Aigeus of Athens claimed to have asked Androgeus to stop a savage bull that was ravaging Marathon and that Androgeus died valiantly against the beast. It was known that Aigeus's brother Pallas, who wanted to be king, had developed a friendship with Androgeus. Pallas claimed that Androgeus was murdered, ambushed by Aigeus's men at Oinoe. Still others say that the Athenian youths who lost at the Panathenaic Games slew the foreigner in rage at their defeat.

When news of the tragedy reached Minos Andraimon, he cursed Hellas. The gods responded and brought drought to the mainland. Minos decided to exact further revenge for the death of his son. The next year, his fleet was prepared for an attack. Minos sailed against Megara first, where the brother of the king of Athens ruled.

Minos's siege of the Megaran port of Nicaia made little progress until the king's daughter Scylla beheld dashing Minos. Love-struck, she secretly sent him a girlish love letter. Seizing the opportunity, Minos responded by professing his love and asking only that she cut her father's strand of purple hair to prove her love. He promised not to harm her father or anyone in the city if she would do this. Innocent Scylla did as she was asked, and with the loss of the purple strand, Nicaia (Megara's port) lost its invulnerability. After taking Nicaia, Minos Andraimon slept with his virgin accomplice. As they sailed off together, cruel Minos drowned her for her treachery. Too much time had been spent on the siege of Megara to make an effective attack on Athens that year.

Minos decided to remain at home while his curse brought drought and pestilence to Attike. The desperate king Aigeus was forced to surrender on terms (1264T/1014R BCE). The Athenians agreed to provide fourteen youths and maidens from the best families. Minos took them to perform bull-leaping rites and serve the Minotaur. Furthermore, the Athenians agreed to provide fourteen youths and maidens every nine years thereafter. The Athenians also honored Androgeus under the name of Eurygyes with games.

---

**1237T/987R BCE**
Theseus kills the Minotaur, and Herakles captures the Cerynitian hind.

## Theseus Fights the Minotaur

Aigeus's rejoicing ended the following spring when the third envoy of Kretans arrived to collect the tribute of seven youths and seven maidens. Theseus volunteered to go despite the pleas of Aigeus.

Theseus reassured his father with boasts that he would defeat the monstrous Minotaur. As the ship prepared to sail, Aigeus gave his son white sails and made Theseus promise to have the sails changed from black to white if he returned safely. The transport ship was provided by noble Skiros of Salamis because his grandson Menestheus, the son of a rich Athenian merchant and his daughter, was among the noble youths selected to go.

King Minos met the captives upon their arrival in the port of Knossos. His heart was immediately chafed with desire, the dreaded gift of the Cyprian goddess, for one of the captive maidens. She, Eeriboia, shouted for the bronze-corseted descendent of Pandion (Theseus) to help her.

Bold Theseus told the king to check his dishonest intent. The angry king demonstrated his lineage by requesting and receiving the sign of a thunderbolt from the cloud lord, Zeus. Minos scoffed at Prince Theseus's claim to be the son of Poseidon and threw his signet ring into the sea. He commanded Theseus to fetch it from the depths if he were who he said he was. Without hesitation, Theseus dove in after it.

> Sea dwelling dolphins swiftly carried great Theseus to the house of his father, god of horses, and he reached the hall of the sea gods. There he was awe struck by the glorious daughters of blessed Nereus, for from their splendid limbs shone a gleam as of fire and round their hair were twirled gold-braided ribbons: and they were delighting their hearts by dancing with liquid feet. And he saw his father's dear wife, august ox-eyed Amphitrite, in the lovely house; she put a purple cloak about him and set on his thick hair the faultless garland which once at her marriage guileful Aphrodite had given her, dark with roses.[163]

King Minos and the others were astonished to see Theseus return in clothes that were dry, with the god's gifts and holding the ring. Minos dropped his advances toward Eeriboia and, his redirected overtures were spurned by youthful Theseus. Meanwhile, a spirited daughter of Minos[164] fell into a deep love for Theseus.

The captives were sent to their appointed destiny in the Labyrinth as an offering to the half-man, half-bull Minotaur. The princess secretly gave Theseus a knife and a ball of string. She explained that he must unravel the string as he entered the Labyrinth in order to find his way out. He knew what the knife she presented him with was for. Theseus promised to take her away and marry her if he was successful.

Theseus faced the Minotaur in the innermost chambers and slew him. Then, rewinding the string, Theseus returned to the light of day, where Minos's daughter rushed to greet him. Together with the other Athenian youths, Theseus and his lover hastened to their waiting ship. Then the

[163] Bakkhylides, "Theseus", in *Greek Lyric.* Translated by David A. Campbell

[164] She is universally called Ariadne, but she could not have become the wife of Dionysos, because some of their children preceded Theseus by several generations.

princess stopped to beg her father's forgiveness. Minos was swayed to forgive the young lovers and let their ship pass in peace. They set sail for Delos. The Minoan admiral Taures took off after them anyway and was slain by Theseus when he overtook them.

On Delos Theseus gave palm branches to Apollo in thanks and danced the crane dance. Next the happy youths sailed to nearby Naxos and spent the night. At dawn Theseus set sail, leaving his sleeping lover behind; never again were his actions unblemished. Whether he just broke his promise or he was told by Dionysos to leave, who knows. Either way it was his preference, for he did not love her and had other dreams for his own life. Her unhappy fate was variously described.

Theseus continued homeward troubled by his own actions. On the one hand custom dictated that heroic action in combat was the path toward everlasting fame. Nevertheless, abandoning a helpless girl who loved him left him feeling a bit hollow in spite of his having slain the Minotaur. Engrossed in internal debate, he forgot to change the sails to white. His father's death shattered his dialogue before he resolved his own moral dilemma.

King Aigeus had spent each passing day watching the sea from the acropolis cliffs, fretting and hoping. When Aigeus saw the tribute ship returning with black sails, he jumped to his death, and the sea that safely brought his son home now bears his name. Theseus became king.

**3) Golden-Horned Cerynitian Doe:** Meanwhile, much-enduring Herakles had spent the whole year tracking the fabled Cerynitian Doe before capturing her with wild Artemis's permission. After displaying the doe outside the gates of Tiryns, Herakles released her unharmed.

In Thebes peerless Lykos, son of Poseidon and the Pleiades Celaino, gambled that Herakles would die trying to complete his labors. Lykos left his homeland on Euboea Island, killed old king Kreon, and set fire to the citadel Kadmeia (this has been confirmed by archaeologists). Then he ruled as king.

**1236T/986R BCE**

Zeus strikes Asclepius dead with a thunderbolt for raising the dead, and furious Apollo retaliates by killing the Cyklopes. Ixion dines on Olympos, and Herakles captures the Erymanthian boar.

## Asclepius Raises the Dead

Apollo's son Asclepius was tutored by the Centaur Kheiron and then excelled as a traveling doctor, a worker of sound-limbed painlessness. His wife, Epione, bore him talented healers who fought valiantly at Troy—Makhaon and Podaleiros. Asclepius used a vial of the gorgon's blood to raise Hymenaios[165] from the dead, for gold. Happy Hymenaios became the god of the marriage hymn, immune from death having once passed through it. Possessive Hades was exceedingly angry over losing one of his subjects without permission and complained bitterly to Zeus, saying that a mortal was bringing men back to life and denying him his due.

Zeus responded by instantly killing golden Apollo's son Asclepius by hurling lightning into his breast, and Apollo, in angry retaliation, slew the Cyklopes who fashioned Zeus's fire. Apollo's fate would surely have been to join the Titans in bleak Tartaros, but Leto persuaded Zeus to lighten the sentence upon their son.

To humiliate Apollo, he, a god, was ordered to serve a man, young king Admetos of Pherai, descendant of Aiolian Pheres (founder and eponym of Pherai) as a slave for one year (or for an eternal year as some say). Admetos wisely treated Lord Apollo with utmost respect, and to reward his pious nature, Apollo helped him secure his wife. Admetos desired lovely Alcestis, eldest daughter of King Pelias of Iolkos. Proud Pelias decreed that the man who could prove his mettle by yoking a lion and a boar to a chariot could claim his lovely daughter as bride. Pelias was impressed when Admetos, with the help of Apollo's invisible hands, performed the feat and Alcestis became his wife.

---

[165] Many heroes were identified as the man whom Asclepius brought back from the dead. Apollodoros's *Library*, iii.9–11, lists the following: Tyndareos (Panyassis); Kapaneus & Lykourgos (Stesikhoros, *Eriphyle*); Hippolytos (*Naupactika* and Pausanias, *Guide to Greece* ii.27); Hymenaios (Orphics—not a bad idea; once having passed through death, Hymenaios never died again); and Glaukos, son of Minos (Melesagoras of Khalkis and Apollodoros, *Library* iii.3.1).

By comparing the generation within which each candidate lived, only Hymenaios emerges as plausible. Lykourgos the Arkadian died before the flood, and Lykourgos the Thracian died at Dionysos's coming, long before Herakles. The sons of Minos died a generation earlier. Besides, as noted above, Polypheides is usually credited with restoring Glaukos. Tyndareos and Kapaneus died a generation later. Hippolytos died when Theseus, a younger contemporary of Herakles, was an older man.

As for Asclepius, for his great feat men began worshipping him as a god.

> I begin to sing of Asclepius, healer of diseases
> And son of Apollo. Noble Koronis, daughter of
> King Phlegyas bore him on the plain of Dotion
> To be a great joy for men and charm evil pains away.[166]

## Ixion Invited to Olympos

The Lapith king Ixion seized control of Magnesia after murdering his father-in-law. He could find no man willing to purify him of his dastardly deed until Lord Zeus, who was quite taken by the king's wife, Dia,[167] agreed to do so. The Cloud-Gatherer even invited Ixion to Olympos.

> Among Kronos' kindly sons
> Lapped in sweet ease, he stayed not long in bliss,
> Fool in his wits!
> Who loved Hera, her that is set apart
> For the mighty joys of Zeus. But pride drove him
> To blind presumptuous folly.
> He suffered soon his due, getting a choice award of woe.
> His two sins live and bring him misery: one that he, a hero, first and with guile
> Bought kindred blood upon men,
>
> The other that in the great darkness of a bridal chamber
> He tempted the wife of Zeus.
> (Let a man, when he measures,
> Remember his own size!). His lawless love
> Cast him into great depths of evil
> When he came to her bed: for he lay by the side of a Cloud (Nephele),
> Clasping a sweet lie, ignorant man.

---

[166] Hesiod, "Homeric Hymn to Asclepius," in *The Homeric Hymns and Homerica.*

[167] Homer, *Iliad*, xiv.317–318, includes her in a list of Zeus's lovers. Eustathios's *On Homer* states that Zeus seduced Dia in the form of a stallion and sired Peirithoos (meaning "course around"). So Ixion's seduction of Hera is no worse than Zeus's action; his crime was that he did not possess the power necessary to carry it off.

Its shape was like the mightiest daughter of Kronos
The son of Heaven.
The hands of Zeus made it,
To snare him, a lovely sorrow.[168]

Ixion was far too drunk to notice the deception. Lord Zeus surprised him in the act and had his keen-eyed messenger Hermes beat him until he said obediently "benefactors deserve honor." Then the son of Kronos had him thrown into Tartaros, where he was bent backward and his ankles, wrists, and neck were attached to a winged wheel that spun incessantly.

The seeded cloud delivered a monstrous offspring, Centauros.[169] He avoided the towns of civilized people and remained in the wild. He mated with Magnesian mares on the foothills of Mount Pelion. Their prodigious offspring, Centaurs, carried the image of both parents: their nether parts of the mother, their father's above.

**4) Erymanthian Boar:** Herakles spent the year chasing and finally overpowering this boar after tracking it down in deep snow. While chasing the boar, Herakles was entertained by the wise Centaur Pholos, but he slew other Centaurs who attacked him.

### 1235T/985R BCE

Herakles wrestles Alcestis away from death and defeats a usurper to the Theban kingdom while completing four labors. Oidipous fulfills a dreadful prophecy by unwittingly killing his father and marrying his mother. Telamon and Peleus are exiled for killing their brother Phokos.

**5) Stables of Augeias:** Herakles was sent to clean the dung from King Augeias's fabled stables in one day. Upon arriving in Elis, Herakles offered to clean the stables for a fee. Augeias, who had succeeded his grandfather Eleios as king of the Epeians, agreed because he was worried that the

---

[168] Pindar, Pythian Ode ii.25–41, in *The Odes*. Translated by C.M. Bowra.

[169] The earliest artistic representation of a Centaur was found at Lefkandi on Euboea and possibly correlates to the earliest horseback riding in Hellas (late tenth century T / early eighth century R BCE). The first representation of battles between half-man, half-horse Centaurs and men depicts their struggle with an archer (eighth or early seventh century BCE). In the Peloponnesos, the archer became identified with Herakles; in Thessalia it may have originally been Caineus. It would be another two hundred years before artists began portraying the famous fight at the wedding of the Lapith king Peirithoos.

thickening dung was causing the crops to fail. In a dark mood, Herakles diverted the local river and washed the stables clean by sunset while avoiding the ignoble task of flinging dung. While Herakles worked, Augeias discovered that Herakles was a servant working on behalf of Eurystheus. Accordingly, Augeias refused to pay, saying that Herakles had already been paid by his owner. Herakles stormed away in anger.

**6) Stymphalian Birds:** These birds had quills as sharp as arrows. Because they were too numerous to drive away, Herakles contrived to bang a bronze rattle, and the loud noise scared them off. They fled Arkadia to roost on an island in the Pontic (Black) Sea.

**7) Kretan Bull:** The first six labors were performed in the Peloponnesos, but afterward Eurystheus sent Herakles farther afield to make his tasks longer and more arduous. On Krete grazed the magnificent white bull that had once been the object of Queen Pasiphae's unnatural desire. King Minos was only too happy to see it hauled away. Surly Herakles released the bull after displaying it in Tiryns. It wandered to Marathon and was killed by Theseus.

Image 10.2
Map of the Last Six Labors of Herakles

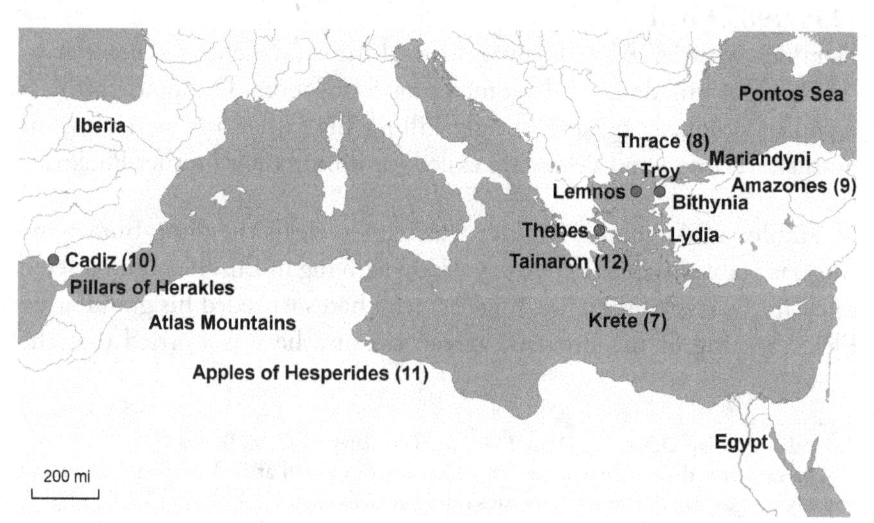


**8) Mares of Diomedes:** Diomedes was a Thracian brute who fed his enemies to his fles-eating horses. On his way to Thrace, Herakles dropped in unexpectedly in Thebes. Herakles killed the usurper Lykos, and Laios, son of the former king Labdakos, was anointed king. (Laios had been sent to Pelops when Amphion and Zethos seized Thebes. He had been permitted to live in Thebes as a private citizen while Pelops's son Kreon ruled Thebes [Lykos had killed King Kreon]). Poseidon transported his beloved son Lykos to the Isle of the Blessed.

Next Herakles stopped in Opus in Lokris and seduced the youth Abderos (Herakles's nephew Iolaos had outgrown that role). Then, accompanied by Abderos, Herakles stopped in Thessalian Pherai, where he was hospitably entertained by the mourning king Admetos. Learning that the wife of his host had just died, Herakles caught and overpowered Thanatos (meaning "death"), gaining her release. Admetos was ecstatic to see his wife, Alcestis, again.

Just the year before, Apollo had helped Admetos win Alcestis. At the end of his year of service, Apollo wished to grant him the privilege of dying old. However, the lord of prophecy knew that although Admetos was young, his death was near at hand. Apollo plied the Moirai with drink and received their permission to let Admetos escape Hades for the present, provided that he offered another willing body to the spirits below. Admetos soon fell into his terminal illness, and he canvassed and solicited all his friends, his aged parents, and his subjects, but he found no one except his wife willing to die and forgo the light of day for his sake.

Alcestis nursed her husband back to health and was shot herself by the arrow of Artemis—that is to say, the unexplained illness. Alcestis moved about the house, supported in her husband's arms and gasping her last, for the day Admetos had been fated to die and quit this life was at hand. Admetos held his dear wife in his arms and wept, beseeching her not to forsake him, asking what was impossible. As she expired, Apollo chided Thanatos that he would lose his quarry.

As the mourning began, Herakles happened to arrive while on his way north to fetch the four-mare team of the Thracian Diomedes. Admetos hid his grief and entertained the hero graciously. When Herakles learned from servants that the queen had just died, he set out immediately, unbeknownst to Admetos, to bring back Alcestis. Herakles caught up with Thanatos before he reached the entrance to Hades and wrestled her away from him.[170]

Meanwhile, Admetos mourned his wife with regret, regarding her fate as happier than his though it might not appear to be so. For no pain would ever touch her again; she had surceased many toils, and with glory. But Admetos feared that any man who was unfriendly to him would bruise his soul by saying, "Look at that guy who stays alive so shamefully; he had not the courage to die, but gave in exchange the woman he married, in his cowardice, and escaped Hades."

A great feast was prepared when Herakles returned with Alcestis. During the feast Herakles told the enraptured court about his other great exploits. Admetos built a shrine to Apollo in the mountains of Euboea Island in thanks for his gifts. Admetos's younger brother Lykourgos figured correctly that since Herakles had killed the man-eating Nemean Lion, the place it once ravaged would now be suitable for settlement. He set out with supporters and founded Nemea in the Peloponnesos.

Then Herakles departed from Hellas and captured the Thracian Diomedes. Herakles fittingly fed Diomedes to his own horses, thereby satisfying their hunger and gaining mastery over them. Unfortunately, the horses ate Herakles's squire Abderos first.

On his way back to Tiryns, Herakles passed the horse-loving Plain of Thessalia and was entertained by Dorian king Aigimios. Herakles helped the king defeat the attacking Lapiths. In thanks, Aigimios promised a third of his kingdom to Herakles.

## Oidipous Fulfills the Dreadful Prophecy

Prince Oidipous of Sicyon grew up unaware of his real parentage. King Polybos and Queen Periboia (Metope) denied that he was adopted, but nagging rumors persisted because he was so courageous while his father was so mild mannered. Finally Oidipous went to Delphi to settle the matter. He received the disturbing answer that he would kill his father

[170] Euripides's *Alcestis* is the source. Apollodoros's *Library*, i.9.15, says Persephone sent her back because it was shameful that a woman should die for a man.

and marry his mother. In horror Oidipous left Delphi by a different road, swearing to avoid his fate by never returning home to Sicyon.

Oidipous was understandably in a foul mood when six men approached and belligerently ordered him to step aside and let them pass by on the narrow road that wound its way up the desolate, majestic slope of Mount Parnassus. Tempers flared, and the herald Polyphontes killed Oidipous's horse. Outnumbered though he was, Oidipous struck back and killed five of the six men. One servant turned tail and escaped on horseback without seeing the transgressor.

Horseless, Oidipous walked on, and King Damasistratos of Boiotia Plataia found and buried the dead men with honors.[171] Meanwhile, the sole surviving servant arrived in Thebes with the bad news. Not wishing to look weak by admitting one man had overpowered the six of them, the servant lied and said that they had been attacked by a large band of pirates and only he had escaped.

Among the dead was Laios, the newly anointed king of Thebes. That a homosexual (Laios) had been allowed to be king displeased the marriage goddess Hera. To punish the Thebans for this sacrilege to family values, she had sent the Sphinx to punish them.[172] The Sphinx was a lioness with a woman's head. Her parents were fiery Typhoeus and his speckled mate, Echidna.

The Sphinx stayed on Mount Phakion and pounced on the youths of Thebes. She would ask them the riddle "What walks on four legs, then two, and then three?" When her flustered victims could not guess it, she killed them.

King Laios had decided to consult the oracle of Apollo at Delphi; he felt that he could surely find the answer to the riddle there. While traveling through Phocis, at the crossroads of the Delphi and Daulis roads, Laios came upon another rider. Laios's herald Polyphontes called out as usual for

---

[171] Damasistratos isn't mentioned before Pausanias and Apollodoros, and perhaps he is a historical man who built a memorial to Laios.

[172] Thebes is at least twice identified with Egypt; first it shares its name with a royal Egyptian city. Second, the Sphinx is an Egyptian motif. We know from Linear B texts that this Boiotian city was called Thebes from an early date.

the stranger to make way for the king of Thebes. The stranger, who was Laios's son, refused to yield.

Oidipous did not know that one of the men he killed was his birth father, Laios. Years earlier, while drunk, Laios could not resist his curiosity to sleep with his wife even though he preferred men. In the morning Laios regretted his action and anxiously awaited the outcome, for an oracle warned him that a child of his would bring him misfortune. Sure enough, Jokaste conceived. When the child was born, Laios had his ankles pierced, and the hapless baby was exposed in the Cithairon Mountains (1252T/1002R BCE). Everyone assumed wrongly that the baby died. Instead, cattlemen of King Polybos of Sicyon found the screaming infant and, noting his noble clothing, gave the child to their king. Polybos and his wife, Periboia, who were unable to produce a child of their own, accepted this one. Polybos named the child Oidipous, meaning ("swollen foot").

Meanwhile, upon hearing of Laios's death, Kreon, son of Menoiceus of the Spartoi (who years before had killed Orkhomenian king Klymenos) and the brother of widowed queen Jokaste, was chosen as temporary ruler. With Laios's death, it was believed that the line of Kadmos had perished. The elders decided to offer the kingship and Jokaste's hand in marriage to the man who could rid Thebes of the Sphinx.

Oidipous arrived on foot several days later, still pondering his future. He decided to go for the prize and confronted the Sphinx. To her riddle, young Oidipous pondered only briefly before answering that it was a man, for man crawls on all fours as a baby, walks on two legs as a youth, and walks with the aid of a cane in old age. The Sphinx was crestfallen that he had correctly answered her riddle and killed herself.

Eighteen-year-old Oidipous returned triumphantly to claim his rewards. Unwittingly he married his thirty-four-year-old mother and became king. In innocence he had fulfilled the cursed prophecy. Oidipous became a wise king who gave Kreon and Jokaste, who were, obviously, much older, considerable power. Thebes prospered.

Oidipous found sweet ecstasy and fatal union in his mother's bed. In an unnatural twist of fate, Oidipous and Jokaste made a good couple. Jokaste now had a husband who was responsive to her needs, someone who instinctively saw the world in the same way she saw it. Jokaste bore

Oidipous four children. The twin boys, Eteokles (meaning "true fame") and Polyneices (meaning "much strife") were born one year into his reign. The Thebans rejoiced that an heir came so quickly. Later Jokaste bore their daughters, Antigone and Ismene.

## Peleus and Telamon Kill Their Half brother Phokos

It is said that Zeus gave might to the sons of Aiakos, wisdom to the sons of Amythaon, and wealth to the sons of Atreus. Aiakos's descendants were among the stoutest warriors ever: Phokos, Telamon, Peleus, Akhilleus, Aias (Ajax), and Neoptolemos. Possibly the most powerful of the rainmaker Aiakos's children was Phokos, whom the lovely Nereid Psamathe bore him after he had helped built the walls of Troy with Apollo and Poseidon. He had caught a glimpse of her while she was peeling off her shiny seal skin to sun her shapely naked form by the sea swell. Clever Aiakos crept close and grabbed the unsuspecting nymph. He held her tight as she struggled against his amorous embrace. Unable to break his hold, she submitted to his desire. In time she recovered her hidden seal skin and leapt joyfully back into the sea, abandoning her lover and their young son, Phokos.[173]

Aiakos then married shapely Endeis, daughter of mighty Skeiron, who was polemarch of Megara and brother-in-law of the Megarean king Pandion (1269T/1019R BCE). Lovely Youth, herald of Aphrodite's celestial loves, was seated on the soft eyelids of the new bride, who bore her lord Telamon[174] and Peleus. It was either Endeis who persuaded Peleus to murder their half brother, Phokos, or it was an evil plan of his own creation; we do not know. Those close to the family said that Telamon and Peleus were so jealous of Phokos, who surpassed them in athletic skill, that they wanted him dead. Telamon reluctantly agreed to go along with the plan. They challenged their brother to a discus-throwing contest, and Peleus killed him with a

[173] This is the first recorded version of the common European myth of the seal-woman who is captured by a man, bears his son, and returns to the sea. Aiakos's son Peleus also captured a seal-woman, and their abandoned child was the great warrior Akhilleus.

[174] It was not universally accepted that Telamon and Peleus were brothers; Pherecydes says Telamon was the son of Aktaios of Salamis, and his wife, Glauce, daughter of the first Salamis king, Cykhreus. Pherecydes, who wrote in Athens, obviously supported the Athenian viewpoint that Telamon was not an Aiginetan hero.

deliberately errant heave. Their grieving father buried his godlike son in an elaborate tomb on Aigina.[175]

Aiakos was not fooled by his sons' deceitful plan to make the shameful deed appear to be an accident. Angered and shamed by his sons' actions, he banished them. Peleus migrated to the ancestral homeland of Myrmidons, Phthia, and never returned. To torment Peleus for murdering her son, the furious Nereid Psamathe sent a great wolf to ravage his flocks. Eventually silver-sandaled Thetis soothed her sister and she relented. Telamon went only as far as Salamis Island, which he had inherited from Skeiron because he was his eldest grandson (Skeiron had no sons).

**1234T/984R BCE**

Herakles retrieves the bronze belt of an Amazonian queen and saves Princess Hesione of Troy.

**9) Hippolyte's Belt:** Eurystheus's daughter whispered into the king's ear that she wanted the famous girdle of the Amazon queen. The king demanded that Herakles fetch it for her. To undertake the perilous journey, Herakles assembled a crew of the finest heroes (including Theseus, and Aiakos's bulky exiled sons Telamon and Peleus) to man a ship that sailed to the land of the Amazones. Along the way, the crew was attacked on Paros Island, and two crewmen were killed. Herakles besieged the islanders until they offered two sons of Androgeus (the prince of Krete killed by the Athenians) as compensation. Farther along, Herakles and his crew assisted the Mariandyni tribe against their enemies the Bebryces.[176] Once the hero arrived in Amazon country, Queen Hippolyte boarded the Hellenic ship for discussions. Herakles made his request to her, and the sympathetic Hippolyte agreed to bring him her girdle. Cow-eyed Hera felt this was too easy and incited the other Amazones to attack. Herakles suspected treachery and slew Hippolyte. The Amazones recovered their queen's

[175] Usually Peleus is named as the murderer, but Apollodoros's *Library*, iii.160, says Telamon lost the lots toss and launched the killing discus throw. Phokos of Aigina was often confused with the king and eponym of the country of Phocis. The son of Aiakos lived in the same generation as Krisos and Panopeus, sons of the other Phokos.

[176] The battle between the Bithynians and the Mariandyni over iron mines must have occurred after iron replaced bronze as the chief metal used (after 1050T/840R BCE). Most likely the struggle occurred during the eleventh century T / eighth century BCE, when the Phrygians expanded out from their home on the Anatolian Plateau to control the precious metal. Early Hellenes merchants noted this struggle and added to their Bronze Age epics.

corpse before the Akhaians rallied and beat them back. The women fled behind their walls and were besieged. Their fortifications held until one of the Amazones fell in love with crew member Theseus. She stole the girdle and fled with the Hellenes before the Amazones discovered their loss.

On the homeward journey, they passed by the great city of Troy and saw a lovely maiden, clothed only in fine jewels, wriggling in terror, chained helplessly to a seaside rock, while a beast rose out of the roaring sea and advanced toward her.[177] Peerless Herakles was quick to size up the situation. He found the king fretting nearby and struck a deal. Laomedon would part with his twelve immortal horses if Herakles could kill the beast and save his daughter.

Dauntless Herakles stepped between the oncoming beast and the fair maiden. He killed the furious serpent and unchained the happy girl. But Laomedon did not take the near disaster as yet another warning to abide by his agreements. Instead he interpreted it to mean that no matter what his transgressions were, he could escape dire consequences. Therefore, over the objections of his youthful son Priamos, he sent Herakles away without payment. The brooding Herakles promised vengeance.

Herakles took out some of his aggression by conquering Thasos Island. He left behind the sons of Androgeus to rule it. Finally, at Torone, Herakles was challenged to a wrestling match, and he defeated two powerful sons of the old man of the sea, Proitos.

**1233T/983R BCE**
The barbaric Centaurs are utterly defeated at the wedding of Peirithoos and Hippodameia, and Herakles steals Geryones's cattle.

## Marriage of Peirithoos and Hippodameia

When the Lapith king Peirithoos, son of foolish Ixion and Dia, chose to marry Hippodameia (meaning "horse tamer"), daughter of the Lapith chieftain Bootes, he invited many distinguished guests from all over Hellas: Theseus of Athens, Peleus of Thessalian Akhaia, Dryas of Aitolia,

[177] A similar story is told about Andromeda and Perseus (great-grandfather of Herakles). Both may be based upon the Babylonian myth of Marduk and the sea monster Tiamat.

Kometes of Thessalia, Krantor of Ormenion, Nestor of Pylos, and the lawless Centaurs, monstrous scions of his bastard half brother Centauros. Most of the Lapith nobility was on hand for the gala event: Elatos's sons Caineus and Polyphemos, Caineus's young sons Koronos and Phaisos, the lords Exadios, Phageros, and Prolokhos, and others.

The sight of the lovely bride, no less than the wine, inflamed the passions of Eurytos, the fiercest of the fierce cloud-born Centaurs. In a lustful drunken frenzy, Eurytos lost self-control and seized the startled bride. Theseus, who was close by, scolded the Centaur and released the girl from his clutches. Angry Eurytos pummeled Theseus's face with his fists until the great hero retaliated by breaking a pot over his assailant's head. "To arms!" the Centaurs shouted, the wine giving them courage. Each grabbed the girl who struck his fancy—or one that he could catch.

The aging warrior Caineus fought with a young heart and single-handedly beat back several fierce assaults, killing six Centaurs in the process. Finally he was overpowered by a group of Centaurs who pummeled him under massive fir tree logs. Though he was invulnerable to weapons, he suffocated under the weight of the trees. The seer Mopsos said he saw his spirit ascend from the pile in the form of a sandy-winged bird. When the corpse was uncovered, it was again female.

Extraordinary Caineus had been born a girl, the daughter of the Lapith king Elatos and the loveliest girl in all of Thessalia. Once, as she wandered along a lonely stretch of the seashore, Cainis was forcibly subjected to the embraces of the sea king Poseidon. After enjoying the pleasures of his new love, dark-haired Poseidon offered a gift to the girl. He told her to speak up and not to fear to ask for what she wanted most. "'The way I have suffered' she replied 'evokes the fervent wish that I may never be able to undergo such an injury again. Grant that I be not a woman, and you will have given me all.'"[178]

Even as she was still finishing her request, her voice lowered and manly limbs replaced her soft curves. Poseidon added another boon; Cainis, now Caineus, was invincible to weapons. Unstated was a third benefit; his youth as a man was doubled to make up for the boyhood he never had, for he lived an extra generation—until his glorious end in battle.

[178] Ovid, *Metamorphoses* xii.

After the death of Caineus, the son of Elatos (meaning "fir tree"), the Aitolian Dryas, Theseus of Athens, Peleus of Phthia, and Peirithoos demonstrated the greatest valor in leading the Lapith guests to victory.

Caineus was not the only one of the guests to die. The Centaur Rhoitos slew the aging warrior Kometes, who lived near the confluences of the Apidanos and Enipeus rivers in Thessalia. News of his death reached his wife (the Aiolian princess Antigone of Pherai, elder sister of Admetos) and their son Asterion in his town called Peiresiai, near Mount Phylleion. Krantor of Ormenion was also slain.

Despite losses to the Lapiths and their guests, the battle proved a disaster for the Centaurs. Finally Apollo brokered a truce. Most of the surviving Centaurs agreed to leave Magnesia in exchange for their safe passage out.

**10) Geryones's Cattle:** Herakles was not at the wedding because he had been ordered to fetch the fabled cattle of Geryones. It took Herakles a year to complete the journey to either Iberia (Spain) or Akarnania and back. It was the last labor on which his nephew Iolaos accompanied him. During his travels, Herakles became so frustrated by the intense heat that he shot an arrow at Helios. The amused god loaned him his golden goblet to float from the mainland out to Geryones Island. Herakles clubbed Geryones's two-headed guard dog, Orthos, to death and stole the cattle. While driving them toward Tiryns, incredible Geryones, who had three bodies in one, caught up to Herakles, but he lost his life trying to recover what was rightfully his.[179] While driving the herd homeward, Eryx of Sicily tried to steal the cattle and was killed for it.

Herakles returned to Tiryns believing that his debt had been paid, but King Eurystheus demanded two more labors. Before the labors began, Eurystheus had proclaimed that each labor was to be completed without assistance or pay. Eurystheus correctly noted that Herakles's nephew Iolaos (whose father was Amphitryon's son Iphikles, twin brother of Herakles) had helped him slay the Hydra and that Herakles had requested payment to clean Augeias's stables. The furious Herakles protested, but he was compelled to comply.

[179] In early Indo-European cultures, the proper role of a warrior was raiding cattle, all the more so against a three-headed foreigner.

**1232T/982R BCE**

Herakles searches for the apples of the Hesperides.

**11) Apples of the Hesperides:** The last two labors seemed impossible: to fetch golden apples from the magical tree Hera had received as a wedding present from all-nourishing Gaia and to bring to Tiryns the hound of hell. Both represented Herakles overcoming death to gain immortality.

Herakles had no idea where to find the mystical apples. The magical tree was tended to by daughters of the Titan Atlas and guarded by the serpent Ladon, son of terrible Typhoeus (whom Zeus vanquished) and Echidna.

Herakles wandered east, searching past the land of the Amazones. Then he who would conquer death saved the savior of man. In the Caucasian Mountains, Herakles freed the Titan Prometheus with Zeus's blessing and killed the eagle that had tormented him. Prometheus told Herakles that the daughters of Zeus and Themis (either the Horai or Moirai) could instruct him as to the whereabouts of the garden holding the apples, and he recommended that Atlas fetch them for him. Prometheus now wears a ring of iron with a small piece of rock attached to it so that Zeus's decree that Prometheus would be bound ever after is not broken.

On the Eridanos River in Illyria, Herakles met up with the daughters of Zeus and Themis, who told him to question the wise sea god Nereus, who could be found in the Aigaian Sea somewhere between Imbros and Samothrace. Herakles returned overland to Hellas, and in Thessalia he met up with the Dorians and killed their enemy, King Theiodamas of Dryopia. Bronze-hearted Herakles took the king's young son Hylas as his latest youthful lover.

After subduing Nereus, who vainly changed into different forms, Herakles learned that the apples were located in the Atlas Mountains of Libya. Then, as Herakles prepared to set out for Libya in pursuit of the apples, he heard of the heroic voyage of the Argonauts and took time out to join them.

**1231T/981R BCE**

The voyage of the Argonauts, the Kalydonian boar hunt, and the completion of the final labors of Herakles mark the pinnacle year of the Heroic Age.

## Voyage of the Argonauts[180]

On the wintry day that marked his twenty-first birthday, stout Jason, son of Aison, determined to reclaim the throne of Iolkos, the northernmost palace city of Hellas, which his uncle Pelias had stolen from his father. The household was overcome with anxiety, fearing for Jason, and all the women wailed while age-stricken Aison added his soft moans to theirs. Undaunted, Jason soothed their sorrows with boastful words and bade them farewell. When he reached the silver-slipping stream Anauros, an old crone—Hera in disguise—tested his nobility by asking to be ferried across. Noble-hearted Jason carried her across, and she approvingly guided him on his quest.

While crossing the rain-swollen stream, Hera ensured that Jason lost one sandal, and so he entered the city amid great hubbub. Word was sent to the king that a tall, long-haired youth wearing the rough trousers and panther-skin cloak of a Magnesian had arrived with one foot bare.

King Pelias leapt into his mule-drawn chariot and, with headlong haste, arrived in the marketplace, demanding to know who the stranger was. Jason calmly told him and demanded his kingdom back. Pelias listened incredulously as Jason quite seriously offered to let Pelias keep his estate in order to avoid civil war.

Pelias was conducting a festival to Poseidon, and to act upon his desires and have Jason killed outright would have been an outrage against the laws of hospitality. Moreover, he feared that Aison still had many supporters in the city that would come to the bold youth's aid. So Pelias asked Jason what he would do if an oracle had told him that a certain man would kill him. Jason replied without hesitation, "I would order him to bring back the Golden Fleece." Pelias promptly commanded Jason to do precisely that before he would relinquish the kingdom. Alternatively it is said that Pelias tricked Jason by saying an oracle demanded that the Golden Fleece be brought to Iolkos and that if young Jason was to be king he needed to prove his merit with the quest. Either way, Jason readily accepted the challenge,

[180] The most important account of the voyage comes from Apollonios in his epic poem *Argonautika*. The only other surviving version of any length is found in Pindar's *Pythian Ode*, iv. Hyginos's *Fabulai*, 12, 14–23, follows Apollonios. Apollodoros's *Library*, i.9–28, and Diodoros's *Library of History*, iv.40–49, give summaries of the voyage; and Ovid's *Metamorphoses*, vii.1, also uses material from the story.

and they bound the agreement with an oath. Pelias never imagined the rash youth would succeed.

## Assembling the Crew

Jason went to Delphi to receive omens about his quest. Encouraged, he sent criers throughout Hellas asking for the most adventurous heroes to join him when he returned to Iolkos. The expert shipbuilder Argos was commissioned to build the *Argos* under Jason's order. Besides his immense carpentry skills, Argos was chosen for the job because of his connection to the fleece; he was a descendent of Phrixos, the man who had flown on the back of the golden-fleeced ram to Colchis and sacrificed it there.

Bright Athena instructed Jason on the ship's construction using timber she cut on Mount Pelion. Athena added a beam of Dodona oak as its prow and empowered it with speech. The best warriors of Hellas were assembled for the voyage in the largest ship that had yet been designed, a ship with fifty oars. A stout crew of fifty-four prepared for the journey.

All marveled at the huge ship when it was completed. The assembled crew unanimously chose bronze-hearted Herakles as their leader, but he declined, saying this was Jason's quest. An offering and feast were prepared that night. Alone after the celebrations were over, Jason brooded over his troubles. When dawn came and the crew prepared to push off, King Pelias's son Akastos and the shipbuilder Argos rushed down from Iolkos to join. They had been forbidden to do so by Pelias, who feared for their lives. In defiance of Pelias's orders, they joined as the ship was set to embark, before Pelias found out and could stop them. After several days of rowing they turned their backs to land, leaving Mount Ossa and Mount Olympos behind, and ventured out onto the open sea. When they landed on Lemnos, they found the isle inhabited only by women, the men having been killed off some time before. The women feared the Argonauts but longed for offspring, and so the queen invited Jason to a conference in order to help her determine her course of action.

## The Lemnian Women

Jason had no sooner entered the gates than the women of town came flooding after him, charmed by his appearance. He was escorted to Queen Hypsipyle's royal palace. He soothed her fears, and she offered to open their homes to the Argonauts. Jason returned with his men, and countless young girls ran up to them from every side and danced in their joy.

Jason set out straight for Hypsipyle's home, while the other men scattered as chance took them. The men stayed many days in a sailor's dream: living on a deserted island surrounded by countless beautiful women who wanted nothing more than merriment and lovemaking. Herakles remained behind to guard the ship, content to stay with his beautiful young squire Hylas, a descendent of the great hunter Orion.

Who knows how long they may have stayed—perhaps forever—but for Herakles. He sent an ironic message admonishing them for the type of glory that they were after, and in shame they returned to their ship. With parting gifts and tears, Hypsipyle invited Jason to come back and live with her after his quest. In due time she bore twins to Jason: Euneos and Nebrophonos (Deipylos).

## On to Colchis

After being initiated in the Samothracian mysteries upon the insistence of Apollo's son Orpheus, the Argonauts sailed past Hellespont and were hospitably entertained by the Doliones. When they sailed off, a dense fog confused them and they landed near where they had departed from. The light was so poor that the Doliones attacked, thinking the Argonauts were Pelasgian pirates. The Argonauts beat them back. The light of day brought a sad realization; the dead were their friends. Among the dead, their king, Cyzikos, was found; his heart had been ripped open by Jason's spear.

For twelve days afterward there was foul weather day and night, and the Argonauts were unable to put out to sea. But toward the next night, as Akastos and the seer Mopsos were on watch, Mopsos saw an omen of good weather. He awoke Jason, who immediately prepared and then performed the prescribed rite. The weather turned, and the voyage resumed.

When much-enduring Herakles's young lover Hylas was abducted by water nymphs in Mysia, Herakles began a frantic search. The godlike band of picked heroes waited impatiently but finally set sail. Then they pulled in their oars, reconsidering their move. They argued fiercely as to whether they should go back or not. Jason was paralyzed with a sense of helplessness, for which King Telamon of Salamis, son of Aiakos, rebuked him sharply. His quandary was ended when the sea god Glaukos appeared to say that Herakles was not fated to go to Colchis.[181] Jason graciously accepted Telamon's apology, and the two became close friends. Then they rowed safely through the blue Clashing Rocks and glided across the Black Sea like an eagle.

Herakles was furious when he discovered that he had been left behind. He took Mysian youths as compensation for lost Hylas and returned to Hellas. He established Dorians and Mysians in the town of Trakhis, which was formerly in Dryopes territory. Then Herakles returned to his labors.

Jason, as oft occurred, saw his resolve fail and sank into despair. Though the Argonauts were lost, the crew managed to keep things going. Then, on Ares Island, Jason welcomed four half dead castaways and discovered they were from Colchis. Jason took heart, and the castaways piloted the *Argo* directly to Colchis.

## King Aietes and the Test

Upon their arrival at Colchis, Jason suggested that they first try to persuade King Aietes to give up the fleece peacefully. Accordingly, he picked his friend Telamon to speak, and to act as guides and interpreters, he chose the descendants of Phrixos whom he had rescued on Ares Island. The Kolkhian princess Medeia was first to see the strangers. She pulled her veil aside and turned a wondering eye upon Jason as love awakened inside her.[182] Barbaric Aietes knew enough of the laws of hospitality to prepare a banquet in the guests' honor. After supper Jason was introduced, and he stated his request. Blunt Aietes accused the visitors of plotting to seize his throne. Jason checked the insulted Telamon, who rose to fight against

[181] Theokritos says he followed the crew to Colchis on foot.

[182] Pindar says Aphrodite invented the magic wheel to make Medeia fall in love with Jason.

overwhelming odds. Then Jason turned to Aietes and, in a conciliatory tone, assured the king that all he wanted was the fleece and that he was prepared to fight Kolkhian enemies to earn it.

Aietes was totally unmoved, and after a moment's thought, he announced his decision. He promised to freely give the fleece if Jason could pass certain tests of strength; he must yoke fire-breathing bulls to a plow, plow a field and sew it with dragon's teeth, and then kill the armed men who would spring up to fight him. Jason listened to this with his eyes fixed upon the floor, without a word, resourceless in the face of his dilemma. Finally he accepted when it became clear that Aietes would accept no other way. They returned to the ship without confidence.

The Argonauts soon recovered their courage, and Telamon's brother Peleus offered to perform the feat if Jason was unwilling. Jason brightened and declined to let anyone else have the honor of performing the task. The prophets foretold victory by laughter-loving Aphrodite, and so Argos (one of the rescued castaways, not the shipbuilder) arranged a secret meeting for Medeia, who wished also to meet Jason.

When Jason arrived at the appointed rendezvous spot, Medeia's twelve maiden attendants discreetly disappeared. Jason sensed her uneasiness and soothed her fears.

> Jason's homage melted Medeia. Turning her eyes aside she smiled divinely and then, uplifted by his praise, she looked him in the face. How to begin, she did not know; she longed so much to tell him everything at once. But with the charm, she did not hesitate; she drew it out from her sweet-scented girdle and he took it in his hands with joy. She reveled in his need of her and would have poured out all her soul to him as well, so captivating was the light of love that streamed from Jason's golden head and held her gleaming eyes. Her heart was warmed and melted like the dew on roses under the morning sun.

> At one moment both of them were staring at the ground in deep embarrassment; at the next they were smiling and glancing at each other with the love-light in their eyes.[183]

Medeia professed her love and told him how to use her magic charm. He promised to take her home with him.

The next morning, Jason obtained the dragon's teeth for sowing, and that night he prayed to Hekate as Medeia had instructed. At dawn Jason anointed himself and his weapons with the drug Medeia gave him, and he was suddenly flooded with strength and confidence. He stepped boldly off the ship and warded off the charging bulls with his shield; the ointment kept him safe from their flaming breath. Then Jason grabbed each in turn by the horn and kicked them to their knees, yoked them to the plow, and tore the earth, sowing the dragon's teeth behind him.

Earthborn men began to shoot up from the furrows, fully armed. Following Medeia's advice, Jason threw a boulder in their midst, and they began fighting among themselves. Jason rushed into the melee, and all the dragon men were dead by the time the sun sank.

Ashen Aietes could not believe it, and without a word he led the Kolkhians into their city to plot treachery. Medeia knew her father would figure out her treacherous role, and in the dead of night she stole out of the palace to where the Argonauts were celebrating. With a toast, Jason announced to the crew the promise he had made to her.

## Hasty Retreat

Medeia warned the crew of treachery and urged the Argonauts to sail immediately to the sacred wood of Ares, where she and Jason disembarked. With incantations and a magic herb, she put the guardian serpent to sleep. Jason pulled the fleece off the nail Phrixos had once affixed it with. He would not let the curious crew touch it, reminding them that they were still in great danger. He ordered the crew to row down the Phasis River and make their escape.

[183] Apollonios, *Argonautika,* iii.

The Kolkhian fleet pursued them under the command of Aietes's noble son Apsyrtos. He overtook the Argonauts at the mouth of the mighty Danube. Apsyrtos and Jason met under a truce on a tiny delta island sacred to Artemis. Apsyrtos agreed to let Jason keep the fleece if he left the maiden behind. When Medeia heard the deal, she boiled with rage, and Jason claimed that he was only stalling for time. She offered to lure her brother into Jason's hands if he had the stomach to kill him. More frightened of an angry sorceress than the Kolkhian fleet, Jason agreed.[184]

Medeia tricked Apsyrtos into returning to Artemis's isle alone, and Jason cut down the defenseless man. Then Medeia cut him into pieces to slow the Kolkhians' pursuit. She knew that the Kolkhians were compelled by custom to retrieve the pieces for proper burial. The Argonauts escaped.

The Argonauts sailed on to Circe's isle. The formidable witch Circe had eyes that shot out sunshine, as did all the children of glowing Helios. The Oceanid Perse bore both King Aietes and Circe; maligned-minded Aietes lived near the dawn, in Colchis, and Circe near the dusk, on the forested island of Aiaia. Jason commanded the men to stay behind, despite Circe's seductive call. Jason and Medeia alone followed Circe's steps until they reached her marvelous home of polished stone. Once inside, they sat at the hearth in the manner of supplicants in distress. Without asking any questions, the witch performed the rites of purification that they requested. Only afterward did she question Midea in the Kolkhian tongue. Medeia answered but said nothing about Apsyrtos.

> Not that Circe was deceived. Nevertheless she felt some pity for her weeping niece. "Poor girl," she said "you have indeed contrived for yourself a shameful and unhappy homecoming; for I am sure you will not long be able to escape your father's wrath. The wrongs you have done him are intolerable, and he will soon be in Hellas itself to avenge his son's murder. However, since you are my suppliant and kinswoman, I will not add to your afflictions now that you are here. But I do demand that

[184] During the Hellenistic age, in which Apollonios wrote, witchcraft was very important. This was not the case during Homer's era. Many of the Argonaut deeds were performed with magic, whereas the deeds of the Homeric heroes were performed through their own strength or the intercession of the gods.

> you should leave my house, you that have linked yourself to this foreigner, whoever he may be, this man of mystery whom you have chosen without your father's consent. And do not kneel to me at my hearth, for I never will approve your conduct and disgraceful flight."[185]

Such was the sacrifice Medeia made for love—to be cut off from her family and become an outcast among foreigners.

Slowed by their trip to Circe's island, the *Argo* was overtaken by the Kolkhians at Kercyra. The island's king decided to end the issue without recourse to arms. Medeia was not convinced of the Argonauts' resolve to protect her and begged with soft words for support at the knees of Queen Arete. The queen told her weary guest that if she were married the king would not send her back to her father. Midea sprang up to tell Jason, and hastily they set about the customary rites: mixing wine, sacrificing sheep, singing hymnal songs, and, of course, preparing a bridal bed. Many fleeces were laid out in a sacred cave, with the Golden Fleece on top. The nymphs brought flowers, and the sight kindled in their eyes a sweet desire. The Argonauts stood guard outside. After the king's decree, the Kolkhians gave up the chase.

## Return to Iolkos

The Argonauts rowed comfortably along the familiar western shores of Hellas until a terrible storm blew them across the terrifying open sea to Libya. Huge waves pushed the mighty craft far inland and then receded.

Stranded on hot desert sand, the demoralized crew sat down alone, apart, each preparing to die. Then the local nymphs appeared to Jason in a vision. Encouraged, he spoke to rouse the men, and on Peleus's urging they lifted the *Argo* onto their backs and carried her back to the sea. They rowed about lost on Lake Tritonis until Jason made an offering to the sea god Triton. Then they discovered their way out onto the open sea. When they reached Krete, they killed a towering bronze man guarding the lush island before returning to Iolkos without further incident.

---

[185] Apollonios, *Argonautika,* iii.

While the Argonauts were away, King Pelias of Iolkos assumed incorrectly that they had perished. Believing his son, too, was gone, he decided it best to protect himself against the other son of bedridden Aison. Aison was sentenced to die, and Pelias allowed him to take his own life by drinking a poison made from bull's blood. His young son Promakhos was brained on the palace floor. Poor Polymede, wife and mother, tasting calamity yet again so late in life, was without hope for her son Jason's return or an unclouded end. She committed suicide by thrusting a dagger into her own heart, cursing Pelias.

## Death of Pelias

When the jubilant Argonauts arrived back in Pegasai, their celebrations were dashed when Jason learned the sad fate of his family. The Argonauts were too few to challenge the great king of Iolkos, and so Jason turned to Medeia for revenge. Medeia transformed herself into an old crone by applying ointment to her hair and skin. She then went to the great palace and said that upon Artemis's order she was restoring youth to the aged nobles of Iolkos. Then she rubbed off her ointment and became the beautiful young sorceress she was. The unmarried daughters of Pelias were impressed and asked her to restore their father.

Medeia instructed the naive girls to cut up their father and put the pieces of him in a boiling pot filled with special herbs. The girls hesitated, as Medeia had anticipated. In a high-stakes magic trick, she chopped up an old ram and put it in a cauldron. Then she made appear a lamb that she had hidden. The sheltered princesses were convinced. Horror bruised their pretty faces when their father did not reappear as planned. Jason restrained them from killing themselves. Repulsed by the hideous deception, the citizens banished Jason, and Akastos succeeded his father, Pelias, as king.

## Herakles Obtains the Golden Apples

Meanwhile, armed with the true foresight of Nereus, Herakles had set out for Libya. Along the way, much-enduring Herakles defeated Emation of Arabia, Bousiris of Egypt, and Antaios of Libya. Antaios's strength was renewed each time he touched Mother Earth, and so finally Herakles held him off the ground and crushed him with a bear hug. Herakles held the world upon his own broad shoulders while the Titan Atlas gathered the golden apples belonging to Queen Hera. The despairing Argonauts saw him in the distance of the Libyan Desert as he was returning to Hellas with the apples, but he was too far ahead for them to catch up to him. Pallas Athena returned the apples to the garden after they were displayed in Tiryns.[186]

## Kalydonian Boar Hunt

The Argonauts returned, each to his own city, and were honored. Prince Meleagros returned to Kalydon, where his father, Oineus, ruled. His mother, Althaia (meaning "truth"), was a Kouretes princess of unsurpassable beauty from the neighboring palace city of Pleuron. Pious Oineus entertained gods and men alike in his splendid palace.[187] The gods Dionysos and Ares were drawn to Kalydon because of the king's wisdom and, more compellingly, because of the queen's beauty. As a reward for his discretion in the matter, Dionysos gave Oineus a vine that produced superior wine.

Wealthy Oineus erected strong walls around Kalydon. He sacrificed his eldest son, Toxeus, when the youth jumped over the fortifications during construction. He was sacrificed either as part of an ancient custom or because of the superstitious belief that by jumping over the walls the leaper would be able to bring them down.[188]

The queen bore many children besides Toxeus. By chariot-riding Ares or noble Oineus she bore Meleagros, and to Oineus she delivered horse-taming Pheres, Agelaos, Purifies, Klymenos, Thyreus, and a half a dozen

---

[186] The Minoan concept of death was not as depressingly dark as was the early Hellenes. The Minoans diminished the terrors of death with concepts of judgment and a happy existence in the Elysian Fields for the worthy. Herakles's success in obtaining the apples may have represented his overcoming the Minoan death. The twelfth labor, with Herakles overcoming Cerberus, may have been added as a victory over a death that the Hellenes could understand. Herakles's victory over Hades at Pylos (meaning "gate") is yet another version of the hero overcoming death.

[187] Homer, in *Iliad*, vi.216, quotes Diomedes as saying his grandfather Oineus once entertained Bellerophontes. This may have been an example of Oineus's legendary hospitality, but it could not have happened. Bellerophontes died before Oineus was born.

[188] Romulus killed his twin brother Remus for jumping over the fortifications of Rome and thus rendering them vulnerable to him.

or so daughters, including Gorge and Perimede.[189] By Dionysos (or Oineus) Althaia bore lovely Deianeira.

King Oineus's second son was red-haired Meleagros (born 1254T/1004R BCE). While Althaia was lying peacefully by the fire, snuggled with her seven-day-old darling, the Moirai appeared beside her and sang his fate. Klotho said he would be noble, and Lakhesis that he would be brave, but Atropos looked at the brand burning on the hearth and proclaimed, "To the log and the new born child we assign the same span of years."[190] As soon as they vanished on the billowing smoke, Althaia sprang from her couch, doused the fire with cold water, and put the log safely away. Meleagros grew into a large man of fiery temperament.

Meleagros might have been the greatest of the Argonauts (after Herakles, of course) had he been a bit older. As it was, the others could see his budding potential and gladly accepted him. He distinguished himself in battle against the Doliones, killing two of the enemy.

Upon his return, Meleagros chose a wife. He married the well-endowed sister of strong king Idas of Triphylian Pylos.[191] Meleagros led his lady, Kleopatra, her eyes lowered, into the bridal chamber, and immediately she conceived.

King Oineus of Kalydon was at the pinnacle of his distinguished career. His laborers brought in a record harvest, and his first grandchild, Polydora, was on the way. Oineus prepared a great autumn feast to celebrate. While the other gods enjoyed hecatombs offered in thanks, the king gave nothing to Artemis (patron goddess of Kalydon)—either forgetfully or carelessly. He quickly realized his mistake and tried to make amends.

---

[189] The sixth-century BCE mythographer Asios of Samos, whose works are lost, is quoted by Pausanias in *Guide to Greece*, vii.4.1, as saying rather fancifully that Perimede married the Phoenician king Phoenix and begat Europa.

[190] This famous version was composed by Ovid (*Metamorphosis*, viii). Pausanias's *Guide to Greece*, x.31, declares that the fifth-century BCE Athenian playwright Phynikhos was the first poet to dramatize the story of the firewood that the Moirai gave to Althaia and that consumed Meleagros. The mythic roots are much older, for evidence of a fire cult in Kalydon date to the Geometric Age (ninth or eighth century BCE).

[191] Homer, *Iliad*, ix.553–596, says Kleopatra was Idas's daughter, not her sister. However, Idas was roughly the same age as Meleagros, who died as a young man, thus making it impossible for Idas to be his father-in-law.

> It is hard for mortal men to turn aside the purpose of the gods; for otherwise horse-smiting Oineus, would have checked the anger of august Artemis, white-armed, bud-garlanded, when he entreated her with sacrifices of many goats and red-backed cattle. But no, the maiden goddess had conceived an unconquerable anger, and she sent a boar of vast strength, a ruthless fighter, rushing on Kalydon with its beautiful plains, where in the flood-tide of his might he hacked down the vine-rows with his tusks and slaughter sheep and any mortal who confronted him.[192]

Artemis remained angry that Oineus had forgotten her alone when he gave his harvest thanksgiving to the Deathless Ones. His strong-armed son Meleagros called upon the best Hellenes to come hunt the boar with him.

Among those who heeded the call was a formidable maiden warrior from Arkadia, Atalante. As soon as the hero of Kalydon saw her, he fell in love, though because of his beautiful young wife he did not act upon his desire, and it remained his secret. When some of the guests threatened not to hunt if a woman was allowed to join in a man's sport, the imposing Meleagros forced them to back down.

After feasting for nine days at Oineus's expense, the heroes waged persistent, hateful war upon the beast for six days. Finally driven from its retreat, it rushed furiously into the midst of the hunters, scattering the yapping hunting dogs with sidelong blows from its mighty tusks. Then, in an unswerving attack, the murderous brute charged straight down on the band of young warriors, cutting down Ancaios of Arkadia and everything else in its path.

The first to draw blood was Atalante, whose well-aimed arrow grazed the top of the boar's back and sent a thin trickle of blood down behind its ear. Meleagros threw two spears, each with a very different effect; the first one struck the ground, but the other lodged in the middle of the boar's back. Without any loss of time, while the beast violently twisted his body round and round, his jaws slavering with foam and blood, Meleagros approached and rousted the beast to fury before burying a death blow into its shoulder.

[192] Bakkhylides, "Olympic Ode for Hiero of Syrakuse", in *Greek Lyric.* Translated by David A. Campbell.

Then they buried the victims of the loud-squealing boar. But deadly fate destroyed more men, for the fierce goddess of the animal had still not put a stop to her anger. A fight broke out for the red-brown hide, which led to war between the Aitolians and Kouretes.

Meleagros shared his glory with Atalante, giving her as a trophy the head with its magnificent tusks and bristling hide. A murmur rang through the palace halls from the jealous hunters who got no part of the spoils. Plexippos, the eldest son of King Thestios of the Kouretes, rose up in rage, and his brother Iphikles stood by him. Plexippos bellowed that as the next of kin he was entitled to the hide if Meleagros relinquished it. With that he grabbed the hide away from the girl. The furious Meleagros slew unsuspecting Plexippos, and while Iphiklos hesitated, Meleagros struck him too. Thus the dear brothers of Queen Althaia (uncles of massive Meleagros) expired.

## Meleagros Defeats the Kouretes

The remaining sons of Thestios, all of whom had been present at the boar hunt and were witnesses of their brothers' deaths, slipped away and left Kalydon. They returned at the head of a Kouretes army, bent on revenge. The Kouretes fought a warlike race, the Aitolians, around the walls of Kalydon, with slaughter on both sides. The Aitolians defended their beloved Kalydon while the Kouretes longed to sack the town.

During the siege, the fierce daughter of Thestios unflinchingly initiated her son's demise by setting fire to the swiftly dooming log that fate had decreed at Meleagros's birth would be the limit of his life. She called upon the Furies to behold her unnatural sacrifice, by which she both avenged and committed a crime: death to atone for death, wickedness to be piled upon wickedness, slaughter upon slaughter. Her son had committed the unspeakable crime of placing love or friendship before family relationship.

> Artemis set on a clash with battle cries between Kouretes and proud Aitolians over the boar's head and shaggy hide. As long, then, as Meleagros, backed by the war god, fought, the Kouretes had the worst of it for all their numbers and could not hold a line outside the walls.

But then a day came when Meleagros was stung by venomous anger that infects the coolest thinker's heart; swollen with rage at his own mother, Althaia, he languished in idleness at home beside his lady, Kleopatra.

This lovely girl was born to Marpessa of ravishing pale ankles, Evenos' child, and Idas, who had been most powerful of men on earth. He drew the bow against the Lord Phoebus Apollo over his love, Marpessa, whom her father and gentle mother called Alcyone, since for her sake her mother gave that sea birds forlorn cry when Apollo ravished her. With Kleopatra lay Meleagros, nursing the bitterness his mother stirred, when in her anguish over a brother slain she cursed her son. She called upon the gods, beating the grassy earth with both her hands as she pitched forward on her knees, with cries to the Lord of undergloom and cold Persephone, while tears wetted her veils - in her entreaty that death come to her son. Inexorable in Erebos a vampire fury listened. Soon then, about the gates of the Aitolians tumult and din of war grew loud; their towers rang with blows. And now the elder men implored Meleagros to leave his room, and sent the high priests of the gods, imploring him to help defend the town. They promised him a large reward: in a green countryside of Kalydon, wherever it was richest, there he might choose a beautiful garden plot of fifty acres, half in vineyard, one half in virgin prairie for the plow to cut. Oineus, master of horsemen, came with prayers upon the door sill of the chamber, often rattling the locked doors, pleading with his son. His sisters, too, and then his gentle mother pleaded with him. Only the more fiercely he turned away. His oldest friends, his dearest, not even they could move him - not until his room was shaken by a hail of stones as Kouretes began to scale the walls and fire the city.

Then at last his lady in her soft-belted gown besought him weeping, speaking of all the ills that come to men whose town is taken: soldiers put to the sword; the city

> razed by fire; alien hands carrying off the children and the women. Hearing these fearful things, his heart was stirred to action: he put on his shining gear and fought off ruin from the Aitolians. Mercy prevailed in him. His folk no longer cared to award him gifts and luxuries, yet even so he saved that terrible day.[193]

He bravely faced his enemy and turned the tide against the invaders, winning a glorious battle. Red-haired Meleagros unwittingly killed the remaining brothers of his mother, though Apollo supported them – for in the heat of a battle hard hearted Ares does not allow a javelin to distinguish a friend from a foe once launched.

Immediately the terminal illness brought on by the burning log hit him. Meleagros was scorched by the flame, and felt a hidden fire consuming his vitals. He endured his agony with indomitable courage; but still, he grieved that he should meet so inglorious an end, that his death involved no bloodshed, and declared Ancaios lucky to have suffered the wounds he did. For the last time he called upon his aged father, his brothers and loving sisters, cried out his wife's name, groaning as he did so, and perhaps his mother's too. As the fire blazed up, so did his agony: then both died down again, and were extinguished together. Gradually his breath dispersed into the thin air, as the white ash gradually settled over the glowing embers.[194]

His mother knew full well the dreadful thing she had done. With her own guilty hand she exacted punishment from herself, driving a sword through her own body. As a final act, Artemis, annoyed at their pitiful grieving, raised the hero's virgin sisters, all except Gorge (the only one already married) and Deianeira (daughter of a god), causing feathers to sprout from their bodies and stretching wings along their arms. She gave them horny beaks as well. When they had so changed to guinea fowl (which bears the species name *meleagrides*), she dispatched them into the sky.

Noble Kleopatra honored her husband in the custom of the bravest wives. She leapt upon the funeral fire of her dead husband and perished in screaming agony. When their infant daughter Polydora came of age, she was married to a valiant prince. After he died bravely in battle, Polydora

---

[193] Homer, *Iliad,* ix.527–600.

[194] Ovid, *Metamorphoses,* viii.

followed the example of her noble mother and died on the pyre of her husband.[195]

The power of the Kouretes was destroyed. The Aitolians of Kalydon razed Pleuron in revenge, the first of these two great palace states to suffer the ills of war. Most of the Kouretes fled westward into Akarnania, escaping as their fair city was sacked.

After the fall of Pleuron, Oineus distracted himself further with a campaign against Olenos, a city on the coast of Akhaia, just across the Gulf of Korinth. Olenos had been part of the great Lapith kingdom of Eleia. The next year, he conquered the city and made it his vassal, putting a man named Dexamenos in charge (1230T/980R BCE). His prize was the Olenian princess Periboia, daughter of Hipponoos. He married her, and she bore him Tydeus and Melanippos (Olenias). [196]

---

Exhibit 10.3
Marriage of Idas and Marpessa

King Agenor of Kalydon had four grandsons, sons of Ares, who grew to be fierce, war-thirsty warriors who rallied the Kouretes into rebellion. The sons of Ares were victorious, and they wrestled the Kouretes' stronghold Pleuron from King Porthaon of Kalydon, son of Agenor. Thestios, eldest of the four brothers, became king. His powerful brother Evenos was the father of lovely Marpessa.[197] Evenos held jurisdiction over Ortygia (later Khalkis) and survived the battle against the Aitolians, which cost Meleagros and the sons of Thestios their lives. Evenos did not want to pay a dowry for his daughter, so like Oinomaos of Pisa, Evenos competed against his

[195] Stasinos or Hegasias of Cyprus, in *Cypria*, says Polydora was the wife of Prince Protesilaos of Thessalian Akhaia, who died in the Trojan War. Polydora could not have been a young bride at that time, and so the assertion by Apollodoros (*Library*, Epitome 3.30) and Hyginos (*Fabulai*, 9.10–4) that Laodameia, youngest daughter of King Akastos of Iolkos, is Protesilaos's wife is better suited.

[196] The sack of Olenos was recorded in the lost epic *Thebaid*, quoted by Apollodoros. Diodoros, in *Library of History*, iv.35, says alternatively that Hipponoos refused to believe his daughter had been impregnated by Ares and sent her to his overlord Oineus for execution. Oineus married her instead. Peisandros called her Gorge, and Pausanias says Tydeus was the son of Oineus and his own daughter Gorge.

[197] Her mother could not have been Alcippe of Athens, as some claimed. To fit Athenian chronology, Alcippe must have lived during the mid fifteenth century T / late thirteenth century R BCE.

daughter's suitors in horse racing. He roofed Artemis's temple with their skulls. As Bakkhylides tells it, Idas carried off the willing Marpessa from Ortygia (1227T/977R BCE).

> She, sitting at home and exceedingly angry with her father and in her affliction she makes supplication to the netherworld Curses, poor wretch, that he complete a bitter and accursed old age for keeping his daughter alone indoors and preventing her from marrying, although the hair will turn white on her head.
>
> Such a father, they say, was the bronze-belted son of gold crested Ares, Evenos, bold of hand and murderous, to his long-robed daughter, bud-eyed Marpessa; but time subdued him and strong avenging necessity against his will; as the sun rose came Idas, prosperous son of Aphareus, driving the swift racing mares of Poseidon; and the hero carried off the beautiful-haired girl, as she wished, from the sanctuary of the lovely-veiled goddess Artemis. [198]

Evenos, slowed by age, raced after Idas in his chariot. But the chariot of Idas was pulled by "winged" horses of Poseidon and he made good speed. Upon reaching the river Lykormas without catching them, Evenos sank down willfully into the river, and ever since then it has been called the Evenos River in his honor. As the happy couple approached Idas's home in Arene, Messenia, long-haired Apollo intercepted them and seized Marpessa. Idas drew his bow, ready to fight even against the gods for his bride, but Zeus intervened as arbitrator and gave Marpessa her choice; she was afraid that golden Apollo would abandon her in her old age, and so she chose Idas. A man who risks his life for one against terrible odds is a difficult man for one to resist.

---

**12) Cerberus of Hades.** In Herakles's bid to overcome death, he first sought initiation into the Eleusinian mysteries. Then he descended into Hades at Tainaron in Lakonia. King Hades faced Herakles at the gate

[198] Bakkhylides, "fragment in the Oxyrhynkhos papyrus", in *Greek Lyric*. Translated by David A. Campbell.

(Pylos) and defended the entrance to his realm. Herakles wounded Hades, who ascended Olympos for restoration. Herakles waited at the entrance until Hades returned. When he did, Hades agreed to let Herakles take Cerberus, but only if he could catch the dog without weapons and so long as he brought the hound back unharmed. While in Hades, Herakles came upon the massive ghost of Meleagros, who had just died in Kalydon. Herakles asked if he had a sister who was of like stature. Meleagros said he did and that she (Deianeira) was still a virgin. Herakles swore he would marry her.

Protected by his lion skin, Herakles grabbed one of the monster's throats and subdued the guard dog of Hades. He displayed him outside of Tiryns. Herakles returned the beast as promised and was freed from his bondage to Eurystheus. It had taken an eternal year (eight years and one month) to atone for his children's death, just as Kadmos had served an eternal year for killing the dragon.

# Sack of Cities

## Late Helladic Bronze Age (LHIIIB); Part of Hesiod's Age of Heroes

> So we find ourselves hopelessly in love with the thing we see, this world of brightness, because we have no experience of any other mode of living, and no proof of the other world; myths merely lead us astray.
>
> —Euripides, *Hippolytos*, fifth century BCE

Between the fall of Troy VI and Troy VII, Hellas underwent a massive disruption. Three centuries of growth ended and ushered in a long decline. Massive migration to Akhaia, Cephallenia Island, Attike, Anatolia, Palestine, and, above all, Cyprus accompanied the decline, and the unified nature of Mycenaian culture broke apart. Beginning with Pylos, most of the palaces of Hellas were destroyed between 1200T/950R and 1190T/940R BCE. Although most of the sacked cities were rebuilt, the palaces were abandoned, and Mycenaian civilization never recovered. The cause for this lack of recovery could be famine, earthquakes, climate change, civil unrest, foreign invasion (Dorians from the north), or a combination thereof. The Hittite conquest of Miletos in Anatolia and the embargo of Akhaian goods could have been factors, although those events occurred some thirty years beforehand.

Hellenic mythology is full of stories explaining the fall of cities. They unequivocally place the blame on their heroic ancestors, who sought power, glory, and loot. No hero was more to blame than Herakles for the self-destructive behavior—and the Hellenes bestowed immortality upon him for these accomplishments. In myth (as in the archaeological record) the cities were rebuilt but did not recover their former glory. Because of the universal belief in a ten-year-long Trojan War, the mythic dates for the sack of cities were pushed back a generation. Myths of massive migration were placed immediately after Troy VII fell.

## Herakles is Free

With his twelve labors completed, Herakles returned to his birthplace, Thebes. Having murdered his own children, it was impossible for him to return to his wife, Megara. He married her to his nephew Iolaos. Iolaos had faithfully served Herakles as squire through many of his twelve labors, and Herakles felt only Iolaos was worthy enough to marry his ex-wife.

Forgetting his vow to the ghost of Meleagros, Herakles sought the hand of Iole, the beautiful daughter of King Eurytos of Oikhalia. After his elder sons Iphitos and Klytios returned from their glorious adventure as Argonauts, Eurytos offered to marry his lovely daughter Iole to anyone who could beat him and his sharp-eyed sons in archery. (Klytios had won renown in battle against the Doliones, the Bithynians, and the Stymphalian birds.) No one could, until Herakles finished his labors and took the challenge.

He won a very close contest. Eurytos then backed away from his promise—not because he was afraid to see his daughter married, but because he feared for her life. Eurytos had heard that Herakles had killed his first wife and children in a fit of madness, and he did not want that to happen to dear Iole. He threw out Herakles (1230T/980R BCE).

Prince Iphitos argued on Herakles's behalf by telling his father that if he had not intended to live up to the terms of the contest, he should never have dueled. When King Eurytos's prize cattle (or twelve of his horses and twelve of his mules) were reported missing a few days later, King Eurytos needled Iphitos, saying, "This shows the true nature of he whom you defend, a slave is he and a cattle rustler too." Iphitos retorted that Hellas's greatest hero was no common thief, and he set out to find the stolen animals.

Iphitos followed their tracks to Tiryns, where Herakles had gone. Iphitos too became suspicious, and he confronted Herakles, asking him if he knew the whereabouts of the missing animals. Herakles professed his innocence—a lie—and asked Iphitos to accompany him up to the top of the mighty Cyklopean walls that surrounded Tiryns to survey the land and prove that the missing herd was not in his possession. Herakles seized the moment when a man's thoughts wander one way and his gaze another and hurled Iphitos from the summit. Herakles kept Iphitos's great bow, which Apollo had given to his father and his father had given to him. Herakles later gave it to young Odysseus. The bow was so hard to string that none of the suitors could do it. Odysseus did and slew many suitors with it.

Father Zeus was angry with Herakles for stooping to such a base act of treachery. Had he wreaked his vengeance openly, Zeus would surely not have taken issue. In punishment, an illness struck Herakles that he could not shake.

Seeking purification, Herakles traveled south to Sparta, accompanied by Oionos, the son of his uncle Licymnios. Along the way they stopped in Tegea, and Herakles secretly raped King Aleos's daughter in the precinct of Athena. Upon reaching Sparta, King Hippokoon refused to purify him of murder.

The humiliated Herakles was jeered by men and snarled at by dogs as he left town. Herakles's cousin Oionos threw a rock and killed one of the tormenting hounds. In response, the sons of Hippokoon killed Oionos, and Herakles could no longer hold back his rage. Like an angry bear pursued by baying hounds who tires of their snapping, he suddenly wheeled about to face his numerous tormentors single-handedly. His assailants were quick and jumped back wherever Herakles lunged to attack. Meanwhile, those behind Herakles would snap to the attack. In this manner they managed to wound the great hero in the hand, pelvis, and thigh without being injured themselves. Herakles could find no advantage and finally beat a hasty retreat.

Asclepius, the deified healing god, hid Herakles in the Taygetos Mountains and cured him of his wounds, though his illness persisted. To cure his illness, Herakles traveled over the mountains to Pylos, where King Neleus also refused to purify him from such a cowardly crime (he was an ally of the Dryopes—bitter enemies of the Dorians and of Herakles—many of whom lived in Messenia). In great pain, Herakles traveled to Delphi seeking a cure.

Because silver-bowed Apollo felt burly Herakles's actions were unbefitting one who had earned a place on Olympos, his priestess refused to grant him an audience. The angry Herakles stole the sacred tripod, which immediately brought Apollo into action. The two fought until Zeus threw a thunderbolt between them. Herakles gave the tripod back, and Apollo told Herakles to be sold as a slave for three years. The slave price paid by Lydian queen Omphale for the great hero was grudgingly sent to Eurytos as restitution, but he refused it. Herakles recovered, and before embarking, he founded the Lakonia port of Gythion with Apollo to demonstrate their new friendship. Thereafter, the shrine of Delphi was considered the highest authority in religious matters by the Herakleids (Dorians).

## Last Great Exploits of Herakles

After completing a second servitude, the brooding Herakles planned revenge on the enemies he had made over the years. Despite Herakles's presence, the battles were fierce and the outcomes in doubt. Numerous Thebans participated in Herakles's expeditions against Troy, Elis, Pylos, and Sparta (1220T/970R–1218T/968R BCE). The spoils enriched Thebes so much that Oidipous constructed a sumptuous royal palace and central marketplace. These structures are among the most impressive Bronze Age buildings discovered in Hellas as of yet.

Oidipous would have been the king of Thebes when, according to Assyrian records, the Assyrians sent an embassy to Thebes to try to circumvent a Hittite embargo (1225T/975R BCE).

Image 11.1
Map of Important Sites in the Later Life of Herakles

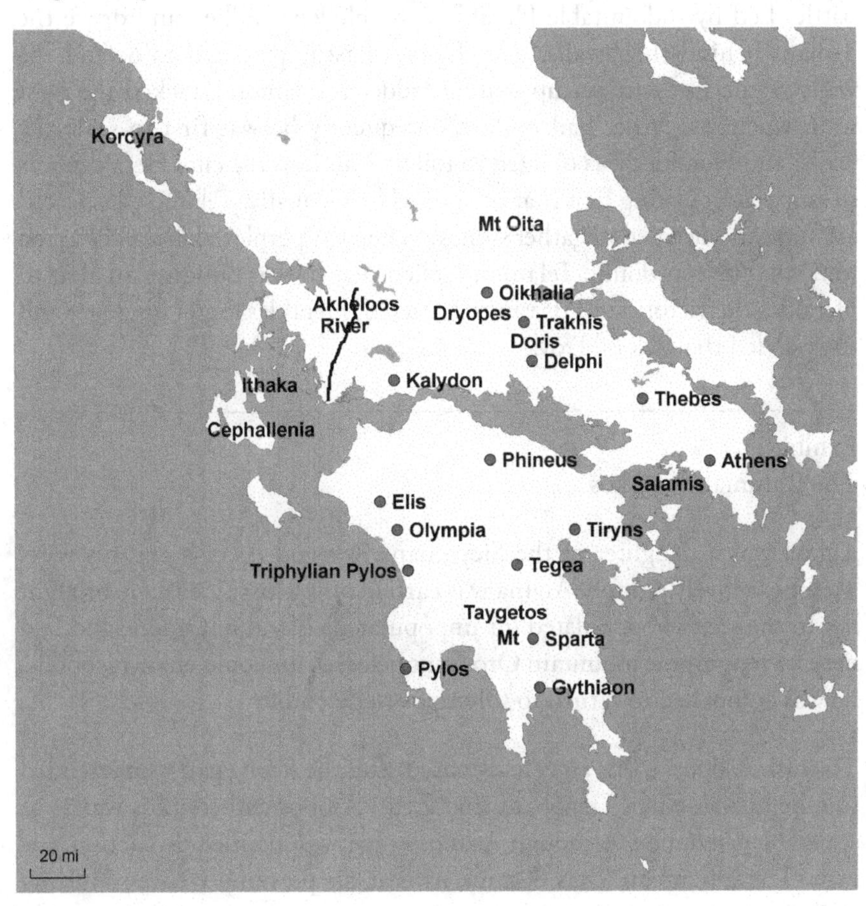


## First Sack of Troy

Herakles first outfitted eighteen fifty-oared ships to sail against Troy. Among his captains were his brother Iphikles and his nephew Iolaos, the rainmaker Aiakos's mighty sons Telamon of Salamis and Peleus of Thessalian Akhaia, and the Boiotia champion Deimakhos. Herakles sent his brother Iphikles and Telamon of Salamis ahead as envoys to demand Hesione and the horses King Laomedon had promised for saving her life. The ambassadors were held in prison until Laomedon's noble son Priamos released them.

The Trojan[199] army then drove Herakles and his forces back to the sea and burned most of the ships. The Boiotian Deimakhos was killed during the battle. Led by indomitable Herakles, the Hellenes rallied and drove the Trojans behind their walls. The Trojans hastily prepared to defend the walls as the Hellenes set up scaling ladders. Telamon attacked the west wall, where his father had built. Consequently he was first to scale the walls, and Herakles was obliged to follow him into the city. Herakles was so angry at not being first that he stalked his own ally. Telamon suspected as much and stooped to gather stones. When the perplexed Herakles asked him what he was doing, Telamon replied that he was building an altar to Herakles the victorious. His vanity flattered, Herakles forgot his anger and the two led the sack of Troy.

---

Exhibit 11.1
The Rainmaker Aiakos

Aigina was a daughter of the Sicyonian river god Asopos and his wife, Metope, a lovely nymph. Aigina was carried off by lusty Zeus. He brought her to the sparsely populated (or unpopulated) island of Oinone and laid her down upon the mountain Oros, but before Zeus could enjoy his spoils, he was compelled to return to Olympos to defend it.

The rash Asopos, in his rage, had chased after the strong god who intended to rape his daughter. Unable to find Zeus, Asopos gathered his waters to scale holy Olympos. Although Asopos's rage was justified, his action was rash. The Olympian Zeus became livid at his presumptiveness. Hurling well-aimed thunderbolts safely from the ramparts, he drove Asopos back, humbled and lamed.

The commotion naturally caught the attention and ire of Zeus's cow-eyed wife, Hera. Zeus placated his wife by not returning to Aigina. The young nymph was left alone and frightened, far from home, knowing Zeus would one day pour down upon her like a storm and take his pleasure with her.

Finally, after many years, Hera's attention wandered elsewhere. The irrepressible Zeus returned disguised as an eagle. While Eros hovered

[199] The term "Trojan" comes to us from Latin. The Hellenes called them Teukrians. For simplicity, the term "Trojan" will be used.

above, administering the gifts of love, Zeus shared a couch with his captive prize. In due time, she bore Aiakos to the god; he was a son who delighted in horses.

When Lord Poseidon and fair Apollo wanted a man to assist them in building the walls of Troy, they could have picked anyone. They chose Aiakos. Zeus commanded Poseidon and Apollo to serve a man, King Laomedon of Troy, in punishment for instigating an unsuccessful palace coup (1272T/1022R BCE). The Stronger Ones were commanded by Laomedon to build impregnable walls, and they enlisted mortal assistance because only the mortal-built portion could be breached. The gods wanted no man's citadel to be invincible. When the work was completed, foolish Laomedon sent the laborers away without paying the agreed-to wage.

---

Herakles killed King Laomedon, and the Trojans surrendered. The city was spared when a ransom was paid. Herakles awarded lovely Hesione to like-minded Telamon as part of his spoils because he had been first into the city. Herakles was happy to let Priamos assume power, since he had supported Herakles's claim to the mares.[200]

During the voyage home, Herakles's ship was separated from the others and blown off course by Hera. Landing on Kos Island, they were assumed to be pirates and attacked by the locals. Herakles killed King Eurypylos but was wounded by the Koan champion Khalkodon. Zeus snatched his beloved son away in time to save him from certain death.

Twelve successful labors had already won immortality for Herakles once he died, but Zeus still needed him alive as a mortal. The Olympians were

[200] Because LHIIIB pottery was found at Troy VI, it is possible to date the fall of the city as somewhere between 1290T/1040R and 1195T/945R BCE. Narrowing the date to the 1260sT/1010sR BCE is tempting given that Hittite records of that time say the royal House of Wilusa fled to a nearby kingdom when the renegade Hittite nobleman Piyamaradu seized the city. Perhaps the mythic Akhaian attack on Troy by Herakles was the Ahhiyawa (Akhaian) support that the Hittite records say Piyamaradu received during his occupation of Wilusa (Troy).

For several reasons, including the fact that two sons of Herakles (Telephos and Tlepolemos) fought against the army of Agamemnon, Hellenic mythology suggests a later date, such as 1220T/970R BCE, the date used in the Clevenger chronology. Either way, the struggles of Piyamaradu probably occurred before the Hittites drove out the Akhaian ruler of Miletos and before the sack of Troy VI.

about to engage the Gigantes, and prophecy had revealed that they would win only with the help of a mortal. Zeus was not confident that anyone other than Herakles would do.

Herakles killed giant Alcyoneus, and a spell of invulnerability to the Olympians was broken. The Olympians then routed the Gigantes (1220T/970R BCE). Cloud-gathering Zeus was furious at big-eyed Hera for her incessant meddling with Herakles and for her having nearly been the cause of his death at such a crucial time. In punishment mighty Zeus hung her from heaven by her feet.

## Competition for the Hand of Deianeira

Remembering his pledge to the ghost of Meleagros, Herakles headed toward Aitolia, where Princess Deianeira had reached a ripe age for marriage. While staying in the Aitolian ruled port of Olenos, where his friend Dexamenos ruled, Herakles saved the king's daughter from being forcibly married to the Centaur Eurytion. Then he sailed across the Gulf of Korinth and walked to Kalydon.

Herakles announced himself to Deianeira's father, King Oineus of Aitolia, as his new son-in-law. Once Herakles announced his intentions, no mortal dared to sue for her hand. The king of the river gods, Akheloos, took the challenge to test Herakles for the right to marry her.

Shapely Deianeira strongly desired Herakles and shuddered at the thought of sleeping with the shape-shifting river, but the decision was not hers. She quietly sat on the side of a hill that could be seen afar, awaiting the husband that would be hers.

Each suitor stated his case. Herakles told of his success in his labors and reminded them that his father was the strongest one, Zeus. Akheloos responded by scolding Oineus for considering a mortal over a god, a stranger for a native son. Then, turning to taunt his opponent, the deep-eddying Akheloos remarked that either your father is not Zeus or your mother is an adulteress.

Herakles had been glowering at Akheloos as he spoke. Instead of controlling his flaring rage, he yelled that he was better with his hands than with his tongue. Akheloos may have won a verbal victory but was about to lose fight! He rushed at the river god, who accepted the challenge. Manly Ares assisted Akheloos, and wise Athena supported Herakles. They struggled for a long time, and when Akheloos was worn down by the hero, he changed from human form to three others: a bull, a speckled serpent, and a Minotaur. When Herakles broke off his horn, which became the horn of plenty, Akheloos conceded.[201]

The god withdrew, and Herakles was married (1226T/976R BCE). Deianeira bore to her champion Hyllos, Glenos, and Onitas. While living in Aitolia, Herakles gathered an army to attack his enemies in the Peloponnesos.

## Sack of Elis

When Herakles attacked the Epeians they gave him considerable trouble. King Augeias realized he had made a powerful enemy by not paying the agreed-to fee for cleaning his stables and had prepared for this day. He invited Molios, the youngest son of the Dryope king Eurytos of Messenian Oikhalia, to build a fort in Eleia and to marry his eldest daughter, auburn-haired Agamede, a sorceress knowledgeable in healing herbs. Next Augeias turned to Amarynceus, lord of Buprasion and son of Pyttios. Augeias enriched Amarynceus by granting him the monopoly over Epeian trade by sea and thereby bought himself an ally. Augeias[202] also depended upon the support of his brother Aktor, the chief of the Lapiths. In battle Aktor had lost the city of Olenos to Herakles's ally, King Oineus of Aitolia, a few years before (1230T/980R BCE). Aktor responded by building the port of Hyrmina on the coast near Buprasion and naming it for his mother. He moved his capital from Olenos to Hyrmina.

---

[201] Strabo, in *Geography*, iv.35, said "wrestling" Akheloos meant diverting his water for irrigation. In Boiotia, Herakles was connected with the dikes and ditches that drain Lake Kopais—as the destroyer of them.

[202] Apollonios, in *Argonautika*, includes Augeias as an Argonaut. Others more reasonably do not, since Augeias had grown sons and was too old. Besides, he was the enemy of another crewman, Herakles.

Aktor was the father of incredible conjoined twins Eurytos and Kteatos, who were connected at the hip. Not only did these twins survive their birth (1247T/997R BCE), but they also grew into a prolific fighting team. They were called the Moliones for their mother, Molione. Because of their strength and miraculous appearance, many wondered if the Moliones were not Lord Poseidon's children. The Moliones married twin daughters of the Centaur Dexamenos of Pisatis.

Herakles returned as expected at the head of a large army of Tirynians, Thebans, Aitolians, Lakonians, and others (1219T/969R BCE). Among his army were the young twins Kastor and Polydeuces.[203] They sailed from Aitolia and landed at Olenos, the beachhead that had recently fallen into Aitolian hands. Amarynceus fought valiantly, and the Moliones carried the Epeians to victory, handing Herakles his only battle defeat. Herakles's twin brother, Iphikles, was mortally wounded by the Moliones, and his close companion Telamon of Salamis received a debilitating injury. Herakles's army appealed for a truce, which the Epeians granted.

Herakles and his defeated army withdrew to Arkadia and wintered in Pheneos. Iphikles was buried there with honors while Telamon recovered—although he would never be able to fight again. Herakles's enemy King Eurystheus of Tiryns sensed weakness and drove out those exiles, including Alkmene, who had returned to Tiryns. They joined Herakles in Pheneos.

As with Orkhomenos years before, Herakles turned to cunning when outright force failed. He ambushed and killed the Moliones as they traveled to Korinth under general truce to compete in the Isthmian Games. Herakles then sacked Elis, although Augeias escaped.

Herakles paused to celebrate his victory with Olympic Games funded by the booty taken from Elis. Herakles won the fighting and wrestling contests, and Iolaos won the horse race.

---

[203] Because of the historic importance of Sparta, the exploits of these twins was exaggerated. They were defeated by the Messenian twins Idas and Lynceus and were part of the forces of Herakles defeated by the Moliones. Despite this, they were added to the crew of the Argonauts and were deified, even though greater twins than they were not.

## Sack of Triphylian Pylos

Because Pylian king Neleus had once incurred Herakles's enmity by refusing to purify him of Iphitos's murder, he marched south into Triphylia, where his army was challenged by Pylian forces led by Periklymenos, the eldest son of Neleus. The Pylians fought valiantly and were aided by the war god Ares himself. Trusting in his enormous strength and ability to change shapes, Periklymenos bravely faced Herakles, in spite of the terrible reputation of that indomitable warrior. When Herakles began to get the upper hand, Periklymenos began changing shapes to find a way to get at Herakles. The relentless Herakles proved invincible, and he eventually overpowered and killed Periklymenos. His ten brothers rushed in a fury to avenge their brother, but even en masse they were no match for Herakles, and they all perished by his sword (1218T/968R BCE).[204] Herakles even wounded Ares, and the Pylian forces withdrew.

The Messenian Pylos was too large for Herakles to attack directly, and Neleus continued to rule. However, Herakles's wrath against Neleus was satiated by the death of his sons. Avenged, he turned his army east to Tegea. There he planned his attack on Sparta, another place he wished to avenge himself upon. Neleus was sorely grieved when he heard the fate of his sons. His wife, pale Khloris, had seen ten siblings die for the vain boast of her mother, Niobe, and now eleven sons died for Herakles's pride (her youngest, Nestor, was too young to fight and survived).

## Sack of Sparta (Ancient Therapne)

Sparta braced for the attack to come. Herakles sought revenge against King Hippokoon for having refused to purify him of Iphitos's murder and for the wound his sons inflicted upon him. Herakles had atoned for his sin by serving Lydian (Arzawan) queen Omphale and was not weakened by illness this time. Knowing that the battle would be fierce, Herakles enlisted additional reinforcements from Sparta's enemy, the Tegeans. King Cepheus

[204] The city of Pylos (meaning "gate") became confused with Herakles's struggle to overcome death at the gates of Hades. The older Triphylian Pylos was first identified with the underworld, but as Messenian Pylos grew, it usurped the older city. Consequently, Herakles battled both the king of Pylos the city and the king of the underworld. Both battles were placed near Triphylian Pylos. Herakles defeated Neleus and war himself (Ares) and then defeated Hades. Both gods withdrew after receiving wounds inflicted by the incredible mortal warrior.

was reluctant to fight the Lacedaimonians again, respecting their prowess in war and fearing a surprise attack on Tegea during his absence. Willful Herakles would not take no for an answer and gave Cepheus's daughter Sterope the lock of Medousa's hair that grey-eyed Athena had given him; he promised that it would repel any enemy if she held it up three times on the city walls. Reassured, Cepheus gathered his sons, assembled his army, and marched with Herakles. Herakles's polyglot army also included Lacedaimonians loyal to the deposed king Tyndareos of Sparta, led by his sons the Dioskouroi. Tegea was not attacked during the king's absence.

Just as Herakles and Cepheus predicted, the battle against the Lacedaimonians was fierce, but after a bloody resistance, they were defeated. Sadly, Cepheus was not around to celebrate; he and all his sons were killed in the hard fought hand-to-hand battle (1218T/968R BCE). The rightful king, Tyndareos, was restored.

Herakles had avenged himself against those whom he had sworn vengeance against. He was now forty-three years old and ready to settle down in Kalydon. But he was not suited to a peaceful life and led the Aitolia into several battles.

Herakles departed Aitolia for the following reason. During supper, the cupbearer Eunomos (Eurynomos), young son of King Oineus's relative Arkhitelos, accidentally spilled water on gruff Herakles. In a fit of anger, Herakles punished the boy so severely that he died from his beating. Although Arkhitelos forgave him, Herakles insisted that he be banished anyway, as custom dictated (1213T/963R BCE).

Herakles decided it was time to claim his third of the kingdom of Doris and traveled east. Many of those who had fought with Herakles chose to pack up their families and go with him. When they reached the raging waters of the Evenos River, the ferryman Nessos offered to carry the women across. He would carry his passengers upon his back and shoulders or in his arms and wade across the strong stream.

Nessos had been a member of the largest band of Centaurs, a backward tribe that lived in the mountains of Hellas. They lived in the hill country of Magnesia until their catastrophic battle with the Lapiths. During the battle, Nessos wounded Cymelos in the groin before managing to escape. Most of the Centaurs who escaped settled in the mountains of the Peloponnesos.

The shaggy-breasted Nessos chose to stop at the Evenos River. He claimed that the Stronger Ones had sanctioned his craft because of his sterling character. This day could have been a profitable one for the Centaur but for the lust that inflamed him.

Deianeira was equally afraid of the river and of Nessos, but Herakles entrusted the Centaur with his precious wife. Upon reaching the far bank, Nessos raped his lovely passenger. Herakles heard her cries and, from across the river, shot an arrow dipped in the poison of the Hydra. The arrow pierced the Centaur in the back as he climaxed. As its barbed tip protruded from his breast, Nessos thought of how not to die un-avenged.

He ripped the tunic from his back and gave it to Deianeira, telling her to smear it with his blood and semen. The dying Nessos professed remorse for the act he had committed and offered to Deianeira the tunic and fluids in atonement, knowing full well it contained deadly poison. He said it would act as a charm for the soul of Herakles, so that once he wore it he would never again look upon another woman to love more than her. Then he gasped his last, and naive Deianeira tucked the shirt away before Herakles caught up to her.

As Herakles and his followers approached Trakhis, warlike Cyknos blocked their path, spoiling for a fight. Cyknos's charioteer was his father, the war god Ares. Herakles and Iolaos mounted their chariot to face the challenge. When the two cars charged, they were forced to yield before the furious onslaught of Cyknos and Ares. Pallas Athena arrived to give encouragement to the dispirited champions and advised them to wound Ares but leave him be. On the next pass, golden Apollo helped guide Herakles's spear, and Cyknos crumpled out of his chariot, dead. Ares attacked in rage, and Herakles wounded him in the thigh; in howling pain he withdrew to Olympos. Then Herakles and Iolaos stripped proud Cyknos of his gleaming armor.

## Sack of Elion

The great hero and his band were welcomed in Trakhis by the grateful kings of Doris and Trakhis. They were given a large tract of land in exchange for their support against the Dryopes and Lapiths. After dealing with those tribes, Herakles sacked the Dolopes city of Elion, near Iolkos.

## Sack of Oikhalia

Herakles settled down but again grew restless. Not content with all that he had earned, Herakles focused only on what he had been denied. The last slight to be avenged was the one by Eurytos, even though his protagonist was dead and he himself had remarried. Eurytos's beautiful daughter Iole had been unable to marry because potential suitors were afraid of offending Herakles, who had rightly won her years before in a competitive archery duel. Herakles easily assembled and led a great force of Dorians, Arkadians, Thaumacians, Aitolians, and Thebans. The campaign was popular. The Dryopes were enemies of the Dorians, and the prospect of booty was enticing. The large force easily overwhelmed the defenses and utterly sacked the city (1207T/957R BCE). The remaining sons of Eurytos won glory by dying valiantly defending their city. It was never rebuilt.

Iole so hated Herakles for killing her brothers and keeping her from marriage that she tried to cheat him of his prize by jumping from the ramparts, but her dress acted as a parachute and broke her fall. She survived unharmed and was captured. Iole uttered not a word to her conqueror but instead suffered continually with her burden of sorrow. She, incessantly wept bitterly from the time she was forced from her windy home.

> The bold-planning hero left behind Oikhalia consumed in fire; and he came to the sea-washed headlands, where he was about to sacrifice from his booty nine deep bellowing bulls to wide-clouded Cenaian Zeus[205] and two to the sea-rouser and earth subduer (Poseidon) and a high-horned

[205] Bakkhylides (*FGrHis,* 15) suggests that, of the five known cities called Oikhalia, the Euboian one was sacked by Herakles. The epitaph to Zeus he used applied to the god in his worship on Mount Cenaion in northwest Euboea.

ox, never yoked, to the maiden with might in her glance,
the virgin Athena.[206]

## Death of Herakles

Brash Herakles sent his herald Likhas with captive Oikhalian maidens to Trakhis and asked him to return with a wedding tunic. Likhas tried to hide his intent from Herakles's lawful wife Deianeira, but she discovered it. Upon hearing the wretched request, sorrowful Deianeira remembered the tunic the Centaur Nessos had given her. She anointed a fresh tunic with the fluids of the Centaur Nessos, hoping to restore Herakles's love for her, and gave it to Likhas. She also sent along her son Hyllos, perhaps to give Herakles pause to consider his actions.

Battle-dauntless Herakles put on his wedding tunic, and heat from the Hydra's poison immediately began to burn him. He tried to rip the tunic off, but it clung to his body at every joint and tore away his flesh. In anger he grabbed Likhas by the foot and hurled him onto the rocks below, dashing his skull into pieces and spattering the mountain with blood. No one dared approach the great hero until he was spent with throwing himself on the ground in his anguish. Then they placed him reverently upon a stretcher, and while he writhed in agony, they pondered about what to do. Finally, long-suffering Herakles sent his nephew Iolaos and his uncle Licymnios to Delphi. They came back with word that his time was at hand and he should build a pyre and die upon it.

Ready to escape the pain, Herakles demanded that the bier holding his great weight be carried up Mount Oite and be placed upon a prepared funeral pyre. Then the mighty son of Zeus cried out out in disbelief that it was not a strong-armed warrior or some giant but a woman, a weak woman, not born with the strength of men, who had vanquished him and not even with a sword. Then he called his son Hyllos to his side and bade him to marry unwilling Iole (the unhappy bride of Hyllos bore him Kleodaios, the ancestor of the Herakleids who later ruled the Peloponnesos.). Then he asked to have the pyre lit, but none dared do it. Finally, Poias of Malis had his son Philoktetes light it. In thanks Herakles gave the boy his famous

[206] Bakkhylides, "Herakles; for Delphi", in *Greek Lyric.* Translated by David A. Campbell.

bow. Then, as the flames took away his body, the immortals took his spirit to heaven (1207T/957R BCE). Herakles was welcomed on Olympos and given Hera's daughter Hebe (meaning "youth") in marriage.[207]

> In the past he wandered endlessly over the boundless earth and sea on missions ordered by lord Eurystheus, and he committed many reckless deeds and himself endured many. But now he joyously dwells in his beautiful abode on snowy Olympos with fair ankled Hebe. Hail, O lord and son of Zeus. Grant me virtue and happiness.[208]
>
> Homeric Hymn to Herakles, sixth century BCE

So it was that in only this one quest, his desire to marry the daughter of Eurytos, did Herakles fail. It was her perverse pleasure to watch him writhe painfully, poisoned accidentally by his second wife, the Aitolian princess Deianeira.

Angry young Hyllos returned home to lambaste his mother, saying that he wished she were dead or, if living, no mother of his, or that some new and better spirit would pass into her bosom. Deianeira recoiled and withdrew, realizing the Centaur's guile and her own naive mistake. With a vehement hand, she loosed the golden brooch from her robe, bearing all her left side, and drove a two-edged sword through to her heart. Hyllos then wept for his mother.

Meanwhile, the Oikhalians who escaped death or enslavement fled to other Dryopes settlements on Euboea and the Cyclades, but most sought the protection of King Eurystheus of Tiryns. Eurystheus gladly accepted Herakles's enemies as his friends and reveled in the death of his enemy. Eurystheus settled them in the cities of Asine, Hermione, and Eion. He feared that the children of Herakles (Herakleids) would grow into

[207] Herakles's demise is deeply woven with Near Eastern epic heroic myths similar to those of Gilgamesh. What he represented to the Hellenes was the hope for divinity. He was the prototype—that which is in all of us and that which transcends the mortal form. By his indomitable will he shattered the limits of religion and broke through the gulf between humanity and divinity. In many Christian households it has become common to cry out the name Jesus when seeking assistance; the Hellenes and Romans called on Herakles.

[208] Hesiod, "Homeric Hymn to Herakles", in *The Homeric Hymns and Homerica*.

powerful men and determined to kill them. He sent his herald Kopreus, son of Pelops, to bring them to him.

The herald Kopreus threatened invasion unless the Herakleids were handed over. Although Herakles's army, now led by Iolaos, swore to defend his children, without Herakles they were not intimidating. Even the support of the armies of King Ceyx of Trakhis and Dorian king Aigimios was not enough. Herakles's enemy and tormentor Eurystheus threatened war against any state that provided hospitality to the Herakleids. So they wandered from city to city like lowly refugees. Kopreus followed with the same threat to whoever gave them hospitality. Every city feared Eurystheus's army and sent them away.

## Sack of Tiryns

The Herakleids were unable to find anyone willing to take them in until they arrived at the altar of Mercy in Athens (1205T/955R BCE). The powerful king Theseus took them in and did not appreciate threats from the Tirynian king. Although not as large as Tiryns, Athens was indeed a strong polis with a proven military leader. With the added forces from Herakles's army (many of whom were from the dead hero's birthplace, Thebes) and the advantage of defense, they were a match for Eurystheus. Kopreus was sent home with a message for the king to bring it on if he dared. The Herakleids' confidence grew knowing the Thebans had defeated an Argeian invasion called the Seven against Thebes, which had been led by King Adrastos of Midea some years before.

After repeated warnings, Eurystheus finally backed up his threat to attack (1202T/952R BCE). Battle lines were drawn at Marathon, one of the few places in Attike flat enough for chariot warfare.[209] Herakles's only daughter, Deianeira's too, virgin Makris, volunteered to be a sacrifice when an oracle said that to do so would bring victory. She became a fountain nymph at Marathon. Her brother Hyllos was very much his father's son, strong and eager for battle.

[209] Euripides embellished the story of Athenian support to the Herakleid rulers of the Argeia at a time when the Athenians sought Argos's support against Sparta during the Peloponnesos War.

Image 11.2
Map of Cities Attacked between Trojan Wars (Including Year and Perpetrator)

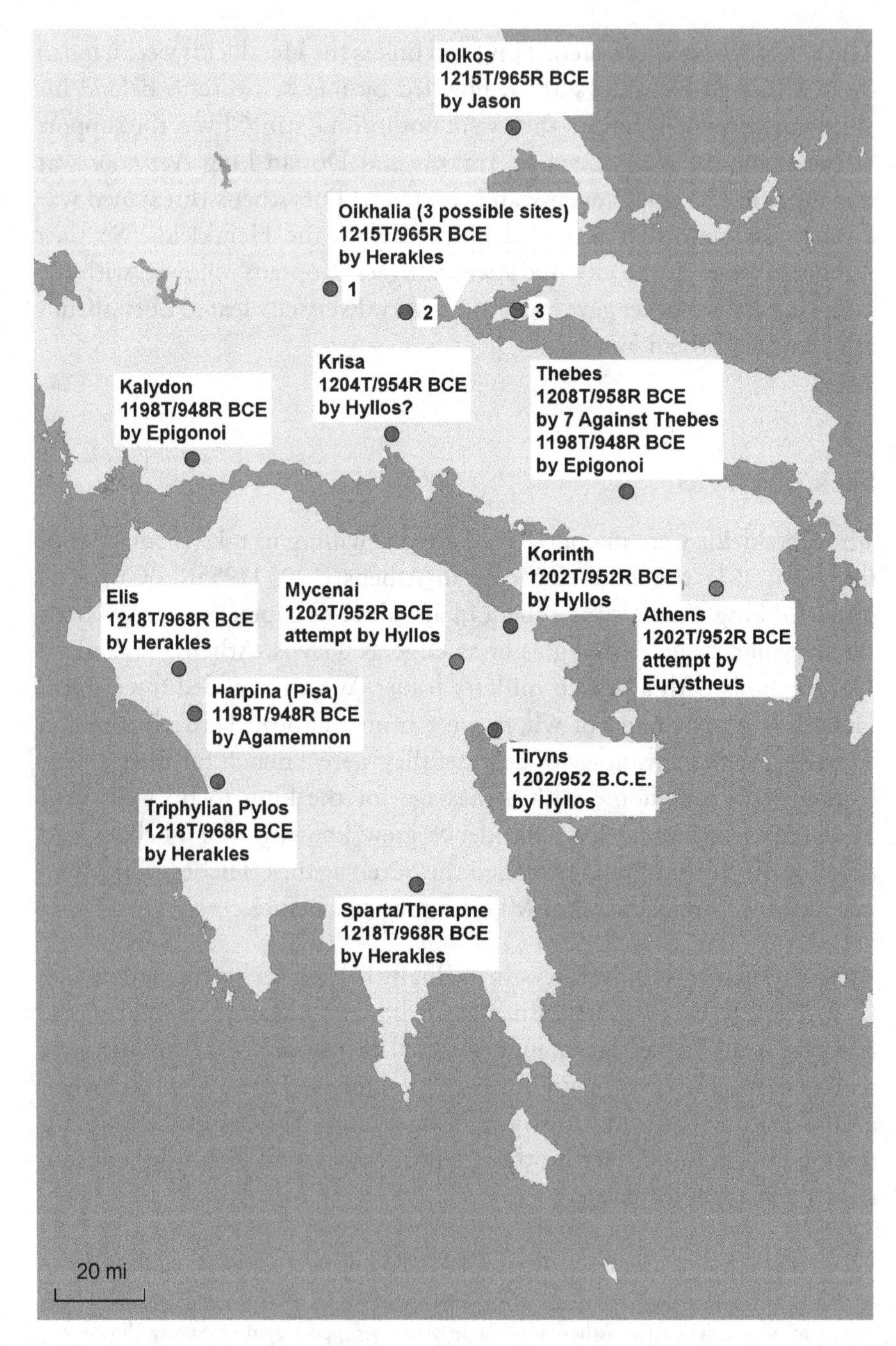

Too old to fight, Eurystheus's five sons by the Tegean princess Antimakhe led the charge. Iolaos, his youth restored for battle by divine Herakles's new wife, Hebe, led the Herakleids in his war chariot with Hyllos serving as his squire. Theseus led the Athenians on the other wing.

The defenders were victorious, and all five of Eurystheus's sons were killed (Mentor, Perimedes, Eurybios, Eurypylos [Alexandros], and Iphimedon). Eurystheus fled in his chariot with the retreating remnants of his army. Herakles's most trusted companion, Iolaos (son of Herakles's twin brother, Iphikles), and Herakles', eldest son, Hyllos, overtook and captured Eurystheus when his chariot crashed. Iolaos had Eurystheus beheaded upon the request of Herakles's mother. The victory was not without cost, as two sons of King Aigimios of Doris (Pamphylos and Dymas) died fighting. The three Dorian subtribes are named for the inheritors of Herakles and Aigimios: Hyllos, Pamphylos, and Dymas.

There was no army prepared to stop the Herakleids, and they marched unopposed into the Peloponnesos and conquered Tiryns. Hyllos assumed his birthright as leader of the Herakleids and was crowned king of Tiryns, the second largest city in all of Europe. One year later, a plague broke out. Hyllos sought the reason in Delphi and was told that the Herakleids had returned too soon. He was instructed to leave and return during the third harvest.

Hyllos led most of the Herakleids back to Marathon, where they waited. Some of the Herakleids chose to remain in Tiryns under Akhaian rule. Herakles's old mother, Alkmene, and his uncle Licymnios were among those who stayed behind in the city of their birth.

## Sack of Iolkos

Meanwhile, in the northern palace city of Iolkos, King Akastos, son of Pelias, ruled. Akastos had been an Argonaut and hunted in the Kalydonian boar hunt. When fellow Argonaut Peleus, son of Aiakos, accidentally killed his benefactor, King Iphitos of Phthia (Thessalian Akhaia), during the boar hunt, Akastos graciously offered him hospitality. When they arrived in Iolkos, Akastos performed the rite of purification for Peleus. When word came that Peleus was to remain in exile for a period of atonement, Akastos let him stay in Iolkos. Akastos's shapely wife, Astydameia, a blood relation of her husband through Kretheus, grew fond of Peleus, but his honor kept him from being seduced.

The spurned Astydameia hissed a lie to Peleus's wife that her husband had agreed to divorce her now that Astydameia's daughter Sterope had come of age. Then the scheming queen told her noble husband Akastos that Peleus had tried to rape her. Akastos was furious but dared not break the laws of hospitality by killing Peleus in his home. Using his friendship, he challenged unsuspecting Peleus to a hunting contest on Mount Pelion,[210] which was still inhabited by hostile Centaurs. Peleus easily won the hunt and celebrated with a large quantity of wine. Then, during the night, Akastos gathered all the weapons and left Peleus behind naked and alone. When Peleus awoke, he found himself surrounded by hostile Centaurs, just as Akastos planned. They remembered the havoc Peleus had wreaked on their brethren during the wedding of Peirithoos, and they would surely have tortured and killed him except for the opportune arrival of the wise Centaur Kheiron. Kheiron intervened on behalf of Peleus, securing his release and finding his sword. The wise Centaur told Peleus that if he were ever to need a wife that he should go to see the old man of the sea. Peleus was married and thought nothing of the remark until he returned home to find that his wife had hanged herself in grief (having believed the malicious lie that Peleus was about to divorce her).

King Akastos returned home to his wife, strong sons, and three daughters (including Sterope). Their daughter Sthenele married Prince Menoitios of Lokris and was the mother of Akhilleus's famous charioteer, Patroklos. Akastos's youngest daughter, Laodameia, never knew her parents, because they died while she was little. She loved her husband, King Protesilaos of Akhaia, and committed suicide upon hearing of his death in the Trojan War.

Peleus's thoughts turned next to revenge, for he was angry over the treachery of Akastos and his queen. He gathered a mighty army that included the Argonaut captain Jason and the Dioskouroi of Sparta, and he attacked Iolkos. Akastos bravely led the resistance but was killed by his former friend Peleus. The battle lost, Iolkos sued for peace (1215T/965R BCE). To spare the city, it was agreed that Astydameia would be executed.

---

[210] The name of the mountain is derived from "Peleus."

A large amount of booty was collected and handed over to Peleus.[211] With Peleus's blessings, a neighboring Pelasgian tribe called the Haimonians took over the city. The Haimonians controlled the city only briefly before the sons of Akastos recovered it.

---

Exhibit 11.2
Marriage of Peleus and Thetis

Both Zeus and Poseidon desired the lovely Nereid Thetis until Prometheus told them that the son of Thetis was destined to be greater than his father. To prevent such a child from threatening the gods, Hera, who had raised Thetis as a girl, was charged with finding a suitable mortal husband for her. She picked heroic Peleus. Peleus pinned down the old man of the sea and learned that the gods had decreed that he should marry beautiful Thetis so long as he could hold on to her. Proitos warned Peleus to wait in ambush at the cave at Sepia on the ocean slopes of Mount Pelion and wrestle her, and to beware that she would assume many forms.

Peleus waited as instructed and watched as the beautiful goddess, whose form had attracted the kings of both heaven and sea, ascended out of the ocean to sun herself naked on the deserted beach. The sensual sight made him weak in a way no battle ever had. He steadied his stout heart, and once she was comfortably situated, he crept forward. He grabbed hold of the tan Nereid and held on tight as the athletic nymph struggled unsuccessfully to break his hold. Then, just as the old man of the sea had warned, she assumed various forms, but Peleus held on through them all. Enamored by his prowess, she returned to her divine form, and their struggle melted into a passionate, salty embrace (1217T/967R BCE)

The greatest mortal wedding since Kadmos had married the daughter of golden-helmeted Ares and laugher-loving Aphrodite was celebrated. Most of the gods and many distinguished mortals attended the reception in front of Kheiron's cave on Mount Pelion. The couple received many splendid gifts. Among the best gifts presented were the immortal pair of talking horses Balios and Xanthos, which the earth-shaker Poseidon gave. The craftsmen god Hephaistos gave Peleus a fabulously inlaid dagger and an

---

[211] Archaeological evidence concurs that Iolkos was sacked during LHIIIC, which began in 1195T/945R BCE).

impressive suit of armor for his new horses, and Kheiron whittled an ashen shaft that bright Athena polished and Hephaistos fitted with a spearhead. The eager groom awaited his chance to clasp his bride again.

But the happy celebrations were marred when Eris (meaning "discord") arrived. She was quite distressed at not having received an invitation, and she arrived unannounced with a gift—an apple she slyly said was for the fairest. Athena, Hera, and Aphrodite each claimed it, and an argument ensued that was not decided until Paris of Troy was made judge. Paris picked golden Aphrodite—who could fault him?—and that led to the Trojan War.

Like the wedding, Peleus and silver-sandaled Thetis's marriage was plagued by discord. Peleus returned home to his envious subjects, all of whom were taken by the beauty of his stupendous wife and by the rich treasures he had taken from Iolkos. To be sure, Thetis was a marvel for the eye to behold, but within their palace her resentment showed. She treated her husband with disdain, for she considered him a brutish mortal, one not worthy of her. Though her lovely form reclined dutifully across his couch, she felt nothing but disgust for the act.

---

## Oidipous's Crime Exposed

Meanwhile, Thebes was beset with calamities of its own (1218T/968R–1217T/967R BCE). As the fifth century playwrite Sophokles of Kolonos wrote of the plague, "By such deaths, past numbering, the city perishes: unpitied, her children lie on the ground, spreading pestilence, with none to mourn." [212]

Wise king Oidipous had ruled for many years over a city that prospered by providing mercenaries to Herakles's armies. But Herakles was dead, and the unwitting crime of Oidipous caused the city's fortunes to decline. The populace beseeched King Oidipous, who sent his brother-in-law Kreon to Delphi to find out why the Stronger Ones were angry with them.

[212] Sophokles, "Oidipous the King", in *The Complete Plays of Sophocles*. Translated by Sir Richard Claverhouse Jebb.

Kreon returned with the message that Laios's murderer, who remained among the Thebans, must be punished. Oidipous figured that if anyone could solve this riddle, it would be blind Teiresias. He summoned the old seer to the palace to question him.

Old Teiresias had figured it out all right, but he hesitated to tell. The prophet discerned that Oidipous himself was the guilty party. Teiresias knew the truth would be devastating and decided the plague was better. Oidipous sensed that grey-haired Teiresias was keeping something from him. He goaded the old man until Teiresias blurted out in anger that the king himself was the murderer.

Oidipous was stunned by Teiresias's declaration. Feeling the weight of his own sad fate pressing down upon him from all around, he reacted with uncustomary rage. Claiming that Teiresias was lying to help Kreon seize the throne, he threw them both in jail for conspiracy. After the guards had taken the prisoners away Jokaste soothed and reassured her king. Realizing his own error, he had the prisoners released and personally apologized. Then Oidipous questioned Jokaste in detail as to what Laios was like. A gnawing struck his belly, as he could no longer deny to himself the possible truth.

News arrived from Sicyon that Oidipous's father, Polybos, had died and the throne was his. Oidipous felt sorrow for the death of his beloved father but was also relieved that the terrible prophecy that he would kill his father had not come to pass. Oidipous declined the throne but questioned the heralds in detail. His relief was dashed when the sad news came out that Polybos was not his natural father. The evidence turned bleak. Jokaste beseeched Oidipous to call off the investigation. The king would not shirk his responsibility, even if the outcome was horrific.

Oidipous's relentless search finally uncovered what they all feared—that he had indeed killed his father and married his mother. The final evidence came when the servant who had escaped at Laios's death changed his story. Under threat of torture, he admitted that only one man had overpowered Laios. Jokaste ran away screaming down the hall to her bedchambers. Oidipous rushed after her, and upon opening the chamber doors,

> there he beheld the woman hanging by the neck in a twisted noose of swinging cords. But he, when he saw her, with a dread deep cry of misery loosed the halter by

> which she hung. When the hapless woman was stretched upon the ground, and then was the sequel dread to see. He tore from her raiment the golden brooches with which she was decked, and lifted them, and smote full on his own eyeballs, uttering words like these: "No more shall you behold such horrors as I was suffering and working! Long enough have you looked on those whom you ought never to have seen, failed in knowledge of those whom I yearned to know: henceforth you shall be dark!"
>
> To such dire refrain not once alone but oft he struck his eyes with lifted hand. At each blow the ensanguined eyeballs bedewed his beard; no sluggish drops of gore were sent forth, but all at once a dark shower of blood came down like hail. [213]

The sons of Oidipous were shamelessly delighted. Blinded by their own greed to rule, they did not listen to the warning given them by the seer Teiresias to not evoke their father's rage. Callously, they had the guards imprison their father until his fate was decided. Angry Oidipous prayed they would never divide their father's goods in loving brotherhood, but instead that war and fighting might ever be the portion of them both.

## Oidipous Banished

Reluctantly, and upon the deposed king's own wishes, Kreon banished Oidipous to end the plague (1217T/967R BCE). Only Oidipous's daughters did not treat the once popular king as some kind or monster or leper. Oidipous was crushed that his own twin sons had no pity whatsoever for their father even when he was banished into the cold. It was as if they had trampled upon his eyes as they fell from his face. Antigone alone accompanied him. Meanwhile, the twin sons of Oidipous plotted misfortune for each other. Wise Teiresias counseled them with gentle words, checking the twins from strife, bidding them to shake lots and for

[213] Sophokles, "Oidipous the King", in *The Complete Plays of Sophocles*. Translated by Sir Richard Claverhouse Jebb.

the loser to take the gold and flocks and depart. The twins agreed to rule in alternate years. Eteokles lost the toss and departed.

Wandering through blistering summer and bitter winter on both sides of the Cithairon Mountains, Oidipous could not rest, for "Unwearied wings, the fierce daylight of the mind hovered around him, and the Avenging Furies of his crimes assailed his heart."[214]

Yet over the years he came to realize that he was not to blame for a crime he had committed in complete innocence. Still the Thebans continued to treat him as if he were a monster and refused to take him back. The abandonment he experienced was nearly unbearable. Antigone cared for him lovingly, and his younger daughter Ismene would come often with news and supplies. The news she brought concerning her brothers was not good. The older (by minutes) and more mature Polyneices ruled for a year (1217T/967R–1216T/966R BCE) as Eteokles went into the agreed-upon exile with the inheritance of Harmonia as collateral. Eteokles returned at the end of the year, and Polyneices handed over the scepter as agreed. Polyneices left with the family heirlooms and traveled to Midea, whose king, Adrastos, was famous for his hospitality.

On a gusty fall evening, King Adrastos was drawn to his gate by the sound of a vicious fight outside. He watched as two proud young noblemen fought fiercely over meager shelter from a gathering storm. As Adrastos watched, he noticed that the emblem on the taller combatant's shield was that of a lion while the other's was a boar. Remembering the oracle's advice to him to marry his daughters to a lion and a boar, Adrastos had the men separated at once. Eagerly the king asked of their lineage. First spoke Polyneices, son of Oidipous. The other knight, who, though smaller in frame, had shown the greater valor despite his young age, was Tydeus, son of King Oineus of Aitolian Kalydon.

Adrastos knew the families of both men well. Oidipous's adopted father, King Polydoros of Sicyon had accepted Adrastos as supplicant when his brother-in-law Amphiaraos seized Midea in a coup and forced him to flee. Polydoros even gave him his kingdom when Oidipous chose to remain in Thebes (1217T/967R BCE). Adrastos did not stay long in Sicyon, as the Midean nobles forced Amphiaraos to allow Adrastos to return as king.

[214] Statios of Neapolis (Naples), "Thebaid" i.

Adrastos was also well aware of King Oineus of Kalydon, whose eldest son, Meleagros, had led the Aitolians to victory over the Kouretes and whose daughter Deianeira had married Herakles.

A great wedding feast was prepared. Argeia was married to Polyneices, and Deipyle to Tydeus[215] (1216T/966R BCE). Both girls had recently begun to menstruate, and that cost them the rest of their childhood. Polyneices left the next spring to rule Thebes as he and his twin brother had agreed. To Polyneices's surprise, the gates were barred to him, and he returned to Midea cursing his brother's treachery and swearing revenge. Adrastos brashly swore to place his sons-in-law back upon their rightful thrones. Adrastos's boastful oath unwittingly promised him a crop of bitter tears.

## Fight for the Kingdom

The problem with Adrastos's oath was that, king though he was, he could not order his army into war without the approval of either his sister Eriphyle or her husband Amphiaraos, son of Oikles and Hypermnestra. Amphiaraos's mother was a princess of the Kouretes (bitter enemies of the Aitolians), and he was not willing to help any Aitolian. Besides not wanting to help Tydeus for tribal reasons, Amphiaraos's clear vision saw trouble in the undertaking. This unique power-sharing arrangement came about as follows.

Amphiaraos, whose father, Oikles, died in battle serving in Herakles's army attacking Troy, gained a reputation for manly prowess because of his exploits during the Kalydon boar hunt. In a competition before the hunt, Amphiaraos won the leaping contest. During the hunt, Amphiaraos distinguished himself by being the second to draw blood. His arrow struck the boar's eye. Unfortunately, an argument flared during festivities after the hunt. Arguments were inevitable between the rival Aitolians and Kouretes. Returning in glory from the hunt, Amphiaraos learned that the argument had led to bloodshed. His uncles had been slain during the battle.

---

[215] Theokritos, in "Young Herakles", in *The Idylls of Theocritus*. Translated by Thelma Sargent. Theokritos says that Tydeus was given the estate of the exiled warrior Kastor, son of Hippalos. Theokritos says, erroneously, that the exiled Kastor taught young Herakles hand-to-hand battle skills in Thebes, but Herakles was nearly a generation older than Tydeus.

These exploits earned Amphiaraos the position of polemarch of Midea and the hand of King Adrastos's sister in marriage. Mighty as he was, Amphiaraos was more famous for his prowess as a seer. Loved by Zeus and Apollo, Amphiaraos first received the grace of divine vision while visiting Prince Oidipous of Sicyon just before he left Sicyon to fulfill his destiny in Thebes. Over the years, he had refined his prophetic skills such that he had become the best seer in Hellas. His specialty was divining dreams.

Amphiaraos's ambitious wife, Eriphyle, convinced him to lead a popular coup against her brother. Adrastos fled in a cart pulled by the great steed Arion to the Mycenaian vassal state Sicyon.[216] He knew that the old king Polybos had only one son, Oidipous, who had chosen to rule in far-off Thebes. Although an exile, Adrastos knew his chance of obtaining the Sicyon crown was good because his maternal grandmother was a Sicyonian noble and because of his ties to the rulers of Mycenai and Midea. Sure enough, when Polybos died and Oidipous declined to abdicate the Theban throne to inherit the Sicyonian crown, Adrastos became the king of Sicyonia and instituted famous games (1217T/967R BCE).[217] Believing Adrastos's success was a sign of his destiny to rule, the nobles of Midea pressured Amphiaraos into a compromise to bring Adrastos home. Under the compromise agreement, Adrastos received his old title as king after only a few months as king of Sicyon. But if his decisions were contrary to Amphiaraos's wishes, then Amphiaraos's wife, Eriphyle, would break the tie. Eriphyle was considered a neutral tiebreaker since she was Adrastos's sister as well as Amphiaraos's wife. This gave Eriphyle unparalleled power for a Hellenic woman in the Bronze Age.

Amphiaraos's specialty was the interpretation of dreams, and his own nightmares told him that Adrastos's swaggering boast would be the cause of his own death. He tried to warn Adrastos, but Adrastos believed Amphiaraos was just saying this to avoid helping his enemy Tydeus. Unable to convince Adrastos otherwise, Amphiaraos forestalled the event by voting

---

[216] Horse-drawn two-wheeled war chariots debuted in Troy around 1735T/1485R BCE but were not commonly used around the Aigaian until the rise of Mycenai (1580T/1330R BCE). Horseback riding did not reach Hellas until sometime after the Trojan War ended (1184T/934R BCE), either just before or just after the Mycenaian civilization collapsed. Chariot warfare is unique to the Late Bronze Age.

[217] The Sicyonian Games, like the Panathenaic Games of Athens and the Heraion Games in Argos, were popular but never quite secured the status awarded to the Panhellenic games at Olympia, Delphi, Nemea, and Korinth (Isthmos).

against the expedition. With the kings divided, Eriphyle sided with her husband, and no war preparations were made. Amphiaraos knew he could not deny fate, but a sly smile crossed his face, as he knew that delaying an undesirable fate was the best that the Olympians themselves could do.

So Adrastos was unable to authorize war. Polyneices and Tydeus waited, exasperated, for the stalemate to end. Amphiaraos did agree to let Tydeus go as ambassador to Eteokles and the elders of Thebes. During games that were held during Tydeus's stay, he demonstrated his physical prowess. At diplomacy, though, Tydeus failed. Polyneices and Adrastos then thought to consult with Herakles, but they learned of his recent death. During the delay, Polyneices raised his young sons Thersandros and Adrastos.

Ill-fated Oidipous became ill during his harsh years in exile. When the oracle of Ismenion Apollo in Thebes predicted that Oidipous was going to die at Kolonos in Attike, King Eteokles sent Kreon to fetch his father, having learned from seers that whichever son had his blessing would prevail. Ismene reached her father with the news before Kreon arrived. Oidipous dispatched a plea for help to King Theseus. Then Kreon arrived and pleaded with Oidipous to come live near Thebes. Kreon said that because of the pollution, though, Oidipous would not be welcomed in the city proper. Oidipous refused to go, saying the Thebans had abandoned him during his exile and that they were still holding back their acceptance.

Meanwhile, impatient Polyneices sought the gods' advice to resolve his predicament. An Argeian oracle gave the same clue as did the Ismenion oracle of Apollo: the son who had his father's blessing would succeed. So he traveled to meet Oidipous, who understood his son's motives for now visiting him. Oidipous refused to meet with his son until Antigone pleaded so adamantly that he consented out of love for her. Polyneices apologized for not coming to his father's aid earlier but promised support now. Oidipous was disgusted with his son's insincerity and cursed both of his sons. Antigone pleaded with Polyneices not to attack the city of his birth, but he said he had to do it to save face. The two siblings hugged and cried. On the way back to Midea Polyneices went to meet the great hero Theseus of Athens out of respect and told him of his father's grave condition.

Kreon, uncle and brother-in-law of Oidipous (as well as his longtime supporter), did not let his feelings get in the way of his duty. He was a good soldier who did not feel his own morals should be different than what the state required. Against his own desire, he seized Oidipous and his two daughters when they refused to come willingly (for Eteokles, too, was acting upon the oracular prediction that victory would come to the son with Oidipous's blessing). Theseus arrived just in time to demand that Kreon leave Athenian territory at once. Back home the Thebans exiled Kreon for failing to bring back Oidipous.

Oidipous died, as foretold, at Kolonos (in Attike) and was believed to have been taken away by the gods (1208T/958R BCE). Only Theseus knew the exact spot from whence he ascended. Oidipous received cult worship at Kolonos.[218] Upon hearing of his death, neither of his sons felt remorse for his actions, and neither felt the need to pay his respects. Antigone returned home to Thebes to try to stop the impending war. There Eteokles sponsored funeral games to try to gain public appeasement from his father's ghost.

The Midean warlord Amphiaraos understood much about his fate and how others were ensnared by it too. Still, no man sees his fate clearly, just as the wind cannot be seen clearly; we only glimpse it in the trees and thereby perceive its strength. Just as men gather around a mighty fallen oak after a gale to reflect in awe at the unseen power that brought it down, so now Amphiaraos went to attend the funeral of Polyneices's mighty old father, Oidipous. Amphiaraos was well aware that current events had been set in place a long time before, back to the day when the Stronger Ones brought gifts to die for at the wedding of Kadmos and Harmonia. Amphiaraos knew that he, like those before him, would fall like a domino in the chain of necessity. A stale breeze raised the hair on his neck as he viewed once mighty Oidipous's crumpled corpse.

[218] The story of Oidipous is the first part of the Theban Cycle, an important early oral myth narrative placed chronologically between the Herakles Cycle and the Trojan War Cycle. The Theban Cycle was written down in four poems, the first about Oidipous (*Oidipodia*), the second regarding the fight over Thebes by his sons (*Thebaid*), the third detailing the sack of Thebes in the next generation (*Epigonoi*), and the last about the madness of the Epigonoi leader Alkmeon (*Alkmeonis*). None of these poems survive. The Theban Cycle was largely preserved by Athenian playwrights Aiskhylos and Sophokles. Aiskhylos wrote a trilogy called Oidipodia (containing *Laios*, *Oidipous*, and the surviving *Seven against Thebes*), and Sophokles wrote a surviving trilogy on Thebes (containing *Oidipous the King*, *Oidipous at Kolonai*, and *Antigone*) and lost plays, such as *Epigonoi* and *Alkmeon*. The Thebans are cast in a poor light, and a noble role for the Athenian hero Theseus was inserted. Statios of Neapolis wrote an epic poem entitled *Thebaid* in the first century CE.

Amphiaraos returned to find the army preparing to march upon Thebes. The furious Amphiaraos demanded to know who had authorized war. He was informed that during his absence, Eriphyle had changed her vote to war. Dumbfounded, Amphiaraos sat and listened to how Polyneices had ended the stalemate. Polyneices had followed the consul of King Iphis of nearby Argos (son of Alektor, son of Anaxagoras, son of Megapenthes, son of Proitos, who had wrestled the city from his twin brother, Akrisios) and bribed Eriphyle, his own wife, with a gorgeous family heirloom, the necklace Harmonia wore on her wedding day. It was none other than the craftsman of the Olympians, Hephaistos himself, who had sculpted it. Eriphyle was so taken by its beauty that she gladly risked her husband's life in battle to possess it.

## Seven against Thebes

Adrastos assembled an impressive army that included many of the leading warriors from the area. Because seven major leaders fought in this army, the expedition was called the Seven against Thebes. Adrastos divided the Midean forces among captains chosen from among the descendants of Talaos.

| | |
|---|---|
| 1) Amphiaraos | Brother-in-law of Adrastos and second in command |
| 2) Mecisteus | Brother of Adrastos |
| 3) Hippomedon | Son of Adrastos's brother Aristomakhos, who lived near Lerne |

Chief among the allies were the Argives, whose king, Iphis, provided the ruse to get the campaign rolling. The allied leaders were the following:

| | |
|---|---|
| 4) Kapaneus | Polemarch of Argos and the tallest soldier |
| 5) Polyneices | Leading his loyal followers from Thebes |
| 6) Tydeus | Leading Aitolian followers and expecting to be restored in Kalydon after Polyneices was restored in Thebes |
| 7) Parthenopaios | Close companion of Telephos who led Arkadian bowmen from Orkhomenos |

Joining the expedition were two young warriors of noble background who were not yet chieftains:

| | |
|---|---|
| Eteokles | The crown prince of Argos went under the tutelage of Kapaneus. |
| Lykourgos | His father, Pronax, brother of Adrastos, had recently died. |

The army's first day's march ended at Nemea, where Amphiaraos's son-in-law Lykourgos ruled. Lykourgos had led Thessalian settlers to repopulate the area after Herakles killed the Nemean Lion on his first labor. Black omens followed the army. While camped in Nemea, King Lykourgos and Queen Eurydice's infant son and heir died of a snakebite. This infant child, Opheltes, had not even learned to crawl yet. They buried him upon a bed of parsley.

---

Exhibit 11.3
Fate of Hypsipyle

Queen Hypsipyle ruled Lemnos when the Argonauts arrived and found the place devoid of men. She bore Jason two sons—Euneos and Nebrophonos. She continued to rule for years after the Argonauts departed until the women of Lemnos discovered that she had saved her father when the other women killed the men off. In anger they sold her off as a slave. She was purchased by the king of Nemea and forced to care for his son. When the boy died from a snakebite, the king decided to have old Hypsipyle killed for neglect. Alerted by Dionysos, Euneos and Nebrophonos arrived and ransomed their mother.

---

Amphiaraos said the child's death was an omen to turn back. Adrastos refused and instead initiated the Nemean Games to appease the baby's ghost. The locals and the army competed. These games became important Panhellenic games during historic times.

The army marched north until they reached Mount Cithairon. There, with Thebes visible in the plain below, they stopped and made camp. Tydeus was sent a second time as an envoy to intimidate the Thebans into capitulating, but the brave Theban warriors did not back down. Instead

Eteokles responded by sending fifty young soldiers under Kreon's grandson Maion to ambush and kill Tydeus after he left. Maion's father, Haimon, had been killed by the Sphinx, and he had been raised by his grandfather Kreon. Tydeus turned the tables and killed his attackers, sparing only Maion to send back word for the Thebans to expect their doom.

Eteokles had been resolutely planning for this war since the day he broke his oath and drove his brother away. He enlisted Phocian and Phlegyan (Minyan) mercenaries to bolster his forces. He recalled Kreon home from exile to advise him. As the battle drew near, Eteokles paused and ordered Kreon not to bury Polyneices should Eteokles die and the Thebans win. Then, fearlessly, he led his forces out to face the Akhaians invaders. When the Thebans saw the size of the army facing them, their spirits sank. Kreon suggested that they had a better chance to prevail if fighting from behind their walls. Quickly overmatched, the Thebans fled behind their walls. Adrastos established a command post on the plain and sent his captains to attack each of the seven gates.

Eteokles exhorted his cowering comrades behind the walls, bellowing for them not to give up. Then he prayed. Finally, rallying behind his command, troops with brave resolve were placed at each gate under a fierce champion:

| **Gate** | **Champions** |
|---|---|
| Elektra (SE) | Melanippos, son of Astakos of the Spartoi |
| Proitos or Proixidian (E) | Periklymenos, son of Poseidon and Historis, and noble Aktor |
| Ogygian (NE) | Ismaros, son of Astakos, and Hyperbios, son of Oinops |
| Homoloides or Krenidan (N) | Megareus, son of Kreon and Lasthenes, who had an old man's heart in a young man's body |
| Neistan (W) | Amphidokos, son of Astakos. |
| Onkredan or Spring (SW) | Leades, son of Astakos |
| Hypsistan or High (S)* | King Eteokles |

* It was from the south that the Akhaians came.

Still, when Eteokles realized the devastation that might befall his kingdom, he reconsidered. He sent word to Polyneices that he would honor their agreement to share the throne. Eteokles also offered his brother compensation for having seized the throne unfairly. Polyneices smelled victory and responded by saying that that it was too late for anything less than unconditional surrender.

Upon hearing Polyneices's reply, the old seer Teiresias was consulted. He gave the city hope by declaring that the city would be saved if the virgin Menoiceus, son of Kreon, were to sacrifice himself. Without hesitation, the youth fell upon his sword.

Eteokles then suggested to the city elders that he face Polyneices alone to decide the issue. The elders did not approve, fearing for their own safety should Eteokles lose. Overriding their concerns, Eteokles reminded Kreon not to bury Polyneices and confidently strode out of the Hypsistan Gate armed and alone. As the Akhaian army bore down on him, Eteokles issued a challenge to face his despised twin brother in single combat to decide the issue. Polyneices was eager to kill his brother and accepted.

As the Akhaians sat down to watch and the Thebans observed from atop of their walls, the twins engaged. Equal in ability and ferocity, they fought. All watched in amazement as each dug deeper into his store of hate and rage to launch yet another attack. Finally, as they pulled each other's hair out with one hand, they stabbed each other with the other. Both died.

Before the stunned Akhaians could regroup, a grandson of Teiresias distinguished himself. Periklymenos's father was Poseidon, and his mother was Teiresias's daughter Historis. Periklymenos threw a well-aimed rock that killed the Arkadian mercenary leader Parthenopaios as he tried to scale the walls. The Akhaians suddenly lost their confidence and began to fall back, believing that the Deathless Ones themselves were against them. The exuberant Thebans jumped down from their walls with a shout and gave pursuit.

Melanippos (meaning "black horse") was first to engage the Akhaians, killing the Midean warrior Mecisteus, brother of King Adrastos. Adrastos's nephew Lykourgos was killed by Ismaros. The Akhaians' withdrawal continued until valiant Tydeus turned upon his attackers like an angry bear will when tormented by snapping hounds. He slew the Theban champion Melanippos. Tydeus was close to winning himself immortal fame but for his affront to bright Athena.

The surprised Akhaians were confident in their numbers and chose to attack and loot the city even with Polyneices gone. They began to scale the walls, and the outlook for Thebes was grim. Kreon's son Megareus was slain, and the Akhaian warlord Kapaneus of Midea became the first to scale the walls. Atop the Elektra Gate, Kapaneus paused to boast that even the Deathless Ones could not stop him now. In the time it takes for lightning to crash, Kapaneus lay crumpled on the ground. Lord Zeus made sure that proud Kapaneus regretted his words as he bit the dust, gasping out his own death. The bolt recharged the Theban warriors, who recognized divine support. Conversely, the Akhaians were seized with foreboding.

The tide of battle may have turned again, except for the self-destructive actions of the seer Amphiaraos. While Tydeus was stripping the armor off of Melanippos, who had slightly wounded Tydeus, Amphiaraos rode up and suggested to the man he despised that he eat the brains of his vanquished foe and gain his power. His wits failed him where his strong arm had not, and Tydeus cut open Melanippos's head and gulped down the bloody gore. Momentarily losing focus on the battle at hand, Tydeus was killed by an arrow shot by an alert Theban archer.

Dark Amphiaraos smiled as Tydeus crashed into the dust, unconcerned by the horror that squeaked from the voices of the Akhaian forces. One and all, they dropped their swords and shields and ran for their lives. The shouting Thebans cut down all that were too slow. Ismaros slew Hippomedon, Leades slew the Argive Eteokles, Periklymenos chased after Amphiaraos, and Midean king Adrastos fled in a gleaming chariot pulled by his fast horse Arion.

Amphiaraos's chariot was slowed by the mud along the river, and the Thebans caught up to him. King Zeus did not wish for Periklymenos to kill the great seer Amphiaraos, who had not wanted this war. So the son of Kronos caused the ground to open and swallow Amphiaraos. On that spot an oracle arose (the Thebans were not allowed to consult it). So it was that Adrastos, alone among the Akhaian leaders, got away safely.

## Tragic Aftermath

The celebrating Thebans named Kreon regent for Eteokles's young son by a Spartoi bride: Laodamas. Kreon kept his word and left Polyneices and the other slain invaders to rot or be eaten by the dogs and vultures. In contrast, Eteokles and the other fallen Thebans were given elaborate funeral honors. Teiresias warned that not allowing proper burials would bring disaster. Kreon countered that to allow burial of Polyneices and his supporters would be condoning those who acted in treason by attacking his own city.

Oidipous's daughter Antigone challenged Kreon, saying the decree was unjust. When he refused her request she stormed out defiantly while her fiancé, Haimon, pleaded with his father, saying that bending trees survive longer than unyielding ones. Kreon would not budge.

Antigone asked her sister Ismene to help bury Polyneices in spite of the consequences. Angry Antigone wanted the whole world to see her pious act. The state was wrong, she said, to deny a family the right to bury their own. Ismene was afraid and tried to talk Antigone out of disobedience, saying it is one's duty to honor the laws of the state. Antigone countered by stating that moral law stands above civil laws. Ismene realized Antigone's mind was made up and convinced her to bury Polyneices secretly, hoping she would escape punishment. Ismene wished to save her sister and correctly pointed out that acting in defiance would be boastful and angry, and therefore morally impure. So Antigone buried Polyneices in a secret, solemn ceremony.[219]

When the Thebans discovered that Polyneices had been buried, Kreon figured that Antigone was to blame and had her arrested. When charged, she freely admitted her guilt. When Kreon also indicted Ismene, Antigone convinced him that she had worked alone. Despite Ismene's pleas for leniency, Kreon had Antigone buried alive in her tomb. Haimon told Kreon the whole town was against him on this one, but Kreon stubbornly refused to back down and lose face. Haimon stormed out, and Ismene offered to share her sister's fate, but Antigone would not have it.

[219] A proper burial was vitally important to the Hellenes. Without one, a soul would sit forever on the far banks of the Styx River, denied access to Hades.

Adrastos, meanwhile, had gone to King Theseus of Athens to protest the sacrilege against his fallen soldiers. Theseus traveled to Thebes and threatened war. With dissidence at home and a new threat from abroad, Kreon could now see the problems Teiresias had warned of and relented.

Kreon hastily opened Antigone's tholos tomb and found Haimon there, crying on Antigone's lifeless body. Haimon had already opened her tomb and found that his beloved had committed suicide. Haimon, with fierce eyes, spit in his father's face and

> drew his cross-hilted sword. As his father rushed forth in flight he missed his aim; then, luckless man, angry with himself he straightaway leaned with all his weight against his sword and drove it, half its length, into his side. While sense lingered he clasped the maiden to his faint embrace, and as he gasped sent forth on her pale cheek the swift stream of his oozing blood.[220]

When Kreon's wife, Eurydice, heard the news, she too blamed Kreon and committed suicide. Kreon's own grandson Maion buried Tydeus in thanks for Tydeus having once spared his life. Kreon remained in the palace, knowing a despair Oidipous had known. He built a tomb to Oidipous outside the city, hoping to appease his ghost but still fearful of polluting the city by building his tomb within the city (fear of pollution also caused the Thebans to build the tomb of King Amphion outside of the city walls).

Adrastos took his fallen comrades to Eleusis and, with Theseus's permission, buried them with honors (except Amphiaraos and his charioteer Baton, whom the earth had swallowed). As the remnant slowly marched home to Argeia, Kreon ruled over Thebes, grimly waiting the day the Akhaians would return with vengeance. A few years later, he died a broken old man. Eteokles's young son Laodamas became king.

## Epigonoi (Sack of Thebes)

Ten years passed and the Epigonoi (meaning "orphaned sons") grew into strong men with an angry purpose. Alone among the Epigonoi, Alkmeon,

[220] Sophokles, *Antigone*.

son of Amphiaraos, did not wish to fight. It was not that he was weak; in fact, he was the best fighter among them. It was just that he did not see a reason to fight other than revenge, which was not enough—especially since his father had opposed the first invasion. The other Epigonoi were eager for battle, but they could not carry out the expedition without Alkmeon's approval, since he had inherited his father's share of the kingdom. Besides, an oracle told Polyneices's son Thersandros that only with Amphiaraos's son Alkmeon in command would the Epigonoi succeed.

| **Epigonoi** | **Father** | **Polis** |
|---|---|---|
| Alkmeon and Amphilokhos | Amphiaraos | Midea |
| Aigialeus | Adrastos | Midea |
| Polydoros | Hippomedon | Midea |
| Sthenelos | Kapaneus | Argos |
| Euryalos | Mecistheus | Midea |
| Thersandros | Polyneices | Thebes |
| Diomedes | Tydeus | Kalydon |
| Promakhos | Parthenopaios | Orkhomenos |

Alkmeon was a powerful warrior, but like his father, he had no wish to fight at Thebes. Amphilokhos, a superb seer like his father had been, encouraged his brother Alkmeon to fight. When his encouragements failed, Thersandros used the tried-and-true trick of bribery that his father had successfully employed. Thersandros gave Alkmeon's mother, Eriphyle, the rest of Harmonia's inheritance (the robe). She then convinced her dutiful son Alkmeon to fight, and King Adrastos of Midea, the only surviving leader of the previous battle, began preparations for war.[221]

Upon arriving in the Theban Plain, the Akhaians razed the surrounding villages and destroyed the fortress of Eutresis (Plataia). Among the

[221] The owners of the inheritance of Harmonia did not fare well. Alkmeon would kill his mother and take the gifts to his first wife. Later, Alkmeon was killed by first wife's brothers after he took them away to give to his second wife. The brothers, sons of Pheneos, were killed by Alkmeon's sons, who recovered the heirlooms. The sons of Alkmeon wisely decided to dedicate them as an offering to the god Apollo. The necklace and robe remained at Delphi until the Phocians sacked Delphi (357 or 355 BCE) and sold the treasures to pay for mercenaries. Phocis was crushed, and the necklace of Harmonia later showed up on Delos.

destroyed villages was that of the ancient Kabeiroi, who were forced to flee. Young Laodamas, Eteokles's son, prepared his army for the defense.

The Theban forces met the Akhaians at Glisas. Hoping for another miracle, Laodamas led the attack, killing Adrastos's son Aigialeus. The Akhaian leader Promakhos also fell in battle. The Thebans did not have long to gloat before their king, Laodamas, was slain by fierce Alkmeon, son of Amphiaraos. The leaderless Thebans fled behind their walls.

In the Akhaian camp that evening, Adrastos, who was too old to fight, learned of his son's death. Revenge lost its sweetness, and he committed suicide in his dark tent. Meanwhile, the Thebans huddled behind their walls and sought the council of old Teiresias. This time the old seer could see no way for the Thebans to win, and so he advised them to run for their lives. (His prophecy was that once all the original attackers were dead, Thebes was fated to fall.) Many gathered their things and fled under cover of darkness (1198T/948R BCE).

Teiresias joined those that fled, but he was too weak for the arduous journey. He died nearby at the spring of Telphousa, having lived the long life Athena had promised for him.

The Queen of Darkness, Persephone, greeted wise Teiresias upon his arrival in the undergloom. She permitted him alone to pass the river of Lethe (meaning "forgetfulness") without drinking, and so he retained his intelligence and prophetic powers in the underworld.

After burying Teiresias, the fleeing Thebans splintered into groups. Some went no further than a few miles and sought protection from the Boiotians. Others settled at Homole in the Thessalia Mountains (in territories near to where sympathetic Boiotians and Herakleids lived), while the remainder moved on to far-off Illyria, where Kadmos had settled long before. Many who settled among the Boiotians nearby and at Homole eventually returned to Thebes.

It did not go well for those who chose to remain and fight for their homes. The Akhaians easily took the city at dawn. Oidipous's daughter Ismene and her lover were among those killed by the marauding victors. Teiresias's daughter Manto was taken as a concubine by Alkmeon.[222]

The Epigonoi led the surviving captives away as the army marched toward Kalydon. Even though Adrastos had committed suicide in his tent, the army was still determined to honor the promise he had uttered long ago to restore Tydeus at Kalydon after restoring Polyneices at Thebes. Along the way, the army stopped at Delphi and left the prisoners behind as an offering to the oracular god Apollo. Manto was among those left behind. Her rape by Alkmeon had filled her womb. At Delphi she bore his twins, Amphilokhos and Tisiphone. At birth they were taken from her and sent on Alkmeon's orders to King Thersandros to be raised in Thebes. Thersandros was married to Alkmeon's sister Demonassa.

Manto was an accomplished prophetess whose powers increased under tutelage in Delphi. This attracted long-haired Apollo, to whom she bore the great seer Mopsos. On Delphic order, the Theban prisoners were sent as settlers to Anatolia. Manto was instructed to go meet and marry the son of Lebes and found an oracle to Apollo. She led the Thebans to Klaros (Kolophon) in Ionia. There the Thebans were defeated in battle by the local Karians, who sent them to a nearby Hellenic king, Rhakios, son of Lebes. Rhakios allowed them to stay and married Manto. She built the oracle as commanded, and her tomb can be seen in Kolophon, according to the locals. The Romans say Manto eventually settled in Italy and that the town of Mantua arose near her tomb. Her son Manto succeeded Rhakios as king of Kolophon.

## Sack of Kalydon

From Delphi, the Epigonoi marched on Kalydon, which they found in a fighting mood. When Tydeus was exiled so long before, he had left his father, Oineus, without protection. Oineus's brother Agrios seized power and threw Oineus into prison. Agrios was long dead; his eight sons fought

[222] Excavators discovered that the Late Bronze Age palace at Thebes was burned twice, and the mythic tradition agrees (by Poseidon's son Lykos and by the Epigonoi). The first historical sack occurred during the fourteenth century T / late twelfth century R BCE—earlier than the purported lifetime of Lykos. The second sack occurred during the late thirteenth century T / early tenth century R BCE, just as in myth.

valiantly against the invaders but lost. Alkmeon and Diomedes led the Akhaian assault, killing six of the eight enemy chieftains in battle. Agrios's sons Onkhestos and Thersites fled, and now it was Kalydon's turn to be sacked (1198T/948R BCE).

After the Epigonoi conquered Kalydon, Diomedes decided to return to Midea instead of taking over Kalydon. The next-highest-ranking member of the royal family still surviving was grey-haired Andraimon, the husband of Oineus's daughter Gorge. He became king.

Diomedes took old Oineus, too feeble to rule, to live out his remaining time with him in Midea. Onkhestos and Thersites ambushed them en route, but all they accomplished was the death of old Oineus at Telphousa in Arkadia. Diomedes carried the remains as far as the Argeia, where he buried him in a large tholos tomb at a town renamed Oinoe in his honor.

Under Andraimon's rule, neither Pleuron nor Kalydon regained their splendor of earlier times. The whole Mycenaian world was in decline, and the Italian trade that gave these palaces much of their wealth dissipated. It appears that former co-kings Thersites and Onkhestos were permitted to return as private citizens.

Dutiful Alkmeon had to fulfill his unwanted destiny. Before departing on the ill-fated first attempt on Thebes, Amphiaraos had demanded that his son Alkmeon swear that one day he would kill his mother for her treachery in voting for the expedition. After the fall of Kalydon, his younger brother Amphilokhos advised him to fulfill his promise. Troubled by the prospect, Alkmeon decided to consult the oracle of Delphi to be sure the gods approved of such a terrible oath. The answer suggested that his mother should die for her behavior.

Reluctantly, solemn Alkmeon carried out his grim task. He faced years of trouble and turmoil afterward, for the avenging Erinyes pursued him. Eventually he married Kallirrhoe, daughter of the river god Akheloos, and found peace from the Erinyes when he settled on lands that had not witnessed his crime. He built his home on the expanding delta of the Akheloos, land that had come into being after his crime had been committed. Among their children was Akarnan, eponym of the Akarnanians.

While Alkmeon fulfilled his terrible destiny, criers from Sparta were sent to the great cities to say that the unsurpassable princess Helene was eligible for marriage (1197T/947R BCE). Helene, daughter of Zeus and Nemesis, was raised by her stepfather, King Tyndareos of Sparta, and his queen, the Kouretes princess Leda. All of the Epigonoi except for Alkmeon competed for her hand in marriage. They were joined by young Thoas, son of the newly anointed king Andraimon of Kalydon. Because her beauty was already legendary, there were not many unmarried princes who did not court her. All of them pledged to assist the successful suitor. Andraimon and his wife died while their son Thoas was fighting at Troy. They were buried side by side in an elaborate tomb in Amphissa.

# The Wanax, King of Kings

## Late Helladic Bronze Age (LHIIIB); Part of Hesiod's Age of Heroes

What human life is desirable without pleasure, or what lordly power? Without it not even the life of the gods is enviable.

—Simonides of Keos, sixth century BCE

### Atreus, King of Kings

King Atreus began his reign during the eternal year, when Mycenaian prestige and wealth were at their greatest. He reigned over some two hundred thousand subjects living in the Argeia. During his reign, the long period of Mycenaian growth and prosperity ended. He ruled Mycenai while Herakles performed his labors, through tumultuous years of warfare when so many of the cities of Hellas were sacked. While the Mycenaian world began its unstoppable decline, the great-king remained preoccupied with a destructive feud with his brother Thyestes.

Atreus sat upon his impressive throne in the great hall of the richest palace in Europe. In his strong right hand, he firmly gripped the finest scepter ever seen. The limping god Hephaistos had made it on the will of all-seeing Zeus. Lord Zeus gave it to the bright pathfinder Hermes to present to Pelops, and when Atreus became king of Mycenai through the direct intervention of the Thunderer-on-High, it was presented to him. Atreus was called *wanax* (king of kings).[223] No king before him held this title, and only his descendants Agamemnon and Orestes (and maybe Tisamenos) did so after him.

The ancient poets suggest the decline was caused by the sly slayer of Argos, Hermes, who ensured that the curse of his son Myrtilos upon Pelops and his descendants was fulfilled. Because of the curse, the poets say, war, plagues, and crop failures buffeted Mycenai. Not to be underestimated for the decline was the Hittites' success in driving the Mycenaian lords from Asia.

Still, there were early successes for King Atreus (1238T/988R–1201T/951R BCE). Three years after Herakles killed the Nemean Lion, the hill country behind Mycenai that led to Korinth was considered safe enough to settle. Atreus commissioned his brother Kleoneus to found Kleonai (Zygouros), and the Aiolian prince Lykourgos of Pheres to found Nemea (Aidonia; 1235T/985R BCE). With those two forts in place, Atreus subdued important cities north of Kleonai: Korinth and Sicyon. Atreus placed the Korinthian nobleman Kreon on the throne, but he sent his brother Skeiron to monitor events and collect taxes.

In his great palace, Atreus pondered how Thyestes had gained possession of the Golden Fleece, which had nearly cost him the kingdom. Atreus and Thyestes had been close as children, but they began their gruesome feud over the scepter of Mycenai. At first, love blinded Atreus to his wife's treachery. In exchange for the Golden Fleece, Airope received the affections of Thyestes. Atreus assumed that the child Airope bore to Thyestes was his own. The child did not survive to manhood.

---

[223] "Wanax" appears to be the Mycenaian word for "king" while "*basileus*" was the Mycenaian term for the master of the guild of smiths. In Classical Hellenic usage, "wanax" was reserved for a premier king, great-king, or king of kings, and only the Mycenaian Atreid Dynasty was accorded that honor. (The Hittites addressed Mycenaian kings as "great-king.") Bronze Age texts mention six great empires whose rulers were awarded the prestigious title great-king: Egypt, Assyria, Mitanni, Hittite, Babylonia, and Ahhiyawa (Akhaia); the last one probably identical to the Akhaian wanax of Mycenai in Hellenic texts.

The Classical Hellenes called the Persian kings "great-king" to indicate their status above other kings. Classical Hellas shed itself of most of its kings, and the word "basileus" evolved into the common term for someone with regal responsibilities in cultic matters.

Alluring Airope had a checkered past. When she was young, her father, Katreus, was warned by an oracle that his death would come by the hands of his own child. Like Akrisios before him, Katreus vainly hoped to thwart his hated fate. Katreus sold his royal daughters to Klytoneus, the merchant and ruler of Nauplia. Klytoneus kept Klymene as his own bride and sold Airope for a bride's fee to lovesick Atreus (1250T/1015R BCE). Klytoneus passed off lovely young Airope as a virgin, neglecting to tell the great king that her father had once caught her in bed with one of her lovers.

Image 12.1
Map of Important Sites of Argeia and Korinthia

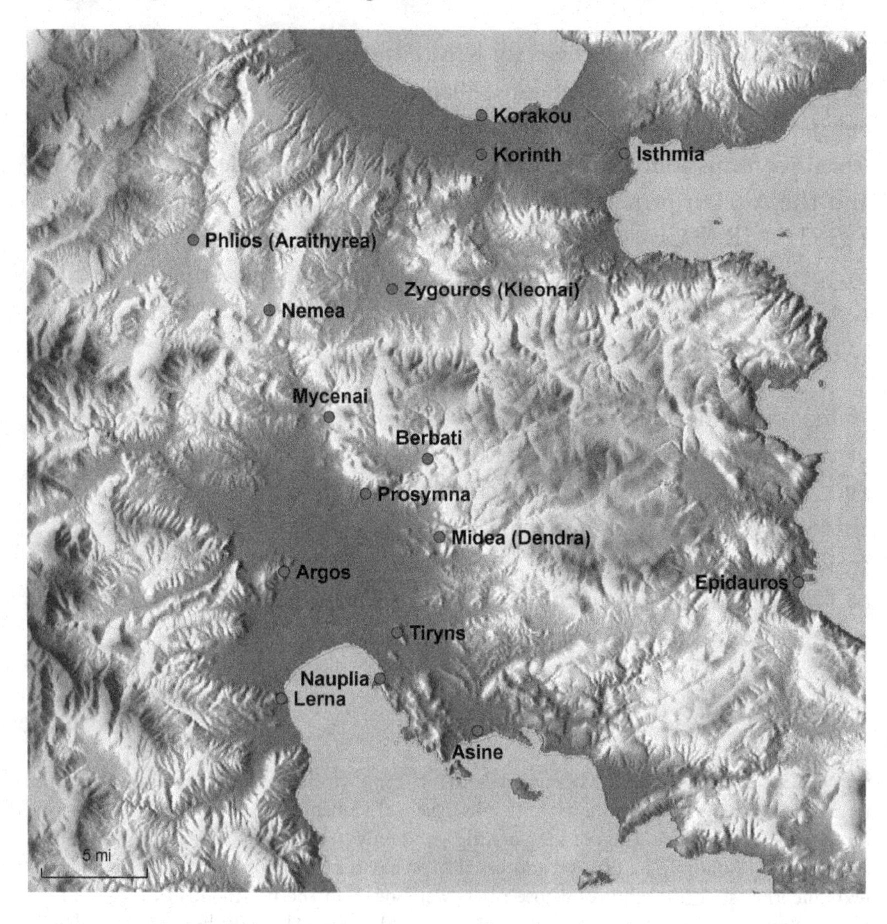

## Atreus and Thyestes Feud Again[224]

After a time, Atreus discovered that it was his wife who had given the Golden Fleece to Thyestes. In screaming rage, he executed her and sent bounty hunters to find Thyestes. Thyestes had always feared this possibility and moved around constantly. He spent several years at the home of the future king of Sicyon, Thesprotos. There he fathered Pelopia, whom he left for Thesprotos to raise (1231T/981R BCE). Then, back on the run again, he met and married a river nymph (naiad) and fathered Agelaos, Kallileon, and Orkhomenos.

With Thyestes on the run, Atreus ruled with supreme confidence. Familiar with the customs of the pharaohs, and considering himself their equal, he arranged the marriage of his son Pleisthenes to his daughter Kleolia (1230T/980R BCE). Pleisthenes was the son of his first wife, Kleolia, who had died in childbirth. Atreus had insisted that his eldest daughter be named Airope after her mother (1247T/997R BCE). Once ripe for marriage, Atreus married her to Pleisthenes. Atreus became the only grandfather to their offspring: Agamemnon (meaning "admirable for standing firm"; 1228T/978R BCE), Menelaos (1226T/976R BCE), and Anaxibia (1227T/977R BCE).

All the while, relentless bounty hunters searched for Thyestes. They eventually found him (1223T/973R BCE). The clever prince tricked the bounty hunters into killing Atreus's son Pleisthenes and escaped. The seething Atreus then raised his young grandchildren by Pleisthenes.

Grief magnified the great king's rage. The most powerful monarch in Europe sent a legion of bounty hunters to capture his despised evil twin brother. For nine years Thyestes eluded them. At last, chained like wild animals, Thyestes and his children by the naiad nymph were brought back to Mycenai and into the great hall, where the sardonic Atreus greeted them. Feigning reconciliation, the great-king ordered their chains removed and welcomed his brother home with a hug. He ordered that baths be prepared

[224] Atreus and Thyestes have brief references in Homer's *Iliad* and Hesiod's *Catalog of Women*, 69. Their feud is the backdrop in Aiskhylos's play *Agamemnon* and is mentioned in Sophokles's play *Elektra*. However, the story does not appear to have been fleshed out until the first century BCE, when the Roman Stoic Seneca wrote a play entitled *Thyestes*. The Roman-era mythographers Apollodoros (*Library*, Epitome 2), and Hyginos (*Fabulai*, 88), provided summaries.

for each of them. When Thyestes returned refreshed and shining like one of the immortals, he was escorted to a lavish banquet prepared in his honor. With grim satisfaction, Atreus watched as Thyestes unwittingly ate the flesh of his own children, whose bath had been a cooking cauldron. After Thyestes had eaten his fill, Atreus gleefully displayed the heads and hands of his brother's children.

Thyestes fell back vomiting and cursing. Atreus ordered guards to throw Thyestes outside the city gates to wander again as an exile. Atreus knew the pain of a lost child and felt that it would be a fate worse than death to live in sorrow, wretched poverty, and lonely exile (1211T/961R BCE).

Thyestes screamed curses at the mighty walls and nearly drove his own sword into his side. He stopped himself with determination to endure his pain for the chance at revenge. The vagabond prince walked barefoot to Delphi and solemnly swore to do anything necessary for revenge—anything. The Stronger Ones demanded a stiff price; to succeed he would have to rape his own daughter. Driven by hateful purpose, Thyestes left holy Delphi for Sicyon, where King Thesprotos had raised his daughter Pelopia as his own.

Thyestes arrived in Sicyon and learned that his daughter Pelopia was now a beautiful young woman and a priestess of virgin Athena. In disguise he stalked her, awaiting his chance. One night she went out with a group to perform a nighttime sacrifice. While he observed from a thicket, Pelopia slipped on the blood of a ram and absentmindedly went alone to wash her tunic in the stream. Thyestes beheld the beauty of his naked daughter and rushed upon her. Pelopia fought furiously, but Thyestes managed to complete his objective and fled. Although she could not identify her assailant, Pelopia had managed to take his gem-studded sword. Fearing discovery, Thyestes fled to his father's ancestral lands of Lydia, leaving behind the seed of revenge.

Atreus did not long gloat over his revenge. Thyestes's curse caused the crops to fail because of Atreus's horrible crime. The seers told Atreus that in order to find relief, he must find his brother. When Atreus arrived in Sicyon, beautiful young Pelopia, so familiar and mysterious, enchanted the old wanax. Airope had been dead many years, and Atreus was ready for another bride. Pelopia was just reaching the bloom of youth and was young enough to be his granddaughter.

Believing Pelopia to be the daughter of King Thesprotos, Atreus demanded that his vassal give her to him in marriage. Atreus returned to Mycenai with his new bride and happily greeted the news of her pregnancy. He did not know that the girl and her baby's father were one and the same—his sworn enemy and brother, Thyestes.

Pelopia knew the rapist had fathered her child and so exposed it. Atreus believed it to be his own and thought Pelopia was suffering from postpartum depression. The baby was found suckling a goat, and so Atreus named him Aigisthos (meaning "goat").

## Mycenaian Setback

Dynastic fighting between Atreus and Thyestes weakened the kingdom as much as the ongoing fighting between city-states. When the Hittites drove the loyal Akhaian ruler from Miletos and replaced him with an Akhaian loyal to them, the Mycenaians were unable to muster a counterattack (1235T/985R BCE).[225] The Hittites had grown increasingly frustrated with Akhaian (Hittite "Ahhiyawan") meddling in the affairs of their Arzawan vassal kingdoms in western Anatolia. The Hittite great-king further punished the Ahhiyawa by banning their goods in Syrian ports. The economic loss to Mycenai must have been dramatic.

Tumultuous events abroad and civic strife throughout Hellas (usually instigated by Herakles and described in heroic terms during the previous chapter) caused Atreus to expend great resources to build strong defensive walls around Mycenai instead of adding to his sumptuous palace or building a great tomb to impress those who came after him. It took twenty years and a great expenditure of resources to complete this fourth and final

[225] It is certainly speculative to suggest that the Hittites installed Thyestes, the arch enemy of the Mycenaian king, as vassal ruler of Milawata (Miletos). We know from Hyginos that Thyestes returned to his father's homeland in Anatolia (he says after raping Pelopia, but to fit the timeline it would have to have been earlier). The Mycenaian kings lost their prestige along with Milawata, for afterward they were no longer referred to as great-kings by the Hittites.

major building works of Mycenaian Hellas.[226] The famous Lion Gate, with the only example of monumental sculpture found in Bronze Age Hellas, was constructed as well.

Exhibit 12.1

Argeian Kings List after Perseus Traded Mycenai for Tiryns (Revisionist Dating)

| Mycenai | Tiryns | Argos | Midea | Nauplia | Kleonai |
|---|---|---|---|---|---|
| Melampous (1075–1050) | Perseus (1075–1047) | Megapenthes (1075–1025) | Bias (1075–1041) | Proitos (1099–1070) | |
| Abas (1050–1015) | Elektryon (1047–1013) | Anaxagoras (1025–1000) | Talos (1041–1005) | Lernos (1070–1039) | |
| Koiranos (1015–988) | Sthenelos (1013–993) | Alektor (1000–975) | Adrastos (1005–948) | Naubolos (1039–1013) | |
| Atreus (988–951) | Eurystheus (993–952) | Iphis (975–947) | | Klytoneus (1013–967) | Kleones (986–957) |
| Agamemnon (951–933) | To Mycenai | Sthenelos (947–922) | Cyanippos* (948–933) | Nauplios (967–931) | Ctesippos (957–935) |
| Aigistheus (933–927) | | Cylarabes (922–913) | To Argos | Oiax (931–924) | Thrasyanor (935–914) |
| Orestes (924–885) | | To Mycenai | | To Mycenai | Antimakhos (914–893) |
| Tisamenos (885–852) | | | | | Amphianax (893–854) |

* Diomedes was regent for Cyanippos, son of Adrastos. The boy died while Diomedes was fighting at Troy, and so the kingdom was his upon his return. He refused it and migrated away.

The Argeia city of Asine was given by Eurystheus to the Dryopes, but their list of kings is lost.

[226] The massive walls replaced older, smaller walls. The new walls enclosed both the citadel (where the palace was) and the Circle A shaft graves, but not the older Circle B shaft graves. A restoration of the shaft graves and older tholos tombs occurred, and they became public cult sites for the first time. An impressive well was dug from within the city.
Throughout Hellas, a new phase of construction began in which massive defensive walls were built. It was a time of retrenchment and paranoia. The great Cyklopean walls of Tiryns are the most impressive example. At Athens, walls, towers, and a double gate were built for the first time to shore up the only accessible route up the Acropolis (ca. 1240T/1005R–1230T/995R BCE). A deep well was dug at considerable expense and inconvenience to provide a reliable water source from within the citadel.

Mycenaian fortunes abroad did not recover, and the kingdom appeared weak and vulnerable to its warlike neighbors. Mycenaian prestige fell further when the forces of vassal-king Adrastos of Midea were utterly defeated during an invasion of Thebes (1208T/958R BCE). That defeat provided encouragement to the Herakleids, who were being persecuted throughout central Hellas on order of Mycenaian vassal-king Eurystheus of Tiryns. They approached King Theseus of Athens as supplicants, and he boldly gave them sanctuary, refusing (as other kings had) to send them away despite threats from Eurystheus. Eurystheus led his mighty army against them, but he died while fleeing in ignominious defeat from pitched battle at Marathon (1202T/952R BCE).

The victorious Herakleids boldly marched into the Peloponnesos. Contrary to the opinion of many, the Herakleids were not foreign invaders; they were descendants of the Tirynians that Amphitryon had led to Thebes in exile many years before. Amphitryon and his stepson Herakles were direct descendants of both Perseus and Pelops. Herakles's son Hyllos led the Herakleids, who were seen as a savior by many Mycenaians disgruntled with the empire's decline. When the Herakleid army reached the Argeian city of Tiryns, the happy citizens opened their gates and welcomed Hyllos as their new king (replacing dead Eurystheus).

This sudden disaster at the principal port of Argeia caught preoccupied Atreus off guard. He was forced to hunker down behind the massive Mycenaian city walls that had been recently completed. The walls held, and the angry hoards were kept out of Mycenai. However, the houses outside of the walls were destroyed.

Fortunately for Atreus, a plague broke out in Tiryns the next year (1201T/951R BCE). The prophets read the signs and blamed that misfortune on the fact that the Herakleids had retaken their ancestral lands in Tiryns before they were entitled to it. When they departed, Atreus asserted direct control over Tiryns in order to keep it from supporting a Herakleid return.

The loss of Miletos, the defeat at Thebes, the short occupation of Tiryns, the burning of houses outside of the walls, and the eminent return of the Herakleids all had a devastating effect upon the kingdom. Many of the displaced Akhaians of Anatolia and disgruntled Mycenaians of Argeia sailed off in search of a better life. They pillaged the coastal cities of Egypt and the Near East. When the pharaoh Merenptah boasted of beating back people of the foreign lands of the Sea, one of the vanquished tribes he mentioned was the Aqaiwasha (Akhaians; 1204T/954R BCE). Many of them settled on Cyprus and lived by plundering merchant ships passing between Hittite and Egyptian ports. The population of Mycenai did not recover, and the houses outside of the city walls were never reoccupied.[227]

## Final Battles between Atreus and Thyestes

The need for people to crowd together behind city walls for safety made it easy for the plague to return. This time the signs pointed to Thyestes's curse. Atreus sent his grandsons Agamemnon and Menelaos to Delphi with orders to find his whereabouts. As fate would have it, Thyestes was in Delphi to learn what the next steps were in order to exact his revenge. The grandsons of Atreus recognized their great-uncle and seized him. They took him back to Mycenai.

While Thyestes slept in a foul prison cell, Atreus sent Aigisthos on his first manly chore—to kill the prisoner. Wary Thyestes awoke and kicked Aigisthos's raised sword away. As he grabbed it, he recognized it as his own—the one he had lost while raping Pelopia. He told the boy to bring Pelopia to him.

When Pelopia arrived and saw her father with the sword she had taken, she knew who her hated assailant was. She grabbed the sword and plunged it deep into her own side, piercing her heart. Thyestes pulled it from her body and grimly told their shocked son to present the bloodied sword to Atreus. Atreus presumed that Thyestes was dead and decided to give thanks and celebrate. As he sacrificed a ram, Aigisthos followed Thyestes's instruction and plunged the sword though Atreus's backside. Thyestes seized control of the palace while Agamemnon and Menelaos fled to King Tyndareos of Sparta (1201T/951R BCE).

---

[227] Archaeological evidence indicates that an attack on Mycenai occurred between the fall of Troy VI and VII, exactly when the Herakleid attack on the city supposedly occurred. All of Argeia was affected: Tiryns, Midea, and Zygoures (Kleonai) were destroyed at this time, and Prosymna and Berbati were abandoned. Mycenai held out but declined afterward, while evidence indicates Tiryns (where the Herakleids reputedly settled) and Asine (where the Dryopes reputedly settled) grew larger.

One day of rule by Thyestes had been followed by thirty-nine years of Atreus's reign. Now Thyestes ruled again and held the great scepter that the craftsmen god Hephaistos had made. This reign too was brief, although longer than a day. Atreus's grandsons Agamemnon and Menelaos returned later that summer with an army of their supporters and troops supplied by King Tyndareos of Sparta (led by the famous Dioskouroi Kastor and Polydeuces). Thyestes fled without giving battle to Cythera Island and promptly died of old age. Agamemnon became wanax and wielder of the scepter of Pelops (1201T/951R–1183T/933R BCE). He and Menelaos buried their father in a great tholos tomb.[228]

## Early Successes of King Agamemnon

Agamemnon was a tall, stately man whose regal appearance seemed well suited to his new position. He excelled as a hunter, and no one in Hellas could match his ability with the javelin. Unfortunately, he was also indecisive and petty.

King Agamemnon started off his rule nobly. His first act as king was to forgive the boy Aigisthos for murdering Atreus, and he granted amnesty to Thyestes's supporters. Agamemnon hoped to thereby end the feud and unify the nation to face the anticipated return of the Herakleids. His gesture healed riffs enough to effectively deal with the crisis at hand, but unfortunately the curses of Pelops's murdered charioteer, Myrtilos, and of wronged Thyestes ran too deep to be extinguished altogether.

In preparing for the inevitable Herakleid invasion, the young wanax led his army to nearby Phlios, Sicyon, and Korinth. He desperately needed the loyalty of these cities, since his plan was to stop the Herakleids at the Isthmos. He could not afford to have enemies behind his defenses. Each city pledged their allegiance without issue. Agamemnon then led his

[228] The ancients called the largest and most splendid tholos tomb built in Mycenai (rivaled only by one built in rich Minyan Orkhomenos) the Tomb of Atreus because he was the richest of the mythic kings of Mycenai. It was probably built a bit earlier than the mythic dates presented here for Atreus. It would more likely have been built during the reign of Koiranos, whom Atreus succeeded (it would fit with Atreus if Troy VI was the one sacked by Agamemnon). With the tomb ascribed to Klytaimnestra, it was one of the last two tholos tombs built in Mycenai, and both were of superb craftsmanship.

assembled army to the Isthmos, where he built fortifications to stop the Herakleids before they could reach the Argeia.

Misinterpreting the oracle, the Herakleids returned in the third spring (1198T/948R BCE). Hyllos felt it best to attack the new king Agamemnon before he could sufficiently consolidate his power.[229] The Herakleid leader Hyllos gave a challenge to decide the issue by single combat. Agamemnon wisely refused. He knew the odds were better for his much larger army to prevail in open battle than for him to fight in single combat against the powerful son of mighty Herakles. But one of his Arkadian allies, King Ekhemos of Tegea, could not face the shame of not accepting such a challenge. He stepped forward and slew Hyllos in single combat. The Herakleids withdrew from their bases in Attike into the mountains of central Hellas. The capture of Princess Helene of Sparta by the Herakleids' ally Theseus might have been one skirmish in this war.

With the Herakleid threat past, Agamemnon departed upon a campaign to restore Mycenaian power throughout the Peloponnesos. His brother Menelaos was his staunchest ally on this campaign, a far cry from the legendary feuding between their grandfather and great-uncle.

Agamemnon wanted to conquer Pisa,[230] his great-grandfather Pelops's kingdom, for when Tyndareos had helped restore Agamemnon to the rule of Mycenai the year before, he had suggested to Agamemnon that he sack Pisa. Tyndareos was unhappy with his son-in-law Tantalos, and he wished to cement his relations with the great-king. Agamemnon did not let the fact that Pisa was ruled by Tantalos, the cousin of his father, Pleisthenes, and son-in-law of his benefactor, Tyndareos, stop him. The attack succeeded; Pisa fell (1200T/950R BCE). Agamemnon killed King Tantalos on the glorious field of battle. The victorious king then ripped Althaimenes, the infant son of his vanquished foe, from his wailing mother's soft breast and brained him. Then he took the grieving mother, Klytaimnestra (daughter of Tyndareos and sister of Helene), to be his own bride.

---

[229] Diodoros, in *Library of History*, iv.58.1, says that Agamemnon's grandfather Atreus led the defense, but there was not general agreement among the ancient writers. Agamemnon's son Orestes was also a candidate. Evidence of a defensive fortification built at the Isthmos during the Late Bronze Age has been uncovered.

[230] The great western Peloponnesian state of Pylos was sacked at this time; Pisa was not then a significant city.

Agamemnon marched from Pisa to Amyklai in Lakonia to bring gifts to Tyndareos from the booty of Pisa. Tyndareos was a practical man with little regard for women. Tyndareos ignored Klytaimnestra's anguish, and he hoped that she would come to understand that this was a better marriage. Later Agamemnon helped his brother Menelaos prevail over a great number of impressive suitors to win the hand of Klytaimnestra's gorgeous sister Helene.

# The Trojan War

## Late Helladic Bronze Age (LHIIIC); Part of Hesiod's Age of Heroes

Muse, tell me those things that never happened before nor shall be hereafter.

—Leskhes of Pyrrha (Lesbos), *Little Iliad*, seventh century BCE

There was a time when the countless tribes of men, though wide-dispersed, oppressed the surface of the deep-bosomed earth, and Zeus saw it and had pity and in his wise heart resolved to relieve the all-nurturing earth of men by causing the great struggle of the Ilian war, that the load of death might empty the world. And so the heroes were slain at Troy, and the plan of Zeus came to pass.

—Stasinos or Hegesias of Cyprus, *Cypria*, seventh century BCE

## Paris Judges Beauty[231]

As was mentioned earlier, a feud between three lovely goddesses began when angry Eris threw a golden apple among the guests at Peleus and the Nereid Thetis's wedding, saying it belonged to the fairest (1217T/967R BCE). Peleus was the mighty son of rainmaker Aiakos of Aigina, the man who had helped the gods built the impregnable walls of Troy. Peleus and his brother Telamon helped Herakles sack Troy and sailed with Jason as Argonauts. Among the splendid wedding gifts the gods gave them that day was the suit of armor Akhilleus[232] would wear to Troy.

While tending livestock on Mount Ida, Paris was approached by the divine. Lord Zeus ordered luck-bringing Hermes to lead the goddesses to him. Hermes told Paris that since he is as handsome as you is wise, Zeus commands you to judge the fairest. Paris reluctantly accepted the golden apple and declared he would divide it evenly. Argos-slaying Hermes shock his head and declared the ruling unacceptable. Paris must use his abilities to decide.

Paris asked whether he was to judge them robed as they were or naked. Sly Hermes smiled discretely and said that it was up to him to establish the rules. Paris promptly asked for the goddesses to disrobe and announced that he would view each one individually. The guide Hermes politely turned his back. Stately Hera approached first, and as she turned around slowly to display her magnificent figure, she told him to consider her carefully and promised to make him king of Asia and the richest man alive. Bright Athena came straight up to Paris next and promised him victory in all battles and to make him the wisest of men. Then laughter-loving Aphrodite sidled up to him, and Paris blushed because she came so close that they almost touched. She offered him the love of one as beautiful as she was herself and no less passionate. Paris chose garland-loving Aphrodite and made enemies of the other two.

Cyprian Aphrodite ordered Paris to go to Troy and said she would guide him from there. Oinone, the nymph who loved him dearly, understood

---

[231] The complete epic cycle concerning the Trojan War is found the following poems: *Cypria, Iliad, Aithiopis, Little Iliad, Sack of Ilion, Nostoi "Returns," Odyssey,* and *Telegony.*

[232] Once Linear B was deciphered, Michael Ventris and John Chadwick quickly identified fifty-eight Homeric names among the texts, including Akirue (Akhilleus), Ekoto (Hektor), Aiwas (Aias or Ajax), and Oreta (Orestes).

why he was leaving. Tearfully she let him go, but she warned him of the danger of his desire. She told him that she alone could save him if he were to be wounded and that he should to return to her if that happened.

Paris was unaware of his own royal heritage; he was the eldest son of King Priamos of Troy and his principal wife, Hekabe, the queen. Hekabe came from the Sangarios River territory, and her father was Dymas of Mygdonia, Cisseus, or the river god Sangarios. Just before the birth of their first son, Hekabe dreamed she gave birth to a faggot from which wriggled countless fiery serpents. She awoke screaming that Troy and wooded Mount Ida were ablaze.

Young Aisakos (Priamos's son from a previous, lesser wife) was called in to interpret the terrible dream and foretold that a noble child born that day would cause Troy's downfall. Only the sacrifice of both the mother and child would prevent it. That morning, Priamos's sister Cilla gave birth to Melanippos. She and her infant were sacrificed as her broken-hearted husband, Thymoites, looked on. Hekabe delivered her baby that evening; she named him Alexandros.

As a precaution, Priamos gave their infant son to the shepherd Agelaos to expose on Mount Ida (1223T/973R BCE). The shepherd dutifully complied but found the hearty child still alive after five days, for a she-bear had suckled him. His resolve broken, Agelaos took him home, named him Paris, and raised him with his own son.

Paris became the handsomest youth of his day. His looks were not just for show, either. He learned the rough arts of a shepherd and ironically received the nickname of Alexandros (meaning "defender of men") because of his ability to protect the flocks from thieves and wild animals. The legend of his prowess grew, and he excelled beyond anyone in Ilion in boxing and archery.

Despite his status as a slave, Paris became the lover of the nymph and prophetess Oinone, daughter of the local river god Cebren. The Great Goddess, Cybele, had taught Oinone prophecy, and Pythian Apollo had taught her the healing arts. She fell desperately in love with Paris while he tended Laomedon's flocks. She bore him two children: Korythos and Daphnis. Paris's affection for her did not go as deep as hers for him.

Paris had been selected to choose because of his fairness in previous dealings. The noble slave took to amusing himself by staging bullfights among the herd. When he noticed that one bull always won, he pitted him against bulls from other herds. His bull always won. Finally he offered the gold crown he had bought with his bets for the bull that could beat his. Stout-hearted Ares took the form of a bull and won. Paris unhesitatingly awarded a crown to the surprised Ares, and it pleased the watchful Olympians.

While Paris lived as a mountain shepherd, Priamos sired fifty sons and twelve daughters by his many wives. His sons and daughters and their spouses lived in adjacent polished stone rooms in his palace. Hekabe alone produced nineteen sons, each taught the noble skills of a soldier. Their second son, Hektor, was heir and became the best in Ilion at war games. His full brothers included Deiphobos, Helenos, Mestor, Polites, Antiphones, Antiphos, Panmon, Hipponoos, Troilos, and Polydoros. Hekabe's daughters were Kreousa, Laodice, Kassandra, and Polyxene. Helenos and Kassandra were twins. Helenos and Kassandra became seers in the following manner: They were once left overnight in the temple of Thymbraian Apollo. They were found in the morning with snakes licking their lips. Afterward they could understand the language of the birds.[233]

Paris was a great athlete in peak condition, and he impressed the citizens when he arrived in Troy. When he learned of games being held, he entered and won every contest. The king and queen observed his performance and recognized him as their son. His brother Helenos saw the danger in his parents' desire to reclaim him. As the state seer, he warned them against it.

Helenos had succeeded his older half brother Aisakos in the role of royal seer for the following reason. When his wife Asterope, daughter of the river god Cebren, died, distraught Aisakos leapt from a sea cliff. When he survived, he leapt again. The sea goddess Tethys, wife of Oceanos, took pity on him and changed him into diver bird, a magus.

---

[233] This myth is recounted by Hyginos. Similarly, the great Hellenic seer Melampous of Triphylia gained his ability when snakes licked his ears.

Priamos and Hekabe were so overjoyed at seeing their son alive and so noble-looking that they ignored Helenos. They dressed Paris in purple and welcomed him back into the family with his given name of Alexandros.[234]

Soon lovely-eyed Aphrodite ordered that he and her son Aineias, son of Ankhises, outfit a ship and sail to Lakonia (1195T/945R BCE). The Trojan Pherekos built the ship (he died in battle in the tenth year of the Trojan War). Helenos's warning against the trip was likewise ignored.

---

Exhibit 13.1
History of Wilusa (Ilion/Troy)

Hittite Version

Wilusa first entered Hittite history when Great-King Mursili II (1321T/1071R–1295T/1045R BCE), son of Supplilumas, defeated Arzawa and advanced as far as the Seha River Land (Teuthrania) just south of the Troad. Like all Arzawa states, Wilusa became a Hittite vassal. Arzawan revolt, instigated in Masa (Mysia), was defeated, and no other trouble in Arzawa was recorded during Mursili's reign.

When the rebel Hittite lord Piyamaradu seized Wilusa (Troy), the Hittite vassal ruler of the Seha River Land attempted to drive him out, presumably on his overlord's behalf. Piyamaradu inflicted a humiliating defeat upon him and countered by attacking what was apparently one of his dependent territories, the island of Lazpa (Lesbos).

Great-King Muwatalli II (1295T/1045R–1272T/1022R BCE), son and successor of Mursili, dispatched General Gassu to drive Piyamaradu from Wilusa. Along the way, the general obtained auxiliary forces led by King Kupanta-Kurunta, vassal ruler of Mira-Kuwaliya (Karia). The exact outcome of the expedition is not recorded, but a subsequent treaty affirms that Wilusa was once again a vassal state. Piyamaradu escaped, probably to his Ahhiyawan (Akhaian) allies.

[234] Hittite records speak of a treaty between their great-king, Muwatalli II, and the Wilusa king, Alaksandu, which sounds a lot like Alexandros. There is also a Luvian tradition of classical times that said Helene's lover was an ally of Muwatalli. Wilusan troops were counted among the Hittite forces that faced the Egyptians at Kadesh, which was near the Phoenician coast Alexandros would visit.

Among the surviving Hittite documents is a treaty between Muwatalli and vassal-king Alaksandu of Wilusa (whose name sounds a lot like Alexandros, or Paris). The Hittite great-king praises Wilusa for being one of the empire's most consistently loyal states. The document also mentions a previous king, Kukunni. Wilusa sent troops to support Muwatalli's army that checked Egyptian expansion into Syria at the Battle of Kadesh (1274T/1024R BCE).

Hittite records indicate that Wilusa suffered from repeated attacks from the mid thirteenth century T / late eleventh century R to the early twelfth century T / mid tenth century R BCE (Hellenic mythology mentions two attacks on Troy during this time). One tantalizing letter says the Hittites and Ahhiyawa nearly went to war over Wilusa during the time Troy VI was destroyed. Wilusa king Wilmu was expelled during the reign of Great-King Hattusili III (1267T/1017R–1237T/987R BCE) or his son Tudhaliya IV (1237T/987R–1209T/959R BCE), fitting well with when Herakles attacked in eighteen ships. After conquering Milawata (Miletos in Ionia) from the Ahhiyawa (Akhaians/Mycenaians), Tudhaliya ordered his new vassal to restore loyal Wilmu.

Hittite control in Arzawa ended with the collapse of the Hittite Kingdom during the rule of Supplilumas II (1207T/957R–ca. 1178T/928R BCE). The late 1180sT / late 930sR BCE saw massive destruction of Hittite cities. It appears the Hittites were brought down by peoples to the north and west, as well as by Ahhiyawans cutting off the food supply from Egypt. The Egyptians say the kingdoms of Arzawa were overwhelmed. Although Troy VII was destroyed, western Anatolia was spared the level of devastation that hit central Anatolia, the heartland of the Hittite Empire.

Hellenic Version

| **King** | **Revised** | **Traditional** |
|---|---|---|
| Teukros | 1150–1120 | 1400–1370 |
| Dardanos | 1120–1100 | 1370–1350 |
| Erikhthonios | 1100–1080 | 1350–1330 |
| Tros | 1080–1067 | 1330–1317 |
| Ilos | 1067–1032 | 1317–1282 |
| Laomedon | 1032–970 | 1282–1220 |
| Priamos | 970–934 | 1220–1184 |

Homer says eponymous Teucros was the first king of Troy, an indigenous chief who was the son of the river god Skamandrios and the mountain nymph Idaia (1400T/1150R BCE).[235] His people, the Teukrians ("Trojans" in Latin), were considered similar to the Hellenes. Homer thought they could understand each other's speech. Artifacts from this era found in both countries have much more in common than not.

Dardanos, the second king of Ilion, was a son of Zeus. He was conceived when the star nymph Elektra clung to a statue of the maiden Pallas in a fruitless attempt to avoid cloud-master Zeus. The king of the Olympians flung the statue (the Palladium) aside and committed the only recorded rape on Olympos. Then dark-clouded Zeus threw the star nymph and the Palladium from Olympos, and they landed on Samothrace Island. Dardanos's mother, Elektra, became deeply involved in the Samothracian mysteries of Cybele/Demeter. Dark-faced Elektra raised her sons Dardanos and Iasion on Samothrace.

Sad-hearted Dardanos left Samothrace during a torrential downpour, grieving the death of his brother Iasion (1375T/1125R BCE). All-seeing Zeus smote his own son Iasion with a thunderbolt for sleeping with one of the Olympians, Demeter. Dardanos clung to the sides of a small raft made of inflated hides with four stones for ballast. Landing where Mount

[235] Excavations at Troy indicate that after a fifty-year lapse, Troy (VI) was inhabited by a new populace that did not revere the earlier inhabitants (1700T/1450R BCE). Thus Teukros would not have been the founder, but a descendent of these new settlers. Strabo, in *Geography*, xiii.1.58, provides a more detailed and slightly different account of the city's founding than Homer. He said the Kretan prince Skamandrios built Troy. Skamandrios named the most important local mountain Ida, in honor of the Kretan mountain with the same name and the reputed birthplace of Zeus. Apollo (presumably through the prophetess of Delphi) told Skamandrios to settle where earthborn people (i.e., natives) attack tents at night. The local Berbycians attacked, and the prince jumped into the Xanthos River to escape them. He returned to defeat them, and the river was renamed for him. He built the Sminthian (meaning "mouse") Apollo temple and the city of Troy. In Strabo's version, this prince, and not the river god, is the husband of Idaia and the father of Teucros. Mice were sacred in Krete—and apparently here as well. The Berbycians are also mentioned as having battled the Tyrrhenians of coastal Lydia.

Ida touches the sea, he gave thanks and initiated the rites of Cybele along the lines of the Samothracian mysteries.[236]

Teucros was a good man, and he welcomed Dardanos. He gave Dardanos his daughter Bateia in marriage. Dardanos founded the first Trojan city, Dardania. In time the term "Dardanian" became synonymous with "Teukrian" ("Trojan"). Dardanos succeeded his father-in-law as king of the Trojans, ruling from Dardania (1370T/1120R BCE). Dardanos became Zeus's favorite mortal offspring (if you do not count Herakles as mortal). That is to say, royal Zeus bestowed upon him the scepter of a great kingdom.

Dardanos's eldest son, Ilos (or Zacynthos), died childless before him. So Erikhthonios, the second son, became the next king (1350T/1100R BCE). Erikhthonios became the richest man in the world and the proud owner of three thousand mares. The north wind, Boreas, impregnated twelve of them, producing twelve immortal foals as fast as the wind and belonging to Zeus. Erikhthonios resided in Troy, married the nymph Astyokhe (daughter of the local river god Simoeis), and fathered Tros.

When Tros became king, he renamed his capital Troy (1330T/1080R BCE). He married Kallirrhoe, daughter of the river god Skamandrios. Tros loved his three sons, Ilos, Assarakos, and Ganymedes, dearly and his lovely daughter Kleopatra as well. The king was, naturally, distraught at the loss of his youngest, Ganymedes (meaning "delighting in genitals"). Zeus became enamored with the boy, the most beautiful youth of his day, and in the form of an eagle, he carried him off to be his lover and the cupbearer of the gods (1321T/1071R BCE). Then the father of gods and men, Zeus, granted that Ganymedes's youth should remain eternal. To compensate the grieving father, Zeus sent luck-bringing Hermes to present Tros with the twelve immortal mares that Boreas had sired, along with a golden vine crafted by the limping god Hephaistos.

Ilos and his younger brother Assarakos divided the kingdom on Tros's death (1317T/1067R BCE). As the eldest son, Ilos received the larger

[236] According to an obscure Athenian version, Dardanos had a son by Khyrse of Arkadia, the daughter of a man named Pallas, before coming to Ilion. This son, Idaios, came later with the Palladium, which was part of Khryse's dowry. Idaios settled on the mountain (and presumably gave it its name) and instituted the mysteries of the Phrygian mother goddess (Cybele). His daughter Idaia was the second wife of Phineus of Thrace, brother of Prince Kadmos of Krete.

kingdom, Troy, as well as the twelve immortal mares. Assarakos received Dardania and married the nymph Hieromnemea, daughter of the river god Simoeis. They begat Kapys and Aisyetes. Kapys married his cousin, Princess Themisto of Troy, and succeeded his father as king of Dardania. His proud sons were Ankhises and Aletes. Aisyetes married Kleomestra and fathered Antenor and Alkathoos.

Ilos traveled east immediately after his ascension to a land that would later be called Phrygia.[237] His connection to Phrygia suggests that he was ousted or that he was an outsider, possibly a Hittite prince, who seized the throne from a disloyal ruling family. Rebellion was common among the Arzawans, although the Trojans seldom joined them. Perhaps rebels sympathetic to Pelops, who led a Panarzawan revolt against the Hittites, forced Ilos out (1317T/1067R–1316T/1066R BCE). In Phrygia, which was then part of the Hittite Empire, Ilos won respect by winning first prize in a wrestling contest. When Pelops advanced into Phrygia, Ilos and Adrastos countered and succeeded in driving him out of Asia altogether.

For his valor, Ilos was rewarded with the hand of the princess Eurydice. Her father, King Adrastos, gave as a dowry fifty youths and fifty maidens, all of them loyal to the Hittites.[238] Ilos then returned to Troy and ruled without further rebellion. His queen, Eurydice, bore him Tithonos, Laomedon, Themisto (who married her cousin, King Kapys of Dardania), and Astyokhe (who married King Telephos of Teuthrania). Laomedon's eldest son, Tithonos,[239] like Ganymedes before him, was so beautiful that

[237] The Anatolian Plateau west of Cappadocia (the Hittite heartland) and east of Aigaian coastal states like Troy was called Phrygia by ancient Hellenic and Roman writers. "Phrygia" was firmly under Hittite control by the fourteenth century T / twelfth century R BCE, long before the Phrygian people arrived in the region. Sketchy archeological evidence suggests the area was probably occupied by Arzawans during the time of Hittite rule or, less likely, occupied by the related Hittites themselves.

[238] According to a late version borrowing from the foundation myth of Thebes, Adrastos commanded Ilos to follow a cow, as Kadmos had done in Thebes, and found a city where it sat down. It sat down at Troy, and Ilos founded the city with his one hundred settlers. In this version, the Palladium fell from heaven into Ilos's outstretched hands upon his prayer to Zeus. He had asked that another sign be sent so that there would be no misunderstanding as to whether he had found the correct place to build his city. Diodoros's *Library of History*, iv.74–75, calls Ilos the eponym and founder of Troy.

[239] Perhaps the abductions of Ganymedes and Tithonos have historical seeds. It was Hittite practice to require their vassal kings to send them one of their sons to ensure loyalty. Diodoros's *Library of History*, iv.75, says Tithonos campaigned as far away as Assyria. The Assyrians had frequent dealings with the Hittites.

he attracted the divine. The dawn goddess Eos carried him off to live as her lover in her splendid eastern palace. She loved him so that she begged Zeus to grant him immortality despite the Olympians' displeasure with mortals who bedded goddesses. The rosy-fingered dawn was surprised when the sly thunderer nodded his approval. Memnon and Emathion were the offspring of their happy union.

Over time, the reason for Zeus's benevolence became apparent. Although immortal, Tithonos aged like a mortal. Eos had forgotten to ask that Tithonos receive eternal youth to accompany his immorality. Even as Tithonos grew old, loving Eos stayed with him, tenderly caring for her lover. Eventually Tithonos was completely bedridden, and still he declined. Finally he shriveled into a grasshopper and jumped out of the palace window.

As a result, it was the second son, Laomedon, who inherited Ilion and the twelve immortal mares of his father, Ilos (1282T/1032R BCE). Knowing the new king's arrogance, the son of Kronos used him to further punish Apollo and Poseidon for their unsuccessful palace revolt. King Zeus humiliated the two gods by demanding they hire themselves out as laborers, promising to improve the imposing fortifications at Troy. The gods required that mortal Aiakos, king of Aigina, assist them, lest Troy become completely impregnable to men. Aiakos assisted the dark-haired lord Poseidon in building the walls, while Phoebus Apollo played his lyre and tended the flocks.

As discussed earlier, when Herakles killed Laomedon, his eldest son, Priamos, succeeded him. Priamos was the father of Alexandros and Hektor, and he died as his mighty city fell.

---

## Helene of Sparta

> May Leto, nurturing Leto, give you fine children
> And Cypris, goddess Cypris, equal love for each other
> And Zeus, Kronian Zeus, prosperity without end.[240]

While Paris was raised in poverty and obscurity, Helene's was brought up in opposite conditions. She was conceived when the Olympian Zeus fell in

[240] Theokritos, "Helene's Wedding Song", in *The Idylls of Theocritus*. Translated by Thelma Sargent.

love with Nemesis, who fled from him, taking the form of a goose. Zeus quickly changed himself into a swan and caught the goddess. As a result, she laid an egg in a grove near Sparta. Shepherds found the egg and took it to Queen Leda of Sparta. Leda knew who the father must have been and raised the child once she hatched (1213T/963R BCE). Her name soon spread smiles on the lips of young men dwelling around the sea-swelling shores of the Aigaian. Her name was Helene.[241]

She was raised by King Tyndareos, and her strong-arm brothers, the Dioskouroi (twins born by Leda; one the son of Zeus, the other of Tyndareos), offered protection; but her beauty and lineage caused her childhood to end abruptly. Once, while the Dioskouroi were away, Theseus, the aging king of Athens who hereto had lived an exemplary life, surpassed in deeds only by Herakles, was talked into acquiring daughters of Lord Zeus as brides by his rough friend Peirithoos of the Lapiths. (Their wives had died.) Hearing of Helene's beauty, they came to Lakonia. They observed Helene running races naked and oiled, as was the custom for maidens only in Lakonia. They carried off twelve-year-old Helene as she was making a sacrifice to the virgin Artemis in thanks for her victory.

Theseus and his coarse companion Peirithoos took the frightened girl to the citadel Aphidnai in Attike. Wishing to preserve her virginity until she was sexually mature, Theseus consummated his marriage by sodomizing her like he would have a youth. Then he left his new bride in the protective custody of his loyal baron Aphidnos with his mother, Aithra, charged with tending to his young bride. Meanwhile, he accompanied Peirithoos into grim Hades to abduct the underworld queen Persephone to be his friend's bride. Theseus and Peirithoos returned to Lakonia and descended into the underworld at Tainaron.[242]

---

[241] Helene was a Non-Hellenic deity, perhaps a tree goddess. The Hellenes incorporated her into their myths, reducing her status to that of a mortal. In Lakonia she retained her divine status; there she helped sailors in distress, as did her divine brothers the Dioskouroi. Her mother is variously reported to have been Leda (possibly a form of the Titan Leto demoted to an Aitolian princess), Nemesis, or an Oceanid.

[242] The "rape" of Helene may originally have been connected to (or a local variation of) the rape of Kore by Hades. Both Kore and Helene were vegetation goddesses. Theseus accompanied Peirithoos during his failed attempt to rape Kore, and she retained her dignified position in a myth of vegetative rebirth. In contrast, Helene was raped and lost her status as a goddess to become an adulterous princess. However, she retained shrines in Lakonia, at Midea (Argeia), and on Rhodes.

The Dioskouroi learned of Helene's whereabouts and gathered together the army. Knowing Theseus's reputation for valor, the twins enlisted allies that included their brother-in-law King Ekhemos of Tegea and the exiled Athenian nobleman Menestheus. Arkadian Ekhemos had not yet won immortal fame by killing Herakles's son Hyllos in single battle, thus forcing the Herakleids to withdraw in defeat from their first attack on the Peloponnesos (1199T/949R BCE).

To entice them into joining their expedition, the Dioskouroi offered Menestheus the Athenian crown, and to Ekhemos, grandson of their deceased ally Cepheus (who died helping Herakles and the Dioskouroi restore Tyndareos in Lakonia), they offered the hand of their lovely sister Timandra. Klytaimnestra was given as bride to King Tantalos of Pisa. Both of these women, like their sister Helene, would one day be unfaithful to their husband. Then Leda would hang herself in grief over the actions of her daughters.

The next spring, the Dioskouroi and their allies besieged Aphidnai, where loyal baron Aphidnos held out, hoping for Theseus's return. Theseus and Peirithoos's quest to obtain Zeus's daughter Persephone for Peirithoos failed when King Hades detained them in his realm. Without Theseus, the Athenians failed to break the siege, and the Dioskouroi entered Aphidnai, killing Aphidnos and recovering their sister (1200T/950R BCE). The wound Kastor received in his thigh could not dampen the happy reunion.

The Athenians, angry at having been abandoned by their great king, willingly accepted the Dioskouroi's demand that Menestheus become their king. Then the army returned home laden with booty from Aphidnai. Among the slaves were Theseus's old mother, Aithra, and Peirithoos's sister Phisadie, both of whom became handmaids to Helene.

## Marriage of Helene

When Tyndareos announced that his unbelievably desirable daughter Helene had reached marriageable age, suitors from all over Hellas came in haste (1197T/947R BCE). Born of a white swan's white egg and exceedingly fair of complexion, many came for her. Menelaos had been completely mesmerized by the beautiful princess when he met her while accompanying Agamemnon to Lakonia after the conquest of Pisa. He joined the suitors, and Agamemnon went with along to help him gain the prize.

Tyndareos began to worry that the great number of inevitable losers might become violent, and he also worried that Agamemnon might divorce Klytaimnestra if his brother were not selected. Pondering how he might avoid a riot, Tyndareos was approached by a short, barrel-chested suitor from the tiny island of Ithake. Old Tyndareos smiled absently at this ungraceful-looking man with limited wealth, knowing full well he would never be the one chosen. The suitor introduced himself as Odysseus, son of Laertes, and mentioned the concern Tyndareos was feeling. This snapped Tyndareos out of his haze, and he paid full attention to the wily stranger.

Odysseus said he had a plan to avoid bloodshed, which he would tell for a price. Tyndareos was eager to learn of it, but not at the price of his daughter. Odysseus said that it was no longer Helene that he wished to marry, but Ikarios's lovely daughter Penelope, who glowed with an inward beauty that only he detected. All the other suitors remained captivated by Helene's physical beauty and seductive charm. If Tyndareos would secure him Penelope, Odysseus would share his plan. Tyndareos agreed to secure her, if no blood was spilled.

Following the clever solution Odysseus offered, Tyndareos called together all the suitors in the great hall of his palace. There he made each stand upon pieces of a sacrificed horse and solemnly swear an oath to defend Helene and her chosen mate from harm, should need arise. All were eager for the prize and agreed. Then Tyndareos withdrew to decide the issue. His sons the Dioskouroi came to him on behalf of King Menestheus of Athens, who had fought with them to recover Helene from Theseus. Menestheus was a wealthy man, a noble choice. Next, his son-in-law Agamemnon came to press his case. Agamemnon was the richest man alive and offered to give many gifts if Tyndareos picked his red-headed brother Menelaos. Unable to decide, he decided to let his daughter pick between the two. Among the suitors, she was given a wreath to put on whomever she wished to marry. She put it on tall, broad-shouldered Menelaos, for he offered more gifts, by far, than any other suitor.

Remembering their oaths, the disappointed suitors held back their anger, packed, and solemnly departed after Menelaos joyfully lifted the veil to kiss the most beautiful woman alive.

> On Sparta, once at the palace of yellow-haired Menelaos,
> Maidens with hyacinth blossoms wreathed in their hair
> Before freshly painted bridal chamber ordered the dance,
> The first twelve of the city, the flower of Lakonian women,
> When the younger of Atreus' sons having courted and won,
> Beloved Helene, shut himself in with Tyndareos' daughter
> All sang on one strain, and with feet interweaving
> Beat out the measure, and the house rang to their hymn.[243]

Agamemnon returned home to rule peacefully while his wife Klytaimnestra, older sister of Helene, bore him four children: Iphigeneia, Elektra, Khrysothemis, and Orestes.

Meanwhile, Tyndareos ordered Ikarios to give his daughter Penelope to Odysseus. Tyndareos and Ikarios offered great villas to their new son-in-laws if they would stay in Lakonia. Menelaos agreed but Odysseus did not wish to forsake his home. Tyndareos gave Menelaos the palace at Therapne while he continued to rule from Amyklai.

Unable to convince Odysseus to stay, Ikarios continued to pressure miserable Penelope to stay, and she was willing. Still her tears could not sway Odysseus to change his mind and he told her that she must choose. Demonstrating the faithfulness that she became famous for, she prepared to leave. When the wagons were packed, Ikarios tried again to dissuade his daughter from leaving, promising to find her another husband. Penelope sweetly kissed her crying father, lowered her veil, and nodded to Odysseus that she was ready.

[243] Theokritos, "Helene's Wedding Song", in *The Idylls of Theocritus*. Translated by Thelma Sargent.

Menelaos deeply loved his beautiful wife and gave her everything he could. She presented to him a beautiful daughter they named Hermione.[244] In these peaceful times, Tyndareos joined his ancestors and the Dioskouroi became co-kings.

## Alexandros (Paris) and Helene Fall in Love

Cytherian Aphrodite told the Trojan prince Alexandros (Paris) to visit Lakonia in order to gain the prize she promised him. She instructed her own son, the great-hearted Dardanian prince Aineias to accompany Alexandros. Aineias was conceived in the following manner:

Lord Zeus cast sweet desire upon laughter-loving Aphrodite to be joined in love with a mortal man so that she would not be innocent of the ordeal that she put others through. So in her heart a sweet desire for the Dardanian prince Ankhises arose, who was tending cattle among the steep hills of many-fountained Ida. The Cypriot withdrew to her sacred precinct at Paphos, and the richly dressed Graces bathed her with heavenly fragrant oil and dressed her in rich clothes. When she had decked herself with gold, she swiftly traveled to Ida. She found Ankhises, as handsome as the gods, in his home alone, playing the lyre. The sweet-smelling goddess appeared before him in mortal form, and Ankhises was seized with love and caught her by the hand.

> And laughter-loving Aphrodite, with face turned away and lovely eyes downcast, crept to the well-spread bed which was already laid with soft coverings for the hero; and upon it lay skins of bears and deep-roaring lions which he himself had slain in the high mountains. And when they had gone up upon the well-fitted bed, first Ankhises took off her bright jewelry of pins and twisted brooches and earrings and necklaces, and loosed her underpants and

[244] Homer specifically says Hermione is Menelaos and Helene's only child, although the renowned lyric poet Stesikhoros of Lokris (late seventh or early sixth century BCE) mentions a son, Nikostratos. Other writers add Maraphios (ancestor to the Persian family Maraphion), Aithiolas, and Pleisthenes, the latter of whom Helene brought with her when she deserted Menelaos (but she left him on Cyprus). Pausanias's *Guide to Greece*, ii.22.6–7, says she bore Iphigeneia to Theseus and gave her to Klytaimnestra to be raised. Helene was also said to have born Aganos and possibly other children to Alexandros.

> stripped off her bright garments and laid them down upon a silver-studded seat. Then by the will of the gods and destiny he laid with her, a mortal man with an immortal goddess, not clearly knowing what he did.[245]

The dashing Asian princes were welcomed in Lakonia by the great co-kings Kastor and Polydeuces. The twins lavishly entertained their guests in their royal palace at Amyklai. Curious Helene came to meet the wealthy visitors and invited them to her husband's palace in Therapne.

When the Dioskouroi left on a cattle raid, they sent their guests to the house of their brother-in law. When Paris laid eyes upon Menelaos's lovely wife, Helene, he knew instantly that she was the one promised to him. She too fell deeply under love's spell. After nine days, unobservant Menelaos was called away for the funeral of his great-grandfather Katreus. He instructed his wife to continue providing hospitality to their guests.

Unsupervised, the two spent their every waking moment together. Paris boldly proposed that she come away with him, and she accepted. They stole as much of Menelaos's treasures as they could load on his ship and set sail. Helene also brought with her five servants, including two former princesses (Theseus's mother, Aithra, and Peirithoos's sister Phesadie) taken by the twins when they seized Aphidnai and recovered abducted Helene. She gave herself to the eager prince at the first port they stopped at. They either returned home directly after three days of good sailing or went by way of Phoenicia/Cyprus to avoid pursuers or because angry Hera, still sore because Alexandros had not picked her, caused a storm to blow them off course to Sidon in Phoenicia. From there they followed the coastline to Troy (1195T/945R BCE).

The Trojans were worried about reprisals when Alexandros returned with a stolen woman and treasure. Helene quickly won their hearts, and they decided she could stay. She married the envied prince in a sumptuous ceremony. Through all the troubles that followed, the two remained close lovers and parents of Aganos, Bunomos, and Idaios, who all died as children when a roof collapsed upon them, as well as a daughter named Helene.

---

[245] Hesiod, "Homeric Hymn to Aphrodite," in *The Homeric Hymns and Homerica.*

Meanwhile, a cattle raid took the Dioskouroi to the far side of the Taygetos Mountains. There they came upon the cattle of their cousins Idas and Lynceus. Those two Triphylians had once helped the Dioskouroi raid cattle in Arkadia and had won the Dioskouroi's share in an eating contest won by Idas (who once successfully stood up to the long-haired god Apollo over his bride, Marpessa). The Dioskouroi were pleased to make the two their victims this time. As they drove their herd up Mount Taygetos, sharp-eyed Lynceus spotted them from afar. Soon the twin sons of Poseidon overtook the twin sons of Zeus.

Men of war settle their differences with weapons. Kastor fell beneath Idas's spear while wine-ruddy Polydeuces dropped Lynceus into heavy, eternal sleep. Idas then faced Polydeuces and knocked him out with a blow to the head. Zeus feared great indiscretion would befall his immortal son, and therefore he killed Idas with a thunderbolt.[246]

When Polydeuces revived, he grieved mightily at the side of his dead brother. He prayed to all-seeing Zeus that they not be separated, and the god nodded his mighty head. From that day forward, the twins together alternated days between Olympos and Hades. Forty years after their death, the Lacedaimonians became aware of their placement in the skies as the constellation Gemini, where they exercised their powers as gods to assist sailors in distress.[247]

## Preparations for War

Lord Zeus sent the messenger goddess Iris to descend on the rainbow that bridges heaven and earth to tell Menelaos that his wife had abandoned him. Hastily, he returned home, where more bad news awaited him. The Dioskouroi were no longer living among men. His coronation brought him little joy. When the ceremony was over, he angrily set off to Mycenai, where he plotted revenge with his brother Agamemnon.

[246] Theokritos, "Dioskouroi", in *The Idylls of Theocritus*. Translated by Thelma Sargent. Theokritos says that the pair of twins fought over the daughters of Leucippos. Kastor killed Lynceus in a duel, and Zeus's thunderbolt dropped Idas as he prepared to hurl the tombstone of Aphareus at Kastor.

[247] During the Hellenistic era, the Gemini came to represent the two halves of the celestial sphere (the one above and below the horizon), hence their alternate days in Olympos and Hades. The Dioskouroi were identified with the Assyrian constellation The Great Twins.

Agamemnon sent his herald Talthybios to deliver messages to the unsuccessful suitors of Helene's abduction and reminded them of their oath. But it was not just their word that compelled the suitors to come; the promise of loot and the fear of offending the great wanax were also powerful motivators. They were ordered to assemble at the Boiotian (Minyan) port of Aulis.[248]

Agamemnon ordered brilliant Palamedes of Nauplia, son of the great sailor Nauplios (descendent of Nauplios the sailor, whom Amymone bore to Poseidon when he gave her the springs of Lerne), to join him and Menelaos as they went to enlist Nestor, the sage king of the greatest Peloponnesian state outside of the Argeia. King Nestor of sandy Pylos was not obliged to go, since he had not been a suitor, but he agreed to do so for wealth and glory (Nestor was the sole surviving son of Neleus because he had been too young to fight against Herakles with his brothers). Hearing from heralds that wily Odysseus was not coming, Agamemnon dispatched Menelaos and Palamedes across the Ionian Sea to force him to do so.

Odysseus was in no mood to have his joyous time with Penelope interrupted, and he pretended to be insane. They found Odysseus wearing the headgear of a madman. He had yoked a horse and an ox and was sowing his fields with salt. He did not acknowledge his guests; nor did he listen to their demand that he honor his pledge to rescue missing Helene.

Bright Palamedes was suspicious of Odysseus's madness and decided to test him. He took Odysseus's infant son Telemakhos from his cradle and placed him in the path of the plow with these words: "Give up your pretense and come and join the allies". Odysseus swerved to miss his son, and thus his sanity was established. With his cover blown, Odysseus dutifully gathered together his forces.

The Hellenes wished to enlist a legendary young fighter: Akhilleus. Like Nestor, he had not been a suitor and therefore was not obliged to go. Akhilleus was born from the union of the sea goddess Thetis, who had submitted to Peleus after their strife-ridden wedding. Because his wife left him, Peleus gave their son, Ligyron, to the wise Centaur Kheiron to raise. Kheiron gave the child a fantastic education and renamed him Akhilleus.

---

[248] Archaeological evidence strongly suggests that nearby Perati in eastern Attike was the principal launching point for expeditions across the Aigaian Sea at that time.

He instilled courage in the boy in part by feeding him the entrails of wild animals. As a boy Akhilleus once chased down a doe; another time he killed a lion.

Silver-sandaled Thetis got wind of the Hellenes' intent and appeared before her young son. She had no intention of sharing the fate of the other Hellen mothers and widows who would be singing dirges for their lost ones around the hearths of every city. So Thetis commanded her son to go hide among the ladies of the court of King Lykomedes on remote Skyros Island. Akhilleus was miserable until he met the princess, Deidameia.

Image 13.1
Map of Troas and Surrounding Area

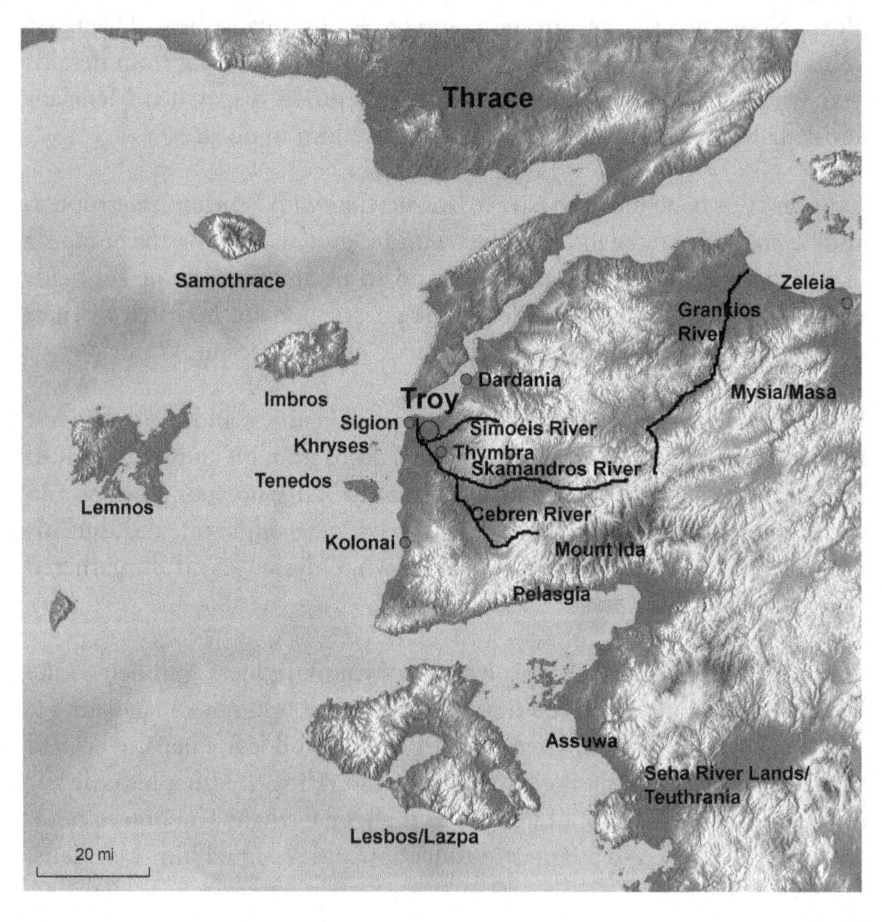

The Hellenes implored the seer Kalkhas to find Akhilleus. (Kalkhas was the son of the Korinthian seer Thestor, son of the seer Idmon, who was killed by a boar on the voyage of the Argonauts.) The seer correctly "saw" that the youth was hiding among the ladies of Skyros. Odysseus was dispatched immediately. Upon his mother's order, Akhilleus did not disclose himself, so wily Odysseus prepared a ruse. Odysseus placed shiny new weapons among feminine trinkets for the ladies of the palace. Then Odysseus sat back and observed the women until he noticed a big woman taking a longing look at the weapons. Odysseus then sprung his trap by signaling for a war trumpet to blow in the distance. Akhilleus instinctively threw off his girlish garments and grabbed the arms. Once discovered, Akhilleus paid no more attention to his mother's fear that he would die young and gloriously instead of old and happy. Young Akhilleus eagerly took Odysseus back to Phthia to ask his father's permission to go. Peleus was proud to let his strong-armed son fight.

Hellenic forces assembled at Aulis on the coast of Boiotia. It was the largest gathering of troops Hellas had ever seen and represented a logistical nightmare. It took a year to inform and assemble the suitors and their forces. The seer Kalkhas predicted the war would swallow nine years after observing a snake eat eight fledglings and then the mother in a bird's nest.

A bit uncertain as to where Troy was, the fleet accidentally landed in nearby Teuthrania (1194T/944R BCE). Marching inland, they pillaged the countryside. King Telephos arrived with his army, and the disoriented Akhaians fell back before his ferocious onslaught. Only the Epigonoi warrior Thersandros of Thebes, son of Polyneices, stood his ground while those around him fled. The two champions dueled until Telephos slew King Thersandros. As the mighty son of Herakles continued to drive back the Akhaians, he slipped on a grape or ivy vine while chasing Odysseus. Alert Akhilleus jabbed Telephos with a spear thrust to the thigh before Telephos recovered his footing.

The Akhaian retreat stopped, but when it became apparent that Telephos was not seriously hurt, the two sides agreed to a truce. The Akhaians discovered their mistake and tried to enlist the great warrior Telephos. When Telephos declined (his wife was a Trojan princess), the Akhaians buried Thersandros and sailed home. During the winter, Akhilleus stayed on Skyros and married Princess Deidameia, the mother of his son Neoptolemos.

---

Exhibit 13.2
Telephos and Teuthrania

Eponymous king Teuthras once killed a boar sacred to Artemis, and in revenge Artemis struck him with a skin disease.[249] After a time the king was able to scrape the disease away using rocks found nearby, because his mother, Leucippe, had appeased the goddess by building her an altar on Mount Teuthras, where the transgression had occurred.

According to tradition, King Teuthras bought his Arkadian bride, Auge, from the Akhaian slave trader Nauplios. It was obvious to the king that this stunning beauty was no ordinary woman. Nauplios noticed the king's instant infatuation and told him she was a Tegean princess whom he had saved from tragic circumstances. Love-struck Teuthras agreed to pay a handsome fee for Auge and promptly married her (1229T/979R BCE).

[249] A mythic Bronze Age king of neighboring Lydia committed the same crime and lost his life for it.

King Teuthras ruled an important state by the time Arkadian Telephos[250] came to his court (1211T/961R BCE). Arkadian Parthenopaios told the interested royal couple about his silent companion Telephos. He had been abandoned as an infant and received his name when shepherds found him suckling an *elephus* (doe). The two became childhood friends, for Parthenopaios too had been exposed upon the same mountain. (Princess Atalante of Arkadian Orkhomenos, the maiden who tried to join the Argonauts and was the first hunter to draw blood on the Kalydonian boar hunt, exposed the child she bore that was sired by either manly Ares or Arkadian Melanion.) Telephos, he said, had not spoken a word since he accidentally killed a Tegean nobleman. (His silence was to avoid detection by the avenging Erinyes.) The two fled to Delphi to discover their ancestry and to find purification for Telephos. They had been ordered to go to Mysia without any explanation.

As Parthenopaios spoke, weeping Auge realized that he was describing her own son. She told the astonished court that her father, King Aleos of Tegea (son of Apheidas, son of Arkas), feared the prophecy that if she bore a son, he would kill his own uncle. In a futile attempt to cheat fate,

[250] The myths concerning Telephos, Auge, and Eurypylos are ancient. Because of the later importance of their Hellenistic city, Pergamese writers localized these tales in Pergamon, a city in the region of Teuthrania. The myth of Eurypylos is the oldest. He was mentioned by Homer (*Odyssey* ix.519) and Leskhes (*Little Iliad* i.8). Telephos is mentioned as Eurypylos's father but otherwise is unmentioned in the Trojan War Cycle. The lives of both Telephos and Auge were first recorded in now lost fifth-century BCE works. Telephos's life was detailed in two plays: *The Mysians*, by Sophokles, and *Telephos*, by Euripides. The fifth-century BCE historian Hekataios of Miletos's telling of Auge's tragic tale is quoted by Pausanias (*Guide to Greece* viii.4.8–9). Late writers, such as Apollodoros (*Library* ii.7.4, iii.19, and Epitome 3.17–20), Diodoros (*Library of History* iv.33.7–12), Hyginos (*Fabulai* 99, 100, and 101), and Strabo (*Geography* xiii.1.69) refer to her story.

Although the Akhaians (Ahhiyawa) were active in western Anatolia during the Late Bronze Age, they did not settle along the coast of Teuthrania until long afterward (despite the above mythic claims to the contrary). This is probably due to the strength of Arzawan kingdom of the Seha River Land, a vassal of the Hittites that was probably based in the region of Teuthrania.

Hittite records may corroborate the existence of these mythic personalities, but they were not Hellenic. It is distinctly possible that Telephos is a Hellenized version of the Hittite royal name Telepines and that Eurypylos is the historical figure Urballa/Warpawplas. Homer (*Odyssey* ix.519) supports this seemingly farfetched connection by asserting that Eurypylos led Ketoi warriors to Troy. The Egyptians called the Hittites the Kheta. It is certainly possible that a Hittite prince from Teuthrania led soldiers to defend besieged Troy. Finally, could Auge be Massanauzzi, the Hittite princess who was married to an Assuwan king when she was too old to bear him children?

King Aleos appointed his daughter to the role of priestess of virgin Athena instead of giving her away in marriage. She recalled with bitter tears how drunken Herakles had raped her in the holy temple of Athena in Tegea. (Her brother Cephelos was unaware of this and had died fighting with Herakles against the Spartans). When her father discovered her pregnancy, he undertook stronger measures to thwart fate and to hide the family disgrace presented by her unwed pregnancy. The king, her own father, paid the slave trader Nauplios to take her to the sea and drown her. While marching to the sea, pangs of childbirth overwhelmed her, and she delivered on Mount Parthenios. Heartlessly, she was forced to get up, abandon her precious baby, and resume her march. The sound of her helpless crying baby haunted her. She had been certain her son had died. Fortunately for her, Nauplios did not kill her as instructed and instead sold her to profit twice from her misfortune.

Telephos wiped away his mother's tears and broke his silence to soothe her. Teuthras rose from his throne and embraced Telephos. He purified him of murder and adopted him as his son. He soon needed the help of his adopted son, and his strong friend Parthenopaios, to thwart a powerful Hellenic raider. Of all the children of Herakles, Telephos most resembled his father in fighting spirit. He proved his mettle while fighting with the Teuthranians against invading Akhaians. With Parthenopaios guiding his chariot, Telephos beat back the great warrior Idas of Messenia (1199T/949R BCE).

Grateful Teuthras, who had no sons of his own, gave his daughter Argiope in marriage to Telephos and made him his heir. Parthenopaios married the Mysian nymph Klymene and stayed awhile in Teuthrania. Then he took his young wife home to Arkadia and died in the glorious but unsuccessful Akhaian attack on Thebes led by Adrastos.

In time Teuthras died and Telephos became king. He sent for Arkadian settlers to help him build a new city at Pergamon. King Priamos of Troy sent his youngest sister, Astyokhe, to the new king to cement relations between the two kingdoms. According to the custom of the east, Telephos was permitted numerous wives, each received in a political arrangement. Astyokhe bore his first son, beloved Eurypylos.

---

## Sacrifice of the Princess

The troops gathered again at Aulis (1193T/943R BCE). They waited for spring to calm the ocean and allow safe passage. While waiting, Agamemnon angered the huntress with shafts of gold, and she responded by sending a series of storms to delay the launch. Either he slew a wild hind sacred to the goddess or he rashly boasted that he was a better hunter than Artemis, who delights in arrows. The seer Kalkhas correctly divined her anger and what was necessary to appease her. The angry goddess demanded no less than the sacrifice of the king's daughter to win her support. Agamemnon wavered at the thought, but Menelaos convinced him that his kingdom was at stake. If he did not perform the required sacrifice, Menelaos said, he would appear weak and risk a rebellion among the army and allies. Euripides says the event was preordained when Agamemnon imprudently vowed to sacrifice to virgin Artemis the fairest thing brought forth the year his daughter was born. Iphigeneia was the fairest one born that year.

Sadly, Agamemnon sent Odysseus and his herald Talthybios to fetch his eldest daughter, Iphigeneia. They were instructed to tell Klytaimnestra that the girl was to marry the great young warrior Akhilleus. Iphigeneia was only ten; her expected bridegroom barely in his teens. Klytaimnestra was thrilled and decided to attend the wedding despite her husband's command to the contrary. She brought with her the heir apparent, their toddler son Orestes.

During a tempest, Kalkhas prepared to sacrifice Iphigeneia to appease Artemis and gain a fair wind. When Iphigenia figured out what was happening, she protested in panic. Once she realized she had no choice, she accepted her fate and decided to die nobly to provide a good omen so that the army could attack the enemy. When the moment arrived, she asked for her father to give her a kiss or a glance goodbye, but her grieving and guilty father was unable to look up. Afterward, the king solemnly paid for the construction of a shrine to Artemis in nearby Megara. Klytaimnestra was infuriated at Agamemnon for sacrificing their daughter for Menelaos's sake.

Agamemnon sacrificed more than his daughter. Akhilleus was angry that his good name had been used deceptively, and Klytaimnestra went home with implacable hatred for her husband. No grief outdoes that of a mother witnessing her child's death. Hermione, the only daughter of Menelaos and

Helene, was left in Mycenai for Klytaimnestra to raise since her parents were absent.

## On to Troy

Despite the sacrifice, there would to be no smooth sailing to Troy. Agamemnon first sailed to Andros Island, where he abducted King Anios's daughters. Dionysos gave these marvelous girls the ability to change soil into oil, grain, and wine, and therefore they could provision the troops. Once out to sea, the girls escaped when Dionysos turned them into doves.

When the fleet reached Tenedos Island, just off of the coast of Ilion, they met resistance. The hopelessly outnumbered natives were defeated despite the valiant efforts of its king, Tenes. Akhilleus killed Tenes for trying to stop the Akhaian ships from landing by throwing stones at them despite his mother's warning before he left that he would not return home alive if he killed the son of Apollo. (Because Tenes was a seer, he was often called a son of Apollo, though his earthly father was King Cyknos of Kolonai). The Akhaians enslaved the inhabitants and ransacked their homes.

Agamemnon ordered the fleet to remain on Tenedos while Menelaos—the aggrieved party—wise Palamedes, and wily Odysseus were sent as an envoy to Troy. Agamemnon passed the time by inviting the Hellenic captains to a feast. Akhilleus felt slighted because his invitation came late, and relations between the two remained strained throughout the rest of the war. Next Philoktetes was bitten by a viper while performing a sacrifice. The stench from his wound became intolerable, and the other captains shipped him off to Lemnos. He survived by hunting with the famous bow of Herakles that the great hero had given him in gratitude for igniting his funeral pyre.

When the envoy reached the rich city of Troy, an angry mob gathered, intent on killing Menelaos, Palamedes, and Odysseus. If it had not been for the forceful intercession of the powerful elder Antenor, they would have met their doom. Kindly Antenor offered them protection and hospitality in his home.

> Wise-counseling Antenor told King Priamos and his sons
> the whole plan of the Hellenes. Then heralds speeding

> through the wide city, gathered the ranks of Trojans into the agora where the army musters, and their loud summons raced everywhere; and they raised their hands to the immortal gods and they prayed for an end to their griefs.[251]

Then the three appeared before the assembled ranks and pleaded their case. Antenor led the peace party, which Priamos favored. However, Priamos changed his decision because his sons adamantly supported war and because the Trojans overwhelmingly supported keeping Helene and the treasures of Menelaos. Antenor escorted the envoy safely out of town. Antenor's kin in Dardania chose to remain neutral, even though Aineias had been with Paris at Sparta.

Fired up by the Trojan response, the bloodthirsty invaders sailed to the coast where Sigion would later rise. The Trojan warmongers stood ready for them. Hektor and Cyknos led the determined Trojan defense. When the Hellenic soldiers saw imposing Hektor in his brightly shining gold-crested helmet, a gift from Apollo, they became afraid. Hektor waited to face whoever leapt ashore first, and even Akhilleus held back. Finally, Prince Protesilaos (meaning "first of the people") of Thessalia (a descendent of Iphikos, whom Melampous cured of impotency) jumped boldly from his ship and faced Hektor on the beach. While Hektor was busy dispatching Protesilaos, other Hellenes waded ashore. Protesilaos's wife, Laodameia, daughter of King Akastos of Iolkos, committed suicide, unable to cope with the news of his death.

The second ashore was Akhilleus, whom Cyknos (meaning "swan") confronted with vengeance on his mind, for he was the father of Tenes. Cyknos was the son of Poseidon and Kalyce, daughter of Hekato. He had been abandoned as a child beside the sea, where he was comforted by a swan. He ruled the Trojan city of Kolonai and prospered by his father's grace on the sea trade that passed by his city. Loud-crashing Poseidon was so fond of this son that he made Cyknos invulnerable to weapons. Cyknos married Prokleia, daughter of the prominent Trojan elder Klytios, brother of King Priamos.

[251] Bakkhylides, "The Sons of Antenor", in *Greek Lyric.* Translated by David A. Campbell.

The pair raised three lovely children: Tenes, Hemitheia, and Glauce. When Prokleia died, Cyknos chose to remarry. He picked a beautiful young maiden named Philonome, daughter of Kragasos. Philonome desired young Tenes but failed to seduce him. Angrily she bribed the flute player Eumolpos into corroborating her story that Tenes had raped her. Cyknos chose to believe his beautiful young bride and put Tenes and Hemitheia, who stood by her brother, into a chest and flung them out into the sea. Glauce was too young to be involved.

Miraculously, innocent Tenes landed safely on nearby Tenedos Island, where he became the king. When Cyknos learned the truth, he buried Philonome alive, stoned Eumolpos, and vainly went to Tenedos seeking forgiveness. Tenes and Hemitheia refused to see him; their disagreement had happened long before the Hellenes arrived. Now Cyknos grieved the loss of a son whom he could never reconcile with. His heart burned against the Akhaian soldiers feasting on the riches Tenedos offered.

Akhilleus was a far better fighter, but he grew frustrated with his failure to slay Cyknos. His weapons bounced uselessly off of Cyknos's body. Finally Akhilleus strangled Cyknos with his own helmet thongs. Loud-roaring Poseidon changed him into a swan, and he flew off. The panicked Trojans withdrew behind their walls.

With Cyknos dead and the Trojans gone, the Hellenes easily sacked Kolonai. Cyknos's daughter Glauce had grown into a beautiful maiden, and she was awarded to big Ajax of Salamis. Ajax had been named by Herakles on the request of his stalwart friend Telamon. Ajax was the cousin of Akhilleus; both were grandsons of Aiakos, the man who had helped the gods build the walls of Troy. Glauce lived in the tent of this conqueror as a concubine while the Hellenes besieged her kin in Troy.

Though reluctant, the elders permitted furious Hektor to lead the army again into open battle. In that battle he challenged Akhilleus below the citadel of Troy. When neither combatant prevailed, the Trojan withdrew behind their walls. Afterward the cautious elders overruled Hektor's call for further battles, preferring to wait them out behind the strong walls. The Akhaians then besieged the city; thrice the two Ajaxes (Telamon's son and Ajax of Lokris), Kretan king Idomeneus (a descendent of Minos), Menelaos, and Agamemnon led assaults on the weakest part of the walls—the west side near a large fig tree. Harassed from above, the walls of Troy proved impenetrable and unassailable.

## The Long Siege

The Akhaians made ramparts to protect their ships, which they pulled up onto the sandy shore. Their strategy was to reduce Troy by strangling the trade coming into the Aigaian Sea out of the Hellespont. They did not (or could not) block trade to the interior or along the seacoast to the north. This strategy failed to bring the Trojans to their knees.

Akhilleus or Ajax usually led the raiding parties. Akhilleus's war parties destroyed twenty-three nearby settlements—twelve by the sea, eleven by land. Most were Trojan settlements or their allies on Lesbos Island. Ajax led war parties against the Pelasgian cities of Mount Ida and in further-off raids against Trojan allies in Thrace, Mysia, and Phrygia. Palamedes reputedly invented dice during this time to occupy soldiers during long periods of boredom.

Akhilleus had not been a suitor of Helene, nor had he ever laid eyes on her. He was curious to see the woman with fabled looks and begged his mother to arrange a meeting. Silver-sandaled Thetis spoke to golden Aphrodite, who arranged for the two to meet briefly and uneventfully. Afterward, when the discouraged Akhaians wished to give up, Akhilleus restrained them.

During the siege, Palamedes demonstrated his wise and innovative mind, one which only Odysseus could match.[252] He once chided his rival Odysseus for failing to secure grain during a raid on Thrace. Odysseus challenged him to do better and, he promptly did. Odysseus, with the support of towering Diomedes (son of Aitolian prince Tydeus, an Epigonoi, and regent of Midea on behalf of Adrastos's grandson Cyanippos) plotted to eliminate this rival to the affections of the wanax and to punish him for uncovering his ruse to avoid the war. They framed Palamedes by coercing

[252] Nauplios and his son Palamedes were not mentioned by Homer. Their exploits appear in the Homeric poems *Cypria* and *Nostoi* (meaoning"returns"). Neither poem survives. Surviving references disagree in detail. Both men appear in plays by Euripides, including the lost play *Palamedes*.

prisoners to carry a false letter accusing him of bribery and hiding gold in his tent. Agamemnon sentenced him to die by stoning (or drowning). His last words were "Truth, I mourn you, who have predeceased me."

Priamos and Hekabe's second-youngest son, Troilos (whom some claim Apollo was the father of) was an incredibly athletic child. Though young, he demonstrated athletic potential beyond that even of his brothers Paris and Hektor. The Hellenes worried about him and set a trap to ambush him, lest he grow to manhood. When the trap was sprung, Troilos ran like the wind, but he was not yet as fast as Akhilleus.

As Akhilleus caught up to the youth, he demanded that he yield or die. Troilos kept running but was overcome at the temple of Thymbraian Apollo. With livid face and crushed ribs, he endured the bearlike embrace of Akhilleus. So the boy, patterned on the gods, was horribly slain by Akhilleus outside the citadel of Troy.[253]

Akhilleus once led a cattle raid on Mount Ida and found a large herd with cowherds commanded by Priamos's son Mestor and Aphrodite's son Aineias. Along with Hektor and Troilos, Mestor was his father's favorite. Akhilleus managed to kill Mestor and the cowherds. He chased Aineias down the wooded slopes, but he got away. While Aineias took refuge in Lyrnessos, word reached the Dardanians that the Akhaians were attacking. The Dardanians fled before Akhilleus to Troy.

Aineias escaped from Lyrnessos and followed the Dardanians to Troy. His lame father accompanied him. Aineias led one of the five companies into battle while his cousin Alkathoos was second in command of Paris's unit. Two sons of Antenor, Akamas and Arkhelokhos, were Aineias's lieutenants.

While Akhilleus was conquering Trojan allies, Ajax led war parties farther afield. When he raided isolated Pelasgian villages on Mount Ida, the people fled to Troy. Hippothoos and Pylaios led the Pelasgians into battle. They were the sons of King Lethos, son of Teutamas, king of Larissa and eponym of Lethos.[254] The Pelasgians were vassals of Troy, as were their Dardanian neighbors.

[253] The romantic myth of Troilos and Kreside began during medieval times, long after ancient Troy, and ancient Rome for that matter, had fallen.

[254] Herodotos said that there were still Pelasgian speakers in Hellespont Phrygia during his time (fifth century BCE).

During winter, when no fighting occurred, the Akhaians passed their time improving the battlements, practicing archery, and gambling with dice. Akhilleus happened to visit the temple of Thymbraian Apollo while Hekabe and her beautiful daughter Polyxene were present. Polyxene had just reached marriageable age, and Akhilleus took note.

After returning to his ship, Akhilleus became vexed with love. He sent kindly Automedon to Hektor, asking for a bride-price. He replied by telling Akhilleus that if he betrayed the Hellenes, Polyxene would be his. Akhilleus would not agree to such terms.

Unable to starve the Trojans into submission, Menelaos, Talthybios, and Odysseus were sent to the Mycenaian settlements on various islands to request support. The pledge of support the Cypriots gave was never delivered as promised.

When the Akhaians sacked Lyrnessos, home of the Alizones tribe, Akhilleus slew King Evenos. His sons Mynes and Epistrophos were also slain by Akhilleus, but a third son, Odious, escaped and led the Alizones survivors at Troy. Akhilleus seized Mynes's lovely bride, Briseis, who became his prize. Her father, Briseus, hung himself in grief. Also captured was Khryses's daughter Khryseis, who was awarded to Agamemnon. Ironically, she had been sent to Lyrnessos for her safety. Khryses ruled the small island of Khryses, sacred to Apollo, but feared that the Hellenes would not honor the holiness of the place after Akhilleus had violated Troilos at Apollo's Thymbraian shrine.

The priest Khryses arrived in the Akhaian camp and tried to ransom Khryseis. Agamemnon turned him away with opprobrious words. On Khryses's fervent prayers, Apollo shot arrows of plague upon the Hellenes in punishment. For ten days men got sick and died. To appease bright Apollo, Agamemnon sent Khryseis back to her father with proprietary gifts. When Akhilleus told Agamemnon to stop grumbling about it, the king of kings angrily demanded Akhilleus's concubine Briseis of Lyrnessos to compensate for his loss.

## Tenth Year of War

The siege of Troy took a toll, and the restless citizens became exceedingly frustrated with the wait-it-out strategy. King Priamos changed plans and dispatched urgent messages for his allies to send armies to help him drive off the invaders. With spring, the allies began arriving: Thracians, Paphlagonians, Mysians, Phrygians, Lydians, Karians, and Lycians.

A nearby vassal of Troy unscathed by war also sent troops. They were the Zeleians, a related tribe living east of the Granikos River. Lykaon ruled over them and called his nation Lycia. His son, a magnificent archer named Pandareos, led the Zeleians to Troy. (Only Paris was a better archer on the Trojan side.) Lykaon suggested he take a chariot and horses, but Pandareos feared there would be short rations of fodder under siege, so he went on foot.

Arriving allies strengthened Troy just as the Hellenes fell to bickering. Akhilleus withdrew from the contest when Agamemnon forced him to give up his concubine Briseis. The Trojans took heart and made a vigorous attack, not waiting for all the allies to arrive. The two sides squared off with tall Hektor as commander-in-chief and general.

In the plain below Troy, the armies met. Brave Paris strode out into the no-man's-land between the armies, eager to face any challenger. It was Menelaos who saw him and eagerly went out to face him. Seeing Menelaos, Paris lost heart and slinked back into the Trojan line. Hektor admonished his brother for cowardice and Paris offered to duel Menelaos to decide the issue. Hektor entered the no-man's-land and threw down his spear, asking for a hearing. Agamemnon commanded his soldiers to hold back. Hektor offered Paris's proposal to duel for the haunted lady and the Spartan treasures.

Both men armed for battle. Fiery Menelaos had been trained since his childhood in the ways of battle, but Paris had only lately been taught the noble art of hand-to-hand combat. After ineffective spear tosses, Menelaos drew his sword, but broke it on Paris's helmet. Cursing his luck, Menelaos grabbed Paris by his helmet strap and dragged him toward the Akhaian lines. When it snapped, Aphrodite whisked Paris away safely into Helene's arms back in Troy. While menacing Menelaos vainly sought his enemy, Paris safely made love to Helene on his ivory-framed bed.

In the confusion that followed, Pandareos of Zeleia shot Menelaos, hoping to end the dispute by taking out the aggrieved party. Menelaos fell back and turned pale until he realized that his armor had saved him. He was only slightly wounded.

The battle resumed, and the Hellenic warrior Diomedes went berserk, killing Pandareos and many others, including Priamos's nephews Aispos and Pedasos. He broke Aineias's hip with a stone toss and stole his fabulous horses. Aphrodite grabbed her son to save him, and impertinent Diomedes wounded her in the wrist. Leto and Artemis cured Aineias for Aphrodite. Then, with Pallas Athena's assistance, Diomedes wounded Ares, god of the bloodcurdling yell.

Elsewhere on the battlefield, King Sarpedon of Lycia, descendent of Pegasos-riding Bellerophontes,[255] was taunted and challenged by Herakles's fierce son Tlepolemos of Rhodes, one of the best spearmen on the field of battle. As their chariots drew near, they raised ashen spears,

> and from their hands in unison long shafts took flight. Sarpedon hit his enemy squarely in the neck with a force enough to drive the point clear through, unending night of death clouded his eyes. Tlepolemos' point hitting the upper leg went jolting through between the two long bones.[256]

As the Lycians carried Sarpedon to safety, the great Trojan prince Hektor drove the Akhaians back. Then tall Hektor returned to Troy to rouse his brother to battle in order to help him stop towering Diomedes.

> There the warmhearted lady came to meet him, running: Andromakhe, whom bold Eetion had borne. Hektor was her lord now, head to foot in bronze; and now she joined him. Behind came the maid, who held the child against her breast, a rosy baby still, son of Hektor, the world's delight, as fresh as a pure shining star. How brilliantly the warrior smiled, in silence, his eyes upon the child!

[255] An Ahhiyawa attack and defeat by a Lycian (Luwian) king was probably incorporated into the Trojan War Cycle.
[256] Homer, *Iliad,* v.748-752

> Andromakhe rested against him, shook away a tear, and pressed his hand in both of her own to say: "Oh, my wild one, your bravery will be your undoing. Bring the soldiers in and fight no more." He told her no and held out his arms to take the baby. But the child squirmed round on the nurse's bosom and began to wail, terrified by his father's great war helmet - the flashing bronze, the crest with horsehair plume tossed like a living thing at every nod. His father began laughing, and his mother laughed as well. Then from his handsome head Hektor lifted off his helmet and bent to place it, bright with sunlight, on the ground. When he had kissed his child and swung him high to dawdle him, he said this prayer: "Oh Zeus and all immortals may this child, my son, become like me a prince among the Trojans. Let him be strong and brave and rule in power at Ilion: then someday men will say this fellow is far better than his father!" After the prayer, into his wife's arms he gave his baby, whom on her fragrant breast she held and cherished, laughing through her tears. Hektor pitied her now. Caressing her, he said: "Unquiet soul, do not be too distressed by thoughts of me. You know no man dispatches me into the undergloom against my fate; no mortal, either, can escape his fate, coward or brave man, once he comes to be." He stooped to recover his helmet as she, his dear wife, drew away, her head turned and her eyes upon him, brimming with tears.[257]

The Trojan bulk ward, Hektor, found Paris not unwilling to fight beside him, and the two boldly marched back into the fray. After Paris wounded Diomedes with a bronze-tipped arrow, the Trojans rallied behind Hektor. Then Hektor proposed a duel against Akhilleus to decide the issue.

Word came back from Akhilleus that he was not fighting for the Akhaians. Big Ajax volunteered to take his place. The combatants fought without pause until nightfall. They separated with gifts and praise for each other.

Without a clear victor, the battle resumed the next day. After a glorious morning where men fell equally on both sides, the Danaans broke through

[257] Homer, *Iliad,* vi.390–500.

the Trojan ranks behind the strong arm of lord Agamemnon. Among his victims were Prince Antiphos and his charioteer Ilos, his bastard half brother. Early in the war the two had been caught and ransomed by the raiding Akhilleus while tending flocks on Mount Ida.

Antenor's eldest son, Iphidamas, challenged Agamemnon. Muscular and athletic Iphidamas had been raised by his grandfather in Thrace and left his new bride behind in Perkote to lead twelve ships to defend Troy. His spear toss bounced off Agamemnon's armor, and Agamemnon's sword cut him. Immediately, Iphidamas's brother Koon attacked Agamemnon from a blind side, cutting the tendons in the king's elbow before the king killed him.

While Agamemnon withdrew, tall Hektor led a furious counterattack. The Akhaians were driven off the plain and behind the barricade they had built to protect their ships. The Trojans followed in hot pursuit. Asios of Arisbe led the charge, foolishly driving his chariot into the camp. King Idomeneus of Krete killed him while Asios's son Adamas fell to Meriones of Krete, son of Idomeneus's half brother Molos. When Hektor received a mild concussion by a rock thrown by Ajax and Meriones killed Antenor's son Akamas, the Trojans withdrew.

Ajax and Akhilleus were the best Akhaian warriors and so had confidently placed their ships on the exposed camp wings. Since Akhilleus was not fighting, the Trojans regrouped, dismounted and charged the battlements on Ajax's wing. King Sarpedon recovered quickly from the wound Tlepolemos had inflicted and was the first to scale the barricade defending the Hellenic ships. He called back to Lycian cocaptain Glaukos, saying, "Ah cousin, could we but survive this war to live forever deathless, without age, I would not ever go again to battle. Nor would I send you there for honor's sake! But now a thousand shapes of death surround us, and no man can escape them, or be safe. Let us attack - whether to give some man glory or to win it from him"[258]

Prince Glaukos hailed from a Lycian kingdom boardering the one Sarpedon ruled. Like Sarpedon, Glaukos was a descendent of Bellerophontes. He readily accepted the challenge but was soon slightly wounded in the arm by one of Teucros's arrows. Teucros was half Trojan; his mother was

[258] Homer, *Iliad* xii.

the Trojan princess Hesione, whom Herakles had saved and awarded to Telamon for being first to scale the walls of Troy in a bygone battle. As Glaukos withdrew, big Ajax and his sharp-shooting half brother Teucros beat Sarpedon back off the wall. Sarpedon would not be denied; he gathered his men and charged again. The two forces battled to a draw until the shaken Hektor revived and rejoined the fray. With Sarpedon he led the breaching of the walls.

The Hellenes desperately fought to save their camp. Ajax slew Antenor's sons Arkhelokhos and Laodamas, but Hektor drove Ajax from his ship and set it ablaze. The casualties were heavy on both sides. Akhilleus stubbornly refused Agamemnon's overtures as the battle raged.

With the smell of ships burning in the air, Patroklos pleaded with Akhilleus to fight or let him lead the Myrmidon troops. Patroklos was the son of Menoitios of Lokris and Sthenele, the daughter of a fellow Argonaut, King Akastos of Iolkos. His family had been forced to flee as a supplicant to Peleus when aggressive Patroklos killed one of his playmates. He had become an inseparable friend of Akhilleus. Now wearing Akhilleus's armor, Patroklos attacked the Trojans while Ajax slightly wounded Hektor. With Hektor absent to have his wound attended to, and thinking Akhilleus was attacking, most of the Trojans fled to their chariots.

Then King Sarpedon of Lycia drove at Patroklos, who was leading the Hellenes out of their camp. Patroklos killed him and wished to rob his corpse. Glaukos rallied the Lycian troops and recovered Sarpedon, saving his corpse from outrage. While Glaukos carried him off, Patroklos killed more Lycians, and the resistance crumbled. Patroklos then chased the Trojans and their allies all the way back to Troy, and three times he tried to scale the walls. Each time the far-shooter Apollo pushed him back.

When the corset of Patroklos's ill-fitted armor came unlaced, the young Dardanian warrior Euphorbos, son of Panthoos, wounded him while he was distracted. Hektor returned to the battle and slew Patroklos with a single blow. The fighting around fallen Patroklos was fierce. Hektor striped the god-made armor Peleus had given Akhilleus off of Patroklos, but he had to yield the corpse to the combined strength of Ajax and Menelaos. The day's carnage ended with the Akhaians withdrawing to their ships.

To avoid another close call, Agamemnon again tried to reenlist Akhilleus. He offered to give back the girl Briseis untouched. He also showered gifts on the great warrior. Although Akhilleus accepted the gifts, he chose to reenter the fray to avenge Patroklos's death, not to help Agamemnon.

That evening, bright Polydamas urged Hektor not to engage in battle the next day because he feared Akhilleus's wrath would spur him on to greater feats. Born the same day as Hektor, Polydamas was a great strategist and good soldier; he was as good in debate as Hektor was in battle. He was Hektor's good friend and second in command of his company. His father, Panthoos, son of Othrys, was the priest of Dardanian Apollo and now an elder in Troy. Although Polydamas was furious with the Hellenes, especially Menelaos, for the death of his brother that day, it did not cloud his judgment.

Hektor would not refrain from battle for fear of any man. He urged war, and because of recent successes, his father agreed. Hektor kissed his wife and his infant son, Astyanax, goodbye, knowing that before each battle, goodbyes may be forever. Hektor had named his son Skamandrios, but he was called Astyanax (meaning "lord of the lower town") because his father was the savior of the city.

To open the battle, Aineias hunted for Akhilleus menacingly out in the no-man's-land between the two advancing armies. Akhilleus was pleased to see a challenger and eagerly stepped out to begin avenging Patroklos. Because Hektor had stripped Patroklos of Akhilleus's old armor, Thetis had asked the limping-god Hephaistos to make her son new, better armor.

Aineias's spear bounced off Akhilleus's new shield, but Akhilleus's mighty toss broke through Aineias's. As Aineias ducked to avoid the piercing shaft, Akhilleus drew his sword and leapt at Aineias with a war cry. Crouching Aineias grabbed a stone two men today could not lift and threw it at the sea goddess's son. It hit Akhilleus squarely in the chest, and if not for the armor of Hephaistos, he might have been gravely wounded. If it had not been for Lord Poseidon's fast action in removing Aineias from the scene, the son of Aphrodite might have been run through by Akhilleus's sword.

With Aineias's departure from the battlefield, furious Akhilleus moved across into the Trojan ranks, slaughtering men like sheep. Among the first was Priamos's young son Polydoros, the fastest of his sons. He was too young to be an effective fighter, and Akhilleus easily killed him. His older brother Lykaon, Leleges Laothoe's son, was next. Akhilleus recognized him as the one he had sold into slavery years before. This time he dealt a harsher sentence. Unable to blunt the fury of the sea goddess's son, the Trojans broke ranks and bolted for Troy.

Antenor's second son, Agenor, saw that Akhilleus might lead the Hellenes into Troy before the gates could be closed. Bravely he called out to Akhilleus, distracting him from the fleeing Trojans. Agenor ran ahead of Akhilleus and veered away from the gates. He managed to escape with only a minor wound while the gates were closed.

Only Hektor remained outside, determined to challenge his enemy. Hektor's plan was to wear down Akhilleus by running around the walls, possibly giving some Trojan archer a chance to shoot him. Even though Akhilleus had not been in recent battles, he remained in excellent shape, and he cut off Hektor each time he tried to get close to the walls. With his plan obviously not working, Hektor stopped to give battle. Akhilleus killed him and dragged the body around the city walls behind his horses. The Trojans did not dare to fight. Still angry, Akhilleus dragged the corpse around the remains of Patroklos every day.

Finally, old Priamos slipped into the Hellenic camp unseen, driven in a cart by his old herald Idaios. Then, alone and unarmed, he entered Akhilleus's tent at night and pleaded for his son's corpse. Remembering his own aged father, Peleus, Akhilleus relented. He agreed to give up the body for an equal weight in gold.

Scales were set up outside of the city walls, and Hektor's huge weight was placed in one pan. Gold filled the other. Then Akhilleus offered for Priamos to keep the gold in exchange for Polyxene in marriage and for Helene to be given back. Priamos countered that he could have Polyxene but not Helene. No deal was struck. Eventually Hektor's bones were taken from Troy to Thebes, where a cult temple to him was raised.

The Trojans had erred by not waiting until all the allies arrived before attacking. The Amazones, Hittites, and Teuthranians had not arrived, and their combined numbers might have been overwhelming.[259] It was an error they would repeat again, for when fierce Amazonian fighters (long ago subdued by Priamos) arrived a few weeks later, the Trojans were eager for the fight. When Queen Penthesileia, daughter of the great-souled Ares, slayer of men, heard of Hektor's death, she changed her mind; only Priamos's bribe convinced her to fight.

The Amazones and Trojans challenged the Hellenes on the open plain. Penthesileia showed great prowess, and several times Akhilleus had to back away from her furious assault. After killing her in battle, Akhilleus felt a sad loss while he stripped her of her armor and admired her beauty. Akhilleus committed necrophilia upon her corpse, and the ugly soldier Thersites mocked him for it. Akhilleus angrily killed him. Akhilleus wished to bury her corpse with honor, but Thersites's cousin Diomedes threw it in the river.

The Trojans hid behind their walls while Odysseus took Akhilleus to Lesbos to purify him of murder. While they were away, the son of a Trojan prince arrived at the head of a massive Aithiopian (Hittite) army consisting of two thousand soldiers and two hundred chariots.[260] He was Memnon, son of the Trojan prince Tithonos and rosy-fingered Eos. Like Akhilleus, Memnon (meaning "resolute") wore armor crafted by Hephaistos into battle. Akhilleus and big Ajax were away at Patroklos's grave, and Memnon routed the Hellenes. As they fled in disarray, old king Nestor of Pylos could not get out of the way fast enough, and Memnon closed in upon him. The old man would have been easy prey except for the action of his valiant son Antilokhos.

Antilokhos wheeled his chariot around to face Memnon. As Nestor got away, Antilokhos died at the hands of a better warrior. Just then Akhilleus

[259] It has been argued convincingly that the Iliad is a compilation of numerous battles between Akhaians and Arzawans during the Late Bronze Age. These unrelated wars were weaved together into one masterpiece.

[260] Homer is clearly identifying Aithiopia with a large kingdom to the east since his mother, Eos, is the dawn. That kingdom is best described as the Hittite Empire. Hittite royal records speak of sending an army to Wilusa's defense during the mid to late thirteenth century T / early tenth century R BCE, which is tempting to identify with Memnon. However, the Hittite force would have been sent in defense of Troy VI, which was the invasion Herakles led. In the myth of Andromeda, Aithiopia is in the east as well, but usually the Hellenes place Aithiopia in Africa.

and Ajax returned; Akhilleus brushed Ajax aside and stabbed Memnon in the heart during single combat, and Memnon's forces fled.

While Eos obtained immortality for her slain son, the Trojans withdrew in a panic. Akhilleus raced ahead of his comrades, eager to enter the city before the gates could be closed. From a safe distance, Paris backpedaled with his eye on the rash hero, waiting for an opportunity. When a clear shot at Akhilleus appeared, Paris shot him dead with a well-aimed arrow. The Trojan flight halted, and the battle flared anew around the body of Akhilleus. Ajax killed the great Lycian warrior Glaukos and slung Akhilleus over his shoulder while Odysseus covered his retreat. Meanwhile, Aineias saved Glaukos's body, and each side retired with their casualties when a sudden tempest arrived. Memnon's body was either buried beside the Aisepos River in Hellespont or was taken home to the east.

The Hellenes held games in honor of their fallen comrade. The ashes of Akhilleus were placed with those of Patroklos in a golden urn made by Hephaistos—he who taught men glorious crafts. Antilokhos's ashes were spread over Akhilleus's tomb. The chiefs decided to honor the best among them with the fabulous armor of Akhilleus. Only Odysseus and Ajax were bold enough to claim the prize, and a bitter rivalry set in. When the armor was awarded to wily Odysseus, huge Ajax slew a flock of sheep in madness, thinking they were the Atreids, Odysseus, and other Hellenes. When he came to his senses with the dawn, he committed suicide in shame. Because he had attempted murder and had not died in battle, Agamemnon decreed he was to receive no honors. His half brother Teucros soon returned from a trading raid and vehemently argued on Ajax's behalf and defiantly began funeral preparations. Odysseus showed his worth by convincing the Atreids to accept a compromise, and Ajax was buried.

With Akhilleus and Ajax dead, the Hellenes began to despair. To raise their spirits, the seer Kalkhas told them that they could still win if they had the bow of Herakles, owned by Philoktetes, the ivory shoulder blade of the old rebel Pelops, and the services of Akhilleus's son Neoptolemos. He also said that the Trojan seer Helenos could tell them what else was needed.

Agamemnon dispatched Diomedes and Odysseus to bring the ivory shoulder of Pelops, the one rich-haired Demeter had made of ivory. The Epeians readily gave it to them. Afterward, the heroes met Phoenix at the court of King Peleus in Phthia to enlist the new recruit. Neoptolemos (meaning "young soldier") readily agreed to come, and Odysseus gave him his father's armor. They then sailed to Lemnos, where they found Philoktetes still suffering from his snakebite and nursing resentment against his comrades for deserting him. Odysseus tricked him and took his bow, but Diomedes and Neoptolemos overruled him and gave it back, urging Philoktetes to come with his bow. Only the intervention of deified Herakles convinced him to go. In camp he was cured by Podaleirios (who was called a "son of Asclepius" because of his talents).

The Teuthranian prince Eurypylos arrived in Ilion just before Diomedes and Odysseus returned with Neoptolemos and Philoktetes. Eurypylos was the son of Telephos and Laomedon's youngest daughter, Astyokhe. King Telephos had defeated the mistaken Akhaian attack upon his kingdom, but he was now dead. So King Priamos sent an urgent plea to his son and successor Eurypylos, a nephew of Priamos, to help him. Astyokhe objected strenuously—until the golden vine Priamos sent to her was unwrapped. She accompanied her son to Troy, where Priamos announced that he would receive Kassandra as his wife, should he be successful in battle. Proudly, Eurypylos led the Trojans and Teuthranians into battle, killing many (including the doctor Makhaon and Peneleos, who had replaced Thersandros as captain of the Thebans after he had been killed by Telephos) and driving the Hellenes back. The advance was not without cost; the great Trojan strategist Polydamas was killed by Ajax of Lokris (son of King Oileus of Lokris and his wife, Eriopos, daughter of Jason and the sorceress Medeia).

The next day, Eurypylos was on the point of entering the Hellenic camp when Neoptolemos, Philoktetes, Diomedes, and Odysseus arrived. Neoptolemos proved to be nearly as good a fighter as his father. He killed Eurypylos in single battle, and the Trojans retreated. Philoktetes proved his worth by shooting four arrows from his famous bow at Paris, connecting with three. Paris staggered back, wounded in the wrist, ankle, and eye socket. Menelaos rushed at Paris, eager to finish off his rival, but he hobbled away safely into the Trojan ranks.

Paris was secretly carried out of Troy on a stretcher under the cover of darkness. On his order, they hastily carried him to the home of his former lover, the nymph Oinoe, on Mount Ida. Oinoe refused to help, for she suffered from inveterate hatred of Helene. Rebuffed, Paris asked his bearers to take him home to die in Helene's arms. He did not make it home. Meanwhile, Oinoe changed her mind and rushed to him with healing herbs, but alas, she was too late. She hanged herself in grief.

When Paris died, golden Aphrodite's spell on Helene was broken. She wished to be returned to Menelaos to face the consequences of her actions. The Trojans, again holed up behind their splendid walls, denied her this. She was still a gorgeous woman, and the two most eligible Trojan princes, Deiphobos and Helenos, quarreled over her. Against her will, Priamos awarded her to Deiphobos, citing his superior valor. Deiphobos, like Ajax, was a strong, warlike man with a sullen and brutish nature. Helene was forced to yield to her third husband (fourth if you count Theseus) while Helenos stood by, bitterly disappointed.

Helenos left the city hastily, heading for Mount Ida. Ever-observant Odysseus followed him and caught up to him at the temple of Thymbraian Apollo, where the priest Khryses was offering him hospitality. (There, as children, he and his sister Kassandra had fallen asleep and been touched by the tongues of serpents and thereby received prophetic powers.) Khryses had left his island for his own safety. Odysseus seized Helenos without a fight. To soothe his smarting wounds over not receiving Helene, and to avoid certain torture and death, Helenos offered to tell secrets about Troy and who now slept with fair Helene. Odysseus swore in the temple to spare his life. Helenos foretold that Troy would not fall as long as the Palladium that had fallen from Olympos was still in the citadel.

## Fall of Troy

Now Odysseus, or some other Hellen, contrived to build the Trojan horse as a ruse to get inside of Troy. While Epeios, son of Panopeus (who had fought with Amphitryon against the Taphians and been caught pilfering the spoils), constructed it, Odysseus slipped into Troy to find the location of the Palladium. Helene spotted him and readily told him its whereabouts in the temple of Athena, for without Paris she wanted to go home. Hekabe then entered, and Odysseus pleaded with her not to yell out. Surprisingly, she did not and agreed to let him pass. In return he promised that should the city fall, no one who did not resist would be hurt. Soon Odysseus returned with Diomedes. Odysseus hoisted Diomedes over the precinct wall, and they returned with the stolen Palladium.

When the construction of the horse was complete, somewhere between twenty-three and fifty of the best fighters were hidden inside. Then Agamemnon burned the camp and set sail, hiding the fleet on Tenedos and the Kalydnai Islands. He planned to return the following night. Only silver-tongued Sinon, cousin of Odysseus, was left behind. It was his job to convince the Trojans to accept the horse and to light a beacon to guide the fleet back.

Advance scouts rushed back to the city at dawn bursting with the news that the Hellenes were gone! Excitedly they all went down to the burned out camp and marveled at the huge horse left behind with the inscription "dedicated to Athena" on its flank. The elder Thymoitos spoke first, saying that the horse should be taken to Troy. The elder Kapys, brother-in-law of Priamos, disagreed, saying it should be burned and its belly inspected. Others suggested pushing it down a rocky cliff.

Then they found huddled Sinon and brought him before the elders. He told them that the horse was a gift to Athena to thank her for a fair wind and to placate her for stealing the Palladium. Bright-eyed Athena, he said, was sorely vexed at them for stealing the Palladium and had sent several ominous signs, and Agamemnon had decided to leave for Hellas and gather a new force under less auspicious circumstances. Sinon went on to say that Odysseus had suggested using him as a blood offering to complete the sacrifice. But his real reason, said Sinon, was that he knew the secret of Palamedes's death, and for this Odysseus wanted to destroy him. Sinon said he had escaped in the confusion of the camp's burning.

The war-weary Trojans wanted to believe, but they were rightly suspicious of the wooden horse. They asked Sinon why it was so big. His gave his rehearsed answer, stating that it was that size so the Trojans could not haul it into Troy. Laokoon bellowed out, saying that Sinon was lying.

Laokoon was the priest of Thymbraian Apollo and the son of Priamos by one of his many wives. He had angered Apollo by denouncing a vow of celibacy and making love to his wife, Antiope, within sight of the god's image. Laokoon struck the horse with his spear, and a sea monster suddenly appeared from the sea and attacked his young twin sons, Thymbraios and

Antiphos (meaning "one who speaks instead [of god]" [i.e., a prophet]). Laokoon defended his children and was killed with at least one of his sons before the beast was driven away. The Trojans took this as a sign that the gods were displeased at his attacking the horse, and so they triumphantly wheeled it into Troy. In truth, either Poseidon sent the beast to confuse the Trojans (he favored the Hellenes), Apollo of the silver bow sent it as a warning not to accept the horse, or Apollo sent it to punish Laokoon for his impiety.

Priamos spoke, saying that his brother-in-law Thymoitos was right and that they should treat the property of Athena with respect. His daughter Kassandra gave a prophetic warning, though it fell on deaf ears. Thymbraian Apollo had once wooed Kassandra, but she resisted. He offered to give her the gift of prophecy if she would sleep with him. When she reneged on her part of the bargain, he begged for one kiss. He spat in her mouth so that though her prophecies would be true, no one would believe her. This is the worst fate that could befall a prophet.

The Trojans hauled the gift horse up on the acropolis of Troy, in front of the temple of Athena. They needed to break down some of the walls to get it through the gates because they were not wide enough. They patched the walls, and a night of mirth and feasting followed. To please her new husband, Helene went round the horse, imitating the voices of the heroes' wives. Odysseus had to restrain Menelaos, Diomedes, and Antielos from jumping out when they heard their wives' voices being imitated. Neoptolemos was the only one unafraid, and he continually nudged Odysseus to start the attack. Patient Odysseus would not consent.

Aineias and his followers were greatly disturbed by the portent of Laokoon's death and refrained from merrymaking. Instead they prepared for a quick flight from Troy if necessary.

It was midnight, and the clear moon was rising before Odysseus gave the command. On the beach Sinon had lit fire signals that guided the fleet back. While the people slept off the festivities, the heroes used a rope ladder to get out of the horse. They slew the guards and opened the gates to the returning army.

So Troy fell after a ten-year campaign (1184T/934R BCE). During the sack, the fighting was fiercest around the house of Deiphobos. Inside,

Deiphobos had gotten so drunk in the victory celebration that he never awoke. Menelaos slew him as he slept. Hekabe warned Menelaos not to look upon his wife if he planned to carry out his intention of running his sword through her. Helene lowered her eyes and bared her breasts before her angry husband, and his heart melted. To Hekabe's great disappointment, he took her back as his wife. "Menelaos at least, when he caught a glimpse somehow of the breasts of Helen unclad, cast away his sword, me thinks." [261]

The strife at Priamos's palace was nearly as great. Neoptolemos killed three of the four sons of Priamos and Hekabe still living at home: Antiphones, Panmon, and Polites. When Neoptolemos struck down Polites in sight of his father, the old king feebly tossed a spear at the young soldier. Neoptolemos either killed him there at the hearth altar or dragged from the hearth and dispatched him offhand at the doors of the house.

Then the bright son of bold Akhilleus led the wife of Hektor to his hollow ship, but her son he snatched from the bosom of the rich-haired nurse. He seizing the child by the foot and cast him from a tower, for as the poet Stasinos said, "He is a simple man who kills the father and lets the children live." Odysseus killed Leokritos, the offspring of Hektor's top strategist, Polydamas.

The fate of Priamos's daughters was not much better. Ajax of Lokris was one of the honored soldiers selected to hide in the horse. He wore a corselet of linen to battle, which he hastily removed to rape Princess Kassandra during the fall of Troy. Kassandra held tightly to the statue secured on the altar of Athena, and Ajax ripped her away with such force that the statue of Athena broke off in her hand. She continued clutching the statue as he roughly defiled her under the holy altar.

Two of Priamos's daughters disappeared in the confusing night, never to be seen again. Kreousa was captured, but golden Aphrodite and all-nourishing Gaia saved her from slavery because she was Aineias's wife; the

[261] Hesiod, "Little Iliad", in *The Homeric Hymns and Homerica.* The Little Iliad was written by Leskhes of Pyrrha or Mitylene.

earth swallowed her. Laodice,[262] the most beautiful of Priamos's daughters and the wife of Antenor's son Helikaon, was lost in the melee, and her body was never recovered. She was reportedly swallowed by the earth on her own prayers. Youngest Polyxene was captured along with her mother, Hekabe.

The story at the house of Antenor was better. Odysseus and Menelaos had rushed there to save Antenor's family in thanks for his hospitality years before. When they arrived they found Antenor's son Helikaon seriously wounded and Glaukos being chased. Odysseus saved them both, and then he and Menelaos saved Antenor, Theano, and two other sons (Eurymakhos and Krino). Unfortunately, Agenor was not among them, as Neoptolemos had killed him while he defended himself.

Aineias and his followers ran at the first sign of danger. Some perished trying to get out, including his wife, Kreousa. Aineias carried his aging father on his back and held his son's hand and escaped in the darkness. Ankhises had been struck lame by Zeus's thunderbolt for revealing the identity of Aineias's mother while drinking wine with his companions. (Aphrodite had raised her girdle to partially deflect it, saving his life.) The survivors fled into the glens of Mount Ida. The Akhaians set fire to the city after taking as much loot as they could carry.

Agamemnon distributed the booty from Troy among the jubilant Hellenes. Polyxene was to be given to the ghost of Akhilleus, his spoils from the victory. She faced her fate nobly as she was led to Neoptolemos, who sacrificed her on the tomb of Akhilleus. Polyxene was then properly buried while the dead king was decapitated and his body left for the dogs and birds at Akhilleus's tomb, unburied. Despite the loss of her husband, most of her children, and her rank, Hekabe was a comfort and an inspiration to the huddled Trojan women who awaited word as to who would take them to satisfy their lusts and work at their looms back home.

---

[262] According to the third-century BCE poet Euphorion of Khalkis, she slept with the Athenian Akamas during the first year of the siege, when he came to Troy with Diomedes as part of an otherwise unrecorded diplomatic mission. She bore him Munites, whom Helene's slave Aithra raised. Munites died of a serpent bite in Thrace during the journey home with his father. The gods granted her prayer during the fall of Troy, and the ground swallowed her up. Pausanias doubts this and says it was more likely she joined her husband in settling in Libya. Others say she was part of Akamas's spoils.

The chiefs were happy to grant Neoptolemos the first choice among the women. Without hesitation, he picked the well-built wife of Hektor, Andromakhe. Their commander, Agamemnon, chose next. He picked the girl whom Apollo had coveted—Kassandra, the sole surviving daughter of Hekabe. Then the other chiefs were allotted their prizes.

Queen Hekabe was given as a slave to Odysseus, for she had once protected him when she spotted him spying in Troy. She was allowed to bury Astyanax. She wailed at his little gravesite thinking how once this little prince was the fire that fueled his great father on a defense that was futile. Once she cuddled him; now she buried him. Aithra was given to the sons of Theseus, her grandsons, on the permission of Helene.

## Troy Rebuilt

Antenor and Aineias led the rebuilding of Troy. Either Aineias[263] or Antenor was king of the much-maligned city, a mere shadow of its former greatness. Aineias's young son Askanios became king afterward and continued the line of the House of Dardanos for generations to come. He is credited with having refounded the city.

There were other, more popular versions of the fate of Aineias[264] and Antenor. Many cities claim that one or the other had been its founder. The Romans said Aineias founded the ruling house of Rome. Along the way Aineias founded Etis and Aphrodisia in Lakonia, towns he named for his daughter and mother. Byzantine scholastic notes say the Sack of Ilion says that Aineias was captured by Neoptolemos and settled at Pharsalia in Thessalia.

Antenor's family is said to have settled in Thrace, Italy, or most commonly in Libya. Part of the fleet of Menelaos and Helene was driven to Libya by the troubling winds. In Cyrenaika he dropped off the Trojan elder

[263] Homer, *Iliad*, xx.300–320, says only that his fate was to survive the war and that he and his descendants would rule the Trojans thereafter.

[264] Virgil gives the famous Roman account of his migration to Italy in his epic poem *Aineid*. He says that Ankhises died before the wanderers reached Italy. The Arkadians claim, improbably, that he died there during the years the refugees were wandering through Hellas and that a mountain near Orkhomenos was named for him.

Antenor. Antenor had been spared at the fall of Troy because of the hospitality he had shown Menelaos and Odysseus years before. With his wife Theano, several of his children, and other Trojan survivors, he settled down. Their descendants welcomed Battos and accepted him as king.[265]

Even before the fall of Troy, the Mycenaian civilization was in decline. After the sack of Troy, trade declined dramatically, and none of the new settlements in Ilion became large enough to be called a city. Myths of Trojans wandering across the sea have support in Egyptian texts. Pharaoh Ramesses III (1183T/933R–1152T/902R BCE) mentions the Teukrian-sounding ("Teukrian" meaning "Trojan") tribe Tjekvaye among the Sea Peoples he defeated. The Tjekvaye settled in Dor (Palestine) and Libya, where many say Antenor settled. The Egyptians say the Sea Peoples had destroyed the nation of the Arzawans (late 1180sT / late 940s R BCE). This corresponds well to the date Troy VIIA was destroyed.

After the war, another people settled peacefully beside the Trojans in their modestly rebuilt city. Less than half a century later, more immigrants arrived, this time from the Balkans. They were probably the ancestors of the Phrygians. The different groups seem to have coexisted peacefully.[266]

---

Exhibit 13.3
Fate of the Palladium

The Palladium was a wood statue standing three or four feet tall; it was an image of the maiden Pallas. She held a spear aloft in her right hand and a distaff and spindle in her left; the aegis was wrapped around her breast. Athena had carved it while grieving over the death of her playmate, the Libyan nymph Pallas. Once, while Pallas and virgin Athena were engrossed in a fierce round of war games, Zeus feared for his daughter's safety and showed Pallas the real aegis, which was terrifying to behold. The poor girl was turned to stone. After carving the Palladium, Athena erected it on a

[265] This version of Antenor's fate was mentioned by Pindar (*Pythian Ode,* v.80–84) and told by the royal family of Cyrene to curry favor with one of the other few remaining monarchies in Hellas—Sparta. The more likely account has Antenor and Aineias rebuilding the smoldering citadel of Troy.

[266] Strabo, in *Geography*, xiv.5.29, claims that the Thracians settled around Troy after its fall. Homer, in *Iliad*, iii.184, says the Phrygians were already living in Anatolia when Troy fell, but they were living north of Troy along the Sangarios River at the time.

pedestal on Olympos. Later, the star nymph Elektra clung to it in a fruitless attempt to avoid cloud-master Zeus. The king of the Olympians flung it aside and committed the only recorded rape on Olympos. Then dark-clouded Zeus threw the star nymph and the Palladium from Olympos and they landed on Samothrace Island. Dardanos was conceived from the unholy rape.

Apollo true prophecy of the statue's role in Troy was that if the Trojans preserve the goddess who fell from the skies, they will preserve their city: for wherever she goes, she carries the empire. So Dardanos took the sacred Palladium with him when he left Samothrace. In thanks for his safe landing in Ilion, Dardanos built the beautiful temple of Athena in Troy to house the Palladium. There it stayed until Diomedes stole it with Odysseus's assistance so that Troy could fall.

The fate of the Palladium after the war was disputed; three cities claimed possession of it. The Argives said Diomedes brought it home with him, the Athenians said Diomedes lost it to Athenian Demophoon when he landed on the coast of Attike during his voyage home, and the Romans said only a replica was stolen and that Aineias took the original to Italy and the Vestal Virgins guarded it in Rome.

---

# The Returns

## Late Helladic Bronze Age (LHIIIC); Part of Hesiod's Age of Heroes

> Gifts beguile men's minds and their deeds as well.
>
> —Agaios of Troizen, *Nostoi*, seventh century BCE

> The votive (vow) offerings at Samothrace could have been even greater if those who died at sea had been able to fulfill their oath.
>
> —Diagoras of Melos, fifth century BCE

Once the spoils were divided, the unruly Akhaians began arguing about when to go home. The discomforting grey sea was choppy, as fall was in the air. Conflicting wisdom, Athena, drove the kings to argue whether to sail immediately, before the storms came, or wait and give offerings to the immortal gods, as was customary. Both courses of action seemed prudent.

As the Hellenes prepared to sail, Kalkhas faced north for a sign as to whether sea travel was advisable. A bird of prey appeared to his left, a bad omen, and warned the Hellenes that the Stronger Ones were angry at them because Ajax the Lesser had raped Kassandra at the holy altar of Athena and because Neoptolemos had killed King Priamos at the altar of silver-bowed Apollo. Kalkhas recommended that travel across the open sea be avoided.

Odysseus argued convincingly that bright-eyed Athena would be appeased if they stoned Ajax the Lokrian for raping Princess Kassandra as she clung to virgin Athena's image. The desperate Ajax grabbed the very same idol, and no one dared to touch him. Impatient Menelaos said time was wasting, and after a heated argument with his brother, he ordered his men to prepare to sail. Agamemnon recommended they stay and make sacrifices to appease the Stronger Ones, particularly angry Athena. Menelaos later regretted that in this, their last meeting, the brothers argued and departed ways angrily.

The Akhaians split into four groups: those who boldly sailed across the open sea with Menelaos, Odysseus, Diomedes, and Nestor; the few who marched west along the coast of Thrace protected by the strong arm of Neoptolemos; those who sailed south, hugging the coast of Anatolia with the seers Kalkhas and Amphilokhos and the Lapith leaders Polypoites and Leonteus; and those who stayed behind with Agamemnon.

## The Myrmidons March Home

While the hasty ones sailed away with Menelaos, those that remained behind sailed only as far as offshore Tenedos Island for safety against the natives. The Nereid Thetis ordered Neoptolemos to join them. On Tenedos, Agamemnon offered sacrifices to appease the Stronger Ones. After the ceremony was completed, Ajax of Lokris sailed off in pursuit of those sailing for Hellas. Neoptolemos followed the good advice of either his divine grandmother or his Trojan slave Helenos (the sole surviving son of King Priamos and Queen Hekabe), a noble seer, and sailed to Thrace and marched homeward briskly.

Those who traveled overland were spared catastrophe and reached their destinations safely. When the Myrmidons arrived in their homeland, the sons of Akastos of Iolkos, who were threatening old Peleus, withdrew.

Neoptolemos did not stay long in his grandfather's kingdom. To reward Helenos for his support in bringing down Troy, Neoptolemos took his army into Epeiros and conquered land for Helenos and the surviving Trojans to settle on. Neoptolemos was impressed with the area and conquered the Molossians of Epeiros and ruled them himself. There his concubine

Andromakhe (wife of Hektor) raised his sons Molossos and Pergamon. Eventually Neoptolemos released Andromakhe and gave her to Helenos in marriage. Upon the death of Helenos, she returned to Asia, to nearby Teuthrania, with her then grown son Pergamon.

## Those Caught in the Storm at Sea

Once those brave Akhaians who sailed for home reached the open sea, divine retribution came in the shape of a great, angry storm, and many a sailor drank dense clouds and sank into his watery tomb. Compounding the sailors' plight were false lights lit by Nauplios the Wrecker on the shore of Euboea, which lured many ships to break up on the rocky coast during the storm. He did so to avenge his son Palamedes, who had been executed by the Hellenic leaders at Troy.

> The lone sailor Nauplios
> Lit his false fire on the Capherian Cape -
> A star turned liar, which lured ten thousand more
> To ram the sunken rocks like fierce jaws agape;
> And watched men die amidst the Aigaian's roar.[267]

Resourceful Ajax of Lokris managed to swim safely to the rocks of Kapherides and clung on. Ajax would have escaped, even though Pallas Athena hated him, had he not gone wildly mad and tossed out words of defiance. Like his friend big Ajax, he took little account of the immortal gods and boasted that he could survive without divine providence. The mover of earth and the fruitless sea, Poseidon, raised furious waves and washed him off the rock, and Ajax died when he swallowed down the salty sea. His body washed ashore on Mykonos Island, where he was buried by Akhilleus's mother, the Nereid Thetis.

[267] Euripides, "Helene" 1122-1131, in *The Bacchae and Other Plays.* Translated by Philip Vellacott.

Image 14.1
Map of the Returns

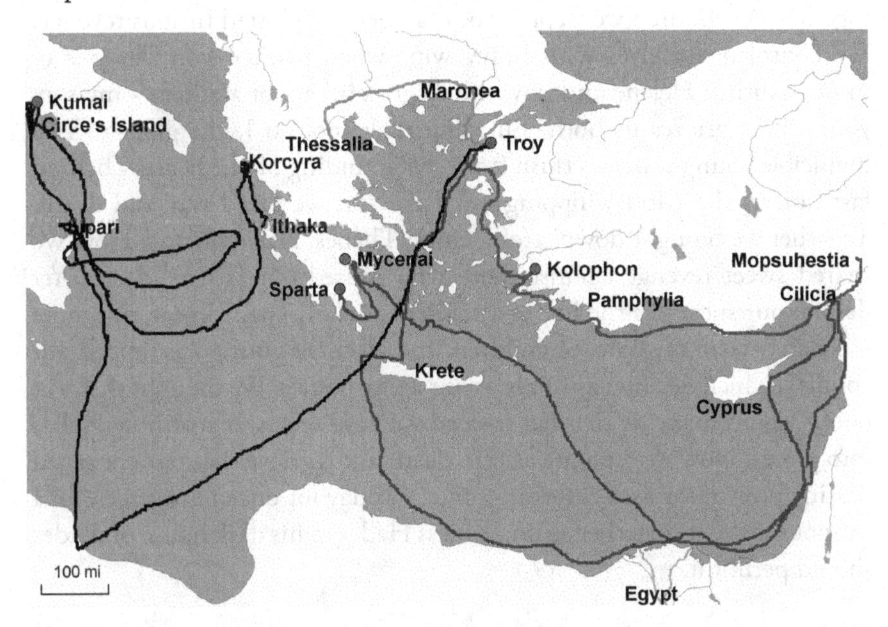


Odysseus's route took him west of Hellas, Menelaos sailed around the Eastern Mediterranean, the Seers hugged the coast of Anatolia, and Neoptolemos took the short overland route through Thrace.

The storm drove Diomedes of Midea and Sthenelos of Argos, friends who fought in the same chariot as Epigonoi and at Troy, onto the shores of Lycia, where the hostile inhabitants tried to kill the crew. They escaped and arrived home safely after just a few days.

Diomedes's homecoming was disappointing. His wife had taken Sthenelos's now grown son as a lover (bitter Nauplios had convinced her to do so), and the citizens of Midea were not thrilled at the soldiers' return. The young grandson of Adrastos, Cyanippos, for whom Diomedes had been acting as regent for ever since his father died in the Epigonoi attack on Thebes, had died. Towering Diomedes decided to sail on, leaving the Midean kingdom that was now his to his charioteer Sthenelos (who already ruled Argos).

One could imagine a departure where Sthenelos said something like - old friend, today I grieve more than if I lost my wife, even my son. Though not a common mother we share, our love and rich tapestry of experiences I find more meaningful. Days of pain, like today, have brought us close together. As children we wept for our fathers and plotted furious revenge. We consoled ourselves with heavy wine when neither won the love of most beautiful Helene and now the disgraceful act of adultery - my son, your wife - grieves us both. But remember too, do I, the glory of two invincible young warriors flush from the pounding of our hearts - behind fast horses, the wind whipping our faces - as we faced war and death. Together we brought down strong cities; Thebes, Kalydon, and Troy. We shared sweet revenge against those who caused our fathers' death. Yet despite our successes the life of a soldier is a hard one. I know you more intimately than my wife, or children, and all this fighting has sapped our country, which declines as surely as our aging bodies. We thought that war booty would make us rich but instead we have seen war tear holy Hellas into pieces. Now we separate as if in death and I grieve that our entwined destiny now unravels, as all things must. Today for once I am a seer, for I cannot foresee us together again - unless Hades in his dark house of shades should permit it.

With that the two men embraced, and Diomedes sailed away for good.

Sthenelos watched the ships disappear and returned home to build a life with the wife he barely knew and the children he had long ago left behind. War had robbed him of the wonder of their childhood, for now they were men.

The great Roman poet Virgil said Diomedes settled in Italy. There he lived quietly, declining to fight remnants of the Trojans that settled under the command of Aineias on a nearby site that would one day be Rome.

Frightened, King Idomeneus of Krete offered rashly to sacrifice the first thing he saw when he arrived on Krete if only he made it through the storm safely. The Stronger Ones made sure that it was his son, Orsilokhos, fleetest of the Kretan youths, who spotted the ships and raced to the shore to greet them. Sadly, Idomeneus complied with his oath. Idomeneus became instantly unpopular with his subjects. Then he discovered that while he was away his wife had been sleeping with a nobleman from court named Leukas. (Like Diomedes's wife, she had also been encouraged to do so by the merchant-king Nauplios.) Idomeneus decided to move on and became the king of Kolophon[268] in Ionia not long after those who left Troy hugging the Anatolian coast had left it (including its king, Mopsos).

## Menelaos

Menelaos was on one of the five ships from his fleet (which numbered sixty at the start of the war) that were pushed before the winds to Egypt; the rest of the ships were either lost at sea or shipwrecked on Krete. In the storm, Menelaos lost all of his recovered treasures and his share of the Trojan booty. So his troops spent seven years wandering along the coasts of Libya, Egypt,[269] Phoenicia, Cyprus, and Cilicia serving as mercenaries. In the service of kings, he more than replaced what had been lost from Troy.

Laden with treasures, Menelaos sought to return home. He prepared to cross the open seas from Pharos Island off the Egyptian coast. A fierce northern gale pinned down his ships for twenty days. The provisions were running low, and the men were getting desperate. Finally the nymph Eidothea took pity upon the crew and told Menelaos how to catch her father, the seal herder Proitos, who could tell him how to end the storm.

The next day, Menelaos sprung on the unsuspecting old man of the sea and wrestled him to the ground as Eidothea instructed. Menelaos held on despite the various forms Proteus assumed to try to break his hold. Subdued, kindly Proteus told Menelaos to return to the mainland and give proper sacrifices to the glorious gods. Shape-shifting Proteus also told Menelaos of Agamemnon's death.

---

[268] The ancient Homeric poem *Nostoi* tells the fate of soldiers after leaving Troy. It is usually ascribed to Agaios of Troizen, but Eustathios of Antioch says the poet was Kolophonian, which would explain why Kolophon plays such a prominent role in the poem. It survives only in fragments, which usually mention only Kalkhas, Polypoites, and Leonteus as having traveled south along the Anatolian coast after the war. Homer's *Iliad*, *Odyssey*, and *Telegony* provide additional details. Apollodoros's *Library*, Epitome 6, provides the most complete surviving account of the returns and adds Amphilokhos.

[269] Stesikhoros is said to have slandered Helene for her actions. He was immediately struck blind by angry Helene. Consequently, he changed his version of the myth to say that it was only a phantom of Helene that accompanied Alexandros to Troy while Hermes spirited the real Helene away to Egypt. There she waited virtuously for Menelaos to rescue her. Further, she is said to have married Akhilleus on the Isle of the Blessed. Helene was so pleased with Stesikhoros's *Palinodia* (meaning "recantation") that she restored his sight. Euripides follows Stesikhoros's version in his play *Helene*.

Carried by the dangerous wind back to Egypt, Menelaos performed the prescribed sacrifice the very next day. Menelaos also sacrificed two Egyptian children and was pursued as far as Libya. The winds calmed, and he enjoyed smooth sailing home. He sailed right past Lakonia to Mycenai, where he had left his darling daughter Hermione for safekeeping. When he finally returned home, only one leader remained unaccounted for.[270]

## The Long Odyssey Home

When Odysseus sailed away, he endured Queen Hekabe's fearlessly uttered hideous invectives for the cruel barbarity of the Hellenes and Odysseus's breach of faith to her. When Odysseus landed on the coast of Thrace, her great spirit was finally broken when hit with a fresh tragedy—one of treachery and death. Before the end of the war, Priamos and Hekabe had sent their youngest son, Polydoros, with a sack of gold to Thracian king Polymestor for safekeeping. After hearing of Troy's fall, the murderous king killed the youth and took the gold. Hekabe happened to find her dead son's body washed up upon the shore. She instigated the death of the killer, but her raving nature remained. She was changed into a fiery-eyed bitch.[271]

When the great storm Poseidon created on the urging of angry Athena hit, the twelve ships from Ithake were tossed about, but because Tritogeneian Athena was not angry with Odysseus, his ships managed to reach Cape Malea safely. They would have safely rounded the cape and reached home had not a strong northerly wind driven them south for nine days, driving them all the way to Libya. Odysseus sent out scouts, who met the friendly Lotus-eaters. When they did not return, Odysseus followed and found them eating the lotus offered them by natives. The drug had robbed them of their ambition. Odysseus feared that if the other men tasted the lotus, they too would lose their will to continue. He dragged his scouts back to the ships and set sail immediately.

---

[270] The population of Lakonia dropped dramatically after Therapne was sacked (1200T/950R BCE). Menelaos may have led these people to raid Anatolia, Syria, and Egypt before their defeat by Ramesses III (1183T/933R BCE). Ramesses settled them in Palestine. They did not return to depopulated Lakonia.

[271] She might have been somehow identified with Hekate, the Hellenic goddess with a similar-sounding name. Dogs were sacred to Hekate. Bitch's Rock on the coast of Thrace was considered her resting place.

## The Cyklops

Blown westward, they landed on a small island off of Sicily. They feasted all the next day on the game they found. The following day, Odysseus decided to cross to Sicily in one ship and explore. Upon landing, Odysseus picked eleven of his best men to investigate with him. They found the cave of the Cyklops Polyphemos and peered inside. Finding no one inside, they entered it and discovered a plentiful store of food, plus bleating lambs and kids. The greedy sailors wished to make off with the goods, but curious Odysseus wanted to know who the owner was. They waited, and at dusk a giant appeared with his flock. After entering the cave, he rolled a huge stone across the entrance, blocking the men's exit.

At the sight of the Cyklops, the men hid in terror. After his eyes adjusted to the dark, the mighty Cyklops caught sight of the men. Odysseus then spoke out, reminding the giant named Polyphemos of the laws of hospitality. The gruff giant scowled and boasted that the Cyklopes recognized neither the gods nor their laws. Then he grabbed two crewmen, dashed their brains out on a rock, and roasted and ate them.

The men wished to kill the Cyklops as he slept, but Odysseus knew that if they did, they would not be able to roll away the stone that blocked their exit. So the wily leader sought another plan. The next morning and evening, the Cyklops roasted and ate two more men. While the remaining men despaired, Odysseus boldly stepped forward and offered the monster strong wine to wash down his despicable meal. The wine supplied by the Thracian vintner Maron pleased the ugly Cyklops, and he offered a gift in exchange for more. Odysseus complied and introduced himself as "Nobody" and asked for his gift. The giant responded by saying he would eat Nobody last. Then he fell into a drunken stupor and vomited up his grisly supper.

Immediately Odysseus and his men carried out their plan. They heated a large stick and drove it into his single eye. The blinded giant roared for his fellow Cyklopes. They gathered about the closed entrance and asked who was hurting him. "Nobody is killing me," he cried. "If nobody is harming you," his neighbors replied, "there is nothing we can do." [272] They went back to their homes.

[272] Homer, *Odyssey,* ix.455.

At dawn the blinded Cyklopes rolled away the stone and sat down in the doorway, hoping to catch the Hellenes as they escaped. Odysseus ingeniously tied together groups of three rams and hid a crewman under the middle one in each group. Strong Odysseus then clung to the underbelly of the largest ram. After his flocks passed, Polyphemos rolled back the stone—vainly, for the men had escaped. The rage of frustrated Polyphemos grew when Odysseus taunted him from the bow of his ship. Polyphemos's father, Poseidon, swore to avenge his son.

Odysseus and the crew from his twelve ships sailed to the Lipari Islands, where they were hospitably entertained by Aiolos and his gentle family. Aiolos tied up all the winds in a bag, except for the west wind, and gave the bag to Odysseus as a parting gift. Odysseus jealously guarded the bag while the west wind gently blew them home. After sailing for ten days, they came into sight of Ithake. Exhausted, Odysseus fell asleep. The other men opened the bag, believing he was hiding great wealth from them. The winds drove them back to Aiolos, who refused to help them again because he had discovered that loud-crashing Poseidon was angry with Odysseus.

The disheartened sailors drifted for seven days before seeing land. Then the tired men beached their ships in the sheltered harbor of the Laistrygonian city of Telepylos. Only Odysseus took the prudent precaution of beaching his ship outside the harbor's narrow entrance. Odysseus sent heralds with the daughter of the king of the Laistrygones after she greeted them hospitably. The cannibals promptly ate one of the men, and the other two escaped and ran screaming back to the ships. The Laistrygones rushed to the hills above the entrance to the harbor and threw rocks down upon the hapless men. Only Odysseus's ship escaped and sailed sorrowfully onward.

## Circe's Island

Before long the somber crew reached lovely Aiaia Island off the Italian coast. Eurylokhos, a near relative of Odysseus, was second in command. He lost a dice toss and led a reluctant search party inland. He was the lone member of the party not lured into the witch Circe's beautiful palace, and he watched in horror while his comrades were changed into swine. He ran back to warn Odysseus.

Only Odysseus was willing to try to rescue his men; the others were too terrified of witches. Along the way, the swift messenger Hermes appeared to Odysseus and gave him a distinctive herb with a white flower and black root. He told Odysseus that the herb, which he called moly, would ward off the magic of even the most powerful witch. Upon keen-eyed Hermes's suggestion, Odysseus marched boldly into Circe's house and drank the drugged wine she offered him. When she touched him with her wand, he did not, as she expected, turn into a groveling hog. Instead, he followed luck-bringing Hermes's advice and drew his sword and threatened to kill her unless she swore to do him no harm. The startled Circe swore as she was commanded and then offered to sleep with him. Odysseus agreed, and afterward she restored his men, at his request. Lovely Circe bore Odysseus a son they named Telegonos.[273]

For a full year, Circe's lovely attendants took care of the men—men accustomed to hardship. Then the men persuaded Odysseus to quit the bed of Circe and lead them home. Circe told him that in order to return home safely, he must first go to the ends of the earth and speak with the spirit of the dead Theban seer Teiresias. She sent him on his way with a gentle breeze behind him. At the stream of Oceanos, which flows around the broad earth, they disembarked and followed Circe's instructions. After making the required sacrifices, the underworld shades appeared, attracted by the smell of blood. With sword in hand, fierce Odysseus kept the spirits away. He cried when he saw his mother's ghost, for she was alive when last he had heard, but he obediently kept her away all the same. After drinking his fill, Teiresias told Odysseus that his ship would return home safely only if the men refrained from eating the cattle of the sun. The shade of Agamemnon warned him to return home cautiously.

Odysseus returned to Circe's island to say his final farewell. She warned him of the dangers ahead, such as the seductive Sirens and terrifying Kharybdis and Scylla. Circe told Odysseus how to avoid the Sirens' enchantment, but she had no advice on how to avoid the twin terrors.

Before long, the ship approached the Sirens' rocky perch. Following Circe's advice, Odysseus filled his crewmen's ears with wax and had himself tied securely to the mast. He listened to their song of wisdom, hearing their melodic understanding of past and future and how they sang with the

[273] Hesiod added Latinos, eponym of the Latin people.

terrible clarity of the mad or enlightened. Later, once they were out of earshot, the men unbound their leader. Odysseus thanked his crew for not releasing him as he had begged and pleaded while he could hear them, but in his words they detected disappointment, as though there were ash in his mouth while he spoke.

Hardly a moment passed before Odysseus and the crew heard the roar of the waters of the terrible whirlpool Kharybdis. Kharybdis and Scylla haunted opposite sides of the straights that divided Italy from Sicily. Kharybdis would suck down whole ships in a single gulp if they happened to pass above her at an inopportune time. The six-headed bitch Scylla could be counted on to prey upon the men. Odysseus chose to accept a certain loss rather than gamble on passing over Kharybdis unharmed. He stood on the prow of his ship, fully armed, waiting to protect his men as they passed by the bitch's lair. Odysseus's attention drifted for a moment, and Scylla snatched six of his crewmen. Odysseus could only watch helplessly as she returned to her lair with the six screaming men dangling from her jowls.

The tired and traumatized crew overruled Odysseus's command to press on and landed on the first island that came into view. It was a pleasant island, rich in cattle and belonging to the sun god Helios. Immediately a prevailing south wind began to blow. The breeze would have driven them back to Kharybdis and Scylla, so it prevented them from sailing. After a month, their provisions ran out. Despite Circe's warning not to kill any of the sacred cattle, the starving men did so while Odysseus was out of sight. For six days they feasted while famished Odysseus alone resisted the tempting smell of freshly roasted meat. On the seventh day a favorable wind arose and they sailed off. Radiant Helios asked loud-thundering Zeus to raise a violent storm and destroy the ship. Everyone was killed, except for Odysseus.

Odysseus survived by lashing the broken keel and mast together, and he floated aimlessly until he reached the island of Ogygia after nine days. There he met the lovely nymph Kalypso. For a while he was pleased to share her cavern bed. She bore him two sons, Nausithoos and Nausinous. He grew restless and declined her offer to obtain immortality for him; he wanted to go home to Penelope. After seven years, grey-eyed Athena convinced Lord Zeus to send luck-bringing Hermes to Kalypso with an order to let Odysseus go.

Odysseus outfitted a raft and sailed eighteen days before his implacable enemy Poseidon spotted him while returning from one of his frequent trips to Aithiopia. The angry god raised a storm and destroyed the raft. The sea goddess Ino provided Odysseus the means to stay afloat, and after two days he washed ashore on Kercyra.

King Alcinoos of Kercyra entertained Odysseus lavishly and offered him his daughter in marriage. When Odysseus declined, the gracious king dispatched a ship to take him home.

Odysseus slept as the sailors dropped him off. He awoke disoriented, fearing that he had been stranded in the wrong place, for after twenty years away, it took him a moment to recognize his homeland. While he was standing perplexed, Pallas Athena came to tell him that rapacious suitors were courting his faithful wife, Penelope. She helped him hide the gifts King Alcinoos had given him. So Odysseus returned home alone, the only survivor from the twelve ships he led to Troy.[274]

## Death of the Suitors

Wily Odysseus did not go home right away, fearing a greeting like the one Agamemnon had received. Disguised as a beggar, he spent two days with his faithful swineherd Eumaios. Then his son Telemakhos arrived, and when they were alone, Odysseus revealed himself to his son. After tearfully rejoicing, they plotted revenge.

Telemakhos was returning from a trip abroad. He had visited King Nestor in sandy Pylos and King Menelaos in Lakonia, hoping to learn of his father's fate. They gave him handsome gifts but had no news concerning his father. The suitor Eurymakhos led a ship that failed to intercept and ambush Telemakhos upon his return from Pylos. The suitors were beginning to fear Telemakhos, who was becoming a strong young man.

[274] The Romans invented two other sailors whom they said survived: Both Virgil and Ovid said one of the twelve men (Arkhimedes) held captive in Polyphemos's cave was accidentally left behind. Aineias rescued him. Ovid added that the sailor Makareus chose to be put ashore on the mainland opposite Circe's island rather than face the perils ahead.

A large number of suitors had assembled in Ithake seven years after Troy fell, each hoping to obtain the queen and her property (1177T/927R BCE. There were fifty-two suitors from Delikion, led by the most pious suitor (Amphinomos); twenty-four from Cephallenia who sought the hand of Penelope, led by Agelaos, Peisandros, and Elatos; twenty suitors from Zacynthos who called on Penelope; and twelve from Ithake, led by Antinoos, son of Eupeithes, and Eurymakhos (Eurylokhos), son of Polybos. Antinoos was the strongest and worst-behaved of the suitors. He was their unofficial leader. Eurymakhos was the second most powerful of all the suitors, and he gave Penelope the most gifts. She liked him best.

For three years Penelope kept the suitors at bay, promising to marry one of them once she finished a shawl for old Laertes. She would weave it by day and secretly unravel it at night. When they uncovered her strategy, they forced her to finish it. She thought she now must choose one.

Telemakhos returned to the palace, and Odysseus arrived later, in his beggar disguise. Only his old hunting dog Argos recognized him; the dog was too old to rise but joyfully wagged his tail. Odysseus feared discovery and could only discreetly wipe away a tear as the dog expired. At Telemakhos's suggestion, he begged food of all the suitors so as to learn about them. Only vulgar Antinoos refused him and instead threw a stool at him.

With two faithful servants, Odysseus and Telemakhos plotted while Penelope announced a contest for her hand. She said she would marry the one who could shoot an arrow from the handsome bow of Iphitos (stolen by Herakles when he murdered Iphitos and later given to young Odysseus) through the handle of twelve iron axes, a feat her first husband had accomplished on numerous occasions. Telemakhos decided to string the bow for the contestants, and he would have on his fourth try, had not his father given him a sign not to. Instead, he laid it down for the suitors to string it. All of the suitors except for Antinoos of Ithake failed to string the bow, and Antinoos cleverly excused himself. They all protested furiously when the lowly "beggar" asked for his turn. Penelope insisted, and all were amazed when he strung it easily and shot through all twelve axes without rising from his stool. Then he shot unsuspecting Antinoos, the strongest of the suitors, dead. It was not long until the last of the suitors followed him to the house of Hades; not a one escaped (1174T/924R BCE).

From the room full of suitors, Odysseus spared only the minstrel and herald, both of whom had been forced to serve the suitors against their will. Odysseus allowed no one in the household to exult over the dead, but he punished those of his own servants who had aided the suitors. The twelve serving girls who had taken suitors as lovers were forced to carry out the corpses and clean the palace hall before Telemakhos hanged them.

Penelope did not recognize her blood-spattered husband and pulled back as he tried to greet her. Only after he bathed and answered her questions about their bedroom did she believe that he had come home at last.[275] They conceived a second son, Arkesilaos (or Poliphorthes).

The next day, Odysseus went to see his father, Laertes, who had withdrawn from the palace after his wife died some years before. He lived alone in a crude hut, mourning the loss of his wife and brooding over a son he believed would never return. Overjoyed at the sight of his son, Laertes dressed himself once more in clothing suited to his dignity, and they sat down to discuss their plan of action. Meanwhile, the parents of the Ithakian suitors buried their sons and confronted Odysseus at Laertes's house.

Laertes killed ungrateful old Eupeithes, father of Antinoos, who had inflamed the elders into seeking retribution. He had fled from his Taphian home after a raid on Thesprotia and had been taken in by Odysseus before the Trojan War. After his death, the shout of Athena drove the others away. Odysseus was stopped from pursuing them when a thunderbolt fired by Zeus crashed between the two parties. Both sides agreed to arbitration to settle their dispute.

[275] In Homer's *Odyssey* and the lost Homeric poem *Thesprotis* (quoted by Pausanias in *Guide to Greece*, viii.12.6), Penelope is unquestionably faithful, though she does enjoy the suitors' attention. Un-Homeric versions doubt her chastity. In one (Apollodoros, *Library,* Epitome 7.31–39), Odysseus kills her for sleeping with Amphinomos, and in another (Pausanias, *Guide to Greece* viii.12.6) he sends her back to Ikarios for sleeping with Antinoos. On her way home, she was supposedly seduced by Hermes in Mantinea and bore the great god Pan. The Mantineans proudly showed off Penelope's tomb to a skeptical Pausanias.

## A Second Odyssey

Odysseus sacrificed to the nymphs and sailed to Eleia to inspect his cattle herds. There he was reunited with a comrade at Troy, Polyxeinos, who had returned home years before and had succeeded his father, Agasthenes, as king of Elis (Agasthenes was the son of King Augeias, the king whose filthy stables Herakles had once cleaned). He entertained Odysseus lavishly and gave him a mixing bowl as a parting gift.

Odysseus returned home and performed the sacrifices to dark-haired Hades and Queen Persephone prescribed by the ghost of Teiresias. Then he rewarded his two faithful servants, Philoitios and the swineherd Eumaios, by making them lords. Philoitios received a great estate on Cephallenia; Eumaios's reward was not recorded.

Neoptolemos arrived to act as arbitrator and decreed a stern sentence, hoping to steal Odysseus's kingdom during his absence. Odysseus was to be exiled ten years for murder. For his part in the affair, Telemakhos was exiled for one year. He spent it on Cephallenia. Neoptolemos's plan did not come to pass, for he was soon murdered in Delphi.

Following Teiresias's advice, Odysseus sailed to Epeiros in order to appease the earth-shaker Poseidon. He was to walk inland carrying an oar until he reached a place where no one knew what it was used for. In Thesprotia he was asked what he was carrying. There he made sacrifices and was forgiven. Since he could not yet return home, he married Kallidice, the widowed queen of the Thesprotians. He lived with her for nine years, once leading the Thesprotians into battle against the Brygoi. Because the god of the bloodcurdling yell, Ares, personally led the enemy, the Thesprotians were routed. As soon as his sentence was over, Odysseus left Kallidice and their son Polypoites, and returned home.

On his way home, Odysseus was entertained graciously by Mentes, now the king of Taphios. This time Odysseus found his house in good order. His son Telemakhos had aptly managed the household while Penelope raised their younger son. Telemakhos married King Nestor of Pylos's youngest daughter, Polykaste, whom he had met while visiting King Nestor to learn about his father. They had several children.

Odysseus ruled peacefully for a number of years. Odysseus was an old man when he mistook his son by Circe for a pirate. He had good reason, for Telegonos was carrying off some cattle to feed his hungry men. Odysseus sounded the alarm, and despite his age, he led the defense. He was killed by Telegonos in self-defense.

Then Telegonos discovered that the man he had killed was the man he had been searching for. Odysseus's son Arkesilaos became king of Ithake because Telegonos took Telemakhos, Penelope, and the corpse of Odysseus to Circe's island. Tearfully they buried Odysseus, and the witch gave Telegonos, Telemakhos, and Penelope immortality. Penelope[276] married Telegonos, and Telemakhos married Circe.

## Those Following the Seers

Those who sailed with the seers Kalkhas of Korinth and Amphilokhos of Midea (one of the Epigonoi) clung to the safety of the shoreline of Asia. Among the heroes sailing in this group were two Lapith warriors who distinguished themselves during the defense of the ships—Polypoites (son of coarse Peirithoos, who was still seated in Hades) and Leonteus (son of Koronos, son of Caineus [the woman changed into a man by Poseidon])—and the Thessalian doctor Podaleiros, scion of deified Asclepius. Kalkhas's esteem grew when the great storm he predicted came to pass and they remained safe.

When the fleet arrived in Kolophon in Ionia (already an Akhaian city), they were entertained by a young Hellenic seer named Mopsos, who ruled the city. During a lively dinner conversation between the guests and hosts, both sides claimed to have the better seer. A contest was arranged between Mopsos and old Kalkhas, the best Akhaian seer. The contest was so one-sided in Mopsos's favor that Kalkhas died of a broken heart. (Kalkhas had guessed a pregnant sow carried eight babies while Mopsos correctly stated there were nine, all boys, and that they would be born without issue the next day).

[276] Either Odysseus (Hyginos, *Fabulai,* 127) or Telemakhos (Homer, *Telegony,* 1013) sired Latinos upon Circe. The Romans said Telegonos and Penelope were the parents of Italos, eponym of Italy.

The troops honored great Kalkhas despite his defeat and buried him after a great ceremony at the site of the contest, Klaros. Mopsos had built the oracle at Klaros in completion of the task Delphi had given his mother, and it served as a testimony to his victory. The shrine's power was enhanced with the grave and ghost of Kalkhas.

Mopsos had succeeded his stepfather as king and defeated a Karian army that besieged Kolophon. That young king Mopsos was a great seer was no surprise. His father, Apollo, had sired him after loving the great Theban prophetess Manto, daughter of the marvelous blind seer Teiresias. After conquering Thebes, the Epigonoi gave the Thebans they captured (including Manto and young Mopsos) to Delphi, hoping to curry divine favor in their attack on Kalydon. Delphi instructed Manto to lead the refugees to Anatolia, where she married Akhaian Rhakios of Kretan Mycene, the founder of Kolophon.

The army convinced Mopsos to assume Kalkhas's leadership position, and many Kolophonians joined him. They continued to sail in a southeasterly direction, hugging the rocky coast tightly lest Poseidon send a sudden swell. Along the way, Mopsos named Pamphylia, the mountainous region between Lycia and Cilicia, for his half sister Pamphyle (daughter of Rhakios and Manto). Many chose to settle there, including the Lapiths and Korinthians. (Mycenaian artifacts uncovered in Pamphylia confirm this claim.)

The rest continued on to Cilicia, where the Akhaians and Danaans settled down. Amphilokhos was credited with founding the trade post Poseidonion at the eastern end of Cilicia below the Syrian Gates road, and Mopsos reputedly established the oracle at Mopsuhestia[277] near the important city of Karatepe, which had early Akhaian ties. Together they founded the city of Mallos away from the native Bronze Age strongholds of Mersin, Tarsos, and Adana.

[277] Archeological evidence indicates that oracles first developed in the Near East and spread westward from there and not, as the arrogant Hellenes boasted, the other way around. Cilicia was indeed one of the regions most heavily settled by the Sea Peoples toward the end of the Bronze Age. The Akhaians are convincingly linked to these people. Hellenic settlements at Karatepe and Poseidonion are of a later date. From Karatepe comes a bilingual Hittite-Phoenician inscription in which King Azitawanda of Karatepe claims to be a descendent of Mopsos (Hittite "Mukshush"; Phoenician "Mpsh").

Mopsos's pairing with Amphilokhos was doomed to fail. After all, Amphilokhos had been a general in the army that sacked Thebes and thereby brought about Mopsos's enslavement as a boy. His mother had been raped by Amphilokhos's brother Alkmeon, and the twins she bore him were taken from her. Little Mopsos must have been enraged while helplessly watching his kin die or be enslaved, but now he cooperated with one of the perpetrators.

Inevitably, a feud broke out between the two seers, and they killed each other in single combat, each one "seeing" the other's death beforehand (1168T/918R BCE). Amphilokhos was a far more experienced warrior, but he was well past his prime. In death they became partners again, sharing an oracle on the spot where they dueled in Mallos. Mopsos and Amphilokhos were buried beside each other at Mallos. An oracle arose beside their tombs.

Image 14.2
Map of Late Bronze Age Mycenaian/Minoan Migrations

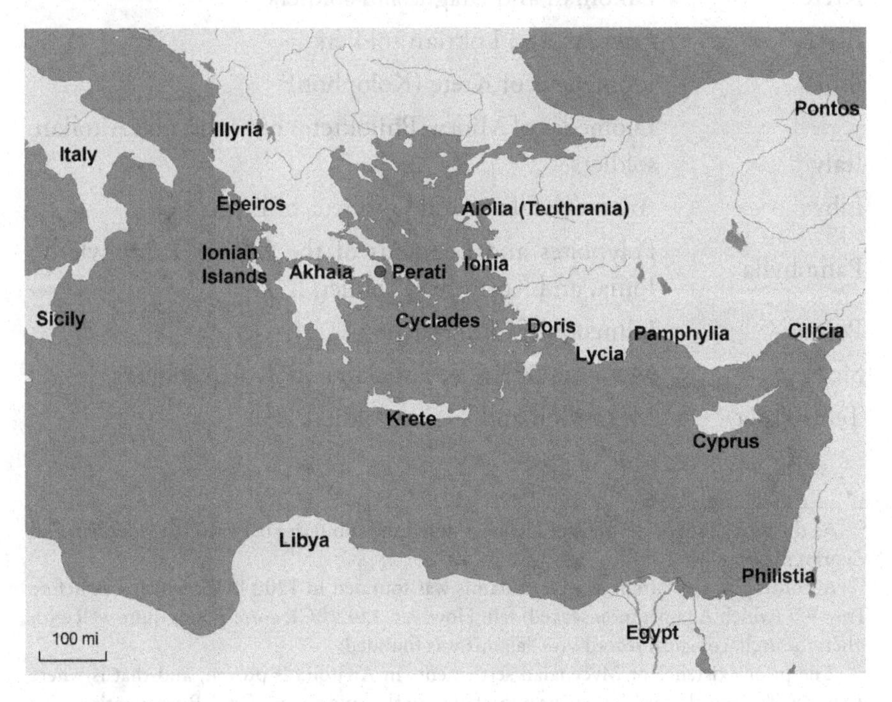

Exhibit 14.1
Where the Akhaians Settled after the Trojan War

| Region | Settlers |
|---|---|
| Akhaia | Eurypylos of Ormenion and soldiers of Thessalian Akhaia |
| Balearic Islands | Rhodian soldiers of the slain leader Tlepolemos |
| Cilicia | Amphilokhos of Midea and Mopsos of Thebes/Ionia |
| Cyclades | Epeios of Phocis and Athenian soldiers |
| Cyprus | Agapenor of Arkadia (Paphos),[278] Akamas of Athens (Soli), Pheidoppos of Kos, and Teucros of Salamis (Salamis)[279] |
| Doris | Podaleiros of Thessalia |
| Epeiros | Helenos of Troy and Neoptolemos of Thessalian Akhaia |
| Krete | Lakonian and Magnesian soldiers |
| Illyria | Euboian and Lokrian soldiers |
| Ionia | Idomeneus of Krete (Kolophon)[280] |
| Italy[281] | Diomedes of Midea, Philoktetes of Malis, and Aitolian soldiers |
| Libya | Antenor of Troy and Gouneus of Epeiros |
| Pamphylia | Polypoites and Leonteus of the Lapith, Pamphyle of Ionia, and Korinthian soldiers |
| Pontos | Ialmenos of Orkhomenos |
| Sicily | Meriones of Krete, Phocian and Trojan soldiers |
| Teuthrania | Myrmidon and Trojan soldiers |

[278] As this story shows, the ancient Hellenes noted the similarity between the Arkadian and Cypriot dialects.

[279] According to the Parian Marble, Salamis was founded in 1202 BCE, which was before Troy VII (which Agamemnon sacked) fell. However, 1202 BCE corresponds quite well with when the archaeological record says Salamis was founded.

[280] The prior existence of Mycenaian settlements in Anatolia is proven, and that is where Agaios of Troizen claims Idomeneus migrated to in the epic poem *Nostoi*. Roman writers like Virgil tied Idomeneus into the myth of Aineias and said he settled in Italy, where Mycenaians traded but didn't settle.

[281] Although the Sea Peoples did attack Italy and Sicily, there were no Mycenaian settlements there despite Roman-era claims to the contrary.

Exhibit 14.2
Early Mythic Settlers—The Sea Peoples of Near Eastern Texts

Archaeological evidence and Near Eastern texts make clear that large numbers of foreigners from the Aigaian Sea basin invaded and settled in the Near East during the Late Bronze Age. The Egyptians called them the "people from the midst of the sea" or "Sea Peoples." The Egyptians listed many tribes among the invaders, including Aqaiwasha (probably the Akhaiwoi of Homer and Ahhiyawa of Hittite records), the Denyans, (possibly Danaans of Homer and Dan tribe of the Hebrews), Keftiu (Kretans or Minoans), Lukka (Lycians), Tjekeryu (possibly Teukrians/ Trojans), and others. Hellenic myths claim that they were the ones who settled in the Near East at that time.

The first overseas Mycenaian conquest was Krete, during the early fourteenth century T / late twelfth century R BCE; this was the mythic rape of Europa. Soon afterward, the Cyclades and Rhodes were heavily colonized and became wholly Akhaian.

From their island bases, the Mycenaians began settling along the western Anatolian coast. When Hittite great-king Tudhaliya I (1400T/1150R–1380T/1130R BCE) first campaigned in western Anatolia, he observed that Attarsiya (meaning "man from Ahhiyawa/Akhaia") was conducting military operations there with infantry and one hundred chariots. In myth, Rhadamanthys and Sarpedon migrated from Krete to the Anatolia coast during the reign of their Akhaian brother Minos. Somewhat later, Xanthos of Mycenai, Aithios of Troizen, Athamas of Orkhomenos, and Bellerophontes of Korinth settled there. The Argonauts Ancaios of Samos and Eriginos of Miletos were Hellenic. Milawata (Hellenic Miletos) held the only Mycenaian palace built outside of Hellas.

The expansive Mycenaians became active in copper-rich Cyprus as well. Almost immediately after Krete fell, the first tholos tombs, a structure common in Hellas, began appearing on Cyprus. Significant Mycenaian settlement of the island began during the fourteenth century T / twelfth century R BCE, when the Hittites held nominal control over the local Alashiya Kingdom. Hittite great-king Tudhaliya I said that Ahhiyawan (Akhaian) Attarsiya was active in Cyprus too. The Akhaians were also active upon the Anatolian shore opposite Cyprus, where the mythic civilizer Triptolemos of Eleusis settled Akhaians from the Argeia at Tarsos, Cilicia.

The continual expansion of the Mycenaians brought them into conflict with other states. Egyptian complaints of piracy correspond to when the Mycenaians began to dominate the coast sites of Cyprus and the native Alashiya Kingdom was clearly in decline.

Hittite great-king Tudhaliya IV (1237T/987R–1209T/959R BCE) tired of Akhaian raids on his Anatolian vassals. He forced the Mycenaian lords out of Miletos (although the populace remained Akhaian), attacked their allies—the Alashiya Kingdom of Cyprus—and closed Anatolian and Syrian ports to Mycenaian goods.

Soon most of the Mycenaian palaces were sacked (the glorious battles of myth) and the greatest eastward migration of Mycenaians began (and it continued for a century). In myth this great migration was thought to have been largely led by the heroes of the Trojan War. However, there are a few stories of slightly earlier movements: some refugees of the Epigonoi sack of Thebes settled on Euboea Island while other refugees settled in Ionia under the prophetess Manto; there she married Rhakios of Krete, who was an Akhaian ruling Kolophon. Euboians fleeing the Thebans settled on Khios Island under Amphikles. These myths support material evidence showing that Cilicia/Pamphylia, Cyprus, and Ionia were heavily settled by the Sea Peoples during the Late Bronze Age (both before and after Troy VII fell). Other than in Palestine, the Mycenaians did not settle along the Syrian coast (nor did they in myth either).

Hittite, Egyptian, and Ugarit royal records mention troublesome Sea Peoples arriving en masse at a time when the population of Hellas declined rapidly (especially in Argeia, Lakonia, and Messenia). Egyptian records speak of whole tribes on the move, no longer just soldiers of fortune. The pharaoh Merenptah boasted of beating back people of the foreign lands of the sea when they invaded the Nile delta (1204T/954R BCE). Hittite great-king Supplilumas II (1207T/957R–1178T/928R BCE) mustered three great armadas and claimed to have defeated the Sea Peoples off the coast of Cyprus. Immediately afterward, Hittite and Ugarit royal records are silent, and their capitals were sacked.

The Egyptians continued to record events and they say the Sea Peoples destroyed Arzawa (western Anatolia), Qode (Cilicia), Alashiya (Cyprus), Ugarit (Phoenicia), and the coastal city-states of Canaan before they were repulsed in the Egyptian delta by Ramesses III (1183T/933R–1152T/902R BCE). Ramesses forced the vanquished invaders to settle down in Canaan. One of the tribes mentioned by the Egyptians was the Peleset, most likely the Philistines (meaning "Palestinians"). The Bible refers to Philistines as Cherethites (possibly Kretans) and the Philistine coast as the Kretan Negev. Philistine ceramic traditions were predominantly Mycenaian of a type common on Krete.

The story of Menelaos's return may contain a trace of the Sea Peoples' defeat by Ramesses. According to Homer, Menelaos and his men served as mercenaries along the eastern Mediterranean shore after the war, and he returned only after a punishing delay in the Egyptian delta. (No heroes were said to have settled in Egypt, but they did settle in Libya, and the Egyptians say the Libyans were allies of the Sea Peoples.)

Although later Hellenic and Latin writers provided stories of war heroes migrating westward, the only evidence of Mycenaian settlements in the west is found on the Ionian Islands just off the west coast of Hellas. Among the mythic settlers were Cephalos of Athens (he fought with Amphitryon against the Taphians) and Zacynthos, son of Dardanos of Psophis (in Arkadia), who led many to the islands that bear their names.

The myths speak of a second major oversea migration led by Neleus and his brothers (in the year 1087T/837R BCE, according to the mid third-century BCE Parian Marble and the fourth-century CE bishop Eusebios of Caesaria). Evidence suggests that there may indeed have been some movement during the Protogeometric Age (1025T/830R–925T/790R BCE), because Miletos in Ionia was enlarged at that time, and Attike-style pottery was introduced. However, Hellas was largely unpopulated at the time and therefore could not have sent many immigrants. The Neleids of Pylos (by way of Athens) would more likely have migrated to Ionia during the great migration about the time Troy VII fell, since sandy Pylos was sacked a few years beforehand.

---

## Those Returning with Agamemnon

Agamemnon and his followers were right to stay behind and spend yet another cold winter on the desolate, windy beaches of Ilion. When spring came, the prudent leaders who had stayed sailed home. They crossed the wine-dark sea safely without incident. As Teucros of Salamis, Demophoon and Akamas of Athens, and others sailed away, Agamemnon remained behind to let his concubine Kassandra bear his twins before undertaking the difficult journey.

Teucros of Salamis, half brother of gigantic Ajax, led his brother's forces home. Teucros had been the best javelin thrower among the Akhaians and had been one of the honored warriors who entered Troy in the wooden horse. But his accomplishments in battle and brave defiance of Agamemnon in giving Ajax a proper burial (despite his having committed suicide) did not impress his hard-hearted father, Telamon. Telamon blamed half-breed Teucros (son of the Trojan princess Hesione) for not preventing the suicide of his brother and for allowing shame to come to Ajax's name by not demanding that Ajax be placed upon a funeral pyre in the armor of Akhilleus. Teucros explained that he had been away on a raiding party at the time and that upon his return he honorably defended his dead brother's rights to a proper burial, at great risk to himself. Telamon was not impressed. Rejected at home, Teucros left Ajax's children by his concubines with Telamon and sailed off.

When Teucros arrived in Phoenicia, King Belos (Baal) of Sidon promised him land on Cyprus. Teucros sailed to the promised lands, and Alashiyan king Cinyras of Cyprus permitted him to found the port of Salamis, not far from the largest Cypriot city, Enkomi. He married Princess Eune, daughter of King Cinyras or Sandokos, and named their firstborn son after his brother Ajax. When Ajax came of age, he founded Olba in Cilicia and started the priestly dynasty of the Teucrids.[282]

The Athenians had remained with Agamemnon as well. Their king, Menestheus, the choice of the Dioskouroi to marry Helene, had been among the best soldiers who hid in the Trojan horse. He must have been

[282] The historic Teucrid kings of Salamis and priests of Olba probably claimed to be descendants of Teucros to bolster their legitimacy and curry favor from powerful Athens. (The people of Salamis Island belonged to the powerful Athenian democracy.)

killed during the fall of Troy, although his body was never recovered. The sons of the great Athenian hero Theseus by his Kretan wife, Phaidra, had fled Athens when Menestheus seized the kingdom, and they had fought at Troy with the Euboians, hoping to recover their grandmother Aithra (who was forced to serve Helene since her capture by the Dioskouroi). Demophoon, the elder of the two, now took command of the Athenian forces and led them home as king. His younger brother Akamas[283] chose to make his fortune elsewhere and reputedly founded Soli on Cyprus. He died when a horse fell on top of him, the result of a curse laid on him by his spurned Thracian lover, Phyllis.

Agamemnon had spent the winter dallying with Princess Kassandra, the lovely virgin daughter of Priamos. The awe-inspiring gods rewarded Agamemnon's prudence with warnings to be cautious. For his piety, the Stronger Ones sent a warning about his homecoming through the prophetess Kassandra, and she repeatedly foretold his doom, but alas, he could not believe her. So the Deathless Ones sent another warning to Agamemnon; they sent the ghost of Akhilleus to warn him in a dream. Determined Agamemnon dismissed the warning and prepared to sail home anyway.

Agamemnon delayed his return until well into the summer to allow Kassandra time to bear her burden—twin sons they named Teledamos and Pelops. Then they sailed home smoothly. Since the Akhaians had begun to arrive in Hellas the fall before, Klytaimnestra and Aigisthos had time to prepare for Agamemnon's return. Oiax, son of Nauplia the Wrecker, brought additional news: Agamemnon was bringing back a Trojan concubine as his wife.

[283] Apollodoros confused and reversed the life stories for Demophoon and Akamas from the usual account. He says Akamas became king and Demophoon the lover of Pyllis.

# The Fall of Mycenai

## Late Helladic Bronze Age (LHIIIC); End of the Age of Heroes

> To our sorrows do not add harsh anxieties, and do not show me heavy hopes for the future. For the immortal gods did not for all time alike establish over the holy earth strife unending for mortals, no, nor friendship either, but the gods establish within one day a different mind.
>
> —Stesikhoros of Lokris, fifth century BCE

While King Agamemnon sailed happily homeward, his queen, Klytaimnestra, prepared for his arrival. Many of the Akhaians had already made it home, and they told her that Agamemnon was waiting for his young concubine to deliver their child before returning. It had been ten years since Klytaimnestra had last seen her husband; it was the tumultuous day that he had sacrificed their brave little daughter Iphigeneia.

During Agamemnon's long absence, his powerful wife Klytaimnestra brooded resentfully against the king for killing her first husband and child as well as for killing Iphigeneia. When she was wooed by Thyestes's young son Aigisthos—the boy once pardoned for killing King Atreus—she resisted the young man's advances, fearing that Agamemnon would soon return. But as the years passed her fear subsided, but her anger at Agamemnon did not. Vassal-king Nauplios of Nauplia lobbied hard for

Klytaimnestra to accept Aigisthos's advances. Nauplios the Wrecker was avenging the execution of his son Palamedes.

All-seeing Zeus sent luck-bringing Hermes to warn Aigisthos not to seduce Klytaimnestra.[284] Blinded by a family curse and the chance to gain a great kingdom, Aigisthos (named for a stubborn goat) did not heed divine warning. He killed the minstrel Agamemnon had left to guard Klytaimnestra and seduced her. The lovers entered their relationship with something very much stronger in common than mutual love—their hatred for Agamemnon (1186T/936R BCE). Together they ruled, with Klytaimnestra holding a dominant role. The couple quickly conceived three kids before she passed her childbearing years: Erigone, Aletes, and Helene. Nauplios and his sons became staunch supporters of the couple.

## Death of the King

Aigisthos and Klytaimnestra arranged a sumptuous feast for the returning soldiers, a hero's welcome. Aigisthos left the scene while Klytaimnestra led the welcoming party. Agamemnon introduced Kassandra as his second wife, having acquired a taste for the oriental custom of polygamy.

Klytaimnestra ordered her lovely slave girls to prepare a warm bath in a silver tub for her travel-weary lord. After a relaxing soak and rubdown, the godlike king stepped out of the tub to partake of the feast prepared for him. Klytaimnestra threw a net over him, and Aigisthos emerged from his hiding place and struck him twice with his sword. Agamemnon fell back into the tub, and Klytaimnestra, to avenge Iphigeneia, beheaded him with a double axe (1183T/933R BCE). She then cut off his hands and feet so that his ghost could not walk or harm her. She remained convinced to the end that her act of revenge was justified. His feasting soldiers were slaughtered next. Only Kassandra died without wide-eyed disbelief, felled by Klytaimnestra with the same bloody double axe. Aigisthos slew her twins.

---

[284] A major earthquake shook the Argeia, and nearby Prosymna and Berbati were abandoned at the end of LHIIIB—the early 1190sT / 940sR BCE. Perhaps the earth-shaker Poseidon was warning the Aigisthos and Klytaimnestra not to get involved, although the poets say that Zeus sent Hermes to deliver the warning. Many Hellenic palace cities were sacked during that decade as well.

During the melee, eighteen-year-old Elektra (daughter of Agamemnon and Klytaimnestra) wisely sent her thirteen-year-old brother Orestes away with protectors to their uncle Strophios, king of the large Phocian city of Krisa. Many years earlier, Agamemnon's sister Anaxibia had married King Strophios and moved into his stately palace. There she had born a noble son, Pylades, who was close in age to Orestes.

Orestes and Pylades quickly became inseparable friends. Orestes spent his exile with both wealth and love. Meanwhile, Elektra, who had remained behind, was punished.

Aigisthos and Klytaimnestra were now officially married in a sumptuous ceremony, and he officially became the king (1183T/933R–1177T/927R BCE). Aigisthos kept foreign bodyguards and never slept a sound night, fearing Orestes's return. For six years Elektra had to bide her time, sending a stream of secret letters to Orestes, goading him to return and avenge his father. Further, she openly displayed hatred toward her mother. Aigisthos feared what she might do and would have killed her. Klytaimnestra refused this, though she was stung by Elektra's obvious hatred. Finally, in a move to both punish and humiliate, they married her off to a peasant. The wise peasant feared repercussions and never slept with her.

## Orestes Avenges his Father

Elektra grew obsessive. She had no respect for her younger sister Khrysothemis, who did not share her zeal. She nursed an all-encompassing fury for revenge, like Atreus and Thyestes had before her. Elektra spent her days in backbreaking toil unfit for one of such noble pedigree, and she lamented for Orestes's return.

Once he became a man, Orestes was tormented by his destiny. He faced two alternatives, neither desirable: avenge a father he never knew by killing his mother, or be saddled with social disgrace and lose the kingdom that was rightfully his. He did not feel hatred for his mother the way Elektra did. The story of Alkmeon of Medeia, who had faced this same problem a generation before and had been deeply tormented by it, worried Orestes. Orestes knew that a dilemma of this magnitude required guidance from the Deathless Ones.

Pylades and Orestes walked up the mountain path to Delphi, where they heard the god's prophecy. The prophetess said his fate was to avenge his father or contract a skin disease and become an outcast in every city. With many misgivings, Orestes set off for Mycenai accompanied by loyal Pylades.

The young men first paid homage at Agamemnon's tomb. While there, Orestes was recognized by his look-alike sister Elektra. The reunited siblings noticed a libation at the tomb sent by Klytaimnestra, who had suffered a disturbing, prophetic dream the night before.

> She dreamed that a serpent appeared
> with blood-dripping scales,
> and from his belly stepped a king
> from the ancient dynasty
> of Pleisthenes and Agamemnon[285]

True to the dream, Agamemnon's children plotted together to kill Aigisthos and Klytaimnestra. They decided to spread rumors that Orestes was dead. Klytaimnestra was saddened by the news but also relieved for her own neck's sake.

Orestes, disguised as a supplicant, arrived at the palace (1177T/927R BCE). Orestes killed unarmed Aigisthos while his back was turned to make an animal sacrifice to the rich-crowned immortals. Meanwhile, to bring Klytaimnestra to the place of ambush, Elektra sent for her mother, feigning illness. Klytaimnestra rushed to the scene hopefully, for she thought her daughter was finally reaching out to her, and she was concerned for her daughter's welfare.

Sadly, the call was a ruse, and hateful Elektra, with twisted pleasure, watched her mother learn the truth. She smiled as Klytaimnestra arrived and was seized by Orestes. Overcome by the memory of himself as a small boy happily rocking in his mother's arms, Orestes halted. Elektra's expression instantly soured and she screamed out for bloody murder while Klytaimnestra pleaded for mercy. Pylades broke the moment by flatly reminding Orestes of the oracle of Delphi. Orestes then struck his mother

[285] Stesikhoros, "On Klytaimenestra", in *Sappho and the Greek Lyric Poets.* Translated by Willis Barnstone.

with a hesitant blow that left Klytaimnestra writhing in pain, cursing before she died.

The killers returned to the palace, and Orestes slew his seven-year-old half sister Helene while Pylades warded off the sons of Nauplios, staunch allies of Aigisthos. The sons of Nauplios managed to rescue Erigone and Aletes (the other children of Aigisthos and Klytaimnestra) before the palace erupted into a general mutiny led by Orestes.

Despite divine sanction for his act, Klytaimnestra's dying curse brought the Erinyes upon Orestes and drove him mad. He was stunned; his deeds overwhelmed him. Orestes sank to the ground and remained prostrate for six days, giving Oiax, son of Nauplios, time to rally a resistance. As fate would have it, Menelaos arrived after wandering seven full years after Troy's fall. He offered to mediate between the two parties in order to avert civil war and ensure that no harm came to his daughter - who had lived in the palace of Mycenai for the seventeen years her parents had been away.

## The Erinyes (Avenging Furies) Chase Orestes

Orestes's position was desperate, and in anger he tried to kill Menelaos's wife, Helene, but Apollo Pytho saved her. So the desperate siblings then tried to gain asylum by capturing Hermione, who had been kindly raised by Klytaimnestra during Helene's absence. The kidnap forced Menelaos to negotiate a compromise to save his daughter. Hermione was pleased to be of help; she had spent much of her childhood in the same palace with Orestes and was betrothed to marry him. Menelaos won a decree of banishment instead of execution for Orestes. Menelaos, Helene, and Hermione then returned home to Lakonia.

Although Hermione had been betrothed to Orestes since they were little, Menelaos had also promised her to Akhilleus's son Neoptolemos in reward for his valor at Troy. When Neoptolemos heard of Menelaos's return, he came to Lakonia to claim his bride (1177T/927R BCE). Hermione, beautiful and arrogant like her mother, wanted to marry Orestes and return to wealthy Mycenai as queen. Menelaos was angry that Orestes had blackmailed him and was justly afraid of Orestes's mental state, pursued as he was by avenging Erinyes on behalf of his mother. Therefore he kept his promise to the brutish Neoptolemos.

Meanwhile, Aigisthos and Klytaimnestra's young son Aletes (meaning "wanderer") (1177T/927R–1174T/924R BCE) became king, and Oiax was appointed regent. For one year Orestes lived in exile, and agony, in Arkadia, as ordered. Pylades married Elektra, but he left his new bride behind and risked defilement to care for mad Orestes.[286] He finally gained some relief, but not before, in a fit of madness, he bit off one of his own fingers.

At the end of the year, Orestes returned to the Argeia and was purified of murder at Troizen. His reprieve did not last long. Unfazed by ritual purification, the Erinyes hounded him relentlessly. Wherever he ran, they followed slowly, stubbornly, always closing in on him. In terror he fled to Delphi and was ordered by Apollo Delphos to stand trial on the Athenian Areiopagos. Phoebus Apollo sent the Argos slayer Hermes to put the Erinyes to sleep so that Orestes could get a head start. Once Orestes was in Athens, silver-bowed Apollo defended him while the Erinyes prosecuted him. The Erinyes offered to willingly leave Orestes alone if he would only swear an oath that he did not kill his mother. Of course he could not. Despite this, Pallas Athena, whom the Erinyes accepted as judge, cast the deciding vote to acquit Orestes.

Still, some of the Erinyes continued to pursue him. In desperation Orestes returned to Delphi and threatened suicide. He felt Apollo Delphinos was personally responsible since his priestess had told him to commit the murder in the first place. This time the entranced priestess told him that if he brought back Artemis's statue from far-off Tauris, he would be free of the Erinyes and the seizures they induced.

Orestes commissioned a fifty-oared warship (a *pentekonter*) and set sail with Pylades (1175T/925R BCE). They sailed through the Bosporos and into the inhospitable Sea of Pontos (Black Sea), just as the Argonauts had

[286] Hellenic custom required that the polluted, which included murderers, be banished and not speak to or stay with anyone lest they bring on defilement (a harsh penalty in a society that honored community). Once the polluted reached his destination, he was allowed to speak and to be accepted as a supplicant and to receive atonement through ritual. By going with Orestes, Pylades risked defilement and therefore demonstrated incredible loyalty (as Parthenopaios once showed Telephos).

done before them. But while the Argonauts had sailed east along the south shores to Colchis, Orestes turned north at Sinope to reach the Tauric Khersonnese (Crimea).

It was the custom of the barbaric Taurians, a Scythian tribe, to sacrifice all strangers to Artemis Tauropolos. Orestes landed and hid his ship and crew before the natives discovered their arrival. Then Orestes and Pylades ventured inland on foot but were captured.

Orestes fell into despair, expecting to die far away from home in a futile quest for peace of mind. But unbeknown to any Akhaian, his sister Iphigeneia was there, alive and well. She had not died during her sacrifice at Aulis as the troops had believed, but instead had been spirited away by virgin Artemis. Apparently the Mistress of Animals had switched Iphigeneia with a hind at the moment she was sacrificed; she would not have her altar stained with human blood.

Iphigeneia was alive but miserable. She was far away from home and forced to perform religious rituals for Hellenic strangers (her own people) before they were sacrificed. Still, she was respected and retained her virginity.

In questioning the new Akhaian sacrificial victims, Iphigeneia and Orestes learned each other's identity. Iphigeneia offered an escape, but only for one. Orestes and Pylades each demanded the other go. Finally, Iphigeneia tricked the king and all three escaped. She used the trust she had earned by having always done the king's biding before.

The three safely got to the hidden ship with the holy statue of awful Artemis. Athena (wisdom) told the barbarian king Thoas not to pursue them. On their return trip, the trio stopped on Sminthes Island, where Khryses served as priest of the long-haired god Apollo. There they met their nine-year-old half brother Khryses, who eventually succeeded his grandfather as Apollo's spokesman. Meanwhile, Tauric king Thoas changed his mind and pursued the fugitives. Orestes killed him when he caught up to them, and the Erinyes stopped haunting him.

The Athenians say bright Athena Parthenia (meaning "virgin") told Iphigeneia to disembark with the statue in Brauron in Attike and become the priestess of Artemis, the one who delighted in arrows. There she lived out her life as a virgin servant devoted to the goddess. The Spartans disputed the Athenian claim and said Orestes kept the statue and clutched it when he felt the madness returning. When he felt strong enough, he discarded the wooden image by the Eurotas River during a trip to Lakonia.

Orestes and Pylades returned to Pylades's home in Krisa but discovered that Elektra was absent. They ascended Mount Parnassus to Delphi and left a votive offering in thanks to the god for his guidance. In Delphi they met up with Elektra, who was seeking word about the fate of her brother and husband, whom she feared were dead. After their joyful reunion, Elektra reminded Orestes that his task was not over. He still had to take the throne that was rightfully his.

## Orestes Becomes King

Orestes had little trouble regaining his kingdom (1174T/924R–1135T/885R BCE). Remembering that his father had been killed by a man he once granted clemency to, Orestes killed the boy-king Aletes (whose father, Aigisthos, son of Thyestes, assassinated both Atreus and Agamemnon). Then Orestes seized his thirteen-year-old half sister, Erigone, and let his rage and lust combine into a furious assault. Intoxicated by the unstable mix of hate and lust, he kept her as concubine until his marriage. Then he sent her to the Attike town of Rhadmos to be the priestess of glorious Artemis. After all, even though he had no further use for her, he could not bear the thought of a less noble man with his hands upon her or letting her womb deliver a potential enemy. He lovingly raised the bastard son she bore him: Penthilos.

With affairs settled in Mycenai, Pylades and his wife, Elektra, returned to Krisa. Often Orestes went to visit, and even more often Pylades and Elektra came and were lavishly entertained in Mycenai.

Orestes discovered that while he was in a state of madness, his promised bride had been married to Neoptolemos, son of Akhilleus. Agamemnon had been Akhilleus's enemy, and Orestes became the enemy of Neoptolemos. When Orestes received word from Pylades that Neoptolemos was in Delphi, he quietly followed. Neoptolemos had come to Delphi seeking restitution: he blamed Apollo, god of the unerring bow, for guiding the arrow that Paris shot to kill Akhilleus. While the locals considered his request, Orestes inflamed their anger and fear by reminding them that Neoptolemos had defiled Apollo's altar at Troy by killing old king Priamos upon it. Then Orestes reminded the people of Neoptolemos's stated hatred of Pythian Apollo.

The far-shooter Apollo made an example out of Neoptolemos as a warning for others. Apollo ensured that he was killed in the same manner as he had killed Priamos, sacrificed at the altar of Apollo. Unsuspecting Neoptolemos was murdered by the mob as he offered sacrifice (1174T/924R BCE). Orestes quickly made off to Phthia and spirited away willing Hermione, who was accustomed to the sumptuous palace life of Mycenai and did not care much for boorish Neoptolemos.

Thetis then appeared to Peleus for the first time since he had beaten her so brutishly long ago. She told the old man of Neoptolemos's death and said, "Give Andromakhe to Helenos and then you will become a god and we will dwell together for all time, god and goddess in the house of Nereus. Wait at the hallow cave of the ancient rock of Sepias and their take your seat and wait for me with my choir of fifty Nereides to fetch you.[287]

Peleus sent Andromakhe and her sons by Neoptolemos (Molossos, Pielos, and Pergamos) to her prophet-brother, Helenos, in Epeiros. As a man, Molossos became eponym of an Epeirot tribe, and Pergamos returned to Assuwa (Asia) with his mother and founded a settlement that would become a great city. The sons of Akastos, enemies of Peleus, ruled Iolkos and now added Phthia to their realm.

---

[287] Euripides, *Andromakhe*. The *Palatine Anthology* says Peleus forfeited his immortality by chartering a vessel to Molossia, where he hoped to find Neoptolemos alive, but he died in a shipwreck off the small island of Ikos in the Peparethos chain. If so, he was like Odysseus—one who excelled in this life but chose not to accept immortality offered him.

When Thessalos, descendent of Jason, drove the descendants of Akastos out of Iolkos, the rightful line of Aison finally gained control of Iolkos.[288] The city became one of the few places to see a population increase at this time. Jason's son Thessalos had spent some time under the tutelage of Kheiron and returned from beyond the Pindos Mountains in Epeiros,[289] where his father had settled and died. Thessalos began uniting the tribes of the plain (Aiolians, Lapiths, Pelasgians, Myrmidons, Kadmeians, Centaurs, and others), and they took his name. [290]

---

Exhibit 15.1
Jason and Medeia

After the voyage of the Argonauts, Akastos succeeded his father, Pelias, as king of Iolkos, and Jason was banished because of Medeia's role in the death of the old king. Jason went to the home of the seer Thestor to tell him that his father, Idmon, had died with the Argonauts and to obtain advice. Thestor suggested that they all move to Korinth, where he had relatives. Thestor correctly foresaw that a sea power like Korinth could use Jason's experience.

---

[288] Excavators have found that Iolkos suffered some damage during an attack. Despite the fact that Iolkos had only modest fortification, the destruction was concentrated on the palace alone; the settlement around it had been spared. Perhaps the citizens overthrew the king. The destruction occurred somewhat later than the ancient writers thought and also later than the sack of most of the palace states farther south (most palaces were destroyed around the end of LHIIIB, ca. 1195T/945R BCE, but Iolkos fell afterward, in LHIIIC, ca. 1125T/875R BCE). The palace was not reoccupied. So archaeology supports the mythic suggestion that Thessalos sacked Iolkos while Peleus merely installed a new ruler. Even so, to fit the later sack date now accepted, Thessalos had to have been a grandson or great-grandson of Jason—not his son, as Apollodoros relates.

[289] Several sources claim that the Thessalians were from Epeiros. This doesn't necessarily mean that they were related to the Epeirot tribes living in Epeiros during historic times. Neoptolemos had led the non-Epeirot Myrmidons to Epeiros, Aiolian Jason had settled in Epeiros, and the Athmantians of the Pindos Mountains in historic times were quite possibly an Aiolic/Minyan tribe and claimed a connection with Kadmos (the tribe's name suggests Aiolian Athamas as its eponym).

[290] Linguistic evidence supports the claim that the Thessalians were descended from a son of Jason, because Jason was an Aiolian and the historic Thessalian dialect was Aiolic in nature. Mycenaian culture was extremely homogeneous, and most of the dialect differences noted by historic Hellenes probably developed during the isolation of the Dark Age. Thessalian differed from Aiolian (which was spoken by colonists who had settled in the islands and near Troy) because it borrowed some from northwestern Hellenes, such as the Akhaians (Myrmidons). The Mycenaian Age ended in Thessalia without the devastation prevalent further south (twelfth century T / early ninth century R BCE). The villages of Thessalia show no signs of destruction (unlike the palace city of Iolkos), and although they contracted, they continued to be inhabited.

King Kreon of Korinth gladly welcomed his kinsman Thestor, famous Jason, and Jason's sorcerer wife, Medeia (1231T/981R BCE). While in Korinth, Jason and his wife Medeia had a daughter named Eriopis followed by four sons: Mermeros, Pheres, and the twins Thessalos (the elder) and Alkimenes. Magical Medeia also built a temple to garland-loving Aphrodite in town. Jason had the ship Argos pulled up onto shore and often went to it to reminisce about his glory days.

Jason became intrigued with blossoming Princess Kreousa and the throne that was her dowry. So, after fourteen years of marriage, Jason callously gave Medeia a decree of divorce. Jason told Medeia that the divorce was in the best interest of their children, for now they would become rulers instead of just merchants. Medeia followed the rules of love, not politics, and deplored Jason's justifications.

The nobles of Korinth, however, were only all too willing to nullify Jason's marriage to a barbarian witch. They were happy to have such a hero as their future king. Medeia feigned acceptance. Nevertheless, Jason knew her temper and the skill with which she had killed her own brother and, upon his request, Pelias of Iolkos. Jason gave Medeia one day to leave town.

Medeia did not spend her day packing. Instead, all of her energy was spent devising revenge—at any cost. Medeia prepared a venomous potion with which she anointed Kreousa's wedding veil and crown. She hoped both Kreon and Jason would embrace her and share in the death she wore.

The wedding began with the bride, as always, looking radiant. Mermeros and Pheres arrived with an airtight box, a gift from Medeia. Despite Kreousa's intuitive objection, Jason persuaded her to accept the gifts, a gown and veil. Once she had put the garments on, they burst into flames while the guests watched in horror.[291] Kreousa rushed to the fountain, but water made it burn hotter. Kreon tried to smoother the flames, but he

[291] By the description of the potion by Euripides (*Medeia,* 431), both Pliny and Plutarch speculated that Medeia used naphtha. Modern scientists point to petroleum, sulfur and lime, flammable materials that were used in the textile industry as dyes, bleaches, cleansers, and softeners. Ordinarily the residues were carefully removed from clothing before wearing. Women's lives were closely monitored, but they did run the textile business and therefore had access to dangerous chemicals. Euripides and Sophokles (writing about Deianeira unwittingly poisoning Herakles with a garment at approximately the same time) wrote what might have been in many a man's thoughts—namely that a woman could kill them by accident or with malice by such means.

too caught fire. The two died in great agony. Aghast, the wedding guests realized what had happened and became angry. Grabbing anything close, they tried to stone Jason's sons for having presenting Kreousa with her death. Jason grabbed his sons and hastily withdrew (1217T/967R BCE).

Medeia was nowhere to be found. She disappeared so quickly that the mob thought only a chariot drawn by dragons could have taken the witch away unnoticed. Raving Medeia rejected her own children because Jason loved them. She left her toddler twins at rich-crowned Hera's altar, hoping divine presence would gain them mercy. Jason learned of their whereabouts in time to save Thessalos, the angry mob having killed tender little Alkimenes already. His ghost kills other infants in Korinth to this day. Jason's daughter Eriopis escaped as well and eventually married King Oileus of Lokris and bore the infamous javelin thrower Ajax the Lesser.

Jason sailed the old ship Argos to Kercyra Island. Knowing he would not be welcome there once word of the king's death reached the island, Jason gathered provisions for his supporters and settled on the wild Epeiros coast nearby. He sent either Mermeros or Thessalos to the wise Centaur Kheiron for instruction. Jason died when the *Argo* fell on him as he rested under it daydreaming.

---

In a great palace ceremony, Orestes married Hermione, who shared her mother's famous beauty. Old Menelaos shrugged and accepted it. When Menelaos died, his illegitimate sons Megapenthes and Nikostratos exiled Helene. She took refuge with Polyxo, widow of Tlepolemos, king of Rhodes (1169T/919R BCE). Tlepolemos had died in the Trojan War, and Danaan Polyxo, who had previously been a friend of Helene (when Helene lived in Mycenai and Polyxo in Tiryns), pretended to welcome her. She ordered her maids to dress themselves as Erinyes and to hang Helene from a tree.

Queen Hera bestowed immortality upon Menelaos, and he was reunited with his wife on the Island of the Blessed. She was honored with a blessed afterlife because she was Zeus's daughter; and he, for being her husband.

The Lakonian lords elected Orestes as their king over Menelaos's bastard son Megapenthes (1170T/920R BCE). They did so because Orestes's wife, Hermione, was the only legitimate surviving heir of Menelaos.

Orestes conducted one last campaign with his close friend Pylades. Supported by Phocian troops under his brother-in-law Pylades, Orestes conquered much of Arkadia (1169T/919R BCE). This conquest was intended, in part, to clear the roads to Sparta and Pisa of highwaymen.

One major concern for the king was producing an heir. For many years, Hermione did not conceive, but Orestes truly loved her and did not want to replace her to produce an heir. Their patience was rewarded with the birth of an heir they named Tisamenos (1165T/915R BCE). With a healthy heir at home, Orestes sent his twenty-year-old bastard son, Penthilos, to govern Lakonia (1153T/903R).

Orestes, like his father, had to ward off an invasion by the Herakleids. Aristomakhos, son of Kleodaios, son of Hyllos, prepared the second Herakleid invasion. He marched south into the Peloponnesos, where the army of Akhaian Orestes blocked his way. When the forces engaged, Orestes's most important ally was slain—vassal-king Cylarabes, son of the Epigonoi Sthenelos. Cylarabes held responsibility over Argos, Tiryns, and Medeia and fought valiantly for his lord, Orestes. When the Herakleid leader Aristomakhos was killed in battle, the outnumbered Herakleids fled (1163T/913R BCE). Aristomakhos left behind a widow, Talaos's daughter Mythidice, and three sons—Temenos, Kresphontes, and Aristodemos—back in Doris.

Image 15.1
Map of the Mycenaian Kingdom

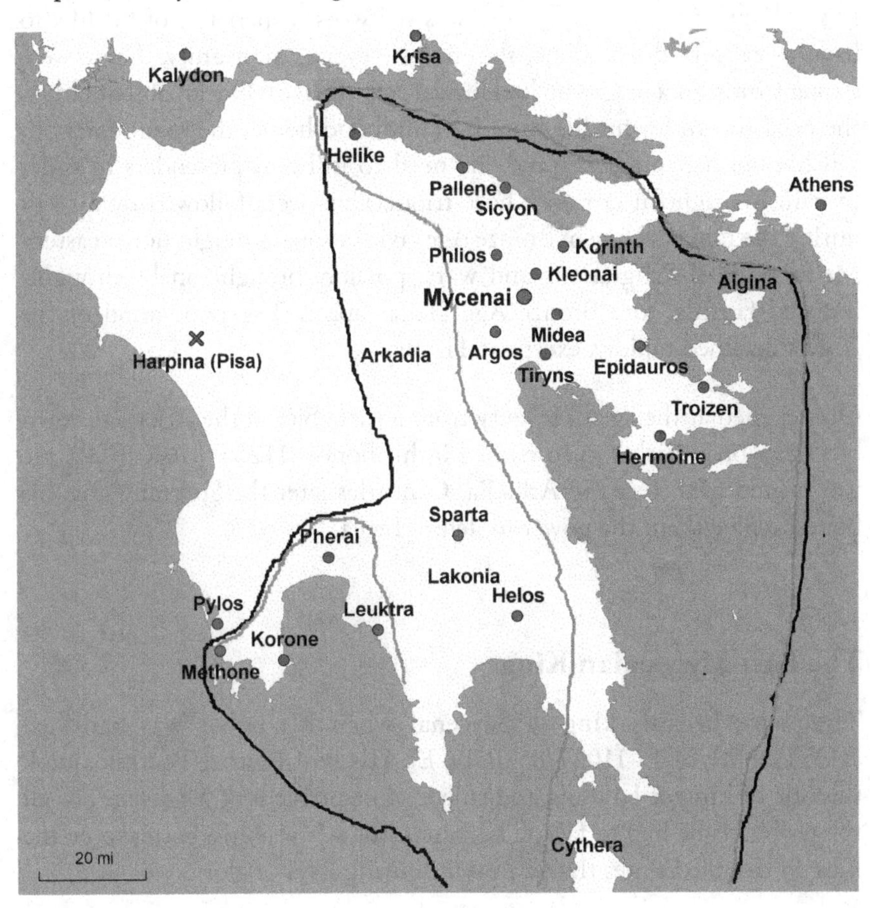


Agamemnon's kingdom in Grey

Orestes's kingdom expanded in Arkadia and Lakonia in Black

## Banishment of Orestes

Future generations remember Orestes for his wise and strong leadership, which enabled him to maintain order in difficult times. Orestes was exiled on command of holy Delphi after a severe earthquake struck the Argeia. The oracle said the quake was a sign from the now divine twins

Dioskouroi (uncles of Hermione) that old Orestes should step down and go to Arkadia, the place where he had been most afflicted by his madness. His old-age banishment, he said, was the worst experience of his life: to have to eat and drink alone, shunned by every community. These were strong words for a man who had lived a very difficult life: an absent father, the need to run for his life from his childhood home, the requirement to kill his mother, madness, and the need to kill two pretenders in order to gain his rightful crown. Those tribulations were followed by a reign during the rapid decline of Bronze Age civilizations throughout the eastern Mediterranean. Migrations and wars, possibly brought on by drought-induced famine, tore Bronze Age Hellas apart. The population of the Argeia declined rapidly, except at Tiryns.

Orestes died at the age of seventy from a snakebite in the Arkadian town of Oresteion, which was so named in his honor (1126T/876R BCE). He was buried near Tegea in Arkadia. Centuries later the Spartans stole his bones to give them the power to defeat Tegea.

## The Last Mycenaian King

Tisamenos became king of Mycenai when his father was banished (1135T/885R BCE–1102T/852R BCE). His half brother Penthilos took the title of king of Lakonia and ruled it independent of Mycenai. For all the problems he had to face, Tisamenos knew it was still better to be the king in troubled times than a peasant during days of glory.

Tisamenos was the last king of Mycenai; his reign ended with the sack of his great city (1102T/852R BCE).[292] If Tisamenos did not die in the battle over Mycenai, he did in the battle for Akhaia, where his sons Kometes (eldest), Daimenes, Sparton, Tellos, and Leontomenes prevailed and ruled. Under a truce, the defeated Ionians were allowed to leave Akhaia. They joined their brethren in Attike, and the Akhaians occupied their

[292] Archaeologists have estimated that the important sites of Mycenai, Tiryns, Asine, and Iria were all razed around 1125T/875R BCE. The first three were immediately reoccupied. Based upon the Alexandrian librarian Eratosthenes of Cyrene's assumption that Troy fell in 1184T/934R BCE and Thucydides's statement that the Herakleids returned eighty years later, then the sack occurred a few years later (1104T/854R BCE). Both dates fit within the latter stages of LHIIIC.

cities. Tisamenos's bastard son Arkhelaos reputedly led Akhaian settlers to found Cyzikos (in Anatolia). Other descendants of Tisamenos migrated to Miletos (Mycenai's colony for over two hundred years).

---

Exhibit 15.2
The Akhaian Migration

The stories of massive migration to Akhaia by Akhaians from other parts of the Peloponnesos and their subsequent movement abroad during the Late Bronze Age fits well with the archaeological record. Before the Akhaian migration, there are correspondingly few myths concerning Akhaia. Similarly, archaeologists have found little evidence of cities of any substance in Akhaia until the last century and a half of the Late Bronze Age. There is ample evidence that Akhaia experienced a population explosion starting in the late thirteenth century T / early tenth century R BCE, just as the myths claim. The settlers came from elsewhere in Hellas, where the population was declining. The places suffering the largest population declines—Messenia, Argeia, and Lakonia—were the very ones said to be sending migrants here. Akhaia was one of the few places in Hellas where the population increased at that time (Akhaia is located in the Peloponnesos, bordering Eleia and just across the Gulf of Korinth from Aitolia).

According to Pausanias, Akhaians moved en masse from Mycenai under King Tisamenos of Mycenai, son of Orestes. Others arrived under Damasios, the son of Tisamenos's half brother Penthilos, king of Sparta, as well as the Lakonian noble Preugenes and his son Patreus. The indigenous Ionians fled to Attike, which also experienced rapid growth at that time. The mythic claim that the earlier populace was driven out and replaced by the invaders, however, is not supported by evidence.

From Korinth and Sicyon, near Akhaia, migrants went to northwest Hellas. The famous Argonaut captain Jason left Korinth and settled in Epeiros (1217T/967R BCE) while Ambrax of Sicyon, son of King Thesprotos, fled Herakleid invaders and settled in the territory of the Thesprotian tribe of Akarnania (1202T/952R BCE).

---

## House of Herakles (1104T/854R–460s BCE)[293]

The Herakleid conquest of so many cities of Hellas represents the end of the Mycenaian Bronze Age and the start of the Dark Age in the Peloponnesos. The arrival of Boiotians and Thessalians in the northern plains and the Neleids in Attike represent the same.

The Herakleid leader who defeated Tisamenos was Temenos, eldest son of Aristomakhos (who had died leading a previous, failed invasion). Although this invasion ultimately succeeded, the campaign was not easy. While preparing another Dorian army of invasion, calamity struck before they even sailed. While assembling in the harbor at Naupaktos, Aristodemos was struck dead by lightning.[294] The expedition was halted as commander-in-chief Temenos went to Delphi wondering if his brother Aristodemos's unusual death was a bad omen. At Delphi he admonished the priestess for giving false prophecies that encouraged his ancestors to engage in disastrous invasions. The priestess said it was not Apollo's fault that they had misinterpreted the message to return during the third harvest. The lord of the silver bow, Apollo, had meant the third generation—Temenos's (the third crop from Hyllos; the first was Kleodaios, the second Aristomakhos, and the third Temenos). The priestess also said that Aristodemos's house must have two kings since he was survived by twins: Prokles and Eurysthenes.

Temenos assembled his fleet again in the harbors along the Gulf of Korinth. Theras the Theban, son of Autesion, took command of Aristodemos's troops and was given custody of Aristodemos's twin sons, whom his sister Argeia bore.

---

[293] The story of the Herakleids was well documented in Hellenic literature. During the fifth century, the historians Herodotos and Thucydides mention it, and playwrights Sophokles (*Trakhian Women*) and Euripides (*Herakleids*) wrote about it. Late writers Apollodoros (*Library*, ii.161–180), Diodoros (*Library of History* iv.58.1–8 and vii.9.1–4), Pausanias (*Guide to Greece*, numerous references), and Strabo (*Geography*, viii–ix) all discuss the Herakleid Return.

[294] Apollodoros, *Library*, ii 8.2, is the source, while Pausanias's *Guide to Greece*, iii.1, says, less plausibly, that the sons of Pylades, king of nearby Krisa, killed Aristodemos. The sons of Pylades would have been too old.

The Herakleids had always included numerous descendants of Theban warriors who had fought for Herakles. When the Boiotians[295] conquered Thebes, most of the citizens fled under ex-king Autesion (the last Theban king from the House of Kadmos and the son of King Tisamenos of Thebes). When Autesion was twenty-three he became the king when his father, Tisamenos (son of Thersandros, the king placed on the Theban throne by the Epigonoi), died during an earlier Boiotia siege (1153T/903R BCE). When the Boiotians finally overwhelmed Thebes, most of the citizens fled with Autesion to Homoloe, including his children Argeia and Theras (1124T/874R BCE). There they joined the Dorians and other Theban refugees who had long ago fled from the Epigonoi.

Unlike the earlier Dorian invasions, Temenos chose to attack by sea instead of marching across the Isthmos. While final preparations were underway, the Herakleid Hippotes killed a strange seer named Karnes, fearing him to be a spy.

After the fleet was destroyed and famine hit the troops, the disheartened Herakleids withdrew. Fuming, Temenos discharged the army and stormed off to Delphi. The oracle upbraided him for doubting his destiny. The cause of his setback, he found out, was due to the seer's death, which angered far-shooter Apollo. Also, a three-eyed guide was needed to assure

[295] As with the Dorian "invasion" of the Peloponnesos, there was no Boiotian "invasion" of Boiotia during the Late Bronze Age. Even the myths suggest this by admitting that the first Boiotians had arrived long before. In neither place did invaders arrive at this time. Instead, the population of both regions declined rapidly, and mass emigration is attested to in both the historic and mythic record. Boiotians/Minyans under the command of Geres, for example, joined the Ionians in settling Teos in Anatolia (twelfth century T / ninth century R BCE). The Boiotians (like the Dorians) must be seen as a new order taking place upon the collapse of the highly bureaucratic palace economy of the Mycenaian era. No central authority remained, and tribal government prevailed. The first king of Thebes under this new order was Damasikhthon, son of Opheltes and grandson of the Boiotian warlord Peneleos. (Peneleos had led the Boiotians to Troy and died there, leaving behind his infant son Opheltes.)

safe passage. To appease the god of seers, Temenos banished Hippotes for ten years and instituted the festival of Karneia.[296]

A new fleet was assembled, and while they made preparations, Temenos noticed a man riding into camp on a one-eyed horse. The chief excitedly asked the man who he was. The reply came that he was Oxylos, son of King Haimon of Aitolia. Haimon was the son of Thoas, who fought at Troy and returned safely. Thoas was the son of Andraimon, whom the Epigonoi installed as king of Kalydon. Prince Oxylos had been recently exiled for killing his brother with an errant discus throw. Temenos offered the prince the job of guiding the Dorians into the Peloponnesos. The agreed-to price was the kingdom of Eleia.

The population of Tiryns had grown during the late twelfth century T / mid tenth century R BCE while the other cities of the Argeia declined; many Herakleids had settled in Tiryns after Hyllos was defeated. All three Herakleid "invasions" started at Tiryns, the ancestral home of Herakles. Because the city fell quickly to Temenos despite its massive cyclopean walls, it might be assumed that the populace was sympathetic to him as one of their own (1104T/854R BCE).

---

Exhibit 15.3
The Dorian Migration

Archaeology evidence supports some, but not all, of the mythic claims. In fact, Late Bronze Age Argeia, Lakonia, and Messenia suffered the most dramatic population decline of any Hellenic region. Argives were said to have gone to Akhaia (under Tisamenos or his sons), Messenians to Ionia via Attike (under the Neleids), and Lakonians to Cyprus (under noble Praxandros) and Akhaia (under Prince Damasios, Preugenes, and Prugenes's son Patreus). Archaeological evidence confirms that a large

[296] The Karneia was the most important pan-Doric festival. At one level it was conducted to appease Apollo for Karnos's/Krios's death. More profoundly it was a military festival about conquest and atonement for the acts of war. The Karneia festival was one of the three great festivals to Apollo. The others were the Hyacinthia, most popular in Lakonia, and the Daphnephoria, popular in northern and central Hellas.
"Krios" (meaning "ram") is a variant of "Karnos." The soothsayer Krios, son of Theokles, told the Dorians how to conquer the place but was murdered. Therefore, a "ram" was the sacrifice that prepared the way for conquest.

group of Late Bronze Age immigrants did migrate to Akhaia, Ionia, and Cyprus.

Image 15.2
Map of Important Dorian Invasion Locations

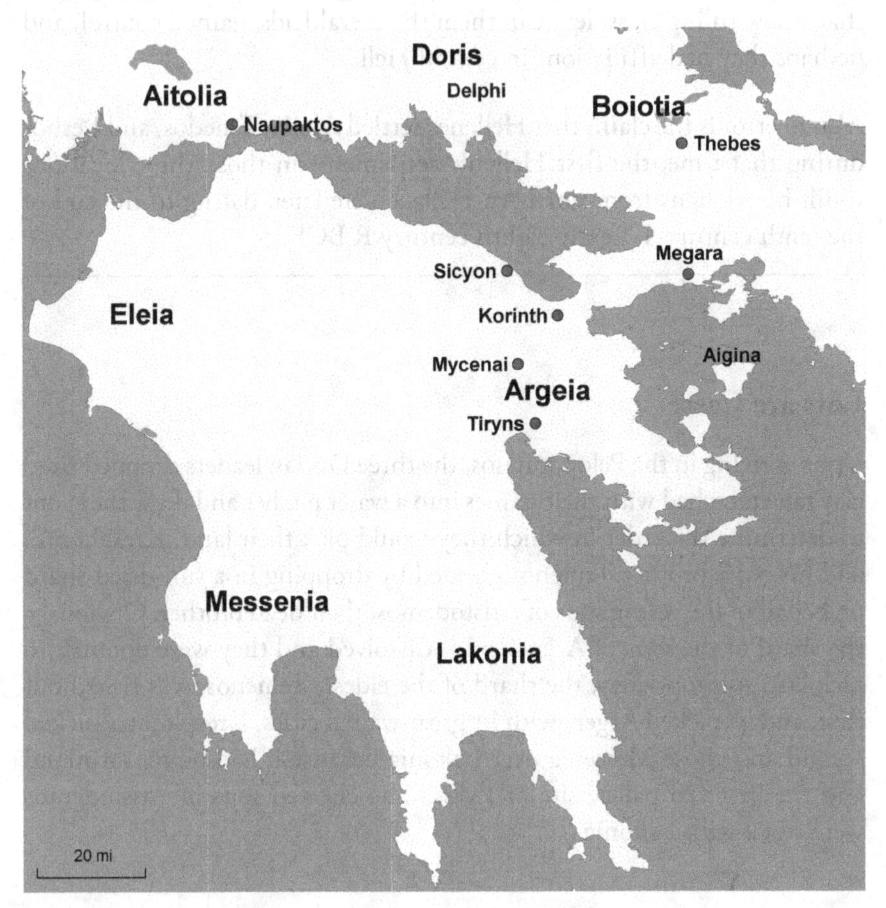


It is also true that central Hellas was depopulated in the Late Bronze Age, roughly the time of the Herakleids' successful invasion of the Peloponnesos. However, archaeological evidence is clear that the Peloponnesos did not receive an influx of people at that time. The people of central Hellas probably settled in Cilicia, Cyprus, Ionia, and other Near East sites, as some myths say.

Despite universal mythic agreement, there is no archaeological evidence of a Herakleid (Dorian) invasion of the Peloponnesos. However, since the population of Argeia was in steep decline (and no foreign pottery is found there) and little or no pottery has been found in nearly deserted Lakonia and Messenia between 1150T/900R–900T/790R BCE, it was certainly not a Herakleid invasion that drove away the locals. It is more likely that what changed in the Peloponnesos at the beginning of the Iron Age was that a new ruling class, let's call them the Herakleids, gained control, and perhaps they had affiliations in central Hellas.

Also in error is the claim that Hellenes settled Aiolia, Tenedos, and Lesbos during that time; the first Hellenic settlements in those three locations (built by Aiolians from northern Hellas) were later, dating to the end of the tenth century T / early eighth century R BCE.

---

## Lots are Caste

Upon arriving in the Peloponnesos, the three Dorian leaders dropped fired clay tablets etched with their names into a water pitcher and drew them out to determine the order in which they would pick their land. Kresphontes and his older brother Temenos cheated by dropping in a sun-dried shard on behalf of the young sons of Aristodemos, their dead brother. Obviously, the shard of the sons of Aristodemos dissolved and they were doomed to pick last. Appropriately, the shard of the eldest, Temenos, was fished out first, and he picked Argeia with its great-walled cities. Kresphontes picked second and chose Messenia over Lakonia because it had better farmland and the deserted palace site of Pylos. The cheated sons of Aristodemos were stuck with Lakonia.

## Dorian Conquest of Tiryns, Lakonia, and Messenia

Tiryns fell quickly, perhaps without a fight. Temenos and his followers remained in Tiryns while the forces of Kresphontes and Theras (as regent for the twin sons of Aristodemos) were led by the guide Oxylos to largely deserted Lakonia. The Herakleids justified their claim to Lakonia by saying that Herakles had restored Tyndareos to the throne only in order to rule it in trust for his descendants. The little resistance they faced collapsed when Akhaian Philonomos betrayed Therapne (Sparta) in exchange for rule over nearby Amyklai. (The last king of Lakonia, Penthilos, had abandoned the area long beforehand [to Lesbos say the ancients, even though that was one Aigaian Island that did not receive Mycenaian settlers].) His son Damasios had led other colonists to Akhaia on the northern coast of the Peloponnesos.

The guide Oxylos led Kresphontes and his Dorian followers through winding passes over the steep Taygetos Mountains and attacked the small Danaan cities of Messenia once promised to Akhilleus by Agamemnon. Kresphontes was largely unchallenged by the remnant populace. His first conquest was Hire, which he renamed Abia in honor of the nurse of Glenos, son of Herakles. Albia had moved to the hamlet of Hire after the first Herakleid invasion of the Peloponnesos failed almost one hundred years earlier. After securing the Danaan cities, Kresphontes marched around the fringes of the marshy Makaria and up the Pamisos River. He built a modest settlement at Stenyklaros to rule from.

Kresphontes married the Arkadian princess Merope of Trapezos, daughter of King Cypseus. When disgruntled nobles led by Polyphontes assassinated Kresphontes, young prince Aipytos was spirited away to Arkadia to be raised by Cypseus. Once he became a man, Aipytos returned. He avenged his father by killing Polyphontes and reclaimed his rightful place as king of Messenia.

---

Exhibit 15.4
Palace of Pylos

The palace of Pylos was burned near the end of LHIIIB (ca. 1195T/945R BCE). Although a calamity for the unfortunate inhabitants, the fire that destroyed the palace fired the clay tablets used to keep track of the Pylian economy, thereby preserving them for archaeologists to discover. Most of the Linear B texts uncovered are inventories of commodities, and numerous deities are listed in them. Most of the Olympian gods are listed, and about half of the Mycenaian gods mentioned were still worshiped by the Classical Hellenes.

What happened to the Pylians? Apparently the citizens received advance warning and escaped; there were no corpses found among the ruins. They may have migrated to the large offshore island of Cephallenia, which received a great influx of people at that time. (Cephallenia may only have been a stopping point, since the population of Cephallenia dropped dramatically within fifty years.) The Hellenic historians say they went to Attike and later to Ionia, which is certainly possible as well.

Although the palace grounds were inhabited by a small contingent afterward, the Pylian state did not recover its splendor. Pylos was sacked again during LH111C, ca. 1150T/900R BCE. Sandy Pylos was nearly deserted after the second calamity, and no city was ever built over it, making it ideal for excavation.

Unlike most of the rest of Hellas, matching historical and mythic dates for Pylos works better assuming that Troy VI was sacked for Helene's sake instead of Troy VII (see Addendum 1, "Clevenger Chronology"). Pottery evidence indicates that Pylos was sacked between Troy VI and Troy VII. If Agamemnon sacked Troy VI, then Neleus would have been the one who made sandy Pylos into a great city (as the myths say) ca. 1310T/1060R BCE. In that case, Neleus and his three successors would have ruled 110 years, or 29 years each, until the city's devastating sack in 1195T/945R BCE. These are slightly long average reigns, but then the myths themselves say that Neleus and Nestor ruled into old age.

The identity of the leader who sacked Pylos is a mystery in myth and fact. If Agamemnon sacked Troy VI, there would not have been enough time to pass for the Herakleids to sack Pylos (eighty years according to the fifth-century BCE historian Thucydides). If Agamemnon sacked Troy VII, then it becomes tempting to blame Herakles for Pylos's destruction. After all, he did defeat the army of King Neleus of Pylos, and some authors say he sacked Messenian Pylos (1218T/968R BCE). More often, however, he is said to have fought stout-hearted Ares and dark-haired Hades at Triphylian Pylos (or allegorically at the Pylos [meaning "gate"] of Hades), and his army did not enter Messenia. An even better fit chronologically is Agamemnon's march into the western Peloponnesos (1198T/948R BCE). After all, Mycenai might have been the only state with resources necessary to sack Pylos. According to myth, Agamemnon sacked Pisa, not Pylos; but Pisa did not exist in the Bronze Age. Perhaps the historic Pisans stole this myth from Pylos. This explanation is not satisfactory given that Agamemnon and Nestor were close friends and allies at Troy.

The identity of the leader who instigated the second sack also remains a mystery (1150T/900R BCE). The final fall of sandy Pylos occurred some forty years too early to have been caused by the Herakleids, despite Pausanias's claim.

---

## Conquest of Eleia

Oxylos was awarded the land of Eleia for successfully guiding the Dorians; but it was up to him to conquer it. It must have taken Oxylos some time to gather a force of Aitolians/Akhaians to conquer Elis, because one of his recruits was Agrios, son of Damasios, the Lakonian who had led Akhaians to Akhaia. Damasios was the son of Penthilos and the cousin of Tisamenos, the Mycenaian king driven out by Temenos.

When Oxylos and his Aitolian followers arrived in Eleia, King Dios (son of Amphimakhos, son of Polyxeinos—the young prince who fought at Troy and returned home safely to succeed his father, Agasthenes [son of Augeias, whose stables Herakles cleaned], as king of Eleia) wished to avoid bloodshed.[297] Dios offered to let the newcomers stay if the Aitolians settled peacefully. As far as who would be king, he proposed an archery duel to decide the issue. Oxylos agreed. The Aitolian marksman Pyraikhmes defeated the Epeian sharpshooter Degmenos, and Oxylos became king.

Oxylos moved the location of the royal capital to Elis to take advantage of its better location.[298] He married pale-ankled Pieria and fathered Aitolos and Laios. Oxylos was the last man of the Bronze Age to host games at Olympia before the Dark Age interrupted the competitions. Aitolos died young, and his tomb stood near Olympia. Laios succeeded his father, but his descendants did not rule after him. With Oxylos and Laios came the end of Mycenaian civilization in Eleia.

---

[297] The Epeians (Epeios) and Aitolians (Aitolos) were kindred tribes, children of Endymion. Linguists agree, lumping Epeian and Aitolian with the northwest Hellenic dialects, which probably broke off from the related Doric dialect during the decline of the Mycenaian civilization.

[298] Scant archaeological evidence supports the founding of Elis during the early Dark Age, though this has yet to be proven conclusively.

## Dorian Conquest of Mycenai, Sicyon and Epidauros

Meanwhile, Temenos settled down to rule in Tiryns and prepare for his showdown with King Tisamenos of Mycenai. He largely abandoned the palace and its rigid, class-based government for a clan-based tribal government. He appointed Deiphontes, the Dorian king of nearby Kleonai, as his chief of staff. He gave Deiphontes his favorite child, Hyrnetho, in marriage (1103T/853R BCE).

It took Temenos two years before he could conquer Akhaian Mycenai. After consolidating power, he besieged and sacked both Mycenai and Argos (1102T/852R BCE).

Temenos raised four sons: Ceisos (Agelaos), Phalces (Eurypylos), Cerynes (Kallias), and Argaios (Isthmos or Arkhelaos). As they grew, Temenos ignored them more and more, favoring his noble son-in-law Deiphontes. In jealousy, the eldest three killed their father and seized the throne (1090T/840R BCE). Only young Argaios disagreed with the plot and refused to join his brothers.

The sons of Temenos feared noble Deiphontes's reaction. They knew that some of the army might support Deiphontes. They tried to curry favor from his wife, their sister, Hyrnetho, and avoid civil war. Cerynes and Phalces approached her, but she refused to speak with them and instead rebuked them sharply for killing their father. Unprepared for harsh rejection, they rashly seized her by force.

Upon hearing this, Deiphontes took after them in a rage. He caught up to the kidnappers, and as he killed Cerynes, Phalces panicked and accidentally slew pregnant Hyrnetho. He got away as Deiphontes stopped to attend to his stricken wife.

The Hellenes believed that burial rites must be strictly followed in order for the deceased to be admitted into the underworld. Otherwise they would wander aimlessly as ghosts on the far side of the implacable river Styx. Deiphontes performed these rites despite his desire to pursue her killers while they were still near. Phalces fled to Dorian Sicyon, which he conquered.

Deiphontes grieved for his wife and was not strong enough to fight Ceisos for the Tirynian throne. Instead he led the portion of the army loyal to him in the conquest of Epidauros.

Ceisos consolidated his rule and exiled his brother Argaios. Argaios had been against his brothers' plans to seize the throne, and he took his followers to Messenia, where he helped reinstate his cousin Aipytos, son of Kresphontes and the rightful king. Then famine struck and he moved on to Macedonia, where he became a tribal chief and reputed ancestor of the historical kings of Macedonia.

## Dorian Conquest of Triphylia and Thera Island

While Theras ruled over the Dorian tribesmen of Lakonia, descendants of the Argonauts and Lemnian women, called Minyans, settled along the Lakonian coast. (There is no more evidence of a Minyan immigration than there is of a Dorian one). Pelasgians from Attike fleeing Ionian invaders from Akhaia drove them off the island of Lemnos (1101T/851R BCE). Among them were grandsons of the Argonaut Euphemos, who insisted that they settle in his ancient home on the rocky coast of Lakonia.

The rival groups nearly came to blows until Theras came up with a compromise. He offered to lead the Minyans, and any Dorians who wished to go, away to find a new home. He said that because the twin sons of Aristodemos had come of age, it was time for him to step down. However, Theras had so loved being in charge that he wanted to leave to start a kingdom of his own elsewhere (1085T/835R BCE).[299] Those joining Theras recalled that Kalliste (Thera) Island had once been promised to Euphemos's descendants. There the two peoples prospered and mingled harmoniously, speaking the Doric dialect. However, most of the Minyans moved to Triphylia, an area of the Peloponnesos where the Minyans had dominated during more prosperous times.

[299] Thucydides says the Dorians conquered Melos Island near Theras seven hundred years before the Athenians conquered it, or 1116 BCE. However, his date is before the Herakleid return and so must be rejected.

## Dorian Conquest of Korinth, Megara, Syme Island, and Krete

During the generation after Temenos conquered Tiryns, the Herakleid chieftain Aletes led Dorian forces against Korinth (1078T/812R BCE). Aletes was the son of Hippotes[300]—the man exiled before the successful invasion for killing the seer Karnos. As a young soldier, he served with his father in the successful Herakleid invasion. When he reached the small settlement of Korinth, he found that it was still ruled by descendants of the Bronze Age kings Doridas and Hyanthidas.[301] By agreeing not to resist, they were permitted to stay as freemen. (In most Dorian cities, the Akhaian populace was enslaved.) Those that chose to fight were defeated in battle and fled. Aletes immediately marched on Megara and Athens. Megara was then a dependent of Athens.

King Kodros of Athens had long prepared for the inevitable Dorian invasion. Because Kodros was too old to fight, he dressed himself as a beggar and allowed himself to be killed by the enemy in a sacrifice to ensure his nation's victory.[302] In the hard-pressed contest the Dorians seized Megara, but their expansion was stopped on mainland Hellas for good (1044T/812R BCE).

The Dorians sailed out to conquer a few Aigaian Islands. One of Hippotes's generals led forces from there to conquer Syme Island. As mentioned above, Theras led Dorians and Minyans from Lakonia to Theras Island (1085T/835R BCE). Althaimenes, grandson of Temenos, led Dorians to Krete (1037T/810R BCE).

---

[300] Pausanias does not mention Aletes's father by name. Hippotes would be Aletes's father following Apollodoros's *Library*, ii.174, which states that Hippotes was the son of Phylas, son of Antikhos, and son of Herakles. Some writers say a daughter of Phylas bore Hippotes, in which case Aletes would be the son of Hippotes and, as Pausanias says, the great-great-grandson of Herakles.

[301] Doridas and Hyanthidas's father, Propodas, was a contemporary of Jason the Argonaut and Herakles. They lived far too early to have surrendered to Aletes as Pausanias's *Guide to Greece*, ii.4.3, says.

[302] The killing of an outcast of society—a beggar or one who is particularly ugly or lame—was called *pharmakos*. It was a rare purification ritual performed by a community to ensure its survival during war, plague, or any other catastrophic event.

## Neleids Seize Athens and Defeat the Dorians

King Kodros of Athens was a descendent of refugees from the initial Herakleid invasion. They had been welcomed to Athens by Thymoites, the last king of the ancient line of Erikhthonios. Thymoites was the great-grandson of Demophoon (the son of Theseus who fought at Troy). Thymoites commissioned some of the last Mycenaian construction projects anywhere. Wells were dug outside of the city walls as relative safety returned. Like his famous ancestor Theseus (who welcomed Herakleid refugees), Thymoites showed kindness to supplicants. He welcomed the refugees led by the House of Neleus who fled fallen Pylos. He also accepted Ionian refugees fleeing from the Akhaians. The growing number of refugees from the Peloponnesos gradually overwhelmed Thymoites's ability to control them. Eventually he lost his kingdom to an insurrection. One of the Pylian (Neleid) nobles, Melantheus, son of Andropompos, killed Thymoites and seized control in a nearly bloodless coup.

Melantheus was a direct descendent of shape-shifting Periklymenos, the eldest son of King Neleus, who had once been a worthy, though ultimately unsuccessful, opponent of Herakles. When Pylos was sacked, its last king, Sillos, a descendent of Neleus's youngest son, Nestor, was killed. Melantheus led the noble class into exile. Melantheus was succeeded by his son Kodros.

After the Dorian invaders withdrew, two sons of the slain king Kodros claimed the right to be king. It was rare for the second son to lay a claim against an older brother, but Neleus felt that Medon was unsuited to be king because he was lame in one foot. An envoy was dispatched to Delphi, and upon its return, the eupatridae (well born) assembled on the Areiopagos to decide the issue. They gave the kingdom to Medon but restricted his royal prerogatives.[303]

---

Exhibit 15.5
The Ionian Migration

Unlike the mythic conquest of the Peloponnesos by the Dorians, the Ionian migration to Asia Minor is supported by archaeological evidence. At

[303] Though the establishment of archonships and curbs to the monarchy actually date to the sixth century BCE, the Athenians believed they began during Medon's reign. The lame king, a weaker man, was the one who lost many royal privileges.

a high level, archaeology and myth concur on the following facts: Hellenes were living in Asia Minor long before the Trojan War, Athens fought off an invasion, Athens received a large influx of immigrants, and two migrations to Ionia occurred. The details do not work out neatly.

Hellenic writers grossly underestimated just how widespread the Akhaian settlement of Asia Minor was. They did note that Rhadamanthys and Sarpedon of Krete, Xanthos of Mycenai, Aithios of Troizen, Athamas of Orkhomenos, and Bellerophontes of Korinth all settled there. However, they did not know that Miletos was a Hellenic city, let alone that it was a major palace site.

Just as the myths say, there is archaeological evidence that an attack on Athens was repelled and that Attike received a large influx of immigrants beginning in LHIIIB. Pylos was sacked about the same time and could very well have been the source of the immigrants. The myths separate these two events. In myth, Theseus or Demophoon defeated the invading army of King Eurystheus of Tiryns in LHIIIB (1202T/952R BCE). The Pylians came much later, and when they did, the Neleid Melantheus seized power in a nearly bloodless coup, not by conquest.

Ionia received a massive influx of Mycenaians during the Late Bronze Age (the first half of LHIIIC [1195T/945R–1075T/850R BCE]). This migration is immortalized in the stories of the "returns," yet the details suggest the migrants were the ones described in the Ionian migration (moving en masse from the Peloponnesos and elsewhere to Attike and then en masse to Ionia). Eastern Attike was one of the few places in Hellas where the population grew during the early twelfth century T / late tenth century R BCE. The east Attike deme of Perati, for example, grew rapidly after 1200T/950R BCE but was deserted by 1100T/850R BCE. It was a more likely launching point for the Trojan War armada than Aulis. The residents of Perati had clear ties with cities farther east, such as Ialysos on Rhodes. As in myth, it is apparent that the residents moved on to places in the eastern Mediterranean within a few generations.

A significant smaller migration to Ionia occurred during the Protogeometric Age (1025T/830R–925T/790R BCE). As Hellas was largely depopulated at this time, there could not have been many migrants. The second migration in myth is the Ionian migration led by the Neleid family.

Since the Ionic dialect was spoken in Attike and Ionia, a connection between the two was obvious to the Hellenes. The belief that Athenian gentry led the migration probably dates to the late sixth century BCE, when the flattering Ionians of Asia were requesting Athenian support against the Persians. The connection continued to be stressed during the fifth century BCE, as Athens looked to justify its hold over the Delian League. However, if the Athenians were involved, their role would have been minimal, for their city was relatively small in the Late Bronze and Early Iron Ages.

Ancient writers correctly state that the Athenians were only one of many people who participated in the Ionian migration. Pylians, Phocians, and Boiotians all played prominent roles in the mythic record, and their citizens did, in fact, emigrate at that time. As discussed above, Pylos was indeed sacked, and much of its citizenry emigrated abroad (ca. 1195T/945R BCE). A strong central Hellas connection is also evident in the myth; the important Phocian port Krisa and the Boiotian citadel Gla were destroyed contemporaneously with Pylos. The important Ionian city of Phocaia was named for the central Hellenic region of Phocis, and one of the most important Miletos families claimed to be descendants of King Kadmos of Thebes. There is also a mountain and a creek near Miletos named Kadmos, and the citizens of Ionian Priene were called Kadmeians (an ancient and poetic name for Thebans).

---

## Ionian Migration[304]

Image 15.3
Map of the Twelve Ionian City-States

[304] The first reference to the Neleids is found in the early sixth-century BCE poetry of Mimnermos of Kolophon or Smyrna. Mimnermos mentions Neleus's arrival in Kolophon. The connection continued to be stressed during the fifth century BCE as Athens looked to justify its hold over the Delian League. Herodotos's uncle Panyassis of Halikarnassos wrote an elegiac poem on the migration of the Ionians under Neleus while Pherecydes, writing mythical history in Athens, covered the same topic (discussing the exploits of Androkles). The influential *Foundation of Khios*, written by the fifth-century BCE historian and poet Ion of Khios provided additional insight into the Ionian migration. Pausanias's, *Guide to Greece*, vii.1–5, is our main surviving source on the migration.

Neleus chose to migrate abroad and sailed away with many followers: Pylians, Athenians, Ionians, Minyans, Abantes, Phocians, Thebans, Akhaians, and others. His target was Miletos, the only Mycenaian palace state in Asia. Neleus marched on Miletos, and after seizing it, he put the men who did not flee to death and took the young women as wives. Those that were spared were made into a helot class (a story refuted by material evidence, which suggests that Miletos, like Athens, was one of the few places not sacked during this tumultuous age; the palace of Miletos was simply abandoned). Then he assisted his brothers in establishing kingdoms throughout Ionia. Two large offshore islands came under Ionian rule as well: Samos and Khios.

| King | City | Comments |
|---|---|---|
| Sons of Kodros | | |
| Neleus | Miletos | The great palace city was conquered first. |
| Androkles | Ephesos | Androkles drove off all natives that did not submit. (In reality, Hellenes occupied Ephesos centuries earlier.) He also conquered Samos but lost it to other Ionians ten years later. |
| Damasikhton and | | |
| Prometheus | Kolophon | Damasikhton and Prometheus conquered this existing Akhaian city. |
| Andraimon | Lebedos | Andraimon founded the city. |
| Cyaretos | Myous | Cyaretos founded the city after driving Karians from the area. |
| Naoklos | Teos | Minyans of Teos and natives living nearby peacefully submitted. |
| Kleopos | Erythrai | Akhaians of Erythrai and natives living nearby peacefully submitted. |
| Sons of Phocian Euktaimon | | |
| Philogenes and Damon | Phocaia | Two Athenians built ships for landlocked Phocian settlers. By treaty they received land from Cyme and named it after Phocis. Their descendants eventually accepted a Neleid as king so they could join the Ionian League. |

| | | |
|---|---|---|
| Son of Neleus | | |
| Aipytos | Priene | During the next generation, he conquered the last Karian city in Ionia with Philotas, son of Theban Damasikhton and descendant of the Boiotia warrior Peneleos, who fought at Troy. |
| Neleid of unknown parentage | | |
| Parphoros | Klazomenai | Parphoros was from Kolophon. He founded the last of the ten Ionian states of Ionia. (A Mycenaian settlement flourished at the site.) |

The long history of Mycenaian overseas migration came to an end with the Ionians. Also at an end was the glorious Age of Heroes. The hard Age of Iron followed.

# Iron Age

## Submycenaian to Geometric Ages

Would that I where not then among the fifth men, but either dead earlier or born later! For now it is a race of iron; and they will never cease from toil and misery by day or night, in constant distress, and the gods will give them harsh troubles.

—Hesiod of Askre, *Works and Days*, seventh century BCE

In Kleobis and Biton the deity clearly showed that it is better for a man to die than to live. It happened on the day they pleased great Hera by yoking themselves to a chariot (the oxen could not be found in time) so that their mother, the priestess, arrived at the Heraion as required. Before the cheering crowd their mother entered the temple and stood before the image and prayed without stretched arms that her sons receive the greatest blessing men can receive. After the sacrifice and feast, the exhausted youths fell asleep in the temple itself and awoke no more.

—Paraphrased from Herodotos, *Histories* i.31, fifth century BCE

## Dark Age

Hesiod and Herodotos give depressing accounts of life during a difficult Early Iron Age. Gone were the hallmarks of the idolized Mycenaian civilization; the great-halled palaces were empty, glorious heroes no longer dueled in gleaming bronze chariots, luxurious Mycenaian jewelry and ivory goods were no longer produced, and exotic goods were no longer imported. Without centralized palace governments, the rigid class hierarchies of rulers, bureaucrats, craftsmen, warriors, and scribes vanished. Without the palaces, there was no need for records, and literacy died out. Men no longer interacted directly with the gods. The Heroic Age was finished.

The Mycenaian Age ended with a chaotic fall of cities throughout Hellas. The men that dwelled in Hellas afterward were identified by Hesiod with the fifth race of men—the men of iron. Indeed iron played a fundamental role in differentiating between his time and the glorious age beforehand. Because of, iron Hellenic civilization was far more egalitarian than the bronze Mycenaian civilization before it. Because iron was locally available and cheap, there was no need for kings to build great bureaucracies in order to procure scarce copper and tin, the elements of bronze, from abroad. Because bronze had been so expensive, only a few wealthy nobles had previously been able to afford the weapons and armor necessary to succeed in battle. Then, the valor of a single strong-armed warrior could change the outcome of a chaotic battle. Now cheaper iron weapons and armor meant that disciplined rows of well-armed farmers tussled in anonymity while aristocratic cavalries played secondary roles.

The period of transformation from Mycenaian (Bronze or Heroic) to Hellenic (Iron) Civilization is aptly named the Dark Age. It was a time devoid of legendary stories, and Hellas became virtually uninhabited; there is no evidence of a single house, tomb, temple, or fortification built in Hellas, Ionia, or Cyprus after the LHIIIC Mycenaian temples of Cyprus and before the Middle Geometric Age construction of walls around the town of Smyrna in Ionia—except for a single tomb built for a remarkable lord at Lefkandi (near Eretria on Euboea). His tomb was not constructed using Mycenaian techniques, but rather was made of mud brick on a stone foundation with wooden columns during the middle of the Protogeometric Age.

Despite the absence of construction, we know some cities remained occupied, primarily because of the pottery they left behind. The Dark Age encompassed three successive pottery styles: submycenaian, protogeometric, and early geometric. Each successive style was superior to its predecessor.

---

Exhibit 16.1
Pottery Dating

Because pottery is abundant and somewhat indestructible, it is used to date time periods. Accurately dating Hellenic pottery is complicated by the fact that pottery styles developed at different rates in different regions. The table below is based upon Athenian pottery dating for submycenaian and protogeometric pottery (since Athens was one of the few cities to survive the Mycenaian Age without being sacked and protogeometric pottery was first developed in Attike) and Korinthian pottery for dating geometric and early mythic painted pottery (both developed in Korinth). Popular Athenian black- and red-figure pottery gave Athens a virtual monopoly on vase production, and distinct regional styles died out after their universal acceptance.

Traditional dates were derived by matching Thucydides's date for the founding of Syrakuse by Korinthians (734/3T BCE) with the earliest pottery found at the site (Korinthian Late Geometric). Fortunately, early pottery from Syrakuse can be dated fairly accurately because contemporary Egyptian goods were found with it. The revisionist timeline pushes these dates back by twenty-five years or so. The calculation of ancient dates is detailed in Addendum 1.

| | Inception (BCE) | | |
|---|---|---|---|
| Period | Traditional | Revised | Comment |
| LHIIIB | 1290 | 1040 | Mycenaian civilization peak |
| LHIIIC | 1195 | 945 | Hellas population drops 50% |
| Submycenaian | 1075 | 850 | Population drops another 67% |
| Protogeometric | 1025 | 830 | |
| Early Geometric | 925 | 790 | In Athens 775 |
| Middle Geometric | 875 | 775 | In Athens 740 |
| Late Geometric | 775 | 725 | In Athens 705 |
| Protokorinthian—Early | 725 | 685 | Proto-Attic—Early 675 |
| Protokorinthian—Middle | 690 | 665 | Proto-Attic—Middle 650 |
| Protokorinthian—Late | 650 | 625 | Proto-Attic—Late 625 |
| Black Figure | 625 | 600 | Korinthian—Early 600 |
| Red Figure | 525 | 500 | Korinthian—Middle 545 |

Other evidence of habitation allowed archaeologists to figure out how the iron industry developed. They believe that the Hittites were the first to experiment with iron tools and weapons during the Late Bronze Age. The superior strength of iron had always been recognized; however, the Hittite Empire collapsed before they figured out how to smelt iron economically. It was left to smiths in Hellas and Cyprus to swap technological improvements until furnaces capable of burning at the higher temperatures needed to cast iron appeared in both places (1050T/840R BCE). Iron's adoption was aided by the massive disruption of trade, which made it nearly impossible to procure tin and copper.

At the darkest moment of the Dark Age, there were only a few settlements in all of Hellas that housed at least a few hundred people. The earlier people had either migrated away or died. It is doubtful that there was any formal government in the small surviving settlements despite the claim of many cities that their local kings ruled throughout the period.

Dwelling in humble settlements where the mighty Mycenaians once ruled, the people could not help but wonder at the impressive monumental architectural standing as a testament to the power of their heroic ancestors. A new religion, with strong emphasis upon ancestor worship, arose beside ancient tholos tombs.[305]

## Mythic Evidence on the Dark Age

The myths clearly mark the beginning of the Dark Age. War and migration brought about the change. (There is ample archaeological evidence of the wars but no evidence for migrations within Hellas.) Every major Hellenic region fell under a new tribe, a new regime, at the end of the Bronze Age: Thessalia to Thessalians, Boiotia to Boiotians, Elis to Aitolians, Akhaia to Akhaians, Attike to Ionians, and most of the Peloponnesos to the Dorians. However, both the new rulers and the conquered were Hellenic-speaking descendants of the glorious Mycenaians.

Whether the Dark Age spanned a few generations or a few centuries is under debate. Homer and Hesiod did not write epics about this period,

[305] There is no evidence of ancestor worship at tholos tombs by the Mycenaians.

and the few relevant mythic references were preserved by ancient historians studying city-state archives from important cities, such as Argos, Korinth, and Sparta.[306] There are no stories for most Dark Age kings; all that is recalled are their names. All were warriors.

**Argos:** Ephoros of Cyme, quoting Argive archives as his source, recorded the names of twelve kings who ruled from the House of Temenos. Each king succeeded his father, without exception. This unlikely boast was proclaimed to legitimize the rule of later monarchs, but no historic dynasty has ever had that kind of stability (the same farfetched claim was made in Sparta, Korinth, and Athens). Besides, for most of the Dark Age, there were too few people for there to be any government to speak of. The works of Ephoros and the Argives are lost, but Pausanias and Diodoros preserved the names of ten kings: Temenos, Ceisos, Medon, Thestios, Merops, Aristodamidas, Eratos, Pheidon, Lakedes, and Meltas. Medon moved the capital inland from Tiryns to Argos for safety and reputedly accepted curbs to his powers (1020T/800R BCE—about the time the tomb at Lefkandi was built [revisionist dating 950T/800R BCE]). Pausanias adds that Eratos sacked Asine (807T/635R BCE) and Damokratidas, the first elected king, conquered Nauplia (745T/553R BCE).[307]

**Sparta:** In Sparta, the descendants of the first Herakleid kings, Eurystheus and Prokles, ruled, impressively, from the late Bronze Age into the Hellenistic Age (1104T/854R–215 BCE). The older, more important line was founded by Agis I, whom the historians said was the son of Eurystheus and Anaxandra. That Agis and Eurypontos were considered the founders of the dual Spartan dynasty instead of their "fathers" Eurystheus and Prokles suggests that some kind of break occurred. Archaeologists have determined that the Spartan plain was devoid of settlements from the Late Helladic (LHIIIB)—well before when Theras reputedly conquered Lakonia on behalf of his nephews Eurystheus and Prokles—to the Early Protogeometric Age. Then signs of settlement reappeared, and soon Agis peacefully unified four neighboring protogeometric villages to become the first king of the newly formed city of Sparta (1037 or 850T/740R BCE).

---

[306] Liberated Hellenistic Messenia created an early kings list to match Sparta's. They were the descendants of Kresphontes, the younger brother of Temenos.

[307] Both the archaeological record and other historical inferences suggest a postmonarchy date for the fall of Nauplia. Pottery finds suggest a traditional date somewhere between 600 and 575 BCE for the conquest of Nauplia, or a generation later by revisionist dating.

Herodotos provides our earliest list of Spartan kings, a complete list of the Agaids kings, which Pausanias follows exactly. He says the father was always succeeded by his son. The semilegendary kings were Agis I, Ekhestratos, Leobotas, Doryssos, Agesilaos I, Arkhelaos, Teleklos, Alkimenes, Polydoros, Eurykrates, Anaxandros, Eurykratidas, Leon, and Anaxandridas II. Alkimenes completed the Spartan conquest of Lakonia by sacking Helos (788T/593R BCE), and his son Polydoros completed the conquest of Messenia (773T/580R–754T/575R BCE). Anaxandros crushed the Messenian revolt in the Second Messenian War (674T/552R–657T/545R BCE), and the Spartan League was formed with the conditional surrender of Tegea during the reign of Anaxandridas II (556T/530R BCE). Kleomenes, son of Anaxandridas II, is the first Agaid king for whom we have a fairly accurate historical account. There were some disagreements among historians regarding the kings list of the lesser Eurypontids House of the dual kingship.

**Korinth:** Aletes and his descendants ruled Korinth for nine generations. The first four kings were Aletes, Ixion, Agelaos, and Praxmnis. The son of Praxmnis was Bakkhais (937T/729R–904T/704R BCE). He was such a great king, developing trade and building the first temples since the Mycenaian Age, that the name of the ruling house was changed to Bakkhais in his honor. Seven Bakkhai kings ruled over five generations: Bakkhais, Agelaos, Eudemos, Aristodemos, Agemon (regent for Telestes), Alexandros (who assassinated Agemon), and Telestes. The Bakkhai claimed to be descendants of the wine god Dionysos; wine festivals throughout Hellas were called Bakkhaides.

**Athens:** The Neleid family of Pylos, which fled the Dorians to Attike and usurped the throne, ruled for fifteen generations. Eusebios provides the list of kings (the son always succeeding his father): Melantheus, Kodros (who stopped the Dorian advance), Medon, Akastos, Arkhippos, Thersippos, Phorbas, Megakles, Diognetos, Pherekles, Ariphron, Thespieios, Agamestor, Aiskhylos, and Alkmaion (who was overthrown after a two-year reign).

**Thessalia:** Emigration had stopped at the end of the Mycenaian Age because Hellas was too sparsely populated to support it. The long tradition of emigrating from poor Hellas to find a better life elsewhere renewed toward the beginning of the Early Geometric Age. Thessalians (speaking the Aiolian dialect) were the first to resume migrations, settling on Lesbos Island (900T/785R BCE) and later on the Anatolian coast near ancient Troy. Thessalia had survived the Dark Age in better shape than the rest of Hellas. Mycenaian palace culture had never reached the Thessalian plain, and so its demise did not cause a significant decline among the self-sufficient farming communities of the plain. The first Aiolian settler, eponymous Lesbos, was said to be the great-grandson of the otherwise unknown Lapith hero Hippotes of Thessalia. Hesiod tells us that poverty drove the migration and that some returned disillusioned.

> Once, long ago, my father crossed far overseas
> In his black ship, and came here, to this place,
> And left Aiolian Cyme far behind;
> He did not flee from riches or success
> But evil poverty, which comes from Zeus.[308]

## Recovery Begins—End of the Dark Age

A brilliant new Hellenic civilization emerged from the germinating Dark Age during the Middle Geometric Age. Historians have labeled it the Arkhaic Age (750T/705R–525T/500R BCE). Existing settlements grew rapidly, and long-abandoned sites were reoccupied. Trade fueled growth and brought in new ideas. The Euboians established the first Panhellenic trade post at Al Mina, strategically located at the mouth of the Orontes River in northern Syria, next to Phoenicia and on the road to Assyria. During the Late Geometric Age, or somewhat earlier, these traders adapted the local proto-Canaanite alphabet[309] to Hellenic and changed some symbols to systematically represent vowels for the first time. The Ionians of Miletos took credit for this invention, although it could have been the Euboians. Unlike Mycenaian writing, which was used to keep palace records, the new alphabet was first used to preserve impressive epic poetic works.

---

[308] Hesiod, *Works and Days*.

[309] The Phoenicians, another Canaanite people, also adapted this script to their own language.

---

Exhibit 16.2
Horseback Riding

The first horses and chariots were introduced into Hellas early in the Middle Helladic (MHI) period of the Bronze Age—the time when Zeus's warlike firstborn son, Ares, played a prominent role. The first horses were no larger than modern ponies, making horseback riding impossible. Once larger horses were bred, horseback-riding aristocrats gained the ability to quickly cross the boundaryless Thessalian plain, and the mosaic of distinct cultures disappeared into the dominant Thessalian/Aiolian tribe. Horseback riding probably gave rise to stories of half-man, half-horse Centaurs, whose earliest artistic representation is found in the Early Geometric Age tomb at Lefkandi. The first recorded horseback-riding nomadic tribe galloped into Anatolia from Scythia and plundered the cities there. These terrifying Kimmerian tribesmen forced the most powerful Anatolian king to commit suicide while plundering his capital at Gordion in 696T/687R BCE. Called Mita in Assyrian records, the Hellenes knew him as Midas. His wealth was legendary, and he was the first barbarian to send a dedication to Delphi—his throne. The Kimmerians lived by plundering the cities of Anatolia for most of the seventh century BCE. They conducted swift raids and rode off before help could arrive. They were finally defeated through the coordinated efforts of the Lydian and Assyrian Empires.

---

The earliest recorded poems were written in the Homeric style of Ionia and the Hesiodic style of Boiotia. These poems record a religion deeply influenced by Near Eastern cosmology and praising the deeds of earthly kings and heroes identified with Mycenaian ruins. These myths were developed by oral poets during the Dark Age, which sat between the Heroic Age and their own. Their poems codified their religion into a form that would be followed for a millennium. Later credited to individual men (Homer and Hesiod), these poems were in fact developed over generations. Poetic schools of each tradition flourished until the poems were written down in final form during the late sixth century BCE.

## City-State Competition

The rapidly growing population quickly outstripped available farmland, especially since a few aristocratic families jealously controlled much of the land. Consequently, the larger settlements began swallowing up their smaller neighbors. Argos, Athens, Elis, Sparta, and Thebes all grew in this manner; only Athens claimed to have done so peacefully.

The explosive growth in territory and population of the leading Hellenic cities drove changes in governance. Three different approaches to government arose. In Argos, King Pheidon consolidated power centrally; the king held strong executive powers (797T/600R BCE). The Korinthians made their kings more accountable by electing a new one each year. After the Bakkhai king Telestes was assassinated by a member of his own clan, he was replaced with an annually elected kingship. The two hundred most powerful families of Korinth voted for the king, who was required to be a member of the Bakkhai clan.[310] The first elected king was Telestes's son Automenes (775T/600R BCE). The reforms of Lykourgos in Sparta balanced power between the unique dual kings and the people by establishing a senate of twenty-eight elders, elected by the assembly (citizens) and the two kings (884T/612R BCE).

## Lelantine War

> Men go to war and in their place urns and ashes return to their home.
>
> —Aiskhylos of Eleusis, fifth century BCE

**Euboea:** Khalkis and Eretria[311] instigated the first recorded Panhellenic war by squabbling over the fertile Lelantine plain located between them (late eighth century T BCE or 597–587R BCE). Because the two states held important trading connections, the battle escalated into a Panhellenic war pitting Khalkis, Samos, Aigina, and Korinth against Eretria, Megara,

[310] A similar sharing of power is documented in Athens, although it probably occurred first in Korinth. In Athens, the office of archon was established to share power with the king during the late seventh or early sixth century BCE, although the Parian Marble dates it to 683/2 BCE.
[311] Lefkandi was abandoned about the time nearby Eretria was reoccupied and the trade post of Al Mina was established.

Miletos, and Khios. Thucydides says it was the greatest war fought between the Trojan and Persian wars. This long trade war, named for the contested Euboian plain, was disruptive but ultimately inconclusive, although it ended slightly in favor of Khalkis and her allies. The war had a profound effect on the Hellenes and was mentioned by early poets.

The late first- / early second-century CE historian Plutarch of Khaironeia says the early hero of the war was wise King Amphidamas of Khalkis, who wreaked much havoc before dying in battle. He identifies this Amphidamas with the man mentioned by Hesiod.

> Then I crossed over to Khalkis, to the games of wise Amphidamas, where the sons of the great-hearted hero arranged for many contests and appointed prizes and there I boast that I gained the victory with a song and carried off a handled tripod which I dedicated to the Muses of Helikon.[312]

Although *Works and Days* presents mythic themes, it is also the first poem dealing with everyday life. The first of the lyric poets, Arkhilokhos, is also said to have written about this war.

> Not even the bows will be repeatedly stretched, not even the teeming slings hurled when Ares gathers the toil of battle on the noisy plain, but there the mournful labor of the sword will start the job of causing many sighs, for in this warfare in which the spear-famed islanders from Euboea are godlike and easily masterful.[313]

The first-century BCE historian Strabo of Amasia in Pontos recorded an inscription that told of an agreement among the short-haired warriors in the Lelantine War (from Khalkis and Eretria), who agreed not to use missile weapons (slings, stones, and throwing spears, which were considered an inferior and less courageous way to fight compared to the phalanx).

[312] Hesiod, *Works and Days.*

[313] Arkhilokhos, in *Greek Lyric.* Translated by David A. Campbell.

## Fall of Kings

Soon after the Lelantine War ended, the first important historic figures of Hellas emerged. They include the statesman Cypselos of Korinth, the philosopher Thales of Miletos, and the lyric poet Arkhilokhos of Paros Island. Most of the monarchies were overthrown by tyrants like Cypselos, who promised building programs to employ the citizens. Thales challenged mythic/religious explanations, using rational explanations to explain the universe. Arkhilokhos turned away from heroic mythic themes to express human emotions and experiences.

These exceptional men initiated great social changes that shattered the old order dominated by kings, prophets, and poets. Kings had represented the earthly dimension of cosmic power (where Zeus was king over the palace city of Olympos). Kings consulted with the gods to determine right actions, and they established ordeals to determine judgments.[314] Prophets shared the kings' ability to interpret the will of the gods. Poets too could see and describe the divine and effected behavior by praising great deeds. These deeds became immortal only if they continued to be praised in verse. Otherwise, all else, like mankind itself, is lost to lethe (forgetfulness or oblivion).

The end of monarchies meant that the social order of man no longer mirrored the gods. Without royal intercessors, men could boldly attempt a direct communion with god—as found in the Bakkhaides and Orphic cults. Educated men began accepting philosophic explanations over prophetic and mythological ones. Oracles continued to be visited, but as the cynic Diogenes said, "Oracles are obscure; they have deceived many." Epic poets continued praising deeds into the Classical Age, which followed the Arkhaic Age, but the rank of poets sank until they were little more than parasites paid to gratify the elite with praise. As the sixth-century Athenian statesman Solon said, "Much the poets lie."

[314] Called incubatory divination, it was the most ancient form of divination.

# Conclusion

The Greek Mythic History provides a comprehensive retelling of the various Hellenic myths in a logical historic sequence. The fact that myth told as a historic narrative flows well should not be surprising, given that mythographers since Pherecydes in the fifth century BCE have rationalized poetic myths into a historic framework.

Hellenic myth is not just good narrative; the myths provide a surprisingly accurate historic account of Hellas during the Late Bronze Age. Before the intrepid entrepreneur Heinrich Schliemann rediscovered Troy, virtually no one believed the myths held any historical value. After 150 years of scientific inquiry, our appreciation of the historic value of myths continues to grow. While some mythic versions clearly do not fit, there are usually one or more versions available that fit the overall historic framework well. Usually, the older the source, the better it correlates with modern findings.

Ancient poets drew mostly from oral traditions in describing religious beliefs, tall tales, and events of their immediate past. Mythic timelines were based upon genealogies; there were no fixed dates. The genealogies provide a historic sequencing of events and relative dates consistent with those calculated by modern historians. The stories were collected around a few broad groups of myths, called cycles. Most influential were the cycles of Herakles, Thebes, and the Trojan War. In addition, the myths of Mycenai were preserved in the archives of Argos. The poets also drew material from the buildings, frescoes, and artifacts available to them even though they did not always understand what they were studying.

Hesiod provided a quick summary of Hellenic cosmology and early technological ages of mankind: men living before the invention of agriculture, Stone Age farmers, and the first men to use metal tools in his Gold, Silver, and Bronze Ages. Each age had a generation of gods in preeminence. Hesiod's Heroic Age came next. A plethora of myths have been preserved by early poets and later mythographers. These myths provide a remarkably accurate representation of Hellas during the Late Bronze (Heroic) Age. A historical outline of myth, as well as our current understanding of Hellenic prehistory, can be summarized as follows:

- An earlier Bronze Age civilization was destroyed by warfare.
- A new, Hellenic-speaking people arose during a difficult period that followed.
- The Hellenes developed an advanced civilization; Mycenai was preeminent.
- The Hellenes conquered Krete and settled in Anatolia.
- Troy was sacked.
- Most of the cities of Hellas were sacked.
- Troy was sacked again.
- The Hellenes emigrated en masse to the eastern Mediterranean.
- Mycenai fell, ending the Bronze (Heroic) Age.
- A greatly impoverished Iron Age followed.

## Historic and Mythic Overlap

In addition to the consistent sequence of events listed above, there are many specific events that are common to both myth and prehistory. A summary of this strong correlation, documented throughout this book, is provided below.

Archaeologists found that a fairly advanced civilization developed in Hellas—a civilization that utilized recently developed bronze tools (Hesiod's Bronze Age). Archaeologists since Marija Gimbutas have identified the destruction of that Bronze Age civilization with the arrival of Indo-European speaking tribes from the north. These Indo-European tribes intermarried with the early inhabitants. The result was a new people, the Hellenes. The linguist J. P. Mallory believed that the Indo-European Hellenic language developed during this time period. Hesiod agreed. He said that after Bronze Age men were decimated through incessant fighting, a new people, the descendants of Deucalion and his son Hellen, arose. Hesiod called the new era the Heroic Age. Modern writers refer to it as the Mycenaian or Late Bronze Age.

After a time, cities developed again; the largest was Mycenai (1580T/1330R BCE). The earliest evidence of the city is its shaft graves. Akusilaos provided details from archives of the city-state of Argos that say Phoroneus founded Mycenai.[315] Akusilaos provided a complete list of Phoroneus's successors down to the sack of Mycenai by the Herakleids. Their rule spanned roughly five centuries. Archaeologists digging at Mycenai, using a time line developed by the eminent Egyptologist William Petrie, came to the same conclusion: Bronze Age Mycenai flourished for five centuries.

For several centuries, Mycenaian Hellas experienced dramatic growth. Archaeology revealed that Mycenaian cities had a homogenous culture, from Iolkos in the northeast to Pylos in the southwest. In myth the unified nature of Mycenaian culture was made clear through the story of twin sons of Poseidon, Pelias, and Neleus. These twins ruled the most distant palaces (Iolkos and Pylos). That Pylos is mentioned in myth is noteworthy given that the site was not occupied during historic times. Homer lists cities providing troops to Troy that had long been abandoned. Unique to the era were men in bronze armor fighting from horse-drawn chariots.

The expanding Mycenaians conquered the Minoan Civilization on Krete (1450T/1200R BCE). The great Kretan archaeologist Arthur Evans (who coined the term "Minoan civilization") and others have found ample proof of this conquest. Later Hellenes completely forgot the early Minoan civilization. What remained in myth was an understanding of the early importance of Krete, a vague understanding of its connection with literacy, and a similarly vague understanding of a Mycenaian conquest.

---

[315] The archives of Argos claimed Phoroneus founded Argos, but they clearly stole the myth from nearby Mycenai. During Arkhaic and Classical times, Mycenai was a relatively unimportant city-state often under Argive dominion.

The historic Hellenes understood that Europa's arrival on Krete resulted in a new dynasty ruling Knossos, the largest city of Krete. What was forgotten was that the rape of Europa was a clear allegory for the Mycenaian conquest of Krete.[316] Europa was the descendant of many Mycenaian kings and a direct descendant of the first king. The nine generations between Phoroneus and Europa fit well with archaeological evidence placing the end of the palace era at Knossos as just over two hundred years after Mycenai was founded. During the early Mycenaian Age, the Minoans were the leading sea power, and they were the source of a writing script adopted by the Bronze Age Hellenes. To Arkhaic and Classical Hellenes, Phoenicia was the preeminent sea power and the source of the Hellenic alphabet.

Although later Hellenes forgot that the Mycenaians were literate, the myths of Kadmos and Bellerophontes indicate that knowledge was not totally lost. Kadmos introduced writing into Hellas while searching for his lost sister Europa. Archaeologists have named the writing script he would have introduced Linear B. It was adapted from a Minoan script by the Mycenaian conquerors of Krete for use in managing the palaces. From Krete it was introduced into the palaces of Hellas. Some of the earliest Linear B texts in Hellas were found at Thebes, where Kadmos settled. Linear B texts include names, such as Akhilleus, Hektor, Ajax, and Orestes, as well as the names of most of the important gods. Poseidon, for example, is the most mentioned deity in texts found at Knossos, and in myth he is the patron of that city. Later Hellenes, following Herodotos, mistakenly assumed that Kadmos introduced the Phoenician alphabet. In fact, the alphabet was introduced into Hellas much later, during the Iron Age, and used by Hellenes thereafter. The other significant reference to ancient writing is found in an obscure line from Homer (*Iliad* vi.174–177). Homer says that King Proitos of Tiryns sent a folding tablet with Bellerophontes to a Luwian (Lycian) king under the pretense of providing a "letter of recommendation." Tablets fitting Homer's description have been

---

[316] Based upon the genealogy of Europa, her rape dates to when the palace at Knossos was abandoned, not when the Mycenaians conquered Krete. The Mycenaians would have conquered Krete during the generation of the Mycenaian prince Epaphos, the great-great-grandfather of Europa. Herein it is assumed that Epaphos, the son of the supreme Hellenic god (Zeus) and the Mycenaian princess Io (great-great-granddaughter of Phoroneus), was a leader in that conquest of Krete. That conquest allowed for expanding Mycenaian trade with Egypt, a place Epaphos is identified with. Egyptian records speak of an envoy being sent to Hellas soon after Krete fell.

found. They were in use during the Late Bronze Age, especially among the Hittites and Luwians.

After Krete fell, the Hellenes rapidly expanded across the islands of the Aigaian and onto the Anatolian coast. Archaeologists have uncovered numerous Mycenaian colonies and even one palace state (Miletos). In myth it is Miletos, the son of Zeus and Europa, and the brother of Minos, who founded Miletos. In myth Rhadamanthys, Sarpedon, Xanthos, Aithios, Athamas, and others also founded colonies in Anatolia. Many of the mythic settlements were established not long after the documented Hellenic conquest of Krete. However, as with the conquest of Krete, the Hellenic writers gradually became less aware of their own deeds.

Mycenaian expansion caught the attention of great civilizations to the east. Surviving Egyptian royal documents indicate that two trade missions were sent to Hellas. The first mission was sent by Pharaoh Thutmose III soon after Krete fell to Mycenaian lords (during the time of Epaphos). Hittite records are replete with references to the Ahhiyawa (Akhaians). Homer calls the Mycenaians by two interchangeable tribal names: Akhaians and Danaans (after Danaos, the uncle of Europa).

Several centuries of frequent interaction between Hittites and Mycenaians was lost to later Hellenes. Well, almost. Homer (*Odyssey* ix.519) says that Eurypylos of Teuthrania led Ketoi warriors in support of the Trojans. The term "Ketoi" is very close to the Egyptian word for the Hittites: "Kheta." It is certainly possible that a Hittite prince from their vassal state (called the Seha River Lands [Teuthrania]) led soldiers to help defend besieged Troy. It is also reasonable to identify Memnon with the Hittites. He led a large army in support of Troy from Aithiopia, a vaguely defined large kingdom that lay to the east (he was the son of Eos, the dawn). The only large kingdom to the east during the time of the Trojan War was the Hittite Empire. The Hittites counted Wilusa (Troy) as a trusted vassal and ally.

Hittite great-king Tudhaliya I led the first recorded Hittite royal expedition into western Anatolia (1390T/1140R BCE). He was the first to mention the men of Ahhiyawa, who have been persuasively identified with the Akhaians.

Somewhat later (calculating by generations) the first Mycenaian hero, Perseus, married the Aithiopian princess Andromeda. The vague term

"Aithiopian" probably referred to the Hittites, but the connection was lost over time. Andromeda was often identified with Cilicia, a coastal region along the underbelly of Anatolia then controlled by the Hittites. As mentioned above, Aithiopian Memnon was most likely leading a Hittite army. Besides, the marriage between Perseus and Andromeda sounds suspiciously like an arranged Hittite political marriage. The Hittites often arranged political marriages to strengthen ties with neighboring states. When Perseus returned to Hellas, he left behind his firstborn son, Perses (eponym of the historic great power to the east, Persia). It was Hittite custom to lavishly care for a son of the neighboring king, one who could generously be called an ambassador. It helped to cement good relations, and the "ambassador" could become a hostage if relationships soured.

The mythic exploits of Bellerophontes in Lukka (Lycia) may be referenced in the annals of the Hittite great-king Mursili II. Mursili apologized to an unnamed great-king from Ahhiyawa for seizing the Mycenaian palace city of Miletos (1318T/1068R BCE). Mursili justified his attack as retaliation for Akhaian attacks on Lukka (Lycia). The timing fits to when Perseus would have been great-king and Bellerophontes was winning many battles in Lycia. Mursili II would have had an open line of communication with Perseus, whose wife was a Hittite princess. According to the Hittites, the Mycenaian general Eteokles fled home across the sea when the Hittites seized Miletos. Eteokles was a common name among the Mycenaians, but who specifically this was is unknown.

There may be one prominent leader specifically identified in both Hittite texts and Hellenic mythology. Hittite royal archives mention a rebellion by their Arzawan vassals of western Anatolia. When the Hittites defeated the rebels, the rebellious Arzawan king Uhhaziti of Arzawa Minor fled to Hellas (1316T/1066R BCE). Arzawa Minor has been identified with Lydia. In Hellenic myth, King Pelops of Lydia was driven from Asia to Hellas and, with Perseus's blessing, became the king of Pisa. The dating of an important Anatolian prince migrating to Hellas is the same time whether using Hellenic mythological genealogically based chronology (Pelops) or Hittite history (Uhhaziti). Granted, Uhhaziti had grown children and Pelops was considered a young man, but the match is compelling.

Archaeological evidence indicates that Mycenaian civilization continued to expand until it peaked two generations before the Trojan War. The population of Hellas was its largest at that time (and Gaia would complain to Zeus about it). New tholos tombs were built, grand palaces remodeled, old shaft and tholos tombs refurbished, and enormous cyclopean walls erected. The myths concur. According to myth, the all-time richest Mycenaian king was Atreus, the grandfather of the leader of the Trojan War expedition, Agamemnon. Atreus was the first to be called wanax, or king of kings, by the Hellenes. Zeus personally intervened during this magical time to ensure that Atreus became king. Zeus commanded that the sun travel the sky backward after Atreus declared it would happen. Atreus became king during the eternal year—an eight-year period when many of the greatest feats of mythology occurred, including the labors of Herakles and Theseus, the battle between the Lapiths and Centaurs, the voyage of the Argonauts, and the Kalydonian boar hunt.

There are many theories for the rapid decline of the Mycenaian civilization. In myth Gaia complained to Zeus about the burden of overpopulation. Zeus responded by starting wars to reduce the population. Many modern theories have been expressed, but none do a better job of explaining what happened. Economic stress brought on by overpopulation and environmental degradation drove the states to fight, and fight they did. The Hellenes were very clear; their own ancestors destroyed their own cities by infighting.

The specific event triggering the decline may have been when the Hittites drove the Akhaian ruler from Miletos and outlawed Mycenaian goods from Hittite ports (1235T/985R BCE). The Mycenaians did not counterattack. Perhaps the epic dynastic fight between Atreus and Thyestes weakened the kingdom so much that a response was never mustered. Never again did the Hittites refer to a great-king of Ahhiyawa. That Thyestes fled for a time to the Hittite vassal state of Arazawa Minor (Lydia) suggests the Hittite great-king may have supported him to undermine Wanax Atreus.

Mycenaian retaliation was against a more remote target, the Hittite vassal state of Wilusa (Troy VI). One informative Hittite document says the Hittites and Ahhiyawa nearly went to war over Wilusa during the time Troy VI was destroyed. Wilusa king Wilmu was expelled but was eventually restored. In myth it was Herakles who led the first successful attack on Troy. However, the sack was not consequential; even the Hellenes admit that the same dynasty continued to rule. (According to myth, the son of the prior king took over; the former king was not restored.)

Between the fall of Troy VI and Troy VII, Hellas underwent a massive disruption. Nearly four centuries of growth ended, abruptly replaced by a rapid and devastating decline. Beginning with Pylos, most of the palaces of Hellas were destroyed between 1200T/950R and 1190T/940R BCE. Although most of the sacked cities were rebuilt, the palaces were mostly abandoned, and Mycenaian civilization never recovered. The myths glorified the destructive battles that ended the Heroic (Mycenaian) Age. Herakles is credited with leading armies to crush a Pylian army and sacking many cities, including Elis, Triphylian Pylos, Therapne (Sparta), and Oikhalia. Peleus pillaged Iolkos. Alkmeon led the Epigonoi in sacking Thebes and Kalydon. Though the strikes were devastating, not all of the cities fell. There is evidence that Mycenai survived an attack exactly when the Herakleids supposedly failed to conquer the city. Athens too was besieged and survived; in myth it was Theseus who defeated an invasion led by Eurystheus.

Because of the beauty of the Iliad, the most famous Hellenic myth is the epic ten-year struggle fought beneath the walls of Troy. The second Troy to fall, Troy VII, was much poorer than the one Herakles conquered. This time the conquest was catastrophic (1180T/830R BCE). Most of the inhabitants either fled abroad or were killed. They were followed abroad by their Akhaian/Danaan attackers, who had little left to go home to.

Massive migrations to Akhaia, Cephallenia Island, Cilicia, Anatolia, Palestine, and, above all, Cyprus are evident in myth and archaeology. Archaeological evidence indicates this migration occurred during the time of the Trojan War and shortly thereafter. As noted in myth, many of the migrants first moved to Attike. The site of Perati in Attike appears to have been the principal launching site for migrants moving eastward. It is unlikely to be a coincidence that the Trojan War expedition set sail from Aulis, just a few miles north of Perati. The arrival of Hellenes (Sea Peoples) were lamented by nations in their path. Hittite and Ugarit (Phoenicia) sources recorded attacks just before their records went silent. The Egyptians say Sea Peoples destroyed Arzawa (Asia Minor), Ailysia (Cyprus), Kobe (Cilicia), and other states as they moved relentlessly toward Egypt. Pharaoh Ramesses III finally defeated the Sea Peoples (1179T/929R

BCE). He did so during the very time that Menelaos spent seven years fighting and collecting booty in the eastern Mediterranean. According to myth, Menelaos had been blown off course on his return home from Troy. The myths are full of stories describing Hellenic settlers moving abroad at this time, including Amphilokhos and Mopsos settling in Cilicia, and Teucros on Cyprus.

The declining population of Hellas could not support a palace-based economic and political system. The fall of Mycenai spelled the end of the era (1102T/852R BCE). In myth, this event occurred two and half generations after the Trojan War, a time frame supported by archaeological evidence. In myth, the last king fled to Akhaia.

The culture that replaced the Mycenaian/Heroic one used more advanced iron weapons and tools; this was Hesiod's Age of Iron. The scant artifacts from this time support Hesiod's depressive account of the era. Petty barons ruled those impoverished sites that were not abandoned. The myths were wrong to imply that the era began with a southern migration of northern Hellenes tribesmen, the Dorians (Herakleids) and Boiotians. The "invasion" is better understood as a poetic way of saying there was a change from the Bronze Age palace civilization to a significantly poorer Iron Age culture. Emigration from Hellas remained a good option. Archaeological evidence confirms a small-scale migration from Attike to Ionia occurred during this era—the mythic migration of Neleus from Athens.

## Final Comments

While the broad outlines of mythic events discussed above read as compelling prehistory, the details are fanciful. It has been argued convincingly that the Iliad is a compilation of numerous battles between Akhaians and Arzawans during the Late Bronze Age. These unrelated wars were weaved together into one masterpiece. For example, Sarpedon of Lycia and Tlepolemos of Rhodes probably dueled in the battlefields of Lycia, not Troy. Menelaos and Nestor could only have led large forces from Lakonia and Pylos, respectively, during the attack led by Herakles. This is because their cities were sacked and largely abandoned between Troy VI and VII. Powerful historic cities stole the glory of smaller sites that had been more important during the earlier age. Argos stole the myths of Mycenai, for example, and Athens exaggerated the importance of Theseus. Every city wanted to claim that Herakles was active there.

Over time the meanings of many things presented orally were lost. Chariot warfare had died out, and the tactics had been forgotten, so warriors usually got off their chariots to fight hand-to-hand in the style of the Iron Age. Kings acted more like petty chieftains than kings managing large, palace-based economies.

One final question posed in the preface was, how long was the Early Iron Age, also descriptively called the Dark Age? Throughout this book, traditional dates based upon the calculations of Petrie were placed alongside revised dates based upon the works of Peter James. While both agree on the length of the Late Bronze Age, they disagree on the length of the Dark Age. Naturally, there is not much mythic material regarding the aptly named Dark Age. Which scholar is right is not important for this book. However, could the myths have retained such a high level of historical accuracy if more than four hundred years elapsed between the fall of Troy and the lifetime of Homer? Half as long, according to revisionist dating, seems a bit more reasonable.

The historic narrative of Hellenic myth is logical and factual. The combination of historic events and great storytelling is awesome!

# Addendum 1
# Clevenger Chronology

## Exhibit A1.1—Clevenger Chronology

| Revised | Traditional | Comments |
|---|---|---|
| Pre-10000 | | ***Hesiod's Age of Gold*** *begins with Kronos creating mankind. The rule of the Titans begins.* The earth provides for mankind. No agriculture is present. |
| 9750 | 10000 | ***Hesiod's Age of Silver*** *begins with the Olympians defeating the Titans.* Slow domestication of cereals, lentils, and peas begins in the Anatolian foothills above the Syrian Desert. Sheep from nearby Tauros and Zagros Mountains are domesticated. |
| 8750 | 9000 | Agriculture reaches Cyprus |
| 7750 | 8000 | First goats, then cattle and pigs are domesticated in Anatolia |
| 7150 | 7400 | First true town arises at Catal Huyuk in Anatolia |
| 6750 | 7000 | Anatolian farmers settle in Hellas: first at Macedonia, Thessalia, and Krete |
| 6250 | 6500 | Early farmers may have first made wine from wild grapes |
| 5950 | 6200 | Catal Huyuk abandoned; new wave of Anatolian farmers bring first pottery to Hellas |
| 5750 | 6000 | Settlers from Cilicia reintroduce farming on Cyprus. |
| 5750 | 6000 | Grape first domesticated for wine production in Caucasians Mountains |

| Revised | Traditional | Comments |
|---|---|---|
| 5500 | 5750 | Dairy farming develops around Sea of Marmara (Anatolia/Thrace), allowing pastoralism |
| 5250 | 5500 | Elataia, Orkhomenos, and Athens are among earliest farm communities below Thermopylai |
| 5000 | 5250 | Farming arrives on the Cyclades |
| 4750 | 5000 | First ores (principally copper) are smelted for tools and trinkets in Iran and the Balkans |
| 4750 | 5000 | Flax domesticated for linen textiles in Anatolia |
| 4250 | 4500 | Proto-Indo-European language develops on the Ukrainian/Russian steppes |
| 4050 | 4300 | Daggers and bows are introduced into Hellas from Thrace |
| 4000 | 4250 | Copper culture of the Balkans collapses amid climate change |
| 3750 | 4000 | First wool sheep breeds and wool textiles in Caucasian Mountains |
| 3450 | 3700 | Proto-Anatolian is first language to split off Indo-European as they move into the Balkans |
| 3350 | 3600 | Wheel invented by Indo-Europeans to use for oxen muscled plough/transport |
| 3250 | 3500 | Bronze Age begins in Anatolia |
| 3250 | 3500 | Indo-Europeans domesticate the horse on the Ukrainian/Russian/Kazakhstan steppes |
| 2750 | 3000 | Olive domesticated in Syria—a most versatile crop (used for perfume, oil, food) |
| 2670 | 2920 | First settlement at Troy built by arriving proto-Anatolians |
| 2550 | 2800 | Early Minoan pottery styles emerge on Krete |
| 2550 | 2800 | ***Hesiod's Bronze Age*** *starts in Hellas with the birth of the younger Olympian gods. Magical guilds of metalworkers introduce the new technology to mankind (Korybantes, Dactyls, etc.).* |
| | | **The Early Helladic Bronze Age (EH)** begins. The first cities arise, and asses are introduced to Hellas. |
| 2450 | 2700 | Most cities of Anatolia destroyed over next century by arriving proto-Anatolians |

| Revised | Traditional | Comments |
|---|---|---|
| 2350 | 2600 | Palace economies provide resources needed for first orchards of grapes, olives, and figs |
| 2350 | 2600 | Big increase in use of elaborate drinking cups and jugs—best evidence for wine use |
| 2285 | 2535 | Wheel-based pottery slowly introduced, improving storage and transport of goods |
| 2285 | 2535 | Most early Cyprus population centers are replaced by bringers of the Bronze Age |
| 2155 | 2405 | Donkeys, domesticated a millennium earlier in North Africa, first appear in Hellas |
| 2125 | 2375 | *King Erikhthonios of Athens invents war chariot and conquers Eleusis* (war carts existed at this time, but war chariots developed later) |
| 2050 | 2300 | Troy briefly abandoned after an attack |
| 2000 | 2250 | After Troy, most cities of West Anatolia and Hellas sacked over next fifty years |
| 2000 | 2250 | Indo-Europeans (proto-Hellenic) arrive in Hellas |
| 1980 | 2230 | Indo-European (proto-Anatolian) invaders from western Anatolia reach Cappadocia |
| 1850 | 2100 | Middle Minoan (MM) pottery style develops on Krete |
| 1775 | 2025 | **Middle Helladic Bronze Age (MH)** begins. The Gray Minyan pottery style develops (but regional differences were far greater than in the fairly homogenized EH Bronze Age). |
| 1750 | 2000 | Faster transport as spoked wheel invented by Indo-Aryan tribes of the steppes |
| 1735 | 1985 | Minoan traders first reach Cilicia |
| 1650 | 1900 | First Kretan palace built at Knossos |
| 1650 | 1900 | Cities of Anatolia and Hellas sacked again |
| 1650 | 1900 | Arrival of pony-sized horse into Hellas (used primarily as a pack animal) and foot-wheeled pottery in Hellas |
| 1650 | 1900 | *Zeus sends great flood, wipes out evil men of Bronze* |
| 1585 | 1835 | ***Hesiod's Heroic Age** begins when Deukalion and Pyrrha repopulate the land as the first "Hellenic" couple.* |

| Revised | Traditional | Comments |
|---|---|---|
| 1550 | 1800 | Influenced by West Semitic scripts, Minoans develop a hieroglyphic writing system |
| 1550 | 1800 | War chariot introduced to Anatolia, probably by the Indo-Aryan Mitanni tribe |
| 1500 | 1750 | First Minoan trade colonies appear, first on Rhodes, then on the Cyclades and Sporades |
| 1450 | 1700 | Horse, chariot, and sword arrive in Troas as its richest site, Troy VI, rises |
| 1450 | 1700 | Palaces of Krete destroyed and quickly rebuilt; volume of Minoan trading grows significantly |
| 1425 | 1675 | Labarna becomes first king of the Hittite nation |
| 1400 | 1650 | Orkhomenos is first Hellenic settlement to become a city |
| 1385 | 1635 | Minoan Linear A syllabic script (syllable sound) replaces cruder hieroglyphic (picture) writing |
| 1350 | 1600 | Time of the second palace era of Krete; towns of Hellas lack monumental buildings |
| 1350 | 1600 | Late Minoan (LM) pottery develops |
| 1343 | 1593 | *Zeus takes first mortal lover, Niobe* |
| 1335 | 1585 | Alashiya Kingdom arises on Cyprus, grand palaces built on Krete |
| 1330 | 1580 | *Phoroneus begins building shaft graves in Mycenai; Mycenai quickly becomes largest Hellenic city* |
| 1330 | 1580 | Earliest evidence of chariots in Hellas comes from Shaft Grave B of Mycenai |
| 1320 | 1570 | Earthquakes damage palaces on Krete; they are quickly repaired, ushering the second palace period |
| 1315 | 1565 | Cypriots adapt Minoan Linear A to their (possibly related) language |
| 1300 | 1550 | **Late Helladic Bronze Age (LHI)** begins, and many cities reappear in Hellas; Phocian Kirra, Messenian Peristeria, and Argeian Lerne are among the first. |
| 1285 | 1535 | *King Argos buried at new shaft grave site—Shaft Grave A in Mycenai* |
| 1274 | 1524 | Rising Hittite Empire begins to challenge Near Eastern powers |
| 1272 | 1522 | *Rape of Io discovered by Hera* |

| Revised | Traditional | Comments |
|---|---|---|
| 1270 | 1520 | Massive volcanic eruption on Theras Island buries a Late Minoan IA settlement [317] |
| 1270 | 1520 | *Mycenaian hero Argo Panoptes slays the monster Echidna* |
| 1269 | 1519 | *Hermes slays Argo Panoptes and frees Io* |
| 1269 | 1519 | *Pelasgos begins to civilize the Arkadians* |
| 1267 | 1517 | *Cyknos of Mycenai reputedly founds first overseas Mycenaian colony at Cyrnos (Iassos) in Anatolia* |
| 1266 | 1516 | *Io gives birth to Zeus's son Epaphos* |
| 1250 | 1500 | **The Late Helladic II Bronze Age (LHII)** begins with monumental construction initiated in Tiryns and Argos, and the first tholos tombs are constructed in Triphylia. Hellas pottery becomes homogenous again, based upon Mycenaian wares. |
| 1239 | 1489 | *Lelex founds Therapne (Sparta), the first city of Lakonia* |
| 1235 | 1485 | *King Triops becomes the first Mycenaian king buried in tholos tomb* |
| 1231 | 1481 | *Polykaon founds Malthi in western Messenia* |
| 1231 | 1481 | Numerous Mycenaian cities begin appearing in western Peloponnesos |
| 1221 | 1471 | Minoan sailors transport Lebanon cedars to Egypt for Pharaoh Thutmose III |
| Mid 1200s | Mid 1450s | Hittites first attack Arzawan states of western Anatolia |
| 1200 | 1450 | Akhaians conquer the Minoans and adapt Minoan script to write first Linear B texts on Krete |
| 1200 | 1450 | A slow, gradual decline on Krete and continues after the Akhaian conquest (it started before the conquest) |
| 1195 | 1445 | First recorded Egyptian envoy to Hellas sent by Thutmose III |
| 1185 | 1435 | Massive Akhaian colonization of Rhodes begins |
| 1162 | 1412 | *Danaos arrives in Mycenai and is awarded the kingdom after a sign—a wolf bringing down a bull* |
| 1140 | 1390 | Hittites advancing west first mention Akhaians; one hundred Akhaian chariots fight in Anatolia |

[317] Late twentieth-century CE scientific evidence suggests that the volcanic eruption on Thera occurred earlier than any archaeological evidence predicted (1650/1600 BCE). The results are hotly debated, but if they prove to be true, Middle and Late Bronze Age dates will need to be revised.

| Revised | Traditional | Comments |
|---|---|---|
| 1138 | 1388 | *Zeus rapes Minoan princess Europa; symbolizes Mycenaian conquest of Krete* |
| 1138 | 1388 | Destruction of Kretan palaces soon followed by the first Mycenaian palaces |
| 1136 | 1386 | *Kadmos slays dragon and founds Thebes* |
| 1132 | 1382 | *Apollo carries Lapith maiden Cyrene to Libya and sires rustic god Aristaios* |
| 1128 | 1378 | *Kadmos marries Harmonia, daughter of Ares and Aphrodite, after serving Ares an eternal year* |
| 1125 | 1375 | **The Late Helladic IIIA Bronze Age (LHIIIA)** begins. The first great palace is built at Mycenai. |
| 1125 | 1375 | *Furious Zeus kills Iasion for sleeping with Demeter; his brother Dardanos flees to Ilion* |
| 1125 | 1375 | *Aithlios, grandson of Deukalion, colonizes Eleia* |
| 1120 | 1370 | Last palace on Krete (Knossos) abandoned; Egyptians no longer mention Keftiu (Kretans) |
| 1120 | 1370 | *Poseidon sends white bull from sea to back Minos's claim to rule Knossos* |
| 1119 | 1369 | *Apollo rapes Kreousa and sires Ion; her brother, King Erekhtheus of Athens, conquers Khalkis* |
| 1115 | 1365 | Important envoy visits Tiryns and Mycenai |
| 1111 | 1361 | *Zeus abducts Aigina, drives back her father with thunderbolts; Sisyphos founds Korinth* |
| 1107 | 1357 | *Athamas becomes first Aiolic (Minyan) ruler of rich Orkhomenos* |
| 1107 | 1357 | *Minos banishes Sarpedon and Miletos; they settle in Anatolia* |
| 1105 | 1355 | Hittite records mention Akhaian-Lycian raids on their vassals |
| 1105 | 1355 | *Proitos challenges older twin brother Akrisios for Mycenaian crown using foot soldiers to accompany chariot warriors for the first time* |
| 1105 | 1355 | *Daidalos flees a murder charge to Krete* |
| 1104 | 1354 | *Phrixos escapes on the back of the flying golden ram* |
| 1104 | 1354 | *Ion and Kreousa reunited in Delphi* |
| 1103 | 1353 | *Semele dies before giving birth to Dionysos* |
| 1103 | 1353 | *Pasiphae produces the Minotaur after an unnatural lust for the white bull that Poseidon sent to Minos* |

| Revised | Traditional | Comments |
|---|---|---|
| 1103 | 1353 | *Tantalos and Pandareos steal golden dog from Zeus's shrine to avenge Iasion* |
| 1102 | 1352 | *Akrisios and Proitos agree to share the Mycenaian Empire* |
| 1101 | 1351 | *Akhaian Miletos conquers the Anatolian city of Milawata (Miletos), the premier Akhaian city of Asia* |
| 1101 | 1351 | *Korinth and Sicyon submit to Proitos of Tiryns* |
| 1100 | 1350 | *Poseidon carries off a Tiynthian princess to the Ionian Islands and sires Taphos* |
| 1100 | 1100 | Assyrian astronomers fix star locations for thirty constellations, including the zodiac |
| 1099 | 1349 | *Hera drives Athamas and Ino mad for harboring Dionysos* |
| 1099 | 1349 | *Amythaon of Iolkos leads the first Aiolian settlers to the western Peloponnesos* |
| 1098 | 1348 | *Athenians recover Eleusis despite death of King Erekhtheus* |
| 1095 | 1345 | *Perseus is conceived when Zeus comes to Danae as a golden light in the tholos tomb her father, King Akrisios of Mycenai, had imprisoned her within* |
| 1094 | 1344 | *King Tantalos of Lydia (Arzawa) becomes first man to dine on Olympos* |
| 1093 | 1343 | *Pandoros, son of King Erekhtheus of Athens, founds Khalkis as an independent state* |
| 1090 | 1340 | *Pirates abduct Dionysos, Hera drives him mad* |
| 1089 | 1339 | *North wind Boreas abducts Athenian princess Oreithyia* |
| 1089 | 1339 | *Aiolian Epopeus conquers Sicyon* |
| 1088 | 1338 | *Daidalos invents wings to flee Krete, his son Ikarios falls to his death* |
| 1087 | 1337 | *Clever Sisyphos temporarily cheats death; Epopeus seizes Korinth* |
| 1086 | 1336 | *Tantalos serves Pelops to the gods* |
| 1085 | 1335 | *Minos pursues Daidalos and is murdered in Sicily* |
| 1085 | 1335 | Evidence of Mycenaian trade posts in Italy and Sicily at this time |
| 1085 | 1335 | After a long fight, Hittite great-king Supplilumas I subdues the Arzawans of western Anatolia |
| 1082 | 1332 | *Apollo kills Krios of Euboea for sacrilege against Delphi* |
| 1081 | 1331 | *Dionysos returns triumphantly to Hellas despite opposition* |

| Revised | Traditional | Comments |
|---|---|---|
| 1080 | 1330 | *Melampous caught stealing cattle of King Phylakos to give as a bride-price for Pero* |
| 1079 | 1329 | *Nykteus of Thebes's attack on Sicyon is repulsed by Epopeus* |
| 1079 | 1329 | *Melampous cures Iphitos and secures Pero as bride for his brother Bias* |
| 1078 | 1328 | *Dionysos marries the Kretan princes Ariadne* |
| 1078 | 1328 | *Melampous cures the daughters of Proitos, whom Hera or Dionysos had driven mad* |
| 1078 | 1328 | *Thebans sack Sicyon; Antiope's twin sons Amphion and Zethos are exposed* |
| 1076 | 1326 | *Perseus slays Gorgon Medousa* |
| 1075 | 1325 | *Perseus accidentally kills his grandfather Akrisios and trades Mycenai for Tiryns* |
| 1073 | 1323 | *Apollo accidentally kills his lover Hyacinthos* |
| 1072 | 1322 | *Endymion chooses eternal sleep* |
| 1071 | 1321 | *Rape of Trojan prince Ganymedes by Zeus* |
| 1071 | 1321 | *Aktaion hunted by his own hounds after leering at bathing Artemis* |
| 1070 | 1320 | *Bellerophontes captures Pegasos and slays the monstrous Chimaera* |
| 1068 | 1318 | Hittites sack Milawata (Miletos) |
| 1067 | 1317 | *Eos abducts Cephalos* |
| 1066 | 1316 | Arzawan (Lydian) king Uhhaziti flees to Hellas after his rebellion from the Hittites fails |
| 1066 | 1316 | *Pelops (Uhhaziti) arrives in Hellas from Lydia, wins the hand of Hippodameia* |
| 1065 | 1315 | *Aitolos banished for killing man at Azan's funeral games* |
| 1061 | 1311 | *Arkhandros and Arkhiteles fail to conquer Sicyon, settle in Mycenai* |
| 1060 | 1310 | Pylos rises; Mycenaian goods appear in the Ionian Islands *(about the same time that Taphios creates a pirate-nation there)* |
| 1059 | 1309 | Hittites subdue a rebellion in Masa (Mysia) |
| 1055 | 1305 | *Ion dies leading Athens to victory over rebellious Eleusis* |
| 1053 | 1303 | *Boiotos (Boiotians) lead settlers from Iolkos onto the Thessalian plain* |
| 1049 | 1299 | *Pelops fails to take Elis* |

| Revised | Traditional | Comments |
|---|---|---|
| 1048 | 1298 | *The Aloadai rescue sister on Naxos, bury mother in Anthedon, and found Askre* |
| 1046 | 1296 | *The Aloadai capture Ares and pile Mount Ossa on Mount Pelion to besiege Olympos* |
| 1043 | 1293 | *King Pylas of Megara is exiled, conquers a harbor town in Messenia, and greatly expands the city of Pylos* |
| 1040 | 1290 | **The Late Helladic IIIB Bronze Age (LHIIIB)** begins. During this time, the regional pottery styles begin to arise again. |
| 1037 | 1287 | *King Labdakos of Thebes defeated and killed during unsuccessful attack upon Athens* |
| 1036 | 1286 | *Sons of Metion seize Athens* |
| 1035 | 1285 | *Amphion and Zethos kill the king and queen of Thebes and free their mother* |
| 1034 | 1284 | *Apollo and Artemis kill giant Tityos for attempting to rape Leto* |
| 1034 | 1284 | *Amphion and Zethos build the walls of Thebes* (archaeology suggests the walls were actually built thirty-five years later) |
| 1033 | 1283 | *Dryopes lead the successful defense of Delphi against Phlegyan attack* |
| 1033 | 1283 | *Pelops conquers Phineus* |
| 1032 | 1282 | *Poseidon raises a blue wave to hide him and Princess Tyro while they make love* |
| 1031 | 1281 | *Prokne and Philomela change to birds after avenging themselves on Thracian Tereus* |
| 1030 | 1280 | *Myrmidons populate Aigina on Aiakos's prayer to Zeus* |
| 1028 | 1278 | The first reference to Sea Peoples made by Pharaoh Ramesses II, who defeats the warriors of the great green sea |
| 1026 | 1276 | *Pelops seizes Azania* |
| 1024 | 1274 | Hellenes fight on both sides of epic battle at Kadesh; Egypt and Hittites fight to a draw |
| 1023 | 1273 | *Pelops conquers Stymphalos* |
| 1022 | 1272 | *Hera, Poseidon, and Apollo lead failed revolt against Zeus; Poseidon and Apollo build the walls of Troy with Aiakos in punishment* |
| 1022 | 1272 | *Aigeus takes Athenian throne from the sons of Metion* |
| 1021 | 1271 | *Orion and Artemis clear Krete of wild beasts; Gaia and Apollo conspire to kill Orion* |

| Revised | Traditional | Comments |
| --- | --- | --- |
| 1018 | 1268 | *Prince Androgeus of Krete murdered in Athens; his father's (King Minos's) curse brings drought to Hellas* |
| 1017 | 1267 | *Queen Niobe of Thebes (wife of Amphion) loses her children after boasting* |
| 1017 | 1267 | *King Minos conquers Megara after a long siege when King Nisos's purple strand is cut* |
| 1017 | 1267 | *Pelops forces Thebes to accept his son Kreon as king after Laios rapes Leucippos* |
| 1016 | 1266 | *Aiakos's prayers bring end to drought brought on by Minos's curse upon son's death* |
| 1016 | 1266 | *Pelops's son Alkathoos kills ferocious lion and is awarded the princess of Megara* |
| 1015 | 1265 | *Artemis kills Koronis for infidelity, Apollo rescues unborn Asclepius from her womb* |
| 1014 | 1264 | *Athens submits to Minos; tribute set at fourteen youths and maidens to be given to the Minotaur every nine years* |
| 1013 | 1263 | *Taphian raiders kill most of the princes of Tiryns* |
| 1012 | 1262 | *Orkhomenian king Klymenos murdered by Thebans; in response Orkhomenos attacks Thebes and forces them to pay annual tribute* |
| 1012 | 1262 | *Amphitryon destroys the pirate nation of Taphios; Zeus makes the sun stay down for a full day to extend his time with Alkmene, who conceives Herakles* |
| 1011 | 1261 | Hittites occupy Miletos and apologize to Mycenaian great-king after withdrawing |
| 1008 | 1258 | *Poseidon raises waterfall over Princess Arete and conceives Idas* |
| 1006 | 1256 | *Atreus and Thyestes flee after murdering Khrysippos, their father's (Pelops's) favorite bastard son* |
| 1005 | 1255 | *Poseidon and King Aigeus of Athens sleep with Aithra and she conceives Theseus* |
| 1002 | 1252 | *Pelias, son of Poseidon and Tyro seizes kingdom of Iolkos from rightful heir Aison; Aison's newborn son Jason is given to Centaur Kheiron to be raised in safety* |
| 1002 | 1252 | *Prince Oidipous of Thebes is exposed at birth* |

| Revised | Traditional | Comments |
|---|---|---|
| 1000 | 1250 | The tholos tombs of Atreus (Mycenai), Klytaimnestra (Mycenai), and Minyas (Orkhomenos) have been built; they are of superb craftsmanship and are the last important ones |
| 1000 | 1250 | *The Fates appear to Althaia at Meleagros's birth, warn her that the log on the fire and her son's destiny are the same* |
| 996 | 1246 | *Amphitryon leads Thebans to victory over invading Euboians under King Khalkodon* |
| 996 | 1246 | *Trojan prince Tithonos abducted by Eos* |
| 995 | 1245 | *Cerkyon wins Eleusis in wrestling match during funeral games of Skeiron of Megara* |
| 993 | 1243 | *Herakles slays Cithairon Lion, sleeps with the fifty daughters of Thespios, cunningly defeats Orkhomenos* |
| 992 | 1242 | *Hippokoon seizes Lakonian kingdom from half brother Tyndareos* |
| 991 | 1241 | *Neleus, son of Poseidon and Tyro, conquers Pylos* |
| 989 | 1239 | *Herakles begins labors by strangling the Nemean Lion* |
| 988 | 1238 | *Zeus ravishes Princess Leda on her wedding day in the form of a swan* |
| 988 | 1238 | *King Koiranos is last Mycenaian king buried in a tholos tomb (the one later attributed to Klytaimnestra)* |
| 988 | 1238 | *Atreus is chosen king of Mycenai over Thyestes when Zeus makes sun reverse course* |
| 988 | 1238 | *Theseus clears out highwaymen and wrestles Eleusis from Cerkyon* |
| 988 | 1238 | *The seer Polyeidos restores dead Kretan prince Glaukos to life* |
| 987 | 1237 | *Theseus kills the Minotaur* |
| 986 | 1236 | *Zeus kills Apollo's son Asclepios with a thunderbolt for raising Hymenaios back to life; Apollo retaliates by killing the Cyklopes; In punishment he must serve mortal Admetos for a year* |
| 986 | 1236 | *Lapith king Ixion is invited to Olympos and attempts to seduce Hera* |
| 985 | 1235 | *Oidipous unwittingly kills his father, Laios, and marries his mother* |
| 985 | 1235 | *Peleus and Telamon kill half brother Phokos* |
| 985 | 1235 | *Herakles wrestles Princess Alcestis away from Thanatos (death)* |

| Revised | Traditional | Comments |
|---|---|---|
| 985 | 1235 | Hittites drive Akhaian ruler from Miletos, ending direct Mycenaian rule in Anatolia |
| 980s | 1230s | Cities of Hellas begin increasing the fortifications around their citadels |
| 984 | 1234 | *Herakles saves Trojan princess Hesione while returning home from ninth labor (girdle of Amazonian Hippolyte)* |
| 983 | 1233 | *War breaks out between Lapiths and Centaurs at wedding of Peirithoos; Centaurs are utterly defeated* |
| 981 | 1231 | *Voyage of the Argonauts* |
| 981 | 1231 | *Herakles overcomes death in his twelfth and final labor (bringing Cerberus from the underworld)* |
| 981 | 1231 | *Kalydonian boar hunt, after which Meleagros defeats the attacking Kouretes and dies; Pleuron sacked in retaliation* |
| 980 | 1230 | *King Oineus of Kalydon conquers Olenos* |
| 980 | 1230 | *Herakles defeats Eurytos and his sons in archery but is denied the prize—Iole; after an illness for treacherously killing Eurytos's son, Zeus separates Herakles and Apollo fighting for tripod* |
| 979 | 1229 | *Auge exposes Telephos and marries King Teuthras of Teuthrania* |
| 977 | 1227 | *Zeus separates Apollo and Idas, lets Marpessa choose; she chooses mortal Idas as husband* |
| 976 | 1226 | *Herakles wrestles Akheloos for Deianeira* |
| 975 | 1225 | The Assyrians send an envoy to Thebes to discuss ways to circumvent Hittite blockade |
| 973 | 1223 | *Thyestes brings about the death of his nephew Pleisthenes, Atreus's son* |
| 970 | 1220 | *Herakles conquers Troy with help of Telamon and helps the Olympians defeat the Gigantes* |
| 970 | 1220 | Troy VI destroyed |
| 969 | 1219 | *Conjoined twins called the Moliones beat back Herakles's invasion of Elis* |
| 968 | 1218 | *Herakles defeats armies of Elis, Pylos, and Sparta* |
| 968 | 1218 | *King Priamos and Queen Hekabe of Troy expose son Paris after bad omens* |
| 967 | 1217 | *Sorceress Medeia kills Jason's new bride, Dioskouroi carry off brides* |

| Revised | Traditional | Comments |
|---|---|---|
| 967 | 1217 | *Oidipous discovers his deed, blinds himself, and goes into exile* |
| 967 | 1217 | *Sea goddess Thetis married to Peleus* |
| 966 | 1216 | *Trojan king Priamos visits Hellas* |
| 966 | 1216 | *Tydeus of Kalydon and Polyneices of Thebes duel outside King Adrastos of Midea's gates* |
| 965 | 1215 | *City of Iolkos is sacked by an army led by Jason, Dioskouroi, and Peleus* |
| 965 | 1215 | *Prince Nestor defeats Epeian invasion of Pylos* |
| 965 | 1215 | Massive walls and Lion Gate completed at Mycenai |
| 964 | 1214 | Zeus *pursues Nemesis, she conceives Helene; Leda raises the child as her own* |
| 963 | 1213 | *Herakles kills Centaur Nessos for raping his Aitolian bride, Deianeira; kills Cyknos in a duel; defeats Lapith-killing Koronos* |
| 963 | 1213 | *Curse of Theseus causes death of his son Hippolytos* |
| 961 | 1211 | *Atreus serves Thyestes his own children at a banquet* |
| 961 | 1211 | *Telephos, exposed son of Herakles, reunited with his mother, Auge, in Teuthrania* |
| 960 | 1210 | *Herakles drives Dryopes from central Hellas* |
| 960 | 1210 | *Thetis deserts Peleus after the birth of Akhilleus* |
| 959 | 1209 | *Nestor wins fame at funeral games of Amarynceus* |
| 959 | 1209 | *Telephos defeats invasion of Teuthrania by Idas* |
| 958 | 1208 | *Oidipous dies at Kolonos just before an army led by seven Argeian leaders is defeated at Thebes* |
| 957 | 1207 | *Herakles dies shortly after sacking Oikhalia* |
| 955 | 1205 | *Theseus gives sanctuary to the Herakleids* |
| 954 | 1204 | Pharaoh Merenptah boasts of beating back people of the foreign lands of the sea |
| 952 | 1202 | *Theseus and Herakleid defeat attack by Eurystheus; Herakleids respond by invading Argeia* |
| 952 | 1202 | Athens and Mycenai are besieged but survive; within ten years, most of the palaces of Hellas are sacked |
| 951 | 1201 | *Atreus is murdered at the instigation of Thyestes; Agamemnon becomes king* |
| 951 | 1201 | *Theseus and Peirithoos abduct Helene and descend into underworld after Persephone* |

| Revised | Traditional | Comments |
|---|---|---|
| 951 | 1201 | *Herakleids withdraw from Tiryns because of a plague* |
| 950 | 1200 | *The Dioskouroi rescue Helene* |
| 949 | 1199 | *Herakleid leader Hyllos is killed in duel, ending the second Herakleid invasion of the Peloponnesos* |
| 949 | 1199 | *Telephos beats back invasion of Teuthrania by Idas of Messenia* |
| 948 | 1198 | *Herakleid Tlepolemos settles on Rhodes, Akhaian Rhakios at Kolophon, and Herakleid Iolaos on Sardinia* |
| 948 | 1198 | *Alkmeon leads the Epigonoi in sacking Thebes and Kalydon* |
| 948 | 1198 | *Agamemnon conquers Harpina (Pisa?) and seizes Helene's sister Klytaimnestra* |
| 947 | 1197 | *Suitors of Helene promise to support the chosen husband; she picks Menelaos* |
| 945 | 1195 | **The Late Helladic IIIC Bronze Age (LHIIIC)** begins right after the destruction of many palaces. Regional pottery dominates, making it harder to date events. |
| 945 | 1195 | *Paris judges Aphrodite the fairest goddess; Helene elopes with Paris* |
| 945 | 1195 | *Dioskouroi and Idas and Polykaon fight and die over cattle* |
| 945 | 1195 | Pylos is sacked, according to radiocarbon dating, and only lightly reoccupied *(However, in myth, Neleids still rule Pylos, but Agamemnon had sacked nearby Harpina)* |
| 944 | 1194 | *Hellenic armada sails mistakenly to Teuthrania, is defeated by Telephos* |
| 943 | 1193 | *Agamemnon sacrifices daughter Iphigeneia at Aulis for a fair wind to sail to Troy* |
| 939 | 1189 | *Alkmeon is murdered* |
| 939 | 1189 | *Palamedes is framed by Odysseus and Diomedes, is executed* |
| 938 | 1188 | *Akhilleus leads sack of Lesbos* |
| 936 | 1186 | *Aigistheus and Agamemnon's wife, Klytaimnestra, become lovers* |
| 934 | 1184 | Fall of Troy VII *to Agamemnon-led Hellenes* |
| 933 | 1183 | *Agamemnon is murdered upon his return home; Aigisthos, son of Thyestes, becomes king* |
| 932 | 1202 | *Teucros founds Salamis on Cyprus* |
| 928 | 1178 | Hittite Empire collapses; Mushki, Kaska, and Sea Peoples play a role in their demise |

| Revised | Traditional | Comments |
|---|---|---|
| 928 | 1178 | *Menelaos active in Egypt delta*; Pharaoh Ramesses III defeats a massive Sea People invasion |
| 827 | 1177 | *Orestes kills Aigistheus and his mother, Klytaimnestra, the murderers of his father* |
| 927 | 1177 | *Menelaos returns home from Egypt and marries daughter Hermione to Neoptolemos* |
| 926 | 1176 | *Orestes acquitted of murder on the Areiopagos* |
| 925 | 1175 | *Orestes and Pylades rescue Iphigeneia in Tauris* |
| 925 | 1175 | A wall is built across the Isthmos—last significant Bronze Age construction job in Hellas; Mycenaian building boom hits Cyprus |
| 925 | 1175 | Rare horse-and-rider figurines suggest horses were ridden by this time in Hellas |
| 925 | 925 | Egyptian pharaoh Ramesses III sacks Jerusalem |
| 924 | 1174 | *Odysseus returns home to Ithake and kills the suitors* |
| 924 | 1174 | *Orestes becomes king of Mycenai* |
| 924 | 1174 | *Neoptolemos killed by mob at Delphi, Orestes marries Hermione* |
| 920 | 1170 | *Orestes inherits Sparta on death of Menelaos through his wife, Hermione* |
| 919 | 1169 | *Helene murdered on Rhodes* |
| 919 | 1169 | *Orestes conquers much of Arkadia* |
| 918 | 1168 | *Mopsos and Amphilokhos kill each other in duel in joint settlement in Cilicia* |
| 917 | 1167 | *Odysseus returns home from exile for killing suitors* |
| 913 | 1163 | *Herakleid leader Aristomakhos killed in failed attempt to conquer Tiryns* |
| 910 | 1160 | Krete only place in Hellas showing continuity; Minoan-Mycenaians build Karphi |
| 910 | 1160 | *Thessalians drive remaining Boiotians from Thessalian Plain* |
| 906 | 1156 | A *Herakleid inherits the kingdom of Sicyon* |
| 903 | 1153 | *Boiotian siege of Thebes fails to take the city* |
| 900 | 1150 | Pylos is sacked *(by Herakleids?)* |
| 890 | 1140 | *Herakleid invasion under Aristomakhos repulsed after Tiryns and Midea sacked* |
| 885 | 1135 | *Orestes forced to abdicate* |

| Revised | Traditional | Comments |
|---|---|---|
| 879 | 1129 | *King Autesion of Thebes joins Herakleids after the Boiotians seize Thebes* |
| 876 | 1126 | *Orestes dies in exile at age seventy* |
| 875 | 1125 | *Jason's descendent Thessalos conquers Iolkos;* evidence that palace was sacked but city was spared |
| 860 | 1100 | Subminoan pottery replaces Late Minoan on Krete |
| 854 | 1104 | *Herakleids conquer Tiryns (Temenos), Pylos (Kresphontes) and Lakonia (Thera); Pylos abandoned and Neleids lead refugees to Athens* |
| 852 | 1102 | Mycenai and Iolkos sacked—Mycenai by *Herakleid Temenos—former king Tisamenos flees with followers to Akhaia* |
| 852 | 1102 | *Neleids seize power in Athens* |
| 851 | 1101 | *Descendants of Argonauts are driven from Lemnos Island* |
| 851 | 1101 | *Herakleid prince Rhegnidas conquers Phlios* |
| 850 | 1075 | **The Submycenaian Age** begins. The final Mycenaian civilization collapses, and the last Hellenes make their way to Cyprus. |
| 850 | 1075 | Evidence that things were not as dire in Thessalia and Krete |
| 850 | 1100 | Thracian-Balkan people settle around Troy (ancestors of the Phrygians) |
| 840 | 1090 | *Temenos murdered and succeeded by son Ceisos; Deiphontes flees and conquers Epidauros* |
| 840 | 1050 | ***Hesiod's Age of Iron*** starts with the development of iron smelting on Cyprus. |
| 837 | 1087 | *Herakleid Deiphontes conquers Aigina* |
| 835 | 1085 | *Eurystheus and Prokles become Spartan co-kings when regent Theras leads Dorians to Thera Island* |
| 834 | 834 | Assyrians complete conquest of Cilicia when Tarsos falls |
| 830 | 1025 | **The Protogeometric Age** begins in Athens. This is an era during which only a few small settlements survive. |
| 830 | 1025 | First evidence of hero worship at ancient sites in Argeia (where mighty Mycenai lay) |

| Revised | Traditional | Comments |
|---|---|---|
| 812 | 1078 | *Herakleid Aletes conquers Korinth and founds Aleteid Dynasty* |
| 812 | 1044 | *Herakleids conquer Megara but are defeated at Athens* |
| 811 | 1043 | *Athenian Neleus leads Ionians to Ionia* |
| 811 | 1043 | Athenian protogeometric pottery arrives in Ionia |
| 810 | 1037 | *Althaimenes of Tiryns, grandson of Temenos, leads Dorians to Krete* |
| 800 | 1020 | *Herakleid king Medon moves capital to Argos from Tiryns* |
| 800 | 975 | Lydian capital of Sardis founded |
| 800 | 950 | Only important protogeometric building in Hellas constructed at Lefkandi on Euboea |
| 795 | 930 | First known representation of Centaurs |
| 790 | 925 | **The Geometric Age** begins in Korinth, so named because geometric designs appear on pottery produced during this age. |
| 785 | 900 | Aiolian settlers from Thessalia begin overseas colonization by settling on Lesbos |
| 760 | 850 | First Phrygian artifacts found in central Anatolia at Gordion |
| 750 | 825 | Phrygians settle at abandoned Hittite capital of Hattasas |
| 744 | 1117 | Assyrian king Tiglath-pileser drives back attacking Mushki (Phrygian) tribes from Anatolia |
| 740 | 850 | Population of Hellas begins to grow rapidly; villages of Sparta unite |
| 740 | 850 | Wall of Smyrna constructed—first Hellenic wall built in Aigaian Sea basin since Bronze Age |
| 730 | 800 | Euboians establish first Hellenic trade post at Al Mina near Phoenicia |
| 729 | 937 | Reign of Bakkhais begins; Korinthians build first Hellenic temple (to Hera) at Perakora |
| 725 | 800 | Korinthians establish first colony on Italian trade route at Ithake |
| 713 | 713 | Assyrians complete conquest of Neo-Hittite states of northern Syria and Cappadocia |
| 710 | 790 | First Hellenic colony of Italy founded at Pithekousai by Euboians to trade with iron-rich Etruria |

| Revised | Traditional | Comments |
|---|---|---|
| 709 | 709 | Assyrians drive Mita from Cappadocia; he enters Hellenic lore as the rich Phrygian king Midas |
| 709 | 709 | Cypriot kings forced to begin paying tribute to Assyrians (who employed Phoenician sailors) |
| 705 | 750 | **The Arkhaic Age** begins, prompted by oriental influences on reviving Hellas. |
| 705 | 750 | Writing reinvented, probably by Euboians altering West Semitic (Phoenician) script to add vowels and create first phonetic (mimicking the sound of voice) writing system |
| 700 | 730 | First representation of Hoplite troops comes from Paros Island (twenty years after last chariot fight scenes) |
| 690 | 775 | Korinthians establish colonies at Kercyra and Syrakuse, two years after first Sicilian colony |
| 687 | 696 | Midas killed in Phrygian capital of Gordion by horseback-riding Kimmerian raiders |
| 687 | 687 | Assyrians' first invasion of Egypt fails |
| 685 | 725 | Painted mythic motifs replace geometric designs on pottery in Korinth |
| 671 | 671 | Assyrians invade weakened Egypt, which is split among twenty kings |
| 665 | 714 | Gyges becomes first tyrant by overthrowing Lydian king, starts the Mermnad Dynasty |
| 664 | 664 | Pharaoh Psammetikhos I begins consolidating Egyptian resistance against invaders |
| 663 | 663 | Assyrians sack Egyptian Thebes |
| 660 | 690 | Lydians begin long effort to conquer Ionia by seizing Kolophon |
| By 655 | 655 | Egyptians drive Libyans and Assyrians out using Hellenic, Lydian, and Karian mercenaries |
| By 650 | 876 | Homeric *Iliad* and *Odyssey* stories set orally |
| 640s | 700 | Euboians establish first colonies of Thrace in Khalkidike; soon after, colonies at Dardanelles |
| 630s | 675 | First colonies built between the Hellespontos and the Bosporos |
| 635 | 807 | Asine abandoned in the Argeia after an Argive siege led by King Eratos of Argos |
| 620 | 650 | First known Hellenic statue sculpted; oldest known law code written on Krete |

| Revised | Traditional | Comments |
|---|---|---|
| 620 | 631 | First Hellenic colonies in Libya |
| 610s | 700 | Hesiod flourishes |
| 616 | 776 | Iphitos of Elis celebrates the first Olympic Games held with a Panhellenic truce |
| 615 | 640 | First stone temple (Doric) built in Korinth, dedicated to Apollo |
| 612 | 884 | Lykourgos institutes reforms in Sparta, curbing monarchy and giving country a unique society |
| 612 | 818 | Agraid Dynasty founded in Macedonia |
| 612 | 804 | Pheidon becomes king in Argos |
| 612 | 612 | Medians and Babylonians conquer Assyrian capital of Nineveh |
| 600 | 797 | King Pheidon of Argos seizes additional powers as first Hellenic tyrant |
| 600 | 775 | King Telestes of Korinth assassinated and replaced by elected kings from Bakkhai clan |
| 600 | 631 | First colony on the Black Sea built at Sinope |
| 600 | 625 | Distinctive black-figure pottery developed in Athens |
| 597 | 735 | Inconclusive Lelantine War—first Panhellenic war—begins |
| 595 | 640 | After defeating invasion by neighboring Pallene, popular Orthagoras becomes tyrant of Sicyon |
| 593 | 788 | King Alkamenes conquers Helos, completing the Spartan conquest of Lakonia |
| 590 | 785 | Pheidon of Argos defeats Spartans |
| 590 | 640 | Work begins on the first Doric stone temple at Olympia (dedicated to Hera) |
| 587 | 615 | Panhellenic trade post of Naukratis established in Egypt as Lelantine War ends |
| 585 | 585 | Thales predicts eclipse that unnerves Medians, who agree to divide Anatolia with Lydia |
| 584 | 776 | Pheidon hosts Olympic Games with Pisa over the objections of Elis |
| 583 | 661 | Pheidon kills supporting Cypselos in a coup that overthrows the Bakkhai in Korinth |
| 583 | 775 | Akhias of the Bakkhai leads defeated Korinthians to Syrakuse |

| Revised | Traditional | Comments |
|---|---|---|
| 580 | 773 | Spartan king Alkamenes invades Messenia, initiating the First Messenian War |
| 575 | 754 | Spartans complete conquest of Messenia |
| 570 | 735 | Spartan king Polydoros assassinated during failed revolt; losing party moves to Taras, Italy |
| 569 | 569 | Miletos agrees to pay tribute to end Lydian attacks |
| 569 | 569 | Pharaoh Adries overthrown after failing to conquer growing Hellenic cities of Libya |
| 565 | 664 | First recorded sea battle fought between Korinth and Kercyra (Corfu) |
| 560 | 610 | Gorgon pediment of Artemis temple on Kercyra created—first Hellenic architectural sculpture since the Lion Gate was built in Mycenai |
| 560 | 575 | Use of money introduced into Hellas from Lydia |
| 556 | 753 | Athenian monarchy abolished and replaced with elected archons |
| 556 | 556 | Phocaia is last Ionian city to fall to the Lydians; many refugees found Alalia on Corsica |
| 555 | 747 | King Meltas overthrown; elected kingship replaces monarchy in Argos |
| 553 | 675 | Elected king Damokratidas of Argos conquers Nauplia |
| 553 | 669 | Argives defeat Spartans at Hyiai |
| 552 | 674 | Messenians revolt under rebel leader Aristomenes, starting Second Messenian War |
| 552 | 672 | Pantaleon of Pisa seizes sponsorship of Olympic Games from Elis |
| 550 | 591 | Krisa sacked, purportedly for obstructing pilgrims to Delphi, ending the Sacred War; spoils used to pay for first Pythian Games |
| 550 | 582 | Isthmian Games founded |
| 550 | 550 | Heraion of Samos completed, becomes the Hellenic standard for temple design |
| 549 | 632 | Aristocrat Cylon fails to seize Athens as tyrant |
| 548 | 624 | Drako develops first law code for Athens (reducing arbitrary aristocratic rulings) |
| 546 | 546 | Persians conquer Lydia, ending Mermnad Dynasty and ending eastern Hellenic expansion |

| Revised | Traditional | Comments |
|---|---|---|
| 545 | 657 | Spartans crush Messenian revolt |
| 544 | 597 | Solon's arguments win Salamis from Megara during arbitration |
| 543 | 573 | Nemean Games, last of the four great Panhellenic games, founded |
| 541 | 541 | Carthaginian/Etrurian fleet drives colonists from Alalia, ending western Hellenic expansion |
| 539 | 539 | Megakles of Athens wins the hand of the daughter of the Sicyon tyrant Kleisthenes |
| 535 | 561 | Megakles, Pisistratos, and Lykourgos lead Athens after Solon retires |
| 535 | 748 | Office of ephors established in Sparta |
| 535 | 789 | Korinthians invent trireme warship, which is moored instead of beached |
| 533 | 606 | Samos and Athens defeat Mitylene and Miletos in trade war over Dardanelles |
| 532 | 566 | Greater Panathenaia is founded in Athens |
| 530 | 556 | Tegea surrenders to Sparta on Khilon's terms, becomes first Spartan League member |
| 529 | 529 | Persians conquer Babylonia |
| 529 | 545 | Pisistratos seizes power as tyrant in Athens |
| 528 | 572 | Tyrant Pyrrhos of Pisa loses Olympic Games sponsorship to Elis,<br>both Pisa and Elis joined the Sparta League |
| 528 | 555 | Pisistratos sends Miltiades to colonize and fortify the Khersonese |
| 527 | 587 | Tyrants of Korinth and Sicyon are expelled, both cities join the Spartan League |
| 527 | 545 | Spartans defeat Argives in Battle of Champions at Boiai, isolating Argos |
| 525 | 525 | Persians conquer Egypt after pressuring Samos and Cypriot kings into providing support |
| 525 | 525 | Hellenic cities of Italy stop Etrurian advance (they had previously conquered Rome) |
| 525/4 | 525/4 | Spartans fail to dislodge Polykrates, tyrant of Samos |
| 524 | 524 | Persians subdue Hellenic cities of Libya |

| Revised | Traditional | Comments |
|---|---|---|
| 520 | 540 | Thessalian attempt to conquer Boiotia fails; Thebes reacts by beginning consolidating Boiotia |
| 519/16 | 519/16 | Persians brutally conquer Samos after crucifying Polykrates |
| 515 | 515 | Lokrians found Naupaktos on best west Hellas harbor (important since ships now moored) |
| 512/11 | 512/11 | Hellenic subjects of Persian Empire support Great-King Darios's failed attack on Scythia |
| 510 | 548 | Fire destroys sacred oracle of Delphi, Alkmaionids of Athens pay for its reconstruction |
| 510 | 520 | Thebes conquers Orkhomenos |
| 510 | 520 | Rich Italian colony of Sybaris is sacked |
| 509 | 519 | Athens checks Thebes's plans to complete the conquest of Boiotia by supporting Plataia |
| 506 | 527 | Tyrant Hippias, son of Pisistratos, becomes paranoid and ruthless after brother's assassination |
| 503 | 510 | First Spartan attack on Athens defeated with help of Thessalian cavalry |
| 502 | 509 | Spartans drive out Hippias from Athens, install aristocratic government |
| 501 | 508 | Athens adopts democracy |
| 500 | 525 | **Classical Age** begins with distinctive red-painted pottery developed in Athens. |

The Clevenger Chronology provides B.C.E. dates for early Hellenic mythic and historic events based upon both traditional and revisionist timeframes. Mythic events are italicized.

**Traditional dates** are largely derived from the works of William Petrie and Eduard Meyer. Petrie cataloged Egyptian pottery and developed a chronological sequence from the time Egypt was unified under one pharaoh down through the time of Kleopatra. Petrie then overlaid his findings with Manetho's kings list, ancient temple monuments, and surviving papyrus scrolls. Meyer used two documented historical events with references to a Sothic calendar to calculate exact dates. The Sothic calendar is an ancient Egyptian calendar based upon the co-occurrence of the rise of the Dog Star, Sothis (Hellenic Sirius), and the annual flooding of the Nile. Two ancient papyrus documents allowed Meyer to calculate the seventh year of the reign of Pharaoh Senusret III as 1872 BCE and the ninth year of Amenhotep I as 1540 BCE. Using those fixed dates, it was relatively easy for Petrie to calculate dates for other pharaohs. By comparing Hellenic pottery found alongside Egyptian wares, Petrie matched the Mycenaian Age with the Egyptian Eighteenth, Nineteenth, and Twentieth Dynasties (1550–1070 BCE). Later discoveries led to a general acceptance of only slightly different dates (1580–1075 BCE). A more detailed discussion of traditional dating is found in section 1, "Traditional Scholarly Derived Dates."

Traditional Clevenger Chronology dates between the Bronze and Classical Ages rely on A. M. Snodgrass for protogeometric pottery dates (1025–900 BCE) and Nicolas Coldstream for geometric pottery dates (900–700 BCE). By default, submycenaian pottery must have been manufactured between 1075 and 1025 BCE. The key assumption by Coldstream was matching a date provided by the late fifth-century BCE historian Thucydides of Athens (*History of the Peloponnesos War*, vi.3) with archaeological discoveries from the Sicilian city-state of Syrakuse. Thucydides calculated that Syrakuse was founded in 734/3 BCE using a genealogy provided by a slightly older source—Antiokhos of Syrakuse. Coldstream, who wrote the hereto definitive work on the Geometric Age, used Thucydides's date to establish when geometric pottery was produced. Because the pottery used by the earliest Hellenic settlers at Syrakuse was of the Late Geometric style, it was assumed that it must have been produced during the mid to late eighth century BCE. More recent discoveries led to assuming the Geometric Era began twenty-five years earlier than assumed by Snodgrass and Coldstream.

Most of the traditional historical, and a few mythic, dates are provided by Eratosthenes of Cyrene (275–194 BCE). Eratosthenes was a royal tutor serving in the court of the Hellenistic pharaoh Ptolemy III of Egypt, and from 234 BCE until his death, he was chief librarian of the Alexandrian Library, the finest in all antiquity. The date Eratosthenes calculated for the fall of Troy became the standard once published (1184T BCE). Petrie's chronology supported Eratosthenes's date for the fall of Troy. However, other dates often conflict with the dating sequence developed by Petrie. There has been no attempt here to reconcile the two. A more detailed discussion of Eratosthenes's dating is found in section 2, "Ancient Historians' Derived Dates."

Finally, where Assyrian dates are available, they are used, since they have been proven to be accurate back to 911 BCE. Assyrian dating is discussed in section 1, "Traditional Scholarly Derived Dates."

**Revisionist dates** are set to fit with dates proposed by Peter James in his book *Centuries of Darkness*. James challenged long-held traditional dating of events prior to the seventh century BCE in Egypt and the fifth century BCE in Hellas. James's premise is that a long Dark Age was invented to fit a faulty Egyptian chronology. Arguments presented for changing dates include fallacies uncovered in the Sothic calendar, evidence that Egypt was divided into multiple fiefs during the Dark Age, and evidence indicating that ancient historians generally exaggerated the ancientness of their heroic and immediate pasts (dates once accepted as supporting the Egyptian chronology). All of these factors led James to propose a downward revision to the long-held dates by roughly 250 years. A plethora of artifacts led him to agree with traditionalists that the Late Bronze Age, between the rise (MHII) and fall (LHIIIC) of Mycenai, was approximately five centuries long. A more detailed discussion of revisionist dating is found in section 3, "Revisionist Dating Proposed by James."

The logic behind revisionist dating for mythic and most historical events is found in section 4, "Deriving Revisionist Clevenger Chronology Dates." A few historical events are based upon Assyrian confirmed dates. All the dates fit within the timelines presented by James.

## Section 1: Traditional Scholarly Derived Dates

Traditional dating of events in the lands surrounding the eastern Mediterranean Sea is largely based upon assumptions concerning Egypt. Specifically, traditional dating derives from ancient Egyptian historical sources, Egyptian pottery chronology, and the Sothic calendar. Ancient Assyrian and Hellenic sources seem to corroborate calculated traditional dates.

**Historical Sources:** The most important historical document used in developing traditional dating is the kings list provided in Manetho's book *Aigyptika* (written in Hellenic). Manetho was an Egyptian priest who lived during the third century BCE—when the Ptolemies ruled Egypt. Manetho's kings list begins with Menes, the man who first unified Egypt and initiated the First Dynasty. Manetho organized his list into thirty dynasties (ruling families) ending with Nectanebo II (360–343 BCE)—the last native pharaoh. Although Manetho's influential book is lost, summaries survive in works by Josephos (first century CE), Julius Africanus (third century CE), Eusebios (fourth century CE), and Syncellus (ca. 800 CE). Egyptian kings lists found on monuments and papyri have largely validated and occasionally augmented the surviving list from Manetho, as have other surviving Egyptian records. Hittite, Hellenic, Assyrian, Biblical, and other records have also been studied for their relevance.

**Pottery Dating:** During the late nineteenth century CE, the British archaeologist William Petrie cataloged Egyptian pottery and developed a chronological sequence from the time Egypt was unified by Menes down through the time of the last Ptolemaic ruler, Kleopatra, who lost her kingdom to the Roman emperor Augustus. Petrie then overlaid his findings with Manetho's kings list. His conclusions through the Twentieth Dynasty have been largely confirmed by later archaeologists, with only minor adjustments. Petrie was the first archaeologist to find Mycenaian pottery at Egyptian sites, and he concluded that the Mycenaian Age occurred during the Eighteenth, Nineteenth, and Twentieth Dynasties of Egypt. Archaeologists continue to develop pottery sequences based upon a combination of stereographical and stylistic analogies, a strategy Petrie first employed.

**Sothic Calendar and Other Astronomical Clues:** The works of Manetho and Petrie provide a solid sequence for Egyptian history; however, neither provides fixed dates. For more than a century prior to Petrie developing his relative chronology, scholars had tried to determine fixed dates by using Egyptian astronomical records. Early Egyptologists were quickly convinced that it was possible to correlate the rising of the Dog Star, Sothis (Sirius), with the beginning of the annual flooding of the Nile River mentioned in Egyptian astronomical texts using modern astronomical calculations. Because the Egyptian Sothic calendar never introduced a leap year, it took 1,460 years to complete a full cycle of years for Sothis to rise on the same date (since the Egyptian year was 365 days but a Sothic year is exactly 365.25 days).

In 1904, C. E. Eduard Meyer proposed the fixed dates that are still used today with very little modification. He derived these dates from a few references. A Roman named Censorinus mentioned that a Sothic Cycle began in 139 CE, meaning that the previous cycle would have started in 1321 BCE. Using that calculated date and two ancient papyrus documents with references to Sothis risings (but not in years that a cycle began), Meyer was able to calculate that the seventh year of the reign of the pharaoh Senusret III was in 1872 BCE, assuming that the Sothic rising occurred in Memphis, Egypt, and the ninth year of Amenhotep I was 1540 BCE at Memphis. Using those fixed dates, it was relatively easy to propose dates for other pharaohs by utilizing the works of Manetho and Petrie. Kings lists from ancient temple monuments and surviving papyrus scrolls were also considered (none dating later than the reign of Ramesses II of the Nineteenth Dynasty). But Egyptologists quickly realized that precisely dating the match of Sothis's rise with the Nile's flooding depends upon where along the river the calculations are made from. If the calculations are computed at Elephantine (Aswan) on the first cataract (and the ancient Egyptian southern border), which Rolf Krauss suggests is a better choice than the capital at Memphis, the fixed dates for Senusret III and Amenhotep I fall in 1830 BCE and 1506 BCE, respectively.

Egyptologists also interpreted lunar cycles for clues to find other fixed dates within the Sothic set dates. Because lunar cycles repeat frequently, the lunar records from the reign of a pharaoh named Thutmose could fit for the years 1504, 1490, or 1479 BCE and for Ramesses II in 1304, 1290, or 1279 BCE. The lowest dates are generally accepted as the most likely to fit the calculation derived from the Sothic calendar.

Sothic derived fixed dates require that the Third Intermediate Period (TIP)—the Twenty-First through Twenty-Fifth Dynasties, which followed the Bronze Age—must be four centuries long. To accommodate this, Egyptologist Kenneth Kitchen[318] had to assume that Manetho did not include coregencies among pharaohs and that dynasties did not overlap; he cited sketchy evidence from Manetho to support these assumptions. However, because of overwhelming evidence to the contrary, Kitchen did allow for some overlap between the Twenty-Second and Twenty-Third Dynasties. The TIP ended when the Assyrians invaded Egypt, a date that can be fixed by Assyrian chronology. Given these facts and assumptions, Kitchen calculated the TIP as lasting between 1070 BCE and 664 BCE.

**Comparison to Hellenic Records:** When Petrie discovered Mycenaian pottery at Egyptian sites along with pottery from the Eighteenth and Nineteenth Dynasties, he was able to conclude that the Mycenaian Age occurred roughly between 1550 and 1070 BCE.[319] Petrie's proposed dates were checked against ancient Hellenic texts and field research at archaeological sites to see if they could corroborate or refute the Egyptian chronology. The famous site of Troy, so beautifully written about by Homer, provided the key. Schliemann proved to a skeptical nineteenth-century CE world that Troy existed beyond Homer's imagination. Archaeologist Wilhelm Dorpfeld, working for Schliemann, identified nine levels of habitation at Troy, which was later confirmed by Carl Blegen. Mycenaian pottery was discovered in two levels of the city, both showing evidence of having been violently destroyed. So Troy was indeed sacked during the later stages of the Mycenaian Age, just as Homer said. But while pottery evidence proved Troy was destroyed during the Mycenaian Age, it did not provide a fixed date other than what could be inferred using Egyptian chronology.

Fixed dates, however, were something amply provided by speculating ancient Hellenic writers (see exhibit below). Most of the early historians proposed dates for the fall of Troy that fit within the timeframe suggested by Egyptian chronology. During the third century BCE, historians such

[318] Kenneth Kitchen, *The Third Intermediate Period in Egypt (1100–650 BC).*

[319] Later discoveries have added to our understanding. Hyksos Period Egyptian objects found in Krete during the Middle Minoan III pottery period provide the first historic cross-reference to Aigaian pottery. The Eighteenth Dynasty pharaoh Ahmose (1550T/1300R–1525T/1275R BCE) drove the Hyksos from Egypt. Because of exchanges between Hellas and Krete, we know that during the Middle Minoan III pottery period, Hellenic pottery was transitioning from Middle Helladic (MH) to Late Helladic I (LHI). Tombs from the Thutmose III era (1479T/1229R–1425T/1175R BCE) contain Hellenic pottery, the latest being LHII. Pharaoh Akhenaten's (1353T/1103R–1334T/1084R BCE) short-lived city holds the first LHIIIA pottery.

as Timaios of Tauromenion, Sosibios the Lakonian (*FGrHis* 595), and Eratosthenes tried to pinpoint dates using chronologies such as Athenian archon lists and Olympic Games. The year 1184 BCE, postulated by Eratosthenes, became the standard once published. The dates postulated by the ancient historians are hardly convincing evidence, but nevertheless, affairs in Krete, Hellas, and Troy seemed to support the traditional dating developed using Egyptian chronology.

Exhibit A1.2—Dating the Trojan War

| Forecaster | Year (BCE) | Comment |
|---|---|---|
| Lokrians (late fourth century BCE) | 1346 | |
| Douris of Samos (340–260 BCE) | 1334 | 1,000 years before Alexandros |
| Herodotos of Halikarnassos (fifth century BCE) | 1235 | 800 years earlier |
| Kleitarkhos of Kolophon (late fourth century BCE) | 1234 | |
| Parian Marble (mid third century BCE) | 1209 | |
| Timaios of Tauromenion, Sicily (ca. 270 BCE) | 1194 | |
| Eratosthenes of Cyrene (275–194 BCE) | 1184 | |
| Sosibios of Lakonia (third century BCE) | 1170 | |
| Pseudo Herodotos, Life of Homer (fourth century BCE?) | 1170 | 168 years before Homer's birth |
| Ephoros of Cyme (mid fourth century BCE) | 1149 | |
| Phanias of Eresos (late fourth century BCE) | 1129 | |
| Kallisthenes of Olynthos (late fourth century BCE)[320] | 1127 | |
| Dikaiarkhos of Messana (late fourth century BCE) | 1082 | |
| Pherecydes of Syros (fifth century BCE)[321] | 966 | |

[320] Kallisthenes and, afterward, Phanias were two students of Aristotle who calculated back seventeen generations of Agiad kings in Sparta from Leonidas, who died fighting the Persians. That gave a date of roughly 1047 BCE, to which they added eighty years. This calculation demonstrates why assuming three generations per century is too long. Ephoros calculated back from 371 BCE and got an earlier date because the four Spartan kings ruling between 480 BCE and 370 BCE did not rule thirty-three and one-third years on average.

[321] Pherecydes (*FGrHis,* 3) says there were thirteen generations in the Philadai family from Ajax to Hippocyides, who was archon in 566 BCE. Assuming, like Herodotos and others, that there were three generations each one hundred years, then the Trojan War ended 966 BCE. Coincidentally, the date for the reign of the mythical Egyptian king Proitos (who entertained Menelaos and Helene) can be calculated from Herodotos (*Histories,* ii.112) as being from 966–933 BCE.

Egyptian chronology required that the manufacture of Hellenic submycenaian, protogeometric, and geometric pottery lasted for nearly four hundred years, 1100–700 BCE. The slightly later date of 1075 BCE is now usually cited as representing the end of the Bronze Age. Two mid twentieth century scholars wrote defining works crystallizing traditional dates for two of the pottery styles; Snodgrass set the various phases of protogeometric pottery (1025–900 BCE) and J. N. Coldstream did the same for the development of geometric pottery styles (900–700 BCE). By default, submycenaian pottery must have been manufactured between 1075 and 1025 BCE. More recent discoveries led to revising the start of the Geometric Age to 925 BCE.

**Bronze Age Correspondences:** With confidence in the Egyptian-based dating growing, scholars were keen to apply it elsewhere. Archaeological sites were scoured for correspondences between the Egyptians and other kingdoms and for Egyptian artifacts buried in the same undisturbed archaeological layer as native goods (as was done to date Mycenaian pottery). Two great discoveries did more than any other to increase our understanding of the Late Bronze Age. First was the discovery of the royal records of the Eighteenth Dynasty pharaohs Amenhotep III, monotheistic Akhenaten, and Tutankhamen, or Tut (whose tomb was unplundered), at el Amarna. The next great discovery was that of the royal records of the Hittite great-kings at Hattusa (modern Boghazkoy) in Anatolia. We are fortunate that no future city was built at either of these sites, as that might have obliterated the ancient record. The el Amarna letters include correspondences between the pharaoh Akhenaten and Assyrian king Assuruballit I (1365T/1115R–1330T/1280R BCE), four Kassite great-kings of Babylonia, and the Hittite great-king Supplilumas I. Versions of a treaty signed by Pharaoh Ramesses II and the Hittite great-king Muwatalli II after they battled to a draw at Kadesh in Syria have been found in the Temple of Amun at Karnak in Egypt and among the Hittite royal records at Hattusa.

Hittite royal records from Hattusa cover Hittite history in some detail from Tudhaliya I/II (1400T/1150R –1380T/1130R BCE) until its destruction at the end of the reign of Supplilumas II (1207T/957R–1178T/928R BCE). Besides relations with the Egyptians, there are correspondences with the Kassite kings of Babylonia and the Assyrians. Hittite great-king Urhi-Teshub corresponded with the Assyrian king Adad-nirari I, Great-King

Hattusili III with Assyrian kings Adad-nirari I and his son Shalmaneser I, and Great-King Tudhaliya IV with Assyrian king Tukulti-Ninurta I. Only the last correspondence is indisputable; the other references are based upon fragments.

Relations between Egypt and both the land of Keftiu (Krete, where the Minoans flourished) and the "Islands in the Midst of the Sea" (Hellas, land of the Akhaians or Mycenaians) are evident from both texts and artifacts. Egyptian monuments mention two specific envoys to Hellas—one sent by Thutmose III and the other by Amenhotep III. However, there is no record of the Mycenaian kings they might have met. Hittite texts are replete with references to the Ahhiyawa (often identified with the Akhaians or Mycenaians), but although they refer to Ahhiyawan great-kings, they do not mention any by name.

**Assyrian Kings List:** An Assyrian kings list written in 738 BCE and found at Khosabad in 1927 CE offered the opportunity to validate or challenge the Egyptian-based chronology. Detailed comparisons with the Egyptian kings list supported traditional dating. The number of kings on the Assyrian list corresponded well with the number on Manetho's list for the long period between Akhenaton's correspondence with Assyrian king Assuruballit I and Assyrian king Esarhaddon's invasion of Egypt in 671 BCE—when the Kushite pharaoh Taharqa (690–664 BCE) fled before him.

**Assyrian and Babylonian Dates:** Babylonian dates found in the Canon of Ptolemy for kings between the ascension of King Nabonassar (747 BCE) and the death of Alexandros the Great (323 BCE) are considered reliable. The Canon is a surviving work of the famous second-century CE astronomer dealing primarily with astronomical observations (especially eclipses), but fortunately it also includes a Babylonian kings list whose reigns are backed up by recordings of heavenly phenomena. Numerous cuneiform texts uncovered in Babylonia support Ptolemy's kings list, and astronomers have been able to fix the dates by calculating astronomical events described by Ptolemy. Claudius Ptolemy's list (no known relationship to the kings of Egypt with that name) has been successfully linked to an Assyrian eponym list (years were named for reigning government officials—eponymous for each year) through numerous uncovered documents. Therefore, Assyrian dates can be accepted back to 911 BCE, the first year of the eponym list.

The eponym list ends with the year 660 BCE. Persian dates are based upon Assyrian/Babylonian dates and can therefore be considered reliable as well.

**Assyrian Connection:** The proven dates for Assyrian kings after 911 BCE can be used to provide definitive dates in Egypt without relying on the Sothic Calendar. Unfortunately, after the El Amara letters to Assyrian king Assuruballit I (1365T/1115R–1330T/1280R BCE), there are no known correspondences between the two empires until Assyrian king Sargon II (722–705 BCE) communicated with Pharaoh Shilkanni (the Assyrian rendering of Osorkon). However, this does not provide a fixed date for the reign of Osorkon, since it could be Osorkon IV by traditional dating or Osorkon III by revisionist dating. Likewise, when Sargon's son and successor Sennacherib says he defeated an Ethiopian/Kushite pharaoh at Eltekeh in Palestine (701 BCE), he does not mention the pharaoh he defeated by name. (The Bible book of Kings says it was Taharqa, but we know from Egyptian records that he did not rule that early; it is possible he was only a prince during that battle.) So the only thing we can conclude is that the Twenty-Fifth Dynasty was ruling in Egypt by the late eighth century BCE. Possibly during a later invasion of Egypt by Sennacherib (687 BCE), and certainly during the campaign of his son Esarhaddon (671 BCE), the Kushite pharaoh Tirhaka (Egyptian "Taharqa") is listed as the main protagonist, and Egyptian dates become independently verifiable. By the Twenty-Sixth Dynasty (664–525 BCE), dates for Egyptian pharaohs can be trusted because of a plethora of Assyrian, Biblical, Hellenic, Egyptian, and Babylonian texts.

**Hellenic Dates:** Based upon ancient sources and the works of the leading Geometric Age pottery expert, Coldstream, most historians have generally accepted that fixed dates for Hellas begin with the colonization of Sicily. It is possible to calculate the foundation dates of certain Hellenic colonies on Sicily using references in the histories of Thucydides and Herodotos. Thucydides (*Peloponnesian War* vi.1–5) says Megara Hyblaiai was founded 245 years before it was destroyed by Gelon of Syrakuse—a date fixed by Herodotos to 483/2 BCE. Therefore, Megara Hyblaiai was founded in 728 BCE. Thucydides added that Syrakuse was founded five years earlier by Korinthians (734/3 BCE). The late fifth-century BCE historian Thucydides and his slightly older sources, Antiokhos of Syrakuse and Hellanikos of Mitylene (Lesbos Island), clearly had no established chronological timeline to base their timetables upon (Hellanikos is said to have been the first historian to date events by Athenian archon lists and

Argive priestess of Hera lists), so they must have based their dates upon genealogies. Coldstream accepted Thucydides's dates and used them to fix pottery timeframes. The earliest pottery found at the Hellenic colonies of Sicily (assuming no trading at the site before colonization) are from the Late Geometric and Early Protokorinthian pottery styles, which were thereby fixed to 734/3 BCE.

In conclusion, traditional dates were developed during the late nineteenth and early twentieth centuries CE by calculating a few fixed dates derived by Eduard Meyer using the Sothic calendar and then deriving other dates using the relative chronology Petrie developed using Manetho's king list and archaeological finds. Archaeologists have been uncovering new evidence for over a hundred years since then, and there has been no evidence uncovered that clearly refutes traditional dates; many findings seem to support them. Given these impressive facts, it will take overwhelming evidence to change the minds of most scholars.

**Arkhaic Age:** Syrakuse was not the first Hellenic colony on Sicily, and so the beginning of Arkhaic Age was traditionally set at 750 BCE. The Arkhaic Age ended with the development of distinctive red-painted pottery in Athens. At this point the difference between the traditional date (525 BCE) and the revisionist date presumed by James (500 BCE) is not much.

**Dark Age:** Mid twentieth-century scholars, such as Vincent Desborough, Snodgrass, and Coldstream, wrote important works attempting to more precisely define traditional Dark Age dates. This task was complicated by the fact that pottery styles were adopted in the various Hellenic regions at different dates. The dates these scholars proposed more or less agreed with one another, and although subsequent scholars have continued to tinker with the dates, the modifications have been very minor. Therefore, traditional Dark Age pottery dates can be roughly summed up in this way: submycenaian pottery was first developed at the end of the Bronze Age (1075 BCE), protogeometric pottery first appeared in Attike ca. 1025 BCE, geometric pottery first appeared in Korinth ca. 925 BCE, and representations of mythic scenes on pottery first appeared in Korinth ca. 725 BCE.

**Fall of Mycenai:** Late nineteenth-century CE excavations at Mycenai led by Schliemann and his able assistant Dorpfeld determined that the city was sacked when LHIIIC pottery was manufactured. Egyptian artifacts uncovered in Mycenai suggest LHIIIC pottery was manufactured during the time of the Sea Peoples' attack on the Twentieth Dynasty of Egypt—traditionally dated to around 1125T BCE.

Alternatively, a date for the fall of Mycenai may be calculated based upon the statement of Eratosthenes that Troy fell in 1184 BCE and that the Herakleids returned to Argeia eighty years after Troy fell. Thus, according to ancient sources, it is possible to calculate the Herakleids' return to 1104 BCE. Mycenai fell shortly thereafter, say 1102 BCE—quite close to the traditional date of 1125 BCE. Both the traditional timeline date of Snodgrass (1125 BCE) and one derived from ancient sources (1102 BCE) fall within the timeframe in which LHIIIC pottery was thought to be in use. For traditional dating, the Clevenger Chronology uses the slightly later date for the fall of Mycenai provided by the ancient sources so that the length of time for the Herakleids is the same for traditional and revisionist dating. The difference is 250 years (1102–852 BCE). For all Late Bronze Age dates, this fixed difference between traditional and revisionist dating is assumed.

According to archaeologists following traditional dating, the use of LHIIIC pottery continued at Mycenai for up to a half a century after Mycenai was sacked (and immediately reoccupied). This fact is consistent with mythic belief that it was Medon, the third Herakleid king of Argeia, who abandoned the last palace, at Tiryns, and settled inland at Argos.[322]

**Fall of Troy:** Based upon pottery evidence, Troy VI is assumed to have fallen while LHIIIB pottery was in use, and Troy VII during the time LHIIIC pottery was manufactured. Because LHIIIC pottery has been found in Egypt, the traditional timeline places the fall of Troy VII in the early twelfth century BCE, and thus Eratosthenes's date of 1184 BCE appears to be reasonable.

**Pelops's Arrival:** Because of the discovery of extensive correspondences between the Hittite and Egyptian kings, Trevor Bryce calculated that the rebellion of Uhhaziti against his Hittite overlords was crushed in 1316 BCE.

---

[322] Revisionist dating requires that the use of LHIIIC pottery stopped soon after Mycenai fell, and so it must be assumed that Medon moved the seat of his kingdom to Argos during the succeeding Iron Age. This is an example of where traditional dating works better, because the abandonment of the last palace (at Tiryns) by Medon corresponds with the end of the Bronze Age.

**Rise of Mycenai:** When Petrie discovered Mycenaian pottery at Egyptian sites along with pottery from the Eighteenth and Nineteenth Dynasties, he was able to date the Mycenaian Age as roughly between 1550 and 1070 BCE. Later discovers have led to a very minor revision (1580–1075 BCE).

## Section 2: Ancient Historians' Derived Dates

The very earliest Hellenic historians assumed that there was a long period of time between the fall of Troy and their own time. The mid fifth-century BCE historian Herodotos of Halikarnassos, the first historian whose book survives, assumed that the Trojan War had taken place some eight hundred years before his own time. Thucydides (*Peloponnesian War* i.18.1) states that the Spartan constitution was written by Lykourgos four hundred years before the end of the Peloponnesian War, or 804 BCE. The late fifth- and early fourth-century BCE Athenian orator Isokrates (vi.12) said that four hundred years of Spartan glory (control over Messenia) ended when the Thebans liberated the Messenians 370/69 BCE. However, there were very few events recorded during that long period.

Ephoros of Cyme, Theopompos of Khios, and Eratosthenes provided the most influential works on sequencing ancient events and establishing fixed dates.[323] Unfortunately, the works of these early historians are lost. Four important surviving Hellenic sources of ancient history are the works of the first-century BCE historians Diodoros of Agyrion on Sicily and Strabo, the late first- / early second-century CE historian Plutarch of Khaironeia, and the obscure second-century CE travel guide writer Pausanias (probably from Ionia). Pausanias usually follows Ephoros, Strabo follows Eratosthenes, and Diodoros takes a compromised middle path. The Roman Christian Era chronicles of Julius Africanus (early third century CE), Bishop Eusebios (early fourth century CE), St. Jerome (late fourth century CE), and George Syncellus (late eighth century CE) preserve some of the assumptions of the early historians.

Ephoros developed the first logical way to date major events. Ephoros, a student of Isokrates in Athens, wrote the first universal history during the middle of the fourth century BCE. His chronological work was based upon reviewing and synchronizing the archives of the leading city-states of Hellas with other documents. He calculated timeframes based upon generations; absolute dates were unavailable.

[323] Mait Koiv's article "Dating of Pheidon in Antiquity" provides clarity around the plethora of ancient dates by demonstrating that ancient historians calculated dates according to the synchronizations of either Ephoros or Theopompos.

Ephoros began his *History of the World* with the return of the Herakleids, which he thought was the first historic event outside of myth. From Herodotos and other sources, Ephoros knew that twenty-one kings, inclusively, ruled Sparta from the Herakleid Eurystheus through Kleombrotos, who had recently been killed in battle at Leuktra in 371 BCE. Like Herodotos (*Histories*, i.66), Ephoros assumed that three kings ruled per century on average. Ephoros calculated that the Herakleids must have returned in 1070/69 BCE. Following Thucydides (who said eighty years separated the fall of Troy and the Herakleids' return), Ephoros calculated the fall of Troy as 1150/49 BCE. The exhibit below depicts his calculations back to the Herakleids' return.

---

Exhibit A1.3—Ephorian Generations[324]

| | Agiad Sparta | Eurypontid Sparta | Argos | Korinth | Ephoros | Eratosthenes |
|---|---|---|---|---|---|---|
| 1 | Aristodemos | Aristodemos | Temenos | | 1070–1036 | 1104–1069 |
| 2 | Eurystheus | Prokles | Ceisos | Aletes | 1036–1002 | 1069–1034 |
| 3 | Agis | Sous | Medon | Ixion | 1002–969 | 1034–999 |
| 4 | Ekhestratos | Eurypon | Thestios | Agelas | 969–936 | 999–964 |
| 5 | Leobotas | Prytanis | Merops | Praxmnis | 936–902 | 964–929 |
| 6 | Doryssos | Eunomos | Aristodamidas | Bakkhais | 902–869 | 929–894 |
| 7 | Agesilaos | Polydeuktes | ? | Agelas | 869–836 | 894–859 |
| 8 | Arkhelaos | Kharillos | ? | Eudemos | 836–802 | 859–824 |
| 9 | Teleklos | Nikandros | Eratos | Aristodemos | 802–769 | 824–789 |
| 10 | Alkimenes | Theopompos | Pheidon | Telestes | 769–736 | 789–754 |
| 11 | Polydoros | Arkhidamos | Lakedes | | 736–702 | 754–719 |
| 12 | Eurykratos | Zeuxidamos | Meltas | | 702–669 | 719–684 |
| 13 | Anaxandros | Anaxidamos | | | 669–636 | 684–649 |
| 14 | Eurykratidas | Arkhidamos | | | 636–602 | 649–614 |

---

[324] Herodotos provides the Agiad kings list that was universally accepted by subsequent writers. The Eurypontid kings list was disputed. Reported herein is the list from Pausanias; he is thought to have used Ephoros as his source. Pausanias also provides the first three and last four Argive kings. Other names are supplemented from Diodoros (*Library of History*, vii.7), quoting Theopompos (Temenos, Ceisos, Thestios, Merops, Aristodamidas, and Pheidon—he omits Medon). Pausanias and Eusebios are the source of the Korinthian generational list. Eratosthenes assumed thirty-five-year generations, pushing back the return to 1104/3 BCE. Ephoros calculates his generations from 369, the year Messenia was liberated. Kleombrotos actually died in the decisive battle at Leuktra two years earlier.

| | | | | |
|---|---|---|---|---|
| 15 Leon | Agesiklos | | 602–569 | 614–579 |
| 16 Anaxandridas | Ariston | | 569–536 | 579–544 |
| 17 Kleomenes | Demartos | | 536–502 | 544–509 |
| 18 Leonidas | Leotykhides | | 502–469 | 509–474 |
| 19 Pleistoanax | Arkhidamos | | 469–436 | 474–439 |
| 20 Pausanias | Agis | | 436–402 | 439–404 |
| 21 Agesipolis | Kleombrotos | | 402–369 | 404–369 |

After establishing the timelines for each generation of Herakleid kings, Ephoros set the chronology for the paltry list of events occurring during their lifetimes. The key early events are included in the exhibit below (as well as the revised dates of Eratosthenes):

Exhibit A1.4—Dark Age Dates from Ephoros's Sequence of Events

| | Derived by: | | |
|---|---|---|---|
| Event (BCE) | Erato-sthenes | Ephoros | Comments |
| Herakleids return | 1104 | 1070 | Theopompos accepted Ephoros's start date. |
| Korinth conquered | 1078 | 1044 | |
| Dorians defeated at Athens | 1044 | 1044 | Did Eratosthenes assume a delay to fit the Athenian kings list? |
| Ionians migrate | 1043 | 1044 | Eratosthenes says this occurred one year after the return. |
| Krete conquered | 1037 | 1003 | This occurred at the beginning of the third generation and was carried out by Dorian Althaimenes. |
| Lykourgos reformed | 884 | 850 | Timaios and Eratosthenes say this occurred three hundred years after Troy fell. Eratosthenes adds that this to 108 years before the first Olympics. Thucydides says it occurred 400 year before the Pelopponesian War ended (804 BCE). |
| Homer writes | 876 | 848 | Ephoros says Homer wrote one hundred years before the first Olympics. |
| Asine sacked | 807 | 786 | Pausanias says the ninth-generation king Eratos sacked Asine. |
| Helos sacked | 788 | 768 | This was an early conquest of the tenth-generation Spartan king Alkamenes. |
| Olympic Games founded | 776 | 776? | Eratosthenes says this occurred 297 years before the Persian invasion. |

| | | | |
|---|---|---|---|
| Pheidon hosts Olympics | 776? | 748 | Isidoros says Pheidon was involved in the first Olympics. Pausanias, following Ephoros, says the Olympics began in 748 BCE. |
| Korinth regime changes | 775 | 747 | Nikolaos says Pheidon died during the Korinth regime change. |
| Syrakuse founded | 775 | 747 | Thucydides calculates the founding of Syrakuse to be 734/3 BCE. |
| First Messenian War occurs | 773–754 | 743–724 | Isokrates says Sparta ruled four hundred years (conquest in 770 BCE.) |
| Nauplia sacked | 675 | 645 | Pausanias says Nauplians fought in the Second Messenian War. |
| Pantaleon hosts Olympics | 672 | 644 | Apollodoros says Pantaleon of Pisa held games 104 years after the first games. Pausanias says 104 years passed between the Pheidon and Pantaleon games. |
| Second Messenian War occurs | 674–657 | 644–627 | The Second Messenian War is generally said to have begun eighty years after the First Messenian War ended. |

Theopompos (Philippika) proposed the only known ancient challenge to Ephoros's sequence of events. Theopompos, a younger contemporary of Ephoros and fellow student of Isokrates, appears to have agreed with Ephoros on most points. However, Theopompos disagreed with Ephoros by associating Pheidon with Lykourgos instead of with the Olympic Games, and he placed the founder of Syrakuse in the same generation as Pheidon.

Theopompos's assumption that Lykourgos and Pheidon were of the same generation makes sense, given that both men are famous for instituting bold reforms to the monarchies of their respective feudal city-states. Lykourgos reputedly wrote the Spartan constitution and instituted militaristic social reforms during the sixth or seventh generation, inclusively, from Temenos's brother Aristodemos.[325] Theopompos said Pheidon flourished during the

[325] Lykourgos's parentage was contrived. Simonides says his father was Prytanis (meaning "president"), but Plutarch said most writers considered him as the son of the Eurypontid king Eunomos (meaning "law-abiding"; eponym of the Eunomia—the social contract that Lykourgos wrote) by his second wife, Dionassa. (Neither king had a history of his own; their names imply they were probably inventions.)

sixth generation, and he may have been the first to suggest Lykourgos's reforms were in response to Pheidon's successes.[326]

Theopompos assumed an earlier foundation of Syrakuse because he places its founder in an earlier generation than Ephoros assumed. Ephoros stated that Telestes, the last Korinthian king, and Arkhias, the founder of Syrakuse, were of the same generation as Pheidon and in the tenth generation after Temenos. Theopompos stated that Arkhias was eleventh in line from Herakles and seventh from Temenos.[327] Thus Theopompos assumed Syrakuse was founded three or four generations earlier than Ephoros did. Theopompos agreed with Ephoros that Arkhias and Pheidon were of the same generation. The Ephorian dates work for traditional dating because the traditional scholar Nicholas Coldstream used Thucydides's date to calculate the age of early Hellenic pottery in Sicily, and Thucydides's dates were close to Ephoros's. Theopompos's hypothesis is that Syrakuse would have been founded during the ninth century BCE, at roughly the same

---

[326] The Parian Marble says that Pheidon introduced weights and measures (a precursor to coinage) into Hellas in 895 BCE; 299 years, or ten generations, from the fall of Troy, according to Timaios. The date follows Theopompos's theory that Pheidon lived during Lykourgos's generation. This date would drop to 884 BCE following Eratosthenes's date for the fall of Troy, well within his seventh generation. The Christian writer Eusebios proposed the later date 797 BCE, but he, too, clearly ties the timing to Lykourgos (whose reforms he proposed as having taken place one year later). But then Eusebios says the event occurred during the reign of the tenth generation Spartan king Alkamenes, the same generation Ephoros places Pheidon in. The date is a bit early for the tenth generation, but Eratosthenes did develop fixed dates that were outside of the generational guidelines to fit other factors.

[327] Most sources support the later Ephorian timeline for the founding of Syrakuse. The Scholiast of Apollonios and the Parian Marble follow Ephoros in stating that Telestes, the last Korinthian king, and Arkhias, the founder of Syrakuse, were of the same generation as Pheidon. The Parian Marble explicitly states that Arkhias was tenth in line from Temenos and adds that Syrakuse was founded during the twenty-first year of the Athenian archon Aiskhylos, which according to the chronology of Kastor of Rhodes is 758 BCE. Diodoros (*Library of History,* xiii.59) agrees with the 758 BCE founding date and adds that Selinos was founded twenty-three years earlier than Thucydides says and that the founding of Selinos helped date the founding of Syrakuse. Ephoros assumed the tenth generation thrived (769–736 BCE). Kastor's date fits within that timeline, and the 734/3T BCE date provided by Thucydides is very close. Eratosthenes apparently dated the settlement to 775 BCE. Eusebios provided a date of 736/5 BCE.

time as Pheidon and Lykourgos flourished. Theopompos's earlier dates are not supported by the archaeological finds at Syrakuse.[328]

Writing a century after Ephoros and Theopompos, Eratosthenes developed the first systematic dating scheme. His lost chronograph provide dates developed by using dating techniques developed over several centuries. The most important methods for dating events were the priestess of Hera lists from Argos, the archon lists from Athens, the ephor and king lists from Sparta, and the Olympiads. Synchronizing the lists was no easy task.

The main problem with these lists used for dating is that none track time reliably before the late fifth century BCE. The earliest fragment of an Athenian archon list uncovered so far dates to the 420s BCE. The archon list was first used for dating by the historian Hellanikos of Mitylene in his Attike history, which was written toward the end of the fifth century BCE. Herodotos, writing in Athens a generation earlier, references only one archon and he does not mention him to help date events. Hellanikos also wrote a lost chronology based upon the list of the priestesses of Hera in Argos. Plutarch says Hippias of Elis, also writing during the late fifth century BCE, drew up the first list of Olympic winners. Names were added later to each of the lists to extend them further back in time, but clearly they cannot be trusted.

Despite earlier references, our first direct evidence of dating by Olympiads is found in Eratosthenes.[329] Eratosthenes closely followed Ephoros's historical chronology but supplemented his findings with lists from the key city-states. One modest, but significant, change was assuming thirty-five years per generation, thereby pushing back the Herakleid return to 1104/3 BCE. His calculation was as follows: The fall of Troy to the Herakleids'

---

[328] Timaios tried to reconcile the two theories. First he suggested that there were twenty-seven Olympiads (108 years) for which the winners were not recorded and so Iphitos really dates to 884 BCE. In that way Pheidon and Lykourgos lived in the seventh generation and they lived during the time Iphitos founded the Olympic Games. Second, Timaios (*FGrHis,* 566) suggested there were two famous Spartans named Lykourgos; one during the time of Homer and the other during the founding of the Olympics. Timaios also tried to synchronize dates by comparing Olympiads, Athenian archons, the priestess of Hera list in Argos, and the list of Spartan ephors.

[329] However, Polybios, in *Histories,* claims that Timaios of Tauromenion (ca. 270 BCE) said Rome was founded 38 years after the first Olympic Games. Even earlier, Aristotle's student Dikaiarkhos of Messena (*FGrHis,* 58) asserted (late fourth century BCE) that Troy fell 306 years before the first Olympiad.

arrival in the Peloponnesos, 80 years; the colonization of Ionia by Ionians arriving from Attike, 60 years; the reforms of Lykourgos in Sparta, 159 years; the years preceding the first Olympiad, 108 years; and from there to Xerxes's invasion of Hellas, 297 years. Xerxes's invasion can confidently be dated to 480/79 BCE, and therefore Troy fell in 1184/3 BCE.

Eratosthenes's absolute dates were generally accepted once published, with some modifications by the second-century BCE historian Apollodoros of Athens. A few later historians could not resist an attempt to reconcile differences between the dates of Eratosthenes and Ephoros or to put forth their own dates within the sequence of events provided by Ephoros or Theopompos.

**Issue with the Dates Provided by Ancient Historians:** Traditional dates were once thought to be supported by the ancient historians. There are many examples of inconsistencies in the dates. The inconsistencies arise when comparing ancient Hellenic texts with traditional dating of the corresponding archaeological record. Kings were said to have fought wars and civil uprisings were said to have occurred during a time when not a single temple, house, or any structure at all was built anywhere in Hellas. Examples of the inconsistencies come from many locales.

**Sparta, Argos, Korinth, and Olympia:** It was counting back by Spartan kings that led Ephoros to assume that the Herakleids returned in 1070/69 BCE (and Eratosthenes to figure 1104/3 BCE). Although the number of generations fits well with traditional dating for the fall of Troy, dates for subsequent events do not work well for Lakonia. The problem is twofold. First, the calculated dates for Lykourgos's reforms and Messenian Wars do not fit with the archaeological record. Second, Sparta, unlike Argos, Korinth, and Athens, was not continually occupied throughout the Dark Age.

Based upon generations, historians following Ephoros's timeline for Pheidon (tenth generation) determined that his reign, the fall of the Korinthian monarchy, and the First Messenian War all occurred during the eighth century BCE. Following Theopompos's assumption (sixth or seventh generation) leads to even earlier ninth-century BCE dates. Either assumption is much too early according to more recent scientific and archaeological discoveries. Sparta, Argos, and Korinth were all very small hamlets and certainly not home to vibrant political struggles during the ninth or eighth centuries BCE; there was no construction of any kind undertaken in the Peloponnesos during that time. Additionally, coinage would not be introduced for two more centuries—something Pheidon is credited with. While there is evidence of a cult at Olympia during the eighth century BCE, there were no temples at that time, and it is highly unlikely that tiny Argos would consider the games valuable and prestigious enough to sponsor. Finally, Bakkhias was thought to have accomplished great things during his reign. What could those great things be if absolutely nothing was built in Korinth during his reign?

**Asine:** After the ninth-generation Spartan king Nikandros withdrew from his raid on Argeia, King Eratos of Argos drove the inhabitants of Asine (supporters of Sparta) from their city. According to ancient historians, this event occurred during the late ninth or early eighth century BCE. Since excavators found Protokorinthian pottery at the site, it could not have been abandoned before 725T BCE, when Protokorinthian pottery first appeared.

**Nauplia:** Pausanias says this city was sacked between the First and Second Messenian Wars. Both Eratosthenes (754–674 BCE) and Ephoros (724–644 BCE) assume eighty years passed between the wars. However, both dates are too early to fit the archaeological record from Nauplia that indicates the city was sacked while Early Korinthian pottery was produced (600–575T BCE).

**Athens and Ionia:** In rare agreement, historians following both Eratosthenes and Ephoros date the Ionian migration to 1044/3 BCE. The Parian Marble dates the event to 1077 BCE, fairly close to the traditional date for the end of the Mycenaian Age. Evidence for two ancient migrations to Ionia has been uncovered in the archaeological record. However, they occurred during the first half of LHIIIC (1195–1075T BCE) and sometime during the Protogeometric Age (1025–925T BCE), neither one supporting any of the proposed dates by ancient sources.

**Cyrene:** According to the foundation myth of Cyrene, the city was founded by Battos, who was reputedly seventeenth in line from the Argonaut Euphemos. According to myth, the Argonaut voyage was of the same generation as the fall of Troy VI, because Herakles and Telamon were involved in both. Traditional dating for the fall of Troy VI is 1220 BCE, and the voyage of the Argonauts happened roughly eleven years before that

(1231 BCE). Following Eratosthenes's assumption on generations, Battos would have founded Cyrene in 636 BCE (1231 BCE minus seventeen generations of thirty-five years each). This is pretty close to Eusebios's traditional date for the founding of Cyrene of 631T BCE. However, with a more reasonable assumption of twenty-five years per generation, Cyrene would have been founded in 807 BCE, nearly two centuries too early.

**Lesbos:** The Heroic (Late Bronze) Age Lapith hero Hippotes is said to have been the great-grandfather of Lesbos, the founder of an Aiolian colony on the large northern Aigaian island named after him. Although determining when the Aiolians first settled on Lesbos has proved difficult, the best indications show that it occurred early in the Geometric Age, which traditionally began in ca. 925T BCE. Thus Lesbos was founded ca. 900T BCE, thereby suggesting that Hippotes would have been born around 1040T BCE—during the bleakest part of the Dark Age and long after the Heroic Bronze Age had ended (900T BCE plus thirty-five years for Lesbos's age when he settled the island plus thirty-five years times three generations). Therefore, traditional dating does not work. By revisionist dating, Lesbos was settled in approximately 785R BCE, and therefore Hippotes would have flourished ca. 895R BCE—toward the end of the Bronze Age, but definitely within it (785R BCE plus thirty-five years plus twenty-five years times three generations).[330]

**Orkhomenos:** One of Europe's earliest historic references provides a powerful argument for a shorter Dark Age. The Amphiktryony of Kalaureia was a confederacy of ports around the Saronic Gulf that clearly cooperated on trade endeavors as sea travel revived during the early seventh century BCE; but the Amphiktryony also included Boiotian Orkhomenos, which was an important trading nation only during the earlier Mycenaian era. Thus it is possible that this alliance survived from the Bronze Age. The problem with traditional dating is that it requires us to believe that this alliance survived from the eleventh century BCE to the seventh century BCE—a span of 400 years. Additionally, traditional dating suggests Orkhomenos was abandoned for 100 years of the time frame of the alliance. Even the revisionist dating is problematic; the alliance would

[330] Assuming three generations per century or thirty-five years per generation doesn't change the date by much. If Lesbos migrated to the same-named island in 785 BCE, then Hippotes would have been active during 885–852 BCE or 890–855 BCE, respectively.

have had to last for 150 years. However, at least Orkhomenos was occupied throughout that period.

**Messenia:** Finally, the Theban general Epiminondas said he freed Messenia after 230 years of Spartan rule in 369 BCE. Thus, according to Epiminondas, the Spartans conquered Messenia in 599 BCE, very close to date suggested by revisionist chronology (and Epiminondas may have been exaggerating). This is much less than the 400 years that Isokrates says the Spartans ruled Messenia.

In conclusion, current archaeological evidence accepted by proponents of the traditional timelines does not support dates provided by ancient historians. The historians' dates are too early.

## Section 3: Revisionist Dating Proposed by Peter James

During the last century, numerous monuments and documents have been uncovered referencing the Late Bronze Age pharaohs of Egypt and the contemporary great-kings of the Hittites, Assyrians, and Babylonians, as well as of numerous smaller kingdoms. These artifacts have largely corroborated Manetho's kings list and the chronology of Petrie. The rich archaeological finds also support the traditional hypothesis that Egypt was united throughout the Late Bronze Age, the time period relevant to the Mycenaian Age of Hellas. Therefore, the traditional dating assumption that the Late Bronze Age period covered roughly five centuries still appears to be reasonable.

However, revisionist historians have challenged the length of the Egyptian TIP that followed the Bronze Age. James's book *Centuries of Darkness* gives a powerful voice to these doubts: his premise is that a long Dark Age was invented to fit a faulty Egyptian chronology. Arguments presented for changing dates include fallacies uncovered in the Sothic calendar, evidence that Egypt was divided into multiple fiefs during the Dark Age, and evidence indicating that ancient historians generally exaggerated the ancientness of their heroic and immediate pasts (dates once accepted as supporting the Egyptian chronology). All of these factors led James to propose a downward revision to the long-held dates by roughly 250 years.

**Sothic Calendar:** James mentions numerous reasons for doubting the accuracy of the Sothic Calendar in providing fixed dates. The most compelling argument against the Sothic Calendar is the need to assume that absolutely no adjustments or recalculations occurred during the several millennia that the calendar was in use. We know, for example, that Hellenistic and Roman officials were constantly tinkering with their own calendars, and the Bubastis stone found in 2004 CE and written in 238 BCE mentions a reform to the ancient Egyptian calendar. Scholars have largely given up trying to fix Mesopotamian dates using the Babylonian calendar, which is richly documented and constantly changed. Perhaps the reason that the Sothic Calendar works at all is that there is so little evidence to test it against. All of the traditional dates before the seventh century BCE were derived using the date provided by Censorinus and two relevant papyrus fragments. Such a small sample size certainly reduces confidence in the findings. Further doubts arise when considering that one of the texts, the Ebers papyrus, only references the convergence of Sothis's rising and the Nile's flooding; it does not give an exact date for the convergence of the two. To accept traditional dates, one must also accept certain assumptions regarding where along the Nile the floods occurred during the rising of Sothis and assumptions regarding lunar cycles, whose variations are difficult to calculate. As discussed above, the el-Lahon papyrus gives a fixed date of 1872 BCE if calculated at Memphis in the north, or 1830 BCE at Elephantine (Aswan) in the south. All of this adds to the uncertainty of Sothic derived dates.

**Egyptian Dark Age:** If the Sothic Calendar is dismissed for absolute dating, it is possible to reevaluate the length of the Dark Age and let the Bronze Age dates drop accordingly. Remember, for Manetho's TIP pharaohs to have ruled for four centuries requires that Egypt remained united throughout most of the period and that the reigns of fathers and sons did not overlap. Scholars following Kitchen's traditional dating admit that some overlaps occurred, but only during the Twenty-Second and Twenty-Third Dynasties.

Rich material evidence from the Bronze Age, the lack of it during the TIP, and historical documents from Hellas and Assyria all suggest the Dark Age was not four centuries long. Numerous monuments and documents dating to the Late Bronze Age indicate that Egypt was indeed unified during the Eighteenth, Nineteenth, and probably Twentieth Dynasties, but they also say that the reigns of fathers and sons usually overlapped. The relatively few monuments and texts uncovered from the TIP, as compared to periods before and afterward, do not support the theory of a unified Egypt and are inconclusive regarding the overlap of reigns. However, there is no reason to assume the practice of overlapping reigns stopped after the Bronze Age. The lack of material evidence is itself evidence that the period is overstated. For instance, some TIP kings have no monuments, such as Osorkon I (924–889 BCE) and Takeloth I (889–874 BCE; mentioned in only one genealogy); and others, such as Smendes[331] (1069–1038 BCE, in two monuments only), are only rarely referred to. The existence of

[331] Smendes started the Twenty-First Dynasty at Tanais while Herihor, priest of Amon, seized control of Upper Egypt to begin the Twenty-First Dynasty at Thebes a few years earlier (ca. 1075T BCE). The rich, unplundered tombs of the Twenty-First Dynasty pharaohs Psusennes I (1039–991T BCE) and Amenemope (993–984T BCE; son of Psusennes I) were found in Tanais in the delta.

kings without monuments is obviously suspicious. (Maybe there were not really four Osorkons and two Takeloths.) Those with few references may have only ruled a small part of Egypt. Assyrian invaders (early seventh century BCE) noted that twenty pharaohs ruled in Egypt at their arrival, at odds with Manetho's claim that the Twenty-Fifth Dynasty Nubian (Kushite) pharaohs Piye and Shabaqo (Shebaka) ruled a unified Egypt. Hellenic historians say the Dodecarchy—a coalition of the twelve kings—ruled Egypt before the foundation of the Twenty-sixth Dynasty by Psammetikhos I (664–610 BCE). Psammetikhos reunited Egypt during the first ten years of his rule. The historian Eusebios clearly stated that Egypt was not ruled by a succession of kings but rather that several kings ruled at the same time in different regions.

TIP inconsistencies with Petrie's chronology and the discovery of genealogy lists for priests, high officials, and the sacred Apis Bulls present additional issues with traditional dating. Petrie's chronology works well for the period of unified Egypt, and its TIP inconsistencies might be the result of Manetho's faulty assumption of a unified Egypt during the TIP. Genealogy lists for TIP priests, high officials, and the sacred Apis Bulls all suggest a considerably shorter TIP than four hundred years.[332] Uncovered texts list the birth date, death date, and life span of each Apis bull back to 664 BCE.

Because Egyptian artifacts were found alongside native artifacts throughout Europe, Anatolia, Nubia, and the Near East, it became necessary to add Dark Ages to those regions as well. In each case, abundant Bronze Age finds are followed by a long period yielding alarmingly few artifacts. In each case, the region becomes nearly uninhabited and then, miraculously (and suspiciously), after hundreds of years, cultures closely related to the long-lost Bronze civilizations arose in the same locations. While it is true

---

[332] According to First Kings 14:25–26, it was the Egyptian pharaoh Shishak who sacked Jerusalem. The fall of Jerusalem can be roughly dated to 925 BCE by way of an Assyrian reference to the event. Traditionally, the Libyan founder of the Twenty-Second Dynasty, Sheshonq I (945–924T BCE), has been identified with Shishak. Records surviving from the reign of Sheshong I state that he campaigned in Palestine, but they don't mention Jerusalem. We also have inscriptions from Byblos (Phoenicia) suggesting that Sheshonq I ruled ca. 800 BCE. By revisionist dating, Ramesses III (933–902R BCE) would be the assailant of Jerusalem mentioned in the book of Kings. Discovered documents indicate that Ramesses III reasserted Egyptian rule in Palestine (after the unruly Sea Peoples arrived). Also, "Shishak" could be an Israelite corruption for "Sessi," a common abbreviation for "Ramesses." This would mean David and Solomon lived during the Bronze Age, not the Iron Age.

that the Bronze Age civilizations collapsed, massive migrations occurred, and a period of relative poverty followed, the length of the impoverished time appears to have been greatly exaggerated. James describes how local histories in every region affected by the Dark Age make more sense without the Egyptian-imposed extended Dark Age.

**Assyrian Kings List:** James challenges the reliability of the Assyrian kings list used to validate the Egyptian kings list (for kings living prior to 911 BCE). As he notes, the purpose of the list was to stress the antiquity and continuity of Assyrian institutions, not to provide a historically accurate account. The lower value placed on accurately presenting the kings is evident in surviving inscriptions that do not agree with the kings list. Some known kings are omitted for having committed offenses, other kings are included who do not have any supporting monumental evidence, and others had their parentage changed to buttress continuity. Finally, two versions of the list have been subsequently found, and they do not completely agree with the first list or with each other.

**Assyrian Constellations:** The Roman-era Hellenic astronomer Ptolemy listed forty-eight constellations. Professor Bradley Schaefer noted that some thirty of these constellations were borrowed from the Assyrians. Schaefer argued that cuneiform texts from Mesopotamia demonstrate that the positions for these constellations can be fixed to the skies over Assyria during the late twelfth century BCE. Since Schaefer provides an absolute date, it can be compared to traditional and revisionist dates. The late twelfth century BCE was a time of great prosperity in Assyria according to revisionist dating, while it represents a time that Assyria was under siege by barbarians at the end of the Bronze Age according to traditional dating. It seems more likely that the development of constellations occurred during a prosperous age.

**Anatolian Dark Age:** Probably the most compelling reason Dark Age dates ought to be revised downward is found in Phrygian history. The Phrygians are first mentioned in connection with the Trojan War, and they settled around the city after the war. From there they spread across the Anatolian plateau, which had been without a central government since the demise of the Hittite Empire. Archaeologist Rodney Young found evidence of (Bronze Age) Hittites and (Iron Age) Phrygians having lived together for some time in the Anatolian city of Gordion. Traditional dating has yet to find a good explanation for how these two peoples could have coexisted.

Archaeologist Blegen found evidence at Troy to confirm assertions from ancient Hellenic historians that settlers arrived in Ilion from Thrace (the Balkans) sometime after the Trojan War. Blegen found cruder Balkan Complex (Thracian) pottery alongside the gray ware pottery of the Trojans sometime after Troy VIIA was destroyed.[333] Apparently the two groups coexisted peacefully. Herodotos provides a name for these people, saying that they were Phrygians, a Thracian people (Strabo's *Geography*, xiv.5.29, concurs). Homer lists Phrygian and Thracian tribes among the allies of the Trojans and says that the Phrygians already lived in their traditional Anatolian homeland before the war. Homer's statements would not necessarily be at odds with Herodotos if the Phrygians entered Anatolia by way of the Sangarios River and later moved into Ilion and onto the Anatolian plateau.

Early Phrygian pottery, ivory, and metalwork shows close parallels to products from the Hellenic Geometric Age and thereby provides confidence in a relative date for their migration inland onto the Anatolian Plateau—a date after the Bronze Age ended. Pottery finds suggest that the migration of these Balkan people, the Phrygians, was unchallenged; no central government had arisen to replace the Hittite Empire, which collapsed shortly after Troy fell. The Phrygians appear to have been peacefully accepted by Hittite inhabitants remaining at Gordion—perhaps because they were allies of the Trojans and the Hittites list Wilusa (early Hellenic "Wilos" or "Ilion") as one of their most loyal vassals. Farther east, sediment layers at Hattusa (capital of the Hittite Empire) indicate that the Phrygians who settled there arrived not long after the Hittites abandoned the city.

Meanwhile, farther east, Assyrian records tell of the Muskhi, who can be identified with the Phrygians who invaded their nation. (It has been suggested that the name "Muskhi" derives from "Mysia," the name of the region in which Ilion/Troy belongs and where the Phrygians settled very early on.) Assyrian king Tiglath-pileser says that the Mushki had ruled bordering lands (Anatolia) for fifty years and had never been defeated. He

[333] Most of the Hellenic pottery found at Troy VIIA just before it was sacked was LHIIIB, but there was some LHIIIC pottery as well. Thus the fall of Troy must have occurred shortly after the LHIIIC pottery era began.

claims to have defeated them in the year of his ascension. Nothing further is mentioned of the Muskhi until Assyrian king Sargon II says that his chief rival in Anatolia was the Muskhi king Mita. King Mita supported the Neo-Hittite kingdoms of southeastern Anatolia and Syria against the Assyrians. (Apparently the two peoples were allies for a very long time, for the Phrygians had been allies of the Trojans and Hittites during the Trojan War.) Sargon defeated Mita and completed his conquest of the Neo-Hittite states. Mita fled to western Anatolia and entered Hellenic literature as the wealthy Phrygian king Midas, clearly identifying the Mushki with the Phrygians. Others fled into the highlands and became the ancestors of the Armenians.[334] Before the Assyrians could press their advantage, nomadic Kimmerian warriors attacked the cities of Anatolia, seeking plunder. Both Midas and Sargon lost their lives fighting against this terrifying tribe, the first horseback-riding invaders.

Traditional dating poorly explains the mythic, physical, and historical references to the Phrygians. The Phrygians first settled in Anatolia along the lower Sangarios River by the early twelfth century BCE. Just as Herodotos says, the Phrygians seem to have settled peacefully among the Trojans sometime after the Trojan War (1184T BCE). They quickly advanced across the central Anatolia plateau, where central government had vanished with the collapse of the Hittite Empire. They settled peacefully among the Hittite citizens of Gordion. The eastern advance of the Phrygians was blocked by the Assyrians, who called them the Mushki. After fifty years of skirmishes, the Assyrian king Tiglath-pileser I (1117–1077T BCE) defeated them (1117T BCE). The Mushki withdrew and apparently vanished. For the next two centuries, the plateau and highlands of Anatolia became virtually uninhabited; there is no archaeological evidence at all. Then, miraculously, around 950T BCE, the Phrygians/Mushki returned to central Anatolia, manufacturing exactly the same pottery they had used two centuries earlier. They mingled with a remnant Hittite population that had somehow survived for two centuries at Gordion without leaving any material evidence during the intervening time. Two centuries after the Phrygians returned to central Anatolia, the Mushki reappeared to challenge the Assyrians, who were themselves recovering from a long period of near nonexistence. The Mushki became allies of the Neo-Hittite states (which were also emerging from a long period without material

[334] In the language of the neighboring Georgians, the Armenians are called Mekhi. Herodotos says the Armenians were Phrygian colonists.

evidence) against the invading Assyrians. Assyrian king Sargon defeated them and completed his conquest of the Neo-Hittite states. Some of the Mushki fled to Phrygia under Mita/Midas,[335] while others remained in the highlands and became the ancestors of the Armenians.

Revisionist dating provides a better explanation of Phrygian history so long as it is assumed that it was Tiglath-pileser III who defeated the Mushki. Thracian-Balkan (proto-Phrygian) people arrived in Anatolia and settled along the lower Sangarios River before the Trojan War and established friendly relations with the Hittites and Trojans. As vassals of the Hittites, they served as allies of the Trojans (934R BCE). After the war, they settled peacefully in Ilion (910R BCE). Clearly influenced by interactions with the Hellenes, the Phrygians migrated onto the central Anatolia plateau, which had suffered significant population decline after the collapse of the Hittite Empire. Among the places they settled was Gordion, where they were peacefully accepted by the Hittite citizens of the city (760R BCE). Their eastern advance met resistance in the highlands east of the Anatolian plateau. There they fought the Urartians and Assyrians. The Assyrian king Tiglath-pileser III (744–727 BCE) defeated them in battle and ended their advance (744 BCE). After Assyrian king Sargon II (727–705 BCE) defeated Mushki king Mita, he completed his conquest of the Neo-Hittite city-states of southeastern Anatolia and northern Syria (713 BCE). Mita withdrew to Gordion, while some Mushki withdrew into the Anatolian highlands, where they conquered the Urartians and evolved into the Armenians. Mita and Sargon both died fighting the nomadic Kimmerians.

The traditional timeline leaves many questions that do not arise with revisionist dating. How could the Phrygians have settled on the Anatolian plateau during the Bronze Age when their earliest pottery is clearly related to Iron Age Hellenic geometric pottery? How could it be that from the Stone Age to today the only time Anatolia was virtually uninhabited was during the Early Iron Age? How could it be that Phrygian and Hittite cultures vanished and then miraculously reappeared after hundreds of years? Although these questions do not arise with revisionist dating, the logic of the revisionist history depends upon the assumption that Tiglath-pileser III (not I) defeated the Mushki. If that assumption is false, then

[335] Midas may have been a titular name. Hittite records mention a King Midash on its northern frontier just before the Hittite demise, which is long before historic King Midas by all accounts.

revisionist dating cannot explain who the Mushki were, where they came from, or how their king Mita became king of the Phrygians, because there is no evidence that any tribe other than the Phrygians settled in Phrygia at that time.

**Hellenic Dark Age:** Traditional dates require a long Dark Age in Hellas as well. Even though archaeologists have been searching for over 150 years, they have uncovered suspiciously little material evidence for such a long epoch. During the three centuries (traditionally) between the use of LHIIIC and Middle Geometric pottery, there is evidence for only one house being built, and no temples, walls, or tombs in all of Hellas. Only a few pottery shards remain to indicate human life existed in Hellas at all. Yet despite claiming Hellas was virtually uninhabited for centuries, the traditional timeline theory maintains that a very similar civilization miraculously sprang up at the same sites after hundreds of years.

Unfortunately, there are no discoveries of contacts with Near Eastern states to help solve this dilemma. During the Dark Age, the Hellenes apparently did not trade with the Egyptians and traded only sparingly with the people living along the Syrian, Phoenician, and Palestinian coasts. The last Egyptian goods associated with Mycenaian pottery come from Palestine and not Egypt; they were goods from the reign of Ramesses III of the Twentieth Dynasty (1183–1152T BCE) and were found with LHIIIC pottery. The next commingled find of Egyptian and Hellenic goods is a scarab from the reign of the Twenty-Fourth Dynasty pharaoh Baken-renef (Hellenic "Bokkhoris"; 720–715T BCE) found buried with very early Protokorinthian pottery in a tomb at Pithekousai, a Hellenic colony off the coast of Italy near Kumai and Neapolis (Naples). Although some trade continued with the Near East, most of the Hellenic pottery discovered there was unfortunately not found in undisturbed sites and therefore cannot be accurately sequenced. Those few that have been uncovered at undisturbed sites cannot be conclusively dated because they were not found together with artifacts with known local kings (who in turn can usually be accurately dated by correspondences with the Assyrians).

**Hellenic Exaggerations:** All of this evidence indicates that the length of the Hellenic Dark Age needs to be shortened and that its end probably occurred later than previously thought. This reduction is necessary because there is evidence that the ancient Hellenes exaggerated the time of their ancestors and because of recent research on early pottery finds. Examples from Italy, Lydia, and Assyria demonstrate this.

Using references from Herodotos and Thucydides, as well as the scholarly conclusions of Coldstream, historians have long accepted that Syrakuse on Sicily was founded in 734/733 BCE. The founding of Syrakuse has been considered a pivotal point in the transition out of the Dark Age and into fixed dates for Hellas. The discovery of an Egyptian scarab at Pithekousai led James to propose a downward revision of Thucydides dates for the founding of Syrakuse. Pottery evidence clearly indicates that Pithekousai was founded before Syrakuse; it is probably the oldest Hellenic colony in the western Mediterranean. A scarab from Bokkhoris's reign would have taken some time to reach Pithekousai and then be interred with one of the earliest settlers to be buried there. Therefore Pithekousai could not have been founded much before 700 BCE, and Syrakuse probably dates to the early seventh century BCE—not 734/3 BCE, as Thucydides stated. James proposed that it is probably safe to assume that Thucydides's dates are at least twenty-five years and possibly as many as forty years too early. Nevertheless, James expressed admiration that Thucydides could have so closely calculated dates three hundred years before his time using the inaccurate, exaggerated, and conflicting records he had to work with. Thucydides was able to do so using genealogies and not, as later (and less accurate) historians did, with chronological dates.

Another reason for reducing the date of the end of the Dark Age comes by comparing references to Lydian king Gyges from Herodotos and Assyrian records. Using Herodotos as a guide, it is possible to calculate the dates of Gyges's reign as 714–686 BCE. Assyrian records speak of Guggi, king of Luddi and ally of Ammetikhos I of Egypt (although he desperately asked Assyrian king Ashurbanipal [668–627 BCE] for assistance against the Kimmerians in 663 BCE). Judging by Assyrian references, Gyges (Guggi) probably died shortly after 650 BCE. Given that Assyrian dates were proven to be accurate for that time period, Herodotos's dates must be some thirty-five years too early.

Even more startling are the Hellenic and Roman dates provided for the fall of the Assyrian Empire. Because Assyrian dates are trustworthy as far back as 911 BCE, we know that the Medes and Babylonians conquered the Assyrian capital of Nineveh in 612 BCE, ending the reign of King

Sin-shar-ishkun (627–612 BCE). Diodoros (*Library of History*, ii.23–27), following the late fifth- / early fourth-century BCE physician Ktesias of Knidos (Persica), calls the last king Sardanapallos, and he was provided with some colorful stories. The Hellenes tied his momentous demise to key events in Hellenic history. The first-century BCE historian Kastor of Rhodes says Sardanapallos ruled from 896–887 BCE, assuming he follows Ktesias chronology. The start of Sardanapallos's reign is then synchronized with Pheidon's date for weights and measures. According to Velleius Paterculus, the Assyrian destruction was synchronized in the same year as Lykourgos's reforms and the founding of the Agraid Dynasty in Macedonia (818 BCE). Alternatively, the seventh-century CE Archbishop Isidoros of Seville ties the Medes' conquest of Assyria to the founding of the Olympics and the founding of the Agriad Dynasty in Macedonia (776 BCE). All of the ancient historian's dates are wide of the mark.

While modern scholars and mythic genealogies agree on a five-century-long Mycenaian Age (as discussed above), the ancient historians exaggerated its length, just as they did for subsequent epochs. Eusebios calculated the time span between the fall of Troy and the ascension of Phoroneus as 622 years, which is 226 years longer than the time frame agreed upon by traditional and revisionist dating (which was 396 years long; 1580/1330 BCE minus 1184/934 BCE). However, recent scientific evidence may support Eusebios.

The book *Centuries of Darkness* presents ample evidence to suggest that traditional dating is flawed and ought to be reassessed. Too much faith has been placed in the absolute dating derived by a few references to the Sothic calendar. Evidence from Phrygia, Hellas, Egypt, and elsewhere points to a Dark Age roughly 250 years shorter than traditionally thought. As indicated above, Hellenic mythical and historical references strongly support revisionist dating. While James deftly showed weaknesses in traditional dating assumptions, his own revisionist dating has been vehemently challenged.

## Section 4: Deriving Revisionist Clevenger Chronology Dates

The meager mythic, genealogical, and historical data available for the period that immediately followed the Bronze Age clearly supports the revisionist theory espoused by James. The length of the time between the sixth century BCE and the Bronze Age appears to have been exaggerated by both ancient historians and the traditional timeline when compared with archaeological finds.

Working backward in time, the key points that the Clevenger Chronology is based upon are when the following events occurred:

- the Persians invaded Hellas
- Pheidon seized power in Argos
- the Herakleids successfully returned to the Peloponnesos
- Troy VII and VI were destroyed (and which one Agamemnon sacked)
- Uhhaziti (Pelops) fled Arzawa (Lydia)
- the first shaft graves were dug at Mycenai (by the first king—Phoroneus)

**Persian Invasions:** The earliest historical events in Hellas that traditional and revisionist theories agree upon are related to the Persian attacks on Hellas. Herodotos and other historians describe events beginning with the reign of Great-King Cyrus (559–531 BCE). The reigns of Persian great-kings can be verified using an Assyrian calendar that has been generally accepted as accurate during that time period. Because Persian records mention Great-King Xerxes's invasion of Hellas in 480 BCE, this date is indisputable. It is upon this fixed date that the Clevenger Chronology hinges.

**Rise of Pheidon:** The lifetime of Pheidon of Argos is pivotal in dating ancient events. He, like the lawgiver Lykourgos of Sparta, whom he is often associated with, belongs to a shadowy time when legend and history meet. The fourth-century BCE philosopher Aristotle of Stagira (*Politics*) tells us that Pheidon was a king who took on tyrannical powers. The genealogy of the Orthagorid family of Korinth recorded by Herodotos provides a means to calculate when King Pheidon of Argos flourished without reference to dates provided by ancient historians such as Ephoros and Eratosthenes. The resulting genealogical dates provide excellent correlations to the discoveries of archaeologists at Hellenic sites, while the dates provided by historians do not (as discussed in section 2: "Ancient Historians' Derived Dates").

Herodotos and others inform us that an Orthagorid named Kleisthenes founded the Athenian democracy a generation before the Persian defeat at Salamis (480 BCE). Aristotle provides the traditional date for the establishment of the Athenian democracy as 508 BCE, the year Isagoras was reputed to be archon. However, according to Athenian custom, aspiring politicians became archon early in their careers as a stepping-stone to real power. Therefore, it should be assumed that Isagoras did not obtain true political muscle until well after his archonship. With Spartan assistance, Isagoras briefly became a tyrant in Athens, but he was driven out by the democrats led by Kleisthenes. Since the Council of Five Hundred, which the great democratic reformer Kleisthenes created, did not swear their first office oath until 501 BCE (according to Aristotle), it is more likely that the democratic reforms were carried out then and not earlier.

The following exhibit works backward in time from the Athenian father of democracy, Kleisthenes, to his great-great-uncle Orthagoras—an early tyrant of Sicyon and, therefore, a likely contemporary of the first Hellenic tyrant, Pheidon of Argos (who was not an Orthagorid). Since we can be certain that Kleisthenes flourished a generation before the Persian War, the exhibit shows that it is reasonable to assume that Orthagoras seized power ca. 595 BCE. Since Pheidon was the first to usurp power as a tyrant, he must have done so somewhat earlier, say ca. 600 BCE.

Exhibit A1.5—Dating Pheidon by the Orthagorids

| Orthagorid | Maturity (BCE)[336] | Comments |
|---|---|---|
| Kleisthenes | 515–490 | This son of Agarista established the Athenian democracy. |
| Agarista | 540–515 | Kleisthenes's daughter married Megakles of Athens. |
| Kleisthenes | 565–540 | This son of Aristonymos restored Orthagorid rule in Sicyon. |
| Aristonymos | 590–565 | The sons of Myron, including Aristonymos, did not rule Sicyon. |
| Myron | 615–590 | Myron succeeded his brother Orthagoras as tyrant of Sicyon. |
| Orthagoras | 615–590 | Orthagoras Seized power in Sicyon in 595 BCE. |

[336] Herein defined as the time of prime political power, which began roughly when a man reached the age of thirty-five.

The Orthagorid family tree provided by Herodotos suggests Pheidon flourished no sooner than the late seventh century BCE and more likely during the early sixth century BCE. There are other historical references about Pheidon suggesting he lived during the sixth century BCE. Ephoros (quoted by Strabo in *Geography*, viii 3.33) and Parian Marble credit Pheidon with introducing currency into Hellas. The earliest electrum coins have been found in the temple of Artemis in Ephesos and date to ca. 560 BCE (or somewhat earlier). The Lydians stamped electrum, a naturally occurring combination of silver and gold collected from the banks of the Paktolos River, into coins of standard weight. The coins were quickly adopted as the median of exchange. However, even using Herodotos-derived dates, Pheidon lived too early to have introduced money, but more plausibly he was also credited with the invention of standard weights and measures—a necessary precursor to the adoption of money. Finally, dating to the middle of the sixth century BCE were Pheidon's son Lakedes's (Leokides's) unsuccessful bid for Kleisthenes's daughter Agarista (to be a suitor would require lowering the dates for Pheidon even further) and the rise to power of Pheidon's grandson Meltas, whom Ephoros says (quoted by Pausanias in *Guide to Greece*, ii.19.2) was the last king of Argos.

Archaeological evidence also supports a late seventh- or early sixth-century BCE date for Pheidon. Excavations at major sites in Hellas all indicate that the emerging cities of Hellas were not of sufficient size to support sophisticated civic institutions much before the late seventh century BCE. The construction of stone temples is probably the best indicator of sophisticated civic development in Hellas. To determine when early temples were constructed, archaeologists have relied on their representation in pottery. The earliest depiction of a stone temple is found on Late Protokorinthian pottery in Korinth and has been dated to the middle seventh century BCE by traditional dating and the late seventh century BCE by revisionist dating. Thus, stone temples were first constructed shortly before the time the Orthagorid genealogy suggests Pheidon flourished. The Olympic Games were probably not economically valuable enough to fight over before stone temples and thesauroi (treasury houses) were built at Olympia—something Pheidon reputedly did.

**Herakleids' Return:** The Dorians (Herakleids) claimed to be descendants of the greatest Hellenic hero, Herakles. According to legend, under the leadership of Temenos the Herakleids sacked Mycenai. They represent the new political order in Hellas that came about at the end of the Bronze Age. Pheidon was one of these kings who took on tyrannical powers. Unfortunately there are no historic or mythic events between the Herakleids' return and Pheidon's rise to help calculate dates.

To determine what date the Dorians first came to power requires an assumption as to how many kings ruled, how long each king ruled, and when Pheidon flourished. Ephoros probably used the work of the fifth-century BCE genealogist Akusilaos of Argos for his list of Argive kings. Akusilaos probably had access to city archives that held the kings list. As with Assyrian kings lists, Hellenic kings lists were meant to stress the continuity of Hellenic institutions; that is why they all claimed that each king was succeeded by his son and unnaturally long reigns were ascribed to them. Nevertheless, there is no other source available, and so the Herakleid kings list from Argos will be used. Following Ephoros, Pausanias (*Guide to Greece*) says twelve Dorian kings ruled Argos, although he lists only the first three (Temenos, Ceisos, and Medon) and the last four (Eratos, Pheidon, Lakedes [Leokides], and Meltas) kings.[337] Following Theopompos, Diodoros (*Library of History,* vii.17) adds three more: Thestios, Merops, and Aristodamidas.

Accepting that there are ten generations, inclusively, between Temenos and Pheidon, and that Pheidon flourished during the early sixth century BCE, the remaining variable to calculate when the Herakleids returned is the length of time each generation ruled. Most ancient historians, including Herodotos and Ephoros, assumed thirty-three and one-third years per generation, which rounds nicely to three kings per century. Eratosthenes assumed slightly longer generations of thirty-five years. However, Herodotos said the twenty-two Herakleid kings of Lydia ruled twenty-three years each on average. Twenty-two mythic kings ruled Mycenai during the Late Bronze Age (from Phoroneus to Tisamenos). These mythic kings covered a span of only nineteen or twenty generations (see Addendum 2, "List of Kings," for details on the Mycenaian kings), thus resulting in twenty-four- to twenty-five-year reigns per generation if, as

[337] According to Pausanias's *Guide to Greece*, ii.19.1–2, ii.36, Meltas, son of Lakedes, was the last hereditary king. Since Ephoros says Pheidon was the tenth king and Lakedes was the eleventh, we can identify Lakedes with Leokides, whom Herodotos, in *Histories*, vi.126, says was the son of Pheidon and suitor of the Orthagorid Agarista. Technically only ten of the Dorian kings ruled from Argos; the first two ruled from Tiryns. Pausanias says Medon, the third Dorian king, moved the capital from Tiryns to Argos.

both traditional and revisionist theories say, five centuries elapsed between the rise and fall of Mycenai. Similarly, the fourteen historic Spartan kings from Kleomenes I (the first who can be dated reliably) to Kleomenes III (who fled before a Macedonian army to Egypt) spanned approximately ten generations, which means each generation ruled for twenty-nine and seven-tenths years on average (see Addendum 2, "List of Kings," for details on the Lakonian kings). These figures exclude King Agesipolis III, who ruled only five years, in exile, after Sparta fell to Macedonia. All of the proposed generation lengths, and presumably any in between, are viable, although it is unlikely that generations during the harsh Dark Age lived as long as ancient historians claimed.

Exhibit A1.6—Argos Dating of the Herakleids' Return

| Years per reign | 21.2 | 25 | 29.7 | 33.3 | 35 |
|---|---|---|---|---|---|
| Pheidon's rule (BCE) | 612 | 612 | 612 | 612 | 612 |
| Nine Dorian kings (years) | 191 | 225 | 267 | 300 | 315 |
| Herakleids' return (BCE) | 803 | 837 | 879 | 912 | 927 |

Since Pheidon is assumed to have ruled some two hundred years later than the historians who derived dates from chronologies thought, obviously none of the dates for the return of the Herakleids in the exhibit above fit with the traditional date of 1125 BCE for the fall of Mycenai, or with Ephoros's (1070 BCE) or Eratosthenes's (1104 BCE) date for the return of the Herakleids. However, within the range above is the date James suggests for the fall of Mycenai—875 BCE, 250 years later than traditionally believed.

While the length of generations provides a range of reasonable timelines, it is necessary to consider the archaeological record and other references to the era to pinpoint the most reasonable date for the return of the Herakleids. Unfortunately there are very few historic or mythic references to the time before Pheidon became tyrant and after the Herakleids returned to Argeia (evidenced in the archaeological record as the sack of Mycenai). Hence, much of this time period is aptly referred to as the Dark Age. A few relevant references concern Libya and Sicily.

The foundation myth for Cyrene in Libya gives intriguing information useful for deriving the length of the Dark Age. Pindar (*Pythian Ode,*

iv) says the founder of Cyrene, Battos, was seventeenth in line from the Argonaut Euphemos. Robin Osborne argues in his book *Greece in the Making 1200–479 BC* that Cyrene was founded in 620 BCE (not far off the date of 631 BCE provided by Eusebios). Assuming the Argonauts sailed 127 years before the return of the Herakleids,[338] the length of generations as above, and a founding date for Cyrene of 620 BCE, the following exhibit gives possible dates for the Herakleids' return.

Exhibit A1.7—Cyrene Dating of the Herakleids' Return

| Years per reign | 21.2 | 25 | 29.7 | 33.3 | 35 |
|---|---|---|---|---|---|
| Founding of Cyrene (BCE) | 620 | 620 | 620 | 620 | 620 |
| 17 generations (years) | 360 | 425 | 505 | 567 | 595 |
| Voyage of the Argos (BCE) | 979 | 1044 | 1124 | 1186 | 1214 |
| Herakleids' return (BCE) | 852 | 917 | 997 | 1059 | 1087 |

The wide range of dates provided in the exhibit above does not support traditional dating at all; however, it does support revisionist dating at the low end. The plausible date range overlap between exhibits A1.5 and A1.6 is between 852 and 923 BCE. These dates fit within the range proposed by James.

So what date is to be chosen for the Herakleid return? Since the entire date range is too late to fit traditional timelines, revisionist dating must be considered. James argues that Troy fell some 250 years later than traditionally believed: 934 BCE. One timeframe the ancient historians agreed upon was that Troy fell 80 years before the Herakleids returned. Therefore, the successful return occurred in 854 BCE—near the low end of the plausible date range suggested by exhibits A1.5 and A1.6. The

[338] To summarize, the myths indicate that the Argonaut voyage was of the same generation as the fall of Troy VI because Herakles and Telamon participated in both events. Traditional dating for the first sack of Troy is 1220 BCE, and the voyage of the Argonauts happened roughly 11 years before that. The second sack of Troy, by Agamemnon, traditionally occurred in 1184 BCE, and Thucydides says the Herakleids returned to the Peloponnesos 80 years later. Thus, the Argonaut voyage occurred 127 years earlier (80 years to the return plus 36 years between the falls of Troy VI and VII plus 11 years earlier for the Argonauts). In other words, the Argos sailed 48 years before Troy VII fell. The Parian Marble assumed the voyage occurred in 1263 BCE (54 years before the fall of Troy VII in 1209 BCE), and Eratosthenes postulated 1225 BCE (41 years before the fall of Troy VII in 1184 BCE).

Bronze Age lingered for only a short time after Mycenai fell, but it must have ended around 840 BCE.

In conclusion, a general timeline for the Arkhaic and Dark Ages has been created using surviving Iron Age genealogies of the fourth-century BCE historian Ephoros but based upon the timeframe for Pheidon inferred by Herodotos. Although originally used to calculate an early date for the fall of Troy, the genealogy provided by Ephoros has been shown to also fit very well with the revisionist dating proposed by James. The revised dates indicate that the Arkhaic and Dark Ages cover 340 years (840–500 BCE), some 185 years less than the 525 years assumed in traditional dating (1050–525 BCE). The date for Pheidon and the length of the generations explain the difference.

**Key Bronze Age Mythic Genealogies:** As with the Dark Age, genealogies provide valuable insights for determining Late Bronze Age timelines. The Late Bronze Age, which immediately preceded the Dark Age, is well documented. Numerous Late Bronze Age discoveries in Egypt, Hellas, and elsewhere have resulted in accepting the time between the rise and fall of Mycenai as lasting approximately five centuries. (However, recent scientific tests may suggest otherwise.) Incredibly, the time line for the mythic kings of Mycenai fits comfortably within that five-century constraint. It may be a coincidence, or as with the discoveries of Troy and Mycenai themselves, the myths may retain kernels of true history. The myths also support a shorter Dark Age and thereby bring the great seventh-century BCE poet Homer of Ionia to within three hundred years of the fabled war he so eloquently described.

The Clevenger Chronology timeline for the Late Bronze Age weaves genealogies with a few important dates. There were two families whose timelines are critical for the whole mythic history to fit the chronological dates derived for the falls of Mycenai, Troy VII, and Troy VI; the arrival of Pelops; and the rise of Mycenai: the families of Akrisios of Mycenai and Laios of Thebes. Working back to King Akrisios, we start with his descendant Temenos, who led the Herakleids' successful return to the Peloponnesos.[339]

Exhibit A1.8—Descendants of Akrisios

| Akrisid | Suggested Birth Year | Comments |
|---|---|---|
| Temenos | 895 | Led successful Herakleid return in 854 BCE |
| Aristomakhos | 925 | Died leading second Herakleid return in 890 BCE |
| Kleodaios | 956 | |
| Hyllos | 975 | Died leading first Herakleid return in 949 BCE |
| Herakles | 1011 | Sacked Troy VI in 970 BCE |
| Alkmene | 1029 | Zeus kept sun down three days to enjoy Alkmene |
| Anaxo | 1046 | |
| Alkaios | 1070 | |
| Perseus | 1094 | Welcomed Pelops to Hellas in 1066 BCE |
| Danae | 1111 | Zeus rained down upon her in the tomb she was shut in |
| Akrisios | 1135 | Fought his twin brother in the womb and for Mycenai |

The timeline presented in the exhibit above matches Classical Hellas custom, in which men married in their early to middle twenties and women in their late teens. Exceptions come from the myths themselves: Perseus started his family at a young age after slaying Medousa, and Hyllos did likewise on the will of his dying father, Herakles. Princess Anaxo was somewhat young, but throughout history there have been examples of girls robbed of their childhood at even younger ages.

The city of Thebes also provides a critical constraint on Late Bronze Age dating. To fit popular stories about Herakles, Pelops's son Kreon had to rule Thebes before Laios, and Herakles had to begin his labors during the reign of Kreon. Laios's descendants Oidipous, Polyneices/Eteokles, and

[339] Given three generations per century, Hyllos was assumed by the ancients to have died one hundred years before the Herakleid return. However, herein it is assumed to be only ninety-five years to fit Pelops's arrival in Hellas in 1316T/1066R BCE and the fall of Troy in 1184T/949R BCE. As Exhibit A1.8 demonstrates, it would be impossible to move Anaxo and Alkmene five years earlier while keeping the date of the arrival of Pelops firm. Already the assumption is that they had children at a very young age. Besides, only three generations per century has been proven to be too long.

Thersandros/Laodamas all had to rule between the labors of Herakles and the gathering of the suitors of fair Helene. See Addendum 2, "List of Kings," for a detailed list of Theban kings.

**Fall of Mycenai:** According to myth, Temenos conquered strong-walled Tiryns upon his return to the Peloponnesos, but Mycenai did not fall immediately. Using the calculations above, Temenos led the successful Herakleid return in 854 BCE, close in line with revisionist dating. Herein it is assumed that Mycenai, twelve miles up the Argeia Valley from Tiryns, fell after a two-year siege (852 BCE).

**Fall of Troy:** Thucydides says that Troy fell to Agamemnon eighty years before the Herakleids returned, thus providing a date of 934 BCE (eighty plus 854 BCE). Given that Troy was sacked twice during the Late Bronze Age, there has been constant speculation as to which one Homer described. As for which Troy was destroyed by Agamemnon, there are strong arguments for either.

Arguments for Troy VI

- Troy VI fits better with Homer's description of Troy as a rich city.
- Archaeological evidence indicates that the palace city of Pylos and the palaces of Lakonia were sacked between Troy VI and VII, which means Nestor of Pylos and Menelaos of Therapne (Sparta) could have led forces only against Troy VI.
- Archaeological evidence indicates that the city of Krisa was deserted between Troy VI and Troy VII. According to myth, Krisa was deserted two generations after Agamemnon.
- According to Lycian myth, the Hittite great-king Muwatalli II was the lover of Helene and lived somewhat before Troy VI fell.
- The Lesbian city of Thermi fell just before Troy VI, and Akhilleus is said to have sacked Lesbos a few years before Troy fell.
- If the wooden horse represents Poseidon's earthquake (god of horses and earthquakes), then Troy VI is a better candidate for a destruction by earthquake.
- The reputed tholos tombs of Atreus and Klytaimnestra were built just before and after Troy VI fell. (However, the tomb of Klytaimnestra's lover Aigisthos was built over a hundred years earlier than Troy VI).

Arguments for Troy VII

- Only Troy VII was destroyed by fire in a hail of arrows, just as Homer describes.
- According to myth, the Hellenes twice conquered Troy, and if Agamemnon sacked Troy VII, then Herakles would have been responsible for the fall of Troy VI.
- The myths are clear that after Troy was sacked, the warriors scattered far and wide; Near Eastern texts make it clear that the Sea Peoples were active right after Troy VII (though the migration of Agamemnon's grandson to Akhaia would fit better with a Troy VI sack).
- Iolkos, Gla, Thebes, and Kalydon were all sacked between Troy VI and Troy VII, and in myth between the sacks of Troy by Herakles and Agamemnon.
- Only with Troy VII does the Mycenaian kings list provided by Apollodoros (*Library*), Pausanias (*Guide to Greece*), and others work within a four and three-quarters century time frame and fit for the family of Akrisios of Mycenai.
- A great-grandson of Pelops/Uhhaziti would have been a mature man only when Troy VII was sacked. (Agamemnon was his great-grandson).
- Thracians (Phrygians) arrived in Ilion after Troy fell to Agamemnon, according to Strabo (*Geography,* xiv.5.29), and according to archaeologist Carl Blegen, who excavated Troy, Balkan (Thracian) tribesmen settled in Ilion only after Troy VII fell.
- Eratosthenes's date for the Homeric sack of Troy fits the traditional archaeological date for the fall of Troy VII.

The Clevenger Chronology assumes Troy VII was sacked by Agamemnon in order to accommodate Pelops's arrival in Hellas, to identify Herakles with a factual fall of Troy (VI), and to fit Eratosthenes's date for the fall of Troy to Agamemnon.

**Pelops's Arrival:** It has proven irresistible to equate mythological Pelops, king of Lydia, with King Uhhaziti of Arzawa Minor (the Hittite name for the region of Lydia). According to Hittite records, Uhhaziti received Ahhiyawan (Akhaian) assistance during his rebellion against the Hittites and fled before the Hittite advance to Ahhiyawa. The Hellenes say Pelops once led his army eastward toward the land of the Hittites, was defeated, and moved to Hellas. Hittite annals include correspondences with Egypt from which the date Uhhaziti fled was traditionally calculated[340] as 1316T BCE (although he was a mature man with grown children, while Pelops of myth was a young man seeking marriage). Thus Uhhaziti fled to Hellas 132 years before Troy fell (1316–1184T BCE, the traditional date for the fall of Troy). Given that this period is so well documented with artifacts and texts, James accepts the length of the Late Bronze Age proposed by Petrie and others. Thus, according to revisionist dating, Uhhaziti must have arrived in 1066R BCE (934 BCE plus 132 years). The Hittite date works well in the Hellenic mythology chronology. Pelops was said to have arrived while Perseus ruled Tiryns. As calculated in exhibit A1.8, Perseus was born in 1094R BCE and would have been a reasonable twenty-seven years old when Pelops arrived.

**Rise of Mycenai:** Excavations at Mycenai have shown that the first flowering of Mycenaian civilization occurred during a period entitled the Middle Helladic II (MHII); this period took place during the early sixteenth T / middle fourteenth R century BCE. The first important structures built in the city were two grave circles now known as shaft graves. The first graves were simple plots with pebbles placed upon them. Subsequent shaft graves were larger, with wooden roofs covering them. Steadily improving technical and artistic skill is obvious. Because artisans became heavily influenced by the alien Minoan civilization of Krete, and because Egyptian goods began appearing in the graves, accurate comparative dating is possible.

The first graves can be identified with Phoroneus, the reputed founder of Mycenai who was afterward deified as the civilizing god. As mentioned above, the length of the Late Bronze Age is not in dispute. According to George Emmanuel Mylonas, Mycenai (more specifically the earliest shaft grave) was founded in 1580 BCE, or 264 years before Pelops arrived (1580 BCE minus 1316 BCE, the year King Uhhaziti fled Arzawa). Thus, by revisionist dating, Mycenai was founded in 1330 BCE (arrival of Pelops in 1066 BCE plus 264 years). The genealogy of the early Mycenaian kings supports this time span (see Addendum 2, "List of Kings," for a Mycenaian kings list). The twelve early kings preceding Perseus (who inherited the kingdom of Mycenai from his grandfather Akrisios in 1075 BCE at the

[340] Bryce, *Kingdom of the Hittites.*

young age of nineteen and traded Mycenai for Tiryns) would have ruled a reasonable 21 years on average (1330 BCE minus 1075 BCE divided by twelve kings).

The exhibit below summarizes the Clevenger Chronology dating of pre-Classical events in Hellas.

Exhibit A1.9—Major Chronology Events

| Event | Date (BCE) | Years After Prior Event | Years After Mycenai Founding |
|---|---|---|---|
| Mycenai founded | 1330 | - | - |
| Pelops's arrival | 1066 | 264 | 264 |
| Troy VII sacked | 934 | 132 | 396 |
| Herakleids' return | 854 | 80 | 476 |
| Pheidon's coup | 600 | 254 | 730 |
| Persian invasion | 480 | 120 | 850 |

Mythic dates are calculated by working back in time from the Persian invasion of Hellas by Great-King Xerxes, the earliest verifiable event in Hellas. Five generations of Orthagorids lived between that momentous invasion and the time of Pheidon. Pheidon seized tyrannical powers ten generations, inclusively, after the Herakleids' return. The Herakleids came to power 80 years after the fall of Troy. The time between the founding of Mycenai and fall of Troy can be fairly accurately determined from the plethora of Bronze Age artifacts and texts. Traditional dating assumes the period is roughly 396 years—between 1580T BCE. and 1184T BCE. Revisionist conclusions and mythic genealogies concur with traditional assumptions of the length of the period.

**Dark Age:** Unlike the preceding Late Bronze Age and the succeeding Arkhaic Age, the aptly named Dark Age has yielded very few artifacts and is therefore very difficult to date using comparative finds from other civilizations. The Dark Age began with the dramatic collapse of centralized palace governments, and the rigid class hierarchies of rulers, bureaucrats, craftsmen, warriors, and scribes vanished. Without the palaces there was no need for records, and literacy died out. The population declined dramatically. Iron replaced bronze as the principal metal of industry. The existence of a prolonged slump in Hellas is not disputed. Historic references to date this epoch are exceedingly rare, as are period artifacts. The most important are found in Ephoros's lost *History of the World.* A sequence of the main events is as follows:

1. Herakleids' return
2. Aletes's conquest of Korinth

3. Herakleids' defeat at Athens
4. Ionian migration
5. Reforms of Lykourgos
6. Homer's period of activity
7. Founding of the Olympics
8. Pheidon's Olympics
9. Regime change in Korinth
10. Founding of Syrakuse
11. Messenian Wars

The Clevenger Chronology follows the sequence of Dark Age events stipulated by Ephoros with two exceptions: Syrakuse was founded before the founding of the Olympic Games and Lykourgos's reforms came afterward. The archaeological record supports an earlier founding of Syrakuse than the revisionist date for the first Olympic Games. Lykourgos's reforms fit well, as Theopompos believed, with the time of Pheidon, which Herodotos dates to a time clearly after Olympia had become an important site. Surviving king lists for Argos (discussed above), Korinth, Athens, and Sparta help to flesh out event dates.[341]

**Dorian Korinth:** Ephoros is the principal source in the surviving works of later historians concerning the Herakleid kings descended from Hippotes. Hippotes had the dubious distinction of having been the one to delay the Herakleids' return to the Peloponnesos under Temenos (who sacked Mycenai) when he killed the seer Karnes. Hippotes was the father of Aletes[342], who conquered Korinth—obviously one generation after the fall of Mycenai, Tiryns, Messenia (Pylos), and Lakonia.

Twelve Herakleid kings ruled Korinth over nine generations. Pausanias (*Guide to Greece,* ii.4.4) says that Aletes and his descendants ruled Korinth for five generations. (Eusebios's *Chronicle* provides the names: Aletes,

[341] Messenia also had a long kings list that was not considered because it was clearly created in Hellenistic times to rival their Spartan enemies.

[342] Pausanias, *Guide to Greece,* ii.4.3, states that Doridas and Hyanthidas, whose father, Propodas, was a contemporary of Jason the Argonaut and Herakles, surrendered Korinth to Aletes; but he also says that Aletes was the great-great-grandson of Herakles. Both statements cannot be. Pausanias does not mention Aletes's father by name. Hippotes would be Aletes's father following Apollodoros (*Library,* ii.174); that Hippotes was the son of Phylas, who was the son of Antikhos, who was the son of Herakles. Some writers say a daughter of Phylas bore Hippotes, in which case Aletes would be the son of Hippotes and, as Pausanias says, the great-great-grandson of Herakles.

Ixion, Agelaos, Praxmnis, and Bakkhais.) The next five generations of kings were called Bakkhai after distinguished Bakkhais. (Eusebios agrees and gives their names: Agelaos, Eudemos, Aristodemos, Telestes, and Automenes). There were two extra kings in the Bakkhai line because Telestes was a child when his father died. His uncle Agemon ruled as regent until he was assassinated by Alexandros. Telestes killed Alexandros but was killed twelve years later by his own relatives. Pausanias says that in a political compromise, annual kings were elected from the Bakkhai clan until Kypselos seized power. Telestes's son Automenes was the first elected king. Diodoros (*Library of History,* vii.9) concurs; Aletes and his descendants ruled for nine generations plus one year in all.

It is assumed that an elected kingship was the Korinthian response to the political crisis affecting monarchies throughout Hellas during the lifetime of Pheidon. In Sparta the power of the kings was reduced by elected officials and the assembly, while in Argos Pheidon seized additional powers. It is herein assumed that the elected kingship started the same year Pheidon seized additional powers (600 BCE).

Exhibit A1.10—Korinthian Kings Timeline

| Event | Years |
|---|---|
| Herakleids' return (BCE) | 854 |
| Advent of elected kings (BCE) | 600 |
| Total Years for ten generations | 254 |

Exhibit A1.6 indicates that each of the ten generation held power for twenty-four and a half years each. Within the intervening two and a half centuries, there were three important events to consider: the Herakleid conquest of Korinth, the Ionian migration, and the rise of Korinth.

**Korinth, Athens and the Ionian Migration:** The Herakleid conqueror Aletes can be directly linked to an Athenian king, making it possible to calculate a date for the Ionian migration. First-century BCE mythographer Konon (*FGrHis,* 26) says that Aletes led the Herakleid attack on Athens, and Eratosthenes adds that the attack occurred one year after Korinth fell. Eratosthenes said that the failed attack on Athens occurred sixty years (or slightly less than two generations, assuming three generations per century) after the Herakleid return. According to Pausanias (*Guide to Greece,* ii.6.6–7), when the Herakleids under Temenos's brother Kresphontes conquered Messenia (including Pylos), the defeated ruling family fled to Athens under Melantheus (presumably shortly after the Argeia fell to Temenos). Melantheus seized power in Athens in a coup shortly after his arrival. He was succeeded by his son Kodros, who had fully grown sons when the Dorians attacked Athens. Thus Eratosthenes's assumption that nearly two generations passed between the Herakleid return and the Ionian migration appears reasonable.

The problem is that most historians (including Ephoros and Pausanias [*Guide to Greece,* ii.4.3]) say Aletes lived only one generation after the Herakleids returned; and Eusebios implies he seized Korinth in the same generation as the Herakleids' return. To fit Aletes and the Pylian kings of Athens, it is assumed that Melantheus was an elder statesman when he arrived in Athens. It follows that Kodros ruled Athens for most of the time between the Herakleids' return and the attack by Aletes. Thus there were one and a half generations between the Herakleids' return and the conquest of Korinth. In other words, Aletes led an attack not immediately upon reaching manhood, but once he had reached middle age. The exhibit below suggests a date in the late ninth century BCE.

Exhibit A1.11—Dating Dorian Attack on Athens

| Reigns | 21.2 | 35 | Average |
|---|---|---|---|
| 1.5 generations | 31 | 53 | 42 |
| Herakleids' return (BCE) | 854 | 854 | 854 |
| Aletes conquest of Korinth (BCE) | 823 | 801 | 812 |
| Attack on Athens (BCE) | 822 | 800 | 811 |

Kodros's death during the attack led to a fight for the throne by two of his sons. Elder Medon prevailed and became king of Athens. Kodros's younger son Neleus lost and immediately led his followers to Ionia (811 BCE). Thus Neleus arrived in Ionia forty-three years after the Herakleids' return, not the sixty years Eratosthenes proposed.

There is archaeological evidence from Ionia to support the genealogically developed date of 811 BCE for the Ionian migration. A migration from Athens may be indicated by the large quantity of Athenian pottery that has been uncovered in Ionia during the Protogeometric Age (unlike earlier submycenaian and later Geometric Ages, when Athenian pottery in Ionia was relatively scarce). This date fits within the proposed dates for the production of protogeometric pottery proposed by James (850–775 BCE), as well as the more stringent dates presented in chapter 16 and the Clevenger Chronology (830–790 BCE). Thus, Neleus led the much smaller second Ionian colonization effort; the main force of Hellenes migrated to Ionia during the turbulent time shortly before and after the Trojan War.

The next significant event in the archaeological record is the rise of Korinth. Archaeological finds have clearly determined that city underwent explosive growth beginning during the Athenian Middle Geometric Age (740–705R BCE). It was understood that Bakkhais must have accomplished extraordinary feats, since the ruling house was renamed for him. So it is reasonable to credit Bakkhais with the rise of Korinth. Most likely he profited from the return of overseas trade, established the first colony on the western trade route at Ithake, and funded the construction of what may be the earliest (wooden) Hellenic temple, which was dedicated to Hera at seaside Perakhora. Assuming twenty-five years per generation, Bakkhais came to power in 725 BCE (812 BCE minus half a generation remaining for Aletes, or roughly twelve years minus three generations of twenty-five years each. Thus the date for the reign of Bakkhais fits well with the archaeological record.

**Athenian Kings:** Eusebios's *Chronicle* lists twelve kings ruling after Kodros died, starting with his eldest son, Medon. In each case the son is said to have succeeded the father: Medon, Akastos, Arkhippos, Thersippos, Phorbas, Megakles, Diognetos, Pherekles, Ariphron, Thespieos, Agamestor, and Aiskhylos. The unlucky thirteenth king, Alkmaion, was deposed after two years.

Exhibit A1.12—Athenian Kings Timeline

| Reigns | 21.2 | 25.8 |
|---|---|---|
| Medon's coronation (BCE) | 812 | 812 |
| Ionian invasion (BCE) | 811 | 811 |
| Reign of the twelve kings (years) | 254 | 310 |
| Death of twelfth king (BCE) | 558 | 501 |
| Deposition of Alkmaion (BCE) | 556 | 499 |

Eusebios stated that the twelve kings ruled 310 years, or a reasonable 25.8 years on average. However, using his timeline provides an unrealistically late date of 499 BCE for the end of the monarchy. Only using the shortest reigns discussed above provides a reasonable date (556 BCE). Athens, like Argos, retained its monarch rather late.

**Sparta:** Unlike Argos, Korinth, and Athens, archaeological evidence from Sparta indicates that the city was not continuously occupied throughout the Dark Age. In fact, Sparta was not a Mycenaian Age city at all; nearby Therapne was. (The Spartans understood this and said Menelaos was buried in Therapne.) Excavations at Therapne revealed that the city was actually sacked before Troy VII fell—and long before the Herakleids "returned." All of the Bronze Age cities of Lakonia were abandoned about the same time (just after 1200T/965R BCE), and the region remained virtually uninhabited for a long time thereafter. Excavators discovered that Sparta was founded during the Middle Geometric Age (850T/740R BCE) by the joining of four small protogeometric-era villages.

The mythic history of Sparta may support the Dark Age founding of the city; the Spartans appear to have retained some recollection that a break occurred. Curiously, it was Agis who was considered the founder of the senior ruling house—not the original Herakleid king, his father, Eurystheus, as would be expected. So Eurystheus can be assumed to have brought down Bronze Age Lakonian civilization, and his "son" Agis founded Sparta. Eurystheus should be thought of as an ancestor of Agis, not his father. Herodotos provides our earliest list of Spartan kings for the older, more important line, which Pausanias follows exactly. The kings are Agis, Ekhestratos, Leobotas, Doryssos, Agesilaos, Arkhelaos, Teleklos, Alkimenes, Polydoros, Eurykrates, Anaxandros, Eurykratidas, Leon, Anaxandridas, and Kleomenes (the first Agaid king whom we have a fairly accurate historical account of). By revisionist dating, the first fourteen Agiad kings ruled an average of sixteen years (740–516 BCE).

**Arkhaic Age:** There is almost no evidence of human activity in Hellas during the traditional Dark Age and very little evidence available to date specific events during the subsequent Arkhaic Age. Traditional dating, following Coldstream, assumed the Arkhaic Age began somewhat before Syrakuse was founded, settling on 750T BCE as the start of the Arkhaic Age and usually agreeing that the era ended in 525T BCE (some twenty-five years later than Coldstream postulated). Adopting a chronology based upon the Orthagorid family causes a reduction in the length of the Arkhaic Age and shifts it later. Archaeologists Michael Vickers and David Francis came to the same conclusion by studying art and architectural styles. To fit mythic genealogical evidence, the Arkhaic Age is herein revised to 705–500R BCE.

The Arkhaic Age was a time of explosive growth and change after a long period of decline. Amid rapid population growth were profound changes in art, pottery, warfare, architecture, and literacy. Contacts were reestablished with advanced eastern civilizations, and overseas colonies were established. The period begins with feudal barons and kings ruling over small settlements—just as they had done during the Dark Age.

**705 BCE:** The reintroduction of the written word was a key factor in ending the Dark Age. Perhaps writing was reintroduced into Hellas by the seafaring Euboians, although the earliest inscription of the Hellenic alphabet is found on a wine jug from the Dipylon workshop in Athens. The jug is associated with Late Geometric pottery (775T/725R–725T/685R BCE); in other words, it is from the very beginning of the Arkhaic Age (750T/705R BCE). Whereas Mycenaian Age writing was used for palace administration, Arkhaic Age writing was principally used to record great poetic works.

**700 BCE:** The way war was waged changed dramatically at the beginning of the Arkhaic Age. The first evidence of hoplite armies fighting in formation is depicted upon an urn found on Paros Island (beginning of Protokorinthian pottery phase, 725T/685R BCE). The last recorded scenes of unique chariot fighting date some twenty years earlier. As iron weapons and protective armor became more affordable, superior citizen hoplite infantry units began replacing aristocratic chariot-based and horseback-based cavalries as the backbone of the army. Indispensable hoplite forces were sought by ambitious leaders—kings and barons alike—to conquer neighboring settlements. In return for their services, these citizens began demanding better governance.

**690 BCE:** Syrakuse, the third-oldest city on Sicily according to Thucydides, was founded. The earliest Hellenic pottery found on Sicily was of the Late Geometric style (775T/725R–725T/685R BCE). Significant overseas trade resumed just before the Arkhaic Age began, and with it came many new ideas imported from abroad. Colonization began during the decade before the Arkhaic Age; for the first time since the Ionians migrated to Ionia, Hellenes were moving abroad in numbers. The Hellenic colonization of Sicily—where Hellenic artifacts are again found with Egyptian ones—clearly showed that a new era had begun.

Given that traders would have brought pottery to Sicily before settlers arrived, it is herein assumed that the first Sicilian cities date to the early seventh century R BCE, toward the end of the Late Geometric Age. Thucydides says the founder of Syrakuse was Arkhias of Korinth. Ephoros adds that Arkhias lived during the time of Pheidon, ten generations from Temenos. Early colonies were not state-sponsored affairs, and there is good reason to doubt that the name of the original colonist is known. There are good arguments (see the year 583 BCE below) for assuming that Arkhias led the defeated Bakkhai party to Syrakuse during the sixth century BCE and not the original colonists. Presumably he gained control over the city and greatly expanded its size.

While most ancient writers accepted Ephoros's chronology (but not his absolute dates), the historian Theopompos proposed an alternative. Theopompos said Pheidon lived during the seventh generation from Temenos, so he would have been in his prime from 689–662R BCE,[343] the very timeframe James proposes for the settlement of Sicily. However, this places Pheidon too early to fit with archaeological facts from Argos.

**650 BCE:** *The Iliad* was largely composed, though the final form would come two centuries later. Judging by Homeric references to objects in use and a reference to the rich Egyptian city of Thebes (which was destroyed in 663 BCE by the Assyrians), it appears that Homer's masterpieces were codified (orally but not yet in final written form) by 650R BCE. Among ancient writers, only Strabo (*Geography* i.2.9) proposed a date as late as the seventh century BCE He said Homer lived while nomadic Kimmerians wreaked havoc in Anatolia.

[343] Based upon Ephoros's generations, it was calculated that Temenos led the returns in 854 BCE and that the reign of Pheidon, the tenth king, started in 612 BCE. So the first nine kings ruled roughly twenty-six and nine-tenths years. Thus, if Pheidon is moved up to the seventh generation to fit King Theopompos, his reign would have been roughly 693–666 BCE.

**635 BCE:** Perhaps the earliest casualty in the movement to consolidate power within geographic areas was the Argeian city of Asine. Pausanias (*Guide to Greece* ii 36.5), following Ephoros, says that the Eurypontid Spartan king Nikandros invaded Argos with the support of Asine. When Nikandros withdrew, King Eratos of Argos retaliated by sacking Asine. While it is extremely unlikely that Sparta had the ability to invade the Argeia that early, the quote is useful in dating the sack of Asine. King Nikandros was the father of Theopompos (the king, not the historian), whose reign overlapped that of King Pheidon of Argos. Archaeological evidence proves convincingly that Asine was indeed sacked during the Arkhaic Age and not reoccupied until Hellenistic times. Coldstream says Asine fell during the Late Geometric Age (775T/725R–725T/685R BCE), but the excavator report from the site states that Protokorinthian pottery was also found. One might infer that the pottery was early Protokorinthian (685–665R BCE), or otherwise Coldstream would have noted it. However, following the sequence of Ephoros, Pausanias implies that Asine was sacked a generation before Pheidon, which argues for middle Protokorinthian (665–625R BCE). It is possible that Korinthian-style pottery did not immediately reach Asine, and therefore the later date, a generation before Pheidon, is herein assumed.

**610s BCE:** Hesiod of Askre flourished. Hesiod made one statement that could be used to determine when he lived; he said he won the poetry contest at the funeral games of Amphidamas in Eretreia. Many have speculated that this meant Hesiod lived during the Lelantine War, but he does not say that. Herein he is assumed to have written sometime between Homer and the Lelantine War, as his literary style seems to be closer in time to Homer than a time when mercantile city-states fought Panhellenic wars.

**616 BCE:** Iphitos of Elis established the sacred truce and refounded the Olympic Games. By decree, every participant and spectator was forbidden to bring arms into the sanctuary, and all hostilities in Hellas were to stop during the games. Aristotle says a bronze discus of Iphitos was kept in the Temple of Hera to commemorate his accomplishment. The discus probably dates to the early fourth century BCE, and its inscription adds, implausibly, that Lykourgos of Sparta and Kleosthenes of Pisa signed the agreement.

Ancient writers mention many games being held at the site before Iphitos restarted the games on a regular four-year cycle. Archaeological findings support this claim; evidence of a cult dates back to the Early Geometric Age (925T/790R–875T/775R BCE). Ephoros says Iphitos thrived during the generation before Pheidon, although Eratosthenes appears to have thought they were of the same generation. By Pheidon's time, temples and treasuries at the site indicate the games were valuable enough to fight over who would host them. The first games are herein dated twenty-eight years before the games Pheidon held; Eratosthenes calculated that the games were founded in 776 BCE, and Ephoros says Pheidon took over the games of 748 BCE, twenty-eight years later. An even later date would fit better with the other Panhellenic games, which were all founded during the middle of the sixth century R BCE.[344]

**615 BCE:** The first stone temples were constructed in Hellas. Doric (stone) temples were first represented on pottery, which often depicted oriental mythic scenes (Late Protokorinthian pottery, 650T/625R–625T/600R BCE). These temples serve as testimonies to the rising power and sophistication of the city-states.

**612 BCE:** Pheidon succeeded his father as king of Argos.

**612 BCE:** The Spartan lawgiver Lykourgos instituted eunomia. Lykourgos wrote a constitution to legally curb the power of the kings and developed social institutions that led to the unique warlike Spartan way of live. The historian Kastor of Rhodes and the Roman historian Velleius Paterculus assumed these reforms were established in the same year that the Medes conquered the Assyrian capital of Nineveh—a date that can be firmly established to 612 BCE. The Arkhaic Age Spartan poet Tyrtaios hints that the constitution became law during the reign of King Theopompos, son of Nikandros. Following Ephoros, most ancient writers said King Theopompos and Pheidon flourished during the tenth generation. This makes sense, as they both were reformers of the Dark Age feudal system. Lykourgos's warlike reforms are generally thought to have been implemented during the reign of his nephew Kharillos, who then initiated attacks on Tegea.

[344] A later date would also fit better with the revised dates for Athenian kings as well. Eusebios says the Olympics were founded in the twelfth year of the reign of King Aiskhylos, which would be 568 BCE by revisionist dating.

Modern archaeology supports a late seventh- or sixth-century BCE date for the reforms. It is only from the last quarter of the seventh century R BCE that there is evidence of city-state governments as sophisticated as those referred to by the myths; they are evidenced by regional consolidation of power, as well as the construction of stone temples and state-sponsored overseas colonies. The constitution Lykourgos authored was called the Great Rhetra. Young Lykourgos reputedly studied law codes under Thales of Gortyn, the city where the oldest Hellenic law code has been found.

There is evidence supporting an even later date for the reforms in Sparta than herein assumed. The Spartans claimed that once Lykourgos instituted his reforms, there were no major changes in governance. However, modern (and some ancient) historians have noted that there were additional reforms. For example, King Polydoros instituted land reforms, and the office of ephors was a later addition. Additionally, there is no sign of a cultural change evident in Sparta during the late seventh century BCE; Spartan arts and architecture continued to flourish down through the early to mid sixth century BCE. Perhaps it took time for the new militaristic society to become firmly entrenched. On the other hand, the changes may have occurred later. A gradual change is assumed herein.

The rapidly growing states challenged the feudal order. In short order, three alternative responses occurred: Lykourgos's reforms to constitutionally limit the powers of the hereditary kings of Sparta, Pheidon expanding his royal powers, and the Korinthians assassinating King Telestes and replaced hereditary kingship with annually elected kings. Some ancient historians thought Lykourgos's reforms were a direct response to Sparta's defeat by Pheidon—a reasonable assumption. However, Ephoros and Eratosthenes clearly placed it beforehand. The historian Theopompos says Lykourgos and Pheidon were of the same generation.

**612 BCE:** In his book *Philippia*, Theopompos glorified his Macedonian patrons by saying the Macedonian Agraid Dynasty was founded the same year that the Assyrian dynasty fell and Pheidon became king of Argos.[345]

[345] The Roman historian Velleius Paterculus (*History of Rome*, i.6) said the fall of Assyria, the start of the Agraid Dynasty and the reforms of Lykourgos all occurred in 818 BCE. Eusebios says the Argiad Dynasty began the same year as the first Olympics, 776 BCE.

**600 BCE:** Based upon the discussion of Herodotos above, it is assumed that Pheidon seized additional power as a tyrant at the end of the seventh century BCE.

**600 BCE:** King Telestes was assassinated in Korinth. Ephoros places Pheidon and Telestes in the tenth generation, and he might have thought Pheidon was responsible for Telestes's death. However, Pausanias says the Bakkhai king Telestes was assassinated by his own relatives, and afterward annual kings were elected from the Bakkhai clan. To allow for a period of elected kings—and, more importantly, because Pheidon is associated with the end of Bakkhai rule in Korinth—it is herein assumed that he did not play a role in Telestes's death.

**597–587 BCE:** The Panhellenic Lelantine War was fought. Very little was written about this struggle in which the city-states of the larger regions fought each other for land and the smaller coastal city-states fought over trade routes and colonial sites. Khalkis and Eretreia's skirmish over a fertile plain located between them escalated into what Thucydides described as the most widespread war in Hellas between the Trojan and Persian wars. The ancient references to the war are of dubious historic value. For example, Hesiod famously claimed to have won the poetry contest at the funeral of the war hero Amphidamas in Eretreia, but he never actually mentions the Lelantine War. Plutarch (*Morals*) claims that Kalkhis ally Korinth drove the Eretreians from Kercyra, but there is no archaeological evidence to corroborate the claim; the end of the war would have resulted in growing commerce. So perhaps the best that can be said is that the war ended before the founding of the Panhellenic Egyptian trade port of Naukratis (see below). Evidence that Eretreian pottery was traded extensively throughout the Mediterranean region during much of the Late Geometric and Early Protokorinthian Ages (775T/725R to 690T/665R BCE) and then virtually disappeared around 700T/660R BCE suggests an earlier date for the war. However, Hellenic city-states were not sophisticated enough to organize Panhellenic warfare at that time. Some other reason must explain the earlier sudden drop-off in Eretreian exports.

**593 BCE:** Agaid king Alkamenes conquered Helos to complete the Spartan conquest of Lakonia. Herodotos and Ephoros place Alkamenes in the tenth generation from Temenos, inclusively; this is the same generation

Ephoros assigns to Pheidon. Alkamenes ruled opposite of Eurypontid king Theopompos.

**590R BCE:** Ephoros (*FGrHis,* 70) says Pheidon robbed Sparta of their hegemony at this time. Pausanias supports Ephoros's claim of an earlier Spartan hegemony by saying that Spartan king Nikandros invaded Argeia shortly before Asine was sacked, although he adds that the invasion accomplished little. Such an early Spartan hegemony seems unlikely; they did not have that kind of power before conquering Messenia, so Pheidon could not have robbed them of it. It was the cities of the Argeia (Mycenai early, Argos later) that were preeminent in the Peloponnesos from Mycenaian times through the early Arkhaic Age. However, Argive support failed to save Helos, and Pheidon may have had to take military action against Sparta to ensure dominance. The details are vague; his opponent and the location of the battle are unknown. Ephoros would not have considered Spartan king Polydoros (as some have speculated) as Pheidon's adversary, since Polydoros belonged to the next generation. Nor would he have placed Pheidon at the battle at Hysiai,[346] which Pausanias says occurred after the First Messenian War.

**587R BCE:** Herodotos says the pharaoh Amasis (569–526 BCE) permitted Hellenic mercenaries to build an autonomous trade port in Egypt at Naukratis at this time. (Amasis succeeded Adries, who was deposed after failing to conquer the Hellenic cities of Libya in 569 BCE). However, the earliest Hellenic pottery uncovered at Naukratis is reliably dated somewhat earlier (ca. 590–585R BCE). Perhaps Amasis officially recognized the reality of an already thriving Hellenic trade center in Egypt. The trade port of Naukratis blossomed after the Lelantine Trade War ended.

[346] Only Pausanias (*Guide to Greece,* ii.24.7) mentions the battle at Hysiai, and he says it was three years after Eurybolos the Athenian was an Olympic victor, or 669 BCE. That date would be one year before the end of the Second Messenian War (685–668 BCE), according to Pausanias (*Guide to Greece,* iv.27.9). However, comments about Tyrtaios and Pantaleon suggest Pausanias followed the war dates of Ephoros (644–627 BCE). Pausanias says Tyrtaios arrived in Sparta during the fourth year of the war (the tenth-century CE Byzantine encyclopedia *Suidas* says he arrived in 640 BCE), and Pausanias indicates Pantaleon of Pisa held Olympic Games in 644 BCE. (It is generally agreed he held the games just before the outbreak of the war.) Thus it is difficult to determine where exactly in the historic sequence the battle of Hysiai took place, but it would have been after the First Messenian War, where Pausanias clearly follows Ephoros (743–724 BCE), and before the end of the Second Messenian War.

**585R BCE:** The poet Arkhilokhos mentions a full solar eclipse that has been identified with known eclipses in 711 BCE and 647 BCE However, if Arkhilokhos wrote about battles in the latter years of the Lelantine War (ca. 597–587R BCE), he must have observed the same eclipse that the scientist Thales[347] of Miletos impressively predicted by interpreting Babylonian sources (May 28, 585 BCE).

**584 BCE:** Assuming that Pheidon rose to power in 612 BCE, based upon the Orthagorid Dynasty, and reigned for roughly a generation, the dates he could have presided over the Olympic Games with the Pisans are 608, 604, 600, 596, 592, 588, and 584 BCE. Because the historians imply Pheidon died one year after holding the Olympic Games, only the latter Olympiads should be considered. To fit a full reign and the date Cypselos became tyrant in Korinth (see below), 584 BCE was chosen.

Pheidon forcefully took over the administration of the games from Elis with the support of Pisa.[348] Even though Pheidon died before the next Olympic Games, the Pisans continued to administer the games for many years; however, there could not have been twenty-six Olympiads separating Pheidon and Pantaleon of Pisa, as the historian Apollodoros of Athens says. Apollodoros expanded and corrected the earlier *Chronicle* of Eratosthenes.

**583R BCE:** Roman-era writer Nikolaos of Damascus says Pheidon of Argos was killed at this time during intense street fighting while supporting a faction in Korinth. Most authors assumed Pheidon helped overthrow King Telestes, who was of the same generation. However, Telestes was overthrown by his own Bakkhai clan, who retained power as elected kings. Elected kingship was an unstable arrangement that lasted until a strong

---

[347] Ephoros is quoted by Strabo (*Geography* vii, 3.9) on the seven sages of ancient Hellas. (Hyginos, in *Fabulai*, 221, concurs.) They were Thales of Miletos, Solon of Athens, Pittakos of Lesbos, Periandros of Korinth, Bias of Priene (Ionia), Khilon of Sparta, and Kleobolos of Rhodes. Thales was an early sixth-century BCE philosopher, while the others were political reformers active between 550 BCE and 530 BCE. Lykourgos of Sparta and Pheidon of Argos were earlier, semimythical reformers not included in this list of luminaries. Anakharis of Scythia replaces Kleobolos on some lists for inventing the potter's wheel, the anchor, and the bellows—things that were actually invented much earlier.

[348] In *Dating of Pheidon in Antiquity*, Mait Koiv lists ancient alternatives for Pisans usurping sponsorship of the Olympics. According to Ephoros, there was a single intervention by Pheidon. Eusebios, following the historian Apollodoros and Eratosthenes, mentions a long Pisan interlude. According to Pausanias, Pheidon's intervention existed side by side with two later Pisan interludes. In all these versions the Spartans helped Elis bring down Pisa.

man emerged. Pheidon was a tyrant who would have been more likely to support a strong man than an elected official. So it is assumed herein that Pheidon died assisting the non-Bakkhai polemarch Cypselos become tyrant, instead of assuming he was helping one Bakkhai faction against another. With Pheidon's involvement, the Bakkhai lost power, and many members of the defeated Bakkhai clan migrated to Syrakuse and Kercyra under Arkhias and Khersikrates.[349] Ephoros says Arkhias was of the same generation as Pheidon.

The date of this coup is set to fit the lifetime of Pheidon, discussed above, and also a comment from Timaios. Timaios says that the Bakkhai Khersikrates was left by his kinsman Arkhias on Kercyra (Corfu) Island with colonists six hundred years after Troy fell, or 594 BCE (given that Timaios assumed Troy fell in 1194 BCE). That date is a bit too early to fit Herodotos's timeline for Pheidon (see above) or Cypselos's children. Herodotos clearly identifies Cypselos's son Periandros with statesmen of the mid to late sixth century BCE (Pisistratos of Athens and King Alyattes of Lydia). Herodotos says Cypselos's great-grandson Miltiades colonized the Khersonessos for Athens—probably not before the 520s BCE, considering pottery finds—and the Megaran poet Theognis curses the Cypselids as one whose angry memory of them was still fresh. Theognis lived to the time of the Persian attack on Marathon (490 BCE). So it is herein assumed that Cypselos seized power six hundred years after Eratosthenes's generally accepted date for Troy's fall. Thus Arkhias (and Khersikrates) were leading Bakkhai families into exile and were not, as Thucydides claims, the original settlers of Syrakuse.

**580–575 BCE:** The First Messenian War began three to five years after Pheidon's death, based upon dates provided by ancient historians. The Argive hegemony collapsed with the death of Pheidon, and Sparta was emboldened to invade its neighbor Messenia. King Alkamenes started the war with a successful nighttime raid on Aphelia; he massacred everyone. The Spartans then used Aphelia as the base camp for subsequent attacks. Agiad king Alkamenes eventually died fighting the Messenians and was succeeded by his son Polydoros. The Eurypontid king Theopompos ruled throughout the war and died of an infection shortly afterward. Although both Messenians and Spartans saw value in considering this an epic struggle,

[349] Strabo says that Syrakuse and Kercyra were settled in the same year. Eusebios says Syrakuse (736 BCE) was settled nearly a generation before Kercyra (707 BCE).

it probably did not take too long to subdue the small country of Messenia. This conflict, like the Lelantine War, was the result of expanding Hellenic city-states competing for increasingly scarce resources—land at home and places to settle and trade abroad. Although Argos began its expansion earlier, it was the Spartans who first succeeded in consolidating regional control in their homeland, which gave them the opportunity to become the first to expand elsewhere. The Korinthian poet Eumelos flourished before and during the early part of the war.

Plutarch (*Morals* 194) says the Theban general Epiminondas claimed to have liberated Messenia after 230 years, giving a date of 599 BCE for the Spartan conquest of Messenia. This date is too early even for the start of the war, but it is closer to the mark than those of the ancient historians. Archaeological evidence does not support the early dates that Eratosthenes assumed for the First Messenian War (773–754 BCE).

**570 BCE:** King Polydoros of Sparta was assassinated. Civil unrest in Sparta followed the Messenian War. Many of the rebels agreed to migrate abroad under Phalanthos. They conquered and ruled Taras in Italy. Other dissenters were mollified with land redistribution. It is after this event that Spartan archaeology looks different than in other states; arts and crafts declined, and the building of temples stopped. Polydoros was murdered by a disgruntled nobleman; the nobility had the most to lose by agreements between the kings and the people.

**565 BCE:** The first recorded sea battle occurred between Korinth and Kercyra. Thucydides (*Peloponnesian War,* i.13.1) says that battle occurred in 664 BCE, 260 years before the end of the Peloponnesian War. However, Kercyra was not large enough to effectively challenge Korinth until the middle of the sixth century BCE. Besides, animosity between the two city-states probably began after the Bakkhai leaders fled Korinth at Kypselos's rise to power. Thucydides thought that triremes were used in this battle, but the shipbuilder who developed them, Ameinokles of Korinth, most likely built ships for the mid to late sixth-century BCE tyrant Polykrates of Samos. Thucydides assumed he built them 300 years before the end of the Peloponnesian War.

**556 BCE:** King Alkmaion was deposed and replaced by elected archons in Athens. This arrangement mirrored an earlier Korinthian policy in which the Bakkhais agreed to an elected kingship to thwart unrest within the clan. As in Korinth, this unstable form of governance lasted only until a strongman came along.[350]

**555 BCE:** Meltas, grandson of Pheidon, pushed the Argives into allegiance with the Arkadians against the resurgent Spartans and led them to victory. However, the costly win discouraged so many Argives (who wondered why they were dying for Arkadians) that Meltas was expelled and Argos withdrew from the alliance. Elected kings replaced Meltas, the last Herakleid king of Temenos's line. The change in policy was a grave error. Without a united front, the Arkadians were unable to suppress the relentless Spartans along the precious route to Messenia.

Meltas can be roughly dated by his grandfather Pheidon. The exact date for his fall was chosen from an obscure fact provided by Diodoros. He says that the Argive kings ruled for 549 years. Assuming he meant just the Herakleids and that he accepted Eratosthenes's date (though usually he seems to have supported the compromise date), then Meltas was ousted in 555 BCE (1104–549 BCE).

**553 BCE:** Pottery finds suggest Nauplia fell during the first half of the time when Early Korinthian pottery was produced (600–575T BCE, or up to twenty-five years later by revisionist dating). It is a little tough to precisely date the fall of Nauplia, since unlike Asine, it was immediately reoccupied by Argives. Pausanias (*Guide to Greece* vi.35.2) says that King Damokratidas expelled the Nauplians between the Messenian Wars. Damokratidas was the first elected king after Meltas was deposed.

**553 BCE:** The Argives defeated the Spartans in battle at Hysiai. Pausanias (*Guide to Greece* ii.24.7) is the only historian to mention this battle, and he clearly states that it occurred sometime after the First Messenian War and before the Second Messenian War ended. Perhaps a Spartan force was coming to the aid of Nauplia. Some have speculated that the Spartan defeat encouraged the Messenians to revolt, which seems reasonable. The names of the Spartan and Argive leaders are not provided by Pausanias.

---

[350] Not the 122 years imagined by Eusebios, but 70 years of archons elected for 10-year terms plus annually elected archons for 52 years down to Cylon's coup in 632T BCE. Eusebios assumed elected kings in Korinth ruled for 90 years.

**552–545 BCE:** After the tyrant Pantaleon of Pisa sponsored the Olympic Games, Aristodemos led the Messenians into revolt from Spartan rule. Pantaleon and King Aristokrates of Arkadian Orkhomenos led allies in support of the rebels. Spartan kings Anaxandros, grandson of Polydoros, and Ariston led the Spartan response, which eventually crushed the rebellion. The Spartans employed Nauplian exiles in the struggle and settled them in Messenia. The lyric poet Tyrtaios moved to Sparta during the fourth year of the revolt.

**550 BCE:** The famous Heraion of Samos temple was reputedly built a generation before the tyrant Polykrates ruled, because he claimed his father was involved in its construction. Polykrates's death can be dated to soon after 520 BCE, when the Persians crucified him. The Heraion became the standard Hellenic temple design for all subsequent generations.

**550 BCE:** The First Sacred War ended and the Delphic Games were founded by Kleisthenes of Sicyon and Eurylockhos of Thessalia. The tyrant Kleisthenes of Sicyon, a member of the Orthagorid clan, is considered to have been in his prime ca. 565–540 BCE (see exhibit A1.5). If the games were always eight years apart, then the games of 564, 558, 550, and 542 BCE fit with Kleisthenes's prime. To narrow the date further requires consideration of the Athenian statesmen Alkmaion and Solon. Plutarch (*Solon* 11) says that Solon argued that all pilgrims should have free passage to Delphi but that it was Alkmaion who led the Athenian forces. Their joint leadership can be assumed to have occurred after the Athenian kingdom was abolished, eliminating the games of 564 and 558 BCE. Alkmaion appears to have been the more important statesman at the time (or else Solon would have led the troops), and he was exiled after the coup of Cylon, eliminating the games of 542 BCE (see below). Therefore, only 550 BCE is a viable date.

The Delphians appealed to Kleisthenes, the Thessalian aristocrat-dominated Amphiktryonic Council, Athens, and others for aid against the Phocian port of Kirrha, which was reputedly accosting pilgrims to the oracle, demanding money in return for safe passage through their territory. The Kirrhans were defeated by the Thessalian cavalry under General Hippias or Eurylokhos. A long seige of Kirrha followed while Kleisthenes (grandson of Sicyon's first tyrant, Orthagoras) led the naval blockade of the port, which lay across the Gulf of Korinth from Sicyon.

The siege ended when the water supply was poisoned and the weakened inhabitants surrendered. No mercy was granted; everyone in the city was put to death. The first games were funded by the pillage of Kirrha. The traditional date provided by the Parian Marble indicates that Kirrha was sacked in 591 BCE.

**549 BCE:** Olympic victor Cylon tried to usurp power to rule Athens as a tyrant. He failed in large part as a result of the resistance of Alkmaion. Thus Cylon and Alkmaion clearly had to live after the kingdom had been abolished in Athens. Alkmaion made his fortune trading with the Lydian Empire and had led Athenian forces to assist Delphi during the Sacred War. Herodotos (*Histories* vi.125) says Alkmaion knew Lydian king Kroisos (reigned 570–546 BCE) personally. He was exiled for the harsh treatment his supporters doled out to Cylon and his supporters.

**548 BCE:** Athenians provided Drako with special powers to establish a written constitution to outline rules of governance and to end the arbitrary justice of nobles.

**544R BCE:** Solon argued convincingly to award Salamis to Athens over Megara. Afterward, he became the leading Athenian statesman. For two reasons, he must date close to the time of Drako. First, Drako and Solon were the men most responsible for initiating the process of codifying laws for the maturing nation. Second, Solon and Alkmaion were Athenian leaders active at the same time, given that both had roles in the Sacred War. (Solon permitted Alkmaion to return from exile.) Second, according to Aristotle, Solon devalued the drachma, and the first Hellenic coins were minted no earlier than the middle of the sixth century BCE. If Solon were involved in currency, it was probably to help introduce its usage. The later date also fits better with Herodotos's claim that Solon visited King Kroisos of Lydia (as did Alkmaion), the pharaoh Amasis (569–526 BCE), and the tyrant Philocyprus of Soli, whose son fought in the Ionian Revolt of the early 490s BCE. However, these legendary visits probably did not occur. Besides, Herodotos also claims that Megakles, who rose to power after Solon, met Kroisos's father. The source of the traditional earlier dates is Eusebios, who says Solon defeated Megara in arbitration for Salamis Island in 597 BCE and gained his archonship a few years later—594/3 BCE.

**535 BCE:** Megakles, son of Alkmaion, Lykourgos, and Pisistratos, shared power after Solon retired. Megakles had recently won the hand of Kleisthenes of Sicyon's daughter Agarista, and as a member of the Orthagorid clan, her prime can be dated to 540–515 BCE (see exhibit A1.5). One of the losing suitors was an Athenian from the powerful Philaidai clan, Hippocyides, who was a grandson of the Korinthian tyrant Cypselos on his mother's side. Pheidon's son Lakedes (Leokides) was implausibly added to the list of suitors. For that to be true, Pheidon would have had to have been active later than the early sixth century BCE assumed above. Besides, the Argive king was not on good terms with the Sicyon tyrant and his son would not have been a likely suitor. When Pisistratos seized power as tyrant, Megakles and Lykourgos regrouped and drove him into exile.

**532 BCE:** Hippocyides founded the Greater Panathenaian Festival in Athens. This festival was traditionally founded in 566 BCE, but he must have founded it after he failed to win Agarista's hand in marriage (as he was not powerful enough to do so as a bachelor).

**530 BCE:** The Spartan (Peloponnesian) League was founded by the ephor Khilon (one of the seven sages and the first ephor mentioned in Spartan history). His proposal to allow Tegea to surrender on terms was accepted by the new king, Anaxandridas, because the Spartans had been unable to conquer the Arkadian city outright. Within a few years, every Arkadian city became a member. Eusebios says implausibly that the office of ephors was founded in 758 BCE.

**529 BCE:** Pisistratos became tyrant of Athens. There are many reasons for assuming his reign began later than traditionally thought. (Eusebios and the Parian Marble say he briefly came to power in 562/1 BCE, and Herodotos says he returned to power the year the Lydian Empire fell, 545 BCE.) First, the dates for Megakles's adulthood can be roughly set by his marriage to Kleisthenes of Sicyon's daughter. Further, Herodotos tells us that Pisistratos's son Hippias did not serve as archon until 526/5 BCE, according to the unreliable Parian Marble. According to Athenian custom, aspiring politicians became archons early in their careers, as a stepping-stone to real power. Since Hippias's father was tyrant, he would probably have been elected archon soon after he met the age requirement of thirty. Herodotos also says Hippias was still politically active in 490 BCE. If, as Herodotos says, Hippias consulted with his dad during his father's exile, his father's banishment could not have occurred much earlier than 535 BCE—not 561 BCE. Herodotos implies that the battle with Mitylene

(Lesvos) over the Dardanelles may have occurred before or during his exile, because the Korinthian tyrant Periandros arbitrated a settlement (and Periandros died three years before Korinth entered the Peloponnesian League). Athens was awarded the Hellespontes port of Sigieon.

**528 BCE:** The tyrant Pyrrhos of Pisa, son of Pantaleon, lost the Olympics to Elis. The Olympics of 528 BCE are assumed for two reasons. First, it is a generation after Pantaleon sponsored the games. Second, it corresponds to the time when most of the Peloponnesos was forced into league with Sparta. Perhaps Sparta offered Elis control over the games as the price for joining the League. There is no evidence that Pisa was sacked at this time, but as an ally of Messenia they were punished with the loss of the Olympics. They were also forbidden to harbor Messenian rebels. The Spartans gained the support of the stronger state (Elis) just as they would later gain Thebes as an ally while cleverly leaving smaller Plataia to be an Athenian ally.

**528 BCE:** Pisistratos sent his popular potential rival Miltiades to fortify and colonize the Khersonese (to control the vital Dardanelles through which grain imports came). Miltiades was from the powerful Philaidai clan and a four-time Olympic champion. He died a couple of years later in an attack on the Miletos colony of Lampsakos in Hellespontes. Pottery finds from the Khersonese corroborate Athenian colonization at this time using revisionist pottery dating.

**527 BCE:** After subduing the Arkadians, the Spartans attacked and defeated Argos in a pitched battle fought at Boiai. Herodotos states that Anaxandridas and Ariston were the Spartan kings when the Battle of Champions was fought at Boiai. Ancient historians liked to link historic events, and Herodotos stated a dubious claim that while preparing for the battle with Argos, the Spartans refused the request of Lydian ambassadors for help against the Persians, citing concerns over the impending battle with Argos. This would date Boiai to 545 BCE. A date of nearly twenty years later fits better because a result of the battle was that Sparta was able to drive the tyrants Aiskhines (Orthagorid) of Sicyon and Psammetikhos (Cypselid) of Korinth from power. Both cities were forced to accept aristocratic overlords sympathetic to Sparta and to join the Sparta League.

**525 BCE:** King Anaxandridas of Sparta led a failed naval attack on Samos to oust the tyrant Polykrates. As a result, Sparta did not pursue naval power, opening the door for Athens. This Spartan failure can be fairly accurately dated via Persia's connection to Samos tyrant Polykrates. The Spartans' attack was in retaliation for Polykrates providing assistance to Persia for its Egyptian invasion in the same year. Presumably this attack occurred after Korinth joined the Peloponnesian League; otherwise, the Spartans would probably not have been bold enough to undertake this naval engagement. The defeated Spartans chose to consolidate their hold on the Peloponnesos and did not venture out again until they entered Athenian politics nearly a generation later.

**501 BCE:** The traditional date given for the establishment of the Athenian democracy is 508 BCE, the year Isagoras was reputed to be archon. However, as noted above regarding Hippias, according to Athenian custom, aspiring politicians became archons early in their careers as a stepping-stone to power. Therefore, it should be assumed that Isagoras did not obtain true political muscle until well after his archonship. Thus, the Spartans would not have installed him as tyrant for some years afterward. Since the Council of Five Hundred, which the great democratic reformer Kleisthenes created, did not swear their first office oath until 501 BCE (according to Aristotle), it is more likely that the democratic reforms were carried out in that year.

In conclusion, the revisionist chronology presents a picture of dramatic growth and change during the sixth century BCE, just as we know Hellas experienced during the fifth and fourth centuries BCE. It suggests that less than a century separated Pheidon's rise as the first Hellenic tyrant and Kleisthenes's development of the world's first democracy in Athens.

The revisionist chronology for mythic and early historical events is based upon Herodotos's date for Pheidon, Ephoros's list of Argive kings, and generations that averaged just over twenty-seven years. The revisionist dating fits well with Early Iron Age discoveries. However, no one can seriously claim that mythic Hellenic genealogies can be used as conclusive evidence in the argument between traditional and revisionist theories. It is not hard to imagine that the genealogies could be wrong. The timeline debate remains unresolved, so the Clevenger Chronology presents both traditional and revisionist dates.

### Section 5: Scientific Dating

After long depending solely upon comparing relative archaeological evidence to determine prehistoric dates, other scientific approaches are now available to help establish ancient dates. While monuments and artifacts yet to be discovered may help, new technical advances will probably be more helpful in deciding if traditional or revisionist archaeological dates—or perhaps neither—are accurate.

Scientists have developed the capacity to date events using radiocarbon, dendrochronology, and other analytical approaches. Radiocarbon analysis measures the half-life of carbon isotopes, and dendrochronology (from Hellenic "*dendron*" [tree] and "*chronos*" [time]) analyzes tree rings. But radiocarbon results are only accurate within a century or two during the Bronze Age, and dendrochronology, like pottery studies, requires artifacts to be viewed in relation to other artifacts found at the site (and wood is not usually available in the desert). Other clues can be deciphered through atmospheric changes captured in ice layers in Greenland.

Radiocarbon dates have consistently yielded dates that are much earlier than traditional dating in both Hellas and the Near East. It suggests that the Bronze Age in Hellas began as early as 3300 BCE and that the MH Age began before 2000 BCE. The exact dates of the volcanic eruption on Thera would provide a fixed point for aligning the entire chronology of the second millennium in the Aigaian, because evidence of the eruption is scattered throughout the region. Recent scientific analyses suggest the eruption occurred during the late seventeenth century BCE; radiocarbon studies suggests a date between 1630 BCE and 1610 BCE, dendrochronology evidence suggests 1628 BCE, and ice cores from Greenland indicate 1645 BCE. However, these dates conflict with traditional dates developed from archaeology, which suggest 1500T BCE or a few years later, based upon Minoan pottery found on the island at the time of the eruption (using Egyptian chronology). The scientific dates are even further out from revisionist archaeological dating, which suggests 1250R BCE.

The accuracy of the scientific findings is being challenged. For example, the eruption of Theras may itself have distorted the finds. The science is new and may not be calibrated correctly. Also, there is evidence suggesting later dates for some events. For example, olive pollen samples indicate that production peaked around 1000–950 BCE before falling off precipitously.

This indicates that the Bronze Age peaked in the late tenth century BCE, which fits well with revisionist dating but not with traditional or other scientific dating. Obviously, additional research is required.

Scientific dating based upon radiocarbon analysis, dendrochronology, and other analytical techniques shows promise in resolving the controversy. However, scientific results so far have raised more questions than answers, and there is as yet no way to provide consistent dating via these scientific means.

# Addendum 2
# List of Kings

| Mycenai (generations) | | Hittites | | Egypt | |
|---|---|---|---|---|---|
| | | Labarna | | | |
| | | Hattusili I | Grandson? | | |
| | | Mursili I | Grandson | | |
| Phoroneus (1) | | Hantili I | Brother-in-law | | |
| Argos (3) | Grandson | Zidanta I | Son-in-law | | |
| | | Ammuna | Son | | |
| | | Huzziya I | By marriage | | |
| Phorbas (4) | Son | Telipinu | Brother-in-law | Amenhotep I | |
| Triops (5) | Son | Alluwamna | Son-in-law | | |
| Agenor (6) | Son | Tahurwaili | Interloper | | |
| Krotopos (7) | Son | Hantili II | Son of Allusamna? | | |
| Sthenelos (8) | Son | Zidanta II | Son? | | |
| Gelanor (9) | Son | Huzziya II | Son? | | |
| Danaos (9) | Interloper | Muwatalli I | Interloper | Amenhotep II | |
| Lynkeus (10) | Son-in-law | Tudhaliya I/II | Grandson of Huzziya | Thumose IV | son |
| Abas I (11) | Son | Arnuwanda I | Son-in-law | Amenhotep III | son |
| | | Hattusili II | Son? | | |
| | | Tudhaliya III | Son? | Akhenaten | son |
| Akrisios (12) | Son | Supplilumas I | Son | | |
| | | Arnuwanda II | Son | | |
| | | Mursili II | Brother | Ramesses I | interloper |
| Melampous (13) | Interloper | Muwatalli II | Son | Sethi I | son |
| Abas II (14) | Son | Urhi-Tesub | Son | Ramesses II | son |
| Koiranos (15) | Son | Hattusili III | Uncle | | |
| Atreus (16) | Interloper | Tudhaliya IV | Son | Merenptah | son |
| Thyestes (16) | Brother | Arnuwanda III | Son | | |
| Agamemnon (18) | Grandnephew | Supplilumas II | Brother | | |
| Aigistheus (18) | Cousin | | | Ramesses III–XI | Not related to Ramesses I |
| Aletes (19) | Son | | | | |
| Orestes (19) | Half brother | | | | |
| Tisamenos (20) | Son | | | | |

There were twenty generations of Mycenaian rulers, assuming that Danaos was of the same generation as Gelanor; they were both great-great-great-great-grandsons of Argos. However, it is nineteen generations if you consider Danaos to be of the generation before, as he was twenty-seven years older than Gelanor.

| Mycenai | Revised | Traditional | Pottery | Construction |
|---|---|---|---|---|
| **House of Inakhos** | | | | |
| Phoroneus | 1330–1320 | 1580–1570 | MHII | Shaft Graves B |
| Argos | 1320–1285 | 1570–1535 | LHI | |
| Phorbas | 1285–1260 | 1535–1510 | | |
| Triops | 1260–1235 | 1510–1485 | | Shaft Graves A |
| Agenor | 1235–1225 | 1485–1475 | LHII | First tholos tombs in Argeia |
| Krotopos | 1225–1183 | 1475–1433 | | |
| Sthenelos | 1183–1163 | 1433–1413 | | |
| Gelanor | 1163–1162 | 1413–1412 | | |
| **House of Danaos** | | | | |
| Danaos | 1162–1153 | 1412–1403 | | |
| Lynceus | 1153–1132 | 1403–1382 | | |
| Abas I | 1132–1105 | 1382–1355 | LHIIIA | Grand palace construction begins |
| Akrisios | 1105–1075 | 1355–1325 | | |
| **House of Amythaon** | | | | |
| Melampous | 1075–1050 | 1325–1300 | | |
| Abas II | 1050–1015 | 1300–1265 | LHIIIB | |
| Koiranos | 1015–988 | 1265–1238 | | Last tholos tomb constructed |
| **House of Pelops** | | | | |
| Atreus | 988–951 | 1238–1201 | | Cyclopean walls and Lion Gate |
| Thyestes | 951 | 1201 | | |
| Agamemnon | 951–933 | 1201–1183 | LHIIIC | |
| Aigistheus | 933–927 | 1183–1177 | | |
| Aletes | 927–924 | 1177–1174 | | |
| Orestes | 924–885 | 1174–1135 | | |
| Tisamenos | 885–852 | 1135–1102 | | |
| **House of Herakles** | 852–460 | 1102–460 | | |

The names of the early kings were provided by the historian/genealogist Akusilaos of Argos, whose lost work was quoted by Pausanias, Apollodoros, and Diodoros. Starting with King Danaos, there was universal agreement on the names and order of Mycenaian kings.

| **Hittites** | **Revised** | **Traditional** | **Egypt** | **Revised** | **Traditional** |
|---|---|---|---|---|---|
| Labarna | –1400 | –1650 | | | |
| Hattusili I | 1400–1370 | 1650–1620 | $15^{th}$–$17^{th}$ Dynasties (overlapping) | 1383–1275 | 1633–1525 |
| Mursili I | 1370–1340 | 1620–1590 | | | |
| Hantili I | 1340–1310 | 1590–1560 | | | |
| Zidanta I | 1310– | 1560– | | | |
| Ammuna | | | Ahmose ($18^{th}$ Dynasty) | 1300–1275 | 1550–1525 |
| Huzziya I | –1275 | –1525 | | | |
| Telipinu | 1275–1250 | 1525–1500 | Amenhotep I | 1275–1254 | 1525–1504 |
| Alluwamna | 1250– | 1500– | Thutmose I | 1254–1242 | 1504–1492 |
| Tahurwaili | | | Thutmose II | 1242–1229 | 1492–1479 |
| Hantili II | | | | | |
| Zidanta II | | | Thutmose III | 1229–1175 | 1479–1425 |
| Huzziya II | | | | | |
| Muwatalli I | –1150 | –1400 | Amenhotep II | 1177–1151 | 1427–1401 |
| Tudhaliya I/II | 1150–1130 | 1400–1380 | Thutmose IV | 1151–1141 | 1401–1391 |
| Arnuwanda I | 1130–1120 | 1380–1370 | Amenhotep III | 1141–1103 | 1391–1353 |
| Hattusili II | 1120–1110 | 1370–1360 | | | |
| Tudhaliya III | 1110–1094 | 1360–1344 | Akhenaten | 1103–1084 | 1353–1334 |
| | | | Smenkhkare | 1086–1084 | 1336–1334 |
| Supplilumas I | 1094–1072 | 1344–1322 | Tutankhamun (Tut) | 1084–1075 | 1334–1325 |
| | | | Ay | 1075–1071 | 1325–1321 |
| Arnuwanda II | 1072–1071 | 1322–1321 | Horemheb | 1071–1042 | 1321–1292 |
| Mursili II | 1071–1045 | 1321–1295 | Ramesses I ($19^{th}$ Dynasty) | 1042–1040 | 1292–1290 |
| Muwatalli II | 1045–1022 | 1295–1272 | Sethi I | 1040–1029 | 1290–1279 |
| Urhi-Tesub | 1022–1017 | 1272–1267 | Ramesses II | 1029–963 | 1279–1213 |
| Hattusili III | 1017–987 | 1267–1237 | | | |
| Tudhaliya IV | 987–959 | 1237–1209 | Merenptah | 963–953 | 1213–1203 |
| Arnuwanda III | 959–957 | 1209–1207 | Amenmesse (usurper) | 953–949 | 1203–1199 |
| Supplilumas II | 957–928 | 1207–1178 | Sethi II | 949–943 | 1199–1193 |
| | | | Siptah | 943–937 | 1193–1187 |
| | | | Twosret | 937–935 | 1187–1185 |
| | | | Sethnakhte ($20^{th}$ Dynasty) | 936–933 | 1186–1183 |
| | | | Ramesses III | 933–902 | 1183–1152 |
| | | | Ramesses IV–XI | 902–845 | 1152–1069 |
| | | | $21^{st}$ Dynasty Tanite | 869–750 | 1069–945 |
| | | | $22^{nd}$–$24^{th}$ Dynasties | 810–664 | 945–715 |
| | | | $25^{th}$ Dynasty (Kush) | 715–655 | 715–664 |
| | | | $26^{th}$ Dynasty | 664–525 | 664–525 |

When the Hittite Empire collapsed, Kuzi-Teshub was the viceroy of Northern Syria (and descendent of Supplilumas I). Various Neo-Hittite kingdoms arose that survived until the Assyrians conquered them during the late eighth century BCE.

Traditional dates from Trevor Bryce

Traditional dates based on Kenneth Kitchen low dates

| Mycenai | Relation to Prior King | Birth (BCE) | Father's Age | Ascension Age | Comments |
|---|---|---|---|---|---|
| Phoroneus | | 1381 | | 51 | |
| Argos | Grandson | 1342 | 39 (grandfather) | 22 | Son of Zeus and Niobe |
| Phorbas | Son | 1320 | 22 | 35 | |
| Triops | Son | 1295 | 25 | 35 | |
| Agenor | Son | 1270 | 25 | 35 | |
| Krotopos | Son | 1235 | 35 | 10 | |
| Sthenelos | Son | 1210 | 25 | 27 | |
| Gelanor | Son | 1187 | 23 | 24 | |
| Danaos | Interloper | 1214 | 21 | 52 | Son of Belos |
| Lynkeus | Son-in-law/ nephew | 1190 | | 37 | Son of Aigyptos, brother of Danaos |
| Abas I | Son | 1160 | 30 | 28 | |
| Akrisios | Son | 1135 | 25 | 30 | |
| Melampous | Interloper | 1105 | | 30 | Son of Amythaon |
| Abas II | Son | 1079 | 26 | 29 | |
| Koiranos | Son | 1049 | 30 | 34 | |
| Atreus | Interloper | 1030 | 51 | 42 | Son of Pelops |
| Thyestes | Brother | 1030 | 51 | 79 | |
| Agamemnon | Grandnephew | 978 | 28 | 27 | Son of Pleisthenes, son of Atreus |
| Aigisthos | Half brother | 965 | 65 | 32 | Son of Thyestes |
| Aletes | Son | 935 | 30 | 8 | |
| Orestes | Half brother | 946 | 32 | 22 | Son of Agamemnon |
| Tisamenos | Son | 915 | 31 | 30 | |

| Korinth | Revised | Traditional |
|---|---|---|
| Sisyphos | 1101–1087 | 1351–1337 |
| Bounes | 1087 | 1347 |
| Epopeus | 1087–1068 | 1337–1318 |
| Glaukos | 1068–1061 | 1318–1311 |
| Ornytion | 1061–1036 | 1311–1286 |
| Korinthos | 1036–1003 | 1286–1253 |
| Demophoon | 1003–983 | 1253–1233 |
| Kreon | 983–967 | 1233–1217 |
| Propedas | 967–952 | 1217–1202 |
| Herakleides | 952–951 | 1202–1201 |
| Kreon II | 951–942 | 1201–1192 |
| Doridas/ | 942– | 1192– |
| Hyantidas and descendants | –812 | –1078 |
| Aletes | 812–800 | 1078–1037 |
| Ixion | 800–775 | 1037–1004 |
| Agelaos | 775–750 | 1004–970 |
| Praxmnis | 750–729 | 970–937 |
| Bakkhais | 729–704 | 937–904 |
| Agelaos II | 704–675 | 904–870 |
| Eudemos | 675–650 | 870–837 |
| Aristodemos | 650–625 | 837–804 |
| Agemon | 625–620 | 804–798 |
| Alexandros | 620–612 | 798–787 |
| Telestes | 612–600 | 787–775 |
| Elected kings[351] | 600–583 | 775–661 |
| Cypselos | 583–561 | 661–633 |
| Periandros | 561–529 | 633–589 |
| Psammetikhos | 529–527 | 589–587 |
| Peloponnesian League afterward | | |

| Sicyon | Revised | Traditional |
|---|---|---|
| Aigialeus and descendants | 1322–1089 | 1572–1339 |
| Epopeus | 1089–1068 | 1339–1318 |
| Laomedon | 1068–1053 | 1318–1303 |
| Sicyon | 1053– | 1303– |
| Polybos | –967 | –1217 |
| Adrastos | 967 | 1217 |
| Thesprotos | 967–952 | 1217–1202 |
| Phaitos | 952–951 | 1202–1201 |
| Ianiskos | 951– | 1201– |
| Zeuxippos | –906 | –1156 |
| Hippolytos | 906–870 | 1156–1120 |
| Lacestades | 870–865 | 1120–1115 |
| Phalces | 865– | 1115– |
| Rhegnidas | | |
| Herakleid kings | –595 | –640 |
| Orthagorids | 595–527 | 640–510 |
| Peloponnesian League afterward | | |

[351] There are many discrepancies in traditional dating. One is that Eusebios says Cypselos became tyrant in 661 BCE after ninety years of elected kings. However, Eratosthenes has Telestes fall right after the first Olympics. Automenes, son of Telestes, was the first elected king.

| Megara | Revised | Traditional |
|---|---|---|
| House of Kar | 1305–1125 | 1555–1375 |
| Lelex | 1125–1102 | 1375–1352 |
| Kleson | 1102–1082 | 1352–1332 |
| Pylas | 1082–1043 | 1332–1293 |
| Pandion | 1043–1025 | 1293–1275 |
| Nisos | 1025–1017 | 1275–1267 |
| Megareus | 1017–1012 | 1267–1262 |
| Alkathoos | 1012–972 | 1262–1222 |
| Theseus | 972–951 | 1222–1201 |
| Telamon | 951–930 | 1201–1180 |
| Demophoon | 930–920 | 1180–1170 |
| Oxyntes | 920–885 | 1170–1135 |
| Apheidas | 885–865 | 1135–1115 |
| Thymoites | 865–850 | 1115–1102 |
| Melantheus | 852–837 | 1102–1080 |
| Kodros | 837–812 | 1080–1043 |
| Herakleid kings | 812–590 | 1043–650 |

| Athens | Revised | Traditional |
|---|---|---|
| Akaios, Kekrops, Kranaos—Middle Bronze Age | | |
| Amphiktyon, Erikhthonios—Late Bronze Age | | |
| Pandion | 1145–1120 | 1395–1370 |
| Erekhtheus | 1120–1098 | 1370–1348 |
| Kekrops II | 1098–1058 | 1348–1308 |
| Pandion II | 1058–1036 | 1308–1286 |
| Sons of Metion | 1036–1022 | 1286–1272 |
| Aigeus | 1022–987 | 1272–1237 |
| Theseus | 987–950 | 1237–1200 |
| Menestheus | 950–934 | 1200–1184 |
| Demophoon | 934–920 | 1184–1170 |
| Oxyntes | 920–885 | 1170–1135 |
| Apheidas | 885–865 | 1135–1115 |
| Thymoites | 865–852 | 1115–1102 |
| Melantheus | 852–837 | 1102–1080 |
| Kodros | 837–811 | 1080–1043 |
| Medon | 811–790 | 1043–1020 |
| Akastos | 790–769 | 1020–997 |
| Arkhippos | 769–748 | 997–973 |
| Thersippos | 748–727 | 973–950 |
| Phorbas | 727–706 | 950–926 |
| Megakles | 706–685 | 926–903 |
| Diognetos | 685–664 | 903–879 |
| Pherekles | 664–643 | 879–856 |
| Ariphron | 643–622 | 856–832 |
| Thespieos | 622–601 | 832–809 |
| Agamestor | 601–580 | 809–788 |
| Aiskhylos | 580–558 | 788–756 |
| Alkmaion | 558–556 | 756–754 |
| Ten–year archons | | 763–683 |
| Elected archons | 556–501 | 683–508 |
| Democracy | 501–336 | 508–336 |

| Sparta | Revised | Traditional | Argos | Revised | Traditional |
|---|---|---|---|---|---|
| Lelex | 1239–1205 | 1489–1455 | | | |
| Myles | 1205–1180 | 1455–1430 | | | |
| Eurotas | 1180–1150 | 1430–1400 | | | |
| Lacedaimon | 1150–1125 | 1400–1375 | | | |
| Amyklas | 1125–1100 | 1375–1350 | | | |
| Argalos | 1100–1090 | 1350–1340 | | | |
| Cynortas | 1090–1070 | 1340–1320 | Melampous | 1078–1075 | 1328–1325 |
| Break in kings list | 1070–1017 | 1320–1267 | Megapenthes | 1075–1025 | 1325–1275 |
| Oibalos | 1017–992 | 1267–1242 | Anaxagoras | 1025–1000 | 1275–1250 |
| Hippokoon | 992–968 | 1242–1218 | Alkestor | 1000–975 | 1250–1225 |
| Tyndareos | 968–945 | 1218–1195 | Iphis | 975–947 | 1225–1197 |
| Menelaos | 945–930 | 1195–1170 | Sthenelos | 947–922 | 1197–1172 |
| Orestes | 930–885 | 1170–1135 | Cylarabes | 922–913 | 1172–1163 |
| | | | Orestes (from Mycenai) | 913–885 | 1163–1135 |
| Penthilos | 885–870 | 1135–1120 | Tisamenos (from Mycenai) | 885–854 | 1135–1104 |
| No king | | | | | |
| Eurystheus | 854–805 | 1104–1037 | Temenos (from Tiryns) | 852–840 | 1102–1090 |
| | | | Ceisos (from Tiryns) | 840–810 | 1090–1037 |
| No kings | | | Medon | 810–780 | 1037–1004 |
| | | | Thestios | 780–750 | 1004–970 |
| Agis I | 740–720 | 1037–1001 | Merops | 750–720 | 970–937 |
| Ekhestratos | 720–700 | 1001–965 | Aristodamidas | 720–690 | 937–904 |
| Leobrotas | 700–679 | 965–930 | | | |
| Doryssos | 679–659 | 930–894 | 7th Herakleid king | 690–660 | 904–870 |
| Agesilaos I | 659–638 | 894–857 | 8th Herakleid king | 660–635 | 870–837 |
| Arkhelaos | 638–618 | 857–822 | Erato | 635–612 | 837–804 |
| Teleklos | 618–598 | 822–793 | Pheidon | 612–583 | 804–775 |
| Alkimenes | 598–577 | 793–760 | | | |
| Polydoros | 577–570 | 760–737 | Leokides (Lakedes) | 583–565 | 775–737 |
| Eurykrates | 570–560 | 737–695 | Meltas | 565–555 | 737–704 |
| Anaxandros | 560–544 | 695–650 | Damokratidas | | |
| Eurykratides | 544–538 | 650–605 | | | |
| Leon | 538–532 | 605–560 | **Historical Generations** | **Relationship** | |
| Anaxandridas II | 532–516 | 560–520 | | | |
| Kleomenes I | 516–491 | 520–491 | 1 (Kleomenes being the first) | | |
| Leonidas | 491–480 | 491–480 | 1.5 | Younger half brother | |
| Pleistarkhos | 480–459 | 480–459 | 2.5 | Son | |
| Pleistoanax | 459–409 | 459–409 | 3 | Younger cousin | |
| Pausanias | 409–395 | 409–395 | 4 | Son | |
| Agesipolis I | 395–380 | 395–380 | 5 | Son | |
| Kleombrotos I | 380–371 | 380–371 | 5 | Brother | |
| Agesipolis II | 371–370 | 371–370 | 6 | Son | |
| Kleomenes II | 370–309 | 370–309 | 6 | Brother | |
| Areus I | 309–265 | 309–265 | 8 | Grandson | |
| Akrotatos | 265–262 | 265–262 | 9 | Son | |
| Areus II | 262–254 | 262–254 | 10 | Son | |
| Leonidas II | 254–236 | 254–236 | 9 | Distant cousin of Akrotatos | |
| Kleomenes III | 236–219 | 236–219 | 10 (tenth from Kleomenes) | Son | |
| Agesipolis III | 220–215 | 220–215 | | | |

| Elis | Revised | Traditional |
|---|---|---|
| Aithalos | 1125–1100 | 1375–1350 |
| Endymion | 1100–1072 | 1350–1322 |
| Eleios | 1072–1053 | 1322–1303 |
| Epeios | 1053–1013 | 1303–1263 |
| Augeias | 1013–968 | 1263–1218 |
| Agasthenes | 968–948 | 1218–1198 |
| Polyxeinos | 948–920 | 1198–1170 |
| Amphimakhos | 920–900 | 1170–1150 |
| Dios | 900–860 | 1150–1110 |
| Oxylos | 860–845 | 1110–1095 |
| Laios | 845–825 | 1095–1075 |

| Pylos | Revised | Traditional |
|---|---|---|
| Pylas | 1043– | 1293– |
| ? | –991 | –1241 |
| Neleus | 991–961 | 1241–1211 |
| Nestor | 961–920 | 1211–1170 |
| Thrasymedes | 920–887 | 1170–1137 |
| Sillos | 887–854 | 1137–1104 |

| Lapiths | | |
|---|---|---|
| Hypseus | –1120 | –1370 |
| Lapithos | 1120–1102 | 1370–1352 |
| Periphas | 1102–1083 | 1352–1333 |
| Antion | 1083–1055 | 1333–1305 |
| Elatos | 1055–1042 | 1305–1292 |
| Phlegyas | 1042–1015 | 1292–1265 |
| Ixion | 1015–986 | 1265–1236 |
| Peirithoos | 986–951 | 1236–1201 |
| Polypoites | 951–934 | 1201–1184 |

| Iolkos | | |
|---|---|---|
| Mimas | 1108–1073 | 1358–1323 |
| Hippotes | 1073–1037 | 1323–1287 |
| Kretheus | 1037–1002 | 1287–1252 |
| Pelias | 1002–981 | 1252–1231 |
| Akastos | 981–965 | 1231–1215 |
| Haimonians | 965–949 | 1215–1199 |
| Descendants of Akastos | 949–875 | 1199–1125 |
| Thessalos | 875– | 1125– |

| Troy | | |
|---|---|---|
| Teukros | 1150–1120 | 1400–1370 |
| Dardanos | 1120–1100 | 1370–1350 |
| Erikhthonios | 1100–1080 | 1350–1330 |
| Tros | 1080–1067 | 1330–1317 |
| Ilos | 1067–1032 | 1317–1282 |
| Laomedon | 1032–970 | 1282–1220 |
| Priamos | 970–934 | 1220–1184 |
| Aineias | 934–910 | 1184–1160 |
| Askanios | 910–885 | 1160–1135 |

| Kalydon | | |
|---|---|---|
| Hippodamas | 1090–1070 | 1340–1320 |
| Chieftains | 1070–1065 | 1320–1315 |
| Aitolos | 1065–1045 | 1315–1295 |
| Kalydon | 1045–1025 | 1295–1275 |
| Agenor | 1025–1010 | 1275–1260 |
| Parthaon | 1010–996 | 1260–1246 |
| Oineus | 996–965 | 1246–1215 |
| Agrios | 965–961 | 1215–1211 |
| Sons of Agrios | 961–948 | 1211–1198 |
| Andraimon | 948–940 | 1198–1190 |
| Thoas | 940–910 | 1190–1160 |
| Haimon | 910–875 | 1165–1125 |

| Thebes | Revised | Traditional | Orkhomenos | Revised | Traditional |
|---|---|---|---|---|---|
| | | | Andreas | 1149–1107 | 1399–1357 |
| Kadmos | 1136–1085 | 1386–1335 | Athamas | 1107–1099 | 1357–1349 |
| Pentheus | 1085–1081 | 1335–1331 | | | |
| Polydoros | 1081–1070 | 1331–1320 | Minyas | 1099–1061 | 1349–1311 |
| Nyktos/Lykos | 1070–1056 | 1320–1306 | | | |
| Labdakos | 1056–1037 | 1306–1287 | Orkhomenos | 1061–1040 | 1311–1290 |
| Lykos II | 1037–1035 | 1287–1285 | | | |
| Amphion and Zethos | 1035–1017 | 1285–1267 | Klymenos | 1040–1012 | 1290–1262 |
| Laios | 1017 | | | | |
| Kreon | 1017–986 | 1267–1236 | | | |
| Lykos III | 986–985 | 1236–1235 | Erigonos | 1012–983 | 1262–1233 |
| Laios | 985 | 1235 | | | |
| Oidipous | 985–967 | 1235–1217 | Azeus | 983– | 1233– |
| Polyneices | 967–966 | 1217–1216 | | | |
| Eteokles | 966–958 | 1216–1208 | Ekhekles | | |
| Kreon | 958–949 | 1208–1199 | | | |
| Laodamas | 949–948 | 1199–1198 | | | |
| Thersandros | 948–944 | 1198–1194 | Askalaphos/ | | |
| Adrastos | 944–928 | 1194–1178 | Ialmenos | –934 | –1184 |
| Tisamenos | 928–903 | 1178–1153 | Leitos | 934– | 1184– |
| Autesion | 903–879 | 1153–1129 | | | |
| Damasikhthon | 879– | 1129– | | | |
| Xanthos | | | | | |

| Thebes | Relation to Prior King | Birth Year (BCE) | Father's Age | Ascension Age | Comments |
|---|---|---|---|---|---|
| Kadmos | | 1160 | | 24 | |
| Pentheus | Nephew | 1110 | | 25 | Son of Ekhion of the Spartoi |
| Polydoros | Cousin | 1121 | 39 | 40 | Son of Kadmos |
| Nykteus | Father-in-law | 1118 | 25 | 48 | Son of Chthonios of the Spartoi, regent for Labdakos |
| Lykos | Brother | 1114 | 29 | 45 | Regent for Labdakos |
| Labdakos | Grandnephew | 1074 | 47 | 18 | Son of Polydoros |
| Lykos II | Second cousin | 1089 | 25 | 52 | Son of Lykos, regent for Laios |
| Amphion and Zethos | Grandnephew | 1068 | | 33 | Sons of Zeus and Nykteus's daughter |
| Kreon | Interloper | 1050 | 36 | 33 | Son of Pelops |
| Lykos III | Interloper | 1016 | | 30 | Son of Poseidon |
| Laios | Interloper | 1038 | 36 | 21, 53 | Son of Labdakos |
| Oidipous | Son | 1002 | 36 | 17 | |
| Polyneices | Son | 984 | 18 | 17 | |
| Eteokles | Brother | 984 | 18 | 18 | Son of Amythaon |
| Kreon II | Uncle | 1017 | 30 | 59 | Descendent of Spartoi |
| Laodamas | Grandnephew | 965 | 19 | 16 | Son of Eteokles |
| Thersandros | Cousin | 965 | 19 | 17 | Son of Polyneices |
| Adrastos | Brother | 963 | 21 | 19 | |
| Tisamenos | Nephew | 945 | 20 | 17 | Son of Thersandros |
| Autesion | Son | 926 | 19 | 23 | |
| Damasikhthon | Interloper | 915 | 25 | 30 | Boiotian chief |

# Addendum 3
# Anatolia Prehistory and Bronze Age

Archaeologists have determined that agriculture first developed in Anatolia c. 10000 BCE. In the rain watered foothills above the Syrian Desert wheat, barley, rye, lintels, and peas were cultivated. Sheep and then goats from the nearly Tarsos and Zagros Mountains were domesticated, followed by local cattle and pigs. From here agriculture spread to Europe, Mesopotamia and Iran.

By the middle of the eight millennium BCE agriculture had advance enough for farming settlements to arise at central Anatolian sites such as Catal Hoyuk, Cafer Hoyuk, and Cayonu. Although these sites were eventually abandoned, the Neolithic farming culture of Anatolia evolved largely unimpeded until the third millennium BCE.

Because the earliest documents concerning Anatolia document many spoken languages, Renfrew proposed that both Indo-European and non Indo-European languages were native to Anatolia. The linguist J. P. Mallory provided a compelling argument to dismiss Anatolian roots for Indo-Europeans. DNA testing proved conclusively that the early Anatolian farmers were not Indo-European.

Mallory argued in his book *In Search of the Indo-Europeans* that a proto-Indo-European language developed in the Ukrainian Steppes ca. 4500

BCE.[352] The proto Indo-Europeans were early adopters of dairy technology, which had been invented by farmers around the Sea of Marmara in western Anatolia a millennium earlier.

The first language to break away from proto-Indo-European was proto-Anatolian. The proto-Anatolians migrated west into the rich pasturelands of the Danube during the early fourth millennium BCE—roughly a millennium before the horse was domesticated. The proto-Anatolians were later pushed southward by Indo-European tribes whose language that would eventually split into closely related Hellenic, Armenian, Phrygian, and Thracian.

The proto-Anatolians arrived into relatively unpopulated northwest Anatolia around the beginning of the third millennium BCE. They founded the first settlement at Troy ca. 2920T/2685R BCE.

Roughly two centuries later the last proto-Anatolians were driven out of the Balkans and into Anatolia. There arrival corresponds with a catastrophic event for the indigenous farming people. Between 2700T/2450R BCE and 2600T/2350R BCE most of the settlements of western Anatolia, as well as many sites further east, were destroyed. The cities were rebuilt with megarons (fortified palaces) similar in style to those already found in Troy. The rebuilt cities were littered with ceramics of a style whose origins were in Troas. The archeological record notes a second disruption occurred between 2300T/2065R BCE and 2230T/1980R BCE.

Mallory believes that proto-Anatolian evolved into Hittite, Luwian, and Palaic—the first three written Indo-European languages. He believes that the three languages are so closely related that they probably split from one another no more than five hundred years before texts in all three languages appear in Hittite archives. Mallory also argues that the three languages evolved separately after the proto-Anatolians arrived in Anatolia, because

[352] The archaeologist Marija Gimbutas first identified the Kurgan Culture of the Ukrainian Steppes with the earliest Indo-Europeans. Mallory provided linguistic evidence in support of Gimbutas's theory. Mallory also gave several reasons to refute Renfrew's assertion that Indo-European languages were native to Anatolia: (1) Non Indo-European languages are attested to in Anatolia from the earliest sources; (2) place names of Hellas and Anatolia are not derived from Indo-European languages; (3) the spread of agriculturalists out of Anatolia at the end of the eighth millennium BCE is far too early for the proto-Indo-European language (which developed in the fifth millennium BCE); (4) the agriculturalists appear to be largely peaceful, and Indo-European languages celebrate war; and (5) it does not explain the close association of Indo-European to languages from the Ural Mountains in Russia.

they all clearly borrowed heavily from local non-Indo-European languages. Thus, linguistic evidence presented by Mallory suggests that the Indo-Europeans first spread throughout Anatolia during the upheavals of the third millennium BCE. Their languages began to evolve separately as a result of geographical distance.

When Assyrian traders arrived in central Anatolia ca. 2000 BCE they traded with locals who spoke langauges both Indo-European (Anatolian) and non Indo-European (Hattic, for example). Judging by their adoption of non Indo-European words, the Indo-Europeans must have already been in central Anatolia for some time before they encountered the Assyrians. The horse arrived in Anatolia during the second millennium BCE.

## First Historical Records of Western Anatolia

The Hittites wrote the first texts describing events in western Anatolia during the late seventeenth century T / early fourteenth century R BCE. The Hittites called the area Lukka after the Luwian people who inhabited it. Their attack was probably in response to incursions by Luwian tribesmen on Hittite territories farther east. Luwian speakers appear to have continually migrated eastward into southern Cappadocia (Hittite Lower Land), Cilicia, and northern Syria during the Late Bronze Age.

According to Hittite records, the most important Luwian tribes were the Arzawans and the Lukka. The Arzawans were the ancestors of the closely related Karians, Lydians, and Mysians (the most famous Mysian tribe being the Teukrians, or Trojans) of the Classical Age. The Lycians were descendants of the Lukka.

After the Hittites withdrew, Luwian speakers resumed their southeastward migration into Hittite territories. The Arzawan kingdoms joined into a loose confederacy and became important enough to carry on diplomatic relations with Egypt (early sixteenth century T / late fourteenth century R BCE). The rugged underbelly of Anatolia made political unification impossible, and the Lukka were divided among numerous principalities.

The Minoans, and to a lesser degree the Hellenes, traded with Luwian tribesmen. After the Hellenes, whom the Hittites may be referring to when they mention the Ahhiyawa (Akhaians/Mycenaians), brought down the Minoan civilization, they became active in Arzawan affairs (mid fifteenth century T / late thirteenth century R BCE). The first Hittite text to mention the Ahhiyawa says Attarsiya (meaning "man of Ahhiyawa") conducted a military operation in Arzawa with infantry and one hundred chariots during the reign of the Hittite great-king Tudhaliya I (1400T/1150R–1380T/1130R BCE). Ahhiyawan traders and colonists began settling along the Anatolian coast during the fourteenth century T / twelfth century R BCE, particularly at Milawata (Miletos). These early traders and colonists named the continent after the Assuwa (Asia[353]) Confederacy of Arzawan states.

The Hittites were recovering from a century of divisive internal strife when they became active in the political affairs of western Anatolia under Great-King Tudhaliya I. The Assuwa Confederacy of Arzawan kingdoms had succeeded in taking Hittite territories south of the Halys River, and the threatened Hittites were forced to counterattack. Tudhaliya opened his reign with a preemptive strike against the Arzawans, hoping to weaken the confederated Assuwa states and thereby secure his southwestern border before invading wealthier Syria. The Hittites identified five important Arzawan kingdoms within the confederacy; from northwest to southeast were Wilusa (Troy), Seha River Lands (Teuthrania), Arzawa (Lydia), Mira-Kuwaliya (Karia), and Hapalla (Phrygia). The kingdom of Arzawa was sometimes called Arzawa Minor to distinguish it from the collective name of the states of Arzawa. There were also many smaller kingdoms.

The great-king's attack proved counterproductive. In response to Hittite campaigns, the Arzawan states strengthened their military alliance under the leadership of Kukkulli. Then the Assuwa Confederacy retaliated with coordinated attacks on Hittite territories.

Tudhaliya was forced to quickly return to face the Assuwa Confederacy, and his victory over the Assuwan army was so complete that the alliance was never reestablished. The great-king carried off ten thousand soldiers, plus chariots and horses, and resettled them in the Hittite homeland in order to reduce the chance of further rebellion. It was a practice carried out by subsequent kings as well. Having gained his objective of weakening the

---

[353] Hesiod, in *Theogony*, 359, says Asia is one of the eldest Oceanides and wife of the Titan Iapetos. To the early Hellenes, "Asia" referred only to the Asia Minor area of Anatolia.

Arzawans, Tudhaliya withdrew without trying to control Arzawan affairs and instead turned his attention upon his enemies to the east and north of the Hittite nation.

Tudhaliya's victory brought relative peace only for a short time. Either Tudhaliya or his son-in-law and successor Arnuwanda (1380T/1130R–1370T/1120R BCE) was forced to lead another army westward. Twice the great-king defeated the Arzawan king Kupanta-Kurunta of Arzawa Minor, who escaped both times and retained his kingdom. While struggling to remain free of the Hittites, the Arzawans were hounded by Ahhiyawan traders, raiders, and settlers. The Ahhiyawan port of Milawata (Miletos) became a major city and palace center. Many hapless Arzawans were seized and sold into slavery in Hellas.

When the Hittites came under attack from the Kaska people invading from the north, the opportunistic pharaoh Amenhotep III (1391T/1141R–1353T/1103R BCE) proposed a two-pronged attack on their vulnerable mutual enemy. The Egyptian pharaoh had his eye on rich Syria and proposed alliance with Arzawan king Tarhundaradu. Although the Arzawans occupied the Hittite Lower Land, cautious Tarhundaradu never advanced across the Halys River into core Hittite territory. This blunder allowed the Hittite great-king Tudhaliya III (1360T/1110R–1344T/1094R BCE) to concentrate on the Kaska and drive them out. Then he sent his son Supplilumas to recover the Lower Land. Interestingly, the Egyptian proposal to Tarhundaradu was written in Nesite (Hittite) instead of Akkadian, then the language for international diplomatic exchange. This probably means that Arzawa was not an established member of the international community and Nesite was a language known to both Egyptian and Arzawan scribes.

Crown Prince Supplilumas retook the important Lower Land city of Tuwanuwa (Tyanna/Tabul) and used it as his springboard for twenty years of campaigning to defeat the Arzawans. He drove the Arzawan chiefs out of the Lower Land, although its population remained largely Luwian. Then he conquered two states immediately west of the Lower Land, Pitassa and Hapalla, the latter an Arzawan kingdom. Some of the Arzawan campaigns occurred after Supplilumas succeeded his father as great-king (1344T/1094R–1322T/1072R BCE).

Supplilumas did not try to conquer additional Arzawan territories (beyond Hapalla). His goal was to protect his southwestern flank while he concentrated on richer Syria. He sent one army deep into the territory of Arzawa Minor to defeat King Anzapahhaddu in a preemptive strike. The Arzawan king defeated the invading Hittite army, and the great-king was forced to lead a larger force in person to subdue the Arzawans. The pacified Arzawans caused no further problems during Supplilumas's reign.

The Arzawans rose in revolt upon Supplilumas's death. King Uhhaziti of Arzawa, based at Apasa (which some identify with Ephesos), secured the help of all of the Arzawan states, as well as the king of the Ahhiyawa, to challenge the Hittites. He forced many Hittite vassals to change allegiance to him. When Great-King Mursili II (1321T/1071R–1295T/1045R BCE), son of Supplilumas, sent a large army to briefly occupy predominately Ahhiyawan Milawata (Miletos), the refugees fled to King Uhhaziti, who refused to turn them over to the Hittites (1318T/1068R BCE). Mursili personally led his forces against King Uhhaziti with his brother Sarri-Kusuh, viceroy of Carchemish (in northern Syria), among his allies (1316T/1066R BCE). Because of illness, King Uhhaziti sent his son Piyama-Kurunta to lead the Arzawan forces. Great-King Mursili defeated Piyama-Kurunta and pressed on into Arzawa Minor, occupying Apasa. Uhhaziti fled across the sea to Ahhiyawan territory (and possibly into Hellenic lore as Pelops). Many of his rebel supporters fled to Mount Arinnanda, which extends out into the sea, and to the city of Puranda.

The Hittites starved out the rebels on Mount Arinnanda and besieged Puranda. It fell the following spring. Then the great-king marched north on Uhhaziti's ally, the Seha River Land, whose king surrendered without giving battle. Mursili returned home with 65,000 rebellious subjects to relocate. With this victory the Hittites began playing an active role in local political affairs and the status of the Arzawan kings dropped from protectorates to vassals. During the march home, Mursili reinstated faithful vassal-kings in Mira and Hapalla.

A few years later, a new Arzawan rebellion began in Masa (Mysia), to the north (1309T/1059R BCE). Great-King Mursili returned to Arzawan lands again. After quickly crushing the rebellion, Mursili had no further troubles in the west during the remainder of his reign.

After King Uhhaziti fled, the coastal settlements took on a predominately Mycenaian character and fell under the control of the Ahhiyawan great-king. The Hittites permitted this, hoping it would satisfy Ahhiyawan territorial ambition and promote regional stability. There is evidence of a pact, or treaty between the Hittites and Ahhiyawa indicating a period of peaceful, perhaps even amicable, relations. The vassal Arzawan kings no longer played important roles.

Several decades of peace ended with the arrival of a renegade Hittite nobleman named Piyamaradu. His ambition led him into alliance with the Ahhiyawa. He married his daughter to Atpa, the Ahhiyawan vassal ruler of Milawata (Miletos). Piyamaradu then conquered Arzawan Wilusa (Troy) outright. Late in his reign, the Hittite great-king Muwatalli II (1295T/1045R–1272T/1022R BCE) was forced to respond to this treasonable act and sent an army to capture him. Piyamaradu escaped and, from Ahhiyawan bases, continued to harass the Hittites' Arzawan vassals. Great-King Hattusili III (1267T/1017R–1237T/987R BCE) briefly occupied Milawata, hoping to seize Piyamaradu. Hattusili apologized to the Ahhiyawan great-king for this act and withdrew empty-handed (ca. 1261T/1011R BCE). When the Hittites withdrew, the attacks resumed. The sack of Troy VI could represent one such attack (1220T/970R BCE).

It was clear to Great-King Tudhaliya IV (1237T/987R–1209T/959R BCE) that there would be no relief from raids in western Anatolia so long as the Ahhiyawa held Anatolian territory. He was able to drive a hostile ruler from Milawata and install the deposed ruler's loyal son, thereby ending Ahhiyawan rule. The great-king sent a Hittite princess to be the bride of the new ruler. Ahhiyawan power in Anatolia was at an end (although the Ahhiyawan settlers remained). The great-king also banished the import of Ahhiyawan goods into Syria. These actions devastated the economy of Hellas, resulting in civic unrest, which led to the sacking of most Hellenic palace cities. Tudhaliya used Milawata as a staging area to reassert Hittite rule in western Anatolia. He gave the ruler of Milawata broad control over all Arzawan kingdoms in order to maintain control.

The last Hittite great-king, Supplilumas II (1207T/957R–1178T/928R BCE), repeatedly campaigned in western Anatolia but was unable to stamp out rebellions. The beleaguered Hittite Empire eventually collapsed under attacks from Luwians, Kaska, Phrygians, and Sea Peoples[354] (primarily Hellenes and Luwians). The Egyptians say the Arzawan kingdoms also

[354] The closeness of the Hellenes and Luwians is implied in Homer (*Iliad*) in that the Trojans and Akhaians could understand each other. Pottery and other artifacts also indicate the closeness. The Phrygians are even more closely related to the Hellenes, as both groups split off of the proto-Hellenic/Thracian languages.

collapsed (Troy VII was one of the casualties). Egypt desperately fought off the Sea Peoples' attacks upon their coast.

The population of Anatolia certainly dropped significantly after the fall of the Arzawan kingdoms. Many migrated east into Cappadocia and Syria. The reason for the sudden migration of so many people at the end of the Bronze Age remains a puzzle.

By traditional dating, it took hundreds of years before Near Eastern economies began to recover from the Late Bronze Age disruptions. This long period at the beginning of the Iron Age is descriptively called the Dark Age. During the Dark Age, Mycenaian ports such as Miletos and Iassos remained Hellenic and the culture of the Arzawan speakers survived in the interior. Herodotos said the Lydians of his day believed Lydos (Lydians) was the brother of Kar (Karians) and Mysos (Mysians), each an eponym of a closely related tribe. These tribes were the descendants of the Arzawans. That they remained culturally close to the Hellenes is evident in the following quote by Herodotos concerning the Lydians: "Working class girls prostituted themselves to gain a dowry and pick their own husbands. Otherwise their way of life is like the Hellenes."[355]

Image A3.1
Map of Bronze Age Anatolia

[355] Herodotos of Halikarnassos, *Histories,* i.94.

# Addendum 4
# Minoan Krete

> Out in the dark blue sea there lies a land called Krete, a rich and lovely land, washed by the waves on every side, densely peopled and boasting ninety cities. Each of the several races of the isle has its own language. First there are the Akhaians; then the EteoKretans "Genuine Kretans," proud of their native stock; next the Cydonians; the Dorians with their three clans; and finally the noble Pelasgians.[356]
>
> —Homer, *Odyssey,* xx, seventh century BCE

Krete, the largest island in the Aigaian, is home to the first European civilization. Since we cannot read their writing, we do not know what they called themselves. The ancient Egyptians called their land Keftiu, and in Mesopotamia they were known as the Kaptara (or Caphtor). The eminent

[356] Hesiod seems to have combined the Eteokretans, Cydonians, and Pelasgians when he said three Hellenic people settled Krete: Pelasgians, Akhaians, and Dorians. Most experts doubt the Pelasgians or Minoans were Hellenic, although it is still debated if they were Indo-European or not. The Cydonians and Eteokretans may be the descendants of the Minoans who lived on the western and eastern parts of the island, respectively. Diodoros, in *Library of History*, v.80, says the Eteokretans arrived first, followed by Pelasgians and, later, the Dorians. Judging by place names, the Pelasgian and Minoan languages were similar. It is doubtful that the Dorians are a different group than the Mycenaian-era Akhaians; they are probably their descendants.

scholar Sir Arthur Evans[357] labeled them "Minoans" after the legendary Kretan king of Hellenic mythology. These Minoans probably did not speak an Indo-European language. They definitely were not Hellenic. Ironically, King Minos ruled Krete after the Hellenes had conquered the Minoans and was a descendent of Mycenaian kings.

The first farmers reached Krete from nearby Southern Anatolia about the same time that the first farmers reached Hellas from Northern Anatolia (late seventh millennium BCE). They found an uninhabited island of 3,200 square miles, eighty miles from the Peloponnesos and 160 miles from Anatolia. It was, as ancient sources tell us, a lush forested island where wild goats (ibex), red deer, hare, and rabbit abounded. Although bears were common, there were no wolves, lions, or snakes to worry about. The upland meadows were thick with oaks and cypress, and the mountains were full of the scent of cedar, pine, poplar, and juniper.

## First Cities (2600T/2350R–2000T/1750R BCE)—Early Minoan Pottery

The first cities on Krete arose during the Early Bronze Age (2600T/2350R BCE) not long after the first Aigaian cities arose at places like Troy and Poliokhni. Within two centuries urban sites had developed throughout the island. Archaeological evidence indicates that the whole island adopted a single culture—that which we call Minoan.

Whereas most of the cities of Hellas and Anatolia were destroyed in the twenty-third century T / twenty-first century R BCE, Krete was spared. Consequently, uninterrupted Minoan culture surpassed that of its related neighbors on the mainland. Minoan culture reached a fairly sophisticated state by the end of the second millennium BCE. Besides improvements in metalwork and pottery, Minoan workmen learned to engrave gems

---

[357] Sir Arthur Evans was also responsible for introducing a tripartite system of chronology for dating pottery. The three Bronze Age pottery eras and their approximate time line are as follows:

- Early Minoan (early third millennium to 2100T/1850R BCE)—prepalace period
- Middle Minoan (2100T/1850R–1650T/1350R BCE)—pre-, first, and early second palace periods
- Late Minoan (1550T/1300R–1100T/860R BCE)—later second and postpalace periods

and manufacture seals. The major ports were all located on the protected northern beaches. The mountains ran straight down to the sea on the south side of the island.

## First Palace Era (1900T/1650R–1700/1450R BCE)—Middle Minoan Pottery[358]

The palace era was one of continuation, a time of economic and cultural growth for the Minoans. The development of palaces was a revolutionary change. Besides serving as the residence for the royal family and their retinue, the palaces also functioned in the administration of the state, religious ceremonies, and in business activities, such as manufacturing, warehousing, and trade. The palaces had the resources to intensely cultivate orchards of grapes, figs, and olives. Many crafts were fostered at the palace. The Minoans performed high-quality architectural feats unheard of around the Aigaian: windows, balconies, and multistory buildings decorated with brightly painted fluid frescoes. In addition, the first beehive-shaped tombs, called tholos tombs, were constructed in the Mesara plain and used by whole clans over many generations.

Exports of manufactured goods (especially wheel-made polychrome pottery with charming plant motifs, statues, purple-dyed cloth, and miniature jewelry of ivory and precious stones) generated the wealth needed to pay for the construction of labyrinthine palaces and tholos tombs of proportions never before seen in the Aigaian. The use of wagons was introduced into Krete to transport ever-larger shipments of goods. The Kretans imported metals (primarily gold, silver, tin, and copper), ivory, jewels, and luxury goods from abroad. Palace walls were decorated with beautiful, boldly painted murals.

[358] Because of palace-era interactions between Krete and the Near East, it is possible to date events on Krete relative to the Near East. Pottery of the first palace period has been found in Phoenicia and Egypt in relation to Egyptian pottery from the early Twelfth Dynasty into the Thirteenth Dynasty (early to mid 1800sT / mid to late 1600sR to early 1600sT / late 1400sR BCE). Radiocarbon samples from Phaistos on Krete and Ayia Irini on the Cyclades island of Keos confirm those dates. The finding of a stone lid bearing a cartouche of Pharaoh Khyan (1637T/1387R–1619T/1369R) in a first-palace-era site indicates the first palace period lasted at least to the end of the seventeenth century T / mid fourteenth century R BCE.

On the religious and cultural front, there were Minoan advancements in music, dance, and other arts. The Minoans played three musical instruments: the lyre, pipe, and sistron (like a tambourine). The Hellenes believed the Minoans invented dancing. Discoveries of two types of cultic activities have been found: processional and dancing rites (to restore the zest for life after the death of a loved one). All the major elements of a Hellenic sacrificial rite, except for fire, are found in Minoan religion: procession to an altar, proprietary offering, flute accompaniment, and catching the victim's blood.

By the nineteenth century T / sixteenth century R BCE, Minoan traders had boldly set up trading relations with the peoples of the Levant. As the cities of Anatolia and Hellas began to recover from their catastrophic upheaval toward the end of the twentieth century T / mid seventeenth century R BCE, trade resumed there as well. Kretan trade colonies began appearing on Rhodes, the Cyclades, and the Sporades after 1750T/1500R BCE. Trade with the Near East is attested to in a text from Zimri-Lim, king of Mari around 1760T/1510R BCE, that mentions the transport from Krete (Kaptara) to Mesopotamia of such goods as daggers encrusted with gold and lapis lazuli, richly decorated vases, and various textiles and articles of clothing. Leather shoes sent to King Hammurabi of Babylon were mysteriously returned. Surprisingly, trade with nearby Hellas remained only sporadic; the Hellenes traded mainly with the Cyclades and Anatolia.

The largest palace was built at Knossos, which had surpassed the cities on the east side of the island in size. Good roads were built to connect the various cities, indicating that the island was either under one government or that various communities were on very friendly terms. The manufacture of foot-wheeled pottery began during the nineteenth century T / seventeenth century R BCE

Under the influence of Mesopotamian scripts, hieroglyphic symbols were first experimented with as the economy grew too large and complex for the bureaucrats to retain records in their heads (1800T/1550R BCE). Two forms of hieroglyphics developed, one based on the other. By the end of the era, a highly developed hieroglyphic system was used. Although undeciphered, it undoubtedly recorded inventories of palace goods and tax transactions.

Religious ceremonies were performed in the palaces and elsewhere as well. Votive offerings were presented on mountain peaks, in caverns, at the bases of sacred trees (usually fig or olive trees), in tiny cult chambers within houses or palaces, and possibly at tiny temples. Women are represented as holding important religious positions and a high place in society in general. Women wore dresses to accentuate their femininity and were shown in scenes of dancing and bull leaping, just as the men were.

## Second Palace Era (1700T/1450R–1400T/1150R BCE)—Middle and Late Minoan Pottery

Just as the original palaces were becoming bustling population centers, they were all destroyed by some natural phenomenon, perhaps earthquakes (ca. 1700T/1450R BCE). Whatever the cause, the people had ample warning of the impending disaster and had fled to the hills. Although the destruction was massive, the resilient Minoans returned, and over the next century they rebuilt the palaces on a more expansive scale. Middle Minoan pottery styles continued for about a century before giving way to Late Minoan styles.[359]

The disaster occurred when the Minoan civilization was nearing its acme and could well afford a grandiose rebuilding program. High-quality Minoan crafts (especially pottery and clothing) were sold throughout the eastern Mediterranean, and their fluid, natural designs contrasted with the stiff and dignified works of Egypt and the Near East. The civilization appears to have been remarkably peaceful, given that no war scenes were

[359] It was once thought that the original palaces were destroyed by the tidal waves and earthquakes associated with the eruption of the volcano on nearby Theras Island. However, examination of the palaces revealed that Middle Minoan pottery was found in the destruction level while Late Minoan IA pottery was found in the Minoan sites destroyed during the eruption on Thera Island. Late Minoan IA is traditionally dated to 1600T-1500T BCE (using comparative Egyptian artifacts). Recent scientific evidence (radiocarbon, dendrochronology, and ice cores from Greenland) suggest a date between 1650 BCE and 1600 BCE. To alter traditional Minoan dates would affect the entire chronology of the Late Bronze Age and our understanding of the archaeology of the eastern Mediterranean. The consequences would be even bigger if revisionist dates were used, because they assume events occurred some 250 years later than traditional dates. What is certain is that the eruption did not bring down the Minoans. The arrival of Mycenaian conquerors is later, at end of the Late Minoan IB pottery period.

commemorated in art and because the cities were all un-walled. The sea provided protection from more warlike peoples, such as the Hellenes.

The innovative Minoans developed better writing systems. Hieroglyphic writing was replaced by Linear A syllabic script (symbols mimicking syllable sounds, ca. 1635T/1385R BCE), which has not been deciphered. Its primary use was in administering the palace economy and not for artistic or religious expression. Because there are numerous palace sites with Linear A records, we can assume that Krete was divided into numerous independent states that, based on the lack of fortifications, must have been on friendly terms with one another.

The Minoans now conducted the first large-scale commercial enterprises in the Aigaian. Minoan culture exerted a profound impact on Hellas—including the building of palaces[360] and tholos tombs there once firm trade relations were established (sixteenth century T / fourteenth century R BCE). Additional markets created greater wealth in Krete, and Minoan trade posts and, later, colonies were established in Sicily, southern Italy, various Aigaian Islands, and the Anatolian coast.

The palaces were destroyed again, probably by an earthquake (which could be related to the eruption of the volcano on nearby Thera Island) but possibly as the result of an invasion (ca. 1570T/1320R BCE). Again they were rebuilt, and Minoan culture suffered no setback. In fact, it entered its golden age. The emerging mainland Mycenaian civilization continued to borrow heavily from its Minoan trading partners.

Minoan influence abroad is attested to by the development of Cypro-Minoan Linear A (ca. 1565T/1315R BCE). It represents an adaptation of the Minoan Linear A to an Eteocypriot language of Cyprus. Although Cyprus was physically closer to the ancient literate societies of the Near East, its culture was clearly related to the people of the first farming village of Anatolia, Catal Huyuk, and to the Minoans.

It had been the Minoans and not, as was widely believed, the Phoenicians who had transported the cedars of Lebanon to Egypt at the behest of

[360] Hellenic megarons differed in that they centered on a great hall, possibly a throne room, while the Minoan labyrinths were built around an open court.

Pharaoh Thutmose III (1471T/1221R BCE). At that time, Minoan mastery of the eastern Mediterranean Sea was unchallenged.

## Hellenes Arrive (shortly after 1500T/1250R BCE)—Late Minoan Pottery

The first archaeological evidence of foreign domination on Krete comes from the period when the palaces were at their peak prosperity, soon after 1500T/1250R BCE. By the middle of the fifteenth century T / late thirteenth century R BCE, the Hellenes were clearly in control of the palaces and most of the cities of Krete. Changes in architecture, a more militaristic artistic expression, the introduction of the horse and chariot, and an adaptation of Linear A to Hellenic Linear B are seen.

The earliest Linear B text discovered on Krete dates to around 1450T/1200R BCE,[361] or a bit later, a time when most of the cities were subject to violent activity but continued to be occupied. All of the palaces except for Knossos were abandoned, however. Linear B is written in the Hellenic Arkado-Cypric dialect. Homer calls the conquerors Akhaians.

Various theories abound to explain the Hellenic conquest of Krete. It seemed logical that the volcanic eruption of Theras brought them down, but we now know the eruption occurred at least a century earlier. Perhaps the Minoans were weakened by earthquakes, which the island is prone to. Maybe the rising Hellenes simply overpowered the Kretans with strong armies assembled around the hereto unseen horse and chariot. Although the actual cause of the Minoans' subjection is lost, the Akhaian conquerors did not behave as brutish barbarians, as was once imagined. The Akhaians had nearly a century of continuous trade relations with the Minoans, and they had worked together as partners in expeditions to ports in the eastern Mediterranean. The two were very familiar with one another, and the

[361] The exact dating of the end of the palace period is problematic. In representations of the Keftiu (Kretans) on tomb paintings in Egypt reliably dated to the reign of Thumose III (1479T/1229R–1427T/1177R BCE), they are depicted dressed in a style paralleled with the second palace period, whereas later paintings of Amenhotep II (1427T/1177R–1401R/1151R BCE) show the Keftiu in a kilt comparable to a Knossos processional thought to be of the Late Minoan II pottery period (which ended before the pharaoh-queen Hatshepsut died in 1457T/1207R BCE).

conquerors wisely chose to rule without disturbing the local economy or sacking the cities. In fact, trade with Egypt peaked soon after their arrival.

## Postpalace Era (1370T/1120R–1075T/850R BCE)—Late Minoan Pottery

The massive palace at Knossos continued to be occupied for a quarter of a century after the other Kretan palaces were abandoned, and its frescoes were redone. Meanwhile, large palaces were built on the mainland, modeled significantly after the ones on Krete. The use of Linear B spread to the mainland once similar economic conditions existed at places like Pylos, Mycenai, and Thebes. Although the island palaces were abandoned, Kretan cities remained vibrant under the Akhaian rulers; it is just that the mainland Mycenaians eclipsed them in importance, took over their foreign trade outposts, and kept them from exerting the power they formerly enjoyed.

There was a steady decline under Mycenaian rule. By the thirteenth century T / eleventh century R BCE, Knossos was a fairly impoverished site and Khania was a larger city. After nearly two centuries of Mycenaian rule, the Bronze Age civilizations of the eastern Mediterranean began to collapse during the early twelfth T / mid tenth century BCE. Herodotos says that after the Trojan War, Krete was decimated by plagues and pestilence. Many chose to migrate abroad.

The Kretans appear to have been among the more important Sea Peoples. After the Egyptian pharaoh Ramesses III (1183T/933R–1152T/902R BCE) defeated the Sea Peoples invasion of the Nile, he settled the invaders in Palestine (Philistine). The Bible refers to Philistines as Cherethites (possibly Kretans and the Sea Peoples tribe of Peleset in Egyptian texts may have been the same) and the Philistine coast as the Kretan Negev. Philistine ceramic traditions were predominantly Mycenaian of a type common on Krete.

Krete fared better than Hellas after the collapse of the Mycenaian civilization. Most of the cities (Knossos, Tylissos, Phaistos, Gortyn, and others) remained occupied, although much of the populace moved to more defensible inland positions (Karphi, Dreros, and Vrokastro, for example). Many Kretans migrated abroad as well, particularly to Cilicia, Syria-Palestine, and Cyprus. The need for Linear B died with central administration and was soon forgotten. The Eteokretans, descendants of the Minoans, kept their writing alive and prospered, primarily in eastern Krete, the site of the first Minoan cities. They also held onto Cydonia in the west. The Dorians dominated the rest of the island. They were probably the descendants of the Akhaians, since there is no evidence of another Hellenic group moving to Krete after them.

When Hellas came out of the Dark Age that followed the Bronze Age, Krete was dotted with numerous city-states. It was one of the more advanced regions of Hellas, but the island's isolation prevented it from playing a major role in Hellenic affairs, and its culture declined. The Romans conquered isolated Krete because it had degenerated into a pirates' den.

# Addendum 5
# Procession of the Stars

Star myths are largely absent from early Hellenic mythology. In fact, before 500 BCE there are only two Hellenic writers who reference the heavens: Homer and Hesiod. Both mention only two constellations (Orion and the Great Bear), two star clusters (Pleiades and Hyades), and two stars (Sirius and Arktauros). The scientist Thales reputedly introduced the Phoenician practice of navigating by the Little Bear (Dipper) during the sixth century BCE.

The Hellenes also borrowed the notion of constellations moving across the heavens. Bradley Schaefer notes, in his article "Origin of the Greek Constellations," that some thirty constellations were borrowed from the Assyrians. Mr. Schaefer used cuneiform texts from Mesopotamia to determine that the positions for these constellations can be fixed to the skies of the late twelfth century BCE over Assyria.

Knowledge of the constellation arrived in Hellas from Mesopotamia during the fifth century BCE. The Hellenes then added constellations of their own. The fifth century BCE playwrights Aiskhylos and Euripides were the first to identify Perseus with a constellation. Of the eighteen constellations added to the original Assyrian six of the eighteen are associated with Perseus (Perseus, Andromeda, Kassiopeia, Cepheus, Cetos, and Pegasos). Others relate to the exploits of Perseus's famous descendent Herakles or to seafaring or Hellenistic-era motifs.

Eudoxos of Knidos's *Phainomena* is the first known work on the constellations, a prose work. He also created a star globe (366 BCE). In the very popular star map poem *Phainomena* (based upon Eudoxos's lost work), Aratos of Soli identified forty-five constellations (275 BCE); Pseudo Eratosthenes and Hyginos, (the latter in *Poetic Astronomy*) list forty-two, while Ptolemy of Alexandria's *Almagest* says the great astronomer Hipparkhos of Nicaia (second century BCE) listed forty-nine, while stating a belief in forty-eight constellations.

Discoveries by Hipparkhos profoundly affected Hellenistic thought. By studying Mesopotamian tests, Hipparkhos realized that the procession of the stars was not fixed; their location moved relative to earth over time. David Ulansey argues in his book *Origins of the Mithraic Mysteries* that Mithraism, the great Roman-era cult that briefly rivaled Christianity in popularity, grew out of Hipparkhos's discovery of the procession of the equinoxes.

Perhaps it was the great first-century BCE Stoic philosopher Poseidonios of Apamea who concluded that Hipparkhos had discovered the workings of a supreme being who could move the cosmos and therefore change fate. Stoic philosophy was profoundly influenced by astrology (which arrived in Hellas from Mesopotamia during the fifth century BCE), and they believed that conflagrations periodically destroyed the world. Thus it was easy for them to accept the new scientific proof of changing epochs.

The philosophers of Tarsos, a great Stoic center in the region of Cilicia, identified the god able to move the heavens with Perseus, the patron god of their city. They did so because of the location of the constellation Perseus. Perseus hovers above the constellation Tauros with sword in hand (it was previously thought he intended to kill Medousa), and they suggested that Perseus was actually poised to kill nearby Tauros, the constellation where the spring equinox resided during the epoch immediately preceding our own. However, the philosophers chose to call the supreme being Mithras instead of Perseus to add an element of mystery. The Persian god Mithras was the namesake of King Mithradates of Pontos, ally of the Cilician pirates (and their allies, the Stoic philosophers who ruled Tarsos) against the Romans. (Coincidentally, King Mithradates believed that he was a descendent of Perseus's son Perses, eponym of the Persians.) The historian/philosopher Plutarch stated that Mithraism was introduced to the Romans by Cilician pirates subdued by the Roman general Pompey during the first century BCE.

# Addendum 6
# Important Mythic Sources and Early Poets

Literacy returned to Hellas during the Arkhaic Age to record poetic religious and mythic works. During the seventh and sixth centuries BCE, rival Homeric and Hesiodic poetic schools flourished. The most important surviving works are the Homeric Trojan War Cycle (especially the *Iliad* and *Odyssey*) and Homeric hymns, and the Hesiodic *Theogony*, *Works and Days*, and *Catalog of Women*. Early Hellenic literature drew heavily upon broad oral narratives, such as the Heraklean, Theban, and Trojan War Cycles and creation myths.

During the fifth century BCE, mythic themes dominated genres such as "history," poetry, and drama. City-states commissioned poems to recant their mythic history; the most influential ones were written by Akusilaos about Argos, and Hellanikos about Athens. Great lyric poets, such as Simonides, Bakkhylides, and Pindar, sang mythic praises. The great playwrights Aiskhylos, Euripides, and Sophokles created dramatic recreations of myth. Pherecydes attempted to rationalize and integrate city-state stories into a coherent mythic Hellenic prehistory.

By the late fifth century BCE, the energy in Hellenic literature moved away from myth and poetry. Herodotos and Thucydides wrote prose accounts of historic events. Profane dramatic themes replaced mythic ones. Philosophy and oratory flourished, but they had little use for myth.

After the fifth century BCE, few works on mythic themes were published. The sulking poet Khoirilos of Samos summed up the reason in an early fourth-century BCE poem:

> Blessed were the poets in the old days
> When the field was still wide open. The arts
> Are all fenced in now. The field parceled out,
> And we, the latecomers, scratched from the race
> No room to bring up a new-yoke chariot.[362]

Poetry experienced a great rebirth during the Hellenistic era, led by Apollonios, Herondas, Kallimakhos, and Theokritos. These inventive poets developed new fields of poetry, but they only occasionally covered mythic themes. The one great exception is the epic poem *Argonautika*, composed by Apollonios during the third century BCE.

The greatest generation of Roman poets flowered during the first century BCE. They were greatly inspired by Hellenic poetry. Among the best were Ovid, Virgil, Horace, Propertios, Terence, and Catallos. Their fresh interpretations breathed new life into the old myths.

As the old works began losing their appeal, some writers wrote prose versions that preserved many myths from oblivion. The most notable synopses are found in works by Strabo, Diodoros, Apollodoros, Pausanias, and Hyginos. Strabo and Diodoros, writing during the first century BCE, wrote comprehensive histories starting with mythic prehistory. Apollodoros probably lived during the first century CE and wrote a lengthy mythological synopsis that was meant to instruct or remind the reader about ancient myths. Pausanias wrote an informative travel guide to Hellas full of mythic references during the second century CE. Finally, the Roman Hyginos recorded highly inaccurate Latin versions of Hellenic myths during the second century CE.

[362] Khoirilos of Samos.

The most influential ancient sources of myth used herein are as follows:

| | |
|---|---|
| Aiskhylos (Aeschylus) of Eleusis | Aiskhylos was the first of the three great fifth-century BCE Athenian playwrights. Aiskhylos, Sophokles, and Euripides prepared dramatic reenactments of mythic themes. Seven of Aiskhylos's more than seventy plays survive. |
| Akusilaos of Argos | The lost mythic history of the Argeia composed by Akusilaos was quoted by later writers. |
| Apollodoros | The Roman-era Hellenic mythographer Apollodoros wrote *The Library*, an important synopsis of Hellenic mythology. |
| Apollonios of Alexandria | Apollonios wrote a popular epic poem entitled *The Argonautika*. He was later surnamed The Rhodian, as his poem first became popular there. |
| Arkhilokhos of Paros | Arkhilokhos is the first poet who is clearly historical. His works represent a break from the mythic, epic past of shadowy Homer and Hesiod. Arkhilokhos speaks from a personal standpoint, not from a heroic one. |
| Bakkhylides of Keos | Little of Bakkhylides's work was thought to have survived until the Oxyrhynkhos papyrus was discovered in 1896 CE. Bakkhylides was the nephew of Simonides and a great lyric poet. |
| Diodoros of Sicily | Diodoros wrote an ambitious history of the world, starting with mythic times and ending in his own time—the first century BCE. |
| Euripides of Salamis | Euripides was the youngest of the three great fifth-century BCE playwrights. Nineteen of his plays survive. |

| | |
|---|---|
| Eumelos of Korinth | Eumelos was a poet of the Arkhaic Age. His lost *Titanomakhy* (meaning "war of the Titans") was an important cosmology source for later Hellenic writers. |
| Hellanikos of Mitylene | Hellanikos was the first Hellenic prose historian whose works covered both the mythic and factual history of Athens down to his lifetime in the mid fifth century BCE. He is quoted by later sources. |
| Hesiod of Askre | After Homer, the most famous and influential early poet was Hesiod. Like Homer, Hesiod may represent a poetic school rather than a person. His *Theogony* is the most important Hellenic creation myth. *The Works and Days* is a personal poem espousing the notion of the five ages of men. Other minor pieces written between the seventh and fifth centuries BCE have been attributed to Hesiod as well. |
| Homer of Ionia | *The Iliad* and *The Odyssey* are the most important poems of the ancient Hellenes. They crystallized a religious form that was largely followed for a thousand years. |
| Homeric Hymns | The Homeric Hymns were Arkhaic Age poems written in praise of the gods by anonymous writers. |
| Hyginos | A Latin writer flourishing in the late second century CE, Hyginos provided a highly inaccurate synopsis of Hellenic mythology that provides a few variations not found elsewhere. His surviving works are *Fabulai* and *Poetic Astronomy.* |

| | |
|---|---|
| Kallimakhos (Callimachus) of Cyrene | Kallimakhos was one of the great Hellenistic poets. He was also an acclaimed scholar who spent much of his life at the library in Alexandria. His hymns and epigrams generally shied away from mythic themes. |
| Ovid of Sulmo | Ovid and Virgil are considered the greatest Roman poets. In *Metamorphoses*, Ovid beautifully retells many Hellenic myths. |
| Panyassis of Halikarnassos | Early historians like Panyassis, the uncle of Herodotos, wrote epic chronologies of ancient myths. His lost poems on the Herakles Cycle and The Ionian migration were quoted by others. |
| Pausanias of Magnesia | The second-century CE *Guide to Greece* by Pausanias is, along with the *Library* of Apollodoros, the greatest synopsis of myth available. Pausanias is a valuable source for archaeology and history as well. |
| Pherecydes of Syros | Pherecydes wrote an influential fifth-century BCE poem on the mythic history of Hellas. He attempted to develop a cohesive story from conflicting local legends. His works are lost but influenced Apollodoros, Pausanias, and others. Pherecydes's specialty appears to have been genealogies. |
| Pindar of Thebes | Pindar was the last great lyric poet singing about mythic themes. His fifth-century BCE odes are a major source of mythic material. Bakkhylides and Simonides, both from Keos, were slightly earlier lyric masters who often drew from mythic themes. |

| | |
|---|---|
| Plutarch of Khaironeia | Plutarch's *Lives* compares great historical Hellenes and Romans. He started his work comparing mythic Theseus of Athens with Romulus of Rome. Plutarch wrote during the late first and early second century CE. |
| Sappho of Lesvos | Sappho was the greatest Hellenic poetess. She was compared with Homer, but sadly only a few fragments of her work survive. |
| Simonides of Keos | Simonides was the first of the great fifth-century BCE lyric poets. Only fragments of his poems survive. |
| Stesikhoros of Lokris | The late sixth- or early fifth-century BCE lyric poet Stesikhoros was said to have been struck blind for slandering Helene. He changed his poem to flatter her, and his sight returned. |
| Sophokles of Kolonos | Sophokles was the most popular of the three great playwrights of the fifth century BCE. Out of his approximately 120 plays, only 7 survive, including an influential trilogy on the family of Oidipous of Thebes. |
| Strabo of Amaseia | Strabo is known for his *Geography* and *Historical Sketches*, ambitious works that partly dealt with prehistoric myths. |
| Theban Cycle | The narrative begins with the birth of future king Oidipous and ends with the madness of Alkmeon, the sacker of Thebes. The story is told in four sagas: *Oidipodia*, *Thebaid*, *Epigonoi*, and *Alkmeonis*. Although none survive, they influenced later writers. |
| Theognis of Megara | Active during the sixth century BCE, Theognis wrote elegiac verse on moral and political themes. |

| | |
|---|---|
| Theokritos of Syrakuse | Theokritos invented pastoral poetry. A few of his Idylls covered mythic figures, including Herakles, Hylas, and the Dioskouroi/Gemini twins. |
| Trojan War Cycle | The complete story of the Trojan War from its cause to the death of the last warrior to the return from its gory battle is found in eight sagas: *Cypria*, *Iliad*, *Aithiopis*, *Little Iliad*, *Sack of Ilion*, *Returns* (*Nostoi*), *Odyssey*, and *Telegony*. Only *Iliad* and *Odyssey* survive. A synopsis of the others was preserved by Proklos of Byzantion during the fifth century CE. |
| Tyrtaios of Sparta | The late seventh- or sixth-century BCE poet Tyrtaios extolled the virtues of war to his Spartan audience. |
| Virgil of Mantua | Virgil, the court poet of Augustus, created a lot of Roman mythology based upon Hellenic themes. His major works were the *Eclogues*, *Georgics*, and *Aineid*. |

The most important sources for the chronology are as follows:

| | |
|---|---|
| Bryce, Trevor | Bryce is a Hittite scholar and the author of *The Kingdom of the Hittites.* |
| Ephoros of Cyme | Ephoros, a student of Isokrates, wrote the first universal history of the world, starting with the return of the Herakleids (Dorian invasion), and is the key source of Dark Age chronology. He wrote during the mid fourth century BCE. |
| Eratosthenes of Cyrene | Eratosthenes was an acclaimed Hellenistic scientist and a longtime chief librarian at Alexandria. His proposed date for the fall of Troy is still widely accepted today. |
| Eusebios of Caesarea | Eusebios was a fourth-century CE bishop whose *Chronicles* was the most important source for early historical dates until the nineteenth century CE. |
| Evans, Sir Arthur | Evans discovered the first European civilization on Krete and named it Minoa. His tripartite splitting of ages is still used for Bronze Age chronologies today. |
| Herodotos of Halikarnassos | Herodotos wrote during the fifth century BCE and is called the father of history. He is the first (excluding Hittite texts) to record historical events. His book *Histories* provides valuable insights into dating ancient events using chronologies. |
| James, Peter | James challenged long-held traditional dates in his late twentieth-century CE book *Centuries of Darkness.* He reduced the length of the Early Iron Age by 250 years. Supporters of traditional dating admit he exposed significant flaws with conventional dating, but they are not ready to accept his dating. |

| | |
|---|---|
| Manetho of Egypt | Manetho was a Hellenistic-era Egyptian whose lost book *Aigyptika* details Egyptian royalty from the first to the last native pharaoh. Fortunately, his kings list survives. |
| Meyer, Eduard | After studying the ancient Egyptian Sothic calendar, in 1904 CE, Professor Meyer proposed fixed dates for a few ancient recorded events. His dates were matched to historical sequences from Manetho and Petrie to develop the traditional historical timelines still widely accepted today. |
| Parian Marble | Two fragments of a marble stele found on Paros Island provide chronological dates from the earliest times to 264 BCE, presumably the date it was erected. |
| Petrie, William | Petrie, a British archaeologist who worked during the late nineteenth century CE, developed a chronological sequence of events in Egypt based upon pottery. He then overlaid his findings with Manetho's list and uncovered inscriptions. He conclusively tied Late Bronze Age pottery from the Aigaian to Egypt. |
| Schliemann, Heinrich | Schliemann was an amateur archaeologist who funded excavations at Mycenai and Troy that proved to a skeptical nineteenth-century CE world that the myths of Homer were not pure fantasy. |
| Thucydides of Athens | Thucydides wrote the first truly objective history during the late fifth century BCE. His *History of the Peloponnesian War* proved information pivotal to dating ancient events. |

# Bibliography

Aeschylus. *Prometheus Bound and Other Plays.* Translated by Philip Vellacott. New York: Penguin Books, 1961.

Aeschylus. *Prometheus Bound and Other Plays.* Translated by Philip Vellacott. New York: Penguin Books, 1961.

Apollodorus. *The Library.* Translated by Sir James George Frazer. Cambridge: Harvard University Press, 1921.

Apollodorus. *The Library of Greek Mythology.* Translated by Keith Aldrich. Lawrence: Coronado Press, 1975.

Apollonius of Rhodes. *The Voyage of Argo.* Translated by E. V. Rieu. New York: Penguin Books, 1959.

Burkert, Walter. *Greek Religion.* Translated by John Raffan. Cambridge: Harvard University Press, 1985.

Bryce, Trevor. *The Kingdom of the Hittites.* New York: Oxford University Press, 1998.

Callimachus. *Callimachus Hymns, Epigrams, Select Fragments.* Translated by Stanley

Lombardo and Diane Rayor. Baltimore: Johns Hopkins University Press, 1988.

Campbell, David A. *Greek Lyric.* Translated by David A. Campbell. Cambridge: Harvard University Press, 1991.

Chadwick, John. *The Mycenaean World.* Cambridge: Cambridge University Press, 1976.

Detienne, Marcel. *The Masters of Truth in Archaic Greece.* Translated by Janet Lloyd. New York: Zone Books, 1996.

Dickinson, Oliver. The Aegean Bronze Age. New York: Cambridge University Press, 1994.

Diodorus. *The Library of History.* Translated by C. H. Oldfather. Cambridge: Loeb Classical Library, 1935.

Euripides. *Euripides V.* Translated by Emily Townsend Vermeule, Elizabeth Wyckoff, and William Arrowsmith. Chicago: University of Chicago Press, 1959.

Euripides. *Orestes and Other Plays.* Translated by Philip Vellacott. New York: Penguin Books, 1972.

Euripides. *Ten Plays.* Translated by Moses Hadad and John McLean. New York: Bantam Books, 1960.

Euripides. *The Bacchae and Other Plays.* Translated by Philip Vellacott. New York: Penguin Books, 1954.

Fornara, Charles W. *Archaic times to the End of the Peloponnesian War.* Translated by Charles W. Fornara. Baltimore: Johns Hopkins University Press, 1977.

Graves, Robert. *The Greek Myths.* New York: Penguin Books, 1955.

Homer. *The Iliad.* Translated by Robert Fitzgerald. New York: Anchor Books, 1963.

Homer. *The Odyssey.* Translated by Richmond Lattimore. New York: Harper & Row Press, 1965.

Horace. *The Complete Odes and Epodes.* Translated by W. G. Shepherd. New York: Penguin Books, 1983.

Herodotus. *The History.* Translated by Aubrey de Selincourt. New York: Penguin Books, 1954.

Hesiod. *Hesiod, The Homeric Hymns and Homerica.* Translated by Hugh G. Evelyn-White. Cambridge: Harvard University Press, 1914.

Hesiod. *Theogony, Works and Days.* Translated by M. L. West. New York: Oxford University Press, 1988.

Hesiod and Theognis. *Hesiod and Theognis.* Translated by Dorothea Wender. New York: Penguin Books, 1973.

Hyginos. *The Myths of Hyginus.* Translated by Mary Grant. Lawrence: University of Kansas Press, 1960.

James, Peter. *Centuries of Darkness.* New Brunswick: Rutgers University Press, 1991.

Mallory, J. P. *In Search of the Indo-Europeans.* New York: Thames & Hudson, 1989.

MacKendrick, Paul. *The Greek Stones Speak.* New York: W. W. Norton & Company, 1962.

Nilsson, Martin P. *The Mycenaean Origin of Greek Mythology.* Berkeley: University of California Press, 1932.

Osborne, Robin. *Greece in the Making 1200–479 BC.* London: Routledge, 1996.

Ovid. *Metamorphoses.* Translated by Mary Innes. New York: Penguin Books, 1955.

Ovid. *The Erotic Poems.* Translated by Peter Green. New York: Penguin Books, 1982.

Pausanias. *Guide to Greece.* Translated by Peter Levi. New York: Penguin Books, 1971.

Pindar. *The Odes.* Translated by C. M. Bowra. New York: Penguin Books, 1969.

Plutarch. *Plutarch's Lives.* Translated by John Dryden. New York: Modern Library, 1967.

Polybius. *The Rise of the Roman Empire.* Translated by Ian Scott-Kilvert. New York: Penguin Books, 1979.

Renfrew, Colin. *Archaeology & Language.* New York: Cambridge University Press, 1988.

Sappho. *Sappho and the Greek Lyric Poets.* Translated by Willis Barnstone. New York: Schocken Books, 1962.

Sophocles. *The Complete Plays of Sophocles.* Translated by Sir Richard Claverhouse Jebb. New York: Bantam Books, 1967.

Strabo. *The Geography.* Translated by Horace Leonard Jones. Cambridge: Loeb Classical Library, 1917.

Taylour, Lord William. *The Mycenaeans.* London: Thames and Hudson, 1964.

Theocritus. *The Idylls of Theocritus,* Translated by Thelma Sargent. New York: W. W. Norton & Company, 1982.

Thucydides. *The Peloponnesian War.* Translated by Rex Warner. New York: Penguin Books, 1954.

Vermeule, Emily. *Greece in the Bronze Age.* Chicago: The University of Chicago Press, 1964.

Virgil. *The Georgics.* Translated by L. P. Wilkinson. New York: Penguin Books, 1982.

Virgil. *The Eclogues.* Translated by Guy Lee. New York: Penguin Books, 1980.

Ancient Sources

| Author | Chapter Quotes | Chapter | Note |
|---|---|---|---|
| Agaios | 14 | | 268, 280 |
| Aiskhylos | 6 (2), 16 | 6, A1, A5, A6 | 66, 71, 82, 83, 127, 128, 218, 224 |
| Aisop | | | 140 |
| Akusilaos | | 6, 17, A2, A6 | 66, 68, 75, 113, 126 |
| Antiokhos | | A1 | |
| Apollodoros | | 6, 9, A1, A2, A6 | 3, 7, 16, 43, 66, 68, 69, 75, 93, 113, 115, 121, 123, 127, 131, 144, 147, 153, 157, 161, 165, 170, 171, 175, 180, 195, 196, 224, 250, 268, 275, 283, 288, 293, 294, 300, 342 |
| Apollodoros (historian) | | A1 | 348 |
| Apollonios | 1, 10 (2) | A6 | 1, 51, 110, 112, 180, 183, 184, 185, 202 |
| Aratos | | A5 | |
| Aristotle | | A1 | 2, 320, 329 |
| Arkhilokhos | 6, 16 | 16, A1, A6 | 313 |
| Asios | | 6 | 189 |
| Asklepiades | | | 75 |
| Athenaios | | | 32 |
| Bakkhylides | 8, 10 (3), 11, 13 | 6, A6 | 90, 113, 131, 163, 192, 198, 205, 206, 251 |
| Bible | | 14, A1, A4 | |
| Catallos | | A6 | |
| Cekrops | | | 75 |
| Censorinus | | A1 | |
| Clement | | | 3, 52 |
| Cypselos | | 16, A1, A2 | |
| Diagoras | 14 | | |
| Dikaiarkhos | | A1 | 329 |
| Diodoros | | 6, 16, A1, A2, A6 | 40, 51, 66, 141, 144, 153, 180, 196, 229, 238, 239, 250, 293, 324, 327, 356 |
| Diogenes | 16 | | |
| Dionysos | | 8 | |
| Dionysios (tyrant) | | 9 | |
| Douris | | A1 | |
| Ephoros | | P, 16, A1, A6 | 51, 320, 323, 324, 326, 327, 337, 343, 346, 347, 348 |
| Epimenides | | | 135 |

| Author | Chapter Quotes | Chapter | Note |
|---|---|---|---|
| Eratosthenes | | A1, A6 | 292, 324, 326, 327, 338, 348, 351 |
| Author | Chapter Quotes | Chapter | Note |
| Euanthes | | | 61, 93 |
| Eubulos | | | 53 |
| Eudoxos | | 1, A5 | |
| Eumelos | | A1, A6 | 3, 5, 7 |
| Euphorion | | | 262 |
| Euripides | 3, 7, 10, 11, 14, 15 | 8, 13, A5, A6 | 57, 104, 128, 170, 209, 250, 252, 267, 269, 287, 291, 293 |
| Eusebios | | 14, 16, A1, A6 | 324, 326, 327, 344, 345, 348, 349, 350, 351 |
| Eustathios | | | 142, 167, 268 |
| Hellanikos | | A1, A6 | |
| Hekataios | | 1 | 250 |
| Herodotos | 16, A3 | P, 9, 16, 17, A1, A6 | 76, 89, 96, 113, 153, 254, 293, 304, 321, 324, 334, 337, 355 |
| Herondas | | A6 | |
| Hesiod | 1 (2), 2, 3, 4 (3), 5, 6, 16 (3), A1 | P, 1, 2, 3, 4, 5, 6, 8, 16, 17, A1, A5, A6 | 3, 4, 7, 8, 9, 10, 18, 23, 29, 38, 43, 47, 49, 52, 57, 63, 68, 73, 78, 90, 113, 124, 135, 224, 273, 308, 312, 353, 356 |
| Hippias | | A1 | |
| Hipparkhos | | A5 | |
| Homer | 8, 9, 10, 11, 13 (3), A4 | P, 1, 5, 6, 7, 8, 9, 13, 14, 16, 17, A1, A5, A6 | 2, 7, 28, 29, 30, 38, 89, 113, 121, 122, 123, 124, 142, 143, 149, 153, 155, 167, 184, 187, 191, 193, 235, 244, 250, 252, 256, 257, 258, 260, 263, 266, 268, 272, 275, 276, 328, 354 |
| Homeric Hymns | 3 (2), 4 (4), 6, 7 (2), 10, 11, 13 | A6 | 19, 23, 24, 25, 33, 34, 73, 102, 166, 208, 245, 261 |
| Horace | | A6 | |
| Hyginos | | P, A5, A6 | 3, 39 ,53, 66, 86, 142, 153, 180, 195, 224, 225, 233, 250, 276, 347 |
| Ion | | | 304 |
| Isidoros | | A1 | |
| Isokrates | | A1, A6 | |
| Jerome | | A1 | |
| Josephos | | A1 | |
| Julius Africanus | | A1 | |
| Kallimakhos | 9 | A6 | 111, 152 |
| Kallisthenes | | A1 | 320 |

| Author | Chapter Quotes | Chapter | Note |
|---|---|---|---|
| Kastor | | A1 | 327 |
| Khoirilos | A6 | | 362 |

| Author | Chapter Quotes | Chapter | Note |
|---|---|---|---|
| Kleitarkhos | | A1 | |
| Konon | | A1 | |
| Ktesias | | A1 | |
| Leskhes | 13 (2) | | 250, 261 |
| Lucian | | | 44 |
| Manetho | | A1, A6 | |
| Matris | | | 153 |
| Melesagoros | | | 165 |
| Menandros | | | 142 |
| Mimnermos | | | 304 |
| Moskhos | | 6 | |
| Nikolaos | | A1 | |
| Nonnos | | | 43 |
| Orphic Hymns | | 1 | 165 |
| Ovid | 1, 4, 10 (2) | 1, 4, 6, A6 | 3, 14, 26, 57, 113, 121, 126, 161, 178, 180, 190, 194, 274 |
| Palatine Anthology | | | 287 |
| Panyassis | | A6 | 153, 165, 304 |
| Parian Marble | | 14, A1, A6 | 52, 279, 310, 326, 327, 338 |
| Paterculus, Velleius | | A1 | 345 |
| Pausanias | | 4, 6, 7, 15, 16, A1, A2, A6 | 3, 27, 61, 66, 95, 126, 127, 135, 161, 165, 171, 189, 190, 196, 244, 250, 262, 275, 293, 294, 300, 301, 304, 324, 337, 342, 346, 348 |
| Peisandros | | | 153, 196 |
| Phanias | | A1 | 320 |
| Pherecydes | | P, 6, 17, A1, A6 | 75, 153, 174, 304, 321 |
| Phynikhos | | | 190 |
| Pindar | 4, 7 (2), 8, 9, 10 | 8, A1, A6 | 97, 107, 110, 123, 135, 168, 180, 182, 265 |
| Pliny | 1 | | 1, 52, 291 |
| Plutarch | | 16, A1, A5, A6 | 291, 325 |
| Polybios | | | 154, 329 |
| Poseidonios | | A5 | |
| Proklos | | A6 | |
| Propertios | | A6 | |

| Author | Chapter Quotes | Chapter | Note |
|---|---|---|---|
| Pseudo Eratosthenes | | A5 | |
| Pseudo Herodotos | | A1 | |
| Ptolemy, Claudios | | A1, A5 | |
| Rhapsodic Theogoneia | | 1 | |
| Sappho | 9 | A6 | |
| Author | Chapter Quotes | Chapter | Note |
| Scholiast on Apollonios | | | 327 |
| Seneca | | | 224 |
| Servius | | | 93 |
| Simonides | 4, 8, 12 | A6 | 32, 120, 325 |
| Solon | 1, 16 | A1 | 347 |
| Sophokles | 11 (4) | A6 | 142, 212, 213, 218, 220, 224, 250, 291, 293 |
| Sosibios | | A1 | |
| Stasinos (or Hegasias) | 13 (2) | | 195 |
| Statios | 11 | | 214, 218 |
| Stesikhoros | 15 (2) | A6 | 165, 244, 269, 285 |
| Strabo | | 16, A1, A6 | 51, 113, 201, 235, 250, 266, 293, 347, 349 |
| Suidas | | | 346 |
| Syncellus, George | | A1 | |
| Tallos | | | 17 |
| Terence | | A6 | |
| Thales | | 16, A1, A5 | 347 |
| Theognis | | A1, A6 | |
| Theokritos | 10, 13 (2) | A6 | 153, 181, 215, 240, 243, 246 |
| Theopompos | | A1 | 323, 324, 326 |
| Thucydides | | 15, 16, A1, A6 | 292, 293, 299, 327, 338 |
| Timaios | | A1 | 326, 328, 329 |
| Tyrtaios | 4, 8 | A1, A6 | 117, 346 |
| Varro | | | 61 |
| Virgil | | 14, A6 | 110, 264, 274, 280 |
| Xenophanes | 1, 7 | | |

Modern References

| Author | Mentioned in Text | Mentioned in Notes |
|---|---|---|
| Blegen, Carl | A1 | |
| Bryce, Trevor | A1, A2, A6 | 340 |
| Bulfinch, Thomas | P | |
| Buxton, Richard | P | |
| Campbell, Joseph | P | |
| Chadwick, John | | 232 |
| Coldstream, J. Nicholas | A1 | |
| Dickinson, Oliver | 6 | |
| Dorpfeld, Wilhelm | A1 | |
| Desborough, Vincent | A1 | |
| Durant, Will | | 2 |
| Evans, Sir Arthur | 17, A4, A6 | 357 |
| Francis, David | A1 | |
| Frazer, James | | 20 |
| Freud, Sigmund | P | |
| Gimbutus, Marija | 3, 4, 5, 17 | 10, 352 |
| Graves, Robert | P | |
| Hamilton, Edith | P | |
| Hood, M.S.F. | 6 | |
| James, Peter | P, 17, A1, A6 | 22 |
| Jung, Carl | P | |
| Koiv, Mait | | 323, 348 |
| Kitchen, Kenneth | A1, A2 | 318 |
| Krauss, Rolf | A1 | |
| Mallory, J.P. | 3, 17, A3 | 63, 352 |
| Meyer, Eduard | A1, A6 | 22 |
| Mylonas, George Emmanuel | 6, A1 | |
| Nilsson, Martin | | 84 |
| Osborne, Robin | A1 | |
| Petrie, William | 17, A1, A6 | 22 |
| Renfrew, Colin | 3, A3 | 352 |
| Schaefer, Bradley | A1, A5 | |
| Schliemann, Heinrich | P, 5, 17, A1, A6 | |
| Snodgrass, Anthony | A1 | |
| Ulansey, David | A5 | |
| Ventris, Michael | | 232 |
| Vickers, Michael | A1 | |
| Young, Rodney | A1 | |

Printed in the United States
By Bookmasters

Printed in the United States
By Bookmasters